# EXODUS
## THE ARK

F6C

# PAUL CHAFE

Exodus: The Ark

A Baen Books Original

Baen Publishing Enterprises
P.O. Box 1403
Riverdale, NY 10471
www.baen.com

ISBN: 978-1-4391-3322-4

Cover art by David Mattingly

First printing, November 2009

Distributed by Simon & Schuster
1230 Avenue of the Americas
New York, NY 10020

Library of Congress Cataloging-in-Publication Data

Chafe, Paul, 1965–
  Exodus : the Ark / Paul Chafe.
      p. cm.
  ISBN 978-1-4391-3322-4 (trade pbk.)
  I. Title.
  PR9199.4.C44E96 2009
  813'.6—dc22

                                            2009034339

10   9   8   7   6   5   4   3   2   1

Pages by Joy Freeman (www.pagesbyjoy.com)
Printed in the United States of America

*Pour Gabrielle, avec amour*

For more on the Ark project visit
http://projectark.net

# Prelude

---

*Thou shalt make no covenant with them, nor with their gods.*

—Exodus 23:32

---

# Shipyear 3809

The steelsmith's son moved carefully through the ancient trees, his rabbit bow at the ready. He was keyed up, focused, and, if he was honest with himself, afraid. The forelanders liked to fight from horseback and rarely came into the forest, but the treeline was getting close. *But I won't show fear.*

He glanced behind him to make sure his friends were still following. They were. It wasn't his first time raiding a forelander farm, but it was his first time leading a raid. He hadn't imagined how much a leader had to think about. There was a clearing ahead, and he skirted around it. The suntube dappled splashes of light through the canopy, and they danced as the leaves rustled in the breeze. The ground was soft beneath his leather shore-shoes, and it smelled rich and earthy. *Every sense is heightened.*

The treeline was ahead and the steelsmith's son dropped into a crouch as he led his small group nearer. Instinctively he reached for his quiver, drew an arrow and nocked it to the string. The steel arrowhead glinted, and he smiled. He'd forged the points himself, honed them razor-sharp. The blade at his belt was steel as well, a luxury only a smith's son could indulge in. His friends came mostly from fishing families and their blades were ironwood, good enough to gut trout but a poor match for inquisitor steel.

The trees grew smaller as the group approached the forest's edge. There was a small bush in the treeline, good cover, and the young man headed for it. It was large enough for his friends to get under as well, and they followed him under. *Not a good thing.* It would have been better for the other three to stay back, to give him cover, but it was too late now. They slid forward on their

3

bellies to look out over the pastureland in front of them. Across the pasture he could see the fences of the farm he wanted to raid.

"Look," The youngest one pointed, and the young man turned to see. A patrol of six mounted inquisitors was coming along the treeline. They were armed with spears and blades, and their red cloaks fluttered in the breeze as they rode.

"Get down," the steelsmith's son said. "We'll let them pass."

The others did as he told them, but he himself kept watching. The enemy rode on without showing any sign they'd noticed his hiding place.

"Let's get them," said the raft-captain's son. He'd raised his head to watch as well.

"Get down," the steelsmith's son repeated, and gave his friend a look. Raiding the forelanders was almost expected behavior for the fisherfolk youth, and the bolder parties even took on the inquisitors, luring them into ambushes in the forest. He resisted the urge to let fly with his bow. *That's not why we're here.* They'd get themselves a couple of sheep and vanish back into the forest. He didn't need the bragging rights, no matter how much his friend wanted them.

The patrol turned foreward, but stopped a few hundred meters away. One of the inquisitors dismounted and set up some kind of instrument on a tripod. It had a long arm that could be rotated and elevated, and the man sighted along it, changed its position, and sighted again. The group moved a dozen meters and he repeated the process. *What are they doing?* Whatever it was, they weren't getting out of the way. The man with the tripod moved again, repeated his ritual, and then drove a stake into the ground. The entire group dismounted then, though they stayed alert.

The steelsmith's son bit his lip, considering his options. They could either wait to see if the patrol left, or move a couple of kilometers and try their luck somewhere else. Before he could decide, movement caught his eye. A convoy of four carts was jolting its way across the pasture. As he watched, one of the inquisitors waved, and the convoy headed for the small group. The carts drew up, and then, off the first one jumped a slave crew, roped together with neck ropes.

The drivers began yelling and the slaves started working on the pasture with shovels. Another group started unloading the bricks from the cart. The Prophetsy was building something. *A new farm?* They couldn't be so foolish; the pastureland beyond the forest was already full of empty farms, some of them burned in the war, some of them abandoned because they were too easily raided. *What then?*

It didn't matter, the inquisitors wouldn't be leaving any time soon, which meant they'd need to get their sheep somewhere else. He looked up the curve of the world to see where else they might try, and saw something he'd overlooked before. There was another group of carts a kilometer antispinward, surrounding a small brick structure half built. *A watchtower!* Further up still there was a third, and perhaps a fourth. The Prophetsy couldn't be hoping to put a ring of towers against the forest edge around the entire world. *Could it?* He looked higher, searching the patchwork fields up and around as the world arched over the suntube, and down the other side. There were towers under construction to spinward as well, also evenly spaced. They hadn't been there last time he'd gone on a farm raid. The inquisitors meant business. *This is important.*

"Let's go," he whispered, and began to back out of the bush.

"But what about—" the raft-captain's son began.

"Forget it." The steelsmith's son cut him off. "We aren't going."

The others followed him in silence, and he led the way back into the forest, heading for the ocean. *Father needs to know this.* Something had changed with the Prophetsy, and he sensed it wasn't for the better.

# Exodus 1

*Therefore he set over them masters of the works, to afflict them with burdens.*

—Exodus 1:11

# Shipyear 3830

"Well, well, well, look what we've caught. A little guppy."

Danil Fougere jumped and spun, taken by surprise. The gang leader was named Hatch. He was three or four years older than Danil, and a lot bigger. He advanced with a confident swagger, a subordinate boy close behind him. At the other end of the alley another pair of gangers appeared, blocking the exit. Danil stole a glance back the way he had come, saw another figure waiting there. He was trapped.

"What you got there?" The leader smirked and pointed at Danil's belt-bag. "Anything I might like?"

"Just an axe head," said Danil, backing away. "I found it."

"Really? Well, I just lost an axe head. Why don't you show me and we'll see if it's mine."

"It's mine." Danil put a hand protectively over his belt bag. The axe head was a prize, tradable to a smith for three or four days of food. Losing it would mean hunger, and Danil was already very hungry. "I found it where the Prophetsy crew works."

Hatch lunged and grabbed him by the shirt front. "Give it here, guppy." His voice was suddenly hard. He was done playing with his prey.

"Alright, alright." The other gang members had closed in, and Danil was surrounded. "Just let me get it untied."

"Do it fast, guppy." Hatch released Danil's shirt front, shoving him backwards at the same time. "You don't want me getting bored."

Danil fumbled with the leather laces that held the bag to his belt. When he had it undone he held it out to the bigger boy. Hatch reached to take it, but when he came close Danil swung the bag, catching him hard in the side of the face. The larger boy yelped in pain, and Danil darted for the far end of the alley. The boys who were blocking his path lunged to grab him but he swung the heavy bag again, smacking the larger one on the skull with an audible *crack*. His assailant went down. The second one snatched at the bag, but Danil drove his knee into his groin and the other collapsed to writhe in agony in the dirt.

Danil ran as shouts rose after him, desperate fear driving him to speed. He swerved into a side alley, caroming off the wall to make the corner. As he did so, he stole a glance back to see Hatch and two more boys chasing him. They were all bigger than he was, and if they caught him now they would do worse than steal his axe head. His breath came in gasps as he forced himself to run faster. He had an escape route, if he could get that far.

Fifty meters further on, he came to a narrow gap, an accidental feature formed where a stable yard and a fishmonger's shop didn't quite meet, not wide enough to be considered an alley, but big enough for him to squeeze in sideways. It was a shortcut he'd discovered, when he'd first come to Far Bay. The pursuing boys nearly caught him then, but they had to squeeze into the narrow space themselves and Danil recovered his lead. He moved as fast as he could, ignoring the small hurts inflicted when the building's sideboards caught at his skin.

"You're not getting away, guppy," Hatch yelled.

Danil ignored him. If he was yelling it was because he was frustrated, and if he was frustrated it was because Danil was getting away. The confined space was more an obstacle for the older boys than it was for him. It dead-ended at a fence that surrounded a cut-yard, and under the fence was a space just large enough for him to slip through. Normally he looked carefully first, to make sure none of the yard hands were watching. This time he thrust his head and shoulders under the fence without so much as a glance. It was a tight squeeze, and he had a moment of panic when his belt caught against the fence boards. It took him precious seconds to wiggle free, and then he felt hands grabbing his ankle, pulling him back. He kicked desperately, felt one foot connect with something solid. There was a grunt of pain and the hands let go, and he pulled himself through to the other side.

He stood up and dusted himself off, breathing hard. While he recovered he watched to see if the gang would try to follow him, but they weren't stupid enough to wedge themselves into the narrow space while he was free to kick them in the head as they came through. Curses and threats came through the fence, but they weren't important. Danil found himself trembling. *That was too close, too close by far.* Coming to Far Bay had been an act of desperation, and the city had no welcome for a lone runaway. He had managed to survive so far on his wits, but the gangs were hard to evade, and every time he ran into one he made more enemies.

The voices on the other side of the fence faded. Danil turned to see if he'd been spotted, crouching behind a pile of timbers to see where the yard team was. Fortunately they were preoccupied, working the big two-man vertical crosscut in the center of the space and stacking the sawn boards in piles. The clean, fresh smell of cut timber filled the yard, somehow making him feel even dirtier in comparison. He crept to the next timber pile and then to the next, keeping them between himself and the hands. At the far end of the yard, a pile of stacked logs formed an impromptu staircase that would take him over the fence to the next street.

He was halfway to it when he spotted a worktable covered in rough hewn boards. It was unattended, with a buck saw and a big chisel lying on top of it. He paused, considering. Either would make a nice prize, both together would feed him for a week. He looked again to where the yard hands were working the crosscut. They were preoccupied, and looking the other way. *It would be so easy . . .* he pushed the temptation aside. It would be easy *this* time, but he needed the cut-yard route. If tools started disappearing the yard hands would look to find the reason. Dock rats like Danil were already assumed to be thieves, and he would be beaten if he were caught in the yard. If he were caught stealing, he might get some bones broken, and that would leave him easy prey to the gangs.

He slipped over to the lumber pile, checked to make sure no one was looking, and scampered to the top. From there it was a short jump to the fence's top rail, and then he swung himself down to a narrow street of hard packed dirt. He checked left and right, just in case Hatch had anticipated his route, but the way was clear. He dodged around a fishmonger's cart, jumped up onto the rough-hewn boardwalk and ran along it to the bridge that crossed the Silver River just before it emptied itself into the ocean. On the other side of the bridge, a brick and timber forge dipped a waterwheel into the lazy current, smoke pouring from the clay-plastered chimney. He heaved a sigh of relief. Era was there, and working. He ran across the bridge and into the open shop front. The broad-shouldered smith was at the furnace hearth, holding a work piece in the coals with a pair of steel tongs.

Danil watched in fascination. He loved to watch the shop's machinery moving. The waterwheel drove a tacklewheel that turned a beltrope to work the furnace bellows. Every blast of air made the furnace roar, and sent a wave of heat rolling into the shop and against Danil's face. When the shipsteel glowed red hot, Era turned to put it on the anvil beneath the drop hammer. He caught sight of Danil then, and threw him a wink. A long wooden lever engaged the waterwheel to the hammer's shaft, and the hammer began to rise and fall, clanging with loud rhythm. Danil watched in fascination as the red-glowing shipsteel yielded to the hammer, trying to determine what it was Era was making. Eventually the blacksmith was satisfied with his handiwork, and thrust the work piece into a bucket of water where it sizzled and steamed. He put down the tongs, and disconnected the waterwheel from the hammer, then moved another lever to disconnect the bellows as well.

"That will do for now." He smiled as broad as his shoulders. "What have you brought today, lad?"

Danil took his prize from his belt bag and held it up. "An axe head."

"Not stolen, I trust?"

"Not from any fisherfolk."

"From a lumber crew?"

"Maybe."

Era laughed. "Young man, you'll live to regret stealing from the Prophetsy."

"I don't steal, I scavenge. It's not my fault they leave so much behind."

"The Prophet already thinks he owns us. He might yet own you, and you'll be hauling those trees instead of climbing them." The blacksmith took the axe head and hefted it. "This is nice. How much do you want?"

"Whatever you think is fair."

"We'll say thirty hooks."

"Thirty? There's a good kilo of shipsteel there."

"Forty, then."

"Islan Keenn would give me sixty."

"Islan wouldn't give his own mother sixty, but you're welcome to ask him."

"Fifty, Era, that's fair."

"I don't have fifty hooks, so let's say thirty hooks and a token, since you drive such a hard bargain." Era went to a shelf filled with ranked wooden boxes, took one down and counted out thirty fishhooks, then added a silvery trade token to the pile.

Danil swept the hooks into his belt bag, careful to avoid pricking himself on the points, and slipped the token into a pocket.

"Thanks, Era." He hesitated. The token alone was worth thirty hooks. He wanted to say more, but he didn't know what to say. Era was the only person who'd been kind to him since he'd come to the city, and his wife Sall would sometimes slip Danil a heel of bread or some dried trout. He wanted to thank Era for that as well, he wanted to find a way to win the big man's friendship, he wanted . . . he wasn't even sure what it was he was looking for. He didn't know what words to say, and didn't want to risk the fragile connection by saying the wrong ones.

"No thanks required for a fair trade." The big man smiled and the transaction was over. It was Danil's cue to leave, but he didn't want to go. Hatch would be angry and looking for him, and the forge was safety for as long as he could stay.

"What's are you working on?" he asked, because he couldn't think of anything else to say.

Era fished the now cooled work piece out of the water with the tongs. "It's a better wheel hub." He handed it to Danil. The piece of shipsteel was round and as big as his hand, with a flange on the outside to hold the spokes and a hole in the center to take the axle. "Try it, see how it works." He pointed to a rounding jig with a finished wheel on it.

Danil put down the hub and took the wheel from the jig, held it by the axle and gave it a spin. It turned smoothly and easily, and he smacked the edge of it to speed it up, until finally the spokes were a blur.

"It's so quiet." Danil had little exposure to wheels or hubs, but every wagon he'd ever seen squeaked and rattled while the wheels went around.

"No other wheel in the world spins like that."

Danil nodded silently, unable to take his eyes off the simple magic he was holding. "How did you do it, Era?"

"A smoother bearing surface. Two pieces of shipsteel, shaped against each other hot so they fit perfectly."

Danil nodded, so engrossed with the motion that at first he didn't notice the subtle force twisting the wheel in his hands, but it grew steadily until finally it threatened to take the axle right out of them.

"What makes it twist like that?" he asked.

"Like what?" Era was puzzled.

Silently Danil handed the wheel back to its creator, spun it up, and watched until the effect manifested itself.

Era's eyes widened. "I don't know what it's doing. It's a perfectly ordinary wheel, I built it myself. The hub spins better, but there's no magic to that."

Danil shook his head. "*Something* is pulling at it." He looked closely at the wheel hub, not really sure what he might be looking for that could explain what he had experienced.

Era nodded. "Something is. I never noticed that, but I've always spun it in the jig."

They spun the wheel again in the jig, which resolved nothing, and then spun it a few more times, taking turns holding it. They found that sometimes the wheel tried to turn itself sideways and sometimes it didn't. It was Era who discovered that if you tried to force it to turn it would always resist the movement, which was strange, but it was Danil who discovered that it twisted most if you faced foreward or aftward, and not at all if you faced spinward or antispinward, which was stranger still.

"How can it know the difference?" he wondered. "It's just a piece of wood and shipsteel."

Era shrugged. "I don't know."

"Do other wheels do it?"

"I don't know that either. Other wheels don't spin so well as mine."

Danil faced foreward and spun the wheel again, and held it as it turned slowly through a full circle. Something about the motion seemed familiar . . .

"Let's take it outside," he said, sudden inspiration in his voice. "I have an idea."

They went out the back into Era's yard, full of piled scrap and ingots of shiny shipsteel. Danil pointed up at the foredome, where the faint stars revolved in the blackness between the central glare where the suntube touched it and the grey mist that shrouded the top of the forewall. "Watch the stars . . ." He faced foreward, held the wheel vertically and spun it up. " . . . and watch the wheel."

They watched and Danil shifted his grip as the wheel twisted, allowing it to move the way it wanted to and spinning it up again when it started to slow down.

"What should I be seeing?" asked Era.

"The wheel stays aligned with the stars. It's moving with them, but we aren't, so to us it looks like it's the wheel that's twisting."

Surprise came into the blacksmith's face. "You're a clever one. How did you guess that?"

"Something seemed familiar, and it was the rate of twist, the same as the speed the stars go around. You could keep time with it, if you could keep it spinning somehow."

"That's clever, though you'd put the timeringers out of business," said the smith. "You could be a mechanographer, young man."

"Do you think so?"

"I do. Now I have that hub to finish, and I'm sure you've got something to trade those hooks for."

Danil nodded. He'd stayed as long as he could. They went back into the forge. Era restarted his bellows, and Danil went out, his hunger returned, and his temporary respite from Hatch over. He checked carefully at the doorway, saw no one hostile, and stepped into the street. It was crowded with horses and wagons, merchants and customers, and he threaded his way through the throng, staying to the side where he was out of the way, less likely to attract attention. Six hooks bought a couple of loaves of dark bread from a baker, three more bought some smoked trout. He split one loaf in half and made a sandwich of the trout, and devoured half of it on the spot. That tamed his immediate hunger, and he put the rest of it under his shirt and made his way back to his nest on the waterfront, hidden behind a fence-board rigged to be a doorway just big enough for him.

His nest wasn't much, just a dilapidated wooden box by a net spinner's shop on the wharf, once used to hold carved balsa floats, and now used to hold nothing. He had made it more comfortable with a section of discarded sail canvas to sleep under. The float box was part of a tangle of disused gear by the side of the shop, most of uncertain purpose and all of it broken. The net spinner was an old man with failing vision, and his business was slowly dying. Neither he nor his customers ever came to Danil's side of the shop, and that suited Danil just fine. He had slept under a wharf his first week in the city, and it hadn't been pleasant.

He climbed into his box and left the lid open. A loose board on the bottom lifted to reveal a tiny, hidden space and he undid his belt bag and put hooks and the token in it. Only then did he lie back to enjoy the rest of his sandwich. He felt safe in his nest, and the suntube was warm on his face. He could look up and around the arch of the world overhead, watch the fishing rafts high up on the ocean's curve, sails bright in the sun. It seemed they should slide down, that all the water arching over his head should slosh down to flood the bottom of the world's cylinder, that the people who lived on the other side of the suntube should fall, as everything fell from a higher place to a lower one. They never did though, regardless of what Danil Fougere thought they should do, so he just looked up at it and wondered. Somewhere up there was Cove, where he'd grown up, and he was suddenly filled with longing for the home he'd had there, for his parents, for his brother and his sister. It was always like that after he had been to Era's. It was nice to spend time with the big blacksmith, to not have to be afraid for those few precious minutes, but it always reminded him of what it was he had lost. A flight of ducks flew over in V formation, and he found himself wishing he could fly as they did, just fly across the world to home and safety. He was suddenly overcome with loss and sadness, and he pulled the lid of his box down over himself, and finished his sandwich in the dark. When it was done he curled up tight in his sail, stomach full, but still empty in a way the meal could not satisfy. He felt that he should be crying, but he had no tears. Instead he closed his eyes and willed himself to go to sleep.

Sleep was slow in coming. The fight with Hatch's gang had been frightening, and he wondered if he should leave Far Bay. For most of his life he'd known the city as nothing more than a shape, an outline blotched in buildings against the ocean shore, halfway up the curve of the world. It was the place he looked to when his father was away to trade their catch, a place the older fishers told stories of, a place that seemed mythical even though he could see it directly. It touched the ocean with a tangle of docks and fishing rafts and the forest with rows of neat houses set into the rising upper shore. The space between was a bewildering maze of merchants and mongers and crafters, smokesheds and warehouses. Danil wasn't comfortable with so many people doing so many things in such close proximity, and moreover the place *smelled*, of dried fish and wood smoke and leather and sweat and too many people in too little space. He didn't like that at all. He'd had a plan, when he first arrived. In Cove, all the children dived for clams. All you had to do was line up at the dock and get on the next raft going out clamming. It was hard work, but fun, and you got a quarter of all you could bring up. He'd gone down to the docks his first day in the city, expecting it to be the same, but in Far Bay there were more children willing to dive than there were spaces on rafts to take them out to the clam beds. Every gang worked with a certain raft captain, and Danil had gotten his first beating for intruding on someone else's turf. He'd gone hungry that first night, and the next as well. He'd had to learn quickly to scavenge for what he could sell, to hide while the city worked and move in the sleeping hours. *At least I'm surviving now.* More than that the world seemed unwilling to grant him.

He fell asleep at last, listening to the gentle waves lapping against the dock pilings, and woke up to the distant chiming of the mid-sleep bells, feeling better. He yawned and stretched, and opened the lid of his nest, squinting his eyes against the suntube's brightness. *Today's work feeds tomorrow's hunger.* His father's words overcame his residual drowsiness, and he climbed out of his nest and went out into the wharf street, idly munching on his second loaf of bread. The shop fronts were closed and shuttered, the streets silent. It felt strange to be alone in the city, but it was safer than going out in the waking hours. He followed the suntube forewards, towards the thick band of forest that separated the ocean from the patchwork farm fields of the Prophetsy. A couple of times he had to duck into doorways or behind fences to stay out of the way of the sleep-watch. Soon he was out of Far Bay, into the forest and away from anyone who might care that he was awake while they slept. For a short distance he followed the trading road. It was a good road, the quickest route through the trees to the forelands, and laid with baked clay bricks to prevent rutting. It was also patrolled by the sleep-watch, and at the forest's edge it met the barricade wall controlled by the Prophetsy's elite inquisitors. Getting caught by either group was not in his plan.

Instead he cut into the woods, following a faint animal track that he knew. This part of the forest had never been logged, and the tall oaks and ironwoods towered overhead, creating a permanent twilight beneath their shade. He kept his eyes open in case he ran into one of the rare leopards, but saw nothing. Occasionally a rustling in the undergrowth told of a squirrel or other small herbivore. Yesterday's rain still dampened the ground, and the air was rich and humid as the moisture steamed from the saturated ground. Some of the ancient trees were hung heavy with kudzu vine, the others had their lower reaches covered in moss. A couple of kilometers foreward the forest changed, with younger trees interspersed with tall bamboo. The underbrush was thicker there, and it made for harder going. He pushed his way forward, until he broke through at a hundred meter wide clearing, broken only by a few low thickets of blackberry. On the other side of it was the tall resined-brick wall that separated the forest and the fisherfolk from the Prophetsy. It was a good five meters high, and every two hundred meters there was a watchtower on the forelander side. At the clearing he paused, looking carefully left and right, because sometimes the inquisitors had spotters patrolling the forest side of the wall as well. He couldn't help but marvel at the way the wall curved up and around the world, gradually thinning to a line as it climbed the world's arch, to a thread as it went vertical in the distance and then circled overhead, until finally it vanished in the glare of the suntube.

He returned his attention to the closest watchtowers. Not every tower was manned all the time, especially in the sleeping hours. When he was satisfied that the coast was clear he ran across and, cat-agile, leapt up to grab for the rough edges of the bricks, climbing as easily as he'd climbed the trees around Cove. He paused as his head cleared the top, checking again for patrolling inquisitors. On the top of the wall there was a walkway three meters wide and a meter and a half down from the top, and when he was sure no one had seen him he pulled himself up and over in one fluid motion, rolled across the walkway and grabbed the lip to flip himself down on the other side of the wall. He held on just long enough to check his fall, let go and rolled again when he hit the ground. He smiled to himself as he came up running. No doubt the forelanders thought their wall was an obstacle, and maybe to the town boys it was, but the children of Cove grew up swimming and climbing, and he had always been the best at both in his peer group. The forelands were mostly a patchwork of cultivated fields, but next to the wall it was all pasture, and five hundred meters foreward there was a plot of woods. He ran hard, made it to the trees, and slowed once he was among them.

The trees were mostly oak and beech, not as big as they were in the aftward forests but big for a foreland forest. He came to a clearing surrounding a crude, rutted road and he slowed, moving cautiously now. Up ahead came the rhythmic ringing of axes on wood. It was still two hours short of the breakfast bell, but the Prophet's slave crews worked sixteen hours a day. He stole closer to the sounds, choosing his route carefully. The road turned a corner, and the clearing widened. At its edges a crew of Prophetsy slaves were felling trees, sweating under the suntube's heat, and Danil crouched down beside a thick oak trunk to watch. There were three dozen or so, and the rhythmic *thunk, thunk* of their axes echoed through the woods. Half a dozen crew-drivers guarded them, occasionally applying their leather short-whips to encourage the work along. He watched the activity for a while, satisfying himself that his arrival hadn't caused any change in the rhythm of their work. Once he was sure they hadn't seen him he clambered up the oak, keeping the trunk between him and the workers. He found a comfortable fork ten meters up and settled himself down to wait.

They kept at it steadily as time slid past. It took two or three backbreaking hours for a pair of men to chop their way through one of the thick trunks, angling their cuts to bring the big trees down onto already cleared land. When the tree fell they could be injured or killed if they didn't get out of the way, a task made difficult by the short neck-rope that linked their shipsteel slave collars together. A buck crew cut the fallen giants into manageable logs to be dragged away by the toiling haul crews, forty or more men yoked into traces and straining under a driver's lash. The crew's passivity puzzled Danil. *Why don't they fight back?* To him it seemed the obvious thing to do. Their axes were only slightly less effective weapons than the spears the drivers carried, and the advantage the guards enjoyed in armor was more than offset by the imbalance in numbers. If the slaves chose they would make short work of their captors. Instead they endured the abuse and worked on. *Why don't they even run away?* All a slave had to do was cut his neck rope and vanish into the forest. *But they don't.* It didn't really matter, the forelanders were strange in a lot of ways. What did matter was that, sooner or later, the food wagon would arrive, and the drivers would herd the slaves over to eat. When that happened the odds were good that someone would leave a tool unguarded, and Danil could be able to keep himself fed for a few more days.

A foraging squirrel caught his attention, and he watched as the small creature diligently scoured acorns from the forest floor and ran them up to its hidden storehouse high in another tree. Unlike the laboring slaves it was well aware of his presence, and carefully avoided coming too close to his tree. He slowly became engrossed in its antics, so much so that the sudden silence in the forest took him by surprise. He looked up to see the clearing emptying, the slaves filtering foreward. The food wagon had arrived. Danil looked around carefully, alert for any stragglers, and then, as agile as the squirrel, swung himself down through the oak's thick branches. The forest floor was soft against his toes, and he crouched instinctively. *It wouldn't be good to get caught.* Carefully he crept towards the work area, keeping to the shadows where the leafy canopy blocked the suntube, and choosing his path for both cover and silence. Still-white stumps dotted the area, and the ground was churned by dragged logs. He could hear voices coming faintly down the crude logging road; the forelanders weren't far. He went to one half-felled forest giant, quickly checked around its base, found nothing. He moved to the next and the next, again coming up empty handed. It seemed the slaves had taken their tools with them. The axe-head he'd traded to Era had come from this very crew, and the slave who'd lost it would have been punished. The rest would be more careful for a while.

He checked the remaining trees the crew had been working on and found nothing. That was disappointing, and there was a temptation to look further, but the key to scavenging shipsteel from the Prophetsy was caution. Impatience would get him caught, sooner or later. He turned to go, and then he saw it, so obvious that he was momentarily astounded that he hadn't before. It was not just an axe but a whole pile of axes, arranged to lean against each other and form a neat pyramid, and he found his heart suddenly pounding. This wasn't just a score, this was *wealth*. The pile was just down the crude road, close to the edge of the clearing, but out of sight of the meal wagon. He ran to it, checking down the road to make sure the slaves weren't on their way back. There were eight axes, and it was immediately apparent he couldn't carry them all in a bunch, not easily anyway. Working quickly and quietly he disassembled the pile, being careful not to let it clatter to the ground. He stacked his prizes head to head and haft to haft, and stripped off his shirt to tie them into a bundle. Once that was done he picked the burden up and turned to steal out of the clearing.

Something slammed into his head, flashing pain and sending him sprawling forward. He scrambled up, ready to run on reflex and found himself facing a leveled spearhead. He saw crimson cloth and shipsteel, and looked up to find hard eyes on his. He froze. Where the crew drivers were to be avoided, the inquisitor warrior-priests earned dread.

"Don't try to run, little boy," his assailant warned, lethal intent clear in his voice. "We've got arrows on you."

Danil darted his eyes left and right, saw the scarlet uniforms in the tree line on either side, bows drawn. He was caught.

"Smart move." The inquisitor nodded approvingly as he saw Danil's realization that he had nowhere to go. "Get on your belly." Danil complied, felt a knee forced into the small of his back, and then his arms yanked back and expertly tied behind him. The soldier cinched the knots tight and secured the rope to Danil's belt. A second length of rope went around his neck in a tight loop.

"Mik!" The man yelled. "Get over here and take him up to the camp."

Another soldier came running, this one shorter and not quite as lean. He took Danil's neck rope and led him up the road. As they came up to the slave crew he saw a familiar face standing beside the head driver, younger than the others, smirking in triumph. *Hatch.* The pile of tools hadn't been left by accident, the inquisitors were no coincidence. Danil had been sold out.

## Shipyear 3839

Prophet Polldor paced impatiently around the confines of the Prophet's tower. The room was sumptuously appointed, the shipsteel floors covered in thick rugs and the walls in intricately dyed quilts. They served both to keep out the damp and the chill of the forewall lands, and to advertise to any visitor the refinement of the Prophet's taste. The tower was the highest point in the

Prophet's temple and, when the mists allowed it, the view was the best in the world, encompassing everything from his temple aftward, over the close-crowded buildings of Charity to the blue ring of the ocean against the aftwall. It was *his* world, every last square meter of it, though the fisherfolk didn't yet acknowledge his rule. *They will though, and soon.* His people outnumbered them by five to one at least. When he was ready, he would move, and when he was finished, his authority over his world would be absolute.

He frowned at the thought. *So why is it I have no authority in my own house?* He shot a glance at his chief slave, who waited silently in his niche to be called for. The man carefully didn't meet his master's gaze, and the Prophet smirked at his subservience. *He knows when to avoid calling attention to himself.* For a moment he considered sending the servant out of the room, but he dismissed the thought. The man had outlived his usefulness anyway.

There was a knock at the door and he looked up sharply. "Enter."

The door opened and his daughter came in, dressed in blue, looking beautiful. Her eyes were quick and intelligent, and she carried herself with the aloof confidence of a woman who knew she aroused desire in every man who saw her.

"You sent for me, Father?"

Polldor looked at his child, momentarily unable to speak. She looked like her mother, who had been by far his most beautiful wife. Also like her mother, she was willful, disobedient and devious, a never-ending source of trouble. She smiled, and his frustration faded. No matter what she did, he found it impossible to stay angry with her. *It's not her fault.* She was his firstborn, and her mother had died in childbirth. *And what did I know of parenting a girl?* She was his firstborn and was still his favorite, and he had spoiled her. He was paying for that now. *But she's not a child anymore, and this needs to end for once and for all.* He suppressed the urge to embrace her in greeting, and turned to look out the windows, to steel himself for what he had to do.

"Father?"

Polldor took a deep breath and turned around. "Annaya, are you pregnant?"

His daughter blushed. *At least she still has the decency for that.* "No, Father, of course not."

"Of course nothing. I know what you've been doing."

"Father! I . . ."

Polldor slashed a hand through the air to silence her. "No. I won't hear you lie about it." He turned away to look out the window again. "Did you think I wouldn't find out? Here in my own temple?"

Her eyes flashed with sudden anger. "I thought you would respect my privacy."

"Privacy? You're the Prophet's daughter, and you expect privacy?" He cut her off before she could answer, his affection overcome by resurging anger. "Nothing you do is private. Nothing!" He pointed at his chief slave. "This man here is witness to everything happening right here, right now. Do you think it won't be all over the temple by the evening bell?"

In his niche the slave stood stock still, his face a mask of fright, and Polldor smirked. *At least someone still fears me.*

"Do you think I care what a slave knows?"

"Do you think nobody listens to slaves? Tell me who he is!"

"I won't." She spat the words, her anger changed to defiance.

Polldor felt his face darken. "You'll regret it if you don't."

"I'll regret it more if I do."

"You stupid little girl!" Polldor shouted, now angry beyond recovery. "You stupid, selfish little girl." He saw the impact of his words in her face and instantly regretted them, but it was too late. *And she gets her temper from me, I can't deny that.*

"Go on, why don't you just hit me and get it over with," she screamed back. "Hit me again, maybe it will make you feel better."

Polldor looked away, his throat working, wondering at how quickly the interview had become a fight. He *had* hit her once, when she was twelve, when she had stolen something—he couldn't even remember what now. She'd lied about it, and he'd hit her and bloodied her nose, and felt guilty about it every day since. She had never, ever let him forget it.

"No, Annaya." He fought to keep his voice calm, to de-escalate the situation. "I won't hit you. I've never been able to punish you, and that's the real problem. I didn't know how to raise a daughter."

"You didn't know how to raise a son either," Annaya shot back.

Polldor's lips compressed at her words. "Don't speak that way about your brother."

"What? Are you going to tell me Olen is everything you ever hoped for in an heir?"

"He's young. He'll mature."

Annaya snorted. "By which you mean he'll grow breasts. He's more of a girl than I am. And he's not my brother."

"Olen is not what we're here to discuss."

"Which is what? My sleeping habits?"

"You are the Prophet's daughter, not some crew-begotten concubine! What do you think the Elder Council will say when they hear about your indiscretions?"

"That collection of dried fruit? They'll all be jealous I wasn't in their beds."

"Annaya! Don't speak like that!"

"What, you don't like that I have sex?"

Her words struck him like a physical blow. "In the name of Noah, please tell me you're not pregnant!"

"What business is it of yours?"

"I'm your father!"

"It's my body, *Father*." She put sarcastic stress on the last word. "I'll do what I want with it. Including get it pregnant, if that's what I want."

Polldor felt his anger return full force. "It is *not* your body. Do you think this is only about you? You think Olen is weak? Well, so what if you're right; he'll be Prophet, weak or strong. And what do you think will happen then?"

"Why would I care?"

"Because you *need* to care. Do you think Bishop Nufell of Sanctity is going to let a weak boy rule the round world from here to the ocean? Do you think the Mertells of Charity will? Olen is going to need support." He pointed his finger at her chest. "He's going to need support from *you*. And *you* are going to get support from the family you're placed with." He held up a hand to forestall her protest. "Which *will* be someone with position and title and something worthwhile to offer, and *not* be some landless second-son inquisitor mark-leader with come-hither eyes." He saw the look of shock come into her eyes. "Oh yes, I know who it is."

Annaya set her jaw. "So why did you bother to ask?"

"Because I wanted your cooperation." Polldor threw his hands in the air. "For once!"

"Well, you aren't going to get it." His daughter folded her arms across her chest with finality. "Are we finished yet?"

"Don't defy me, girl." A note of warning crept into the Prophet's voice.

"Or what? You're going to take my dolls away?"

Polldor sighed heavily. "I'm not going to punish you, Annaya."

"Well then, I think we're done." She turned up her nose and turned to go.

"No, we're not done." Polldor's voice was suddenly cold, and he jerked his head at his chief slave. "Bring him."

The slave bowed. "At once, your Holiness." He came out of his niche and pulled a bell-rope fastened to the wall beside it. The ropes led over a set of small tacklewheels and out one of the windows, down to the servitor level below. A minute later the doors burst open in front of two drivers. They were dragging a crucifix with a third man nailed to it, blood crusted on his wrists and ankles. He was dressed in the remnants of an inquisitor's cloak, what was left of it hanging in shreds, and had a mark-leader's scarf still fastened at his neck. He had been savagely beaten, his body covered in bruises, bleeding where short-whips had stripped off his skin. He hung there semi-conscious, his eyes swollen shut.

"Sem!" Annaya's eyes flew wide in horror.

Polldor made a gesture and the drivers dropped their captive on the floor, and his daughter ran to his side and knelt by him, putting a hand to his cheek. The beaten man looked up at her and tried to say something, but couldn't form the words. "Sem!" She looked up at her father. "You bastard! It wasn't his fault."

"Someone has to be punished, Annaya." Polldor gestured to the drivers. "Finish him."

"What? No!" Annaya screamed and threw herself on top of the prostrate figure. The senior driver lifted his spear at the Prophet's command, but hesitated. Annaya looked up at him, eyes blazing. "Touch him and I'll kill you myself."

"Finish him!" Polldor commanded again, but still the driver hesitated, looking for an angle where he could thrust his spear without committing the fatal error of injuring the Prophet's daughter. Polldor spat in disgust and advanced on the tableau. He wrenched the spear from the hapless slave keeper's grasp. "Get her off him."

Relieved to have an easier command to obey, the drivers grabbed Annaya and hauled her, struggling and kicking, up and away from her lover's body. Polldor took the spear and drove it into the crucified man's throat. He convulsed and his eyes flew open in sudden recognition that he was about to die. Blood gurgled as he struggled to breathe, thrashing against the nails in his wrists and ankles, until finally his body twitched and went limp.

"NO!" Annaya tore herself free of the drivers and leapt at Polldor, knocking him over in her fury. He cracked the side of his head hard against the table on the way down, and then the guards were on her, pulling her back.

Polldor stood up slowly, putting a hand to his head where it'd struck the table. "Let her go." He waved a hand, feeling suddenly tired. "Let her go."

The drivers did as they were told, and Annaya went to her lover's body and knelt there, sobbing, putting her arms around him as though she could bring him back to life, oblivious to the blood soaking into her clothes.

"You two, go down to the first watch post and wait there. Discuss this with no one. I'll be down shortly." Polldor turned to his chief slave. "You, back to your alcove." He didn't bother to watch them obey. His anger had evaporated, leaving him feeling . . . hollow. Annaya was still crying, and he wanted, more than anything, to go to her and comfort her, as he had when she was small. He fought down the urge. *The last thing she wants right now is anything from me.* Instead he turned and went out the main door, down the stairs to the antechamber below, absently rubbing his chest where she'd slammed into him in her charge. It hurt almost as much as his skull did. *And she fought off two drivers to do that.* He was proud of his daughter, despite the trouble she caused him, proud of her ferocity and her strength. *If Olen had her spirit, I wouldn't have to worry so much about who she was placed with.* But Olen's mother was a woman of exceptional beauty and little substance, and he had inherited none of his father's strength of will. He went through another door into his day-room. One wall was layered with ironwood boxes ranked on polished shelves, each containing the ashes of one of his ancestors. A lone crucifix adorned the opposite wall, weapons and crimson inquisitorial banners adorned the other two. A heavy chair sat facing the encircling windows, a carved oak side table beside it. Most of the windows were glass, but two of them had been broken long ago, and wooden shutters covered the empty spaces.

He went to the chair and sat down heavily. "You heard, Balak?" he asked.

"Enough, your Holiness." A figure moved from where it had

been standing, so still it seemed merely part of the furniture. Polldor's High Inquisitor came forward to stand beside his Prophet. He was not a large man, but he was corded tight with muscle and his calm face held dangerous eyes.

"Such a waste. Sem Vesely was a fine leader." Polldor poured himself a mug of wine from the baked clay flask on the table, and swallowed it in a gulp.

"He broke his vows, Prophet. He sullied the holy flesh of your daughter." There was an edge in Balak's words. "His life and soul are forfeit."

"No doubt." Polldor poured himself another mug of wine. "Also no doubt it was Annaya's idea."

"What must I do?"

"The slave needs to die. He'll be waiting in his place."

The High Inquisitor bowed, a deference he gave only to the son of Noah. "And the drivers?"

"Them too."

"Noah's hand guides you, Prophet."

Polldor nodded. *Noah's hand guides me, and the fate of the man who touched Annaya will go around the gallery by the evening-meal bell.* He smiled to himself. Fear was not his preferred tool of rulership, but there was no questioning its effectiveness. *And Balak will reinforce that.* No redcloak would dare touch his daughter again.

Balak had turned to go, but he paused. "You're concerned?"

"Annaya . . ." The Prophet sighed heavily and drained the wine mug again. "I only pray she isn't carrying that man's child."

"God has not willed it so."

"I wish I was as certain as you, Balak. Just watch her. We need to make sure this problem doesn't occur again."

"That's impossible."

"Impossible?" Polldor looked sharply at his High Inquisitor. "I'll lock her up if I have to."

"That will only delay the inevitable. Do you think the man you place her with will be able to control her? She is of Noah's line. Her will is celestial, subservient only to you and her brother."

"Not subservient enough to me, that's one thing I'm certain of. She's ripe and she knows it, and she'll bear children for the man *she* chooses, regardless of the man I choose for her." Polldor mopped his brow. "I just need her to wait until after she's placed."

Balak raised an eyebrow. "Why not place her now?"

"Her value is in the desire of the senior families to tie their lineages to mine. As long as they're competing for her she brings me power, and they'll compete as long as they think she's still untouched." The Prophet bit his lip. "Once she's placed she can do what she wants. In fact I hope she does. Not one of the Elder Council is fit to sire me a grandson, inbred bootlicks, all of them."

"None of them are worthy, but whatever child she bears will be exalted, Holiness. The chosen family will be honored no matter who the father."

"Yes. And more important, no senior son of a senior family is going to admit he's been made cuckold by the Prophet's daughter. His humiliation would be total. Whatever she does, they'll hush it up. They'll have to. No, she needs to be controlled until she's placed. After that, I don't care."

"Controlling her will be difficult, even for that much time."

Polldor turned to examine one of the tapestries. "I know. It's my own fault. I should never have allowed her to play in the gallery, but she loved the horses, and the inquisitors. She wanted to shoot and ride. She had such spirit! And it seemed so innocent when she was young."

"I'm sure it was innocent, Prophet. When she was young."

The Prophet looked back to Balak. "She's grown up so fast. What was I thinking?"

"Could you have stopped her?"

Polldor pursed his lips. "Perhaps not. She's so headstrong. And I suppose I encouraged her. I saw in her what Olen lacks. I wish I could let her do what she wanted. What a waste."

"He betrayed his oath to Noah's line." Balak's tone carried the weight of final judgement.

Polldor gave his High Inquisitor a look. "Your strength and your weakness is your faith, Balak." He threw his hands up. "I'm cursed, do you know that? I've got a dozen wives, mounted more women than any man in this *Ark*, and what have I sired? Two children, that's all. Two children, a weak boy and a willful girl, Noah's idea of a joke. She could do what she wanted if I had more daughters, or a single son with yats." He brought his arms down and paced impatiently. "If word of this gets out, what can I offer the senior families?"

"They should follow you because of who you are, Holiness. It is unseemly that they require more than that."

"Unseemly perhaps, but that's the reality."

"Those who don't recognize the ascendance of Noah's line should be punished, not rewarded."

"Also true, but I can't unleash your blade on all of them. No. I need Annaya. I need their competition for Annaya."

"You have land enough, and soon you'll have much more. Offer them that instead."

"If I give them my daughter, I get their land and their allegiance together. If I give them my land—they get my land and still owe little allegiance. Better they supplicate for the chance to marry into it. No, she'll stay pure until I'm ready to place her. She'll *obey*. By my name, I'm her father!"

"As she should. The Prophet's word is as sacred as his line." There was something intense behind Balak's eyes, something dangerous. "Take my word that no inquisitor will dare touch her again." Balak moved and suddenly his blade was in his hand, shipsteel glinting. "I'll cleanse the slave now, and the others."

Polldor nodded, and his High Inquisitor went out. For a long time the Prophet just sat where he was, contemplating the shutters where the broken windows had been. From upstairs he could still hear Annaya sobbing. *It was necessary.* He repeated the thought to himself. *It was a lesson she had to learn, and she'll be thankful, eventually.* But he couldn't shake the feeling that in winning this last battle with her he had lost everything.

"Wake up you sons of dogs, wake up!" The head driver walked down the line of slave pens, drumming his spear haft against the bars. "Today is a beautiful day to serve the Prophet."

In his pen Danil stretched and stood, along with the other half dozen slaves in his crew, blinking sleep from his eyes. With well practiced motions he folded the worn flax tarp that served him as a blanket and tucked it into the accidental niche between the board that served as his bed and the corner of the cage. Already the ropemaster was coming down the line. Obediently the men lined up against the bars and held their leash-lines out through the harnessing slot. When the ropemaster got to them he deftly threaded the harness line through the loops. The other ends of the leash lines were spliced to their shipsteel slave collars. Behind him came the drivers with their keys, unlocking the cage doors and leading their charges out for breakfast. Danil's crew had a new driver that day, a heavyset, muscular man of about his own age. Something about him seemed familiar, but it wasn't until he spoke that Danil recognized him. *Hatch!* At first he couldn't believe it, but there was no question that it was his childhood nemesis. The man had the same arrogant swagger as the boy he had known. It was Hatch, no question. *But what is he doing here?*

Their new driver prodded them out of the slave shed. Breakfast was already waiting for them, boiled grain and boiled yam and boiled pork. It was unappetizing fare, but filling. The Prophetsy's slaves ate well enough, if only because the Prophet recognized that starving slaves did little work. The cooks ladled out the food into wooden bowls, which were passed down the line as each crew filed past. The men gulped down their morning meal standing up, and the bowls were passed back to be used by the next group. Hatch herded them along to the road that led down to the brickworks. He didn't seem to have recognized Danil, and Danil was content to leave it that way. As they walked, Danil looked longingly aftward, to the green band of the forest, and the blue of the ocean beyond it. He could recognize Far Bay, halfway up the curve of the world, but his home village of Cove was too small, and too close to the suntube to see at this distance. *And there's nothing left for me in Cove anyway.* In truth there was nothing for him in Far Bay either. He'd had little enough when he was there, and he hadn't been there long enough even to consider it home. *How many years has it been?* Too many to count.

It was still an hour before the breakfast bell when they got to the brickworks, and the overseer assigned the crews to their jobs as they came in the gate, gesturing with the staff that was his badge of authority, and his tool of control should any slave step out of line. Danil's crew was assigned to the digging, shovelling heavy bottom-clay from the dig pit into wooden wheelbarrows so the carriers could push it up to the worksite above. When he'd first come to the forelands Danil had been surprised to find houses built of brick, like the Prophetsy wall. It took so much more work to build with brick than timber, the way the fisherfolk did. Only slowly had he come to realize the underlying reality. The Prophetsy had only a few patches of woodlot left, and the fisherfolk controlled the aftward forests. That made brick cheap and lumber expensive. The brickworks were a good three kilometers from the forewall, as close to the Prophet's temple as it could be without having the foredome mists interfere with the drying of the bricks. For the slaves it meant laboring under the suntube's relentless glare, and longing for the fleecy clouds that spiralled up from the aftwall to bring a cooling rain.

Hatch let them know he intended to set a production record that shift, and laid on his short-whip to reinforce the point. In a bell their smocks were caked in mud, in two they were barely recognizable beneath it. Four of the six slave crews worked at once, on overlapping shifts of sixteen hours. At the noon bell the crew that had been on before theirs was replaced, and they had time to gulp another quick ration of yam and pork stew before moving up from the clay pit to take their turn at the mixing trough, churning cut straw into the clay with paddles until it was ready for the molders, then carrying the finished bricks off so they could dry in the suntube's heat.

It was gruelling work, and by the evening-meal bell sheer exhaustion had slowed their pace, though there were still two hours to go before shift-end. Hatch grew more impatient as the bells passed, determined to see his crew exceed the day's quota, plying his whip so hard he was sweating almost as much as the slaves. He constantly threatened to send them to the finish crew, who did the backbreaking job of hauling the dried bricks to the resin soak to be waterproofed and stacking them on the shipping carts. *But he won't do it.* Much as the driver would have liked to punish someone with the finish crew, sending slaves away would only put the driver farther from his quota. Finally the overseer blew his horn, and the welcome sight of the relief crews came through the gates. They began the cleanup routine, shuffling down to the river to rinse their paddles and themselves, and then to fill buckets to wash the dried mud off the mixing trough. It was on the second trip that Hatch brought Danil up short with tap of the whip-handle against his chest.

"Do I know you?"

Danil shook his head, trying to suppress his sudden fear. "I don't think so, sir."

Hatch looked him up and down slowly, settled his eyes on Danil's face. "I do know you. Where are you from?"

"The aftlands," Danil answered. It was technically true, though in Prophetsy usage the aftlands ended at the Prophetsy wall.

"The aftlands." Hatch considered that. "No, I don't think so . . ."

Recognition slowly dawned in his eyes. "You're from Far Bay, that thieving guppy . . ." He smirked. "Well guppy, it's been a long time. I'm going to have a lot of fun with you."

Perhaps it was the cruelty in Hatch's smile, perhaps the remembered humiliation of being bullied and chased, but something in Danil snapped, and in an instant his fear was replaced by red rage. He brought his full bucket up and around, catching Hatch in the side of the face, knocking him sprawling and soaking him at the same time.

"You son of a dog!" Hatch spat in anger and advanced on Danil, short-whip upraised. "You're going to die today, guppy."

Danil took a step back and put his arms up as if to fend off the coming blow. Hatch brought the whip down, and as he did so Danil brought his own arm down to intersect the lash. It hit his forearm and wrapped around it to cut painfully against his side. He ignored the pain and grabbed the whip handle, yanking hard. The move caught Hatch off guard and he fell forward, stumbling. As soon as his enemy was in range Danil swung his now-empty bucket, catching Hatch across the side of the head and sending him sprawling. Danil advanced on him until his collar brought him up short. The driver was still too far away to hit with the bucket again so Danil dropped it and pulled the whip handle into his hand. He raised the lash and swung, bringing it down hard on Hatch's back. Hatch screamed in pain and rolled over, and Danil brought the lash down again, once, twice, three times before the other man managed to scramble out of range. Hands grabbed him from behind, the slaves behind him, and he fought to get free. It seemed a betrayal of the deepest kind for them to do it, though some distant part of him realized they were only trying to avoid sharing in his inevitable punishment.

Hatch was already up and coming at him, his face contorted in fury. He drove a fist into Danil's face, drove another into his solar plexus and Danil doubled over in agony. The other man brought his elbow down on Danil's skull and pain exploded through his head. He saw stars and fell forward, his collar again choking him as the rope to the next slave brought him up short. The man behind him fell too, and Danil tumbled the rest of the way to the ground. He drew his knees up in front of him and put his arms over his head as Hatch started kicking at him. Other drivers came running, drawn by the commotion. Behind them the overseer stepped down from his shack. Work across the site came to a halt as the other crews stopped to watch. For a slave to be whipped, even beaten was a mundane occurrence. For it to happen because the slave had assaulted a driver was very rare indeed.

Eventually Hatch tired of punishing Danil, and the overseer stepped forward.

"What happened here?" His voice was sharp.

"This sooksan hit me. Took my own short-whip and swung it." His anger returned, Hatch landed another kick in the small of Danil's back.

"That so? Cut him loose."

One of the other drivers pulled his blade from his belt sheath and bent down to slice the rope connecting Danil to the other slaves. He hauled Danil roughly to his feet and a second driver grabbed him as well. The overseer looked him up and down, and stretched out his staff to poke Danil in the chest.

"Name?"

"Fougere."

"Fougere," The overseer nodded slowly. "I remember you, never saw you as a troublemaker. Hitting a freeman. I could have you crucified, you know that?" He jabbed his staff into Danil's gut, hard.

"I'm . . . the Prophet's property," Danil gasped out around the pain.

"Smart one too, yes?" The overseer raised his staff and brought it down again, this time across Danil's face. "You think you're too expensive to kill? I do it just to show what happens to smart ones."

"It would be God's mercy."

"That what you want? The easy way out?" The staff rose and fell again, hard enough to break the skin this time, and Danil sagged between the restraining guards. "For you the cross is too easy. We send you to the timber crew, you can die there. But not easy." He gestured with his staff. "Brand him."

The drivers holding Danil dragged him off and Hatch spat at him as they did. His captors hauled him past the drying tables where the fresh made bricks were baking beneath the suntube, to the high wall that surrounded the brickworks. There were a pair of crucifixes on either side of the entry gate, a constant reminder to the slaves of their ultimate master, and of the penalty they faced for rebellion. They yanked him up the stairs, tied ropes to his wrists and hauled him up to dangle from the cross arm. The pain in his arms was excruciating, and he watched without really seeing as they built a fire in the firebowl set into the wall's parapet. *Death would be a mercy.* But his tormentors were not that merciful. The overseer came to watch as the fire was stoked high, until the coals at the bottom flared white-orange, until the branding steel thrust into them glowed red. Danil was lowered again, and a thicker rope passed around his neck, to force his head back against the cross's hard wood. It was chokingly tight, and he struggled to breathe against its constriction. One of the drivers held the rope, the second raised the burning steel.

"Hold still for it, sooksan, or you'll make a mess and we'll do it again."

The instruction was wasted, Danil couldn't move his head a hand span in either direction, though he instinctively strained away from the approaching heat. The driver pressed it against his cheek and the seared flesh exploded into agony. The branding took only a second, but the pain went on and on, an intense, steady throbbing that suffused his skull. The driver holding the neck rope let go and Danil sagged as far as the ropes at his wrists would allow. The other put down the steel and examined his handiwork. Satisfied he gestured to the first, and together they hauled Danil back up to dangle from the cross arm once more.

"Two days on the cross." The overseer gave a satisfied smirk. "You're marked now. Out of line again and I'll nail you to it. No coming down then."

Danil didn't answer, he wasn't expected to. He was expected only to suffer. After a while the pain in his face faded to something that allowed thought, and a while after that his wrists went numb. There was no one on the cross on the opposite side of the gate, and so he suffered alone. A long time later he watched his crew trudge out, back to the slave shed. The next shift of slaves was already heading in to take over where they'd left off, twenty-four bells in a day were barely enough to labor for the Prophet's glory.

Danil barely registered the change. He had been exhausted from the work shift, and already in pain thanks to the beating Hatch had given him. The cross's tortures were progressive, as his wrists had become insensible the pain began to seep into his shoulders until they burned in agony, and as they in turn went numb the pain spread to his back. Soon hunger and thirst added to his miseries.

Despite his fatigue sleep was impossible, and time seemed to slow down and stop. There was nothing he could do but hang there. The new shift ended, and another came to replace it. The overseer came by, once, and Danil briefly hoped that his time of punishment might be over, but the man simply looked him over and then went back to supervising the work. He started counting bells, but they came so far apart that he lost track.

His mind drifted, wandering back to the time in Cove, the time before his father had died, before his mother had remarried. He remembered her tucking him into bed, and singing to him until he fell asleep. It was a time so long ago that it seemed to belong to another life, lived by another person. The suntube beat down on him relentlessly, and he began to dream of the cool, fresh water of the ocean. He could see it clearly, blue and inviting against the aftwall, seeming so close and yet so far away. He would have wept in frustration, but he couldn't spare the tears. Another shift came and went, and he wondered what had happened to his mother, to his sisters, and dreamed that they were all together again, that his father was there too.

The sharp *crack* of the overseer's staff against his shins shocked him back to the present. *How many bells have gone by?* It was impossible to know. At least a day's worth, which meant the overseer had gone home and come back again. It felt like it had been an eternity.

"So, a little calmer now, yes?" The overseer looked up at him smugly. "Ready for the lumber crew?"

Danil said nothing. The overseer had brought a driver with him, a man Danil hadn't seen before. Together they undid the ropes and lowered him, and unexpected fire shot through his feet when they touched down. He staggered and fell as his exhausted muscles took his weight. They unceremoniously clamped steel wristbands onto him and shackled them to his collar. A rope was securely knotted to the end of his leash line, and the driver led him away, past the rectangular ranks of sun-dried bricks and the laboring crews. A horse was waiting at the brickyard gate, and the driver lashed his neck rope to the saddle, then turned to Danil.

"It's like this. I'm already late for my wife, and we've got fifteen kilometers to go so I'm not stopping. Walk or be dragged, I don't care."

Without waiting for a reply he swung himself up into the saddle and stirred up his mount. The rope pulled taut and Danil was nearly yanked off his feet. He stumbled but didn't fall, and then they were off. Mercifully the driver kept the horse to a walk, but Danil's strained muscles found even that a challenge, especially as he was unable to swing his arms to balance his gait. He concentrated on moving fast enough to keep the rope slack, but time and again it tightened, earning him an unpleasant jerk on the collar. Pain shot though his abused joints with every step but there was nothing he could do but keep moving, doing his best to keep up. On the cross, he could at least escape into the refuge of delirium, but here he couldn't even do that. Every step demanded a maximum effort and soon sweat was soaking into his mud-stiffened shirt. He legs felt steel-heavy, and his bare feet throbbed under the abuse they were taking.

The driver had been serious when he'd said they weren't stopping, and Danil was utterly spent by the time they reached their destination, a slave stockade by a cut-yard full of half-finished timber. The driver turned Danil over to the cut-yard boss, who took him to a stack of felled logs. He was given an ironwood adze and put to stripping bark from the logs alongside a half dozen other slaves. His leash line was tethered to a rope that ran along another line that strung overhead, well out of reach. The arrangement gave him enough freedom of movement to do the job, but ensured he couldn't use his tool to cut the rope and run. There were six other slaves on the barking crew, and their condition wasn't encouraging. All bore cross-brands on their cheeks, and they were gaunt and listless, moving just fast enough to avoid the lash. Their eyes were dull, and they didn't speak as they mechanically went through the motions necessary to carry out their task. Danil emulated them, trying not to draw any extra attention to himself. The Prophetsy's lumber camps were notorious. Those who came back from them were changed men, broken in body and spirit, but few ever came back. Danil bit his lip. *I'm going to have to get out fast if I'm going to get out at all.*

It took Danil a while to realize that he'd made a decision to escape or die trying, and with the decision came a strange feeling of freedom. How he might carry it out in his present condition was another question. Fortunately the driver in charge of them was a fat and lazy man, who sat on an already stripped log and only bestirred himself when a slave actually stopped working. His slothfulness allowed Danil that day to recover somewhat. As long as he kept his aching limbs moving he was spared further punishment. The hardest part was simply keeping his eyes open, and he took to closing them as he worked, catching snatches of not-quite-sleep five or ten seconds at a time. Once he actually fell asleep standing up, and was rudely awakened when his collar caught him falling and nearly broke his neck.

The shift dragged on to the evening-meal bell, but there was no pause for food. The lazy driver was replaced by a younger man with something to prove, and the pace of work picked up as he plied his lash. Danil found himself unable to keep up and earned a new set of stripes for his slowness. The pain brought tears to his eyes, but he swallowed hard and refused to break down. *This is a test, and if I show weakness now I'll mark myself as a victim.* Survival depended on being tough, and how he behaved would mean the difference between getting strong enough to escape and dying slowly in his collar. *And I need a plan.* His crew was working by the forewall, where the constant mists still nourished a few stands of fast growing dougfir, and he had a long way to go to get free.

Finally the shift ended and the slaves were herded back to the pen, a crude stockade of heavy pine poles that surrounded the slaveshed, the cookhouse and a couple of other buildings of uncertain purpose. Danil was so exhausted he could barely think, but he retained the presence of mind to bring a short stick back with him, scavenged from the pile of bark and wood scraps where he'd been working. He didn't yet know what purpose he might put it to, but even in the brickyard survival had depended on seizing the smallest opportunity the instant it presented itself. They were fed the standard slave fare of boiled grain, boiled yam, and boiled pork, but the ration was half what it had been at the brickworks. The slaveshed was even more primitive than the one he had left behind. The floor was dirt and instead of separate cages there were only low shelves, three tiers of them, running around the walls of the building and covered in dirty straw. There was not even a separate latrine, just a barrel in a corner, and the place stank of urine and excrement and unwashed bodies. The preferred sleeping spaces were those far away from the barrel, but Danil lacked any status within the lumber crew hierarchy, and also lacked the strength to fight for it. He wound up right next to the stinking container, but by then he was far beyond caring. He fell immediately into a deep and dreamless sleep.

Sudden pain woke him, and it seemed he hadn't slept at all. He opened his eyes to find himself looking up at a muscular driver, his short-whip upraised.

"Get up." The guard's voice was curt and impersonal. Danil struggled to his feet. The rest of the slaves were already shuffling into crew lines to be harnessed for the day's work. He left his stick lying in a small gap between the sleeping boards and got up to join them. At the brickworks the drivers were well disciplined, and had taken great care to make sure that the slaves were always, always under control, but here they seemed lackadaisical. As Danil looked around at the gaunt, cowed faces of the other slaves he understood. The omnipresent cheek brands meant every man there had once had the will to rebel. The Prophetsy had sent them to the lumber crew to be broken of that, and it did that job very effectively, through brutality, backbreaking labor, and semi-starvation. *But lazy guards are an advantage to me.* He took note of the fence as they filed past. It was four meters high and made of pine poles, each as thick as his thigh, driven vertically into the ground side by side. It would be easy enough to climb in one of the corners, where he could brace himself against opposite walls. *First I need to recover my strength.* His stomach growled as the familiar scent of breakfast rose in the air, and the drivers ordered them out to the cookhouse. He was ravenous, but when he filed past the meal line the ration was no larger than it had been the night before. Recovering himself was going to be difficult.

He was assigned to the haul crew, yoked up with sixty others and marched past the cut-yard where he had worked the other day. They passed a squad of inquisitors on horseback, their striking crimson uniforms and evident discipline putting them in marked contrast with the sloppy drivers. Behind them was a small, well-kept building with the white, square inquisitor Cross on it, and Danil could see by their expressions that the soldiers considered themselves superior to the drivers and kept themselves apart from them. The building passed behind, and they trudged up the crude logging road to a huge dougfir trunk already levered up onto a logging arch. Their job was to drag it back down to the cut-yard to be bucked into boards and beams. They were marched around it and back, to get the array of yoked slaves facing in the right direction.

"Stop there! Hook up the lines," the overseer barked, and a couple of the drivers took the drag lines from the back of the yoke array. The heavy ropes ended in shipsteel hooks that were run into rope loops on the arch's harness.

"Take slack!" the overseer yelled, and the haul crew shuffled forward, pulling the drag lines taut while the drivers moved into place alongside the group.

"Brace!" The slaves leaned into their harness bars, ready for the next command.

"*Heave!* Heave *hard!*" the overseer yelled, and sixty bodies dug in their feet and grunted with the strain. After a second's hesitation Danil's harness bar lurched forward half a meter as they hauled the heavy tree forward. Up and down the line came the sound of whips, and the pained cries of the men who hadn't satisfied the drivers that they were pulling hard enough.

"Brace!" the overseer yelled again, and once more Danil set himself against the yoke.

"*Heave!* Heave *hard!*" Again sixty men strained to haul the huge trunk another arm's length. "Work fast, go home early."

Nobody laughed at the overseer's black humor, and nobody was going home early. The haul crew was the worst job in the camp, and the drivers needed little excuse to mete out punishment. The man behind Danil slipped and stumbled on the next pull, and the nearest driver cursed and cracked his short-whip down. Most of the stroke caught the fallen slave across the back, but the tail of the lash curled around to burn Danil's shoulder. He ignored the unexpected pain. Pain didn't matter, only survival. The man beside him was tall, with sticklike arms and legs and hollow eyes. Danil tried to start a conversation with him, hoping to get some sense of how the camp worked and what the security was like, but the slave's answers were monosyllabic and his expression was far, far away. The slave responded only to the driver's commands, and then only to the extent necessary to avoid the crack of the lash. His body functioned, but inside he was already gone. And he was one of the better off ones, as Danil looked around between pulls and realized most of the other slaves were beyond the point of no return, walking dead, waiting only for the final peace of the pyre.

The day became a blur. The overseer's voice rose and fell in steady rhythm, and Danil set his feet, leaned into the yoke and pushed in time with it, trying to move with a maximum economy of effort. A few bells into the day a man collapsed in his harness, and the drivers lashed him until it was clear he was dead. They cut his body from the traces and left it by the side of the logging trail. Danil found himself strangely unmoved, thankful only for the brief respite the incident had given from the grinding rhythm of the work. The work resumed, until at long last they were led once more to the slave pen, given their meager meal and herded into the shed. Again Danil kept his eyes open, noting the way the stockade gate was hinged and barred. From the outside he could see a walkway that ran around the entire fence, a place for guards to patrol and look down into the compound. That presented a problem, and once they got inside he took care to note where the outbuildings might provide cover for a man to hide. The problem wouldn't be getting over the wall, it would be getting over it unseen. Still, the passivity of the slaves meant that escape attempts must be vanishingly rare. Given endless sleep-shifts of stultifying lookout duty and the evident lack of discipline, the drivers on watch would be slack. It was possible that they'd be asleep themselves. He had planned to wait until he better understood how the lumber crew was guarded before he tried to escape, but he realized he couldn't afford to do that. Every day, every bell that he stayed cost him strength that he would never recover. *It has to be now.*

The guards closed the door behind them, and he took the same place he had before, lying down beside the malodorous waste barrel. He waited there, eyes wide open in the dim suntube light that filtered through the cracks in the walls, until the sounds of breathing and movement around him slowed and quieted. When he was sure the other slaves were asleep he went to the door. He had seen the heavy wooden bar used to close it from the other side, and he didn't expect it would open. It didn't, but closer inspection showed a narrow crack between the door and the frame. If he could get something thin enough to slide into the crack, he could possibly lift the bar out of its cleats and get out into the stockade, at least. *And now I know why I saved that stick.* He went back to his bed space and got it from where he had left it the previous night. He slid it into the crack and the narrow end fit, but the stick thickened along its length, and it stuck a thumb length in. Danil made a face, sat down cross legged in front of the door and began moving the stick rhythmically back and forth in the crack, wearing it down where it was too wide. He was making steady progress when the stick was suddenly snatched from his hands. There was an aggressive *growl* from the other side of the door, and Danil jumped back, startled. When he had recovered himself he looked through the crack, saw a nose, teeth, an eye. A large, black dog had taken his tool in its teeth and was pulling at it, snarling. A sudden realization struck him. *Those other buildings are kennels.* The guards were lazy because they could afford to be, with the dogs let loose in the slave pen while the slaves were asleep they had no need to worry that someone would get out unseen.

A second dog joined the first, and Danil yanked the stick out of the crack and went back to his bed space. There was nothing to do now but sleep, but sleep was elusive. The dogs changed the equation. *How to get out?* Digging a tunnel was out of the question, he had neither time nor energy, nor any way to hide the work in progress. *Maybe get some rope, get up on the roof . . .* If he got a length of rope long enough to reach from the roof to the slave pen fence . . . *Perhaps . . .* He got up again and climbed up to the top tier of the sleeping shelves, trying to avoid stepping on any of the other sleeping slaves. From the top tier he grabbed an overhead beam and pulled himself into the rafters. It was harder than it should have been, and his weakened muscles ached, but he made it up, scraping a knee and an ankle in the process. What he found was encouraging. The roof was a single layer of dougfir shingles laid over poles, and poorly maintained. He pushed gently and felt them yield. Getting through them would be easy. The roof beams themselves were substantial enough to hold his weight. *As long as the dogs don't bark when I go across.* It remained only to find a way to secure a rope to the opposite side of the fence. *And to find some rope . . .*

He climbed back down and went back to his sleeping space. This time exhaustion overcame him, and he slept at once. The next day began as the previous one had, with a shouting guard and the stroke of the short-whip. There were paw prints in the dirt outside the slave shed, more paw prints in the yard by the cookhouse, and he was surprised he hadn't noticed them before. *I'm overtired, and I'm missing things, making mistakes.* That could be fatal, and he resolved himself to pay full attention to his surroundings every waking moment. They were fed their inadequate morning meal, and he took care to examine the fence more closely as they trudged past to the day's labor. From the outside horizontal cross braces tied the vertical poles together at the level of the walkway. Climbing down from the top would be simple. The top of the fence line was uneven, with gaps where shorter poles came between taller ones. That offered a possibility. If he could get something wedged into one of the gaps, it would hold a rope.

They were led away before he had time to carry the thought further, but he had the seeds of a plan. It made the day easier, despite the barking overseer and the driver's curses and lashes. He ignored them, moving unconsciously to the rhythm of the commands, and focused his efforts on the ropes that connected his yoke on the dragline. There were three—two heavy ones to carry the load and a slightly smaller one to stabilize the yoke. He focused on that one, picking at it steadily, breaking a few more strands between every "Brace!" and "Heave!" Another man died on the shift, but Danil barely noticed. Before the mid-day meal he had one end of the rope free. Without it the yoke was harder to control, and several times it twisted as he hauled forward, causing him to slip and catch a bruise when it smacked against his ribs. It was also harder to work on the other end of the rope, where it was tied into the dragline, but he persisted, and by the end of the shift he had his first meter of line tucked into his shirtsleeve. That night he got a better space to sleep, the dead man's place, further from the waste bucket, and on the top tier. He used his short coil of rope as a pillow, and slept better than he had since he'd struck Hatch.

The next morning he put the rope up in the rafters, praying no one would find it, and worried about what he would find when he got to the dragline. The rope-work was maintained by Prophetsy saddlers, who had their own shop near the cut-yard. It couldn't be that unusual to have a line break and need repair, but the dangling, broken piece should still be attached. To have something like that go missing altogether would have been grounds for a search at the brickyard. If that happened his plan would be uncovered before it even began.

As they were lined up, he made sure to get himself into a different yoke on the haul gang, so at least no one could connect the missing rope with him. He got away with the change, which gave him hope. At the brickyard every slave was put in the same position every day, and any attempt to deviate from the routine was immediately punished. Here there weren't even any headcounts. If he could somehow manage to cover the evidence of his escape they might not even notice him missing. He got himself through the gruelling day by focusing on how soon it would be over, and came back from the shift with another length of rope. He found a better way to hide both ropes, laid out along the rough hewn top beam of the wall by his sleeping space, hidden between the curve of the timber and the wall.

As he was settling himself to sleep there was a commotion by the door, a small altercation over who was going to spend the night by the waste barrel. Two new slaves had joined them that day, young men with hard expressions, their cheek brands still healing. Their attempt to force themselves up in the timber crew's internal pecking order brought on what the Prophetsy's systematic brutality could not—a unified front among the slave population. Men who Danil had not heard a word from since he'd arrived suddenly stood up to back up the man who the newcomers had tried to displace. The new arrivals were still fresh, not yet wasted by the punishing routine. They could have held off any two, any four of the other slaves, but as more and more men stood up it became clear they'd have to take on the whole shed. The newcomers backed down and accepted their place, but deep anger smoldered in their eyes. It was an energy wholly lacking in the rest of the crew, who returned to their places and went to bed as soon as the incident was over. The new pair had not yet been broken, whereas the one thing the lumber crew veterans were willing to fight for was their right to rest. It occurred to Danil to wonder what his own face looked like, and his hand moved to his own still-healing brand. *They might prove useful, if I need allies.*

The following day he watched the newcomers. They kept together and talked quietly, and he could see them sizing up the situation, evaluating the guards, and the structures and routine of the lumber crew. He resolved himself to wait and see what they made of themselves. On the haul crew they were defiant, cursing the drivers, and the drivers matter-of-factly whipped them into submission. They lapsed into sullen obedience, which was the only sensible choice under the circumstances, but what surprised Danil was the change in their eyes. They were no longer looking around, not taking in what was around them. They were not *thinking* any longer, and he was taken aback at the rapidity of the change. He had begun to hope that he might take them into his confidence, because he could accumulate rope three times faster if he could get them to help. *But using them could be dangerous, if they're so easily defeated.* He had seen the results of that at the brickyard, where collaborators could earn themselves privileges. It was the most fearful, the most easily hurt, who were quickest to see advantage in working for their enemies. By the end of the day he had his third length of rope, but on his way back to the slave pen he stumbled, not because he had tripped over something but because his knees were suddenly too weak to support him. He recovered immediately, but the incident was a warning. He was losing strength fast. It would take another week for him to get enough rope to go from the roof of the slave shed to the fence, and by the time he had it, he might be too weak to actually make the climb.

And that meant he needed help. After the evening meal he approached them. They were mismatched, one shorter and lean, and with a quickness of movement that the harsh treatment had not yet stripped him of. The taller one was heavyset, almost pudgy, and slower. The smaller one was definitely the brains of the operation, and Danil addressed himself to him.

"What's your name?"

"Bran, you?" The man was reserved, but open. *A good sign.*

"Danil. I've been watching you two." He nodded to the other man to include him in the conversation. "I'm thinking you don't want to stay here."

"Who would?" The man raised an eyebrow.

"If you want out you'll have to do it soon. Nobody lasts long here."

The pair traded a glance, and Bran spoke. "We're listening."

"I need rope. Take it from the haul yokes, the center line. Work it loose, and give it to me, this time tomorrow."

"How do you plan to get out?"

Danil shook his head. "Rope first." He gestured to the rest of the slave shed, where most of the spent slaves where already asleep. "Unless you think you can get a better deal with someone else."

Bran considered it, traded another glance with the larger man, then looked back to Danil. "How soon?"

"Soon. Are you in?"

Bran nodded. "We're in." He gestured to his friend. "This is Jordan."

Danil shook hands with both of them, then climbed up to his sleeping space. Sleep was vital, and he had far too little of it recently.

The next day dragged by endlessly as he worked to free another length of rope from his yoke. He finally got it free and started on the other end when a driver noticed Danil's broken line, and he stopped the gang to inspect it. Danil's blood ran cold. It was a new section of rope, a replacement for a section he'd already stolen, put in by the saddlers that very morning. Even casual inspection would show that it had been deliberately abraded rather than simply worn out. The driver stopped the haul, and Danil watched his eyes, trying to keep his expression blank and expecting immediate and harsh punishment, but the driver simply reaved the broken piece back through the eye on the yoke and retied it.

"There. That should hold you until the end of the day." The driver didn't wait for a reply, just signalled the overseer to restart the haul, and Danil braced and heaved as the familiar litany of commands washed over him again. He looked at the driver who'd helped him, trying to make sense of the event. The driver had returned to his normal role, shouting and plying his short-whip as required to extract the maximum effort from the slaves, as if the pause hadn't ever happened. The event was so incongruous that Danil sensed a trap, and so left the repaired section of rope in place rather than trying to free it a second time. At the end of the day, as they were unharnessed, he watched to see if the driver would check the rope, but he didn't. Stopping the haul, fixing the line, had been an act of kindness. The driver had acted to spare Danil the hardship of a free yoke. *The man is human, after all.* The thought didn't sit comfortably in Danil's mind. The drivers were the *enemy*, and to see one act out of simple human compassion, even for an instant, added a depth and dimension to them that he didn't want to see. Beyond that, it was frustrating to lose the day's rope to the incident, but as they were herded back to the shed Bran and Jordan each handed him a folded length of line, which meant that rather than losing a day he had gained one. *So long as they don't do anything to mess this up.* Bringing them into the plan was a calculated risk. So far it was paying off.

The next day it paid off again, and when they returned to the shed that night he added three more rope sections to his growing collection. *And none too soon.* The brickyard had left him lean but physically strong, but he was hungry all the time now and his body was burning muscle to fuel the haul crew's demands. There was also the risk that the saddlers would notice the sudden increase in the repairs they had to make. He lay awake as the rest of the slaves drifted off to sleep, and then got up and very carefully rearranged the way he'd hidden his treasured cache, laying the individual strands end-to-end behind the eaves of the shed, stepping carefully over snoring bodies on the top sleeping tier. If there was a search he might not lose the whole cache that way, and it would be harder for the guards to prove that he was the one responsible. *I just need one more day.* Occasionally the dogs outside would sniff at the door, but they didn't seem inclined to bark unless they were confronted with something, whether through training or instinct Danil didn't know. *As long as they don't bark when we go over their heads.*

He didn't sleep well, and the next shift was inhumanly hard. The driver responsible for his section of the haul gang screamed like a leopard, laying on his lash with a will. Still, at the noon meal Danil managed to pick up a stray piece of pine, as long and thick as his forearm. It would serve, he hoped, to anchor the far end of his pieced-together rope, by catching in one of the gaps at the top of the fence. *And we'll see how well that works tonight.* The afternoon was as hard as the forenoon, and by the end of the shift Danil's back was striped red and his muscles were so sore it hurt to move. Even so, he felt almost giddy as they marched back to the stockade. He had another length of rope hidden beneath his clothing, and when the exhausted slaves filed back into the slave shed to be locked in for the night, Bran and Jordan gave him two more.

"This is it," Danil told them. "We'll do it after everyone's asleep. Be ready."

And then there was nothing to do but wait, counting one, two, three bells. Time for the guards to get bored and, hopefully, to go to sleep. The time dragged interminably, but eventually he got up and, being careful not to disturb the men sleeping next to him, he recovered his lengths of rope and tied them together with double-loop knots, testing each one to make sure it would hold. He tied his length of pine to one end, and then went to get Bran and Jordan. They were both sound asleep, and he momentarily considered leaving them behind. Getting three over the wall was riskier than getting one. *But I brought them in, and they've kept their end of the bargain.*

He shook them awake, motioning for silence, and quickly explained the full plan in a whisper. They nodded, and waited on the floor beneath his sleeping space while he climbed back up to the third tier bunk and into the rafters. Danil pushed carefully against the shingling, wincing as aged wood splintered, and then he was blinking as the suntube's light flooded into the dim interior of the slave shed. He hadn't considered that, and was suddenly worried that the sudden brightness might wake the other slaves.

A few stirred in their sleep, but none woke. Below him he could suddenly see the faces of his accomplices, looking up in silent concern. *There's no point in looking back.* He cautiously put his head through the opening, squinting while his eyes adjusted, and ready to duck back if he saw a guard. There were none, and he waited, watching patiently, in case any appeared. He saw a dog, black and shaggy, sunning itself beside the cookhouse. It didn't seem to have noticed him. A second dog came around the corner of the slave shed, sniffing lazily at the ground. The kennel was big enough to hold a dozen that size, but there didn't seem to be enough paw prints on the ground for there to be that many. *And dogs have to be fed.* Danil wasn't sure of the monetary arrangements behind the slave crews, but this one seemed to be run on the cheap. It seemed there should be more dogs, but it was possible there were not.

*And there's no sense in waiting further.* Satisfied that the guards weren't paying attention, he gathered his makeshift rope with its improvised anchor and tossed it over the fence. The piece of pine made a muffled *clunk* on the other side, and Danil instinctively ducked back beneath the level of the roof, but nobody came to investigate. When he was sure no one had noticed he carefully pulled the rope taut, and was gratified when the pine section caught crosswise in one of the fence-top gaps.

Working quickly, he secured the free end of the rope to the cross point where a rafter and a roof-pole came together. He tested it, hung his weight on it, and it held. For a moment he just looked at the rope, hardly daring to believe his plan had worked, and on the first attempt. He turned around and gave a nod to his accomplices before climbing out through the narrow hole he had made. He had to be careful to keep his weight over the rafters, it wouldn't do to crash a hole through the roof and wake up the rest of the slaves. Some would certainly try to follow them, and with so many trying to make it across the rope, the dogs would surely respond and alert the guards.

The need for caution made movement awkward, and the rope wasn't at a particularly good angle, but he managed to get onto it, lying on top of it so the rope ran down his chest to his groin. He hooked one ankle over it to stabilize himself, let the other leg dangle as a counterweight and pulled himself along hand

over hand. The rope sagged under his weight and swayed, and
he fought to stay balanced. One of the dogs noticed him, and
his blood froze when it came over, but it didn't bark or leap. It
seemed confused rather than angry. It cocked an ear and tilted its
head, as if trying to decide what he was and how he'd gotten there.

The first part of the journey was easy, though the knots were
painful as he dragged himself over them. However the sag in the
rope meant he had to pull himself uphill after he'd passed the
midpoint. By that time there were half a dozen dogs sitting below
him, looking up quizzically. He had hoped—planned—that they
wouldn't notice him at all, which was perhaps wishful thinking on
his part, but they still weren't barking, which was good enough.
He reached the fence, got a grip on it and hauled himself up
and over. His heart was pounding, but it nearly stopped when he
saw a pair of guards at the corner, not fifteen meters distant. The
walkway there expanded into a small platform and they were both
asleep, their headgear pulled down to keep the suntube's light out
of their eyes, their weapons laid down beside them.

He turned to watch as Bran came out through the hole in the
roof and got himself established on the rope. He hadn't thought
to instruct the other men in how to cross, but Bran had obviously
paid attention, though he had a more difficult time of it than Danil
had. He had trouble at the halfway point, where the rope swayed
the most with every movement. His stabilizing ankle came free
and he nearly flipped upside down. The rope rocked violently as he
fought to keep himself upright, and Danil could see the fear in his
face. One of the dogs yipped, and the sound seemed to echo from
the world overhead. For a horrible instant it looked like another
would start barking, which would have set all of them off, but it
didn't. He looked to the sleeping guards, but they didn't react. On
the rope, Bran recovered himself, his face now a mask of fear, and
pulled himself the rest of the way across. Danil grabbed his wrist
and pulled, helping him up and over the fence and onto the walkway.

"Thanks," Bran put a hand on his shoulder and gave it a quick
squeeze. The meaning of the gesture wasn't lost on Danil. Five
minutes before, there had been two separate groups, Danil himself,
and Bran and Jordan together, brought together only by mutual
self-interest. Now they all shared a bond. Danil's risk had paid
off. On the roof of the slave shed Jordan was preparing to make
his own crossing. The big man was heavier than either of them,

and the rope sagged more under his weight. All went well until he came to the middle. What happened exactly Danil couldn't say for sure. It seemed as though a knot caught on part of his clothing. Whatever it was, he stopped moving. He saw surprise come into Jordan's face, then concern. The dangling man tried to reverse himself, but there was no way he could push himself backwards on the rope, uphill against the sag. He tried to pull himself forward again, but couldn't. He was stuck. His look of concern deepened, and he seemed about to say something. Hurriedly Danil put a finger to his lips, warning the other man to silence. Jordan nodded, then carefully, delicately, reached a hand under himself to try and free whatever had hung him up.

That was all it took. The shift in weight made the rope sway, and when Jordan tried to grab it again he overbalanced himself. He caught it, but he was already falling, and then he hung there, dangling. Danil might have been able to swing himself back up and get on the rope, but the heavier man wasn't strong enough to support his own weight. He tried though, struggling upwards, and then his grip slipped and he fell. The encircling dogs immediately erupted in a chorus of snarls and barks, and one of them lunged at the fallen man, teeth bared.

Danil didn't wait to see more. The guards were already scrambling to stand up, grabbing for their weapons. Without thought he jumped to the ground, rolling when he hit. His roll wasn't all it should have been, and the fall hurt more than he expected it to. He got up and started running, glancing over his shoulder just long enough to see Bran following him. Behind him the drivers were shouting. He ran into the forest, his heart pounding in his ears. He deliberately avoided the road. It would take the guards time to organize a chase, and he had to use that time to put as much distance between himself and pursuit as possible. If they thought to set the dogs on him he might not get far, but he was going to go down fighting. *And I'm free!* The realization gave him wings and he ran on, ignoring hunger and pain and the ache of fatigue that set into his muscles almost at once. He glanced back to see where Bran was, but the other man was nowhere to be seen. Danil felt betrayed somehow. *But splitting up is the smartest thing, give them more trails to follow.*

The stand they'd been logging wasn't as large as he'd thought, perhaps a half a kilometer across, and he broke out from under the forewall mists as he jogged. The woods ended at a road, and on the opposite side of it was a field of ripening flax. *Decision time.* If he took the road he ran the risk of running into an inquisitor patrol, but cutting across the field would leave a distinct trail for the guards to follow. Instinctively he looked over his shoulder, but there was no sign of pursuit. Beyond the flax was a field of corn, growing beneath an overstory of olive trees. The high crop would cover his movement, if he could get into it without leaving a trace. The road ran aftward and spinward, and there were more overstoried cornfields in that direction.

*Good enough.* He took to the road, settling into a steady lope designed to cover ground with the maximum possible efficiency, forcing the movement despite the pain that was already shooting through his legs. He hadn't been running long when a rhythmic sound forced itself into his consciousness. *Hoofbeats.* He looked wildly around and saw half a dozen red-cloaked riders coming down on him from around the edge of the woods. *Inquisitors!* He hadn't imagined that they could respond so quickly. Without thinking he turned and sprinted into the flax field. The corn was three hundred meters distant. *If I can make it there . . .*

"Halt!" The riders had spotted him, but the shout only spurred Danil to greater speed. The tall flax made running difficult, and it slowed him more than it would slow the horses. The drumming hoofbeats grew louder, and he risked a glance backwards just in time to see the lead inquisitor loose an arrow at him. The shaft buzzed past, wide and long. Zigzagging would spoil their aim, perhaps, but it would slow him down too much. *Fifty meters to go . . .* A second shaft went by, stabbing the ground right in front of him, and then a third, and then something slammed into him from behind, knocking him sprawling, and a blur of legs and hooves went overhead. He tumbled painfully, and when he recovered himself he was surrounded by levelled spears and drawn bows. *Caught.*

"That wasn't smart," said the leader. "Not smart at all." He gestured to one of the others. "Take him."

Danil waited, panting, his eyes searching for gap in the circle like a hunted animal at bay. One of the inquisitors dismounted and came towards him with a rope. "Get on your knees, slave," he commanded.

Danil didn't move, and the inquisitor repeated the command. The leader shoved his spear forward to underline the point. Danil could make it easy or hard, but he wasn't getting away. He looked up at the circle of hostile eyes. *This time it's crucifixion.* He took a deep breath, and measured the short distance to the corn. Another few seconds would have seen him running through the stalks. That was no guarantee of escape, but he would have had a chance. *So close . . .*

"On your knees." The dismounted inquisitor's voice was harsh.

In response Danil hit him hard in the nose. The man reeled back, grunting in pain, and Danil dashed and rolled under the closest horse. Shouts rose around him, and an arrow stung his ear, but he was into the cornfield before his pursuers could bring their horses around to give chase. He had bought himself a few seconds at most. From horseback the riders would be able to see him running through the tall crop, but they'd have to duck low to avoid hitting the olive branches, and perhaps that would give him enough of an advantage. He went twenty meters in and threw himself down. Seconds later the inquisitors were galloping past, one nearly running him over in his haste to catch him. Danil's blood froze, thinking he'd been caught again, but the rider didn't slow down. He heard the leader shouting to the others as he directed the search. They stopped and began quartering the area, and that was a problem. He had cut across the grain of the corn rows, but his pursuers could see a long way down the line of the furrows, and they were organizing themselves to systematically cover the area. If he was going to make a clean break, it had to be now.

He got up to a low crouch, and immediately found another problem. The corn was understoried with squash vines, and he couldn't move without disturbing them. The inquisitors would quickly find his trail and track him.

*But I'm free and they were going to crucify me anyway.* He caught a glimpse of a red cloak through the cornstalks and crouched lower. Fortunately the rider was facing in the wrong direction to see him. He took a careful step over the furrow, putting his foot down between the vines and listening carefully, gauging the location of the horsemen. His chosen path took him directly behind one of them, posted there by the leader to prevent him getting away in that direction. The inquisitor was just two rows over, so close he could hear the horse breathing as he crept past, but he was able to slip by. Once he was past he broke into a lope, heedless of the track he left, trying not to trip on the ripening squash gourds. The ground grew softer and harder to run in, but he forced himself onwards.

At the edge of the field there was an irrigation canal, with a big bucketwheel turning slowly in the gentle current. The wheel spilled its buckets into a wooden water trough that ran along the edge of the uphill end of the field, and the trough in turn supplied a steady flow to the smaller troughs that ran the length of the field to trickle water into the furrows. The line of the canal was marked by trees and a few stands of young bamboo. He could swim across, but the next field was full of waist high flax, which didn't offer enough cover. He glanced over his shoulder, but there was no sign of pursuit. That wouldn't last long; once they found his footprints they'd be after him at a full gallop.

*Think Danil, think.* He looked left and right. He'd leave less of a trail along the vegetated canal bank than in the cultivated fields, but there wasn't enough cover there to hide a running man. If he stopped moving he could get into the dense bamboo, but the inquisitors weren't stupid. They'd search the treelike stand thoroughly because it was the only place he could hide.

A rustle in the grass drew his eye, and he looked just in time to see a tiny button shrew vanish beneath a leaf. He lifted the leaf but the tiny creature was gone, lost among shafts of grass that seemed unable to hide anything. *Little sister, I need to be like you.*

Shouts rose in the field behind him: they'd found his trail. He had to do *something*, and he had only seconds to do it. He looked down again at the line of his footprints and cursed the soft earth. *But maybe I can use that . . .* He turned parallel to the canal and ran, keeping to moist ground so his trail would be distinct. Twenty meters along he angled up and over the canal bank, crouching low so his pursuers wouldn't see him as he came across the crest. On the other side he ran to a stand of young poplar and stopped. From there he carefully picked a path down to the water that would leave neither footprints nor crushed grass to give him away, jumping from the roots of one tree to the next. At the edge of the canal he slipped carefully into the cool, muddy water. He stirred sediment from the bottom, an unavoidable telltale of his passage, but with luck the dark swirls he'd created would have blended into the larger flow before the inquisitors realized they'd lost his track. The canal was straight sided and placid, and if they came down to the water they would be able to see him in either direction for hundreds of meters. *Except . . .* He faced back the way he had come, towards the slowly milling bucketwheel, dived and swam, using an efficient clam diver's body-wave to move fast underwater. No one Prophetsy born could hope to compete in the water with a fisherfolk. *And with luck they won't even realize how far I can go underwater.*

The water was too murky to see anything, so he kept his eyes closed and navigated by the steady *splash-splash-splash* of the bucketwheel. Danil had hoped to cover the hundred meters to it in a single breath, but he'd lost a lot of air discipline in the years that he'd slaved for the Prophet, and he was fifty meters short of it when he came up to fill his lungs. He glanced back and saw a horse and rider at the bank where he'd entered the canal. He couldn't tell if the inquisitor was looking in his direction, and he didn't wait to find out, just inhaled deeply and dove again, as quietly as he could. He went deep and swam until his lungs burned, came up within arm's reach of the bucketwheel. His fingers found timber, slimy with algae, and he pulled himself to one of the structure's support pilings, and around behind it. The buckets spilled part of their contents as they emptied into the trough, and there was a veil of falling water between him and the place where the horseman had been. *And that can only be a good thing.* They knew he'd gone into the water, but hopefully they'd think he'd swum right across the canal and was hiding in the wheat field beyond. There would be a bridge over the canal somewhere, and his hope was they'd ride hard for it, get on the other side and then get frustrated trying to pick up his trail there.

He wasn't that lucky. Through the intermittent cascade he could see the man who'd followed him to the canal bank riding slowly in his direction, eyes searching. Danil couldn't see any of the other inquisitors, and the splashing of the bucketwheel drowned out any noise they might be making. It didn't seem to have occurred to them that he might be hiding *in* the water, but the horseman's path would take him right over his position, and the wheel was the only place in the canal that it was even *possible* to hide. Once the man reached it, the splashing water would be scant cover. It was too much to hope that he wouldn't be spotted. Danil breathed deep, once, twice, three times and pushed himself down and under again. Diving for clams he'd been able to hold his breath for a count of three hundred, and he counted the time to himself. He'd only reached eighty when his bursting lungs forced him to come up and breathe again. He surfaced as gently as he could, suppressing the urge to gasp for air, and found himself looking straight up at the horse. It seemed certain that the inquisitor would see him, but a horn signal sounded in the distance, and the rider raised his own horn to answer it. Danil took the opportunity to breathe deep and go under again.

The next time he came up the mounted inquisitor had been joined by another on foot, this one with a pair of dogs on long leashes. They weren't the big black guard dogs; they were a different breed, and they snuffed the ground eagerly. He'd heard of the inquisitor tracking dogs that could follow a person by scent alone. He didn't stay up to get a closer look, just breathed deep once more and resubmerged.

He came up, breathed and went down again. Both inquisitors and the dogs were gone when he resurfaced, but he went under again anyway, once more, twice more, a dozen times more, long enough for the water to steal enough heat to make him shiver. *Better to stay longer and be sure they're gone.* Finally he stayed up long enough to look cautiously around. He could still see no one, and so he cautiously went to the bank and climbed out of the water.

The inquisitors had left, though the number of hoof prints along the edge of the cornfield showed that he had been wise to stay hidden as long as he had. The undergrowth was heavily trampled along the canal as well. There was too much traffic for just six horses. They'd managed to get reinforcements very quickly, and they had searched for him long and hard. A church bell in the distance sounded the mid-day meal, and he realized he was famished.

He stole back into the cornfield. Neither the olives, the corn or the squash were ripe, but each cornstalk supported a twining runner bean, and he feasted on them. *It could be a long time before I eat again.* His hunger satisfied, Danil moved to what he figured was the center of the field, following the path that had been left by one of the horses. His instincts urged him to press on, to get aftward and out of forelanders' territory, into the forests where he'd be safe. *But that's not the smart thing to do.* Better to move after the midnight bell, when people were sleeping.

In anticipation of walking from the midnight bell to the breakfast bell he lay down in the dirt to get some sleep. He had hardly settled down when he heard something, motion in the cornstalks, coming closer, and voices. *They've come back, still hunting me.* All he could do was try to burrow himself under the leaves of the squash vines as best he could, then lie there and listen while they systematically quartered the corn. A rider came by just one row over, and he held his breath and willed the man to pass without seeing him. The rider paused while Danil's heart thudded hard in his chest. It seemed impossible that he wouldn't be spotted, but after what seemed to be an eternity the inquisitors moved on. The Prophet's soldier-priests were trained to track, but the tall corn made it difficult. *As long as they haven't got the dogs with them.* Danil breathed out, slowly. A second inquisitor followed the first, and Danil listened hard for a bark or a whimper, anything to tell him that the dogs were looking for him too. The silence was unnerving.

*It was a mistake to come back to this field.* He couldn't risk moving out of it now, he had to wait out his pursuers. A flash of light caught his eye, high up on the curve of the world. It blinked in rapid succession, a mirror signal from an outlying inquisitor station. Their flash code was a close kept secret, but he didn't need to be able to read the message to know the news of his escape would be at the Prophetsy wall by the next bell.

He waited. Time passed and the bells rang by, and eventually he decided that the last sweep of the field really had been the last and that the chase had moved away. What he really needed to do was sleep, to conserve his energy for the hike he had in front of him. But while he was exhausted, he was also too keyed up. For a long time he lay among the squash vines looking up at the suntube through the tall green corn stalks and the gently swaying branches of the olive trees. A peregrine falcon soared overhead and he watched it wheeling in the breeze until it slid out of sight. Something moved and caught the corner of his eye, and he saw a green bug climbing one of the runner beans. It was a near perfect match for the plant in color and texture, only its motion had revealed it to him, and it vanished again as soon as it stopped, visible under close inspection only as a smooth bump on the stalk. *That's what I need to do, blend in so perfectly no one can see me.* He reached out to poke the bug, encouraging it out of hiding, and it ventured another tenth-meter.

The bug had left a trail, he realized, a line of tiny holes it had drilled in the twining beanstalk to suck out the juices. The lowest ones had turned brown already, as the plant sought to heal itself. The more recent ones were visible only as tiny droplets of oozed sap. *We all leave trails, no matter how well we hide.* There was a lesson in that. It moved again, and he watched it until its path took it around to the other side of the stalk and out of sight. He finally dozed off and when he awoke the forewall mists had drifted down to shroud the suntube. His throat was parched, and so he stole down to the irrigation canal again.

At the edge of the corn he stopped, checked carefully to make sure no one was watching, and then slipped down to the water to drink. The bucketwheel was still turning, and, less concerned with pursuit now, he slipped into a bamboo thicket and watched it as he had watched the bug. It was a simple device, two wheels mounted on the same axle. The wheels were made of ironwood to stand up to continuous immersion, while the frame that supported it was built of oak. The first wheel had paddles around its circumference, and the force of the current against them made it turn. The second wheel went around with it, carrying the buckets. At the top of the circle the buckets hit a horizontal bar that tipped them to spill into the trough. The emptied buckets came down the other side of the wheel to dip into the canal and start the process over again.

The motion was hypnotic, but hunger soon replaced his thirst and he went back to the field. Raw beans weren't a satisfying meal, but they filled him, and as he travelled aftward there would be more farms with more palatable crops. The midnight bell sounded. *Time to move.* He put his back to it and started walking, back into the corn and away from the irrigation ditch, aftward towards home. There was a town halfway up the curve of the world, its buildings barely resolvable as separate structures. He didn't know its name, but he knew the inquisitors were there; it was where the mirror-code flashes had come from. He felt suddenly naked, as though they could see him from their perch up there. He walked, over roads and through fields, until he was once more out from under the mists. At the edge of an orange field he looked back.

Above the line of the mist foredome loomed large, its apex almost straight overhead. The stars revolved within its blackness until they vanished in the reflected glare of the suntube, and they reminded him of his last moment with Era, on his last day of freedom so long ago.

He was free again, but home was very, very far away.

———————————

The Prophet's Temple was a cold place, built of solid shipsteel and subject to the near-constant mist and drizzles of the forewall lands. The heavy wall-quilts went only so far in warming it up. Her Holiness Annaya, daughter of Polldor, son of Noah and Prophet of God, shivered as she hurried through the vast hall of the Prophet's audience room, and pulled her cloak tighter around herself and her hood down over her eyes. It hadn't always been an audience room, she was sure of that. The room was a hundred meters square, far larger than necessary, and it opened into the outer courtyard through a set of sliding doors thirty meters high, now perpetually closed. A set of stairs, dimly lit with light filtering down from above, took her up into the heart of the temple, past the offices of the functionaries who made the Prophetsy run, past the dark and poorly ventilated slave quarters, up to the top level and the chambers of the highest servants of the Prophet.

It made no sense that to reach his closest allies and advisors the Prophet should have to go all the way down his tower, and then all the way back up to the top of the temple, but that was the way the temple was laid out, and as it was built of solid shipsteel it was beyond the ability of any mere human to alter it. She reached the top level at last. It was warmer, being built of wood atop the steel of the main structure, and large oiled-linen windows let in lots of light while keeping most of the damp at bay. She went down a corridor, climbed another short staircase, and opened a door.

"Balak?" she called. The room she'd entered was spacious and spartan. A pair of crossed spears adorned one wall, a pair of crossed blades the one opposite, a wooden cross the third. Two reclining pillows and a low tea-table were the only furnishings. The remains of the evening meal were still on the table. The slaves had not yet come back for them.

A door opened and her father's High Inquisitor appeared, his expression carefully neutral. "Your Holiness? How may I serve you?"

There were no chairs, so Annaya availed herself of a floor cushion, throwing back her hood as she did so. "You shouldn't call me your Holiness."

"You are the daughter of Noah's line."

"And don't tell me you believe my father is truly the descended son of Noah."

"What I believe is between myself and God."

"What you believe . . ." Annaya snorted. "My father is a man, and I am a woman, no more. Noah built the *Ark,* and we can do nothing close to that. Whoever, or whatever, he was, he wasn't human. He couldn't have been. We aren't his descendants, if he even had any."

The faintest hint of a smile came to Balak's lips, though it didn't climb as high as his eyes. "I'll defer questions of faith to the bishops, your Holiness."

The prophet's daughter sighed. "Annaya. My name is Annaya. Please call me that."

"As you wish, Annaya. How may I serve you?"

Annaya shrugged off her cloak and leaned back on her cushion. "You can sit down, for a beginning." Her host nodded and sat on the floor, crossing his legs. "What a strange creature you are, Balak," she continued. "I come in here and disturb you, in your own chambers. I don't even knock. I demand your time and attention and insult what you profess to believe in, and you ask politely how you may serve me. I would laugh, if it weren't so sad."

Balak made the tiniest shrug. "It is my role to serve, and my convenience is unimportant."

The Prophet's daughter laughed. "Is there no way I can annoy you? No, don't answer, I shouldn't be annoying you anyway. I'm ill-disciplined, as my father will be the first to tell you. In truth, I've come to thank you."

"For what, Annaya?"

"For killing the men who killed my lover."

"It was your father's command, and so God's will. I won't accept thanks for that."

Annaya sighed again, extravagantly this time. "Accept my thanks then, for whatever you would like to be thanked for. For your handsome face, if nothing else."

"Of course, Annaya."

"And please, don't say Annaya as if you were saying 'your Holiness.' Can't we just be friends?"

"As you wish."

"You're impossible, do you know that?" Balak remained silent, and after a pause she went on. "Don't you think the gratitude of the Prophet's daughter is worth having?"

"Of course."

Annaya stretched out, catlike, and gave him an inviting smile. "Then avail yourself of it." She put her hands behind her head, knowing it would raise and accentuate her breasts. The motion erected her nipples as they rubbed against the flax of her top-blouse. It was modest in design, closing at the neck and wrists, but it was cut to reveal in contour what it hid in detail.

But Balak's only response was to raise an eyebrow. "It would go against your father's wishes."

Annaya pursed her lips, slowly. "My father wishes me to be a virgin, and it is far too late for that. The next best thing he could wish for is for my liaisons to be very, very discreet. Your whole life is a secret, what better lover could he ask for me?" She gave him a half smile. "Or I for myself? Won't you accept the thanks of a grateful young woman?"

"I can accept your thanks, your Holiness, but not your . . ." Balak looked away, searching for the right word. ". . . offer."

Prophet's daughter pouted and rolled over onto her stomach. "And we're back to 'your Holiness.' Don't you find me attractive?"

"Your beauty is celestial."

"How close you came to answering the question, and yet how far. Do I threaten you? Have I upset your reflex to pursue? Or do you simply prefer men to women?"

"I've sworn an oath of chastity, as you know."

"The inquisitor creed." Annaya snorted. "That's for your ranked soldiers, not the head of the order. Mark-leader Vesley wasn't the first who broke his oath for me you know."

"Your Holiness . . ." Balak looked away, lost for words.

"Have I upset you? Then we're even. You disappoint me, Balak."

"I am very sorry, your Holiness. I wish only to serve."

"You do?" Annaya raised an eyebrow. "Your oath includes obedience too, doesn't it? What if I commanded you to mount me, to take me, right here and now?"

"As much as it pains me to disappoint you again, I must serve your father before you."

There was a tension in Balak's eyes now, something dangerous revealed beneath his supernatural calm. It frightened Annaya, who was unused to being frightened of anything. *And yet it shows that I'm getting to him, perhaps.* "And I suppose that goes for my so-called half-brother too." She carried on the game.

Balak nodded. "Noah's line flows first through him."

She stood up and went over to him, lay down on the floor and rested her head in his lap. "Don't you ever get lonely, Balak?"

"Faith sustains me."

"Faith." She looked up at him. "If you have such faith, how is it you break the sixth commandment so easily? Thou shalt not kill, sayeth the Lord. When the world arrives at Heaven, will you be admitted?"

"My soul is pure when I do as the Prophet commands."

"Are you serious? You could *be* Prophet you know. My father is old, my brother is weak. A man with your strength could rule the Elder Council."

"I am not the son of Noah."

"Silly man, the Prophet's daughter is throwing herself at you." She put a hand on his belly and ran it up to his chest. "Your son could be of Noah's line, and the world would be yours until he came of age. Must I spell it out for you?" She slid her hand back down to his belly, slid it lower still. "I can't believe you don't find me desirable."

"Annaya." He lifted her head and stood up, turning away from her. "I am your father's servant, the High Inquisitor." His voice was tense. "You must not say, must not *do* these things."

She smirked. "Isn't my will celestial, High Inquisitor?"

"It would be wise if this went no further." There was a definite strain in Balak's voice now. "You put me in an impossible position."

Annaya looked at his back for a long time, letting the silence stretch out, unwilling to accept defeat, but unable to think of a way to advance her plan. *What a fool he is, to waste this opportunity.* Finally she gave up, stood up and picked up her cloak. "Then I'll waste no more of our time." She put the cloak over her shoulders and pulled the hood over her head. "Speak to no one of this, Balak. Not even my father." She took a step forward, standing over him. "*Especially* not my father, do you understand? If you do I'll crucify you myself. He won't live forever, and I'll have power enough for that when he's gone, whatever happens." She leaned forward. "Am I clear?"

Balak bowed his head, his equanimity restored. "As your Holiness commands."

"Hmmph. If only it were true." Annaya turned on her heel and went out, nearly knocking over the slave who'd come to clear away the evening meal dishes, and leaving it to him to close the door after her. Outwardly she was calm, but inwardly she seethed. *I was a fool to go to him like that, and he made me twice as much a fool. He'll suffer for that, before we're done. And who would have thought he was such a stoic.*

Had she managed to seduce him she would have gained a great deal of power in the game that was developing between her father, her brother and herself. Had she at least managed to pick a fight with him she would have been able to muddy the waters a little, to gain some leverage, or at least some freedom from the oppressive surveillance of his minions. As it was she had nothing to show for her efforts but a humiliating rejection.

*The man is so infuriating.* She took a deep breath to calm herself. Still, what mattered was not her current embarrassment but her future, and that hinged on what Balak would do next. *Will he tell?* She couldn't know. *And what does he want? Power?* But for men, most men, power was just an efficient way of getting sex, and he'd turned that down too easily. *What else then?* She had no easy answer. Balak was a mystery, but if nothing else she had put him off balance. *That's worth something, but I need more, much more.*

She went back down the stairs to her father's audience chamber, and then down to the gallery. The gallery was separated from the great room by a wooden curtain wall, but Noah had built it as one space. In truth the audience chamber, large as it was, had once been only a small annex to the gallery, which went on for over a kilometer. It was well lit, with most of the glass windows high up on its outside wall still intact. What purpose it had originally been put to no one knew, but now it was the headquarters for the inquisitors, and two full parishas were quartered in the glare. To accommodate them the huge space had been divided up into barracks and store-rooms and offices and stables. She threw back her hood and walked upright, and the uniformed guards stood to give her the Salutation to the Holy as she swept along the corridors.

She went to the Blessing's parisha's chapel, where she had first met Sem, where Sem's peers would still be. She found them there, and watched in silence from an alcove as they intoned the rituals of their order. They were ranked in order of seniority from front to back, kneeling on the cold steel floor in front of their parishan. The rites of the inquisitor were well-hidden secrets. *But I am Noah's daughter.* She had seen them before.

"Your Holiness." Annaya turned, startled, and found mark-leader Klassen standing beside her. He was darkly handsome, an excellent horseman and outstanding shot.

"Mark-leader." She smiled broadly. She had toyed with the idea of seducing Jared Klassen rather than Sem. *And I'm still not sure why I made that choice.* "I was hoping to find you here."

"May I speak to you privately, your Holiness?"

"We're private enough here," Annaya kept her tone light, but something was wrong, and she already had a good idea what.

"Your Holiness," Klassen began, then stopped, searching for words. "Your Holiness, we've been given orders . . ."

"Not to talk to me, is that it?"

"Orders directly from the parishan. And to him from the High Inquisitor." Klassen paused, considering. "Perhaps, after Sem, it's better . . ."

"After Sem?" Annaya's eyes flashed. "What about Sem?"

"I want to assure you, we all appreciate your presence. It's an honor to know the daughter of Noah's line. It's just . . ."

"It's just you're afraid." Annaya snorted contemptuously. "Well, why wouldn't you be, after all?"

"Afraid?" The mark-leader's face darkened, and he came forward again, his jaw set in sudden anger. "I'm not afraid of Heaven nor Hell nor anything in the living world. Sem was my friend, a man of faith and honor. What you did to him . . ." He cut the words short, and his hand went to the shipsteel blade at his belt. "You shoot and ride like a man, your Holiness. Do you duel like one?"

*Is he challenging me?* Sudden fear shot through Annaya. "So much as touch me and my father would have you on the cross."

"Then I'd die pure." Klassen breathed in, and breathed out, slowly. "The ritual is ending. It's better that you go, your Holiness. Now."

He met her gaze, his eyes level, and she could see she had lost. "Don't bother yourself with apologies, flank-captain." Annaya turned on her heel, then shot back over her shoulder. "I came to talk to men. I can see now there aren't any here."

She stalked out, now in a foul temper. She was used to deference from the inquisitors, and she was good at playing their desire for her against their avowed chastity, but her father had changed the game. He knew he couldn't control her, but he could certainly put fear into his soldiers. She could feel her cheeks flush red, and pulled her hood up and over to put her face in shadow, though she refused to lower her head.

*At least now I know why I chose Sem; he never would have let a stupid order stand in his way. Twice humiliated in one day, outrageous.* Her jaw clenched. *And they knew about Sem.*

Of course she should have realized they would have had to know. Her father had found out about it somehow. Had Sem talked to the other inquisitors? Even bragged? *Surely he was smarter than that!* It hardly mattered now. She was truly trapped in her father's plan. Olen would become Prophet and in the meantime she would be traded off like a brood mare to some family her father deemed essential to propping him up. *What I need is power, and I need it now.* The only question was how to get it.

Danil made good time going aftward, avoiding the roads, and keeping to the margins of the tilled fields. Once, as he crossed a road, he saw what looked like a mounted spotter patrol riding the sleep watch, but they were a good kilometer distant and moving away from him. Later he had a fright when he climbed a fence into a field that happened to be owned by a bull. He'd had no experience with cattle in his life, but he knew when he was unwelcome. The bull pawed the ground and started for him, and Danil made it back over the fence with a meter to spare. Detouring around the field cost him time, but it led him to a farmer's vegetable patch. He feasted on ripe cucumbers, a much better meal than the raw beans he'd had earlier. Before he'd finished the churches were ringing the breakfast bell, and he left hurriedly before the farmer's family woke up and caught him. Beyond the cucumbers he found an orchard of ripening peaches and pears, with kiwi vines twining around their trunks, and picked a few of them to carry with him. The orchard bordered a broad, swift-flowing river, and he found a place to hide and rest beneath a wild tea bush. The river gave him confidence, because if he were surprised he could just dive and swim downstream underwater. He carefully arranged the grass around his hiding spot, and pulled a few branches off the bushes to form a natural screen to hide his chosen spot from any casual passer-by.

Once he'd finished he lay back and looked up. The tea bush was in blossom, and through the flowers he could see the over-arching curve of the world. The ocean was luring him onward, and getting a lot closer than it had been the previous day. He had travelled half the length of the world in a single hike. Tomorrow would see him to the Prophetsy wall.

He slept easily, woke for the evening-meal bell and found himself almost nose to nose with a goat. The goat was one of a dozen on a flat-raft being poled steadily upstream by a crew of slaves. They were poling in a steady, easy cadence to the rhythmic, almost musical calls of the overseer. They were unharnessed, and he could see neither drivers nor whips. Only their shipsteel collars give away their status. Apart from the goat, no one on the raft noticed him as it passed, upstream and around a bend in the river, leaving only ripples in its wake. *They could escape so easily, just dive into the water and vanish.* The chains of slavery bound more than the body? Would he have run had the brickyard been less well guarded, if the threat of slow death on the haul crew hadn't forced him to it?

*It doesn't matter, I'm free now.* He decided to wait until the midnight bell before proceeding again, and spent the time watching the river flow by. Several more flat-rafts passed him, laden down with unknown wealth in barrels and boxes, one even carried horses and wagons. For some reason most of the cargo seemed bound downstream, the up-bound rafts were mostly empty. Overhead he saw more mirror messages flashing from inquisitor outposts, and he wondered which ones might concern the search for the slave who had escaped from the Prophet's lumber crew. At least part of the answer to the acceptance of slavery by the enslaved was the tremendous energy the inquisitors devoted to hunting down escapers. The Prophetsy wall loomed large in his thoughts. *They'll be on alert there, that's for certain.* It occurred to him that the river was the solution to the problem of the wall. *All rivers flow to the ocean.* They couldn't block the river, and he could dive and swim past the wall underwater. He smiled to himself. It was a simple solution, and once he was out of the Prophetsy he would be safe.

He looked up the curve of the world to Far Bay. Era would be there still, he was sure, and Era would remember him and cut the collar off his neck, and he would be free. He smiled. Era would probably even buy the collar for its steel.

At the midnight bell he started moving again, following the riverbank aftward. He travelled carefully, alert for the sleep-watch and seeing no one but a lone farmer in the distance, for some reason plowing his fields in the sleeping hours. At one point he had to wade a tributary, and a while later a thorny blackberry thicket forced him away from the river.

Further along, the river curved sharply to counterspinward, and he had to choose between following the bank and continuing due aftward, over a small rise and through another cultivated field. He looked up the curve of the world, to judge what might lie ahead. It was just a couple of kilometers to the Prophetsy wall now, and after looping counterspinward the river angled back in his direction. He estimated that he'd save several kilometers in taking the direct route and, after some hesitation, he decided to take the risk and save the time.

It turned out to be a wise decision. Beyond the hill was a little valley, with a rill leading down to the river. The hill on the other side was larger, a good twenty meters high, and it was nearly a kilometer to its crest. When he reached it he froze. In front of him, not a thousand meters away was the wall, dark against the green of the forest. Also in front of him, and much closer, was a sea of white tents, set up in neat rows in the open pastureland. Horses cropped the grass in temporary corrals, and over every tent a pyramid of spears supported the fluttering crimson banners of the inquisitors.

The river, completing its looping course, curved in and through the wall, and he could see now that swimming past it wouldn't be as simple as he thought. There was a structure there, some sort of low dam with a bridge over it, with watchtowers on either flank overlooking it. There was a raft dock there too, piled high with boxes and barrels, which at least explained where all the river traffic had been going. Had he followed the river's curve the trees and brush at its edge would have hidden everything from his view until he was almost under the watchtowers, and had he been spotted there he would have little chance of escape, even in the water. *What's going on here?* He dropped to his belly and counted tents. If each held ten inquisitors there had to be—he counted rows and columns—*thousands of them. Why?*

Ultimately, it didn't matter. He crawled back down the rise until he was sure he'd be hidden from view, and hiked back down to the point he'd left the river. It was obvious he wasn't going to get across the wall before the breakfast bell. He went back to the brush along the riverbank and slept fitfully through the day. He was awake again for the midnight bell, and he chose a path spinward and away from the river, keeping to the low ground and the tree lines that divided the fields. It made him nervous to leave the river behind him, but with the curve of the world rising ahead of him he could at least see the terrain before he got to it.

One thing he saw was disturbing. There were six more tented camps set at intervals all the way around the Prophetsy wall. Far Bay was just high enough on the curve to see, and the largest encampment was immediately opposite the fisherfolk city. *The inquisitors are here in force, but why?* There was no love lost between the Prophetsy and the fisherfolk, between slave raids on the one hand and banditry on the other. That was why there was a wall in the first place. *Has something happened?* There was no easy answer, and all he could do was choose a crossing point as far from the main encampments as possible.

It took him only a bell to position himself where he wanted to be, but two more to crawl cautiously forward through a field of high pasture to a point where he could get a good view of the wall. Even while the rest of the world slept, mounted inquisitor spotters were patrolling it, and it seemed the watchtowers were all manned. Five hundred meters short of the wall the high grass ended, and from there on there was no cover beyond the occasional small bush.

*And there's nothing I can do except to go for it.* He knew from his shipsteel scavenging experience that he could get over the wall and be gone before anyone knew what was happening. *As long as they don't see me before I start climbing.*

He looked carefully left and right. There were inquisitor patrols here and there, both on the walkway and on horseback in the open area in front of the wall, but none were very close. He gathered himself, checked both directions one last time, and sprinted for the wall. It seemed to take forever to cover the distance, and his heart was pounding in his ears by the time he reached the barrier. He had grown tall and strong since the last time he'd sprinted the distance, but the abuse of crew-slavery and days of hunger had taken their toll. He had planned to just grab the bricks and start climbing as he had when he was younger, but he had to pause to breathe, and when he tried to pull himself up he found the easy grace of childhood had abandoned him. He heard hoofbeats, and turned around to see six mounted inquisitors bearing down on him, spears lowered.

Panic gave him strength, and he pulled himself up the wall, tearing his fingers on the baked clay, heedless of the pain. A spear clattered off the bricks as he pulled himself over the top, and he caught a glimpse of the inquisitors below as they reined up below him, shouting to the watchtowers. Guards armed with bows and arrows piled out of the towers on either side and came running. Without hesitation Danil vaulted over the far side of the wall. He hit the ground and rolled automatically.

An arrow stuck itself into the ground by his head as he came back to his feet, but he ignored it and started running. The distance across the cleared strip on the other side of the wall was mercifully short, but the archers were firing steadily, and something tugged at his right bicep as he made the tree line. He dodged behind an ancient maple, safe at last, and looked down to see an inquisitor arrow running straight through the back of his upper arm and out the front. Blood was running freely from the wound, dripping down his arm and covering his hand. Only when he saw it did the pain hit him. He started to examine the wound, but another arrow *thunked* into the maple trunk, and he looked up to see an inquisitor up on the wall, nocking his next shot. They'd changed their position to get a firing angle on him. Danil turned and ran deeper into the woods. A hundred meters later he was deep enough in that he couldn't see the wall anymore. There were no more arrows. *Safe!*

And then it dawned on him. He was not only safe but *free!* It was an exciting realization, but celebration would have to wait. He returned his attention to his wound, and all of a sudden his head was spinning. He dropped to his knees. *The first thing is to stop the bleeding.*

"Freeze!" The voice was harsh, and Danil looked up to find himself facing another drawn bow, this one carried by a young woman. She was wearing a rafter's quartercoat and had two quivers slung on her back. Danil froze.

"Who are you?" The woman's voice held a fisherfolk accent.

"Danil Fougere. I'm trying to . . . I have . . ." The words were hard to form, as the pain in his arm intensified to a point where it interfered with his ability to think. *How was it that I didn't even feel it going in?* "I'm Danil Fougere . . ." He started again, and then his ears were ringing and the world faded to shades of grey, and he felt himself falling.

He couldn't have been out for long, because when his eyes fluttered open he was looking up at a man. The man was holding a broken, blood-soaked arrow shaft. Someone else was binding his wound, and it took him a moment realize that it was the same young woman who had challenged him. He hadn't looked past the point of her arrow before, but he suddenly realized she was stunningly beautiful. Sudden and intense desire flooded over him, and he felt himself blushing despite his wooziness. *I was a boy last time I saw a woman.*

He had seen sex on the slave crews, always furtive and often violent, and it was something he'd felt lucky to avoid. His embarrassment was somewhat relieved when she cinched the binding cloth tight and the pain distracted him from her beauty.

There was a third man there too, and Danil turned to face him, just to hide the flood of emotions the girl unleashed in him. The man's face seemed strangely familiar.

The third man knelt down and put a hand to Danil's cheek, where the Prophet's brand was. "Slave crew, branded. They kill you the second time, on the cross."

The man looked somehow familiar but Danil couldn't quite place his face. Then all of a sudden recognition dawned. "Era. Era the blacksmith."

The man looked surprised. "Do you know me?"

"I'm Danil, Danil Fougere. I used to scavenge shipsteel for you in Far Bay."

For a long moment there was no response, and then Era smiled. "I do remember you, it's been years. You've certainly grown." The smile faded. "I was afraid the Prophetsy had got you. It looks like I was right."

"I'm . . . free now."

"Free." The man laughed without humor. "You picked a poor time to run."

"Why?"

"Why? You just came across the wall, you saw all those inquisitors. Don't you know what's happening here?"

Danil winced as the girl put his bandaged arm down, and shook his head.

Era grimaced. "Hmmm. Well, it's war, nothing less. The Prophetsy means to have our trees, our land, our fish, everything. You're probably too young to remember last time. Can you stand?" He put out a hand to help Danil up.

Danil took the hand with his left arm, and stood, feeling slightly weak kneed. "What last time?"

Era waved a hand foreward. "Do you think that wall was always there? They tried before, I was a young man then. They came into the forest and tried to take it from us, but horses don't fight so well in the trees, and fisherfolk do. We wiped them out in a day, piecemeal. I don't know how many died, but it was thousands on thousands, most of the inquisitor force. I killed four myself. After that it was our turn, raiding the aftward farms for whatever we could carry back, though we couldn't keep the land against mounted troops, not that we wanted it. Things settled eventually. There's just too many of them for us to take the whole Prophetsy, and we'd bled them too hard for them to try again. They built the wall to keep us out, and it worked as well for us as it did for them." His expression grew grim. "But they've gotten greedy again, they've been readying for war for a year now. We'll beat them this time too, but it's going to cost. Do you remember Sall?"

"Your wife. I remember."

Era nodded. "She'll be glad to hear that you do. She's our surgeon now." He turned to the young woman. "Cira, that wound needs honey or it's going to fester. Take him back and get Sall to look after him. He can fight with us once that's done."

She nodded and slung her bow. "Come with me," she said, and led Danil deeper into the forest, past a line of several more fisherfolk he hadn't noticed before, each armed with a bow, kneeling on the forest floor in silent watchfulness. Unable to ignore her presence, he found himself fascinated with her shape, her voice, her scent, with her fundamental *femaleness*. He wanted to reach out and touch her, explore the curves concealed beneath her leather quartercoat, though he instinctively knew he should not. He could not imagine anything in the world more beautiful than she was, and his breathing quickened as his body reacted to her presence. It seemed that he should say something to her, but when he tried to speak he found himself lost for words.

She led him quickly down the winding forest trails until they came to a clearing. A series of low shelters had been built around its circumference, thickly roofed in leaves and brush. A handful of fisherfolk fighters were there, men and women, old and young, armed with a hodgepodge of weapons. They hardly looked like a force to match the uniformed, disciplined legions arrayed on the other side of the wall, but that was an issue beyond Danil's immediate concern. Cira brought him to one of the shelters, where an older woman was hanging strips of flax to dry on a branch. Sall.

A shipsteel pot steamed over a fire, and a neat wooden shelf held an array of clay jars, as well as various small implements of uncertain purpose. Cira quickly explained the situation.

"Danil, is it really you?" Sal held him at arm's length, looking him over. "I'm glad to have you back." He started to answer but she held a finger to her lips. "No, we'll talk later. We have to deal with your arm first. Cira, take him inside." The girl-warrior nodded and took him into the shelter and had him lie down on the straw bedding there.

"Good luck," she said, and turned to go back to Era's guardian band at the forest's edge. Danil watched her go over his shoulder, unable to take his eyes off her.

"Hold still," said Sall, who had followed Cira in, and Danil tore his attention away from the girl. Deftly she undid his bandage, and he winced as clotted blood pulled free of the wound. More blood oozed from it, but the serious bleeding had stopped. She probed at it and he gasped. Although she was gentle, her attentions hurt more than the original wound had.

"It's good news," she said.

Danil's eyebrows went up. "It is?"

"You had your sleeves up, the arrow didn't go through your shirt. If it had, there'd be little fragments of cloth all through the wound and it would get infected. You could have lost your arm." She saw his shocked expression. "As it is we'll just clean this out and let it heal."

"Why are you so kind to me?" he asked her.

"You're wounded. It's my job to help you get better." She poured water over the wound, cleaned away the blood, then took one the jars from the rack and spooned sweet-smelling goo onto his wound, working it into the torn flesh.

"You were kind even in Far Bay, giving me bread and fish. I wasn't wounded then."

"Not your body, but your soul was." Sall smiled a sad smile. "You were so small then, I used to worry about you. Era and I have no children and we wanted to take you in."

"Why didn't you?"

"Would you have let us, or would that have frightened you off?" Sall took one of the cloth strips that she'd been drying and bound the wound with it.

Danil looked away, thinking back. *I was so scared then, of everything.* "I don't know . . ." he answered slowly.

She nodded. "We wanted to be sure, and for you to be sure of us." She reached over to ruffle his hair. "We didn't know you'd vanish. You gave me a lot of sleepless nights."

And for some reason Danil found himself choking back tears. He looked away, not wanting her to see them. For a long time he just sat. Eventually she put a hand on his shoulder. "Come on, I need more black mushrooms. You can help me find some."

He nodded, grateful for the respite from emotions too raw to expose, and they walked into the forest in silence, seeking the fallen oak logs that the mushrooms grew from. They said little, and the moment that had passed between them faded into the background. Still, something had changed, and from that point forward he moved naturally into the role of Sall's assistant.

As his own injuries healed, he learned how to clean wounds and set broken bones, how to make tea from Valerian leaves as a sedative, and from certain lichens as an anti-infective. There were fresh reports that the inquisitors were readying an attack, followed by more rumors that nothing was going to happen after all.

As the time passed some of the warrior groups went to go back to their fishing, while new ones arrived to take over from them. The atmosphere was an unpleasant combination of tension and boredom. Everyone recognized the need to defend the forest lands from the Prophetsy. Nobody liked to be away from their rafts and their families to do it. He'd been there over a month when Era's group came in, just before the evening-meal bell. The older man came to speak to him.

"How's the arm?"

Danil flexed his injured limb. It still hurt, but far less than a driver's lash. "Improving. Sall says I'll keep the scars."

"Hmmm. I'm sure you will. And you'll feel it there the rest of your life, I'll wager. Still, that arrow saved your life."

Danil looked at him askance. "How's that?"

"Slaves always run to the fisherfolk, and the Prophetsy knows that. They've sent a few spies over, men in smocks with slave collars and a story to tell, but too well fed. They didn't last long. After a while they learned, and sent real slaves, promised them freedom if they came back with information. They'd leap the wall and the inquisitors would be bad shots that day. It took us a while to catch on to that. Later they came with cheek brands." Era's expression grew grim. "Now only blood is convincing."

"And if they hadn't hit me?"

Era shrugged. "If they hadn't Cira would have shot you right there, and not in the arm." He paused and looked Danil up and down. "Think you're well enough to come fight with us?"

Danil remembered the big man's words the day he'd jumped the wall, his automatic assumption that he would come to fight with his group. It certainly hadn't been his plan to go along with that, to accept leadership when he had just won his freedom. At the same time he owed Era his life now, twice. He nodded. "I can fight. What do I have to do?"

"Are you a good shot?"

Danil shook his head. "They don't teach those things to slaves."

"Handled a blade?"

Danil shook his head again, expecting the older man to be disappointed, but Era just pursed his lips. "We'll have to train you. Come with me."

"I have to help Sall."

Era shook his head. "There's people sicker than you who can do that now. We're shorthanded at the wall as it is."

There was no room for disagreement, and when Danil told Sall she smiled and nodded and wished him luck. Era took Danil over to his group, twenty or so men and women armed with anything from rabbit bows and throwing spears with ironwood heads to wicked looking all-shipsteel blades.

For a moment he hoped that Cira would be assigned to help him, but Era handled that himself, drilling him relentlessly that day in the use of the bow, with only short breaks for rest, food and water. He found the rabbit bow most difficult, because the arrow's trajectory changed depending on the direction you were shooting. If you shot counterspinward it went farther than if you shot spinward. Shooting foreward made it spiral to the left, shooting aftward made it spiral to the right, and he had to learn to check the angle of the suntube to make the final correction before he released the string.

"Why does it do that?" he asked, after one arrow went particularly far off course.

Era shrugged. "I don't know. I don't think anyone knows." The evening-meal bell rang, and the older man looked back towards the camp, where cooking smells were wafting through the forest. "We'll save the blade lessons for later. No sense in working too hard the first day." The meal was roasted rabbit and fish stew, and Danil gorged himself to the point of feeling sick. The exercise and plentiful food had him gaining muscle daily. His arm still bothered him, but the next day Era had him out working just as hard as before, this time with an ironwood blade. It surprised Danil that a blacksmith would be so skilled with weapons, though he supposed that a man who made blades for a living would at least have to know how to use them, and he quickly learned that the weapon had its own complications. Era started him with the basics of grip and stance, and then moved on to the intricacies of thrust, parry and counterthrust. He worked Danil to exhaustion and beyond, but by the evening-meal bell he was gaining competence, able to execute a handful of moves with reasonable deftness.

"You're a natural with a blade," Era told him as they sat down with the group for the evening meal. "I don't think I've ever seen someone learn so quickly, especially starting from nothing. It's the bow you have to work on."

Danil shrugged, secretly flattered, and he looked to see if Cira had overheard the remark. He was still trying to figure out the group's social structure, now that he could put names to some of the faces: short, stocky Jorj, laughing Suli, and tall Manal. There was an easy camaraderie in the group, but also some tension. The confrontation with the Prophetsy was dragging on, and everyone had a family back at the shore and a job they were neglecting. After evening meal, the various group leaders would gather to discuss their plans. The defensive effort seemed well organized, though it wasn't clear at all to Danil who was in overall charge. *And to me, it doesn't matter.* He worked diligently with the rabbit bow, trying to turn the required directional compensation into instinct. Something about the way the arrow flew tweaked a memory, the way the wheel had spun on Era's upgraded axle, that last day he'd come to the smithy so many years before. *Of course!* The arrow twisted in the air the same way the spinning wheel had twisted in his hands. *Why?* He looked to the distant foredome and watched the stars as they turned. *What if the stars were fixed, and the world is turning?* He tried to visualize how a spinning world would interact with an arrow as it rose and fell along its trajectory, and failed. *But I can find out practically.* He took a quiver and his rabbit bow into a clearing and, trying hard to keep the shots aimed flat and the string pull the same, he fired arrows straight fore and aftward, to spinward and anti-spinward and to each half-angle between them, and paced out the distances and deflections. They fell in a distorted oval, and he marked the shape around himself with stakes, at a distance of ten meters. Using the stakes to offset his aim improved his accuracy markedly. *Better.*

On the fifth day, another group came back from the wall, and Era led his small band into the forest to take their place. Danil moved behind him, in the long spaced out single file the group used to move through the forest, and Cira showed him how to sling his quiver and his bow so they didn't knock together as they moved. He appreciated her attention, and it was strange to realize that he was part of a group now, a group whose members looked out for each other, helped each other to achieve their common task. It was the first time since he'd left Cove that he felt he could rely on anyone but himself.

Era stopped them in the trees before the clearing in front of the wall, keeping the obstacle itself out of sight. Danil saw then what pain and fatigue had prevented him from noticing when he'd first come into the forest. There were ropes strung through the trees, at heights chosen to unseat riders and trip horses. Lines of sharpened poles had been driven into the ground, angled, to turn a mounted charge and force it into areas overwatched by firing platforms hidden high in the trees. The fisherfolk were well-prepared for war.

*The Prophetsy's wall is more impressive, but this is just as good, or better.* Having seen the ruthless martial efficiency of the inquisitors firsthand he had found it hard to believe that anything the outnumbered fisherfolk could do would hold them off for long. Now he understood where Era's confidence came from. The fisherfolk could never beat the Prophetsy's troops in open battle—the inquisitors had numbers, training, shipsteel and horses—but neither could the inquisitors hope to prevail in the close terrain of the aftward forest, where the fisherfolk could ambush them with rabbit bows and then vanish into the trees before they could react.

The group settled into the routine of watching the wall, a duty which quickly became as tedious as life in the clearing camp. The monotony was broken only by mealtimes and sleep, though Era continued to drill him every day with bow and blade when he wasn't on watch. *And it's far, far better than the haul crew.* Soon Danil was putting arrows into targets with instinctive accuracy, and good enough at sparring to take on most of the others on even terms. Unfortunately, they could only spare him an ironwood blade, which wouldn't hold long in combat against inquisitor steel.

"What's the point in learning to fight with the blade if I have no blade to fight with?" he asked Era.

"When we start fighting, trust me, there'll be a blade or two lying around for you to pick up. What you have is to get you through till then." Era gave him a grim smile as he said it, and Danil suddenly absorbed the fact that no matter how good the defenses were, when the Prophetsy attacked people were going to die. It was a sobering realization, though it still seemed a very remote possibility. The war, if that's what it was, seemed permanently stalemated. Danil contemplated that, as he lay on an ambush platform in an ancient oak. The platform had a leaf-veiled view of one of the Prophetsy's watchtowers, and he was ostensibly watching to see what the inquisitors were doing.

In reality he was bored out of his mind, and thinking of Cira. He still found himself too overwhelmed by the feelings she raised to actually talk to her much. She attracted him, she scared him, she . . . *I can't even express what she does to me.* He imagined what it would be like to be close to her, to make her laugh, to feel her touch, and he was completely unprepared when a shower of arrows came arcing through the branches, every one of them burning.

———————

The forest was in flames, and Prophet Polldor smiled grimly from his mount as he watched his inquisitors advance through the half-kilometer of the Prophetsy wall they'd pulled down under the cover of the smoke. The sounds of the fighting came faintly to his ears, and he pursed his lips. There was little he could do to influence the battle now, with the fighting among the trees it was up to his flank-leaders. All he could do was watch, and order forward the reserves when he thought the moment was right.

*And how will I know when the moment is right?* All he knew of armies and battle had come from the Bible, and it was woefully vague on the details. His inquisitors were efficient and well drilled in small units, but even in training it had been clear that large scale troop movement required thinking on a whole different level than that required to lead a mark patrol. It had taken years to develop those skills, mostly by trial and error, and today was the first time the whole system would be put to the test. The smoke was drifting up and afterward, spiralling towards the suntube. He put a finger to his lips, silencing a thought before he spoke it aloud. *It's a crime to burn all that timber.*

Beside him the high bishop was mumbling incantations in favor of victory, and Polldor urged his horse forward a few steps so he wouldn't have to listen. On his other side his son followed.

"What do you think?" Polldor asked.

"I think it's boring," Olen answered sullenly.

"Boring." Polldor restrained the urge to hit the boy. "You stupid little sooksan. This is about power, and there is nothing boring about power. This is your legacy, and if you don't learn how to command, how to lead, how to *fight* yourself, then when you inherit the Prophetsy you will lose in a day what it's taken me a lifetime to build. Why do you think I'm doing this, if not for you?"

Olen remained silent, staring resentfully into the distance, and Polldor watched him for a long moment. *He doesn't even ride well.* It occurred to him to wonder, not for the first time, if Olen was even really his son. The boy was so—docile. *But he has the widow's peak.* In truth the Prophet Unrisen had more than the distinctive hairline of Noah's descendents. He had Polldor's sharply hooked nose and eyes, his strong jaw, his voice, and even some of his mannerisms. He was a handsome young man, and a perfect blend of his father and his mother. *And that's the problem.* Elen had been the ideal wife, too devoted, too obedient to consider straying even if she had had the opportunity. Olen's personality came from his mother's side, and what Polldor had found endearing in a wife he found despicable in a son.

Polldor turned around in his saddle. "High Bishop," he commanded. "Take yourself forward, and pray where it might do some good." The bishop's expression showed that he didn't much like an order that would take him within arrow range of the fisherfolk, but he dug his heels into his mount and obeyed without question. Polldor turned to Olen. "Go with him. Move among the men and let them see you. And in Noah's name, sit straight in the saddle when you do."

Wordlessly Olen sat up, stirred up his horse and moved off. Before he'd gone twenty meters he was slouching again and Polldor turned away in disgust. Balak had been watching from a respectful distance, and now came forward.

"And what do you think, now we've opened the battle?"

Balak shrugged. "It's early yet. We have numbers and surprise. I doubt they expected the fire."

"Pine pitch on arrows, brilliant."

"I live to serve, your Holiness." Balak bowed, ever so slightly.

Polldor urged his horse forward, anxious to get a closer view of the battle. "I can't see anything. Are we winning?"

"I think we will win. To know if I'm right, we have to wait."

"Hmmph. I wait poorly. Where are the messengers?"

"It's early yet. Wait . . ." Balak put a hand over his brow to shield his vision from the suntube's glare. "Here comes one, I think."

A rider had appeared from the pall of smoke at the gap in the wall, and galloped towards them through the ranked parishas of the reserves formed up in close order behind the breach. Polldor waited impatiently until he arrived and pulled up his horse.

"What's happening?" he snapped, before the man had a chance to draw breath.

"Noah's Grace, your Holiness. The fire is pushing them back, but they're still fighting hard. We've taken their first positions." The banner on the rider's spear was red, blazened with the double crosses of Hope's parisha.

"How many have we lost?"

"A dozen that I know of. The mice are good with their bows."

Polldor nodded slowly. "Well done, rider. Tell parishan Hance to press on."

"We'll need reinforcements, your Holiness."

"They'll come. Go!" Polldor barked the last word, and the rider turned and spurred his mount to gallop back into the fray. Ahead battle horns were sounding back and forth. After the man had gone he beckoned over one of his own messengers, but before he could give the man orders Balak held up a hand.

"Are you going to send those reinforcements now?"

"I was going to. Shouldn't I?"

Balak shook his head. "We should wait. Right now we only have one piece of information. We need to know how the other parishas are doing, and give our support to the one that is farthest advanced. We need to drive to the ocean and take their villages. Once we do that they'll stop fighting in the forest."

Polldor nodded and waved away the messenger again. "Yes. Once we've got their women . . ."

"Their women?" Balak laughed without humor. "Prophet, their women are fighting with the men. It's their children we want for hostages."

"Are you sure of that?"

"It's the fisherfolk way. And really they have no choice. We outnumber them ten to one. They need every body they can get."

"They are godless," put in the bishop, who had come back from the front lines, if he'd even reached them in the first place. "A woman's place . . ."

Polldor whirled around and cut him short with a violent gesture. "In Noah's name *be quiet.*" The bishop looked stunned but fell silent, though suppressed anger crept into his eyes. Polldor tried to keep the contempt off his face. *All I need is an offended sheep on my hands in the middle of my war.* "I told you to get up there," he pointed to the ranked troops ahead. "Now get up there. I'll tell you when you can come back."

"You can't . . ."

"I can, and I am, now get up there or we'll find out if the high bishop fights better than the High Inquisitor."

The bishop left in silence, trailing resentment. *At least Olen didn't come back with him.* The thought was little comfort. Polldor returned his attention to Balak.

"You'll tell me now I shouldn't offend the bishop."

"I don't think I need to, your Holiness."

"And yet you do disapprove."

Balak dipped his head, very slightly. "I serve my Prophet as best I can."

"Very tactful. You serve me well, Balak. I hope my disrespect for our clergy doesn't offend your beliefs."

"Robes don't make a believer. That bishop is unworthy. I don't need him to tell me what God commands."

Polldor turned to face him. "And what do you think of my own lack of belief?"

Balak shrugged. "You are the son of Noah, so descended. What you *believe* doesn't matter. I follow you because of who you *are*."

"Sometimes you frighten me, Balak."

"I am sorry if I do, your Holiness. You should know my loyalty to Noah's line is absolute."

"That's what frightens me. Look, I think we have another messenger."

In fact there were two more riders coming across the battlefield. When they had reported Polldor saw the wisdom of waiting for the full picture. Tidings' parisha was heavily engaged in fighting, like Hope's, but Purity's parisha had encountered almost no resistance and had cleared a path through the forest almost all the way to Far Bay. He called up one of his own riders, and gave him orders to send the reserves forward through the gap to exploit the success. He sent the second messenger forward as well, to act as a guide. When they were gone he called over his signaller to order the march. The signaller took his polished steel mirror and began sending flash code to the inquisitor camps around the arch of the world. The other parishas had been spaced around the wall at regular intervals in order to make it impossible for the fisherfolk to know where the actual attack would fall, now they would move to the breach as further reinforcements. He had twenty-two parishas of five hundred men each, but that was too many to lead. The six that he had here for the main assault was already a handful. *I'll have to give some to Balak to command directly, when they arrive.* Even that wouldn't be enough delegation, he needed another commander of Balak's rank.

*Time for that later.* Right now it was time to turn success into victory. He beckoned his command group forward and rode to the gap in the wall. The scene there was beyond apocalyptic, a vista of burned and burning trees wreathed in choking smoke.

His surgeons had set up a tent right beneath the wall, and the wounded were being sent there for treatment. The lucky few who had been first to fall were lying on litters, the rest on the ground, their clothing soaked with their own blood where they'd been stabbed by arrows or laid open with a blade stroke. Some had been caught by the fire, and burned flesh hung in loose shreds wherever it had touched them. They were coughing from the smoke and moaning in their pain and there were far, far too many of them for the surgeons to handle. Out in the burned landscape there were more bodies, these lying crumpled and lifeless, and those the fire had reached were charred beyond easy recognition as human. A bitter smell hung over the scene, penetrating even the smoke. It was a sickening combination of blood, spilled guts and burned flesh, and Polldor had to fight down the urge to vomit. Shouts and the sound of fighting sounded from the distant trees, but he could see nothing of the actual battle.

*And perhaps I'm lucky for that.* Polldor had seen men die violently, but nothing like this. For a moment it crossed his mind that perhaps Olen was right in his reluctance to join battle. He pushed the thought away as a weakness, but turned away from the carnage to get his stomach under control. *It won't do to let anyone see me vomit.* "Balak!" he yelled. "Take Blessed's parisha forward. Take Virtue's as well. Push through to the ocean."

"I will, your Holiness." Balak bowed his head and dismounted his horse. The inquisitors were mounted soldiers but they'd drilled to fight on foot in the close terrain of the forest, they'd learned that lesson the hard way in the first aftward war. This time only the leaders and the messengers rode, and even the leaders dismounted before taking their troops into the trees.

Ahead of him Balak had gathered the parishans and mark-leaders of the two parishas and was giving them orders for the advance. Polldor watched him for a long moment. *And am I making the right decision in sending him forward?* He wouldn't have Balak's advice by his side for the rest of the battle, worse yet he might lose his most important political asset. The Elder Council feared prophet Polldor, but they were terrified of his High Inquisitor. Losing Balak would be a disaster, even if the sacrifice won him the war.

*But there's no point in second-guessing myself now.* He had to move forward himself, to see what was going to happen in the next phase of the battle. Another messenger was riding out of the smoke, and Polldor ordered his spear bearer to wave his banner high so the man could find the command group. As he drew close an arrow spiralled out of nowhere and took the man's horse in the flank. The wounded animal reared up and the messenger fell, to be crushed a moment later when his mount came down on top of him. Whatever report he'd been carrying was lost forever now. A hundred meters away a pair of inquisitor archers had already shot down the fisherfolk woman who'd played dead until she saw a target worth trading her life for.

*They are nothing if not tenacious.* Polldor nodded in silent acknowledgment of the woman's courage. *We need to win this quickly, before we destroy the prize we're fighting for.* Ram's horns sounded as Balak's leaders rallied their forces for the advance. Polldor drew his blade and advanced into the smoke, signalling for his messengers to follow him. Already he could taste his victory.

Danil knew the battle plan. If the inquisitors came in force, Era's group would let them come into the trees and onto the obstacles. When their tight, mounted formations started to break up the fisherfolk would snipe at them with arrows, appearing to shoot and then vanishing into the trees again before the enemy could respond. There was a network of paths with prepared positions leading through the forest all the way back to the camp. The inquisitors relied on mass and discipline, and once those were broken the superior woodcraft of the fisherfolk would carry the day. When the first flaming arrows came into the trees he knew that plan wouldn't work.

Era knew it too. Before the first trees were alight he came running down the path behind Danil's ambush platform. "Get down, get down!" he yelled.

Danil needed no more urging than that. Already the trunk of his tree was alight, and he half fell out of it trying to avoid the flames. Before he was down several trees were blazing, and more burning arrows were raining down around them. He followed Era down the path as the blacksmith collected the rest of the group. He led them back a hundred meters to a second line of ambush positions and spread them along it. These were less sophisticated than the prepared defenses they'd just abandoned, just piled logs covering the open areas, with aiming stakes set to indicate the

ranges. By using fire as a weapon the inquisitors had eliminated
the trenches and trip lines as obstacles and thereby gained a
powerful advantage. *And we might have to fall back from here as
well.* If the fires really took hold the situation could get very bad
indeed. Danil watched through the screening foliage as puddles
of flame spread and grew and merged. Fire climbed the trunk
of an old beech, seizing each branch as it reached it, until the
tree's crown exploded into flame. From there the fire leapt to the
neighboring trees almost at once. The leaf litter on the ground
was burning too, sending dense clouds of smoke into the air. The
forest was dry and there was nothing to stop the advancing blaze.
The inquisitors were still firing flame arrows and a pair of them
landed directly in front of Danil. He dashed forward and grabbed
them before they could start the leaf litter burning.

"Fire through the smoke!" Era was yelling. "They're right there,
just fire."

Danil couldn't see anything, but he shot both the arrows he'd
just picked up, and sent a few more after them into the murk. A
gap in the smoke revealed a line of inquisitors advancing on foot
immediately behind the burning trees, and he picked a target and
fired. His shot went wide, but the inquisitor who he'd aimed at
saw him and fired back, yelling and pointing to his companions at
the same time. More arrows came at Danil, some of them burning, and he ducked behind a tree. He wasn't hit, but the arrows
that missed set a fire behind him and he was forced to fall back
or risk being surrounded by flames.

He moved back another fifty meters, then looked around for
Era and the rest of the group. He saw no one. *But they'll have to
move through this way, they can't stay where they are.* He picked
a tree and got behind it to wait, watching the fire as it came
towards him. It was moving at a slow walking pace, except where
inquisitor flame arrows helped it along. He caught a glimpse of
one of the others off to his left, a woman named Nans. Like him
she had been forced back by the fire. He considered calling out
to her, but didn't. The enemy wasn't so far away that he wanted
to call attention to his position. At least the volleys of burning
arrows seemed to have subsided. He watched for targets, but
the next gap in the smoke found him face-to-face with a sudden inferno. The fire had reached an area of low, dry scrub and
roared up, hitting him with waves of heat so intense they were

painful. The flame-front came at him so quickly that he nearly dropped his bow, and he had to run backwards again.

Shouts rose behind him as he did, and a fusillade of arrows followed him, but the smoke was spoiling the enemy's aim as much as his own, and they went wide. Era was gone, and he could see none of the rest of the group around. He found cover again behind a thick fallen log and looked back the way he had come, to see nothing but a solid wall of fire. The trees burned with a supernatural roar, and the heat was painful at fifty meters. He couldn't see any inquisitors either. *I should just run, get to the ocean and hide there.* He was suddenly acutely aware of the Prophet's cross branded onto his cheek. It would not be good to be taken prisoner. Still, something in him kept him where he was, and it took him a long time to identify what it was. *Pride.* It was something he'd had little of as an orphan, and less of as a slave, but he was a free man now, and a warrior, and that was something worth fighting for. *If they catch me it won't be cowering in the water.* He nocked another arrow and waited, until a wave of thick black smoke forced him to fall back again, coughing and rubbing his stinging eyes. *But I'm not running away.* He found another log fifty meters back and took position again, looking for a target.

"Danil!" He looked up at the shout. "Over here!" It was Cira. She was beckoning him, but his cover was better so he waved her over instead.

"Where's Era?" she asked.

"I don't know, I lost track of him in the smoke. Have you seen anyone?"

"Only Sall." She pointed to an area now consumed in the fire. "She was killed."

A sudden constriction came into Danil's throat at her words. *It can't be true.* Even as the thought went through his brain he realized that it was. That quickly Sall, her kind words, her care, was gone from his life. He swallowed hard against the lump in his throat. *Tears can come later.* "And the inquisitors?"

"They're over there." She pointed at back where she had come from. "There's a lot of them." As she said it a gap opened in the smoke to reveal an extended line of the Prophetsy's troops. Instinctively Danil fired, and saw his arrow take one of the second rank in the neck. It was the first time he'd seen one of his arrows strike home, and he found himself standing and staring at the dead man, even as a storm of arrows fell around him. *I've just killed someone.* He felt sick, angry, proud . . .

"Danil, get down." Cira yanked him back behind the log, gave him a quick smile. "Good work." She rose to a knee, fired and ducked down again.

*And they killed Sall.* The anger took over and he went up on a knee, aimed and fired. His arrow bounced off an inquisitor's breast plate, but the doubt was gone. He'd kill to protect his own.

"Now what?"

"Wait for them to give up on shooting, run, and do it again."

Arrows imbedded themselves in the log in front of them and buzzed overhead, and Danil waited for the fusillade to stop. The arrows kept coming though, and all of a sudden he was worried. They were safe enough where they were, but the flames were coming fast. He risked a quick glance over the log, to see the front rank of inquisitor bowmen kneeling and firing in orderly succession. The rank behind them was full of spearmen, and all of a sudden he understood the enemy plan. The fire would flush the fisherfolk out of their prepared positions, and the bowmen would harass them as they fell back, hoping to trap them as he and Cira were now trapped, pinned down under cover while the fire burned closer and closer. The spearmen provided close defense to the archers, in case the fisherfolk rallied and fought their way through the fire. *But there'll be no rally here, there's just two of us.* An arrow glanced off a branch overhead and hit him in the shoulder. It was hard enough to hurt, but fortunately the ricochet took enough force out of it that it didn't penetrate. He rubbed his arm where his previous wound was still healing. *I don't want to be shot again.* The roar of the fire grew louder, and wisps of smoke began to rise around the bottom of the log. He could feel the heat beginning to radiate from fire on the other side.

He grabbed Cira's arm. "We have to go, right now."

"They're still shooting!"

"And they're going to keep shooting until we burn. Come on!"

Without waiting for an answer he grabbed her hand, yanked her up and started running, pulling her after him, dodging around tree trunks while arrows zipped around them. They jumped a dry creek bed and found a position on the rise behind it. Danil hoped the small gap in the trees on either side of the gully would be enough to stop the fire, and as they waited he even began to hope that the fires would die out on their own.

*What we need is rain, a good heavy rain.* Unlike the steady mist and drizzle at the forewall, aftward downpours were sudden and heavy. He looked upward for the telltale spiralling billows of cloud-fleece that presaged a coming storm, but the suntube was brilliant through the canopy overhead, its brightness dimmed only by a blue haze of smoke. The world was not about to oblige them with rain.

All too soon he heard the crackle of flame in the distance. The sound grew louder, became a roar, and then the flame-front was at the other side of the gully. The blaze did stop there, and Danil hoped that it had stopped for good. The roar diminished as it consumed the trees in front of them, and then died down enough that he could hear the shouts of the advancing enemy behind it. He and Cira drew their bows, waiting for a target. A flash of red cloak showed itself and he fired. A heartbeat later she fired too. Shouts and screams answered them, and a volley of arrows sang overhead, clattering against branches and tree trunks. He could tell they were unaimed though, and none came close enough to be a risk. They hadn't been spotted.

For a moment he thought they could hold their position, for a while at least, but then the fire jumped the gully, not at ground-level but up in the tree crowns. The upper branches on the near side of the dry creek burst into flame, and the fire started to spread to other trees. *But fire likes to rise, and so perhaps it won't come down to the ground.* A pair of inquisitor spotters came into view, moving by bounds and covering each other as they sought out the threat. He and Cira fired. His own shaft bounced off his target's chest armor again, but Cira got hers in the meat of his thigh and the spotter fell. Danil quickly nocked another arrow and fired again, this time scoring in the man's belly. The wind picked up, an artificial updraft brought on as the burning upper stories of the forest sucked in air to feed the flames. A wave of heat struck him as the tree they were beneath started to burn, and it rapidly grew to painful intensity. He had thought to let the fire pass them overhead. He hadn't realized it would cook them if it did.

"Come on, let's go!" he said. Cira had an arrow nocked and a look of determination on her face. A second later she fired into the smoke. Danil didn't wait to see what she was aiming at or whether she'd hit her target. He pulled her to her feet and they ran, but before they'd gone twenty meters she gave an anguished cry and fell. He stopped and turned, to find her face down with an arrow lodged in the back of her thigh.

Without thinking Danil knelt down, grabbed it and pulled hard. It resisted more than it should have, then gave all at once. Cira screamed, and then he was holding the bloody shaft in his hand. The head was a wicked shipsteel double-barb, and it had probably done as much damage coming out as going in. *No time to worry about that now.* Another shower of arrows sliced in the air around them, backspace. He glanced around, saw a fallen tree trunk and dragged her, half crawling, behind it. The back of her legging was already soaked in blood.

"Can you walk?" Danil glanced back the way they had come. *Not far enough.* The fire was still up in the treetops, burning branches had fallen and set the leaf litter burning as well, and the flames were spreading rapidly towards them. He could hear shouted commands as the inquisitor advanced across the dry gully.

She shook her head. "I don't think so. I felt it hit the bone." He could see the fear in her eyes, and feel the heat from the still-spreading fire behind them even as he quickly tied a bandage over the wound to staunch the bleeding.

He nodded, looked back again to where the fire and the inquisitor were advancing together. "I'll carry you."

"Can you? Fast enough to get away?"

"Watch me." Awkwardly he picked her up and put her over his shoulder. It was harder than he'd expected, not because she was heavy but because she was awkward. They were a target again when they stood up, but fortunately the log they'd sheltered behind was now on fire, and because it was rotted and damp it was giving off a lot of smoke. He found he couldn't run with her on his back, but he managed a rapid trot. All thought of holding off the attackers was now gone. His immediate aim was to get Cira to safety, and after that . . . after that they would have to survive as best they could.

*I can't let them catch me again.* The forest floor was uneven and twice he nearly stumbled and dropped her, but eventually they were far enough away that he felt safe to stop. Danil put her down and turned her over so he could do something more about her injury.

He drew his ironwood blade and cut away her leggings around the wound. It wasn't pretty. He grabbed a handful of leaves off a nearby ash sapling and cleaned away as much of the blood as he could. There was vicious gash on the back of her thigh, the torn muscle exposed and bleeding.

She looked back over her shoulder. "How bad is it?"

"Not too bad," he lied.

"It hurts. A lot."

"That's a good thing. If it didn't hurt, then it would be really bad." Fresh blood was welling from the damaged tissue, and he cut a strip of cloth from his shirt to make a compress to stop it. He tied it as he had seen Sall do.

"That should hold it."

Cira made a face. "It still hurts."

"It's going to." He stood up and reached a hand down to her. "Here, let's see if you can walk. We'll go faster if you can."

She stood, and winced. "I don't think I can."

"I'll help you." Danil put her arm around his neck, and his arm around her waist. "Just lean on me, don't put any weight on it."

"I'll try."

They stepped off, and all at once Danil realized what had escaped his awareness in the heat of the battle. It was Cira in his arms, Cira, whose mere presence had once rendered him speechless, and he was touching her, holding her, talking to her. As if struck by lightning he became aware of her as a woman and he stopped dead in his tracks.

"What's wrong?" Cira's voice was suddenly worried.

Danil started to answer her and found that he had no words, nothing to say to express what had happened. Her eyes were big and wide and he kissed her, full on the lips. At first she pulled away, startled, and then she kissed him back. He kissed her for a long time and would've kissed her longer, but the roar of the approaching fire reminded him that they were still very much in danger. He broke away, and her eyes caught his, her expression open, fearful and trusting in the same measure. All at once the desire to kiss her again was overwhelming. *But there's no time for that now, Danil.* He tore his eyes from hers and looked ahead into the forest. "Come on," he said. "Let's get you to the surgeons."

Even with him helping her, she couldn't move very fast. They were off the paths that he knew, and he glanced overhead to check the suntube, to make sure they were heading aftwards. Once they saw another group of defenders moving forward in the distance, and Danil took them in that direction on the theory that they were probably using a path that would lead back to camp.

He was wrong about that, or else he missed the trail. Cira was hurting, and moving more slowly all the time. There were shouts in the distance, screams of pain and anger, the smell of smoke and the sound of shipsteel on shipsteel. Somewhere nearby the battle had been truly joined. He urged her on, not daring to let her rest in case the fighting or the fire caught up to them. Once they saw a flash of red cloaks through the trees to the right. Danil's heart caught in his mouth and he pulled Cira down behind a bush, but the inquisitors were moving away from them. Even so, it was a bad sign. *They've gotten ahead of the fire, cut through the defenses.* The enemy had planned well and the fisherfolk, outnumbered and outmaneuvered, were going to lose. The only question was, would they hold on long enough for him to get help for Cira.

They found the camp by accident, having missed all the trails. They came through a line of shrubs and there it was.

"You're safe now," he told Cira. "We'll get you looked after."

The arrow took her in the chest at that instant, and suddenly the clearing was full of red cloaks and steel armor. Before he could react a line of spearmen came out of the forest by his side. He was surrounded, and Cira was dying in his arms, blood gurgling as she tried to breathe.

One of the inquisitors, a big man with a golden scarf at his neck, stepped forward, gloating. "A cross brand. Well, well, there's a bounty on escapers. Noah's been good to us. The parishan is going to be pleased."

Danil didn't look up. He was trying to get the arrow out of Cira's wound, even though some distant part of his mind knew she was beyond saving. The arrow's head was lodged behind her ribs, and he broke off the point and pulled the shaft free. Blood spurted, and he tried to staunch the wound but it came too fast, too forcefully, and she gurgled, her frightened eyes locked on his. He was crying, he realized, and he couldn't remember starting to cry, but he worried that his tears might sting her where her flesh was torn. He felt a hand on his shoulder and shook it off, heedless of the fact that it was an enemy's hand, a man who might kill him for any sign of resistance. The light was fading fast from Cira's eyes and there was nothing he could do.

"You're going to be fine," he lied, and smiled at her, trying to convey a confidence that had no grounding in reality. She tried to smile back and her eyelids fluttered, her lips moving to form words she couldn't speak. "You're going to be fine."

He bent forward and kissed her gently on the cheek, and he felt her tremble, heard her gasp. Her muscles tensed and then relaxed, tensed and relaxed, and then she fell limp in his arms. Even then he didn't let go, holding her close, feeling her blood soak into his clothing, into his skin, into his soul. Beneath his breath he said her name, over and over and over, as though that might somehow bring her back to life.

One of the inquisitors moved to haul him to his feet, but the one with the golden scarf stopped him with a raised hand. Eventually he stepped forward to kneel beside Danil. "She's gone. You have to come with us." His voice was no longer harsh. Danil looked up to meet his gaze and saw not an enemy, just a man who had seen too much death for one day. He stood, numb, and went where they led him, not caring where that might be.

The rain was steady on Annaya Polldor's windows, and smelled of burnt wood. It was not the heavy mist or drizzle that were constants at the forewall, it was a heavy downpour, and it had been steady for a week now, long enough that some of the bishops were starting to talk about another Flood. That it had started the third day after her father's attack on the fisherfolk seemed to be an omen, though Annaya was not usually one to believe in omens.

Outside a gang of sodden slaves were laboring in the mud, digging a drainage channel to carry away the water that was transforming the temple's inner courtyard into a swamp. The channel led to the Silver River, and the rain had cleared the forewall mist enough that she could see up the world's curve to the next two rivers as well. All three were brown and heavy with mud. It occurred to her to wonder where all the water came from, and where it all went. Rain and the outfalls filled the rivers, and the rivers filled the ocean. The ocean never got any higher, so clearly the water had to go somewhere else from there, but where?

It was an idle question with an idle answer. *And you've got larger problems than that, Annaya, so think about them instead.* With her father's campaign against the fisherfolk nearly complete the senior families were already jockeying to carve up the spoils. Her hand in marriage had suddenly become an even more desirable commodity, and she had no doubt that when Polldor returned the first thing he would do was cement his newly enhanced position by placing her. If she was going to stop that she was going to have to stop him, but short of killing him herself she couldn't imagine how to make that happen.

*I would have to kill both him and Olen, and then the Elder Council would just fight over me themselves.* She needed an ally, but her father had effectively ensured that no one was willing to take the risk, no matter that the reward was not only her infinitely desirable self but the very Prophetsy. It was unfair that her world allowed no power to women, but as her father himself had taught her—*use the levers you've got to move the levers you don't.* The problem was, at the moment she didn't have any levers at all.

The rain smelled of burnt wood, but at least it had taken the smoke out of the air. For the first week after the attack all of the world had been full of a stinging yellow-blue haze, and everyone had gone around red-eyed and sneezing. The fisherfolk had finally been conquered, the long ambition of her father, and her grandfather, and probably her great-grandfather. All of the world belonged to the Prophetsy now. *And Olen is going to inherit it.* The thought galled her almost as much as the thought of being married off as a bribe to the man whose loyalty her father most prized. Impatiently she turned away from the window and went down the stairs, to her father's audience chamber and to the great doors that lead out into the courtyard. There was a smaller door that allowed access to the outside without opening the large doors, and she paused there. In truth she didn't even think the large doors *could* be opened any longer, certainly she had never seen them opened. *Who built these, and why?* It was obvious the room's original intent hadn't been to assemble the Prophet's worshipers to sing his praises, but as with most of the Prophet's temple, its original purpose was a mystery. *Whoever it was had more power than my father could ever dream of.*

Her intent had been to go outside, to go for a long solitary walk to relieve some of her stress. It had been an impulse, and at the moment it struck the rain had seemed irrelevant. Looking out at the torrent changed her mind, and she turned away. The gallery held no attraction for her; she was done with inquisitors, no matter how dashing.

Instead she went to the staircase that led up into the bowels of the temple and went up. On the top level she chose a door at random and went through into an area occupied by the tithe-counters and scribes who answered to the Elder Council. She paced down the hallway with a scowl on her face, taking petty gratification in the way the bland men who worked there scurried out of her way.

*I could just let myself be placed . . .* It was an option. The man she was placed with would be powerful, and with her support he could overcome Olen, and perhaps even her father. *Except I'd have to deal with his senior wives.* She would have youth, beauty and her power as the Prophet's daughter, but against a flock of women who'd spent years doing nothing but competing for their husband's favor, those advantages might not be enough. Too much would depend on internal household politics she couldn't hope to know in advance, and even if she succeeded, she'd still only have such influence as her husband allowed her. *Unacceptable.* She had to find a better option.

She went past the tally rooms, where the tithecounters labored over ink and paper, and into the deeper and dimmer back-sections where the erranders waited for their seniors to call on them. Suntube light only penetrated so far into the temple, and the rooms behind the erranders were used only for sleeping. The deepest recesses of the temple were too dark even for that, and nobody used them anymore. *And how anyone ever could have is another mystery.* On a whim she turned down a corridor that led past the erranders into the darkness. At first there was enough light that she could dimly see her way forward, but it quickly faded. After twenty meters there was a corner, and around it there was no more light. *What secrets Noah must have hidden in here.* The darkness was strange and forbidding but she took a deep breath, put a hand on the wall and, feeling her way a pace at a time, went into the blackness.

It was difficult to judge how far she had gone, just sixty small steps by the count she kept, but it felt much, much farther. There was a doorway in the wall at that point, and she went through into what she could sense was a large open space. It was not the first time she'd come to this point, but it always felt new and strange and mysterious.

When she was younger she had come into the darkness to escape her father's anger. Now she came to escape her life. In a world where her soul was not her own it was good to have a place where no one could find her.

She felt around with her feet until they made contact with something soft. It was a blanket she'd left there the last time she'd come this way, and she sat down with her back against the cold shipsteel and wrapped it around herself. It was musty, but it kept off the chill that pervaded the dark depths of the structure.

*If I could stay here I would.* To be free of her father and his plans, to be free of the burden of being her Holiness, the daughter of Noah, to simply be *free*. It was more than she could wish for.

*And I still need an ally.* She closed her eyes in the darkness, and tried to imagine who that might be. It would have to be a man, because she couldn't rule the Prophetsy as a woman. It would have to be a man she could ultimately control, which wouldn't be hard to find. It would have to be a man who could make happen what would need to happen, and those were rarer. The real challenge was finding a man who didn't already belong to her father.

She opened her eyes again and stared into the depths of the invisible room. *What secrets do you hold?* Noah must have had a way to light his halls for his builders, or perhaps they simply didn't need light to see. *If I could bring light here I might find something useful.* It was a thought she had had before, but never before had she needed something, *anything* so badly. With sudden decision, she got up and dropped the blanket where she had found it, put her hand to the wall again and followed it back to the doorway, to the corridor and the light of the outside world.

*Fire gives light.* If she could find a way to carry a flame into the darkness she could see what was hidden there. What she might find she couldn't imagine, but the ancient builders had been a people of great power, and perhaps they had left behind something she could use. Back in her rooms she pondered on the problem. She needed something that would burn slowly and reliably. She summoned a slave and had him build a fire in her firebowl, then set him to fetching what she needed for her experiment.

Her first thought was to burn a pine branch, and that took some time to test because the branches he brought were all well soaked and needed to be dried. Once they were she found they burned far too quickly. After that she tried a thicker pine bough, stripped of smaller branches and needles. That burned with satisfactory slowness, but it tended to gutter and go out if she didn't hold it in just the right way. Its unreliability was a warning, and she realized she'd need a foolproof way of finding her way out of the darkness, in case the light she brought failed and left her stranded. She sent the slave for a ball of strong flax yarn that she could unroll behind her as she went. If something went wrong it would serve as a guide to get her out again.

She tried burning cloth in a clay jar, but it simply charred and smoldered without giving off any useful light. Paper burned well, but like pine boughs too quickly. She spent the rest of the day experimenting with different combinations of flammable material and ways of carrying it.

The answer, when it came, was brilliantly simple. The inquisitors had made flame arrows for their attack on the aftward forest, nothing more than a twist of flax wrapped behind the head of the arrow and impregnated with pine pitch. She sent the slave for some, and then spent a bell at her father's range putting shafts into targets just in case anyone was suspicious. Normally she enjoyed her archery sessions, but this time she was impatient to get on with her exploration, and left as soon as she felt she'd stayed long enough to allay any suspicions. She quickly learned that the flame arrows were perfect for light carriers. A bundle of them bound tight with yarn would burn steadily for almost a bell. Perfecting the design took her most of the day, and she stayed up well past the midnight bell making more. It was work fit for slaves, but while she was willing to have them bring her the ingredients she was determined that they would not know what she was doing with them. Some of her slaves would be spies for her father, she was certain of it. *Or for Balak, which would be worse.* There was no need to let anyone know what she was doing.

She slept poorly and was up before the breakfast bell, eager to try her new invention and explore spaces which had lain empty for a thousand years or more. Her first firebrand flared alive in her fireplace, and she went up the well-worn stairs quickly, hoping to avoid meeting anyone who might wonder why she was carrying a burning stick. The ancient shipsteel of the temple seemed alive, seemed to watch her, as she went again to the halls of the Elder Council's functionaries.

She went down the corridor that led to the darkness, and tied her string to a small projection in the wall, at the corner where the last light faded into nothingness. The flame in her hand lit the way ahead with a yellow flickering glow, revealing nothing more mysterious than another corridor, no different from any in the outer portions of the temple. She hadn't anticipated how difficult it would be to unwind the yarn while holding her flame over her head, and her progress wasn't fast. Still there was something exciting in exploring the empty, silent maze of the inner temple. It quickly became clear that she had not been the first to come this way since the builders had abandoned the structure.

Here and there she found bundles of reeds, tied together and burned down, someone else's design for a light carrier. There were smears of soot on the ceiling, and the rooms had been stripped bare, with marks on the walls and floors as the only clue that anything had ever been attached to them. Still, it had been a very long time since anyone had come this way. Everywhere she walked the dust was caked thick on the floor.

Her first firebrand began to go out, and she quickly lit a second from it, eager to go on. She found a pair of sliding shipsteel doors that opened onto a vertical shaft so deep that her light would not reach the bottom of it. Someone had pried the doors open, and it had taken them a great deal of effort. The shipsteel was still scratched and warped where they had forced their tools into the gap to lever them open.

Further on she found a place where the ceiling and walls were not just smeared but heavily caked in soot, and curiosity drew her in that direction. The blackened ceiling led to a doorway, and the soot was crusted in thick layers outside it, the pattern of the flames that had caused it written in the swirls.

There had been a fire in the room beyond, a big one. She went through the door and found a large space full of metal shelves too heavy to loot, though marks on them showed where more portable fittings had been removed. A pile of charcoaled debris four meters around sat in the center of the room, and told her the fire had been deliberately set, intended to destroy whatever had been piled there. It had spread to the rest of the room from there and consumed it.

She nudged the pile with a toe. There were footprints in it, though she could only guess whether they were made the day of the fire or five hundred years later. She walked around the room, trying to imagine what it had contained, and why someone had decided to destroy it. Nothing she saw gave her any insight.

It was no secret that Noah and his disciples had commanded powers unreachable by any present priest or Prophet. Here was evidence that they had fought each other—or fought *something* as powerful as they. She shuddered to think that perhaps that *something* might still be lurking there, perhaps even watching her. *Don't be foolish, Annaya.*

The thought was easy to dismiss, but the feeling of unease it brought didn't go away. She backed out of the room and carried on with her exploration. As she went deeper into the complex she began to understand that it not been built all at once. At first the rooms were the same as any she had seen in the lived-in part of the temple, and the doorways were identical in size and shape to those she had grown up with.

However at one point she went through a pair of much smaller doors, which sealed with heavy shipsteel lugs that had to be undone by spinning a shipsteel wheel. On the other side of them in the corridors were not square but hexagonal in cross-section, and had round cleats set in all six sides at two meter intervals.

In this area there were no staircases, but vertical shafts with ladders in them, of the same size and shape as the corridors. She climbed one of the ladders up a level, and saw how it had been attached to the wall by whatever power it was the ancients had used to melt the very shipsteel together. The ladder's position interfered with access to the cleats, it had obviously been added as an afterthought. *What did they do to get up and down the shafts before it was installed?* It seemed to her that they must have had to been able to fly, but if that were true, why install the ladders?

Yet another mystery. She climbed up and came to a room, larger than the others, where the walls were inscribed with writing. Some of the letters were familiar, others were completely strange, and none of the words made sense.

Light filtered down the sloped corridor to the room beyond, so faint and cold that at first she didn't notice it over the flickering illumination of her firebrand. What finally drew her attention to it was that it was *blue. No, not blue, but blue white.*

Whatever its cast, it was unlike anything she'd ever seen before, and her nameless fears of a nameless watching *something* returned full force.

*But you can't stop now, Annaya, not this close.* Heart pounding and hands trembling, she went up the corridor. The space she found there was larger, and higher. The bluish light came from the ceiling, where a rectangular panel glowed faintly, just enough to fill the room with ghostly shadows. It wasn't fire, wasn't suntubelight, and it filled her with awe.

*This is proof of Noah's power, the real temple.* Annaya had never believed for a second the pious and self-serving prattlings of the bishops. *But they were right after all.*

On one wall there were faces, etched in relief into the very shipsteel. The one at the top was larger than the others, and for a moment she thought it must be the image of Noah himself, but when she came closer she saw that each face had a name beneath it. She ran her fingers over the ancient steel lettering. *Joshua Crewe.* On the opposite wall she found more names, these with no faces and ranked by the thousand. She went over and found that some she could read, others used the strange letters from the inscriptions in the antechamber, and still others were strings of symbols that didn't look like letters at all.

*These were the people of Noah.* She turned back to look at the images again. Joshua Crewe and the others did not look noticeably unhuman, though some of them had distinctly strange facial structures. *But perhaps they had wings like angels.* The silent faces couldn't answer that question and it was a tempting theory to explain the vertical shafts, but when she thought about it more deeply it seemed unlikely—angel's wings would not fit comfortably in the hexagonal corridors.

Her fourth firebrand was almost out, and she lit her fifth and last one. If she wanted to get out with light she had to leave immediately, and the thought of climbing down the ladder in the dark was not appealing. She looped the free end of her yarn around one of the wall cleats, then turned and retraced her steps down to the lower level. It had been her intent to simply follow her trail back out, but as she went through the heavy, wheel-sealed doors into what she had decided must be the more recent section, something she hadn't noticed before caught her eye. There was a pattern on the ceiling, rectangles the same size and shape as the one that emitted the blue-tinged light in the hall of Noah's people.

*Of course, that's how they saw. The whole place was lit like that.* Most of the panels had failed over the centuries, but the one in the central temple still had a little life left in it. It became harder to see; her last firebrand was burning down. It guttered and went out fifty meters later, leaving her in total darkness.

It was a frightening moment, though she knew the yarn would lead her out. Taking small steps and keeping one hand on the string she made her way back the way she had come in, her heart pounding with long buried fears of being lost in the darkness. When she finally came to the corner where the suntube's light dimly penetrated she breathed out in palpable relief. She left the string where it was and went back out to the other corridor and to the windows, to look past the rain to the suntube with newfound appreciation. Her heart was pounding with unexpressed fear, and with the excitement of discovery and possibility. *I have a secret now, and the heart of the temple is mine.*

The half sympathetic treatment Danil had gotten from the inquisitors who captured him ended as soon as they turned him over to the prison guards. They were drivers, not inquisitors, and they handled him with casual brutality, putting him in steel shackles and pushing him into a hastily fenced enclosure built against the Prophetsy wall with a hundred other captured fisherfolk.

As the hours wore past more captured fighters were brought in. Many of them were wounded, some of them critically, but with their hands manacled there was nothing the other prisoners could do for them. The helpless moaning of the injured added misery to the tense uncertainty of the captured fisherfolk, but Danil found himself strangely unconcerned with his fate.

All he could think of was Cira, the touch her skin, the magic of the single kiss they had shared, and the look in her eyes as she died in his arms.

*She's dead.*

The thought wouldn't leave his brain. He found a place where he could lean against the Prophetsy wall and sat, withdrawn into himself. *Cira is dead.*

The stinging smoke of the still burning fires brought tears to his eyes, but he was too numb to weep. As more prisoners came in the enclosure grew increasingly crowded, but they were given no food or water. Hunger and thirst set in, and on the third day the rain began, and it didn't stop. The grass they sat on gradually turned into mud, and the mud stank of urine and excrement, because the degraded prisoners were given nowhere else to relieve themselves. On the fourth day they were given soggy bread to eat, and the drivers hauled away the dead, and those who were close to it. After that he lost track of time, immersed in an internal darkness so bleak that the miserable conditions seemed irrelevant.

They were fed at intervals, nothing more. From time to time an overseer came through the enclosure with a trio of drivers. He checked each prisoner, poking them with his staff if they were unresponsive. Some he ordered taken away, some he didn't. The days dragged past, and slowly the enclosure emptied again, until there were only a handful of prisoners left. The rain continued, a steady, dreary downpour that only added to their misery. And then they came for Danil.

"Branded," the overseer said when he got to him. "Take him."

The drivers hauled Danil to his feet and took him out of the compound. He was loaded into a cage built on the back of a wagon, and in due time two more prisoners were thrown in with him. They were both considerably older than he was, both of the Prophetsy to judge by their accents, and they both had cross brands on their cheeks. Eventually a driver arrived and hitched a team to the cart. They were driven over a rough track, past the tented inquisitor camps to the trading road, and from there foreward. The journey took hours, but neither of the other men spoke to him, or to each other. They all knew what they were there for, and there was nothing to say.

They passed through Charity, where the baked-brick cobbling was starting to break down in the constant torrent. Foreward of the city the road surface gave way to resined logs laid sideways, designed to withstand the forewall mists and thus impervious to the rain. The new surface added an unpleasant rhythmic jolting to the cart's motion. Danil withdrew into himself even further, and only looked up when the jolting stopped.

When he did he was shocked. They were in a field of crucifixes in front of a high wall, each one bearing a man either dead or dying. Behind the wall a solid steel tower loomed overhead. *The Prophet's tower.* Behind the tower the forewall soared vertically up into the clouds overhead. The field of crosses was a ghastly sight, designed to inspire fear, but Danil was far beyond fear.

He recognized one of the bodies. It was Jordan, Bran's partner, his own companion in his escape from the lumber crew, his face pasty white and shrivelled in death but still recognizable.

*I wonder what happened to Bran?* It seemed like a lifetime since he'd fled from the lumber crew, but when he cast his mind back he realized it had only been a few months. It didn't matter. Soon enough Danil would be on one of those crosses himself, and even that seemed unimportant. All he could think of was Cira.

The temple wall was resined brick, with a thick layer of pitch added as extra protection from the constant rain and mist, and topped by a log palisade. Danil had probably made some of those bricks, and the irony wasn't lost on him. The lead driver had stopped outside the heavy, steel bound beams of the main gates, and there was a pause while he talked to the inquisitors who guarded it. Soon enough the gates were swung open, the horses stirred up, and the cart brought into the temple courtyard.

Danil had never been so close to the seat of the Prophet's power before, and despite his misery couldn't help but stare in wonder at the spectacle. The structure was huge, far bigger than anything he'd seen before, and made entirely of shipsteel. The wooden additions that had been added on top of the edifice only served to underscore the raw power involved in creating it. It was built into the very forewall, indeed it seemed to be merely an extension of the world's body, and its lines drew the eye inexorably upwards to the Prophet's tower. Even the great wall looked insignificant beside it.

*What men can build is nothing next to Noah's creation.* He had never really believed in the religion the Prophetsy taught, never thought that Noah literally built the world to save his people from the flood, or lit the suntube or fought the leopard. To him those stories were just a convenient way to explain the existence of the world for those who felt that it needed explaining.

*But this temple was built of more shipsteel than I would have believed existed, and it's no accident, not something that can be dismissed without explanation.*

For the first time since Cira had died Danil felt something, a soul-filling awe at the power of the man who had built the world. The forewall and the aftwall, the foredome and the suntube and the ocean could all be accepted as simply part of the natural order of things, but not the temple. Deep in his heart Danil felt a fear that the gruesome crucifixes had been unable to raise in him. It was not fear of the death that was being prepared for him, but of the unknown that he might face after death. *Are we really bound for Heaven?*

The drivers, oblivious to his sudden shock, opened the cage and unceremoniously hauled the prisoners out. A tall inquisitor mark-leader in an immaculate crimson cloak looked them over, sizing them up like a trader buying cattle.

"This one first." He pointed a finger at Danil.

There were half a dozen wooden crosses lying on the ground in the middle of the courtyard. Danil's arms were jerked up behind him, a tool was produced and his manacles taken off. An instant later burning pain filled them as his circulation returned.

The pain shocked him out of his depression, and suddenly the will to live surged in his heart. His eyes darted left and right, but he was surrounded by high walls and the looming steel bulk of the Temple. Rough hands grabbed him, dragged him to one of the crosses, and forced him down on it.

"Put his hands flat." It was a new voice, and Danil looked up to see a black-bearded man with well muscled arms looming over him, a hammer in one hand, a fistful of steel spikes in the other. He struggled against the hands restraining him, but the guards held him too firmly. The man with a hammer knelt down, Danil's hands were wrenched into position, the steel spike forced into his palm. The hammer came down, just hard enough to drive the steel through the flesh of his hand and set it into the wood. He clenched his teeth, refusing to scream at the pain. The hammer rose again to drive the spike home.

"Kneel! kneel for her Holiness!" The mark-leader aimed a cuff at the head of one of the guards when he was slow to respond. The hands holding Danil released him. He looked up in surprise to see a young woman on horseback cantering past, hooded and cloaked against the rain. Everywhere activity in the courtyard had stopped as workers and inquisitors alike knelt down and faced her with heads lowered as she went by. Ahead of her the gates were opening.

Hope surged in Danil's heart. His guards were kneeling in front of him, looking the other way and relying on the single spike in his palm to hold him. He rolled over, grabbed the top of the spike with his good hand and wrenched. The spike was set harder than he'd thought and didn't budge, so he wrenched harder. The effort sent agonizing pain through his injured hand but he ignored it, working the spike back and forth, feeling it give, at first a little, then more, and then finally coming free.

*Free!* The odds were a hundred to one against him in the courtyard, but he had a weapon now and the gate was open. He rolled to his feet and started running.

"Hey!" The mark-leader's voice rose after him. "Stop him! Stop him!"

It was under a hundred meters to the gate, and all Danil could hear was his heart pounding in his ears as he sprinted. He didn't bother to look back at who was chasing him, he knew they couldn't catch him. It was the ones in front who mattered, and they had yet to figure out what was going on. Some of them looked up from their positions of obescience as he ran past, but once he was past them they didn't matter. A pair of inquisitors jumped up in front of him, but he dodged around them and kept going.

"Close the gate! Close the gate!" Ahead of him the gate guards started to react, and Danil put everything he had into every step, moving so fast he seemed to be flying. The world seemed to slow down around him, and he dodged around another intercepting inquisitor as though the man were standing still. The gates were closing but not fast enough, and he was going to make it through them.

*And then they'll be after me on horses, and with arrows from the towers.* It was too soon to worry about those problems. He could see now the gates weren't going to close in time, but the inquisitors there had recognized that too and had given up trying to close them. Instead they lined up in front of the gap to stop him, four of them. They didn't have their blades out. They wanted him alive for the cross.

Danil didn't slow down as he came to them, he just slammed his shoulder into the closest. The man sprawled backwards and pain blossomed in Danil's shoulder where it had hit his enemy's armored breastplate. The next guard grabbed at him, got a hand on his arm, but Danil swung round with his spike and caught his attacker in the shoulder. The guard cursed and fell back, bleeding. Someone grabbed his leg and Danil kicked out, felt one foot connect with something soft, heard a grunt of pain and was free again.

He turned to keep running, but the guard he'd knocked over

tripped him and he stumbled and fell to one knee. He managed to regain his feet, but he'd lost too much time. The fourth guard lunged to bring him down and Danil swung his spike again. The weapon skidded off the guard's armor, and Danil raised it and brought it down again. Once again he hit steel and not flesh, but the ferocity of his attack had driven the guard back, and Danil turned to run again. He had five hundred meters to cover to the tree line and safety, and in some distant part of his mind it occurred to him that he spent far too much of his life running away.

Someone tackled him from behind and he hit the ground, painfully hard. He rolled and kicked, and then a second guard was standing over him, spear cocked back to strike. Instinctively Danil grabbed the spear shaft and yanked it, twisting it out of his adversary's hands. He swung it around, catching the one who tackled him across his helmet and stunning him, though not managing to knock him clear. He stabbed out at the one he taken the spear from, forcing the man back. Someone else grabbed the weapon from behind him and then he was in a tug-of-war for the spear. The one he taken it from came back to grab his arm, and then a fourth inquisitor, the one whose arm he'd stabbed with the spike, was standing over him, blade upraised and ready for the killing stroke. The reality of death gave Danil strength and he let go the spear to grab the man behind it, pulling him down to use a human shield.

The move worked to prevent the blade blow, but neither did the inquisitor kill his comrade, as Danil had hoped. Instead he changed his stance to give himself a clear shot at Danil's throat. The blade went up again, and with the man he'd pulled on top of him now actively holding him down, Danil was out of options.

"Stop." The voice was harsh, commanding, and the soldier with the blade hesitated and looked up. The mark-leader had caught up, with his man behind him. "Joshil! Stand down."

Reluctantly the inquisitor with the blade fell back, keeping his eyes locked on Danil. "He cut me, mark-leader. His blood is mine."

"No. His blood is the Prophet's, and he's not going to die today." The mark-leader's face was hard. "He's just going to wish he did." He kneeled down, his face in front of Danil's, lowered his voice until it was almost a whisper, his words intense in their ferocity.

"You made me look a fool in front of the Prophet's daughter.

By this time tomorrow, you're going to be begging for the cross. *Begging.*" The mark-leader stood up. "Take him to the cages," he ordered. "Make sure he's reminded of his insolence."

They tied Danil again, and herded him to a set of stairs to spinward of the Prophet's tower. The stairs were shipsteel like the rest of the temple, and the treads were worn shiny, dished out in the center by the countless thousands of feet that climbed them over who-knew how much time. The guards took him to the very top of the temple, prodding him with their spear butts when he climbed too slowly. He was taken through a door and down a corridor that was only dimly lit by the light that filtered in from outside.

It was impossible to know what purpose the corridor had originally served, but it had been transformed into a prison. Rows of wooden cages lined the walls. Some of them held prisoners, others were empty. The place stank like the lumber crew shed had, and beneath that there was another smell. *Death.*

Most of the prisoners stared blankly into the semidarkness, some were moaning in pain or despair, one was babbling, talking nonsense to himself in a voice so fast that Danil couldn't make out the words.

They were met by four drivers, who took him and unceremoniously dragged him into the depths of the prison, to the very end of the row of cages. One of the guards opened the last one, and two more dragged him in and tied him to the wooden bars at the back. They yanked the ropes hard, lifting his feet off the ground and securing him with ropes tied tight at his shoulders and elbows.

They closed the door and barred it and went out the way they had come, leaving him to suffer. *At least I'm not nailed here.* The distinction quickly faded as the ache in his shoulders quickly grew to a level that made him forget about the wound in his palm. His mouth was parched dry from his exertion, and hunger again gnawed at his stomach, but as when he had been put on the cross at the brickyard, the real torture was that he was unable to sleep.

He was spent, and he wanted nothing more than to escape into dreamless oblivion, but his position simply wouldn't allow it. Time after time he would drift off, but his head would fall forward every time, and when his chin hit his chest it would force him awake again. His thoughts began to wander, back to his childhood, and his short time in Far Bay, back to his time at the brickworks, and on the lumber crew, back to his escape, and to Era and the fisherfolk who had befriended him. And back to Cira.

*Cira.* Her kiss came back to him vividly, and her smile, and the way she moved. *Did I love her? I must have.* He had seen enough death in his life, but it had never hurt him like this, not even when his father had died.

*Cira.*

It didn't seem right that he had desired her for so long, and lost her so quickly.

There was barely enough light for him to see the cage on the opposite wall, and the darkness began to play tricks on his eyes. He imagined he saw people, talking and walking, but when he tried to look more closely they vanished into the gloom. Several times he tried to call to them, but though it seemed he was speaking, he couldn't hear his own voice. At other times he could hear their words, but no matter how he tried he could never quite understand.

*I'm losing my mind.*

It was a frightening thought, for some reason more frightening than the realization that however the inquisitors made him die tomorrow, he would die unknown and unmourned. He tried leaning his head back so it would be supported against the bars behind him, but still every time sleep started, his head would fall forward and wake him. Eventually he entered a kind of waking delirium, and then suddenly he was back in the forest in the fire as the flames leapt up, and Cira came towards him.

*Cira, I love you.* The thought came unbidden, and then he realized that it wasn't Cira in front of him but another young woman, and it wasn't the forest that was on fire but only a stick in her hand. She put it down on the floor, opened his cage and came inside.

"Do you know who I am?" she asked.

"No." His voice came out as a barely audible croak and so he shook his head so she would understand. She seemed ghostly in the dim light. *A dream, no more.* She couldn't be real.

"Good." She took a step forward and touched his cheek, tracing the brand there. "You don't make life easy on yourself, do you?"

Even her touch seemed real, and Danil squeezed his eyes shut and then opened them again to see if she had disappeared. She was still there, and he swallowed hard, managed to form a sentence. "Who are you?"

"It doesn't matter. Do you know you're going to be broken tomorrow?"

Danil shook his head. "I don't know what that means." Whoever she was, she was beautiful, and just a hint of her scent came to him through the cloth of her cloak, overriding even the horrid stench of the prison.

"Tsk. Such a waste of a fine body." She ran a hand over his chest and down to his abdomen, where the muscles built with years of hard labor were corded tight. She reached down further to find him responding to her touch and giggled. "How long since you've had a woman?"

Danil looked at her, uncomprehending, unable to find the words to answer.

"Well then, you'll enjoy this." She said it as though he had answered anyway, then stood on tiptoes and kissed him on the lips, gently, teasingly. The contact went through him like fire, and his heart was suddenly pounding. *What is she doing? What does she want?* None of it made sense, but her mouth was soft on his, and he felt her shudder, and long suppressed desire overrode every other thought in his brain.

"Would you like more?" she whispered, grazing his ear with her words, grazing his naked chest with her nipples, already erect and poking through the fabric beneath her cloak.

Danil still couldn't speak and so he simply nodded, not quite believing what was happening. She put her hands on his shoulders and pulled herself up, moved over him, mounted him. The sensation was incredible and the pleasure overrode his body's hurts. His hips moved on their own as she rode him, until finally his orgasm struck and then finally, mercifully, the world spun and went black.

When he woke up he was lying on the floor in the cage and she was shaking him. "Wake up, we have to go."

She was still there, she was real, and she'd cut him free.

"Where?" Danil tried to stand, but his knees gave out and he stumbled. She caught his arm to steady him. He felt strange, a combination of pain and exhaustion and a vague sense of satisfaction.

"Away. You want to live, don't you?" She picked up her burning stick, which was guttering on the ground. It blazed to life again when she held it up. "Follow me."

Danil followed her, not towards the entrance as he'd anticipated, but deeper into the darkness. She led him through dank shipsteel corridors deep into the temple, and it was obvious that these places hadn't been used in years, or centuries. She took him to a hatchway with a ladder leading down, and then through another maze of corridors. He quickly lost his sense of direction, but the woman seemed to know exactly where she was going. Finally they came to a ladder, to a room with strange writing on the wall. She left the firebrand there and led him to another, larger space that was lit with a strange blue light.

"Are you hungry?" she asked, pointing to a basket. "There's bread there, and cheese and meat."

Danil didn't wait to be asked twice. There was a small cask there too, full of water, and he guzzled it directly from the spigot until his thirst was slaked, then fell upon the food in the basket like a starving man. *Which is exactly what I am.* It was all high-quality food, the bread crusty and delicious, the cheese sharp tasting, and the meat well cooked and fresh. He ate until his stomach hurt. The girl watched him, arranging a thick quilt on the cold floor and sitting down while he finished.

Finally he looked up from the food. "Who are you?"

"It doesn't matter who I am." She reached for him and drew him close, down beside her on the quilt. "What matters is that you want me, don't you?" She leaned in to kiss him, and then suddenly he was mounting her again, taking her and she was thrusting up against him, urging him on. Some distant part of his brain watched his body's responses with something like amazement. He had no experience with women, and now that he was having one, it seemed it was happening to someone else. She was beautiful in the flickering firelight, she was beautiful and, whoever she was, for one incredible instant she was entirely his.

He didn't quite black out this time, though his vision went red and his ears rang. Afterwards she cuddled close to him, resting her cheek on his chest, and once more tracing the cross brand on his cheek.

"I watched you fight," she said, after a long time. "I've seen a lot of men fight. Not many can stand up to four inquisitors."

"I'm tired of fighting," Danil answered. There were faces looking down from the walls overhead, and the place had a sense of infinite age to it, somehow making what they had just shared that much more sacred.

"That's too bad. I need you to fight. That's why I chose you."

"Why?"

"Why? Why did you fight the guards?"

He nodded. "I had to, or die."

"Most die without fighting."

For a long time she lay quietly, and Danil listened to her breathe. Finally she asked, "Did you really think you'd get away?"

"I had to try." He paused. "I did get away before. I got over the Prophetsy wall. If the inquisitors hadn't attacked us, I'd still be free."

She nodded. "Freedom." She looked up at the illuminating blue rectangle overhead, and her eyes were far, far away for a long time. Finally she raised herself on an elbow to look into his eyes. "Will you fight for my freedom?"

Danil laughed. "You seem to have all the freedom you need."

"Appearances can be deceiving. Do you love me?"

Danil looked better, trying to find her eyes in the dim light. "I don't even know you. I want more of you. Is that love?"

She laughed. "Men confuse love and lust so easily. I don't love you. You should know that."

"Then why . . . ?"

"I don't love you." She said it fiercely, almost bitterly. "My father killed the man I loved."

Danil didn't know what to say, and so stayed silent.

"My father will have you killed too, if he finds you here."

"You've saved me once. I'm sure if you tell him . . ."

"Tell him?" She laughed humorlessly. "You'd be dead before I finished speaking. My precious virginity is being saved." She smirked. "Or at least the illusion is being saved." She put her hands together to imitate a flying bird. "The virginity itself has long ago flown to Heaven."

"Why would he care so much?"

"I'm to be traded for the power and influence my halfwit half-brother will need to hold on to the Prophetsy. Traded like a pretty carving, wed to some man of wealth and position, to take my place by his side as the first wife of the Prophetsy." Her voice was angry, and she looked away. "I've said too much."

"Your father is the Prophet?"

"Yes."

"Why would he do that to his own daughter?"

She laughed, briefly. "You think the Prophet rules by Noah's word? Perhaps, but only while he's got support from the more powerful bishops. In placing me, he's going to buy loyalty with blood. He wants his dynasty to outlast him, so I'm meant to make my weakling half-brother strong enough to rule."

"What he wants for you doesn't sound so bad."

"To be bartered over like a slave doesn't sound bad?" She looked at him through narrowed eyes. "Perhaps I misjudged you. Maybe you liked being someone else's property."

Danil looked away to the faces on the wall. "Forgive me if I don't see any suffering in a life lived in the Prophet's temple."

"You wouldn't, would you?" She put her fingers to the brand on his cheek again. "Tell me, why did you run away? You knew you were taking your life in your hands."

Danil snorted. "If you were whipped from before the breakfast bell until you went to sleep, if you spent your days toiling for someone else's wealth, if your very body were not your own, you would run too."

"My body isn't my own. In giving it to you, I'm stealing it from the man I'm to marry."

"What's your name?"

"Annaya. And you?"

"Danil. Thank you for saving me. And for . . ." Danil groped for words. "For you."

"Do you love me?"

"You asked that already."

"I'm asking again."

He looked at her, and all at once had an answer to her question, and his own. *I love Cira, which doesn't mean I don't desire this woman very much.* "Is that what you want, to be loved?" He asked not so much because he wanted the answer but because he didn't want to answer hers.

"I need to know you won't betray me."

Danil raised his eyebrows and shook his head. It wasn't the response he'd been expecting. "I don't love you, but I won't betray you."

"If you don't love me, I can't trust you." Annaya looked angry, and then looked away. "Why didn't you lie? All men lie about love."

"You can trust me because I don't lie. I owe you my life."

"And I should believe you?" There was doubt in her voice.

"What higher debt could I owe you?"

"Love." She turned to face him. "I'm used to men wanting to do things for me because they want me."

Danil laughed. "Did you love the man your father killed, or was he just good at doing what you wanted?"

Annaya's eyes flashed. "How dare you ask me that?"

"What is it you want me to do?"

She studied his face intently. "Do you love me?"

"No." He shook his head slowly. "I owe you my life, and I want you, I desire you more than anything. I don't think I love you."

"You think?" She sounded surprised. "Don't you know?"

"I love someone else. I don't think I can love you at the same time."

"More truth." Annaya laughed bitterly. "You should learn to lie, it works better with women."

"Whatever I owe you, it starts with truth."

Annaya looked away and was silent for a long time, long enough that Danil began to think that he'd offended, but when she finally spoke her voice was softer. "She's a lucky woman, to have a man like you."

"She's dead. The inquisitors killed her."

Annaya said nothing. She was thinking, he could tell. What she was thinking, he couldn't know. He reached over to rub her shoulders and her back, appreciating the touch of her skin.

Finally she turned back to face him. "We have something in common, you and I."

"What's that?"

"My father has killed the ones we loved."

Danil nodded slowly. "I hadn't thought of that, but I suppose it's true."

"Of course it's true. And that's what I need you for. I need you to kill my father."

Danil's eyebrows went up. "The Prophet?"

"Not just him, but him first."

"I'm not a warrior, not really."

"Can you use a blade?"

"I can but . . ."

"Don't you want to avenge your woman's death?"

Her words took Danil by surprise. "She wasn't my woman, she

was her own," he answered, just to buy time to think. *Don't I want revenge? I should want that, shouldn't I?*

But what he remembered, when he thought of Cira, was the inquisitor mark-leader who had stopped his men to let her die in his arms. What he remembered was a man whose eyes had seen too much death. *I would kill Hatch, if I saw him, kill the overseers and the drivers, but . . .* He shook his head softly, a gesture meant more for himself than for Annaya.

"No," he answered. "I don't want vengeance. I just want her back."

"So kill him for me then." Annaya's voice was suddenly harsh. "You said you owed me your life. You said I had your loyalty."

"Yes . . ." Danil hesitated, not sure how the conversation had come to this point.

"Let me tell you something." Her words came fast and angrily. "I am not a brood mare, not a trinket to be bartered. I am not a tool for my father to use to fix my half-brother's faults. I'm not a prize to be fought over by those hogs on the Elder Council, another wife to be put on a string. Do you think you were my first choice, some random slave condemned to death, strung up like a gutted chicken in a cage to wait for the cross? Everyone else has failed me. Everyone—but my father is going to die, and so is my brother, and anyone else who stands between me and what is rightfully mine."

There was a lethal ferocity in her voice. "I'll do it myself if I have to. I don't hesitate because I'm afraid to kill. I'm only involving you because it will be safer for me. You get your life in return. You get your life and the gratitude of the woman who is going to rule the round world from here to the aftwall."

She put her face close to his, looked in his eyes. "All you need is the yats to act."

Danil met her gaze and realized he was holding his breath against the intensity of her words. "How would you have me do it?"

She shrugged. "It's simple. I'll get you made a house slave for my father. I'll get you a blade. Sooner or later you'll get your chance. Once he's gone we'll find my brother and kill him too."

Danil shook his head. "No."

"What do you mean? Are you scared?"

"No, I'm not scared, because this plan isn't going to happen."

"You are scared." Annaya's anger was suddenly focused on him. "I can't believe I thought you were a man."

"It's got nothing to do with fear. Yes, I'll die if I do this." He smiled cynically. "I'd like to believe that would break your heart, but somehow I don't think it will. But what do you want out of this? Imagine I succeed. Your father's dead, your brother's dead. What happens then?"

"I'm the eldest daughter, the sole heir to the Prophetsy. It falls to me. I can't rule but you can, if you do what I say."

Danil snorted. "I'm just a fisherfolk, but even I know better than that. Do you think the Elder Council is going to just allow a slave to be Prophet, even if the Prophet's daughter says so? If he's dead, they'll seize power for themselves."

"You think I haven't thought of that? I have plans for them."

"What are they?"

"Why should I tell you?"

"Because you need me."

"Not as much as you think." Annaya's words were bitter. "What makes you think you know anything about the Elder Council."

"I know you won't have as much power with them as your father does, and he already doesn't have enough. Why do you think he's using you to bargain in the first place?"

"Why do I care? It's what he's doing."

"Well you should care, because you're going to bring his plan down in ruins. If you don't have something to replace it ready to go the moment the blade goes into his back, you're going to find yourself being placed by the Council, and you'll probably like that even less than who your father chooses. With your brother dead and your father dead, *you* are going to be the key to the rulership. They'll kill me and fight over you like wild dogs with a bone."

"What am I supposed to do, build an army?"

"You need allies."

Annaya laughed bitterly. "Do you think I don't know that? I had allies, on the Council, in the inquisitors. My father has taken them away, quite deliberately. You're the best I could get."

Danil shook his head. "You aren't doing very well are you?"

"No."

They sat in silence for a while, and Danil looked up at the silent faces looking down on them, then turned to look at Annaya. She was beautiful, compelling, and yet . . . dangerous. Dangerous because she was shallow, and greedy. Dangerous because she lacked any scruple, because anything she did, even make love to him, was aimed at her own goals with no consideration for anyone else.

*Yet she has saved my life, and she has given me her body, and she genuinely wants her freedom, just as I did, just as I do.* Finally he spoke. "So build an army."

"You're funny."

"I'm serious."

"And how am I supposed to do this?"

"How did you get me? There's ten thousand new slaves in the Prophetsy today, fisherfolk who were free a week ago. That's an army right there, if you can manage to organize it."

"And who's going to lead it? You?"

Danil shook his head. "Not me. I know a man who can, if he's still alive. If we can find him."

Annaya looked at him for a long time. "You are serious, aren't you?"

"Completely. How much time do you have before you're placed?"

"I don't know. A while, I think. Father uses me as a bargaining chip, he's not anxious to trade me away until he has to."

"Will he give you slaves?"

Annaya shook her head. "No, not to a woman," she answered slowly, pensively, and then a slow smile came over her face. "But he'll give them to my brother."

Danil pursed his lips, thinking. "Tell me about your brother."

"Conquest is a messy business, Prophet." Bishop Nufell turned to face Polldor. He was a heavyset man, fat but powerful, head of the Nufell family of Sanctity Parish and a power on the Elder Council. Polldor didn't like him much, but he respected him, and he sensed the feeling was mutual.

"Our victory was ordained by God and guided by Noah," Polldor answered the expected answer. The two were walking through the well-manicured orchards of Nufell's farm. The immediate object of the bishop's comment was the undisciplined crew of newly enslaved fisherfolk being trained to harvest mangoes by his drivers in the still-muddy fields, but the still-lingering taint of wood smoke gave the comment a broader context. Halfway up the curve of the world, a full sixth of the aftward forest been burned, everything between the Silver River and the Golden River. The fires were long out now, but a fading blue haze still surrounded the suntube.

"And yet it still had its costs."

"Nothing worth doing comes without cost, Bishop." Polldor waited patiently. *He'll name his price soon enough.*

"The price for Sanctity Parish has been especially high. Our parisha lost two hundred men."

"God will receive their souls."

"What concerns me is who will receive their land."

"Whatever do you mean, Bishop?" Polldor asked, knowing perfectly well what the man meant. *But I'll make him come out and say it, he'll be weaker for using the words.*

The bishop looked uncomfortable. "There's been a rumor among the Elder Council . . ."

"Yes?"

"There has been a rumor that you intend to attach the land of slain inquisitors to the Prophetsy."

Polldor laughed. "Is this your concern, Bishop? Men don't become inquisitors because they have land but can't think of anything to do with it. I doubt there's a hundred tares in question in the world."

The bishop nodded slowly. "True, but even so, for those who do have land it should properly return to the parish, not the Prophetsy."

"Is that what you think? Do the Elder Council share your views?"

"I haven't spoken of it with them. When I heard the rumor . . . well, that's why I asked you here. I can't imagine that they would disagree with me."

"Is that all?"

"Isn't that enough?"

"How long have I known you, Bishop Nufell of Sanctity? Nearly thirty years now. In all that time, I have never known you to act with just one motive."

"You imply I have a hidden agenda."

Polldor stroked his chin. "You're your father's seventh son, and in your father's day the Bishopsy of Sanctity Parish didn't belong to the Nufell family. And yet here you are in the bishop's robes while your older brothers work farms that you own. You didn't obtain your position by being unaware of the deeper implications of . . . anything. If a man like you hasn't got his eyes on the high bishop's staff then . . ." Polldor suppressed a smile. " . . . then he isn't a man like you, is he?"

Bishop Nufell shrugged. "I worked hard and invested the fruits of my effort wisely. The Bible commands as much. A man can't be faulted for that. If the Elder Council decides to reward me in the fullness of time, that's nothing more than you would expect."

"A wise and hard-working bishop might still have more than one thing to ask of his Prophet on a private visit." Polldor smiled. "In fact, that's what *I* would expect. But please forgive me if I'm wrong."

The bishop stood silent for a moment and Polldor smiled to himself. *I've outmaneuvered him, and he knows it.* Nufell would either have to deny he had anything else he wanted, or make his pitch directly.

Finally the bishop spoke. "There is one other matter. It hardly seems the time to bring it up . . ."

"Better to bring it up now while I'm here, Bishop. You have my undivided attention."

"Your daughter is ready for placement . . ."

"And . . . ?"

"Prophet, a lot of the parish leaders are going to object if you really intend to attach parish land to the Prophetsy." He held up a hand to forestall Polldor's interjection. "You're right that inquisitors in general have little. That isn't what concerns them. They are concerned with the precedent."

"And . . . ?"

"And you're going to need support before the Elder Council, if you really want to make this happen. I do have some influence, as you know . . ."

"Influence you'd be willing to exert on my behalf, in return for my daughter's hand?"

"More than that, Prophet. My own daughter is not much younger than your son. If our families were bound by blood, our interests would be completely aligned. I could hardly object to an increase in the Prophetsy's power if my own grandson were to become Prophet."

"And if not?"

"Then I would have to stand for the interests of Sanctity parish. I would have to do all I could on the Elder Council to ensure the parishes retain their land." He paused. "And enjoy the proper share of what their parishas have won for them."

Polldor nodded slowly. "And what would you do?"

"One thing I would do is propose the disbandment of the inquisitors. The fisherfolk are conquered now, we have no further need of an army. The soldiers should be given land in the aftward forest. They should be given wives from the fisherfolk women and slaves from the men, and they should be free to put down the spear and the cross to take up the lives they have thus far devoted to God and the Prophetsy. Of course each inquisitor will tithe to the parish he belongs to."

Polldor laughed. "Sanctity parish is hardly the best represented among the inquisitors. Every slave, every wife they gain will be one you do not. You stand to lose more through this policy than I do."

"Prophet, let me be frank. The Elder Council fears you. Most of them don't yet fear you enough. I didn't understand what you were doing myself until it was far too late. You have put us all in a position where we cannot hope to win, we can only limit our losses."

"Oh? And what have I done to engender this fear, and to cause you all such grievous loss?"

"What have you done? Do I have to say it? In your father's time the parishas belonged to their bishops, and the Prophet was a figurehead. Today the parishas serve the Prophet, and you've made your position too strong for any single bishop to oppose."

"Yet we all serve the same God."

"Do we? The bishops still pretend that's true, at least to your face. Your parishans and half-parishans are all second sons, and they owe their loyalty to you for giving them status they otherwise would have been denied. I commend you for that; it was a wise move, and a subtle one. Balak leads a force so strong that no one can stand against it. Now you've defeated your enemy, and you still have an army to do with as you will. Now you've created a reason to take both land and power from the Elder Council and accrue it to yourself."

"You give me too much credit, Bishop. The conquest of the fisherfolk was God's will, to bring the Word to every part of Ark. Everything else . . ." Polldor shrugged. "I'm too simple a man for such intrigue."

"So most believe, more through their own denial rather than your deception, I admit. I won't believe you are so simple that you didn't plan this from the start. May I offer you some advice?"

"Go ahead."

"Take what you want, consolidate your power. You've earned that. Don't take so much that you leave the bishops with nothing left to lose. They're mostly old men, and cautious ones. They'll accept what you've done, they'll even give it their blessing if you let them save their dignity.

"But if you take too much, if they believe they'll be left with nothing, then they'll fight. You're not yet so powerful that you can defeat the whole Elder Council on your own. At least some of the parishas will side with their parishes. The inquisitors will be destroyed, and the Prophetsy with them."

"You've given this a lot of thought."

"I'm an ambitious man, Prophet. I recognize my own weaknesses in you. Recognize your strengths in me. I'm half your age and your son, if I can say this without disrespect, is no leader. He's going to need a strong guidance after you're gone, or he'll lose everything you've worked for."

"You aren't the only ambitious man on the Elder Council."

"I am the smartest, and the best positioned to help you." Bishop Nufell paused. "Or to hinder you."

Polldor nodded slowly, considering. *This one is dangerous, more dangerous than I thought.* "How many wives do you have, Bishop?"

"Six now."

"And how many children?"

"Seventeen."

"Do you seriously think I'd allow my daughter to become a seventh wife?"

"She would be first in rank in my household."

"So you say, but I doubt your senior wives would allow that."

"It's their place to obey me."

"It's their place to obey you, but it's their instinct to ensure that their own children aren't displaced in the order of Sanctity Parish. If you give the time to the Prophetsy that you are implicitly offering, if you spend your energy supporting Olen against the Elder Council, then I guarantee your wives will find a way to destroy Annaya behind your back."

"They wouldn't dare. I'll divorce them all if I have to."

"And destroy your relationships on the Elder Council? Even the most cautious bishop would have to respond if you divorced his daughter. Your carefully spun alliances would fall apart."

"Prophet, think carefully of what I've said. My offer is very serious."

"I'm sure it is, Bishop. When the time comes to place Annaya, I'll give it the consideration it's due." Polldor gave Bishop Nufell a smile that didn't reach his eyes. "Right now, what you've said is intriguing, but how much consideration it gets will depend on how you act on the council over the next months. I think that's a very fair offer."

Nufell opened his mouth and then closed it. "I think, Prophet, that you are expecting my support without offering anything in return. Why should I give it to you?"

"Because you still have something left to lose, Bishop. Show me you're an ally and you'll be rewarded, perhaps with everything you wish. Show me that you're an enemy . . ." Polldor let the sentence hang in the air, and turned to walk on ahead without waiting to see if his host would follow. *He knows he can't do anything, yet. But this bishop will need watching.*

"I think I should have a logging crew, Father," Olen Polldor said. Behind him Danil traded a surreptitious glance with Annaya. If they were to build an army they needed slaves and resources they could only get with the Prophet's support. The logging crew was their cover story, and the Prophet's heir was their front.

Prophet Polldor raised his eyebrows. "Can it be you're taking an interest in rulership?" His voice carried a hint of suspicion.

"I am, Father." Olen sounded defensive. "You've always said I should."

"Of course, of course. I just . . . Well, never mind." Polldor smiled wide. "Come here and sit down, my boy. Tell me your plan."

Polldor led his son to a table at the side of his opulently appointed day room. Annaya went with them, but lacking invitation, Danil stayed where he was. He carefully kept his head lowered, and wondered if he should move into one of the slave alcoves, the better to stay out of the way. He decided it was better to be reprimanded for not moving than punished for moving without permission, and so stayed where he was. He watched as best he could, as the father sat down with his son to discuss the details of the new venture.

Annaya sat with them, to fill in any blanks that Olen might miss. It was what had worried them most, because it had taken all her wiles just to convince Olen that if he showed an interest in the new conquests his father might relent on insisting that he train as an inquisitor. Olen was frustratingly lacking in attention span, and Danil had worried that the Prophet might see that Annaya was the driving force behind the idea—and then choose to wonder why. However, Polldor didn't seem inclined to ask too many questions about the sudden transformation of his son's ambitions, and from what Danil could see, Olen was holding his own.

"Over here, slave." Danil looked up to see a lean man with hard eyes looking at him. He wore a crimson inquisitor's cape, and his title scarf was dark blue with elaborate embroidery. His tone brooked no disobedience, and Danil went over to him. "What, no obeisance? You're no house slave, are you?"

Belatedly Danil dropped to his knee and bowed his head, as Annaya had taught him to. He bit his lip, wondering who the stranger was, and worrying that his slip might have cost him the entire plan. *I was so concerned about how Olen would do. I need to focus on my own tasks.* The man walked around him, looking him over. "Stand." He ordered.

Silently Danil stood.

The man put out a hand and raised Danil's chin, turning it so he could inspect the cross brand on his cheek. "So you've earned yourself a brand."

"Yes, sir," Danil answered, trying to keep his voice neutral.

"How?"

"I hit a driver, sir."

"Why did his Holiness pick you?"

"I don't know, sir."

"Because I can control him, Balak." Olen spoke up from the other side of the room. "And because he's worked a lumber crew before."

"Really?" The man called Balak turned to Prophet Polldor. "Your Holiness, I'm sure we have unbranded slaves with lumber crew experience."

"We chose him for that reason," Annaya put in. "We have ten thousand new slaves and nowhere near enough drivers in the Prophetsy. Everyone is using head slaves now. This one hasn't had the initiative beaten out of him. We need that."

"We?" Polldor's gaze moved to Annaya. "I wondered why you'd come. I thought this was Olen's idea."

"It was, Father. He asked my advice and I gave it. You always said I should support my brother."

The Prophet nodded slowly. "Very well." He stood and came over to Danil, looking him up and down, assessing him. "We'll use this one," he said finally, then moved closer to Danil. "Name?"

"Danil Fougere, sir."

Pain flared as Balak smacked Danil across the back of the head. "The Prophet is addressed as 'your Holiness.'"

"Danil Fougere, your Holiness."

"You have an opportunity here, Danil Fougere," the Prophet said. "Work well and you can earn yourself a place in the Prophetsy. Betray me . . ." His eyes narrowed. ". . . and you'll find yourself begging for the cross before I'm done with you."

Danil swallowed hard. "I appreciate the chance, your Holiness, and your faith in me."

"Faith." Polldor smirked. "Save that for your crew." The man called Balak said nothing, but Danil could feel his eyes on him even after they'd left his presence.

The next days were hectic, as he and Annaya made the arrangements to start the new lumber crew in the aftward forests. Danil was surprised to learn that it wasn't just a matter of ordering what was needed in the Prophet's name. Polldor's authority was great but not unlimited. They were given a budget to buy slaves, food, and equipment, and then they had to go out and bargain for what they wanted.

At first they tried to work through Olen, but the Prophet Unrisen's initial interest had quickly waned once he realized there was real work required. Fortunately Danil's new status as a head slave gave him much more freedom of action. Because of his brand he couldn't walk the market square in Charity without risking arrest, so Annaya got him a Prophet's Cross sigil to wear around his neck, which warned everyone he dealt with that he was speaking with the Prophet's authority.

In form it was identical to the one on his cheek, and when she gave it to him Danil spent a long time looking at the small shipsteel token, turning it over in his hands. *How strange that the same symbol both enslaves and empowers.* Even the inquisitors who stopped him in the streets changed their demeanor when they saw the sigil, though they stopped short of the respectful deference the common people gave him.

It was only as he began to learn the intricacies of the market that he realized how small the Prophetsy's timber supply had become. There were few logable stands of mature trees foreward of the Prophetsy wall, and the price of wood in the markets was prohibitively high for the average commoner. Logging tools were expensive too, because the wealth of timber the conquest had opened up had started a rush. On the other hand, once expensive slaves were now quite cheap, and the cost of horses had fallen through the floor, because haul crews now cost less than horse teams. He went to the auction houses daily, picking and choosing what he needed in equipment, animals, and human beings, in the process learning how to bargain, and then how to bargain hard.

Quite soon he had the nucleus of his army—thirty workhorses, some logging tools and a ragtag group of thirty recently purchased fisherfolk slaves. It was not even a full mark, and even he had to admit they didn't look like much of a force. The youngest was a boy named Fredir, only thirteen, but even his oldest was just twenty-two, and though all of them had fought the Prophetsy during the attack none of them were warriors in any realistic sense of the word. *But neither am I a war leader.*

He had hoped to locate Era in the slave auctions and put him in charge of the force, but he hadn't. It was going to fall to him to train the army until a real leader could be found, and he was realizing that he had no clue how to do that.

"Why so many horses? You should have bought more bodies," complained Annaya.

"I've worked a haul crew. I'm not going to subject my soldiers to that."

"And you call them soldiers—half of them are women. This isn't an army, it's a picnic for boys and girls."

"They're what I need, for now. Give me time." They were lying in the bed she had made in their secret room in the temple darkness, and Danil ran his hand over the skin of her back, pale in the ghostly light.

"Women cost more and work less," she scoffed.

"Women fight as well as men, and if you want your own freedom women are going to have to fight for it."

"You couldn't turn them into soldiers in a hundred years. And even your men are just boys."

"I can't lead veterans, they wouldn't follow me."

"You aren't supposed to lead them. Where's this great warrior you said you'd have lead my army?"

Danil spread his arms. "I haven't found him. If you want this to work we have to produce a functional timber camp. Do you want me to stop doing that and go search every slave crew in every parish for him?"

"This is taking too much time," Annaya pouted.

"As for time, we seem to spend a great deal of it in bed."

"Are you complaining?"

There was no good answer to that, and so he kissed her, and then after a while he mounted her, while she moaned and shuddered beneath him. *And yet something isn't right.* It wasn't that he didn't enjoy sex with Annaya, he enjoyed it very much. *It's just that she's insatiable, and there's so much to do, and so little time.*

Somehow it seemed like a distraction from more important things, though he had to admit it was a distraction he very much enjoyed. Afterwards he held her the way she liked to be held, and looked up at the etched faces that looked down on their secret space, as he always did to regain his balance after her passion. *We're taking such risks here.*

He laughed at himself for thinking in terms of *we*, implicitly Annaya and himself. He didn't like to think like that, partially because he sensed that Annaya thought purely in terms of herself, but more because it made him feel disloyal to Cira. *But I owe Annaya my life.* Whether he enjoyed it or not, or felt guilty about it or not, made no difference. *It's what I have to do, and so I'm going to do it.*

"Aren't you afraid I'll get you pregnant?" he asked after a while.

"Why would you care?"

"Because it would ruin our plan. You'd be caught and I'd be crucified."

She snorted. "You have a lot to learn about women, don't you? You should say 'Because I love you, Annaya. And even though I know it's wrong, I want you to carry my child.'"

"Why do you care if I love you? Sex is a tool for you, you've said as much."

"Because if you love me, then I know it's working."

"You wouldn't believe me even if I said I did."

"I know what bloodberries are for," she answered, looking

away and avoiding his point. "You don't have to worry about me catching a child."

Danil reached over and turned her face until he was looking into her eyes. "I care for you, Annaya. I'm bound to you. I'll fight for you, and die for your freedom, and my own. I'll swear that on my grandmother's pyre, but if you want me to love you, you're going to have to start loving yourself."

She didn't answer, but he didn't let her turn away either. A tear formed in the corner of her eye, and then she was crying, sobbing in his arms, and suddenly he did love her, and he didn't know what to say or do except hold her and tell her it would be alright.

It was well into the sleeping hours that they came back into the suntube's brightness and went their separate ways. Danil had been given a cubicle with the temple's drivers, a luxury he was not at all comfortable accepting. Once he thought he saw Hatch in the corridor, and turned away shaken, and he hurried back to his quarters. From the window he could look up to the Prophet's Tower, where Annaya lived. Its height seemed only to emphasize the distance between them. *It would be nice to think that we could be together.* They had a long way to go before that could even become a possibility, and the odds were long against such a happy ending.

He went back to planning the timber operation. Prophet Polldor, Danil had learned, had claimed all the forest that had once belonged to the fisherfolk in his own name. One sixth of that, everything between the Silver River and the White River, had been burned in the war. A sixth was divided between the landed bishops, a further sixth given to the inquisitors who'd done the fighting, and the rest he had kept for himself. It was in this section that Olen Polldor's logging camp was to be set up, on the opposite side of the trading road from Polldor's own operation. The burnt out remains of Far Bay were also in the Prophet's sector, and Danil considered that a good thing. *We can hide things in the ruins, if we have to, and we'll probably have to.*

At the next morning-meal bell, he was ready to start. It took until the mid-day meal to get the group organized, wagons loaded with tools and supplies, horses harnessed, slaves roped into line. Once they were, Danil led them aftward down the trading road. In addition to the supply wagons they had a pair of timber carriers, big, skeletal frames with beam cranes mounted at front and back. They rode on oversized, extra-wide steel-shod wheels and were rigged for a twelve horse team, capable of hauling a sixty foot trunk over a rutted logging road. They were Danil's own design, and he'd insisted on them being built despite the cost and time required, because his experience on the haul crew had taught him the hard way of the foolish inefficiency of dragging heavy trees over soft ground.

The trip took them almost until the midnight Bell. When they arrived, after the drivers and hostlers had left, he told his exhausted charges that they were soldiers and not slaves. They went from disbelief to cheers, and Danil went to sleep that night a hero in his small world.

The new-minted soldiers' enthusiasm diminished rapidly the next day, once they understood that being soldiers meant more work, not less. The first order of business was to set up their camp, which meant stripping the brush from a forest clearing and building shelters, simple frames with waxed flax covers to start with.

Danil found even that was a challenge to organize, and he only won their cooperation by making it clear that no one would eat until the work was done. The easy leadership that Era had exercised seemed beyond him. The next day was even harder. Two of his recruits vanished in the sleeping hours, and a half-dozen of the remainder tried to bully their way into the food wagon. It might have meant the end of the project right there, but he appointed Avel, the largest of the group, as his second-in-command, and nobody wanted to fight Avel. With his backing Danil was able to keep the work moving, but at the same time he began to realize that there was far more to be done than he had ever imagined. By the end of the first week all they had for their efforts was a primitive camp and a rough routine to keep it running. Not a single tree had been felled for timber, let alone any effort put into developing tactics for an army and training on them.

Still, the routine at least gave him something on which he could base his organization, a hierarchy of command and the group cohesion necessary to get jobs done. He appointed two flank-captains and four mark-leaders, who led marks of five or six. Avel became his half-parishan, which by default made Danil parishan. It was a ridiculously over-organized structure, but it worked.

*And I have to plan for expansion.* The plan with Annaya was to expand the army to a full parisha, and there was no way he could lead such a force single-handed. *The time to start developing sub-commanders is now.* That brought up the question of training them in tactics and formations once more, and Danil himself knew little enough of that. *But that's a problem for later, and hopefully a problem for Era, if I can find him.*

Discipline and motivation remained problematic, but on the ninth day things were running well enough that he felt comfortable leaving Avel in charge. He took a beltbag of dried mutton and hard bread, and hiked down to Far Bay to see what he might find. The inquisitors had burned and looted the fisherfolk city, but neither operation had been really finished. It was as if the Prophetsy had forgotten the city existed after they'd set their fires. *And perhaps that's exactly what happened.* Poking around the ruins he found a lot that could be salvaged, though nothing that was immediately useful. The net weaver's shop where he had had his secret nest was gone, burned to the ground, but Era's forge was built largely of resined brick and thus was still partially standing. The easy-to-carry tools were gone, but the big waterwheel was still turning, and the tacklewheels and beltropes that drove the forge bellows and the drop hammer were intact. He found the alleyway where he'd first escaped from Hatch, and the cut-yard he'd fled through. The buildings there were levelled, but though the stocks of wood there had been set alight, the flames had burned themselves out, and most of the lumber was still useable.

*That will be useful, when the time comes.* His timber crew was going to have to function as a timber crew in order to stay beneath the notice of Polldor and the frightening Balak. Creating an army would have to happen in the background, in whatever time they could spare, and the already-cut lumber would buy a lot of time. They had only to build a track through the forest and clear some debris to get the big timber-carriers down to the city. He moved on from the cut-yard, through the blackened skeletons of burned out houses. It was strange to be walking streets he had almost forgotten, stranger still that they were destroyed and empty. He looked up the curve of the world to where Cove had once been. The inquisitors had burned it too, and now all he could see was a blackened patch. His throat constricted at the sight, and he felt a cold anger rise in him.

He turned to go back to the lumber camp. When he arrived he cancelled the work shift, and took all his nascent soldiers to the ruins to see for themselves what he had seen. After that, discipline was no longer a problem. A grim determination settled over the small group. They had a purpose now.

It took a month to get the timber camp working as some kind of productive entity, but he had an advantage in his long experience in slave crews and soon they were felling timber. It wasn't a moment too soon. On the thirtieth day, just after the evening-meal bell, a group of inquisitor riders came down the rough track that led to their camp. Balak was at their head.

"Danil Fougere." Balak reined to a halt behind him. "His Holiness the Prophet Unrisen wants to see lumber for sale in the Charity markets."

"We have the first twenty tons ready . . ." Danil hesitated. ". . . I'm sorry, I don't know your title."

"You don't need to answer," said Balak. "Your obedience is taken for granted. You'll have fifty dressed tons there by market-open tomorrow." Danil bowed his head as the only possible response, and tried to keep the fear off his face. Balak nudged his horse and moved off to inspect the worksite. Danil watched him, unsure of what to do next. A man like Balak didn't ride from the forewall to the aftward forests just to deliver a message. He had come to follow up on the suspicions that had been written in his face when Olen had first come to Prophet Polldor with the idea for a lumber crew. The other inquisitors had dismounted and were moving around the camp, looking into the crude shelters they'd built, inspecting the stacked logs and the tools.

*His Holiness the Prophet Unrisen.* That was the formal term for the Prophet's son, but it could not be the lazy and disinterested Olen who was demanding results, it could only be Balak himself, doing it for reasons of his own. *I'm getting caught up in Prophetsy politics, and that's dangerous.* Balak made a signal, and the inquisitors went back to their horses and mounted. *Fifty tons by market open.* They didn't even have that much cut, and half what they did have still needed dressing. They would need time to get the carriers loaded, and more time to move them the twenty kilometers up the trading road to Charity. He was being asked for the impossible.

Balak knew that, he was deliberately setting up Danil to fail.

*But he doesn't know about the lumber still in Far Bay. I can use that and succeed, maybe.* Unexpected success would make an enemy of the High Inquisitor. *But he's already an enemy, and he's the one who's set the rules.* Era would have known how to handle the situation, but Era wasn't there, and there was no point in wasting time.

"Avel!" Danil raised his voice. "Get everyone together, we've got work to do." None of them would sleep that night.

"What did you find, Balak?" Prophet Polldor slung his rabbit bow and reined his horse up as Balak drew level with him. He would rather have gone hunting in his newly won lands by the ocean. There would be deer aplenty there, perhaps even a leopard, but he couldn't spare the time to ride there, hunt, and return.

"Nothing, your Holiness. The slaves are there, the lumber is there. My men searched and found everything as it should be."

"And yet you're still not convinced."

Balak shook his head. "You know me too well, Prophet."

"It's my job to know you well. What makes you suspicious?" Polldor hung the reins and dismounted. A brace of rabbits and a fat pheasant hung from his game tree. It had been a good morning's hunt, even without a deer.

"It doesn't ring true, Prophet," said Balak, swinging down to join him. Together they walked the horses to a nearby beech tree and threw the hitch lines over a convenient branch.

"Explain."

The High Inquisitor put up his hands. "Your son. He asked for this venture, but now he shows no interest in it. Your daughter shows far too much."

"I've asked Annaya to support Olen before. It's a relief that she's finally doing it."

"Is she? Or does she have her own motives?"

"What other motive could she have?" Polldor turned to lead his friend and advisor away from the horses, down to the bank of the Golden River. It was one of his favorite places, to hunt, to ride, to hike, and most of all to get away from the confines of the Tower, where intrigue and politicking consumed far too much time and effort.

"Power."

"Over Olen? She has it already."

"Over you, Prophet. She doesn't accept the order of Noah's line."

Polldor laughed. "And how would she gain power with a timber camp?"

"I don't know. I do know that people don't change, or change little. The Prophet Unrisen changed just long enough to start this venture, and I suspect if we look deeper we'll find her Holiness put him up to it. Now that it's started she runs it, make no mistake. She sends her erranders into the market, to sell your steel and buy tools with the tokens. She watches the accounts, so closely that the tithecounters now dread the sound of her voice. I think she plans to oppose you, Prophet."

"Oppose me?" Polldor laughed. "That's hardly news. She's opposed me every day since her second birthday."

"Not like this." Balak put a hand to his chin, considering what he was about to say. "And then there's her chief slave. He's branded, and I don't trust him."

"Why not?"

"I ordered him to bring fifty tons of timber to the market. He didn't have that much ready, I'm sure of that."

"He's only beginning production."

"Exactly, Prophet! And yet the next day he produced the full fifty tons, cut, dressed and sawn. Where did they come from?"

"Perhaps you overlooked them."

"Perhaps." Balak hesitated. "I should have left watchers in place. I *would* have, except I expected him only to fail."

"What happened to the proceeds?"

"One of your son's erranders was there for the market, and brought the proceeds to the tithemaster."

"And are the figures correct?"

Balak nodded. "To the token, Prophet."

"Hmmm." Polldor stroked his beard. "I trust your instincts, old friend, but what I see here is this. My son is at last turning his head to rulership, and my daughter is at last turning her rulership to support him. They've chosen a smart enterprise, one she can run while letting him have the credit. She's watching his affairs closely, and she's chosen a chief slave who can produce under stress, who's shown loyalty despite his brand, and who is thus far honest."

"Prophet, there is something *wrong* about this, I can taste it. I know her Holiness, better than you think. She . . ." Balak hesitated. ". . . she was more effected by her lover's death than you know."

A pained expression crossed Polldor's face. "You may be right. It won't matter long, though. I'm going to place her soon enough."

"Who with, your Holiness?"

"Bishop Nufell."

Balak paused, considering that. "Are you sure you want to do that, Holiness? He has a reputation for squeezing his parish."

"And now he's squeezing the Elder Council just as hard, on my behalf. He thinks he's gaining power, but soon they'll fear him more than I. He's ambitious, but young. He'll be useful as an ally, and more useful to show the council there are worse potentials than my own rule."

"But will he give her Holiness due reverence?"

"Unlikely." Polldor smirked. "But he may yet live to regret his ambition. It's hard enough to be Annaya's father. To be her husband . . . Let's just say I pity the man."

They had reached the river bank, and Polldor sat down on the roots of an ancient willow. "I need you to watch him, Balak, as closely as you can without giving it away. How loyal is the Sanctity parisha?"

"With land of their own now? More loyal to you than to him, though a lot are eager to leave the ranks, take wives and start their own timber camps. They won't wait forever. It's like that in all the parishas. The war is over, and they want their share." Balak paused. "I apologize, Prophet."

"For what?"

"I would like to think my inquisitors weren't so easily swayed from your service."

"They're second sons who thought they'd never have the chance. I don't blame them, or you. I'll soon release those who want to go, but not yet. Right now good wood is fetching a premium, and we hold most of the market. We'll keep it that way until the price falls, and then they can do what they want with the land."

"You're subtle, Prophet."

"I have to be." Polldor paused, thinking. "Be careful watching the bishop; I don't want him to know you're doing it. There's one who *is* determined to have power."

"And your daughter?"

"Keep watching her too. And this chief slave of hers. I want no surprises coming before I tell her she's placed."

"As you wish, Prophet." Something stirred in the bushes, and

Balak raised his rabbit bow and released the shaft with one fluid motion. Polldor turned in time to see it catch a fat red-tailed squirrel.

"Good shot," he said.

Balak bowed his head. "By your blessing, Prophet."

Era paused to wipe the sweat from his brow, a pointless gesture since he was drenched in it. The field was low lying, and much of it was still sodden from the previous month's rain. The suntube relentlessly boiled out the moisture, which hung in the air like a blanket. Even without the humidity the work was hard and heavy, and raising his arm above his shoulder brought pain to the newly healed scar tissue on his chest.

*At that I was lucky . . . if you can call it luck.* At the end of his row, a driver stepped forward menacingly. Era bent over again to carry on pulling shafts of ripe flax from the ground. The tree that had fallen on him in the battle had burned him badly, but by rights he should have died. The fire had burned itself out, but he'd lain trapped under it for two days before an inquisitor spotter patrol stumbled on him and took him prisoner.

The Prophetsy was well-organized for conquest. It was less well-organized to handle a sudden doubling of its slave population. For Era that meant he had yet to be subjected to the humiliation of a slave collar, because there weren't enough to go around. It also meant that he was poorly fed, poorly housed, and poorly treated. There weren't enough drivers to handle all the new slave crews, especially since none of the newly captured fisherfolk were accustomed to a life of subservience. That meant the frequent application of the lash for problems that had been caused by the drivers themselves.

Era's crew had been given to the Bishop of Ascension Parish and assigned to harvest flax from the parish fields. None of them had ever done it before, and neither had their driver. It was unsurprising that their first day's effort damaged most of the crop they managed to harvest. It was equally unsurprising that they were punished for it.

*But I don't care about that, I just want to see Sall again.*

His first instinct after capture was simply to run. They were kept in a hastily built compound and getting out of it would not have been hard. He chose to wait.

The inquisitors were patrolling the countryside in half-mark strength. The first day he'd seen ten escapers brought in with fresh cross brands burned onto their cheeks. By the third day so many fisherfolk were escaping they started riding down the fugitives and killing them on the spot. When that didn't work they started putting crucifixes up around the slave pens as a warning, and after that people stopped trying to run.

There was nowhere to go in any case. The Prophetsy had put Far Bay to the torch, and around the curve of the ocean's shoreline he could see the smoldering ruins of every fisherfolk village. He had nearly wept when he'd seen the smoke, thinking of his forge, the years of work he'd put into it.

*And my father and grandfather . . .* He had first courted Sall there, proposed to her there. *And we're still young enough for children, if she could bear.* He pushed the thought away. He wouldn't see her again, he knew. He'd seen her die. Far Bay was gone, his life was gone. Prophet Polldor intended his victory to be permanent.

Era finished his row and moved to the next. His crew was better at harvesting now. They had learned how to pull the plants up by their roots without damaging the stem, and how to properly pile the harvested flax on the ground to be retted. It was backbreaking stoop labor, unworthy of a craftsman, unworthy of a battle leader, but he swallowed his pride and worked steadily. There would come a time when he could escape, and a time after that when he could avenge his wife, but not now. While he waited there was no point in gaining a reputation as a problem. When the time came it would be easier to get away if his captors were unsuspecting.

"Keep moving there, you're falling behind." Three rows over a driver raised his stick in warning, and Era bent over again and put some more effort into his motions, though his aching back paid for the exertion. He said nothing, but he knew the man, knew his face. The driver hadn't been a driver the day before, and he had a stick because there was no short-whip for him. *He is fisherfolk.*

The Bishop of Ascension had decided to solve his slave control problem by promoting some of his new workers to oversee the rest. It was not an option Era would have considered for a heartbeat, and it would have been better for all of fisherfolk if no one took the offer. Unfortunately some had, but Era took that in stride too. Sooner or later the tables would turn, and those who had turned their back on their people would pay the price for their opportunism then.

There was a commotion at the top of the field, and Era looked up to see men on horses with crimson cloaks. There was shouting, commands were barked and then all of a sudden the drivers were herding their crews out of the fields, forming them into lines, leading them up to the area beside their pen. The break from the monotonous work was welcome, but the relief in Era's back was balanced by the realization that whatever was happening was probably not going to be good.

When his crew arrived they were put into line with the others. Most of the newcomers were mounted inquisitors, with parish banners fluttering from their spears. Behind them, also mounted, was a young man in splendid white robes. Something was happening down on the far right of the line, a group on foot moving along the long row of slaves.

Era took a risk, took a step forward to look and see what was happening, and then stepped back as a driver raised his short-whip. He saw enough to understand what was happening. Slaves were being selected, taken out of line and sent to another area, for what purpose he could only guess. The ones chosen seemed to be the younger and stronger, but whether it was a good thing to be chosen or not was unknowable. He took another step forward and back to confirm what he was seeing, and this time earned a stripe from the short-whip for his trouble. He accepted it with equanimity.

A whisper came down the line. "It's the Prophet's son . . ." Era touched his tongue to his lips, thinking fast, assessing the white robed figure as though he could somehow read the boy's intent in his face. It might be better to be in the Prophet's service directly, or it might be worse. To the extent that he could influence the choice about to be made for him he could influence his fate. *To be chosen or not?*

On balance it seemed that being chosen must be a bad thing. The youngest and strongest would only be selected for particularly arduous labor. As the group grew close he bent to the ground and picked up a fist full of dirt, ran it over his face and beard and into his hair. He let himself slouch forward, rounding his shoulders, letting his face go slack. He was older than most of the others anyway, it seemed likely that he'd escape whatever it was awaiting the chosen. The group came to him, but he kept his eyes on the ground, trying to look tired and defeated. It was a performance that took little effort.

"Look up." The voice was commanding, imperious, and he recognized it. He looked up to meet the eyes of Danil Fougere. He saw the other's eyes widen in recognition, but otherwise the young man gave no sign. Despite his desire to keep his own expression neutral, Era felt his jaw tighten. He had seen none of his group since the battle, but he would've liked to believe that none of them would betray the fisherfolk. It cut him to the core to see one of his own working for the Prophetsy. *He sold us out.* Unconsciously his hands balled into fists.

"This one." Danil jerked his thumb in the direction of the group that was growing off to the side of the line. He gave no other sign that he'd recognized Era, just moved to the next slave, and the next. An inquisitor herded Era away from his crew, away from the flax field, and towards an uncertain future. The Prophet's son, if that's who the boy in the robes truly was, wasn't even paying attention. Era found that galling somehow, but he reserved his anger for Danil. *He'll pay for this, I swear it.*

Unceremoniously he was roped into a slave crew thirty strong, and marched aftward under the escort of a half-mark of mounted inquisitors. Several bells later they arrived at the Prophetsy wall. There had been fighting in the area, and clustered arrow shafts still spiked up from the ground, but the grass had grown up long since the battle, and there was no other indication that hundreds of soldiers had died on that very ground such a short time ago.

A gap had been cut in the wall, bricks and timbers torn out to make an opening, and they were marched through it into the forest, following a recently cut track to a crude encampment, nothing more than a few hastily constructed shacks in a clearing. Fresh cut tree trunks, haul lines and logging gear told him all he needed to know. *This is a lumber crew.*

Something close to horror seeped into his soul at the revelation. The Prophetsy's lumber crews were notorious for their brutality, even in Far Bay. At the same time he felt a measure of hope. He was in the aftward forest, territory he knew intimately.

Escape would be easy: he needed a hundred meters of head start and they would never find him.

The inquisitor escorting them handed them over to a tall man named Avel who was carrying an ironwood club. Era's jaw clenched; Avel was also fisherfolk. *How easily our own betray us.* Avel moved to the head of the line and watched as the inquisitor rode off through the trees. When they were gone he turned to the group.

"Fisherfolk, the Prophetsy has made you slaves." His voice was strong, commanding. "I came here as a slave, but I didn't like slavery, so I became a soldier. They took my honor, and now I've taken it back. As slaves you have no honor. As slaves you're tied into crews, and lashed like animals." He walked up and down the line, looking each man in the eye. "Well, as of this moment you aren't slaves any longer, you're soldiers. You are soldiers in the army that is going to take back what rightfully belongs to the fisherfolk. The Prophetsy doesn't have your honor anymore. It's right there in front of you. It's up to you to pick it up again."

Era looked at Avel in utter disbelief, then looked around to confirm that they were in a barely established lumber camp. What the big man was saying seemed impossible. There were no weapons, no armor, no nothing, not even as much organization as they'd had before the Prophetsy attacked. And yet already other slaves . . . *No, soldiers!* . . . were coming down the line, unharnessing the newcomers. His own neck rope was undone, and reflexively he looked up the track where the inquisitors had left, but there was nothing there. He looked in the other direction, aftward into the forest and towards the ocean. *I could still disappear.*

"Era!" The voice was familiar, and Era turned to face the speaker.

"Danil! What's going on here?" Era stepped from the line as Avel called the rest of the newly released fisherfolk to follow him.

"Just what Avel said. We're building an army. I'm the parishan."

"Parishan? That's an inquisitor rank."

"We're using their formations, their tactics. We have to if we want to take the battle out of the forest."

"Hmmph. The day I call you parishan is the day I die."

"You won't have to. I want you to lead."

Era raised his eyebrows, his doubt clear in his face.

"Who better, Era? We need you."

The blacksmith nodded slowly, absorbing his sudden change in circumstance. "Then show me what you've got."

———————————

Sanctity Parish Hall was a small fortress in its own right, with high walls topped with arrow towers, and heavy timber gates. Sanctity's parisha was drawn up in ordered ranks in the courtyard, and Bishop Nufell looked down from his balcony on the third floor as the parishan read out the Prophet's proclamation. Each inquisitor would be free to leave the order, if he so chose, and take up a farm in the newly conquered forests. Each inquisitor would be entitled to a wife from the newly captured women. Those who took land would be subject to recall service on the Prophet's order, for no more than six months in a year. Nufell's lips curled into a frown. The Prophet had effectively stolen the loyalty of Sanctity's own soldiers for himself, and there was little the bishop could do about it. *But I will yet have power.* He turned to the young man standing beside him.

"You can see I'm loyal to your father, your Holiness. His proclamation is read exactly as he requires."

"I'm sure you are. Why wouldn't you be?" Olen Polldor sounded earnest, and Nufell smiled a smile that was as contrived on the inside as it was sincere on the outside.

"Ah, young Olen, there's a lot you have to learn."

The Prophet's son made a face. "I wish you didn't sound so much like my father."

Nufell laughed. "I promise I won't make you study. I've asked you here to pledge loyalty to you."

"Well yes, of course," answered Olen, although his expression showed he really didn't understand what Nufell was driving at.

*I'm going to have to be more direct.* "Not 'of course,' your Holiness. Unfortunately, not everyone supports the Prophetsy the way they should." Nufell clapped his hands, and two of his wives came in carrying platters with bowls of berries, rich clotted cream, fresh buttered breads and filtered wine in fine-glazed flasks. "Eat with me and let me explain." He offered the Prophet's son a chair, and the young man sat. "There are those on the Elder Council who believe they could do a better job as Prophet."

"A better job?" Olen seemed half puzzled, half offended. "To be Prophet they'd have to be of Noah's line, and that's my father, and then me. Me." He put stress on the last word. "No one else can be Prophet."

"Are you sure your father agrees?" Nufell raised his flask. "Blessings, your Holiness."

"What do you mean by that?" asked Olen, ignoring the pleasantry.

Nufell shrugged. "It's no secret your father questions your fitness to rule." He leaned forward. "I've heard he's been asking some of the Elder Council if they'll follow his daughter."

Olen looked shocked. "The Prophet can't be a woman!"

"I agree, your Holiness. But it's no secret your father favors your sister over you."

"But he couldn't . . . Annaya . . ." Olen spluttered, suddenly lost for words.

"I'm sure you're right, your Holiness," Nufell went on. "I'm sorry I brought it up. It's not my place to . . ."

"Never mind that. Tell me what you've heard."

"Only what I've told you. But your right, the Prophet can't be a woman, and your father knows that."

"It would be like him to try to put Annaya in my place. He's always favored her. Always." Olen looked away, trying not to pout, and Nufell smiled a small smile. He had the young man just where he wanted him.

"Well, the Prophet's will isn't to be denied. Unless . . ."

"Unless what?" Olen snapped his attention back to the bishop.

"Unless it conflicts with the will of God."

"Hmmph. My father won't care about that. So far as he's concerned he *is* the will of God. He thinks I'm useless, I can't do anything well enough for him." Olen looked to the older man. "It isn't my fault I don't like to shoot and ride. Why would I? Why should I?"

"No reason at all. You're the Prophet's son. Other people should do these things for you."

Olen nodded. "Exactly."

"And you are entitled to be Prophet, when your time comes. God ordains it."

"Yes, yes, exactly right."

"It would be a sin for your father to put your sister in your place. You can't allow that."

"How can I prevent it?" Olen threw his arms up. "He'll do what he wants, he always does."

"Then you'll have to take what you're entitled to." Nufell leaned forward and lowered his voice. "Seize it."

"How?" Olen leaned forward, suddenly interested.

"I've pledged loyalty to you, your Holiness. Do you trust me now? Trust me with your life?"

"Yes, yes I do."

"Well then, I have a way, perhaps." Bishop Nufell leaned closer still. "You'll have to do just what I say."

"Tell me what I have to do."

Nufell smiled. "The inquisitors are the key, and the High Inquisitor is key to the inquisitors."

Olen snorted. "Balak? There's no getting around him. If he were any more loyal he'd be a dog."

"Perhaps. Or perhaps not. I've watched Balak, and the one thing I know to be true about him is—he *believes*. That's his blade and his shield, but belief is a two-edged weapon, and even the largest shield can't cover everything."

"What do you mean?"

"A man can only have one loyalty. The High Inquisitor is loyal to his faith, not your father. We can use that."

"My father *is* his faith."

"Almost true but not quite. We need to find the place where that's false. That's where we slide the blade in."

Olen nodded, thinking that over, but Nufell could tell he had the young man captivated. He smiled to himself. *Polldor has the inquisitors, but I have the Prophet's son.*

"Spear fence, now!" Danil yelled to his flank-captains, "Skirmishers out!"

"Spear fence, skirmishers out!" The flank-captains relayed his orders down the line, and the formation moved. Danil turned to see Era's expression, to read there what he thought of the army Danil had built for him, but the older man's face was impassive. In seconds his parisha had adopted the formation, three ranks with spears planted to receive a horse charge, with a fourth rank carrying rabbit bows deployed ten meters forward.

"Move to double lines!" Danil yelled, and again the flank-captains echoed his words and the formation moved. At first it moved well, but then something went wrong on the left flank. Both marks there had moved, and marched straight into another, causing them to dissolve into a milling mob. Danil turned away, not wanting to watch, or to see Era's reaction. He'd grown his army to a full parisha in just four months, but the slaves-turned-soldiers were still a ragtag group. They had only sharpened poles to represent spears, with no armor, and not even ironwood blades.

More importantly they had only the shakiest grasp on the formation drills required to function as a cohesive unit. It wasn't his fault, he knew, but he also knew that issues of fault would make no difference in the face of the well drilled inquisitors.

The fact was they couldn't train in the open. As a result, they'd spent the first two months just clearing a space large enough to train out of the forest, cutting trees, hauling logs and digging out the stumps eight bells a day, and practicing with their improvised weapons for another six. It had been gruelling work, but his little band had worked hard, and Danil had been proud of them, and himself. Now, with Era watching beside him, they seemed amateurish and unskilled.

The shouting subsided, and Danil turned around to see if the chaos had been sorted out. It hadn't. *At least it's no worse than before.* The mark-leaders of the involved marks were arguing over something, while their charges watched in a gaggle. Their flank-captain was descending on them, already yelling.

"Dismiss them," said Era.

"What?"

"Dismiss them. We're done here. I can't lead this group."

"But Era . . ."

But Era was already walking away. "Flank-captains! Half-parishan, dismiss the ranks!" Danil yelled, then turned to catch up. Behind him he could hear Avel yelling, and then the sudden babble of voices as the ranks dissolved. Era walked to a tree at the edge of their clearing and waited there for him.

"That was a bad example, we've done much better . . ." Danil began.

Era shook his head. "Danil, I appreciate your confidence in me, but I can't be parishan here. Look at the way they follow you. You built this army, it's yours now."

Danil looked at the older man, stunned. He had expected criticism of the failure of the maneuver, not praise for his leadership. "I don't know anything about this or . . ."

"Evidently you've learned."

"Era, you saw what problems we have. I'm already at my limit, and we need to be much, much better to stand in battle with the inquisitors."

Era put out his hands, palm up. "Danil, I led an ambush party against the Prophetsy, but I'm a blacksmith by trade. I can help you with blade and bow, but you credit me with too much. I don't know anything about formation tactics."

"But . . ." Danil was at a loss for words. He had pinned every hope on Era. "You see what we have here. They—*we* need more than I can give them."

Era nodded. "Probably. Still, you're the leader, and you have to keep leading."

"Why do you think I searched you out? I chose *you* to be the leader. What do I know of fighting but what you taught me?"

"You're the one who put this together, Danil. It has to be you. I'm a stranger to most of these people. They won't follow me. And even if they would, that won't make what you've got capable of taking on the inquisitors. It took Polldor twenty years to build his army."

"We don't have that kind of time."

"How much do you have?"

Danil looked away, wondering how much to take Era into his confidence. A few meters away a box turtle was making stately progress across the forest floor, and he watched the small creature while he thought. *Era doesn't need to know, and the fewer people who know the safer we all are. At the same time, he does need to know I trust him. And I need his advice.*

"Not much time," he said. "We have a patron supporting this, a Prophetsy woman. She has power to help us now, but she's being placed for marriage soon and she'll lose it, and us with it. If we aren't able to fight and win by then, we'll all be slaves again."

"How long before your woman is placed?"

"I don't know, and she doesn't either. It could be tomorrow, it could be six months. We can't afford to wait."

Era picked up a fallen branch and idly stripped the twigs from it. "Even if you could produce a parisha as disciplined as any of theirs, they have shipsteel, and we have wood. And the Prophet Polldor has a lot of parishas."

"We'll take them on one by one, that was always the plan."

"You'll lose people every time, and eventually you'll lose the battle. And what if *they* don't choose to take us one parisha at a time. You'll be slaughtered."

"Era." Danil groped for words. "That's why we need you to lead us. I was a slave, and the worst part of that is feeling worthless. You, *you*, are the one who gave me pride, taught me to fight."

He waved a hand at the bustling encampment, where men and women were taking advantage of the unexpected break to improve their shelters, sharpen the ends of their poles, repair their clothing and do the hundred other little tasks that usually went undone in order to meet the demands of the training schedule. "You can't abandon these people."

"They aren't mine to abandon, they're yours. But even assuming they'd follow me, where can I lead them? Back into slavery? To defeat and death. You're trying to make an army like the Prophet's but it's never going to be as good or as large as his. You need to find another way, an advantage they haven't thought of."

"They've thought of horses, spears, blades and bows. They've thought of armor and ordered formations. What else is there to think of?"

Era shrugged. "I don't know. In the first war we beat them, because the trees were our advantage. Their tactics work best in the open. This time they beat us, because they used fire against the trees."

"I can't fill the Prophetsy with trees."

"No, you need something new."

"Hmmm." Danil nodded, thinking. The box turtle had found a cluster of white-capped mushrooms, and he watched while it chomped them down with evident satisfaction. *An advantage against the inquisitors.* He had been so optimistic, so pleased with his army. Whatever flaws it had he had counted on Era to rectify, but he could see now that he'd been deluding himself. *And every fisherfolk who's chosen to follow me.* It was so obvious now how pathetic his efforts were. They lacked the numbers, the resources, the experience to put up any kind of opposition to the disciplined inquisitors. *It's easy to say we need an advantage. Much harder to find one.* The turtle finished the mushrooms and started to move off, and then inspiration dawned on Danil. *Yes . . .*

"Loan me your stick," he asked Era, and took the piece of wood the other man had been playing with before he could answer. He went over to the turtle and tapped it on the back. The small creature promptly pulled its head and legs into its shell, and Danil picked it up.

"This is what we need."

"Turtles?"

"No, we need armor, like the inquisitors. *Better* than the inquisitors."

"We haven't got the shipsteel."

"We'll use wood." He held up the turtle. "Imagine, a wooden turtle, big enough to hold twenty soldiers, maybe more, with walls thick enough that no spear can break them. It's too big and heavy for a horse to overrun. It's on wheels, big, wide wheels like our timber-carriers, with archers here and here . . ." He pointed to the openings in the turtle's shell. "The soldiers inside push it forward, safe from arrows, from anything."

"If it's wood it'll burn, and they know how to use fire."

"So before we begin we soak it with water, and carry more with us. We make the bows bigger, so big it takes two to draw them, maybe three. They can shoot a heavier shaft farther, and penetrate an inquisitor's armor. Even if the shaft doesn't get through it'll hit hard enough to knock a man off his horse." Danil's words came in a rush as his idea gained shape in his mind.

"I think you've lost your mind."

"No, I've only just regained it. Try to think of what else we need. Eventually we'll have to storm the Prophet's temple, we need a way to deal with the walls. Maybe a bow even bigger, just one per turtle, mounted on the top, able to throw a whole treetrunk. A turtle with a ladder built onto its top, so it can be ridden right up to the wall of the Prophet's temple and the soldiers can just run up and jump over. What else might work?"

"Do you know what it would take to build even one of these things?"

Danil laughed. "I've got a whole timber crew. I can get you all the wood you need."

"It's going to take steel, for fittings, for the wheels . . . They'll be better crank-driven than pushed, and that'll take gears . . ."

"You're a blacksmith. I'll get you the steel. Your forge is still standing, or most of it."

Era's eyes were suddenly very intense. "They burned Far Bay. Are you sure of that?"

"I've seen it myself."

The older man nodded slowly, a new determination in his expression. "Take me there."

---

Annaya's footsteps echoed in the empty, dark corridor. She knew the way to the place she called Noah's Temple so well now that she no longer needed torches to light her way, even her flaxen yarn was unnecessary. It was simpler, and safer, to navigate there in the darkness, using just her hand on the wall to count doorways. It was still an eerie feeling, feeling her way through darkness so complete it made no difference if she closed her eyes or kept them open. It was a little trickier after she'd gone through the heavy doors that led to the hexagonal corridors, because she couldn't easily touch the wall with her hand and so had to count footsteps, but she found the ladder, as she always did. Twelve rungs up, a measured pace count, and she could see the faint blue-tinged glow from the sacred place.

It was not actually Noah's shrine—she had searched all the names beneath the faces etched into the wall and found none that even approximated to Noah, but that didn't matter too much. The place had belonged to those who had built the temple, perhaps by the Joshua Crewe whose name and face were so prominent among those etched into the shipsteel walls. Whether Crewe had built the world she couldn't know, but she knew his people had been powerful beyond the imagination of any who had followed them. *What I would do for such power . . .*

She had no illusions that such a dream might come true, but still, she would seize what she could. She followed the blue light with careful footsteps until she came to the corridor that led to the chamber of faces, where it was bright enough to walk normally. Danil was there, waiting for her.

"Danil, it's been so long since you've come." Annaya came towards him.

"There's a problem, we need to talk . . ." he began.

"There's no problem that won't wait."

She put a finger to his lips to stifle his protest, and pulled him close with her other arm. It wasn't what he wanted, she could sense that, but he didn't object. *He never objects, and I always make it worth his while.* She kissed him hard and pushed him back on the soft bed that she'd put there, enjoying his automatic, male response. His tight-corded muscles were hard against her, but his eyes were soft as he looked into hers, open and vulnerable in a way she'd never experienced before, not even with Sem.

*He's still a boy in a man's body.* Sex was her weapon, not his, but she had to admit his innocence had an allure she found hard to resist. *It's necessary.* She told herself that every time. *Necessary to ensure his loyalty, to get what I want from him.* She meant the words to remind herself that he was a tool and not a lover, but in her more honest moments she had to admit that the truth was more complicated. She stripped off his trousers to mount him, and his body responded as it always did as she urged him on.

Afterwards he rolled away from her, and she knew he was feeling the need to recover some distance, some independence. She allowed him that, if only because she needed the space for herself as well. Still, she was relieved when he reached out for her across the gap he had opened to pull her back again, and it was comforting to feel small in his arms. It was also dangerous. *I need to be able to betray him in a heartbeat.* She was growing less sure that she could, and that was a risk she could ill afford.

*All the more reason to change this game.* She turned over and kissed him.

"And now my heroic warrior, tell me what troubles my army."

"The army . . ." Danil turned over on his back. "The army is training well, working hard. The problem is it can't win."

Annaya's pretty features darkened in the flickering light and she pushed herself away from him. "Well fix it. This can't go on any further. Bishop Nufell is pushing my father hard. I'm going to be placed any time."

"I need steel, or tokens to buy it."

"I gave you steel."

"I need more."

Annaya snorted. "Well, you can't have it."

"Then we can't win."

"What do you mean, you lying *sooksan*?" Sudden anger flooded Annaya. "You promised me an army. You *promised* me."

"You have an army. What you don't have is an army that can win."

"You came all this way to tell me this?" She stood up, suddenly angry. "Did I pick the wrong man? Tell me if I need to choose another."

"You have no time to choose another. What we have here is what we're going to deal with. You, me, the soldiers we have. Nothing more. The problem is not with the training, not the soldiers, not with me. The problem is we've set ourselves an impossible task. There's no way I can field a force to defeat the inquisitors. We've been lying to ourselves." Danil stood up and paced. "I have a weapon that can change that, perhaps, but it takes a lot of steel."

"I'm already getting you everything I can. Balak is watching me, did you know that? Every day he's in with the tithemaster. I can't get you more steel. I can't get you more anything."

"Your father controls the steel-falls. Not a kilogram enters this world that doesn't come through this temple."

"In case you hadn't noticed, I'm not my father. Are you afraid to die, is that it?" Annaya laced her voice with contempt.

"Anyone who tells you otherwise is a liar, or madman. I'm not afraid to risk my life, but I'm not stupid either." Danil quirked a smile. "Or at least, I'm getting smarter. Get me the steel and I'll give you a victory, or at least a good chance at it."

"A good chance? My father has to die, and my brother, and a great many bishops. That has to *happen*. Don't you want to be free? Don't you want your people to be free?"

"Of course I do. Get me the steel."

"And you're only figuring this out now? We went over steel when we talked about this. You already wanted more than I could get you. What do you think has changed I can get it now? This was your idea. *Yours*."

"Then I accept responsibility for my mistake." Danil's voice was calm in the face of Annaya's tirade, which only made her angrier. "The question that faces us now is how to move forward."

"What do you want steel for anyway?"

"War turtles. Armored battle machines on wheels."

Annaya snorted. "War turtles? You can come up with a better lie than that."

"The problem is that the inquisitors are better skilled, better equipped and they outnumber us. War turtles are my solution to that problem, but if you have a better idea I'll listen."

"My idea was trust you." Annaya pouted, angry because he was so reasonable, angrier because she couldn't break his calm, and angriest of all because she recognized that she was being difficult for no good reason, and was doing it anyway. "Obviously a mistake."

"We want to rework the world. If you want an effective army, this is the price. How else can we exert influence?"

"Sex, bribery, blackmail, deception."

Danil gave her a look. "Those came to you easily."

She shrugged. "What else do I have in my life? I watch men struggle for power every day."

"And struggle for them yourself."

"Do you think I want power? Really?" Annaya shook her head and turned away. "Power is an empty ambition, nobody knows that more than I do." She thought she was lying as she said the words, because power was what she had fought for since she was old enough to fight for anything, but as she heard her voice say them she realized it was true.

"Then what do you want?"

"The same as you." Annaya's anger faded with her realization and she turned back to face Danil, came close. "Freedom."

"But you—"

"Shhh . . ." She came into his arms, regretting her tantrum. "Don't tell me what I have, how lucky I am. You were a slave. I am still." She looked up into his eyes, feeling suddenly sad. "Will you hold me for a while, Danil? I'm sorry I was angry."

He did as she asked, and all of a sudden she was crying in his arms, hating herself for showing weakness to a man, and at the same time feeling comforted that she could. After a while he picked her up and laid her on the bed, pulling her close. It made her feel better, and eventually she spoke. "Maybe I could come away with you."

"What do you mean?"

"Just leave this, leave my father, the elder Council, plots and plans and war. My father wants my brother to run the Prophetsy. Why should I stop him? I could come with you, be your woman."

"What about the army?"

"Forget about it. I can't get you more steel. I would if I could, Danil." She turned over to look into his eyes. "I would if I could, but I can't. Every day I think Balak will catch me."

Danil looked at her and she felt naked before him in a way she never had before. *Will he choose me?* His eyes were deep and she let herself be lost in them. *Could it be he really loves me?* She wanted it to be true, and hated herself for being so weak. She wanted him to kiss her, to tell her she was his, to take her away and keep her.

Danil shook his head slowly. "I won't abandon the army. They'll be slaves again if I don't lead them."

"Better slaves than dead." He was rejecting her, gently, caringly, but rejecting her. "And we would be together," she pleaded.

"No, it isn't better to be a slave than to be dead, and they need leadership. I am . . . no, *we* are the ones who put this together. We can't give up."

Annaya sat quietly, trying to get a hold of herself. *This isn't me. I reject men, they don't reject me.* And yet she couldn't help latching on to the word "we" the way he'd used it. "We" meant they were together, a unit. *Didn't it?* She wanted to ask him, and couldn't. After a long time she spoke. "How big is a war turtle?"

"Big enough to hold twenty, maybe more."

She laughed. "There isn't enough steel in the world to armor something so big."

Danil shook his head. "Their armor is wooden. The steel is for fittings, for gears, for the axles and holdbolts, springs for the bows."

"Springs for the bows?"

"They're going to be big bows."

"How much are you going to need?"

"I don't know yet. A lot. My smith thinks a hundred kilos a turtle, and I want to put my whole army in turtles, if I can."

"*My* whole army," Annaya countered.

"Ours, if you like."

"Ours." There was more comfort in the word than Annaya wanted to admit, even to herself. She pursed her lips, considering. "How many turtles is that?"

"Twenty or thirty."

"That's a lot of steel."

"Yes, it is."

"Getting it is going to be dangerous. I might get caught."

"This whole idea is dangerous, and we're all taking risks."

"And it's going to take time."

"How much time?"

"I don't know." Annaya looked away, considering. "It's six weeks to the ceremony of the Incarnation. The Bishop of Sanctity has been pressuring my father to have me placed with him. If I'm going to be married this year then that's when he'll proclaim it."

"Two months? We can't be ready by then. It's impossible."

"You have to be. Danil, promise me." She kissed him and he kissed her back, which made her smile. *I still have my power over him.* She moved her hands over him, pulled him to her, and for a while his touch made her forget about her father, and Bishop Nufell, forget about power and the Prophetsy. It was blissful, but it frightened her too. *Sex is my weapon, I have to remember that.* It was hard to keep herself detached when she felt his passion for her, saw his genuine enjoyment of their pairing. She had fought the duel of love with much more sophisticated opponents than Danil Fougere, but his very innocence, and the sincerity that came with it, engaged her affections in the way she'd never experienced before.

"I promise to do my best," he said afterwards, caressing her. "Whatever happens I'll come get you, whatever it takes."

"Will you?"

"You have to get me the steel."

"I'll get it, somehow. I'll send it down with your supply wagons. I'll send you all I can, as fast as I can." She smiled bitterly, trying to raise her courage. "Why should I worry about being caught? What's the worst my father will do? Place me with some wrinkled bishop?"

"I'll expect it then." Danil stood up. "I should be going."

Annaya shook her head and pulled him back down to her. "Stay, Danil, just a little while longer." He protested at first, and then stayed longer, but in the end he had to leave. And in the end, she still felt empty once he was gone.

"Prophet! Prophet! Prophet!" chanted the crowd, and Prophet Polldor stood and waved from his ornate travel cart, receiving the crowd's adulation as his due. *Let the bishops see my popularity.* It was important to show the people the symbol of their worship, important that they knew him to be real. Two full marks of red-cloaked riders preceded him through the streets of Charity, and hundreds more lined the route. They served to keep back the common people, and to remind any who doubted that his power came from men as well as from God.

Ahead, the procession turned right into the main square.

The bishops were waiting there, to lead the procession into the church, and Polldor smiled to himself. There were those on the Elder Council who desired his power for themselves, but he had humbled some, and tamed the rest. *But where is Balak?* His High Inquisitor was supposed to lead the honor guard, but he wasn't there. It was a minor annoyance. The important thing was that the bishops feared his inquisitors more than they hated his usurpation of their traditional authority.

*The truth is the bishops need me.* The bishops could only claim divine power themselves by teaching that it flowed from God to Noah's living descendent. As long as he controlled the inquisitors there was nothing they could do but bleat like so many sheep about the perceived inadequacy of their share of the world's wealth. Bishop Nufell was the exception, the leopard hiding in the flock, a man too smart and dangerous to be allowed to choose his own path, but he'd been safely neutralized. *Annaya needed to be placed anyway.* By giving his daughter to his enemy Polldor was sealing an alliance, assuring himself, and more importantly Olen, of Nufell's support. He looked to his son, still obediently waving, and repressed the urge to tell him to stand straight for the fourth time that day. *The boy has so little backbone.* It would probably be Annaya's son by the bishop who stepped up to wear the Prophet's robes, after Polldor himself was gone. Olen would have sons when the time came, but he doubted they would have the mettle to hold the Prophetsy against Nufell's ambition to see his own blood lead the descendents of Noah.

*And little matter.* The important thing was that they would be Polldor's grandsons either way. His close guards followed the lead ranks into the main square, and as Polldor's cart turned the corner he saw it was jammed with chanting supporters. He took the opportunity to look behind him, to Olen's cart. His son was standing up in the top door as well, looking pleased and comfortable with the crowd, if not exactly commanding. There had been a change in Olen recently, starting with his idea for the timber camp. He was showing himself to be more assertive, taking more of an interest in rulership.

*Perhaps in time, he'll be able to control the bishops.* Ahead of him the Elder Council was waiting in the square on a raised dais, and they fell into step behind him as he went past. The symbolism was important. When his father had been the Son of

Noah the bishops had preceded the Prophet on the slow advance to the ceremony of the Incarnation, and the Prophet had walked as well. Polldor had changed that. He wanted the commoners to know without question who led the Prophetsy. Now there was no one in the world who wasn't aware of the need to show loyalty to their Prophet, or of the penalties that could fall to those who were insufficiently enthusiastic in their worship.

"Prophet! Prophet! Prophet!" The crowd grew denser and the chanting louder. The spire of Charity church rose at the end of the processional way, the tallest structure in the world next to his own tower. The doors were open, red-cloaked inquisitors on guard there too. He'd given some consideration to holding the ceremony at the Temple, but had decided against it. It was better to keep his inner sanctum a mystery and let the common people see him descend among them as Noah had descended from the suntube. He leaned back, enjoying the spectacle as the procession made its way forward. The ceremony of Incarnation was a necessary reinforcement of the Prophetsy's power, but it was also a tremendous validation of all Polldor had worked for since his father's death.

*Why pursue power if you don't enjoy the exercise of it?* He smiled broadly and waved at the masses. Young girls with baskets were spreading flowers on the baked-brick road ahead of his horse team. Every year the pageantry grew more elaborate.

It was Charity parish's responsibility to stage the incarnation, and Bishop Braman's chance to demonstrate his loyalty, his power, and his wealth to both Polldor and the Elder Council. Braman never failed to make the most of his opportunity, and this time was no exception. Charity parish had more than the largest church in the world, it had five times the population of the next largest parish, more than half of the crafters and traders, the principal markets, the only two smithies capable of making large castings, a third of the Prophetsy's grain stores. Charity fielded not one but three parishas, and taken together those factors gave Braman considerable power. *He would be a dangerous adversary, if he had a spine.* Fortunately he did not, and he exercised his power only to show Polldor how loyal he really was.

The procession came to the church doors. A pair of ornately cloaked erranders ran up to open the door to Polldor's travel cart and placed the step so he could descend. He left the cart and climbed the stairs into the church, leaving the chanting crowd behind. Behind him, Olen was doing the same.

The church itself was full of the Prophetsy's elite, dressed in their churchgoing best to bear witness to the miracle about to happen. *And to show their importance to their neighbors, and demonstrate their worthiness to receive Prophetsy largess.* Prophet Polldor had not always had such a hard-edged view of human nature, but it was impossible to fill the role he filled without quickly learning that no one's motives were entirely pure.

When his father had died, he had been surprised at the number of people who became his friend. Perhaps he shouldn't have been surprised at the number who turned out to be cultivating his friendship only because it suited their own interests. Power came with its own imperatives, and one reason he had set out to bring all of the world under his command was the realization that to stagnate was to die. The fisherfolk had made a convenient enemy, and the conquest of them had united the Elder Council and the commoners beneath him.

*But now the war is over.* For a time the consolidation of gains would occupy the Prophetsy's collective attention, but after that he would have to find another way to stay on top of the restive bishops. The inquisitors would have to evolve as well. A lot of them would go willingly to clear and farm their newly granted lands, but the organization needed a new purpose.

*I have time to solve that problem.* Polldor advanced down the center aisle. Unlike the throngs that lined the roads outside, the crowd in the church was hushed. Huge patterned quilts hung from the walls and polished wood crucifixes stood in niches. The window shutters were closed, dimming the interior for the miracle to follow. He walked to the altar, and the choir stood and began to sing as he passed it. When he reached the altar he turned to face the congregation. Olen, still following him, moved to his appointed place on the raised platform behind the pulpit, as the bishops filed in to form two rows on his other side. When they were in place Polldor spread his arms wide, which was the signal for a waiting errander to pull a cord that released a curtain from the ceiling overhead. The curtain fell, hiding him from the watching crowd. Covered from view, he lowered his arms and went to the back wall of the church. There was a small door there that led to Bishop Braman's rooms. An errander opened it for him, and he went in to wait there while the assembled clergy went through the incantations necessary to invoke the Incarnation.

For the next four bells, each bishop would rise and read his own part of the story of Noah, imbuing it with life and meaning. For the next four bells the elite of the world would pay homage to their Prophet, while looking up at his anointed son. For the next four bells Prophet Polldor would wait out of sight and suffer the necessary boredom until the ritual was finished and he would come out and stand behind the curtain again. As the choir reached a crescendo the errander would pull a second rope, dropping the curtain to the floor to to reveal him standing there in all his glory. The miracle would be deemed complete, the Incarnation renewed for another year. He would walk back down the church aisle, his son and the bishops would follow, and the procession would reverse itself, back through the main square of Charity, back out of the city, back to the temple.

Waiting was not something Polldor did well, but it was a something that had to be done. *And it's better than standing there listening.* The curtain was another innovation he had added to the ceremony, to spare himself the mindnumbing tedium of listening to the bishops droning on. He had long contemplated having a woman waiting for him in Braman's quarters, one of his junior wives or even a serving girl. It would be a more pleasant way to pass the time, but he also knew that sooner or later news of the dalliance would leak, and it would undermine the impact of the solemn ritual if those watching it knew their Prophet was having sex while it went on. The same reasoning prevented him from simply leaving the building and spending a couple of hours hunting. He went into the bishop's sitting room, and found his High Inquisitor waiting for him there.

"Balak," Polldor frowned in surprise. "You were supposed to be leading the guard in the procession."

Balak bowed his head. "My apologies, Prophet. I was delayed on a matter of critical importance. I couldn't get back to the temple in time, I came here to meet you as soon as possible."

Polldor raised an eyebrow. "What is it?" He went over to the bishop's reception couch and reclined on the well padded sheepskin.

"It's private." Balak looked at the errander, who had followed Polldor into the room, ready to do the Prophet's bidding.

"Leave us," Polldor said. "Come back in a bell. We'll be done by then."

The errander scurried out a side door and Polldor returned his attention to Balak. "Tell me."

Balak didn't answer right away. Instead he walked to the window at the back of the room. The shutters were open but the curtains were closed, and the light that filtered through them was patterned red and white. Balak parted them and peeked outside, as though looking for eavesdroppers. He let them drop, turned again to face Polldor, opened his mouth and closed it again. Polldor waited, until finally the other man spoke.

"You are Noah's son, Prophet. I know this is true."

"Go on."

"Faith commands me . . ." Balak halted, groping for words. "Prophet, I don't know how to say this."

"Just say it, Balak. There's no one's loyalty I value as much as yours. You can't offend me."

"I'm honored by your faith, Prophet, but it isn't . . ." Balak stopped himself, took a deep breath. "Prophet, I've had Bishop Nufell watched, as you instructed. And I've been watching your daughter myself. There's no one else I would trust with that."

"What have you found?"

"Not what I expected. Your daughter is . . . willful. Well, we already knew that, but it's your son who has . . ." The High Inquisitor seemed in physical pain as he spoke the words. ". . . who has betrayed you."

"What?" Polldor stood up, suddenly angry. "My son? Olen? Impossible."

"Prophet, I assure you, this is why I've come late. I had to go and see for myself. Your son is plotting against you with Bishop Nufell, and he's raising an army."

"An army? Olen? He hasn't got the yats to lead an army."

"He isn't leading it, his chief slave is, and your son has sent them tons of steel, stolen from your own stocks. Tons! That timber camp is a pretense. I watched them doing formation drills, forging weapons. At first I thought it was her Holiness who was responsible, but it's the Prophet Unrisen who's the common factor."

Polldor sat down again, shocked. "Is this true, Balak? I can barely credit it."

"I saw myself, your Holiness. Your son is building an army of slaves. What purpose could it have except to take your power?"

"But Olen—why would he? I can hardly get him to take an interest in command."

"I don't know. Perhaps his indifference is a cover."

"And Nufell. I promised him my daughter." Polldor felt anger creeping into his words. "He got everything he asked for."

"He wanted more than he made clear, Prophet. Perhaps that too was a cover. I know they're conspiring against you."

"Are you sure, Balak?"

"I confronted the bishop. He admitted it himself, though he denied the army."

Polldor stood again, his anger working in his face. "We'll arrest them. Now."

"Prophet!" Balak seemed shocked. "The Incarnation is in progress. You can't interrupt that."

"By Noah's name I can. Watch me."

"Prophet!"

Polldor's eyes met Balak's and saw the anguish there. *I have to remember the strength of Balak's faith.* Polldor himself saw the trappings of his position as nothing more than tools that were useful to maintain power. He found church doctrine as inconsistent as it was high-minded, and had too much experience with the political machinations of the bishops to be anything but cynical about their pious protestations.

Balak was different. He *believed,* with a fervor that Polldor had never understood, and unlike the bishops his belief was in no way self-serving. His devotion to Polldor, his commitment to the Prophetsy flowed naturally from that belief. Because Balak believed, Balak sacrificed, but Polldor could not bring himself to put his High Inquisitor in the same category as the commoners who tithed because they had been convinced their souls would be consigned to Hell if they did not. Balak derived a certain peace-fulness of spirit from his belief, and Polldor sensed that without it he would be a tormented and dangerous man.

And it struck at the core of Balak's belief to see his Prophet so casually dismiss the central ritual of his faith. The High Inquisitor's eyes were almost imploring, and they held a strange vulnerability that Polldor had never seen before. For him the incarnation *was* both sacred and necessary, the reinvigoration of the Prophet's holy link with his ancestors, and with God. If the ceremony wasn't completed the foundations of his world would be shattered.

Polldor clenched his teeth and looked away from his subordinate. There was something innocent in Balak's fervent belief, and it would be almost vandalism to destroy it. *And foolish. Who else can I trust as much as Balak?* The Prophet breathed out slowly. *It will do no harm to wait.*

"We'll arrest them after the ceremony. Until then, tell me more."

Balak's face relaxed, his relief palpable. "Thank you, Prophet. What more is there to tell you? Your daughter has some hideaway in the temple depths. I haven't found it yet, but I will."

"What does she do there?"

"I don't know yet. Perhaps nothing . . ." Balak's words were cut off by a clatter from beneath the window. Polldor strode to the curtain and yanked it open. Outside he caught a glimpse of a fleeing boy. "That errander was listening, a spy for Nufell." Polldor felt his anger grow hot. "I'll have them both on the cross. If they die in a week it'll be a mercy."

"The servant and the bishop, you mean," said Balak, and there was something strange in his voice.

"The bishop and my son. Come on, we have to move now before that little *sooksan* warns them."

"Not your son, Prophet." Balak's eyes were imploring again. "He's your line, Noah's line."

"His blood is going to be all over the altar as soon as I get in there. Get the inquisitors in the street to surround the church. Nobody gets in or out. I want a half mark with me. We'll beat confessions out of them if we have to."

"His blood is as holy as yours." Balak was pleading. "He's the future of Noah's line."

"I can have more sons."

"I wish I could believe that, Prophet."

Polldor rounded on Balak, his rage suddenly refocused. "What did you say? What are you implying?"

"Prophet, I'm sure it's God's will." Balak wrung his hands together, anguished. "God's will. All those wives, all those women and only Olen to carry Noah's blood. Surely you see he's the one. The *one* . . ." His voice trailed away though his lips kept moving, no longer talking to Polldor but only to himself.

Polldor wasn't listening. "You insolent cur!" He backhanded Balak across the face, knocking him sideways to the ground. "You want to spare that useless pup I sired because you think I'm sterile, is that it? Enough of this, get the inquisitors, the ceremony ends now. I want those traitors on the cross in a bell."

Balak stood, rubbing his face where he'd been struck. He nodded slowly, still talking to himself, his expression far away. "I see now how God is testing me."

"Balak!" Polldor made his voice stern. "I gave you an order."

The High Inquisitor's eyes were still distant. "Yes, yes, the bishop said you would. He saw . . . *foresaw* . . . It was the Prophet Unrisen of course . . ." Balak drew his blade and met Polldor's gaze again, and his voice strengthened. "I apologize, Prophet. I know what I have to do now."

"Good." The Prophet turned to the small door, to go through it, to confront his son and the traitorous Bishup Nufell, to demonstrate to them the exercise of *power*. And suddenly Balak was in front of him, blade in hand and pointed at him. "Balak, what are you . . ."

The blade moved and pain blossomed in Polldor's belly as the steel drove in and up, searching behind his ribs for his heart. The rest of his sentence came out as a gurgle, and he dropped to his knees as he felt wetness spreading from the wound. Balak knelt with him, his hand still on the blade's handle. The Prophet inhaled sharply, felt the hurt sharpen. "Balak . . ." The word came out in a hoarse whisper.

"God will welcome you, Prophet. God will embrace you in his love." Balak smiled a small, sad smile. "Noah's line is safe now, safe with Olen. Please forgive me the pain, I'll make it short." He shoved the blade higher, and Polldor stiffened as he felt its cold bite up inside his chest. Balak was still speaking, but there was a roaring in his ears now, and his vision was blurring, going grey. The room spun, and he felt himself falling over. The pain began to recede, replaced by a chill that spread from his chest to his limbs. He shivered once, closed his eyes, and relaxed into the onrushing darkness.

Annaya sighed and looked up from her script sheets, letting her eyes follow the elaborate geometric tracings on her wall-quilts. She had gone looking for the secret of Noah's temple in the Prophetsy's archives and found it there. It was ancient text, elaborately scribed on sheepskin pages, a copy of an even more ancient document called

*Physical Constants and Formulae, 14th edition.* The scriptkeeper she'd asked about it said it was supposed to contain all the knowledge of Noah's people. Unfortunately the language had changed considerably since it was written. Half the words were foreign to her, and she understood none of the symbology that occupied the better part of every page. She strongly suspected that the scribe who'd copied it hadn't understood it either, and a second layer of incomprehension couldn't be helpful. She'd puzzled out enough to understand that tremendous power was locked up in its pages, but she couldn't figure out how to put it into use.

*Which is purely frustrating.* She alone had access to Noah's chamber in the heart of the temple, and the strange blue light that lit it was evidence enough of the ancients' power. If she could somehow turn the words in front of her into a prayer, a ceremony, a ritual that she could perform in that space then the power could be hers. But she couldn't.

There was a knock on the door, and Annaya looked up from her script sheets. "Enter," she said.

The door opened to reveal Balak. "You are summoned to the Prophet's tower, your Holiness," he said. He bowed as he always did, but there was something changed in his manner, his usual calm-over-tension replaced by something else, though Annaya couldn't quite finger it.

"Is the incarnation over already?" She'd lost track of time.

Balak's expression didn't change. "I'm to bring you to the tower," he repeated.

Annaya sighed in annoyance and looked back to the script sheets. The chapter she was trying to read was entitled "Light as a Wave." She'd thought she might make a connection between it and the perpetual ghostly glow in Noah's chamber, but the entire chapter was as cryptic as its title. There was no point in beating her brain further, and no point in making her father wait. *He can't have found out about the steel.* She had covered her tracks well, and even if he'd discovered the missing trade tokens, the clues would point back to Olen. She closed the book and stood up. "Let's go then."

She followed him in silence down to the gallery, and then up the tower to her father's chambers. He opened the door for her, and she went through, steeling herself for whatever it was that Polldor was angry about this time. To her surprise it was Olen who was waiting for her. She opened her mouth to ask where their father was, and then closed it again. Olen was wearing the Prophet's robes, Polldor's robes, and Bishop Nufell was standing beside him. The atmosphere was tense, and something was very wrong.

"It's time for you to be placed, Annaya," Olen said, his young face overlaid with a pompous gravity he couldn't quite pull off.

"Placed? What do you mean? Where's Father?"

"He's dead. Your brother is Prophet now," the bishop answered for Olen.

"Dead?" Annaya felt her throat constrict. *It can't be . . .* She had hated her father, wanted him dead herself, and yet the news struck her heart like a knife. There was a ringing in her ears, and from a long way away she heard her own voice. "How?"

The bishop's eyes met hers and then slid away. "It doesn't matter. What we're here to discuss—"

"Balak, what happened?"

"Your Holiness . . ." Balak struggled with the words. "Your Holiness, your father was a fine man . . ."

"A fine man?" Annaya blurted the words incredulously. "He was *Prophet!* What happened to your loyalty, High Inquisitor? Don't tell me you're involved in this."

Balak was silent, and wouldn't meet her eyes.

"Go on, tell her," said the bishop. Balak's jaw worked, but no words came. "Well, if you won't, I will." There was a note of smug triumph in the Nufell's words, and Balak turned away, walked to the large windows to look out into the mist.

"You don't need to tell me," Annaya snapped. "It's written in your eyes, *sooksan*. You killed my father, and you've convinced my weakling brother to save you from Balak's blade."

The bishop laughed. "You malign me, your Holiness. It wasn't me who killed the Prophet."

"No, you don't have the yats to dirty your hands in person." Annaya spat at his feet. "Some underling did it for you, I'm sure."

The bishop's face darkened in anger, but before he could answer Balak turned back from the window. "It was me, your Holiness." His expression was tortured. "Forgive me. I had to."

"Balak?" Annaya looked at him, her anger replaced with shock. "*You?* Why?"

"For Noah's line." The High Inquisitor looked at the floor. "He . . . he gave me no choice."

Annaya could see that something had happened to Balak. For as long as she had known him his equanimity had been unbreakable, his commitment to the Prophet unquestionable. Now he was . . . *shattered*. Annaya couldn't find words.

"He was going to put your brother on the cross," Balak went on. "The holy line would have ended." He looked up again, his eyes anguished with her. "I made it quick, Holiness. He was purified in his own blood."

"You did that for *Olen?*" Annaya looked in astonishment at her half-brother. Her father's robes were a half-size too large for him, and the pathetic authority he'd tried to assume when she'd come in was gone. "He's unworthy of my father's name." Olen shrank back from her words, a frightened child caught playing a man's game that had gone too far. "Balak, how . . ." She couldn't finish the sentence, it was too unbelievable.

"He's the Prophet's son," said the bishop. "Polldor's mistake was to confuse the High Inquisitor's faith for loyalty." He smirked. "I suggest you don't make the same one. And as for worthiness, we know all about your own plan to overthrow your father."

Fear shot through Annaya. *They know!* She suppressed her reaction but the bishop must have caught a hint of it in her eyes, for he smiled a wide and dangerous smile. "Oh yes, we know all about the pathetic little army you've been building at your lumber camp. Clever of you to make it look like your brother's work, and ironic. You fooled Balak, which cost your father's life. It took us a while to figure out what you'd done. It could have been quite messy, but Olen is Prophet now, and he'll be a good one with my strong tutelage. The inquisitors will be taking care of your lumber camp soon enough, and in the meantime . . ." His smile got wider. ". . . you're going to be placed with me."

"I'll die first," Annaya snarled, feeling her face flush with anger.

The bishop chortled. "I doubt that's necessary. You're not the first new wife I've had to break."

He reached out to take her hand, and Annaya smacked him across the side of his head as hard as she could, cupping her hand to rupture his eardrum. The bishop sprawled sideways, and when he got to his feet his face was a mask of rage. He came at her then, his fist cocked back, and Annaya twisted to receive his attack, not caring that she'd started a fight she could only lose.

There was a blur and suddenly Balak was between them, his

blade at the Nufell's throat. "She's Noah's daughter, Bishop." The High Inquisitor's voice was quiet, but the anguished uncertainty was gone from his eyes. In its place was the burning zeal that Annaya had always seen hidden in their depths. "Until the Prophet declares the placement, you won't put a hand on her."

Nufell looked shocked, fear replacing the arrogance he'd carried a second ago. He breathed in, breathed out, getting himself under control. He put his hands out to show he was no threat, and took a step backwards. When he had a little distance he turned his head towards Olen, though his eyes stayed locked on the blade in front of him. "Well, Prophet," he said, his voice controlled but not quite hiding his unease. "Declare the placement. Just as we discussed, declare the placement."

Olen opened his mouth to answer and Annaya pointed a finger at him. "Olen, don't you *dare* speak a word. Don't you dare or I swear on our father's pyre I'll have your yats on a stick."

Olen's eyes darted back and forth between Annaya and Nufell, but it was Annaya who could hold them, while the bishop's were still fixated on Balak's weapon. "Balak," she said. "Kill him."

Nufell's eyes widened in fear, and Balak looked to Olen. "Shall I, Prophet?"

Olen swallowed hard, his jaw working as he tried to speak, his own expression showing more fear than Nufell's. Annaya let her face show her disgust. *He can't even say yes or no. He's just as useless as he's always been.* She shook her finger at her brother's chest. "I will *not* be wed to this . . . this animal. I will *not*, and take my promise, Olen." She lowered her voice, barely containing her rage. "If you let this inbred *sooksan* talk you into that declaration I will make you suffer every single day for the rest of your miserable life."

She turned on her heel and left, shaking with reaction. As soon as the door closed behind her she started running, her head spinning with what had just happened. *My father . . .* Her throat tightened as she thought of Polldor dying on Balak's blade.

*They know about Danil, how did they find out?* She'd been so careful. With an effort she pushed the question out of her mind. The immediate problem was getting away. Olen feared her instinctively, just as he always had, but it wouldn't take the bishop long to get him back under his thumb. She had to be long, long gone when that happened.

She went into the gallery, through the wood-partitioned halls of the vast steel space. The stables were at the far end, and as she went through the troop areas as the inquisitors on guard jumped to give her the salutation as she passed. She grabbed a blade from one, a bow and quiver from another, leaving the men staring open-mouthed after her. The familiar scent of horses and hay filled the air, pungent but somehow inviting.

She hadn't been into the gallery since the day after Sem was killed, and she'd forgotten how much she liked to ride. *And today I'm going to ride.* The stablemaster was sitting at a workshelf in his small office, writing something with quill, ink and a painfully careful hand. He leapt up when Annaya came in, his face a study in surprise.

"Your Holiness!"

"I need a horse saddled this instant," she said. "The fastest short-horse you've got."

"Your Holiness, your father has forbidden—"

"My father is dead," Annaya cut him off. "You may be next. Saddle my horse."

The stablemaster's eyes grew big, and he looked uncertain, and Annaya realized that the news of Polldor's death was not yet widespread. It was even possible Olen and Nufell were keeping it secret for some purpose of their own. She pressed her lips together and gave the stablemaster a look that could well have killed him all by itself. His resolve collapsed and he scurried out, shouting for the horsehands. Minutes later she was astride a dark-grey and high-strung stallion, trotting out of the gallery towards the outer wall of the Temple courtyard and the great, steelbound gates that closed its entrance.

"Open the gate," she commanded as she came closer, and the detachment of inquisitors there gave her the salutation as they obeyed. She breathed a sigh of relief as she came outside the Temple walls, but couldn't help looking over her shoulder as she did. A boy with a yellow errander's scarf was running across the courtyard from the base of the Prophet's Tower, waving his arms and shouting. Annaya didn't bother trying to understand what he was saying, she just spurred her horse and rode, out of the cleared area around the Temple, following the log-laid trading road into the forest of sapling dougfir beyond.

Ahead of her was Charity, the aftward forest, and Danil, and she planned as she went. Two bells of hard riding would take her to the aftward forest, if nothing stopped her, but as soon as the errander told Nufell that she'd escaped an alert would go out in mirror code to every inquisitor station. The overcast and mist were too heavy for them to use the big, polished steel reflector on the forewall ledge above the temple, which meant they'd have to send a rider with the message to Charity, to use the mirror at the station there. Her lead over the messenger would only be the time it took to saddle his horse, and it wouldn't take long to flash the message ahead of her. *I can ride as far as Charity, but after that they'll be watching for me.* She'd have to abandon the horse there and find another way aftward. That would take time, and if Nufell knew about Danil's army he'd be ordering Balak to march against it immediately.

*Or rather, ordering Olen to order Balak.* Balak was another mystery. What possibly could have happened to make him turn against Polldor? *I would never have doubted his loyalty.*

She came out of the forest and into the cultivated fields that surrounded Charity, and paused long enough to look back and listen for pursuing hoofbeats. There were none, but she didn't allow herself to relax. The mist thinned at the treeline, and the crops were growing tall and green beneath their overstory of olive trees, thriving on the perfect combination of light and moisture they got along the border of the forelands. If she rode on through open fields and the city itself there would be witnesses aplenty to testify to the flight of a young woman on a dark-grey horse, but if she abandoned the horse and took to the fields she'd be easy prey for a mounted search. She bit her lip, considered the fields again. They'd hide her, but . . .

*No time to delay.* Speed counted, and she'd have to accept the risk of witnesses. She dug her heels in again, and her mount snorted and leapt forward. She could see the buildings of Charity, three kilometers ahead, and she had to get there. The wind rose in her hair as her mount accelerated, and despite the danger she was in she found herself smiling.

*I'm free, finally free.* Riding always gave her that sense of freedom, but this time it wasn't going to end when she brought the horse back to the stables. Her life as the Prophet's daughter was over, and all the restrictions and expectations that came with it were gone. She laughed out loud at the realization, and leaned forward in the saddle. The trading road surface changed from logs to fired-clay cobbles just beyond the start of the fields, and the rapid drumbeat of her mount's hooves set her blood racing. Ahead a farmer was harvesting squash from a truck field, piling the ripe gourds on an open cart driven by a boy. They stopped working as she galloped past, and then a thought struck her. She reined up, turned the horse and trotted back to the cart. The man was elderly, but still fit and strong. His face was lined above his graying beard, and his clothing, worn but serviceable, seemed to make him as much a part of the land as his crop.

"Would you like this horse?"

He looked at her with a raised eyebrow. "That's a generous offer, young woman."

Annaya smiled to herself. *He doesn't recognize me. That's helpful.* "It is. There's a price of course."

He laughed. "I doubt I can afford your price."

"It's cheap enough. I need to travel aftward. Take me in your cart and I'll give you the horse."

He gave her a sideways look. "Why bother with the cart? You can get there yourself faster than I can take you."

Annaya hesitated, but there was no point in deceiving him. If he was going to help her he needed to know all the facts. "The inquisitors are chasing me. I need to hide as well as travel."

The man nodded, considering, and looked back the way she'd come, perhaps looking for her pursuers. After what seemed like an excruciatingly long time he spoke.

"I'll take you. Get in the cart. Kesalem, take her horse," he said to the boy. "And give her your cloak." Annaya demounted the horse and the boy took off his rough brown field-cloak and gave it to her as he climbed down from the cart. She climbed up, and the farmer did too, heaving his last squash onto the back. "Now, fast as you can to the upper pasture. Leave the horse there, by the spinward trail, and take the treeline back to the barn. They'll track the horse, but they'll miss you. If they come looking, tell them you've seen nothing, and let them search all they want. Leave the horse there until tomorrow, then take it into the barn yourself. I should be back by then."

"Yes, grandfather," said the boy. He mounted Annaya's stallion and galloped away.

The farmer turned to Annaya. "Now get under the gourds."

He cleared a space for her to lie flat, laid the cloak over her and started piling the ripe squash over her. Their weight pressed lumpily against her, but there was no point in complaining. Still, it was nerve wracking being unable to see anything. When she was covered she felt the cart shift as he climbed off. After a while the cart shifted again, and it took her a moment to realize that he'd gone back to loading his crop. Some time after that she heard hoofbeats on the hard road surface.

"A young woman on horseback came this way just now." The voice carried authority and the expectation of obedience. *Certainly an inquisitor.* Annaya tightened her grip on her blade.

"She went through my fields, that's where," the old man answered. "I told her to stop. Who's going to pay—"

The inquisitor cut him off with a barked command to his subordinates, and hoofbeats sounded again. The old man's voice rose plaintively. "Not there, those are my crops! Come back! Who's going to pay for this? Who's going to pay?" He kept it up until Annaya could no longer hear the horses. After a pause the cart shifted again as he climbed up to take the driver's seat. She heard him stir the reins, the horse whinnied and the cart lurched forward.

"The signal mirrors are blinking," the man said a little while later. "Is that for you?"

"I'm sure it is."

"They're eager to get you back."

"Can I come out now?"

"No, let's wait until we're in Charity and those soldiers are well away."

Annaya grimaced to herself but didn't answer. Her head was pressed uncomfortably against the cart floor, and the piled gourds didn't help. Every jolt banged her teeth together, but she wasn't about to second-guess her benefactor. Eventually the cart slowed and she heard more hoofbeats, not the pounding of galloping inquisitors but the slow clop-clop of farm carts. They were entering Charity.

Her heart stopped once, when another authoritarian voice ordered the old man to stop, but whoever it was must have waved him on without further investigation. More voices rose, and soon the pungent and competing odors of the main market reached her nostrils, the savory scent of cooking meat mingling with the sweetish smell of ripe fruit and the earthy tones of stacked root vegetables. She caught a hint of fresh-cut pine, the sourish smell of a mash tent, and everywhere the musk of horse and human, blended together into the omnipresent background. There was music and laughter everywhere—the Festival of the Incarnation was in full swing. It seemed amazing that it would continue when Polldor had just died, until she heard a street-preacher declaiming praise for the newly incarnated Prophet Olen.

*They turn my father's death into a celebration, and to the commoners one celebration is as good as another. Did the bishop plan this, or just seize the opportunity?* She couldn't know. *And it doesn't matter in the end.* The cart stopped, and there were more voices as the old man unloaded it, tossing the heavy gourds down to someone below. The weight came off Annaya, but she knew better than to move until she was told to.

There were more voices, too low for her to quite make out the words, and then the cart creaked forwards once more. It stopped again soon afterwards.

"Take off your gown, put on the cloak, but stay down doing it," the old man told her.

Annaya obeyed, trying to not only stay down but to stay under the cloak while she got her fine white-flax gown off, a maneuver that involved a lot of uncomfortable wriggling. When she'd succeeded she stood up, and saw that the farmer was looking the other way. *He respects my privacy, that's good.* He'd parked the cart in a narrow alley, and between that and the high sides of the cart she could have changed with less effort. *But I didn't know that.* "Thank you," she said. "I owe you more than I can easily say."

"You can thank me when we get to the aftward forest. We aren't there yet."

"How did you know I was going that far aftward?" She climbed up to the front seat to sit beside him.

"Where else would you run? The fisherfolk are gone, but the trees are still there." He stirred the reins, the horse took the strain, and they moved off. Annaya started to tell him that she wasn't a slave, then thought better of it. *The less he knows the better, for his own safety and mine.* "I'm Moren," the man went on as he twitched the reins. The horse wearily started forward again. It was an old and tired mare, a work-horse, pulling alone a cart made for a team of two. She could only imagine that her fine, fast short-horse was worth a lot to him.

"I'm . . ." Annaya hesitated.

"You're Annaya, the Prophet's daughter."

She gave him a look. "You know who I am?"

"Am I wrong?"

"No, I'm just surprised you'd take the risk to help me knowing who I am. You must know what you're risking."

"I had a daughter once. I didn't like the man she was placed with, but . . ." He shrugged. "The bishop's word is law. She didn't like him either. She ran from him, and was caught and beaten. She ran again, was caught again . . ." Moren looked up to the suntube, his expression distant. "You've got your own reason for running. I've got my own reason for helping you."

"I'm grateful."

"Pull your hood up, like a modest girl should. Keep your eyes down. We're going to Hope, anti-spinward of here and then we'll head aftward."

She did as he asked, and they rode in silence through the busy streets. Once a full mark of inquisitors galloped by, parting the crowd as Moses parted the ocean. She stiffened as they went past, but they showed no interest in her.

"They'll be putting a watch on the trading road first," said Moren. "But they're going to get in front of us too."

"What should I do?"

"Sit there, stay quiet, leave the talking to me."

Before long they came to the edge of Charity, and there was a mounted inquisitor there, armored and cloaked, watching the traffic. He was stopping carts, questioning people, and Annaya's heart raced as they drew close. Her throat tightened hard when a half dozen more inquisitors rode up just as they were coming up to him. They were setting up a checkpoint, and she fully expected to be stopped, but the mark-leader with the new group was talking to the first soldier, and she and Moren clopped past without incident. She imagined their eyes on her back as they continued through the open fields, and didn't relax until they were a kilometer down the road. The road antispinward rose up and ahead of them, and she followed it up towards the suntube, squinting to make out the circular blotch that was Hope. After a while she relaxed.

*I'm safe, for now. And free.* The horse plodded on, pulling them past fields of cheerful sunflowers and pastures full of peacefully grazing sheep and cattle. She took a deep breath, feeling suddenly renewed. *Freedom.* It felt strange. Her father was dead. *How did that happen?* She felt a deep sadness in the pit of her stomach, a feeling entirely at odds with the joy of escape and release, and she didn't know whether to laugh or cry.

Moren left her alone with her thoughts, and Hope had moved well down the world before he spoke. "Do you know anyone you can go to?"

She nodded. "There's a man I know, aftward. In Far Bay."

"Far Bay has been burned."

"I know."

"What will you do when you get there?"

"Retake what my brother stole from me." The answer surprised Annaya even as she said it. She hadn't made a plan beyond immediate escape, and if anything she'd imagined simply hiding with Danil for the rest of her life. And yet as soon as Moren asked, she knew with crystal certainty that her destiny was bigger than that.

The farmer's eyebrows went up. "What did he take?"

"My father, and my birthright." Her voice was harder than she meant it to be.

Moren nodded slowly. "I wondered why they were celebrating Prophet Olen in the market."

"Olen is a puppet, nothing more than that, but I'll still have him on the cross for his part in it."

Moren nodded, slowly. "Vengeance is a poor staff to lean your life on."

"Vengeance." Annaya laughed bitterly. "What else have I got now?"

"This man you're running to."

Annaya pressed her lips together. "He doesn't love me, he just finds me useful."

Moren was silent a long moment. "Do you love yourself, Annaya?"

She looked at him sharply. "Why do you ask that?"

"When you reach my age you gain a certain amount of insight into people. You don't have to answer."

Annaya pressed her lips together. "Danil asked me that once."

"Danil, is that the one you're running to?"

She nodded. "Yes."

"What did you answer?"

"I didn't."

He nodded silently, and the conversation lagged as Hope grew lower, closer, larger. The frantic blinking of the signal mirrors around the world had subsided by then. A bell later they crossed the bridge over the Golden River, and then another over the River of Joy, and finally they came to the outskirts of Hope. There was an inquisitor checkpoint there, and again Annaya felt herself tense up as they drew near. The soldiers were dismounted, but their horses were tethered nearby. There would be no running, they would have to brazen their way through.

*But I knew we'd be here, I knew we would face this.* Strangely she felt worried not for herself, but for Moren. If she were caught she'd be placed with Nufell, but Moren would be crucified. She pulled her hood down and did her best to think like a demure farmer's daughter.

One of the men held up a hand as they approached, and Moren reined their horse to a stop. Annaya peered from beneath the edge of the hood to see if she recognized any of the soldiers, but she didn't. *Which is no guarantee that none of them will recognize me.* Most of the inquisitors quartered in the gallery were from Charity and the parishes aftward of it. Hope was three quarters of the way around the world, but the odds were good that at least some of the officers in Hope's parisha would know her on sight. *And all I can do is hope.*

"Where are you from?" asked the one who'd halted them, climbing up on the wagon's footboard. Two more inquisitors came over to check the back of the wagon.

"Charity parish, inquisitor," answered Moren.

"You've come a long way." Annaya kept her head down, but she could feel the unfriendly eyes on her. The inquisitor climbed up on the wagon. "Who's this?" he asked Moren.

"My daughter Suleen, inquisitor."

"Suleen." The soldier raised the edge of her hood, looking down into her face and Annaya avoided meeting his gaze. "You're a pretty one." He turned again to Moren. "She'll have to come with us."

"Why, inquisitor?" Moren asked. "She's late as it is."

"Orders. Any woman her age coming into Hope is to be brought to Charity as soon as possible. The High Inquisitor is looking for someone."

Fear shot through Annaya, and she swallowed hard to control

it. *We've been caught.* She stood and started to climb down from the cart. There was nowhere to run, and no point in further endangering Moren.

"Of course, of course." Moren got up to help her down. "I'll tell Bishop Hern at once."

"The bishop? Why would he care?"

"He's going to be angry already, just because we're so late. Suleen is here to be placed with him."

The inquisitor paused, and when he spoke he sounded suspicious. "The bishop isn't back from the Incarnation yet."

"He must still be at the Festival." There was relief in Moren's voice. "It took so long to get through the crowds I was afraid . . . well, never mind. He's probably looking for another new wife." The old farmer lowered his voice. "Although I'm sure he won't find one as fine as Suleen, or pay a higher brideprice. Show them your hands, Suleen." Moren sounded proud. "She hasn't spent a day in the fields. We knew we'd get a high placement for her."

Obediently Annaya put her hands out for inspection, inwardly marveling at Moren's brilliant performance. Not only had he very subtly maneuvered the soldier into an untenable position, but he had explained away her callous-free fingers before the inquisitor even thought to check them.

The soldier glanced at her hands, but he wasn't really looking at them. His eyes were distant, his expression unhappy as he considered his options. His didn't want to back down in front of his comrades, but his bishop wouldn't be pleased to discover that his fresh new bride wasn't waiting for him when he got back from the Festival. The calculation was simple. If he let the fugitive Prophet's daughter escape he'd lose the glory of the capture. If he turned back Bishop Hern's new wife his punishment would be severe.

"Get back on the wagon," he told Annaya. "Take her to the bishop," he added to Moren. He stepped back and waved them forward. "I'll tell him she's waiting when he comes through."

"As you order, inquisitor," Moren answered, helping Annaya back up with one hand and stirring the horse with the other. She sat back down beside him and they moved off.

"That was too close," she said when they were out of earshot. "You can leave me in the market square. I'll make my own way aft from there."

He shook his head. "No. I'll get you where you need to go."

She tried to protest, and he calmly insisted until she gave in.

Hope wasn't as large as Charity, the buildings less grand, the church less impressive, but the streets were still crowded with post-Incarnation revelers, eating and drinking and dancing. There were inquisitors on the streets, both on horseback and on foot, but they didn't seem to be looking for anyone in particular. They made their way through the throng, turned aftward at the market square and left Hope behind them. The bells rang past from the forewall to the churches, and to the churches beyond them as they traveled. The evening meal came and went and Annaya grew hungry, but didn't complain.

Several times they were stopped by inquisitor patrols. Each time Moren repeated the same routine, substituting the name of the bishop in the next parish as Annaya's newly betrothed husband. Each time they got away with with the deception. They angled back towards the trading road at Benediction parish, and when they came to it turned aftward again. Eventually they came to the Prophetsy wall, where the huge gates stood abandoned and open, the arrow towers empty, the once-neat guard posts surrounded by weeds and already showing signs of neglect.

"This is as far as I can take you," said Moren. "Good luck."

"I'll remember this, always," Annaya said, and hugged her benefactor before stepping down from the cart. He turned the cart around and she watched him go, then turned herself and went into the forest.

The trees were much bigger in the aftward forest, towering giants that spoke of calm ages. Grass was already growing between the resined brick cobbles of the trading road, evidence that the merchants no longer traveled it. She walked down the middle, wondering how she would find Danil, until she came around a corner and saw Far Bay. *The city my father destroyed.* She had never been there, but there was no mistaking it, blackened timbers, collapsed roofs set against the blue of the ocean and the looming gray disc of the aftwall. She remembered the smell of burnt wood falling out of the sky with the murky rains that had poured down after the conquest, the funeral pyre for the fisherfolk. *My father will have his own pyre soon enough. Perhaps he would have made different choices if he'd known he was going to die so soon.*

As she grew closer she could see the ruins were softening, weeds showing through the collapsed frames of burnt out buildings, the hard black of burnt timber fading to a subtler shade. She went to the ocean shore, found ruined wharves sinking slowly. The water was reclaiming the fisherfolk city. She passed the market stalls where Prophetsy merchants had once traded steel for fish, incongruously undamaged amid the devastation. *But it makes no difference.* The merchants were gone, the city dead. It was as if the fires had burned it out of the memory of the conquerors. *But Danil is here, somewhere.* She knew that instinctively.

She also knew he'd have his sentinels watching the approaches to his stronghold. Ahead of her a plume of smoke rose, a single sign of life in the otherwise abandoned ruins. It was what she was looking for, but at the same time it worried her. It was possible it was just the last smoldering fire in the ruined city. *But it isn't, it can't be.* She walked towards it, carefully, slowly, keeping to the middle of the road. The sentinels would have rabbit bows, and she wanted to give them no reason to fire. She went as far into the city as she dared, and stopped, sat down in the road and waited.

There were no bells in the aftward forest, and that was strange. Had there ever been? Had the fisherfolk echoed in their own towers the peals that drifted down from the most aftward parishes of the Prophetsy? She couldn't know. With no way to tell time she let her mind drift, looking up the curve of the ocean, watching the waves. Eventually she lay back, exhaustion overcoming her. She slept then, throwing her arm over her eyes to screen out the suntube, too tired to notice the hard, uneven bricks beneath her.

She woke up with a foot in her ribs, and opened her eyes to a drawn bow. A man stood over her, looking down. "Who are you?" he asked.

"Annaya. I'm here for Danil. Danil Fougere."

"The parishan?" The man's eyes registered surprise. "How do you know him?" He wore leather armor, a wickedly curved fighting blade on his hip, and a red title scarf at his neck.

Annaya pointed to the blade. "I got him the steel to make that."

"So?" The man backed up a few paces. "Get up, we'll see what he says."

She got up, and saw that he wasn't alone. There was another man, down on one knee, his back turned to her, watching up the road. The first man made a clicking sound, and the second looked back over his shoulder. A crisp gesture brought him to his feet. As he moved more figures appeared around her, four men, two women, deployed in a circle around her. They moved with silence, purpose, and discipline, falling into a file, moving down the road, eyes alert, bows ready with arrows nocked. *This is Danil's army. This is my army.* She felt a kind of safety, despite the implicit threat of the weapons, and something else as well.

*Pride.*

They moved through the destroyed city in silence, heading for the plume of smoke. Eventually they came to a bridge, unburned. On the other side of it a waterwheel turned in the river flow, and the smoke plume she'd followed was coming from the building it was attached to. The structure was an utter ruin, the torched roof fallen in over the resined brick walls at the back, a skeletal frame of blackened timbers was all that was left of the front. For a moment she thought she'd made a mistake, that the curl of smoke really was nothing more than the last-smoldering fire in the destroyed city, but then she caught a sound, a rhythmic *clang clang clang* rising over the otherwise silent scene, the sound of steel on steel. The building was a forge, and despite all evidence to the contrary, it was working. *My steel, my risk, my gift to Danil.* They crossed the bridge and she saw that the forge wasn't actually a ruin. Its roof had been burned, but the bricks beneath had held. What had been lost had been rebuilt, using partially charcoaled timbers arranged to look like the ruins of a larger building almost entirely collapsed, just one more skeletal frame on a deserted street that had once bustled with life.

Her escort halted his group with a gesture, and went alone into the forge. After a while he came out with a man she felt she should recognize, leather armor, a blade on his hip, dark blue title scarf . . . "Danil!"

"Annaya!"

She ran to him, threw her arms around him. "Danil."

He hugged her back, lifted her, put her down. She wanted to kiss him, but somehow sensed that wasn't the right thing to do with his soldiers watching.

Perhaps it wasn't, but he kissed her anyway. "What are you doing here?" he asked when he'd finished. "Why have you come?"

"There's a lot to explain. The High Inquisitor killed my father. My brother is Prophet. They know about the army. I don't know how much."

"Are they coming?"

"I don't know, Danil. If they aren't now, they will soon. Bishop Nufell has taken over."

"Who?"

"The man I was to be placed with. I don't think they have everything figured out yet, but it won't be long."

Danil frowned. "This is bad." He looked away, thinking, then turned to the sentinel leader who'd brought her in. "Coss, go up to the main camp, find Avel. Tell him we need sentinels forward as far as Tidings. Tell him to assign a mark to it, in groups of four, with a horse each. If they see the inquisitors coming in force, the rider is to report back, the remainder to keep watching. I need to know how many parishas, and which ones, speed of march, everything."

"At once, parishan." The other man nodded, signaled his followers and they moved off.

"This is early, too early." Danil continued. "We aren't ready." He paused and looked off after the departing patrol. His brow furrowed in concentration, as though with sufficient effort he could see through the burned out buildings and the forest to spot the advance of his enemies. He stood there watching until the last person in the patrol had vanished from view, and then he relaxed and looked back to Annaya. "But come and see what we've got."

He led her into the ruined forge. Inside it was a hive of activity. There were dozens of people there, most in leather smocks, firing steel, beating it, lathing it to shape. A broad-shouldered man was directing the work. "Six more, just like that . . ." he said, examining an angled steel fitting. ". . . and we'll be in good shape for today." His apprentice nodded and went back to her work table, and the broad-shouldered man turned around as Danil and Annaya came up to him.

"Era," Danil said, "we have a problem." He quickly outlined what Annaya had told him. "We have a day, I think, certainly not much more. How many turtles can we get finished in that time?"

"Finished?" Era looked dubious. "I'll put everyone on it, but realistically only one."

Danil shook his head. "We need more than that. Forget everything but the basics, how many are close?"

"Half a dozen that have wheels and gears, but . . ."

"I need them all finished."

"Danil, three of those are just frames with wheels, we need—"

"Finish them, Era. At least to the point where they can carry soldiers. I'll send you a full flank, will that help?"

"If I can get them organized, if they don't break more than they build." Era made a face. "Send them, Danil. I'll do what I can. . . ."

"Good man."

The big blacksmith turned back to his work and Danil led Annaya back out of the forge, and over the bridge to what had once been a cutyard. Like the forge, it had been arranged to look like a complete ruin from the outside. Like the forge, it was a hive of activity inside, with workers lifting timber, sawing beams, hammering chocks. Eight timber structures, overbuilt three-axle wagons on huge, wide wheels, filled the center of the space. The first was no more than a frame, the next five in various stages of construction, the wood and steel of their bodies only hinting at what they would become, but the last two were finished war turtles, and Annaya found them amazing. They were six meters long, three wide and two and half high, slope-sided boxes with harness bars for a horse team at the front, controlled by a horsedriver who sat behind the wooden armor. Sharp wooden spines protruded from the sides like porcupine quills, to dissuade the enemy from trying to climb on top. There were two huge bows mounted on either flank, their steel-sprung limbs mounted horizontally. Each was aimed by a single soldier who stood in a protected well behind it. How they were cocked was another question, they seemed far too big for a single person to operate.

"Would you like to see inside?" asked Danil.

Annaya nodded, and Danil took her around to the back of the war machine. Access was through a heavy timber ramp, which would be raised or lowered by a rope pulled from the interior. Despite the huge size of the turtle, the inside was claustrophobic. Low benches ran along each wall, each facing a row of hand-cranks linked to foot-pedals, and cramped in by the slope of the sides. There was room for ten on each side, and each crank-line drove a wooden gear train. The gear train turned the huge wheels that took up much of the compartment, and the fighting wells for the springbow archers encroached further on the available space. She ran a hand over the steel fittings that held the structure together.

*My steel. Now I see why he needed so much of it.* The pride she felt when she'd seen the first soldier's blade grew stronger. She had taken a lot of risks to get the steel smuggled to Danil. It was good to know they had been worthwhile. The design used steel only where absolutely necessary, but even so the turtle was so large there had to be a hundred kilos in it. She went deeper into the beast, saw how the huge bows were to be cocked. Haul lines ran through tacklewheels to their mainstrings so the whole team inside could apply their muscle to them. Storage for food, water and supplies took up the forward section, ranked around the hatch where the horsedriver stood. The platform above the central gear train opened to a small pulpit where the turtle's captain could command the whole contraption.

"Impressive." Annaya sat down on one of the benches and put a hand to the wheel cranks. It moved reluctantly and she put her back into the effort. Even with all her strength she could barely shift the turtle, and it was immediately obvious that even with twenty soldiers on the cranks the war machine would be slow and ungainly.

*But I knew that. It's the protection that matters here.* She turned back to Danil. "How do you steer?"

"The wheels on each side are independent. The horsedriver tells one side or the other to stop cranking, and the turtle will turn to that side. We'll only use the cranks in battle, when we have to disconnect the horses."

Annaya nodded and made her way forward to the horsedriver's hatch, crouched beneath the machine's low ceiling. "How many of these do you have?"

"Twenty-two, not counting these. The real challenge is going to be getting enough horses."

"How many?"

"We need an eight horse team for each one, at least. Ten would be better, even twelve."

She looked at him askance. "That's a parishan's worth. You could mount half your force."

"But we can't train them to fight mounted. Not well enough to take on inquisitors even one for one, and it won't be one for one." Danil smiled. "That's why we've built the turtles."

"No, you're right of course." Annaya put her head out the horsedriver's hatch, and saw how it was cleverly hinged upwards to protect the driver from above even when it was open. Wooden shields protected the position on either side as well, but the view forward was adequate to control the horse team. Short lines ran down to the hitching points, quick releases, to cut loose the team in a hurry should the horses be killed or fouled on an obstacle. *Danil really has thought of everything. I chose well when I chose him.* "But will these win for us?" she asked.

"Mechanically, they work well. In battle, who knows? We have protection and strong weapons, but not speed. We have two other versions, one is an assault turtle, with a ladder tower on top to get over the temple walls. The other is a ball thrower to knock them down."

"A ball thrower?" Annaya turned around and made her way out of the beast's belly and back down the rear ramp.

"Baked clay balls, fifty kilos each, with a four hundred meter range. When we get to the temple we'll take down the towers on the outer wall, and kill the rest of their archers with springbows. Then the assault turtles move to the outer ditch, put their ladders over it and up the wall."

Annaya nodded, looking over the machine's lines. "You've thought this out."

Danil nodded slowly. "I hope so. Unfortunately part of my thinking was that we'd have more time." He bit his lip, looking at the unfinished war machines, and Annaya could feel his worry.

The armor breastplate was heavy and the straps rubbed uncomfortably on Bishop Nufell's shoulders. Nevertheless, he smiled in satisfaction as he walked out into the Temple courtyard. Six full parishas were drawn up beneath the tall walls, a sea of horses, spears, and red cloaks in ordered ranks. It was galling that Polldor's daughter had managed to escape him, but there was only one place she could run, and she couldn't hide there long.

*I'm going to enjoy taming her.* He shouldn't have allowed her the opportunity, but he had underestimated how callow the newly ascended Prophet Olen really was. Nufell frowned. It wasn't the first mistake he'd made, and he wasn't a man who forgave mistakes easily, least of all in himself. It should have had been immediately obvious that Olen had neither the intelligence nor the ambition to put together the scheme of rebellion that Balak had uncovered. Nufell frowned. He *hadn't* known right away, and he *had* thought Olen's protestations of ignorance and innocence were disingenuous.

*But I was right about Balak when it counted.* In fact, everything was working out rather well. Annaya's secret army provided the perfect excuse to solidify his control. The inquisitor ranks had dwindled as they went to collect their aftward farms. Now he had an excuse to bring them back under his own command. Without the threat Annaya posed there was no way they'd follow weak Olen, even with Balak leading them.

*Perhaps if Polldor hadn't been so involved with leadership him- self . . .* But he had, and Olen could not fail to disappoint in trying to follow in his father's footsteps. Balak was necessary now, to show the soldier-priests that the new Prophet would be only a figurehead. In time they would learn that Nufell's strong hand was behind the Prophetsy's rule, and they would learn to obey him directly. Of course Balak would have to die after this last campaign. His faith made him uncontrollable, and that made him too dangerous to live.

*Time to worry about that later.* First the rabble had to be destroyed, and then Annaya found and brought to heel. The woman was smart, and dangerous herself, but he couldn't just kill her; she was the key to his dynasty. Once she bore him a son he could dispose of Olen. With his own line blended with the descendents of Noah his sons and his son's sons would rule the world for the indefinite future.

At the gallery stables, the stablehands had his horse ready. He mounted and rode to the gate, then out to where the troops were assembling. Balak was there, two message riders and a signaler by his side.

"How soon will you be ready?" Nufell asked.

Balak turned in the saddle. "We're ready to leave now. We'll be meeting the other parishas aftward of Charity." His eyes were bright and hard, focused on his mission. Whatever inner conflict he had felt over killing his master seemed to have vanished.

Nufell nodded. "I'll ride as your bishop."

"No, you won't. Bless the soldiers if you must, but I have enough to worry about without having to look after you. Stay here and keep the Prophet safe." Balak turned away without waiting for an answer. "Signaler, sound for the parishans to come to me."

The signaler blew five quick notes on his steel-trimmed ram's horn, and a moment later he repeated them.

Anger surged through Nufell at Balak's brusque dismissal and he felt his jaw clench, but he turned his mount and urged it forward, away from a confrontation. *For now.*

There was no point in trying to impose his will on the High Inquisitor. Balak had made it clear that he followed only Olen's orders, and Nufell remembered only too well the scratch of Balak's blade point against his throat. Fortunately the new Prophet had proved himself easy to control, and so long as Nufell's words came out of Olen's mouth, Balak had shown himself willing to obey. He considered going to Olen to force Balak to take him on the attack, but decided against it.

*Still, I'm going to enjoy that man's death.* It couldn't be anything obvious or the inquisitors themselves would revolt, but that didn't mean it couldn't be painful. Nufell smiled a hard smile to himself. With Balak out of the way he'd appoint a pliable parishan to be High Inquisitor, and he'd have nothing to fear from the order when the time came for Olen to go as well.

He guided his horse into the ordered ranks, offering blessings left and right. Going into battle wasn't necessary anyway. What was necessary was that he show himself. It was important that the inquisitors know his face, and got used to seeing him in a position of authority, and for that purpose he didn't really need to leave the Temple courtyard. He had worked his way well towards the front ranks when the signaler's horn blew again. He didn't know what the signal meant, but the mark-leaders and flank-captains started getting their troops into line, and the parishans were riding back from their conference with their commander.

The horn blew again and the front ranks moved off, forming themselves into a four-wide column on the trading road. Spotters galloped past, no doubt on their way to find the enemy and report their strength. Nufell was nearly caught up in the movement, but managed to maneuver his horse to the sidelines. Balak's command group followed the lead parishan with battle banners flying, and Nufell watched them go in silence. He was used to being in charge, and it felt strange to be on the sidelines at such a pivotal moment.

*Never mind that. It's going to be Balak's battle. But it will be my victory.*

"Advance!" Danil Fougere shouted the order down from his command pulpit to his war turtle's driver. Simultaneously he brought his arm forward over his head, signalling the following machines to move with his. The driver stirred up his eight-horse team, and the turtle lurched and moved forward at something less than a walking pace. At the same instant Annaya, now acting as Danil's signaler, ran the green battle pennant up the signal mast. Behind them the other turtle captains echoed his commands, and the great column moved off. The ponderous war turtles lived up to the sedate reputation of their namesakes, and the slow pace of the machine was somewhat anticlimactic. There was no immediate threat, no sign the Prophetsy had any idea it was now under attack. The frantic effort which had gone into preparing for the coming war gave way to a kind of nervous boredom. It took them a full bell just to reach the Prophetsy wall, and when they did Danil found everything there peaceful. *That won't last long.* It was a wish almost as much as a prediction. The sooner the battle was joined the sooner it would be over, and the waiting seemed interminable.

He bit his lip, trying to imagine what he had overlooked. *Not that I can fix it now.* There were so many unknowns in the assault, from how well the war turtles would perform to how well his soldiers would. *And how well their commander will.*

He swallowed hard and reminded himself that no one else in the world had ever led an army of battle machines either. He had structured his force so all the springbow turtles were at the forefront, with the heavier ball throwers and assault towers coming up behind. At their current rate of advance it would take nearly forty bells to reach the Prophet's temple, and that was if the inquisitors didn't find some way to stop them. *Like digging up the road.* The war turtles could negotiate pastureland, at something even slower than their already sluggish speed, but even a ploughed field was a serious obstacle. The trading road was the key to victory. If he was lucky the inquisitors wouldn't realize that.

"Signal open formation," Danil told Annaya.

She nodded and, somewhat inexpertly, blew her ram's horn. Nobody in Danil's army had slept in the last twenty-four hours, and Annaya had spent a lot of her time learning the army signals. He would rather have left her behind, but she had protested with her typical ferocity. She was an expert bow shot and an excellent rider. He may have trained the fisherfolk army, but she had paid for it, and she was not going to be left behind at the critical moment. Making her his signaler was a compromise he'd made only because he didn't think she would manage to master the horn in time. *And I should have known she would.* She was just that headstrong.

Slowly the war turtles spilled through the trading road gates and expanded into formation. Danil watched, his tension dissipating somewhat. The turtles were strongest in extended array, when they could mutually support each other. Strung out in a long line through the forest they were very vulnerable. He had plans to deal with the various obstacles his army would face in its advance. *But hopefully the inquisitors won't understand our weaknesses until it's too late.*

Around the world's cylinder he could see the flashes of inquisitor signal mirrors. He had no doubt the coded messages were all about him. It was the second time in his life he'd been the focus of the undivided attention of the Prophetsy's warrior priests, and it was flattering in a way. *But I wish I could read the messages.*

It took a whole bell for the trudging turtles to deploy, while Danil fretted that the enemy would come before his force was ready. Finally the last turtle moved through the gates and into the open pastureland beyond, and he could finally tell Annaya to signal the advance once more. The turtle's wheels were huge, half a meter wide and two around, with steel spikes set into them for traction. The arrangement allowed them to move their massive bulk on ground too soft and uneven for a conventional wagon, but their speed on the fields was less than a walking pace. It was going to be a slow war. They'd advanced another kilometer when one of his sentinels came into view, riding down the trading road at a gallop.

Annaya waved Danil's black command flag, and the rider angled towards them across the field. It was a woman by her stature; most of the sentinels were. They could ride faster than men, and men were better on the war turtle's cranklines.

She drew her horse up beside the turtle. "Parishan, the inquisitors are ahead."

"How many?"

"I make it six parishas. They're over the next rise, making camp. I don't think they know you're coming."

"Did they see you?"

"No. I've got my people still watching them." She pointed. "We're in that orchard, where the lane turns forward from the road."

"Good work. Go back to them, and then move to where you can watch Tidings parish. They haven't sent all their strength against us, so there'll be more parishas on the move soon. Let me know as soon as you see anything."

"I will, parishan. Good luck." The rider spurred her mount and rode off, and Danil contemplated what he should do. The ground rose gently to the low ridge she had indicated, half a kilometer ahead. It would be hard going to cover that distance of soft pasture under crank power . . . *but if they catch us with our horse teams still connected* . . . it would be less than optimal to fight the battle with his soldiers tired from cranking, but the horses were vulnerable as the turtles were not, and if they lost them his soldiers would be turning cranks all the way to the forewall.

"Cut loose the horses," Danil ordered the war turtle's horsedriver. He turned to Annaya. "Signal that to the rest of the army." She ran up a new set of signal flags, but didn't sound her horn. Danil was about to mention that to her, when he realized she was doing it to avoid alerting the unsuspecting enemy ahead of them. The horsedriver unhitched the team from the war turtle's yoke, and was leading them back to the war wagons that followed behind the turtles. "Advance on cranks," he called into the turtle's belly. Down on the wheel deck the mark-leader echoed the order, and the soldiers took up the wheel cranks. There was a pause while they got themselves coordinated, and then the battle machine lurched forward, moving even more slowly now. For a moment Danil was tempted to send ground skirmishers forward instead. With luck they could lure the bishop's forces into bringing the battle to them instead. *Except that would give them time to prepare, and I don't want that.* Better to take them by surprise when he could. He was somewhat surprised that the inquisitors hadn't taken a basic step of putting out spotters. *But they've always brought the attack to their enemies. Their arrogance is my advantage.*

He kept the turtles moving forward until he could just see over the rise, and then had Annaya signal the halt. The front rank of turtles all carried springbows, the second rank were ball throwers, with the assault towers ringing up the rear. He hadn't been sure if that was the best arrangement, but now it proved its worth.

There was still no sign that the enemy had seen them, and he climbed down from the command pulpit and moved forward on his own. When he got to the top of the rise he dropped to his hands and knees and crawled the last few meters. He could hear the enemy before he saw them, and sure enough on the other side the ground fell away into a broad, shallow bowl, full of white tents and fluttering banners, and several thousand red cloaks. Once he was satisfied that he knew where the enemy was, he crawled back down the rise until he was low enough that he could stand and jog back to his turtle. He climbed back to the pulpit, and had Annaya run up the signal flags to command the ball throwers to fire. A minute later the heavy *kachunk* of their throwing arms sounded, and the heavy clay balls soared over Danil's head to crash into the enemy camp beyond.

"Signal the springbows forward," Danil said, and Annaya ran up the flags and blew her horn. Her signal was echoed by the other turtles, and the weary soldiers inside started cranking again. Even before they got to the rise Danil could hear the chaos the surprise attack had caused, with leaders yelling orders and horns sounding. When they cleared the rise the camp was in chaos. The heavy balls tore through tents and bodies with indifferent ease. Frightened horses had stampeded, trampling men and overturning wagons.

"Springbows, fire!" he yelled, and the archers in the lead turtles responded even before Annaya blew the signal.

The sharp *twangsnap* of the steel-sprung bows echoed over the battle, and the heavy bolts cut into the confused mass of the inquisitors. He told Annaya to order the ball throwers to stop firing. The enemy was fleeing in all directions now, leaving their dead and wounded where they lay, and they were no longer clustered close enough to be a worthwhile target for the heavy weapons. A few arrows rose up against them, but there was no organized resistance. Most of the inquisitors were running, those who'd managed to mount their horses were already gone. Minutes later the enemy encampment was abandoned, save only the dead and those too wounded to flee.

"Advance the rear turtles to this line," Danil ordered, and Annaya set the flags to transmit his command. "Dismount the troops," he yelled across to the neighboring springbow turtles. "Have them search for . . ."

"Danil!" Annaya shouted. "They're coming back."

Danil looked to where she was pointing. Ahead of them a formation of horses was drawing up, just out of springbow range.

As he watched more joined them. "Cancel that order," he yelled to the springbows. "We aren't finished yet."

"There's so many of them," said Annaya, her eyes big as she took in the ranked horses. A second formation joined the first as she said it. The inquisitors had rallied their forces.

"We've beaten them once," Danil said, with a confidence he hoped was warranted. "We can do it again."

"They can wait us out."

Danil nodded, and considered his options. His soldiers had already been awake forty-eight bells preparing for the battle, and he couldn't afford to exhaust them. At the same time he had to advance in order to win, and there was no sense letting his enemy consolidate their reorganization. Time was on the inquisitor's side. He had to bring the battle to them, no matter what the cost. "Advance," he shouted. Annaya blew her horn to send the signal. The war turtle lurched forward as the sweating soldiers inside bent to their cranks once more.

The turtles went faster on the downslope, but still the range closed with painful slowness, to eight hundred meters, to seven, and then to six. The big springbows could throw a bolt that far, but not with any accuracy. Nevertheless one of the leading turtles fired, the *twangsnap* echoing over the field. The big bolt cut the air, arcing high and curving spinward as it did. As Danil watched it fly, the turtle's second springbow fired as well. Both of the missiles fell short of the enemy, though the closest landed within fifty meters. The springbows sounded again, and then the turtle on Danil's right flank joined in. It was exhilarating to watch the bolts flying, but . . . *We're wasting them, and warning the enemy.*

"Stop firing!" Danil yelled. "Stop firing, you *sooksans*. Let them get close!" He heard the order being passed down the line, not fast enough to stop another volley of springbow bolts from being launched, with two more turtles farther down the line letting fly, but finally his eager springbow archers obeyed. He had a signal flag to command them to start firing, but none to command them to stop.

*Something I didn't think of.* There would be other things he hadn't thought of, and some of them might lose him the battle. He looked across to the enemy. Three full parishas had rallied from the chaos of his assault and were drawn up with their horses in battle order. Clusters of banners marked the command groups, though he was still too far away to spot the insignia on their chest plates. He held his breath, afraid his over-eager archers had given the game away. The inquisitor parishans now knew they were badly out-ranged. The smart thing for them to do would be to withdraw just a little, to force the war turtles to keep advancing on crank power until Danil's troops were exhausted. They were so much more mobile than Danil's force, and it occurred to him that they could simply sweep around the edges of the war turtles to attack the vulnerable horse teams and supply wagons from behind.

*But it's too late to do anything about that.* The entire attack was a gamble and there was no turning back now. Mobility was the enemy's strength, protection was his. Even as he considered what he might do in the face of incremental withdrawals by the enemy, a horn sounded from the enemy ranks. There was a collective shout from the massed horsemen, a warcry that chilled Danil's blood, and then the center parisha charged. It seemed that it was an independent decision by the center parishan, though Danil couldn't be sure. *It will be good if they come one at a time.* For the first long seconds he dared hope the inquisitors would make that mistake, but then more horns sounded and the two flanking parishas followed the first. Six hundred horses came bearing down on Danil, spears lowered, and the ground trembled beneath the impact of their hooves. He had an instant vision of himself fleeing the lumber crew as the mounted inquisitors chased him down, and the image paralyzed him. Time seemed to slow down as the horses charged into range, and then finally he found his voice.

"All archers, rapid fire! Ball throwers, rapid fire!"

Annaya blew her horn, and yanked up the red ball and arrow flags to convey the command. He heard the other turtle captain's echoing it up and down the line, the *twangsnap* of heavy springbows filled the air. The big bolts spiraled into the oncoming horde, and one, two, four horsemen were down. From behind him the heavier *chunk* of the ball throwers told him the following turtles were also engaging, and seconds later the heavy clay balls arced over his head. Most of them went wide, and Danil's heart sank. He had imagined his heavy weapons cutting down the enemy in droves, but it wasn't happening. Charging horses were much harder targets than stationary tents, and all of a sudden his awkward array of lurching wooden battle machines looked wholly vulnerable to the descending mass of horses and armor. *We'll be swept away.* His own springbow archers cut loose, and one of the heavy bolts took an inquisitor in the chest. Danil couldn't tell if the shaft had penetrated the enemy's armor, but the man was knocked clean off his horse, to vanish beneath the pounding hooves of those following.

"Yes!" The archer pumped his fist in the air in exhultation.

"Don't cheer! Fire!" Danil snapped, and the man reloaded, aimed and fired again. The bolts were striking home hard now, the distance already down to two hundred meters, and the springbows were more effective. *So close it's hard to miss.* An answering shower of arrows came up from the enemy ranks as they closed to rabbit-bow range, and he ducked behind the command pulpit's shields as they rained down, spiking themselves into *Victory's* wooden flanks. The war turtle's archers swiveled their weapons to face the onslaught, firing steadily while the troops below hauled on the cocking ropes so the archers could reload. Their bolts were hitting home harder now, opening gaps in the inquisitor ranks, and then the charge was on them in a hail of arrows, and Danil ducked behind the pulpit to peer through the narrow slot beneath its rim, bracing for impact. The momentum of the charge seemed unstoppable, but as the horses came upon the strange, slope-sided war machines they balked, and ran to the side. One brave man leapt from his mount to grab the downsloping defensive spikes on the turtle's side. He made it, and used them to climb hand over hand to the top deck. His attack was so fast and so unexpected that Danil barely had time to bring his own blade up before the man was climbing into the command pulpit. Reflexively Danil swung, and the heavy shipsteel cut through flesh and bone. The inquisitor screamed and fell away. A gurgling cry behind him made him spin around, to see a second red-cloaked figure falling backwards with an arrow in his groin. Annaya didn't have her bow in her hands, and it took Danil a moment to realize that she had simply stabbed him with the shaft.

Danil grabbed up his own rabbit bow and put an arrow to the string, determined not to let another inquisitor get so close, but most of the riders were simply flowing through his formation, unwilling or unable to mount the steep-sided war machines against their bristling layer of spines.

He picked a target to his front and fired, saw his arrow bounce from an armored chest plate. He fired again, this time taking his target's horse in the flank. The horse whinnied and reared, throwing its rider off backwards. The wounded horse galloped off, following the rest of the charge and the inquisitor disappeared from Danil's view, hidden by the war turtle's massive prow. Danil picked another target and fired again. His arrow went wide, and then the turtle lurched violently and a blood-curdling scream came from beneath him. The thrown inquisitor had been unable to get out of the way of the huge wheels, and the turtle was running him over. Bones crackled sickeningly, and the scream seemed to go on forever until it suddenly cut off. *What a horrible way to die.* There was no time to reflect on the fate of his enemies, but he was reminded that his army was still advancing when there was no longer any need. The inquisitors had brought the battle to him.

"Halt!" he yelled, and his horsedriver echoed the command into the war turtle's belly, but there was no way his voice would carry even to the next turtle over the sound of the battle. "Annaya, signal the halt."

She hauled at her flag ropes, and blew her horn, and Danil took a deep breath, and looked to assess the situation. Around the battlefield the other war turtles were stopping too. The heavy springbows were still in action, though not at their best at the close ranges, and the horsedrivers were engaging with rabbit bows. His ball throwers had stopped firing altogether, unable to engage an enemy closer than a hundred meters, and having scored few hits firing on moving targets. It was unexpectedly the assault tower turtles who were dealing the most damage. Avel was in charge of them, and he'd ordered the rear turtle captains to put their troops up into the protected ladder towers. From there they were firing down into the milling red mass of inquisitors with terrible effect.

Another brave inquisitor leapt on to the side of the neighboring turtle, and Danil put an arrow to his string and fired reflexively. The arrow took the man in the back, and he fell. A second inquisitor had joined the first, but before Danil could fire again he slipped, to be impaled on the protective spines.

"Danil!" Annaya grabbed him and hauled him down into the pulpit, just as a shower of arrows flew through the space where his head had been, some smacking into the pulpit shields. Danil stuck his head back up to see one of the trailing parishans drawn up short, its archers firing volleys at the ranked war turtles.

"Signal the ball throwers to fire left front."

Annaya nodded. The red ball flag was still up, and she blew her horn and pointed to show the thrower captains where to fire. Nothing happened, and Annaya cursed and shouted at them, a pointless gesture. The nearest thrower turtle was a hundred meters behind him and its captain was surrounded by inquisitors and firing his rabbit bow, oblivious to the danger of the incoming arrows. Danil cursed himself, and turned to direct his own springbow archers to direct their fire at the target, but something struck him from behind and he fell, staggering into Annaya. They both crumpled to the bottom of the pulpit in a tangled heap. He struggled to get to his feet, and found himself looking up at an inquisitor who'd managed to make it onto the war turtle's back. The other man had his spear upraised, ready to drive it down into Danil's chest, and Danil desperately tried to push himself out of the path of the weapon.

There was no room in the cramped pulpit, and Annaya was blocking the narrow space that led down into the turtle's belly, but unable to get through it with Danil's weight on top of her. He saw the man smile in triumph, and then an arrow bounced off his chest armor. The inquisitor looked up, surprised, and a second arrow took him in the forehead. He fell forward, the spearpoint coming down hard on Danil's chest. A second later the soldier's body fell on top of him, blood gushing from the man's impaled skull and all over Danil. Danil tasted blood and spat it out, struggling to get the man's dead weight off of himself in the cramped space. With he and Annaya helpless there was nothing to stop another inquisitor from gaining the back of the war turtle, and if that happened they would certainly die.

He heaved himself upwards, his feet slipping on wood made slippery with his enemy's blood, and managed to get out from underneath the body. He struggled to his knees, and hauled himself up to the pulpit's rim, keeping his head low against the possibility of another volley of arrows. None came, and when he looked over the top he saw that the ball throwers had found the new threat. The heavy clay balls were arcing overhead into the halted parisha, tearing huge gaps in the ranks and leaving crushed men and horses in their wake. The center of the formation had dissolved into milling chaos. The flanks were still in good order, but they'd stopped firing as their flank-captains tried to maneuver them sideways and out of the line of fire. As Danil watched, a springbow volley cut into the left hand flank, killing the flank-captain there and perhaps one of the mark-leaders as well. A second volley speared into the ranks, and that was all it took. A wounded horse screamed in pain, rearing and bucking and turning to bolt. The horses beside it turned to follow, though Danil couldn't tell if that was in spite of their riders or because of them, and then suddenly the parisha's whole left flank was in full flight, with the remnants of the center following them. The right hand flank-captain already had his flank moving out from the killing zone in the center, and he simply wheeled his formation around to retreat in good order. The ball throwers and springbows shifted fire to follow them, but the horsemen were out of range before they could have much effect.

With their departure there were no more enemy in front of him, and Danil turned to see that behind him the charge had been completely broken up. Most of the enemy force was now fleeing in all directions, with springbow bolts flying after the stragglers. Behind the battle line a determined inquisitor flank-captain was still trying to rally his troops against the war wagons, but the fisherfolk there had formed a spear wedge, and the rattled inquisitors failed to press home the charge. Having finished with the remnants of the parisha in the middle of the formation of war turtles, the archers up in the assault towers switched their fire to the group trying to break the spear wedge. The turtle captains were shouting orders, directing the fire on the hapless Prophetsy troops. Only three or four turtles were within good rabbit-bow range of the enemy, but their archers were deadly accurate from the protected elevation of the assault towers. The inquisitor armor turned many of the arrows, but their horses were vulnerable and a horseman thrown to the ground was no longer a soldier but a target. Those who turned to flee were vulnerable, because their armor offered no protection from behind. As Danil watched the heroic flank-captain died, crushed beneath his fallen horse, with half a dozen feathered shafts skewering his body.

That quickly, it was over. The attack had lasted a few minutes at most, and it was a total victory for Danil's force. A cheer went up from the fisherfolk as the last inquisitor galloped out of range, leaving the terrain strewn with dead men and horses.

Danil found himself shaking, and grabbed the edge of the pulpit to steady himself. "Signal a war council," he told Annaya, then yelled down into *Victory*'s belly, "It's over, we won this one."

More cheers answered him, and he hoped what he said was true. He clambered down from the turtle's back to meet his leaders. It took them a while to gather, and Danil kept his eyes moving in case the enemy brought forward fresh parishas. *It would be a bad thing to be caught with all the commanders outside their turtles.* The hardest part of being a commander, he was learning, was not the actual fighting but organizing the force so that when the fight came it was ready.

Avel was the first to arrive, a broad smile on his weathered face. "Three parishas, Danil. We beat three parishas in open combat." The half-parishan was exultant. "War turtles! What a wonderful idea."

Danil nodded, and he fought down the urge to succumb to his own exhilaration. *We beat them, but they'll have learned from this and the next time won't be so easy.* He kept the thought to himself and slapped his half-parishan on the back. "You did a fine job, putting the archers in the towers was brilliant."

His other turtle captains were coming up, all of them equally excited. Danil let them talk for a moment before calling for their attention. It did seem to be a great victory. The inquisitor dead numbered in the hundreds, and the fisherfolk had lost only three killed and half a dozen injured, along with some twenty-three horses. All of their losses were with the supply wagons. The turtles had proved themselves invulnerable. *And yet we can't afford to lose so many horses each time.* The turtles were invulnerable, but his army wasn't.

"We've done a great thing today," he told his captains. "But it's still a long way to the forewall. We've beaten three parishas, they've got nearly twenty still to come at us. Bury your dead, get your wounded back to the war wagons so they can be looked after, and make sure your soldiers rest and eat. In the meantime I want all the springbows and ball throwers ready to fire, and archers up in those towers. Understood? They came back once. They might come back again."

There were murmurs of assent from the group, and Danil turned to Era, who was commanding the war wagons. "Priority for horses goes to the turtles, so Era, that means you're going to have to give up some. You're in charge of making sure that teams are hitched and ready to go."

Era nodded. "We'll be slower. I'll be down to three horses for almost every wagon."

"I know, you'll just have to do what you can to keep up. These turtles aren't fast."

"Oh, we'll do it, don't you worry about that."

"Good." Danil smiled. "For the rest of you, get gathering parties out to recover arrows, and let them take what they want from the inquisitor dead. The priority is weapons and armor, and it should go to whoever can use it best. I'll leave that to your judgment."

"What about trade tokens?" asked one of the springbow captains, a tall lanky woman named Mira. "And anything else of value."

"Everything else goes back with the wagons. When this is over, it'll all be shared out equally." He looked around his assembled leaders, meeting their eyes. "Make sure everyone gets some sleep, yourselves included. We're going to move again at the morning-meal bell. Hitch the horses back to your turtles and be ready to go by then. Any questions?"

There were none, and the meeting broke up. Danil clambered back up onto his turtle and then down into the command pulpit.

The rear ramps on the leading turtles went down and the marks unloaded to go forward and search their fallen enemies. One of the inquisitors nearby wasn't dead, though he had a heavy springbow bolt through his belly. A fisherfolk raised his blade, and before Danil could object the weapon came down. Blood spattered, and the man was dead. Reflexively Danil looked away, and was immediately disgusted with himself for his reaction.

*War is a hard thing, and I must be hard to win it.* He forced himself to look back to the now headless body, and strangely he found himself angry, not at his enemy but at his own soldier. A feeling rose in him, a motivation, an idea only half formed, and he climbed out of the command pulpit. The soldiers had found another wounded inquisitor, this one trapped under a dead horse. The man had been playing dead, but now was pleading for his life as the blade rose for the killing stroke.

And Danil found himself jumping down from his turtle's top

deck in the grip of something very close to rage. "Stop!" he yelled, letting his anger show. "What do you think you're doing?"

The soldiers looked up at him, surprised more than anything. "He was still alive," said the man with the blade, as though that explained everything.

"I know that." Danil strode towards the group. The other soldiers gave him room. "Do you know what you've done here?"

The soldier mutely shook his head.

"The Prophetsy will be back, you can count on that. And when they come, how hard do you want them to fight?"

"I . . . I don't know . . ." The man looked confused.

"Well, think about it," Danil snapped. "Think about how hard they're *going* to fight if they learn we kill their wounded."

The man's face was blank, and Danil cuffed him, hard. "Try that again and I'll kill you myself." He looked back over his shoulder. "Flank-captain!"

"Parishan!" The flank-captain moved to be by him.

Danil met her gaze. "See this man is looked after and taken back to the surgeon. Tell the other captains that all our prisoners are to be treated well. And tell the surgeon that once this one's wounds are dressed he's to be sent back to his parishan to let the Prophetsy know we treat our prisoners well."

"At once, parishan." The flank-captain began yelling instructions to her troops, and Danil turned to the captured inquisitor, moved close to the man's face, looked him straight in his frightened eyes. "And when you get back to your comrades, tell them that Danil Fougere is coming with the wrath of Noah in his right hand. Make sure they know."

The man's eyes grew wide with fear, and Danil turned to walk back to his turtle without waiting for an answer. As he climbed back on he found himself shaking with reaction.

*Did I do the right thing?* He had acted on instinct, and he wasn't used to that. Annaya's eyes were big and he looked away from her, not wanting her to see the uncertainty in his face.

"Annaya, I need you to go to each turtle. Let the turtle captains know we'll be making camp here. We've won some time, and everyone needs sleep. Make sure they keep a good watch. We don't want the Prophetsy surprising us the way we did them."

"I will," she said, and Danil watched as she climbed out of the pulpit and jumped down to deliver his message. He was afraid she would be difficult, as she always had been before, but she seemed to understand whatever disagreement she might have with Danil Fougere, she could have none with the parishan of the fisherfolk army.

Danil watched her go, and then sagged against the side of the pulpit. Annaya's errand was probably unnecessary, a simple confirmation of what the turtle captains should be doing anyway. He'd sent her so he could have some time to himself. *I can't let her see doubts, I can't let any of them see doubts.* There was thankfully little for him to do as his army dealt with the aftermath of the attack, and he had time to recover himself.

His footing was unstable, and he suddenly realized that he was standing on the body of the inquisitor who'd nearly speared him. The inside of the command pulpit was smeared red with blood, and the man's brains were splattered on the shields. Danil felt suddenly sick, but his stomach was too empty to actually vomit.

The episode left him weak and shaky, and then he had to heave the body up and out of his pulpit. The limp corpse was a cumbersome, uncooperative burden, and the man's dead eyes stared at him with empty accusation. When it was gone he looked out over the battlefield, where fisherfolk troops were sorting the living from the dead, collecting unbroken arrows and bolts, and those balls that hadn't shattered on impact.

He became aware of a soreness in his chest, and looked down to find his shirt ripped open and blood soaked. Most of the blood was the inquisitor's, but beneath the tear there was a nasty gash in his chest. The soldier's spearpoint had sliced almost to the bone. If it had come down full force he would have been dead in that instant. The blood was already clotting, and the forming scabs pulled away painfully as he separated the fabric from the wound.

*My enemy's blood and my own, blending his death and my survival.* Reflexively his hand went to the scar on his arm where the arrow had pierced him as he fled slavery across the Prophetsy wall. He would have two battle scars now. *And I'll be very pleased if I never earn another mark on my body.*

He looked foreward, to the distant forewall, and the still invisible temple he hoped to assail. It was a long way to go with the lumbering war turtles, and it seemed unlikely he would cover all that distance without another injury.

He studied the ground ahead, ground he thought he had already learned in his many journeys up and down the trading road. Now at the head of his army a host of new details came to his attention. An irrigation ditch at the edge of the next field was an obstacle that required consideration. A clump of shrubs might shelter an enemy spotter, or offer cover for one of his own.

*I have so much to learn, and an error would be disastrous.* High on the curve of the world he could see the flashes of inquisitor mirror code, flickering news of his victory to his enemies. He had chosen to take on the Prophetsy, and now the Prophetsy would respond to his challenge. There was no sign of the parishas he had defeated, the survivors had fled out of sight, but the next parishans he faced would know the impact of the war turtles. The element of surprise was gone, at least from his side. The fisherfolk could have no other strategy than to advance up the trading road with their ponderous war machines to assault the Prophet's temple, and any halfway rational parishan or bishop would realize that. What surprise the enemy came up with as a counter to the power of his turtles he would not know until they sprung it on him.

"Danil, are you all right?" It was Annaya, returned from her errand.

"Yes, of course." Danil wasn't sure it was true, but he assumed the mantle of surety that was a requirement of command.

"You were . . ." Annaya stopped, not wanting to question him, perhaps not wanting to acknowledge in her own mind that he might not know what he was doing. "I've told the turtle commanders, and they're getting their people food and sleep."

Danil nodded. "Good."

"And you need sleep too." Danil opened his mouth to object but Annaya held up a hand. "Don't argue with me, we need you at your best."

She was right. He nodded, and climbed out of the bloodsoaked pulpit to lie on the war turtle's top deck. He wrapped his cloak around himself, threw an arm over his eyes to block out the suntube, and was asleep in seconds.

It seemed like he'd barely closed his eyes when Annaya was shaking him awake.

"Danil, get up. We're moving out."

He was awake instantly, looking around to see the war turtles loaded with their troops aboard, the horse teams are hitched, and the war wagons lined up to the rear in good formation, the battle flags flying to show his army was ready to move.

Annaya handed him some hard bread and dried cheese. "Your morning meal, parishan."

"Why didn't you wake me earlier?"

"Avel and Era had it well in hand, and you still haven't slept enough."

Danil nodded slowly. He would have rather been up before his turtle captains, to demonstrate leadership if for no other reason, but Annaya was right. He would be no good to his army if he exhausted himself on the first day of the war. "Signal the advance," he said, and watched as Annaya ran up the flags. The horse teams were stirred up, and the formation of war machines moved off. A great many soldiers had chosen to walk behind their turtles rather than ride in the cramped compartments. *Not a bad idea, as long as we have enough warning before the Prophetsy comes again.*

"Any news from the sentinels?" he asked Annaya.

"They're in position. Four parishas are forming up at the Temple."

Danil nodded, thinking. The inquisitors were so much more mobile than his force. They could concentrate almost anywhere, and attack from any direction, while he was constrained to advance in a straight line at a predictable speed. There was no sign of attack as they moved across the aftward fields, though lone riders did appear in the distance, keeping well out of springbow range. *They won't be surprised again.*

A layer of low cloud shrouded most of the suntube, blocking the inquisitor mirror signals, but that wouldn't make much difference at this stage. A kilometer ahead the irrigation ditch he'd noticed loomed as an obstacle. He chewed his lower lip, considering how to get his force across it. Annaya brought up some dried fish from the rations below and he ate it while he ran different scenarios through his mind. It took a whole bell for them to advance to the ditch. The trading road crossed it over a culvert, and another five hundred meters down there was another where a farmer had connected his fields. Danil bit his lower lip as he studied the ground. If the Prophetsy managed to disable a turtle *right there* it would paralyze his whole force. *And yet the risk must be accepted, all I can do is try to control it.* He had Annaya signal a halt, and dismounted. On foot he went to the springbow turtles on either flank, and ordered the two on each side to release their horse teams and cross the narrow chokepoints under crank power. He climbed back up on his turtle, watched with his stomach tight as they did. Behind him the ball throwers maneuvered into position to support the lead elements. The ground offered little cover for a Prophetsy ambush, but the mounted inquisitors moved so much faster than his own awkward force than they could essentially engage at will.

The springbows crossed without incident at both points, though it took almost a bell for them to complete the movement. Once across they advanced a hundred meters beyond the irrigation ditch to cover the remainder of the army as it moved over the culverts. Then Danil had to rearrange his force from the battle line it was deployed in, to two single files to make the crossing. It took an excruciatingly long time. The plowed field was dangerously soft, and most of the turtle captains lowered their back ramps and ordered their soldiers out of the war machines to walk along behind them. That lightened the load for the toiling horses, and gave some much needed air and exercise to the cramped troops. It was a wise, even necessary decision, but Danil worried about what would happen if a parisha suddenly appeared to charge down on their flank. The midday-meal bell had sounded before the last turtle had crossed, and it was almost the evening meal before they'd managed to reform the battle line on the other side of the obstacle. He ordered a halt at that point, with sentries deployed and soldiers building cook fires around their machines. The day's advance had covered only five kilometers, half what he had hoped to achieve. That was worrisome, because the turtles only carried food and water for two days, with another two days of rations carried on the war wagons. There could be no question of sending the wagons back for more supplies, without the protection of the turtles they would be easy prey for the Prophetsy's riders.

Danil held another war council once the sentries had been posted, but confined the discussion to the details necessary to organize the next advance and kept his larger concerns to himself. He couldn't get the face of the inquisitor who'd nearly speared him out of his mind. *He died so that I could live.*

It had been an inquisitor arrow that killed the man, one of

those random accidents of battle that could turn the tide of a war. His chest throbbed where the spearpoint had gouged the flesh, and now that the immediate stress of battle command was gone, the pain surged with every movement. *The line between life and death is so narrow.* The lack of further enemy action worried him, but there was nothing he could do about it. The inquisitors would attack when they were ready, and all he could do was wait.

"Again," said Bishop Nufell, and the driver brought his short-whip down. The man roped to the cross grunted, his face contorted as he clenched his teeth against the pain.

"Again." The whip fell again, and the man's body convulsed, though he managed to bear the stroke in silence this time. Tears were starting from his eyes, but still he said nothing. The bishop stepped forward to take his face in one hand, squeezing. "You can stop this any time you know."

The man shook his head, his eyes hard with defiance. The bishop squeezed harder. "God *wants* to forgive you. Why won't you let him?"

In reply the man spat in the bishop's face. Angered, Nufell backhanded him. "Break him, learn all he knows," he snarled to the driver, and turned on his heel. He heard the whip come down again, harder this time. The prisoner gave a strangled cry, and Nufell smiled as he wiped the spittle from his cheek. *He won't last long.* His smile faded as he went to the Temple's outer wall and climbed the stairs to the palisade. He had learned much in his long quest for power, but the most important thing was information, and information was exactly what he lacked. Waiting for it was not something he enjoyed.

And he was waiting for more than his enemy's confession. He watched aftward impatiently, until far down the road a rider on horseback appeared. He watched as the shape grew closer, resolved a red cloak, a heavy curved blade. The courtyard gates opened as the rider approached. *Balak.* The High Inquisitor was moving at a rapid trot, but Nufell found it annoying that he wasn't coming at a gallop. Nufell went down the stairs to meet him.

"Where have you been?"

"I've been fighting your war, Bishop." Balak's eye twitched, a signal that Nufell had learned that he was going to be unreasonable.

"I hope that hasn't inconvenienced you." There was a nasty looking cut on the side of the warrior-priest's face.

"Inconvenienced." Nufell snorted. "What inconveniences me is the fact that this rabble has put six full parishas to flight."

"The material is unimportant. God has ordained our victory."

"God has ordained, God has ordained." Nufell slammed his fist on the table. "I don't want to hear what God has ordained, I want to hear that these *sooksans* have been crushed." He stood and turned away. "I'm disappointed, Balak. Deeply disappointed."

"Your lack of faith disturbs me."

"So?" Nufell spun around to meet Balak's gaze. "Your lack of success disturbs me."

"You forget that I battle for the Prophet, not you, Bishop." There was a warning in Balak's tone, and his hand moved to the handle of his blade.

The implied threat behind the motion wasn't lost on Nufell. *But he knows his treasured Prophet needs me.* He sat down at the table again. "Then let's pretend for a moment that Olen Polldor isn't a spineless child who wouldn't survive a bell in front of the Elder Council without me behind him. And while we're pretending that you and I can discuss the problem like adults."

Balak ignored the sarcasm, but he sat down at the table. "The problem will be resolved, shortly. I reorganized the lead parishas, and the rest of our strength is gathering."

"We can't afford to throw all the parishas into this. Rumors are already spreading in the slave crews, did you know that?"

"I've ordered a recall of those who've left the order. It will take time for them to gather and be organized, but they can handle the slaves, if necessary."

"Can they? The Elder Council is in a panic."

"The Elder Council is your concern, not mine."

"They'll become your concern if their slaves rebel. If your vaunted inquisitors can't handle a few hundred fisherfolk, I invite you to imagine facing thousands."

"God has ordained the Prophet's victory, Bishop."

"I would feel better if I thought you understood the forces at play here."

"God has ordained the Prophet's victory, Bishop," Balak repeated, and stood up with his eyes blazing. His voice grew intense. "I hear your doubts, I see the falsity of the faith you profess, but mark my words, I will destroy this threat to Noah's line. I will purify the world with holy fire, and I will not stop with the godless rabble you call your enemy."

Balak drew his blade and Nufell started back, almost falling out of his chair. "I know your ambitions, Bishop. I see your contempt for the power God has imbued in our new Prophet, but do not mistake weakness in the vessel for weakness in the wine." He leaned forward and locked his eyes on Nufell's. "You find me useful, for now. So too does God find you useful, for now.

"But know this, Bishop, know this. The time is coming when God will demand penance for your apostasy, and when that time comes I pray, *I pray* he will choose me to be the instrument of your destruction."

Balak yanked at a buckle and his breastplate fell to the floor. "God is my blade and my shield, Bishop." The High Inquisitor slammed the weapon down point first, burying it in the oak tabletop. "If you don't believe that, pick up that blade and kill me while you still can."

There was a look in Balak's eyes that wasn't fully human, a look almost feral in its paralyzing intensity. Nufell instinctively pushed himself back in his chair to get farther away from him. He found he wasn't breathing, and he inhaled consciously, slowly. "There's no need for us to argue. We're on the same side."

"We'll see." Balak reached over and pulled his blade from the table. He reached down and picked up his armor. "You keep the Elder Council in line and out of my way. I have a war to win."

He turned on his heel and left, and Nufell watched him go. His hands were trembling, and he laid them flat on the table while he tried to get his swirling thoughts under control.

*He's dangerous, too dangerous.* He had thought he could control Balak because he controlled Olen, but the High Inquisitor was more complex than that. Yes, his devotion to the Prophet's line was absolute, but he was still a man. He knew he'd been manipulated into killing Polldor, though he couldn't express that anger directly. And he blamed Nufell for the unresolvable anguish that had brought him.

*And if I can't get him under control, I'm going to have to kill him, more quickly than I expected.* He wouldn't do it himself of course. No, that would be more risk than Nufell really felt like undertaking. *I need an assassin . . .* There would be time to solve that problem. For now there was a rebellion to crush, and Balak still had his uses.

There was battle in the air, Danil could smell it. The cloud that had shrouded the suntube had spiraled forward and dissipated, and inquisitor mirror code flickered back and forth around the curve of the world. His sentinels were skirmishing with inquisitor spotters on every flank. At least eight parishas were on the move, probably more. The enemy was gathering, and from the thoroughness of the reconnaissance he was quite sure that when the battle came it wouldn't hand him victory as easy as the last one.

His army had advanced halfway to Charity, and his life had been reduced to a series of tactical decisions. Some of those decisions had cost him sentinels, and he was acutely aware that every loss weakened him. The inquisitors' advantage in numbers meant that they could win just by trading body for body, and they were using that advantage to press his reconnaissance forces hard. Danil agonized over the steady trickle of losses, but he couldn't give up his eyes forward. The cumbersome war turtles were powerful, but he needed all the advance warning he could get to make sure they were ready when the attack came.

*And it will come.*

His concentration was total, not a single aspect of his army's advance was too small for him to take notice of, though he tried not to interfere with the judgment of his captains. *They need to know I trust them, if they're going to trust themselves at the critical moment.* He didn't even eat unless Annaya reminded him to, and when he did he barely tasted his food. Sleep became a matter of a bell snatched here, another there.

The bells wore into days and the attack still didn't come. Even so the turtles advanced a couple of kilometers a day at best, and it was frustrating to call their evening-meal halt an easy walk from where they'd started at the breakfast bell. And the fourth day they reached the orchards surrounding the town of Praise. The fragrance of ripening citrus and mango filled the air, incongruously pleasant, but the close-spaced trees posed Danil a problem he hadn't faced before. The orchard floor was level enough for the turtles to roll, but maneuvering would be difficult at best. The springbows would have hardly any field of fire, and even communication would be difficult.

*We'll be vulnerable from the trees at close range.* He contemplated sending two turtles a side into the orchards under crank power and putting the rest of the army into single file on the road, a maneuver similar to what he'd done at the irrigation ditches, but on further contemplation he realized it wouldn't work. Controlling the movement would be all but impossible, and the turtles in the trees would be almost helpless to defend themselves against foot troops.

Fortunately he had time to ponder the problem as the war turtles lumbered slowly towards the obstacle, and before the first one had reached the edge of the orchards he had the solution. He had Annaya signal a halt and a war council, and outlined his plan to his gathered turtle captains. It didn't take long, everyone knew the drill now, and the captains ran back to their war machines to implement the plan. *We're gaining skill, and that's good.*

Annaya signaled the advance again and the mark-leaders led their units down the back ramps into battle order and filtered into the trees with spears ready. Archers moved farther out into the orchards to provide early warning. The fisherfolk had already proved they could beat the mounted inquisitors in the trees, and if their enemy came into the orchards they would prove it again. *They could still try to use fire against us, but well kept orchards won't burn the way the forest with dead undergrowth did.*

Still he held his breath as the first turtle reached the edge of the orange trees. If it did come to a battle there would be almost nothing he could do to command it. It would all come down to his mark-leaders and the individual turtle captains. The road curved, and with the turtles spaced twenty meters apart he could see only the one in front of him and the one behind.

It was far too late to change his deployment, but still he fretted over it. With their soldiers deployed the turtles had to be pulled by their horse teams. If the inquisitors managed to break through his flank guards they could kill the horses and take on the turtles one by one, and his army would be destroyed piecemeal. *But how else could I have done it?* In war every choice carried risks, and there was no way to know in advance which choices were the critical ones. He bit his lower lip, and waited.

There was no attack, and a bell later a runner came panting back to tell him that the lead turtles were entering Praise, and it was deserted. He sent word back ordering that the houses be left undisturbed. They should only gather food and water for resupply.

*I used the destruction of Far Bay to fuel anger at the Prophetsy. I will not make the Prophetsy's mistake, and hand them a weapon so powerful.* Beyond Praise was Charity, and while his army had the strength to take Praise in the face of its inhabitants' resistance, Charity was too big. If its people fought, the fisherfolk advance would stop there.

Soon enough his own turtle was moving through the village. As reported, it was completely deserted, without even a sleep watch on the main road.

*Did the people run, or are they hiding in their houses?* They hadn't been gone for long, to judge from the smoke rising from the blacksmith's forge. Where they'd gone didn't matter so much; it was enough that they weren't interfering with his advance. When he came at last to the far end of the town he was pleased to see that the lead turtles had moved forward and to the sides to cover the advance as it redeployed into open formation. It was well past the mid-day bell, but they were past the dangerous choke-point and once more into the rolling fields where the turtles could cover each other. They advanced another kilometer by the evening-meal bell, and Danil called the halt.

The advance through the orchards and village had the side benefit of allowing the army to restock itself, which took away the worry that their slow advance would cause them to run out of supplies before they could reach the Prophet's temple. The sleeping hours passed without any sign of the enemy, and the silence made Danil nervous. Even allowing for their first victory, the Prophetsy still commanded eighteen parishas of inquisitors. Their spotters were all around, keeping just out of springbow range and still skirmishing with his sentinels. They wouldn't allow the fisherfolk to simply walk into the temple unchallenged. He noticed almost absently that his jaw ached, and he realized he'd been unconsciously grinding his teeth together. *Stress reaction.*

He told Annaya to signal the advance, and just at that moment a cloud of dust appeared on the road beyond the next treeline, resolved itself into a sentinel rider, galloping hard. The sentinel stopped only briefly at the lead turtle, and then rode to Danil.

"Parishan! The Prophetsy is coming!" The rider was breathing hard and her horse was covered in sweat. Danil noticed an arrow shaft caught in her shield, another protruding from the back of her saddle.

"How many?"

"A dozen parishas at least, maybe more. They're five kilometers ahead and coming fast. They're staying off the road, coming through the fields, with heavy skirmishers forward. We've lost two sentinels at least."

"Are they mounted?"

"Yes, parishan."

Danil nodded. "Good job." He paused to survey the treeline ahead, as though through hard enough scrutiny he could see through it and straight into the mind of the High Inquisitor. "I need you to ride back, keep a close watch on their advance. I need a kilometer's warning before we make contact, and I need to know if they moved to either flank."

The sentinel's eyes widened, a trace of fear crossed her expression, and for just that instant Danil saw her not as a soldier but as a young woman, one who had just survived a dangerous encounter with the enemy, and one who he'd just asked to risk her life again. The moment passed, the sentinel nodded and rode off the way she had come, and Danil pressed his lips together. *What right do I have to play with people's lives like this?* He had no good answer to that. He watched the rider vanish through the trees, then turned to Annaya.

"Signal for the horse teams to be disconnected," he said. "Get the troops back in the turtles. We'll advance on crank power until they come."

"At once, Danil." She busied himself with her flags, and Danil watched as his army began to respond. While they moved, he contemplated his options.

*They've come with all their force, they intend to force a battle.* If that were true, the best thing to do would be to take positions and wait for the enemy. If the enemy didn't advance, he could always start forward again. The treeline ahead was thin, really just a windbreak between adjacent fields of ripening wheat, but it was the best cover available. He let his army advance until the springbow turtles were four hundred meters short of the trees. That would put the inquisitors under effective fire from the moment they broke into his field. He halted the ball throwers a hundred meters behind the springbows, so they could fire into the farther field. If the inquisitors tried to use the space to adopt battle formation he would make them pay. He left the tower turtles behind, in a circular formation around the supply wagons. He didn't want to repeat the heavy horse losses he'd suffered in the first battle. He barely had his disposition set when the sentinel came riding back to report the enemy dismounting in the next field, five thousand strong.

"Already?" Danil raised an eyebrow.

"Yes, parishan." Two more arrows were stuck in her shield, and her horse had a gash in its hindquarters where another had grazed it. "I'm sorry. I wanted to give you more warning, but some spotters got on my flank and pinned me down."

"Don't apologize. You did well. They've learned mounted troops can't stand against war turtles, so they're going to attack on foot." Danil stopped. What he needed was more eyes forward, to keep him apprised as the enemy advanced. *But I can't ask this woman to risk her life again.*

"Ride back to the war wagons. Help them keep the horse teams safe," he told her.

She didn't get a chance to reply. A sudden shower of burning arrows came over arcing over the trees. They left trails of smoke in their wake, but they were too far out of range to be any danger. They stabbed themselves into the ground three hundred meters in front of the closest turtle. The enemy had miscalculated.

"Annaya, get the ball throwers firing over those trees."

The enemy *had* to be there, drawn up in close ranks for volley fire with the spear-marks right behind him waiting to advance. His heavy weapons would force them to retreat or come forward, and when they broke the treeline the springbows would be waiting.

Annaya blew her horn, the notes crisp in the humid air. *She's learned fast.* Danil had been so focused on leading his army that he'd had no room for his emotions towards her, but all of a sudden he saw her once more as his partner, and his lover, the woman who had saved his life and made the whole enterprise possible. With an effort he pushed the feelings down and looked to the treeline. There would be time for that after the victory. *If there is a victory.*

Smoke was beginning to curl up from the dry wheat where the flame arrows had landed, and all of a sudden Danil realized that perhaps the inquisitors hadn't miscalculated after all. They were going to use fire the way they used it in the aftward forests. His turtles were all up to their wheels in dry tinder, and with the horse teams disconnected there was no way they could get out of the coming conflagration in time. Licks of flame rose beneath the smoke, and the fire began to take hold. The steady aftward breeze was blowing it straight towards Danil's stationary army. Danil smiled to himself. *In the forest, fire was a surprise weapon. This time I'm ready.*

"Water barrels," he shouted to the neighboring turtles. "Water barrels." He heard the message being passed on, and saw the back ramps coming down as the soldiers inside hauled out the heavy water barrels. Quickly they were passed up to the top decks and dumped over the wooden superstructures. The turtles were built mostly of greenwood, and soaked down they wouldn't burn easily. More barrels were left on top of the turtles, to deal with any flames that took hold despite the precautions. The *chunk* of the ball throwers sounded, and he heard the low *whoosh* of the heavy balls passing over his head. They vanished over the trees and Danil couldn't tell what damage they were doing. *But the inquisitors will be feeling it, I'm certain of that.*

A second volley of flame arrows followed the first, but the wheat was already burning well. Pungent smoke drifted over their position, and Danil's eyes stung. He blinked away the tears, watching for the enemy to make their move. The effort quickly became useless as the smoke and flame rose up in a solid wall, but the enemy would have to advance right behind the burning wheat or lose the benefit of its cover. Horns sounded from the enemy lines, and he knew the inquisitors were moving. He waited, visualizing what was happening on the other side of the trees. The enemy parishans would have waited until the smoke cover was complete before advancing, and they'd be delayed slightly coming to the treeline. A parisha on foot in four ranks would have fifty meters of frontage and four in depth, which meant the leading formations would be fully into the springbows field of fire . . .

"*Now!* Springbows free fire!" he yelled. "Ball throwers, fire short." Annaya ran the flags up and sounded her horn, though it was doubtful that anyone could see the signals through the smoke. He heard his order being passed down the line though, and then the steady *twangsnap* of the big bows as they fired blindly into the murk. The screams of injured redcloaks came through the smoke, and he knew he'd judged the moment right.

The flame front came on, roaring and crackling and faster than Danil would have imagined possible. He ducked behind the pulpit shields as the heat rose, colliding with Annaya in the cramped space. The noise grew to a roar and the choking smoke swirled so densely that Danil thought they might suffocate even if they didn't burn. He coughed hard, squeezing his eyes shut, and then the flames were past.

"We're on fire," Annaya yelled, pointing, and Danil saw small licks of flame creeping up their turtle's flank, where the intense heat had dried the damp wood and set it alight.

"Water!" he yelled, but she was already out of the pulpit, dumping one of the barrels down to douse the flames. With the fire behind him Danil could see the inquisitors advancing. They were still two hundred meters distant. They too had been taken by surprise by the speed of the fire. As he watched they halted, drew bows and fired.

"Annaya! Arrows!" Their turtle was still burning, and Annaya was maneuvering the second barrel to dump it down on the flames. Danil lunged to pull her back into the pulpit. She was out of his reach, and the burning arrows stabbed down around them. Fire flared up from one of them, and without a second thought Danil grabbed up his cloak, climbed out of the pulpit, and snuffed it out. Even through the fabric the heat burned his hand, but he ignored the pain, grabbed Annaya and shoved her bodily back into the safety of the pulpit, just as another burning volley rained down around them. He stuck his head up again to assess the situation, in time to see one of the springbow archers beating out another flaming projectile with his bare hands. The turtle captains on either side of him had also kept their machines from catching fire, though farther down the line a pillar of smoke told him that at least one of his war turtles had fallen to the fire attack.

And the enemy was still advancing, a hundred meters away now, with a second wave coming up behind them.

"All springbows fire!" Danil yelled, though not one of them had stopped. The heavy bolts were cutting into the advancing ranks of the enemy, but there were too many inquisitors and not enough springbows. Another volley of flame arrows rained down, and a second pillar of smoke told Danil he'd lost another turtle. The inquisitors had measured the threat his war machines represented, and they'd had found a response. They would burn the fisherfolk army where it stood. Once the inquisitors were in close the springbows would be useless. A volley of balls soared overhead, but the missiles fell between the first inquisitor wave and the second.

"Dismount! Dismount!" he yelled to either side, then turned to Annaya. "Get the ball throwers to drop fire. Let's try and shut down those archers."

"I'll try."

Danil heard the other turtle captains passing his order up the line, the back ramps came down, and his soldiers piled out to face the enemy one-to-one. The mark-leaders shouted commands, and with well-drilled precision they formed a spear wall in front of the halted springbow turtles. They were heavily outnumbered by the advancing parishas and Danil felt a surge of pride in his troops. Flame arrows were still coming down, and his soldiers raised their shields to ward them off. An arrow stuck itself into the edge of the command pulpit, just inches from Danil's face and he jumped back, startled. Without thinking he grabbed it and threw it, still burning, over the side. More burning arrows protruded from *Victory*'s flanks, too many to deal with at once. Some of the soldier's shields had been set on fire too, and they had to lower their protection to stamp out the flames. An incoming arrow took one of them in the chest and the man fell out of ranks, killed on the spot. At fifty meters, the front rank of the first inquisitor wave lowered their spears, and Danil realized that the second rank was carrying lit torches. A third wave was advancing through the trees. It was going to come down to a ground fight, with the enemy having the advantage in armor and numbers. His springbows fired again as the red-cloaked ranks came on. At that short range, every bolt killed at least one man or wounded several, but the disciplined inquisitors didn't waver.

*They've got courage themselves; it's important to remember that.* Behind Danil the ball-throwers had the range on the second wave now, the big clay balls wreaking havoc wherever they landed. He glanced up to see Annaya's command flags still flying. He'd wanted the ball throwers to fire over the trees, but they'd misinterpreted the order.

*And they're probably doing more good this way.* There was no use leaving an obsolete order in force. "Annaya! Get those flags down. Order the tower turtles forward." *I have an advantage here, if I can use it.* He'd set himself up to defend against a horse charge, expecting it to flow through his formation to the rear as it had in the last battle, but the foot battle would be fought at the front. The tower turtles had to come up to bring their archers to bear.

*I nearly overlooked that.* He bit his lip hard as he realized how closely he had come to making a crucial error. *I have to remember there is no second chance here.* At twenty-five meters he heard the enemy flank-captains command the charge, and a blood chilling battle-cry went up from the massed inquisitors as they broke into a run, spears lowered. The steady rain of flame arrows stopped, but they'd had a telling effect. More turtles were burning, and there were gaps in the fisherfolk battle line. Danil looked behind him to see the assault turtles slowly crawling forward, and willed them to come faster. Annaya had her rabbit bow in hand and was loosing arrows as fast as she could put them on the string.

"Set spears!" Danil yelled, and his flank-captains echoed him. The fisherfolk braced their spear hafts against the ground to receive the inquisitor charge, and seconds later the opposing forces slammed into each other. The battlefield filled with the sound of metal biting into wood, the shouted commands of the leaders, cries of rage and pain.

The first rank of inquisitors suffered grievously against the fisherfolk spear fence, but the defenders were forced back, and the second rank stepped forward to fight where they had stood, while the fire-bearers started throwing their torches. Those in front of Danil were still too far back, and the firebrands went wide or fell short of his turtle, but more flames rose to the right and left of Danil. *We've lost four turtles at least, maybe five.* He looked ahead to where the second and third inquisitor waves were still advancing with a sick feeling in the pit of his stomach. A fourth wave emerged from the treeline, and Danil's heart sank.

"Springbows, take them in depth!" The bolts from the turtle's heavy weapons were coming dangerously close to the thin line of defenders. On Danil's command they lifted their fire to the follow-ing waves, and their sharp *twangsnap* sounded in steady rhythm. The field ahead was littered with broken bodies. The springbows and the spear fence had broken the first wave, but the defenses had been torn open where the enemy had set the covering war turtles alight, and the second wave was already charging towards the gaps. Annaya dropped her bow to run up the signal flags, and the other springbow turtles lifted their fire as well. It was a gamble, because it meant what was left of the spear fence had to handle the remnants of the first wave by themselves. *But a necessary gamble, because if the enemy isn't broken in depth they'll sweep us away.*

"Ball throwers, concentrate on the gaps!" Danil shouted over the din of the battle, but there was no way the turtles in depth could hear him.

"What signals, Danil?" asked Annaya, now shooting again. The spear fence in front of their turtle was shattered, but her arrows were keeping the enemy at bay. Danil paused, paralyzed as he tried to think of how to signal his command. *It's impossible.* There was simply no way to direct the throwers' fire with sufficient precision by signal flag alone, the battle was too fluid for that.

"No signals. Run back and tell them, we need them to shoot where we've lost turtles."

"I should be protecting you . . ."

"So help me win the battle. Run!"

Still she hesitated, and then she grabbed him, kissed him, and vaulted out of the command pulpit. She ran to the back of the turtle and jumped to the ground. Enemy arrows followed her, and Danil grabbed his rabbit bow and began shooting to give her cover. The second wave of inquisitors had been shot ragged by springbows and ball throwers, but their charge collapsed what was left of the spear fence, and knots of red cloaks had gotten past the burning turtles on Danil's left flank. He took aim at an enemy flank-captain and hit the white inquisitor cross blazoned on the man's chest, but the arrow bounced off the inquisitor's armor. He cursed and fired again, this time taking the man through the shoulder.

His target dropped, writhing in pain but the rest of his group charged the war turtle. Danil nocked and fired again, took another one, and then the inquisitors were climbing the turtle's side, using the downsloping defense spines as climbing aids. His springbow archers had taken up their hand bows as well, abandoning their big weapons to fight off the close assault. Even as he absorbed that development the smell of smoke snatched his attention to the other side of the turtle. The right-forward springbow archer lay sprawled over the side of his weapon, the right-rear archer had vanished, and the enemy had thrown torches into the weapon pulpits. The flames had taken hold and were crackling up the war machine's side.

On the left side an inquisitor hauled himself onto the war turtle's top deck and came at Danil with his spear. Danil dropped his rabbit bow, grabbed his blade and swung. Metal met wood, deflecting the spear shaft enough that the point went past Danil's ear instead of into his face. The inquisitor was unable to check his momentum. Danil stabbed at the man's stomach and connected. The blow was awkward, but the enemy warrior grunted in pain and fell. Danil struck again as he came past, and the blade bit deep into the back of the man's thigh. He howled in pain and rolled away and over the war turtle's side, knocking another climbing enemy off in the process.

Heat boiled up from the crew compartment below, and the crackle of flames rose beneath Danil. The fire had spread from the right side springbow pulpits to the turtle's interior. An arrow hissed past and he ducked behind the pulpit shields as another one sliced through the space where his head had been a half second before. Smoke began to rise up around him, and the heat grew.

*I have a minute here, maybe.* After that he'd have to choose between roasting and getting skewered by the inquisitors. It wasn't a pleasant decision, but at least Annaya wasn't there to make it with him. *And I pray she stays safe to the end of this.* His rabbit bow jumped in front of him like a live thing, and he started back in surprise before realizing that the string had caught fire, burned through and released the tension from the limbs. A sudden cry drew his attention, and he stood up again to see one of the left side springbow archers jump from his position with his clothing on fire. He fell to the ground, rolled, and died before he'd stopped moving, run through the chest with an inquisitor's spear. Flame gouted from the pulpit he'd jumped from, and the smoke that was rising around Danil reversed itself as the new fire sucked in air through the turtle's openings. A heartbeat later it exploded out again as the fire in the war machine's belly roared up like a bellows-pumped forge. Pain burned wherever the flame touched his skin, and Danil leapt out of the pulpit before he could be burned alive.

He looked wildly left and right, but the inquisitors who'd been climbing the war turtle's sides had abandoned the effort in the face of the flames, though they still swarmed on either side as their flank-captain rallied them to push forward to the ball throwers. He threw himself flat on the deck to avoid their arrows. The signal mast was burning now, the flags blazing into ash, and the planks of the top deck were hot and starting to smolder.

He crawled towards the rear of the war machine to escape the heat. Fire roared up behind him and he glanced backwards to see a pillar of flame shooting up from the pulpit he'd just abandoned. Smoke billowed out and over him and he kept crawling, squeezing his eyes shut and trying not to breathe. He reached the rear of the turtle, and then there was nowhere to go but down. He rolled and fell from the burning deck, instinctively throwing out his arms to check his fall. Something snapped painfully as he landed and a split second later his skull hit the ground. The world spun wildly and he shook himself, tried to stand, and found he couldn't get his balance.

*The best thing to do right now is play dead.* He saw red cloaks through the thickening smoke, but nobody seemed to have noticed him, so he stayed where he was and closed his eyes. He shivered, suddenly cold despite the burning war turtle just a meter away.

*Strange to be cold so close to a fire.* It was a curious thought and he would have considered it further, but he felt suddenly sleepy, languid. That too was a strange thing in the middle of a battle, but it was difficult to think at all, and the lure of sleep was too powerful to ignore, and so he let himself drift away into darkness.

The courtyard of the Temple was crowded with injured and dying inquisitors, some on litters, most lying on the ground and Balak walked among them, kneeling beside those he knew, sometimes bestowing a prayer, other times just putting a hand on a shoulder, knowing the wounded man would feel God's power in his touch. *The Prophet's word is with me now.*

"Will I live, High Inquisitor?" asked one, his words coming in gasps. The red of his cloak concealed the red of his blood, but one of the slave's heavy bolts had punctured his chest armor.

Balak looked into his eyes. "You'll reach Heaven before any of us," he said.

"I don't want to die, please. . . ." The soldier was young, barely more than a boy. He had the triple-armed cross of Tribulation parish embroidered into his cloak.

"Death in God's name is a blessing. The Prophet knows your sacrifice." Balak moved the bolt and the young man gasped in pain. Gently he slid a hand behind the soldier's breastplate. Behind the armor the shaft was driven deep into his ribcage. It had torn into his lungs on the right-hand side, and Balak could feel the blood seeping from the wound. The shaft itself was all that was stopping an all-out hemorrhage. The soldier would die the instant it was removed, but he could not live the way he was.

"Tell my mother to come . . ." The soldier's eyes slid closed. With an effort he wet his dry lips, summoning the strength to speak again, and his eyes fluttered open. "Tell my mother . . ."

"God is coming," Balak answered. The young inquisitor stared blankly, not understanding, and then his eyes widened in fear as the meaning of Balak's words sank in. The High Inquisitor smiled gently to calm him. "Be brave and know God's love," he said, and stroked the man's forehead with one hand while he took the protruding shaft with the other.

"You are blessed to die in his service." With a sudden motion he yanked the bolt free. The man gave a short, strangled cry and convulsed, blood spurting from the now-open wound. His eyes registered pain, and then loss, and then peace as his jaw grew slack and his body relaxed into death. Balak stood and moved on. *Today, God's mercy flows through me.*

"High Inquisitor!"

Balak turned to see an errander coming towards him, picking his way around the scattered bodies.

"High Inquisitor, the bishop is looking for you."

"Which one?" Balak asked.

"Bishop Nufell," said the errander.

"I answer to the Prophet. Tell him that." Balak felt his eye twitch. Everyone knew *the bishop* didn't mean the high bishop anymore. Nufell had elevated himself above him. He acted as though he had elevated himself above the Prophet.

The errander's face showed worry. The bishop was likely to blame the messenger for the news that Balak was not scurrying to his presence. Still, it was not his place to question the decisions of the High Inquisitor. He bowed and left.

Balak watched him go and felt the need to kill rise in his heart.

He sat down beside the now-dead inquisitor, crossed his legs, closed his eyes, breathed deep and sought the holy place within himself, where his will was subsumed in tranquility. The bishop would come, and it would be best to be prepared.

He didn't have long to wait. "What's your excuse this time?" an angry voice demanded. "I thought God had ordained your victory."

Balak pressed his lips together and breathed deep before he opened his eyes, still seeking calm. God had willed that he respect Nufell, willed it in the Prophet's voice. *But some commands are harder than others.*

"God has ordained the *Prophet's* victory, Bishop," Balak said, when he had regained control of himself. He stood up to face the other man. "I am only his instrument. And God has kept his promise. They have lost. We have reserves, and their strength is spent."

"You call this victory?" The bishop snorted and swept an arm to take in the bloody scene. "How am I supposed to explain this to the Elder Council?"

"Their souls will precede us to Heaven." Balak let a note of warning creep into his voice. "I'm committing our remaining parishas. The rabble will soon be crushed."

"What do you mean, committing the last of our parishas?"

"As it sounds, Bishop. The Prophet has commanded the destruction of our enemy. I'm going to drown them in their own blood."

"The Prophet commands, the Prophet commands. Are you really such a fool? You watched me tell the Prophet to give you those orders."

Balak felt his eyelid twitch at the bishop's near-blasphemy. *The day will come when Noah will command this man's death.* "His will is celestial. Do not flatter yourself that his words come from you."

"Must I make him tell you this, too? Is that what you want?"

"What the Prophet says is law," Balak cut the words off short and turned away, annoyed. It was likely the bishop would do exactly as he said. Olen Polldor wasn't the man his father had been . . .

*But he is the future of Noah's line.* He felt himself losing control, though he'd just finished praying, and breathed deep again to keep the darkness at bay. The bishop was a trial. He let his hand fall to the blade at his side. Though his desire was to slice open the bishop's belly in holy sacrifice, he only pressed his thumb against the cutting edge.

The bishop was saying something, but his words faded and grew distant as Balak slowly increased the pressure on his thumb. The pounding of his own pulse surged in his ears, washing out the other man's words, until he felt the short, sharp pain that meant he'd drawn blood. *I must never forget that I am the instrument of God's will.* God demanded obedience, not understanding. He raised his hand to see the blood spill in a small, bright stream from the self-inflicted wound.

". . . I've got half the Elder Council in the tower, demanding their parishas back," Nufell was still speaking. "They're afraid of their own slaves. If you waste what we've got left we'll have a slave revolt on our hands."

"All the more reason to strike the enemy now." Balak focused on the dripping blood, keeping his gaze away from the bishop.

"No. Let them come to us, let them waste their strength against the walls."

"The Prophet commands me, Bishop, not you."

"You *are* a fool." The bishop's voice was somewhere between angry and exasperated. "Fine, if you want the words to come from his mouth, I'll go and tell him what to say." He turned and left.

Balak watched him go. *He should not so disrespect the Son of Noah.* The day would come when God will command him to gut the bishop like a feast lamb. *Not today, but soon.*

Danil awoke to pain, throbbing in his shoulder, his legs, his head, and found himself looking up at Avel. "What happened?"

"Danil, thank Noah you're alive."

"The inquisitors?" Danil struggled to sit up and the pain in his shoulder spiked when he tried to use it. His arm dangled uselessly.

"Gone, for now at least. Annaya got the ball throwers on target in time to break the fourth wave. We got the assault towers up to the front line to deal with the third. Barely."

"How many did we lose? There was a pile of burnt timber beside Danil, and it took him a moment to realize it was all that was left of his war turtle.

"A hundred and fifty dead, two hundred too hurt to go on. More or less."

"More than half . . ." Danil gingerly felt his injured shoulder with his good hand and felt bone grate against bone. *No time to worry about that now.*

Avel nodded, his expression somber. "Well over half. We're done, Danil, we haven't got enough left to go on."

Danil shook his head. "We have to finish this." He looked around the battlefield, still strewn with red-cloaked corpses. "We beat them here. Whatever it cost us, it cost them more. We'll beat them again." His calves and ankles were crusted red, raw and tender, and he vaguely remembered the lick of flame and the pungent smell of his own burned flesh.

Avel gave him a look. "How hard did you hit your head, Danil? We've got four ballthrowers, three tower turtles, and a springbow left. War turtles aren't a surprise anymore either, they'll come with fire again."

Danil stood, and staggered. Avel caught him and Danil pushed him away. "I can stand on my own, and I haven't come this far to surrender. Have you? We won, by Noah's name!"

"We won the battle Danil, but we can't hope—"

Danil cut him off. "We've always got hope, and hope works better if we help it. How soon can we move?"

"We're still burying dead, treating the wounded, recovering arrows. It'll be bells."

"Two bells, no more. We can't give them time to regroup. Tell the turtle-captains we'll have a war council at the next bell at . . ." Danil paused. He had been about to say "my turtle," but his turtle was gone. ". . . at that turtle there." He pointed. "Have you seen Annaya?"

"She's at the war wagons, helping with the injured."

Danil breathed out slowly. *Would it be wrong to show my relief, with so many others dead?* "I'm going to go and see the army for myself," he said, and and started walking before Avel could say more, ignoring the pain in his legs. *And so he can't see my face.* He was dizzy with the pain. *I can't let my soldiers see that.* At least it was his left shoulder that was injured; he could still swing a blade with his right.

His army was in sorry shape, struggling to recover in the aftermath of the battle. The ebb and flow of the battle was there to read. The skeletal remains of war turtles still smoldered where they'd burned, and in front of them piles of bodies showed where the spear-fence had stood, and where it had fallen. The burned-over ground was porcupined with hundreds, thousands of arrows, and in the field in front of the line clusters of red cloaks and the grey-white of thrower balls showed where the last enemy waves had been broken.

Danil felt no exultation at the slaughter the inquisitors, just exhaustion as he realized how many more he had to kill before he could claim victory. *Is this even worth it?* It was a question with no answer. They were doing it, *had* to do it because the alternative was death anyway.

War, he was learning, had its own logic, and it didn't bend for the mere desires of those who fought it. His soldiers were going about their tasks mechanically, their faces strained and distant. Some just sat, staring at nothing, while their comrades worked around them. His leaders had suffered heavily, and there were a lot of new faces wearing title scarves, some of them just bits of cloth torn to the approximate length. He traded words with them as he passed, hiding his injury and trying to be encouraging, but what he saw struck hard at his own heart. *We always have hope.* Maybe true, but they didn't have much.

The mood grew worse as he worked his way back to the wagons. Era was organizing the scene, allowing the overworked surgeons to concentrate on saving lives. He had the wounded arranged in ranks, bloodied, limbs broken, flesh laid open by blades or impaled by spear and arrow, faces contorted with pain. Many of them were semi-concious, moaning or calling for their mothers. Others lay quietly as death stole up on them, bleeding slowly into bandages. He recognized one, Fredir, one of his first soldiers, and still one of the youngest. He knelt by the young man, put a hand on his shoulder.

Fredir's eyes flickered open. "Have we won?"

Danil nodded. "We're going to."

Fredir gave a small, weak smile, and his eyes closed again. Danil watched him breathe for a long moment, and then moved on. At the surgeon's wagon, Danil found Annaya, her clothing soaked in blood that Danil hoped wasn't her own, putting a dressing on the stump where a woman had lost her forearm. He had thought to call her forward, to once again be his signaler . . . *But they need her here more than I do.* More than that, she would be safer here, and for some reason that had become very important to Danil. He didn't interrupt her, just found a surgeon.

It didn't feel right, somehow, getting treatment when so many of his army were suffering so much worse than he was. *But I can't lead them properly like this.* The surgeon dressed his burns, then moved to look at Danil's injured shoulder, running strong fingers up and down his arm.

He winced as the surgeon came near the injured joint. "I don't think you've broken it, but it's certainly dislocated." He bent Danil's elbow to form a right angle. "Can you make a fist?"

Danil nodded, and did as he was asked. The surgeon held his elbow firmly and moved his clenched hand until it touched his belly button, then reversed the motion, turning his elbow in and using his forearm as a lever to move his shoulder joint.

Danil bit his lip. "That hurts. A lot."

"It's going to, but not much longer." The surgeon put pressure on the elbow, gently rotating it, and Danil gritted his teeth as he felt the bones grind against each other. All of a sudden there was a sharp pop, a spike of pain, and the joint slid back into place. The sharp pain went away, and Danil breathed out in relief.

"Better?"

"Much better." Danil flexed his shoulder and tried to rotate it. It hurt, but not nearly so much as it had.

He again resisted the urge to talk to Annaya, and went back to the forefront of his Army. The turtle he'd picked for his war council was one of only two surviving springbow turtles. The back ramp was down, and he clambered in to tell the turtle captain he was taking it over. It was all he could do to climb up to the command pulpit, and he banged his burned calf on a projecting beam hard enough to make him woozy with the pain. The turtle's original captain was dead, and the replacement was a young man Danil didn't know, who was half relieved to have the parishan take over. *A parishan with no parisha. I've got two understrength flanks left, maybe.*

From the turtle's pulpit the battlefield gave lessons, and he understood now what he should have realized earlier. The assault tower turtles had to be grouped in with the ball throwers and the springbows. He had envisioned them as coming into play only for the final attack on the temple walls, but now he could see how important they were for the close defense of the longer ranged weapons. Had he done that right at the beginning he wouldn't have lost so many turtles to the dismounted attack. *But I didn't, and I can't do it over again.*

It took his captains some time to gather, and he used it to think, about formations and movement and exactly how to deploy his much diminished force for the renewed onslaught the Prophetsy would doubtless unleash very soon. When they were all together he briefly outlined his intentions. Every turtle would be fully crewed, and put under double draft since they now had a surplus of horses. The formation would be tightened to two ranks, with the two surviving springbows and the assault towers in the front, the ball throwers behind. Sentinel riders would continue forward, then move to the flanks as they approached the temple. They would advance to ball-thrower range of the temple walls, and once they were there the assault could begin in earnest.

"We can't do this," a ball-thrower captain objected. "All we're going to do is die."

"We won today."

The captain swept a hand to take in the battlefield. "You call this victory? We haven't got enough left to go on with."

Danil have him a look. "Would you rather the inquisitors hunt you down like a forest dog?"

"I'd rather not throw my life away for nothing." The turtle captain had a heavy steel blade on his belt and a red soaked bandage on his chest. "I'm not saying it wasn't right to try, Danil, but we're beaten."

Danil looked at the man, took his measure. "Your freedom is worth nothing?" he asked. *Appeal to his sense of pride.*

The turtle captain didn't answer him, but his face was full of doubt, and Danil could see the same uncertainty in the expressions of the others.

"What about the wounded?" asked another captain before the first could reply. "We can't carry them into battle."

"We can't leave them behind," Era put in. "The inquisitors will come around behind us and take them. They'll be crucified."

The turtle captain who'd spoken rounded on Era. "The inquisitors will be crucifying us all before tomorrow's done. You want to handicap us like that?"

Era's jaw clenched, but before he could answer Danil raised a hand. "The wounded who are able are going to look after those who can't, right where they are now. They're going to do what they can to get them back to the forest, independently. If we win, they'll be fine. If we lose, we're all dead anyway."

A babble of voices answered him. *I'm losing control of this group, if I don't get it back my army is finished.* Before he could address the question a sentinel rider came up at the trot. "Parishan, there's a group of Prophetsy slaves here, forty of them. They say they want to join us."

"The inquisitors have tried this trick before," said the belligerent turtle captain. "I say kill them. We're weak enough now, we can't afford spies."

"No," said Danil. "Era, bring them in, get them food and water."

The turtle captain's face darkened. "Are you out of your mind? They'll slit our throats the second they get the chance."

Danil looked at him. "Did you like being a slave?" He raised his voice so the whole group could hear him. "Did anyone here like it? The inquisitors might find men so desperate for his favor they'll volunteer to betray us. They won't find forty of them at once. You want to know what we've won here today? Not the war, maybe not even the battle, but we've won the hope of every slave who hears we're fighting the Prophetsy. And hope is what's going to win this war, nothing else." He turned to Era.

"You're in charge of getting them food, water and weapons. Get groups out to gather up everything you can from the inquisitor dead, armor and blades especially. Get a foraging party together and get back to those orchards, get everything you can carry. Take sentinels with you. If you see inquisitors don't hold your ground, get back here as quickly as you can. We can't afford to lose anyone." He turned to Avel. "There are going to be more escaping slaves coming in, you can depend on it. They need to know how to fight in formation, so get your best people and get ready to start training, just the very basics."

He looked over his assembled captains, meeting their eyes one by one by one. *And this is where I win their loyalty, or lose it.* "We've come a long way, we've paid a high price, but our dead have paid a higher one. To me, there's no option but to go forward, no matter what the risk. I know we might die doing it. But I've lived as a slave long enough to know I'd rather die free. If any of you don't believe that, if any of you think you stand a better chance hiding from the inquisitors in the forest, there's nothing holding you here. Anyone who wants to go will be assigned to escort the wounded back, and you can stay there. That goes for your soldiers as well.

"There are going to be a lot more slaves coming to us, as news of what we've done here spreads. And I'd rather have untrained slaves willing to fight than soldiers who don't believe in themselves. Now, does everyone know what they're doing?" He met their eyes one more time. *It will only take one to challenge me now.* None did, and the moment was over.

"Then let's do it," he said. "Avel, come with me."

Danil and Avel followed the sentinel to where the new arrivals had been taken. They were lying face down by the road, being guarded by a half-mark of fisherfolk. As they came close one of them made to stand up. One of the guards moved to push him back down, but he persisted.

"Danil! Danil Fougere! Remember me? Danil!"

Startled, Danil looked at him. He had a cross brand on his cheek, but Danil didn't recognize him.

"Danil! In Noah's name, tell them I'm not an inquisitor."

"I . . ?" *Why does his face seem familiar?* Suddenly recognition dawned. "Bran! You got away!" Danil waved to the mark-leader. "Let him up."

The mark-leader nodded and the guards fell back, and Bran stood and came over to embrace him. "Danil, thank Noah."

"You know this man, parishan?" Avel asked, as though he doubted the evidence of his senses.

Bran looked surprised. "Parishan? You?"

Danil nodded. "Parishan, for all it's worth." He turned to Avel. "Bran and I escaped a lumber crew together."

Bran nodded. "Barely escaped. They hunted me so hard I had to hide out with a grain crew." He smiled a lopsided smile. "A slave pretending to be a slave to escape slavery. I thought you were dead." He paused, and his smile went away. "They crucified Jordan."

"I saw him . . . I'm sorry." For a moment Danil looked away, unsure of what he should be feeling. He had barely known Jordan, but they had risked their lives together. After a moment he went on. "We'll call you a mark-leader," Danil told Bran. "You've picked a bad time to join us, but we're glad to have you."

The hope he'd been clinging to grew stronger. The unexpected arrival of forty untrained slaves wasn't enough of a miracle to bring victory back into the realm of the possible, but there were tens of thousands of slaves in the Prophetsy, half of them fisherfolk used to their independence. If even a fraction of those came to fight they'd be unstoppable. *Hope is what will win this war.*

He left Bran in Avel's care and went back to his war turtle. Annaya was waiting for him at the war turtle's flank.

"I thought you were back helping with the surgeons," he said, repressing the urge to embrace her and kiss her. *After this is over, I can stop being parishan, but not yet.*

"They don't need me anymore, and you do."

"Who told you I was here?"

"Era did."

Danil looked around, considering what he should do next. The post-battle chaos was slowly coming under control, but it would still be bells before they were ready to advance again. His leg throbbed painfully and his arm felt numb, and he suddenly felt overwhelmed. *There's so much to do, and so much more beyond my influence.* He became aware of Annaya watching him, silent but with concern written on her face. His instinct was to send her back, but it was good to have him with her. *And why give her an order she'll refuse to follow.*

"You're right," he said. "I do need you." The emotions he'd been holding in check through the long advance broke through and he embraced her. "I need you so much."

He let her go when a sentinel rider came up to tell him the inquisitors seemed to have pulled all the way back to the Temple of the Prophet. Danil couldn't decide if that was good news or not. It meant that they would have all the time they needed to regroup, but it also meant that they would face the enemy's full remaining strength in the stronghold of the Temple. *Still, we're fortunate; one more solid attack would overwhelm us right now.* Another sentinel came to tell him that a group of thirty slaves had appeared three kilometers spinward, and wanted to join the army.

"Tell them they're welcome, and bring them to Era. He'll get them equipped."

The rider nodded and rode off, and Danil smiled. *That's two crews now.* One group of slaves escaping to join his army might have been a chance occurrence. Two hinted at a movement. A bell later a third crew came in, this one twenty-two women, the wives of the half-bishop of Purity parish. The senior wife told him they hadn't killed their husband, just strung him up on his own cross and castrated him.

By the time Danil's army was ready to defend itself, two more groups had arrived, one just five strong, the other sixty. *And that is a movement.* He had started something. Now, he just had to finish it.

A hundred arrived over the sleeping hours, and Avel trained them to the breakfast bell. There simply wasn't enough room to put all the newly recruited slave-soldiers into their remaining turtles, so they formed up on the flank, with marks commanded by soldiers who'd been spear carriers just the day before.

Danil told Annaya to signal the advance, and she smiled wide as she blew her horn, the notes sounding crisp and clear. Seconds later the war flags were up on the war turtle's mast. The wind had risen and they streamed aftward, fluttering. The horsedrivers stirred up their horses, and the ponderous wooden beasts began to move. As they advanced it became clear to Danil that their second victory, as costly as it had been, as weak as it had left them, had wrought a fundamental change in the Prophetsy. The farms they passed had been abandoned by their masters, sometimes because their slaves had forced the issue, more often simply in fear of the fisherfolk. Everywhere slave crews came out to cheer as they passed, and to join them when they learned that they could. The inquisitor weapons they had collected from the battlefield were soon exhausted, and Danil commanded an army twice as large as the one he'd started with. His concern moved from having not the strength to face the temple walls to the subtler issues of how to command, and even how to feed, such a large force. The influx continued, and by the evening-meal bell so many rebelling slaves had come to join his army that actual movement slowed to a crawl. Danil's new-minted soldiers were full of enthusiasm, talking loudly of the carnage they would wreak on the inquisitors, but most of them were armed with nothing more than farming tools, and they knew nothing of how to move or fight as a group. *Half of them will run at the first arrow volley.* A mark of riders could strip off all the strength he'd gained with a single charge.

By the next day's noon bell they'd come to the edge of Charity and he was forced to call a halt to try to impose some order on his formation before it devolved into a mob. The bell had a deeper, stronger note than the bells he was used to, but it took him a moment to recognize it was the timekeeper's bell, the standard by which all the other bells were struck, rung by the priests who counted the turning stars from the spire of the steeple of Charity's church. In the distance he heard other bells answering it, spreading the time-mark around the world.

*The whole Prophetsy is collapsing, and the bellringers are still at their posts.* Their dedication was inspiring. He called his sentinel captain forward, and had her organize a patrol into the city to find out was happening there. The patrol was back by the evening-meal bell, with news that through most of the city the streets were deserted, while most of the populace had either left or barricaded themselves in their houses. The exception was in the market district, where gangs of street guppies were ransacking the shops and stalls, grabbing anything they could carry.

"They've got yats, that's certain," the patrol leader told him. "They'd stop only when we were right on top of them, and they were back at it the second we left."

Danil nodded. "When we go in, I want some sentinels left there. We need to show the people we can protect them."

"I've already sent another patrol."

"Good work." He turned to go, then turned back. "And send another one to the church. Protect the timekeepers."

"It's done."

Danil watched her go, and wondered if he could afford the strength he'd just committed to keeping order. *One more thing to worry about.* The departure of the inquisitors had left a power vacuum, and those on the bottom of the social order were taking advantage of it to advance their position at the expense of those at the top.

*And I won't have the inquisitors to keep order with.* That thought brought up the question of what to do with the warrior-cult itself. *We'll need order, some kind of law, a way to rule that's fair to people.* He pushed it away. He knew nothing of governance, but Annaya did, and together they could establish a new system. *Once I've beaten the old one.* Looking around at the ragtag, half-organized mass that was his army that possibility still seemed remote, but less remote now than it had the day before.

The sentinel captain had pushed her patrols well past Charity, and fortunately they could still report that the inquisitors were licking their wounds behind the Temple walls. *That respite will only be temporary.* He'd struck fear into his enemy's hearts, but they'd learned how to use fire to beat his war turtles. It wouldn't be long before they'd regrouped enough to come out and face him again. *I have to use the time I've got wisely.* The first thing he did was organize a command structure, making his flank-captains into parishans and his mark-leaders into flank-captains, promoting his best soldiers to leadership positions. When he was done he found he was leading a full five parishas, though none were as good as the one he had started with. He set the new leaders to giving their troops some basic training in movement and weapons. Era somehow managed to forage enough food from the abandoned fields to feed his expanded army.

Halting the advance again was a calculated risk, an inquisitor attack with his force so disorganized would be disastrous. Danil put the turtles on his perimeter, manned by half the survivors of his original force on permanent guard duty. That left the other half to train the newcomers.

*I need only a day. Please, Noah, let me have it.* In fact a day turned out to be a very optimistic estimate. The simplest issues now demanded his attention, from how to feed soldiers who'd brought no bowls to how to equip his new formations with signal flags and horns. And when that problem was solved he had to teach his new recruits to use and understand them.

No sooner did he have one issue resolved than another group of slaves-turned-soldiers would arrive, setting the whole process back. The day turned into two, and two became four. Each day he got stronger, but the enemy was recovering too. Inquisitor spotters began to probe his sentinel posts with increasing vigor, and a large slave crew was reported digging a defensive ditch across the trading road foreward of Charity. Danil spent the days moving from parisha to parisha, pushing his new leaders to push their soldiers. Weeks of work had to be compressed into hours, and though Danil demanded perfection, he did it only to hasten the moment he could claim his force was minimally functional.

At the end of a week Danil was satisfied, barely. He gave his commanders twelve hours to feed and rest their soldiers, and then he told Annaya to signal the advance again. Once again, the war turtles creaked forward. They moved through Charity without incident, though many of the population had returned once they realized that the approaching army wasn't a threat to them personally.

On the far side of the city they encountered the inquisitors' ditch, but the slave crew that dug it had fled and no inquisitors defended it. He issued a few quick orders to his captains, and a parisha moved forward to fill it in, covered by the springbow turtles. Some few had ironwood shovels, others less useful tools, but whatever his new soldiers lacked in equipment they made up for in numbers, and the obstacle caused no more than a bell's delay. The turtles advanced again, and not long after, passed past the brickworks, where Danil had grown up hauling mud for the Prophet.

The slaves who'd worked there were now part of his army, and they'd strung their drivers up from the walls when they'd revolted. Danil recognized the overseer who'd sent him to the lumber crew. Another face took a moment to place. *Hatch.* He looked into the dead man's vacant eyes as his war-turtle ground slowly past the scene.

*There should be some emotion attached to this.* Hatch had tormented him, betrayed him, victimized him, but Danil could only look at the husk that had once been his nemesis and think how Hatch had ultimately destroyed himself. Danil bit his lip, absorbing the lesson. *Best not to grow too fond of power.*

The forewall mists were heavy ahead, and they'd come all the way down to the ground so the lower part of the foredome and the forewall itself were invisible. The trading road changed from cobbles to resined logs, and their progress slowed as the war turtle jolted uncomfortably over the rough surface. It reminded Danil of the first time he had come this way, as a prisoner marked for death in the back of an inquisitor wagon. The road was lined with saplings and a few young trees. They were nothing compared to the ancient giants of the aftward forests, but they were still enough to hide a substantial force, and if the inquisitors ambushed them at close range they could cut his army in half before he could even respond.

"Annaya, signal a halt, then take a message to the second parisha, and the third. Tell them I want their soldiers to fan out through the forest, second parisha on the left, third on the right."

"Yes, parishan." Annaya ran up the halt flag, then climbed down from the war turtle's back to deliver Danil's instructions. Soon enough the soldiers were moving past, sweeping the woods on either side in advance of the road. Annaya returned, and once the flanking troops had moved a hundred meters ahead Danil had her signal the advance. His turtle jolted into motion again, and Danil bit his lip.

They were protected now from a surprise flank attack, but he he had no illusions about the ability of his ill-trained auxillaries to take on an inquisitor force in close quarters. Time seemed to slow down to a painful crawl. Rain began to drizzle through the mist, soaking everything and making everyone miserable. *But at least they can't use fire again.* He strained his eyes to see forward through the mists. And then, sooner than he expected it, he saw the Prophet's tower looming out of the gloom.

It was an imposing site, a grey steel spire rising from the vast gallery behind it, protected behind its pallisaded walls of resined brick and heavy timber. The wall was studded with guard towers, and the red Prophet's Cross fluttered on banners hung from them. The same symbol adorned the sealed gates. Danil put a hand to the brand on his cheek.

*Today the Prophetsy dies, or I do.*

The leading marks of his flanking parishas were already moving through the field of crucifixes in front of the walls, but there was no other sign of life. The enemy was on the other side of the wall, waiting for him.

"The bishop will be in my father's tower," Annaya said.

Danil nodded, taking the measure of the looming structure, awed by what he was about to attempt. Slowly his army moved forward and deployed, setting up on an angle spinward of the fortress, so his archers would be on the right side of the anti-spinward range advantage. He positioned his war machine with the other springbow turtle in the center front of the formation, angled towards the gates. The ball-throwers lined up to either side of them, and the assault towers in a second rank just ten meters back. His veterans drew up just behind them, with the formations of newly escaped slaves moving to take up positions on the left and right, two parishas on each side.

"Danil! To the right!" Annaya yelled, and pointed.

Danil looked around to see a patrol of his sentinels burst out of the trees on his right wing, with a flank of mounted inquisitors in full charge half a second behind them, spears lowered and cloaks flying. The parisha there was trying to swing to face the threat, but the formation of poorly drilled slave-soldiers was already falling apart. Seconds later the inquisitor charge slammed into the disorganized ranks with lethal effect. It took just seconds for them to rip through the line, scattering the parisha like doves before a falcon, and leaving a wake of trampled bodies. The second parisha fared no better. His depleted veteran parisha was next in line, and Avel managed to get them turned to face the enemy with spears set, but they lacked the depth to halt the charge and the attacking inquisitors broke through the line almost without loss as Danil watched in paralyzed horror.

*They hid their horses in the trees.* The enemy had used surprise to stunning advantage, and the shock of the unexpected attack could destroy his entire stitched-together force in one stroke.

"Springbows! Right flank! Shoot!" he yelled, but the turtle archers were already swinging their weapons to bear. The heavy bolts arced up and over the approaching enemy to land among the scattered troops now behind them. "Spinward!" Danil shouted. "Drop your aim!" By the time he said it there was no need, the horsemen were on them and the ranges were too short to worry about the niceties of trajectory. The two shattered parishas were dissolving now, their cohesion broken. They were reduced to a mob of individuals, all fleeing aftward, even though they no longer faced any immediate danger. A few of the inquisitors had fallen to the springbows, and his half-parisha of veterans were trying to reform a spear fence behind the line of the tower turtles, ready to receive the attack should it veer that way. The most powerful move for the enemy would be to race across the entire frontage of Danil's army and vanish again into the trees on the other side. That would certainly break the raw parishas on Danil's right wing too, and leave a formidable force on Danil's flanks, able to sweep down and disrupt any assault on the walls. With the superior mobility their horses gave the inquisitors, there would be nothing he could do about them. *And now is too late to think about strategy.*

Danil grabbed up his rabbit bow and shot at the closest rider. He missed his target, but managed to catch his horse in the haunch. The animal screamed and stumbled, and the rider fell to the ground, to be trampled by the horses behind him. If Danil had his archers up in the tower turtles the inquisitors would have been slaughtered, but they weren't, and by the time they got into position to fire the attack would be past the turtles and into the vulnerable parishas on the other side. The ball-throwers were useless against fast moving targets at close range, and with only two springbow turtles his army was helpless.

As the charge thundered past him it seemed that was exactly what was going to happen, but then a horn sounded from the inquisitor ranks, and the attackers veered towards the temple. The gates were opening, and the red-cloaked riders galloped for them at full tilt. At the same instant red cloaks and helmets appeared all along the top of the palisade, and a shower of arrows arced through the air. Danil had thought his force out of arrow range, but the temple walls gave the inquisitors archer's another fifty meters. At the last instant he realized the missiles weren't going to fall short, and he ducked into the pulpit's shelter, pulling Annaya after him. He realized he had his bow still cocked, and relaxed the string. He'd nocked another arrow by reflex, and only then did he notice that the hand that held the string was shaking. The shaking got worse and he put the bow down to grab the wooden edge of the command pulpit to steady himself. *And I don't have time for that now.*

He stood up again. More arrows were raining down from the inquisitors, but the enemy wasn't used to shooting with a height advantage, and their fire wasn't very accurate. "Annaya, signal the assault," he ordered, but even as he said it the ball-throwers were launching their missiles at the guard towers on either side of the gate. His turtle captains weren't waiting for orders.

The first shots soared over the wall, but the next ones came closer, and the fourth volley caught the right hand tower and splintered it. The tower turtles ground forward slowly, as the ball throwers continued shooting, smashing first the other gate tower, and then moving along the wall to target the others. Volleys crashed into the wooden palisade atop the main wall, tearing it loose and throwing the red-cloaked soldiers manning it to the ground. The two springbow turtles were targeting individual archers, and the incoming storm of arrows began to abate. They had little effect on the turtles anyway, and his dismounted troops were just out of effective range. As Annaya ran up her flags a cheer went up from the fisherfolk ranks. The assault turtles began to grind forward, and his far left parisha started to advance as well, though they couldn't do anything useful until the towers were in place.

"Halt the left flank," he shouted, and Annaya blew her horn to signal the errant parisha to stop, but it kept advancing.

"Halt them!" he repeated, but now the other left-flank parisha was following the first one forward. His slave-soldiers had their blood up, and they weren't going to stop. *They'll be trapped against the wall.* All he could do now was support them, and hope it worked.

"Ball throwers, concentrate on the gates," he shouted back to the attacking turtles. "Tower turtles, full speed!"

He heard his commands being echoed down the line, and the ball throwers shifted fire again. Danil had wanted the assault to go over the walls, so that his archers would have a height advantage as his blades advanced across the open ground to the walls of the temple itself, but he learned enough as a commander to know what he could control and what he could not. Most of the enemy had been swept from the wall tops, and the attack had gained momentum all its own.

Despite his order the tower turtles didn't speed up, because they were already advancing as fast as they could. The assault would have to go through the gates or his army would pile up at the bottom of the wall. If that happened the ball throwers would have to cease fire for fear of hitting their own soldiers, the inquisitors could regain the top of the wall and slaughter them from above.

*And now they need leadership more than anything.* "Take the walls!" he yelled to Avel in the tower turtle behind him, then turned to Annaya. "Stay here. Keep the springbows firing."

She started to protest, but he put a finger to his lips, took her hand and squeezed it.

She closed her mouth, but her eyes showed her worry. With an effort Danil turned away and climbed out of the command pulpit. There were still a few archers shooting down from the palisade, and as he ran out in front of the advancing turtles he suddenly became an inviting target. He dodged left and right as he angled himself to get in front of his advancing left wing. "With me!" he shouted. "This way!" He made eye contact with the lead parishan, waved an arm to emphasize his words, then turned and started for the temple gates without looking back to see if they were following. He wanted to sprint, but he kept himself to a rapid walk. If he ran the parishas would charge after him.

*Give the ball throwers time to work.* If he arrived at the base of the gates before they'd broken them down, he'd be in exactly the position he was trying to avoid. His heart leapt as a ball sailed ponderously over his head to impact the middle of the left-hand gate, but it shattered when it struck and left the gate undamaged. The gates were more heavily built than the upper palisade, and it suddenly occurred to Danil that the heavy clay balls might not be enough. Two more balls arced overhead, and they too broke up when they hit.

He looked back over his shoulder to see his veterans had rallied in the wake of the inquisitor charge and were advancing as well. The flank-captains had formed them into assault lines, and he knew he was committed. If he tried to turn the army around now it would dissolve into chaos. The inquisitors had responded to the shift in fire, and already more arrows were coming down from the surviving sections of palisade. Danil slowed his pace as much as he dared, and then inspiration struck. He turned around to face his army.

"Archers, by ranks, fire!" he shouted.

Behind him his archers drew, nocked arrows, and fired in successive ranks. The shower of arrows that went up against the palisade didn't kill many inquisitors, but it stopped them from putting down their own much more accurate fire.

More importantly, his advancing parishas had to wait while the archers carried out their orders. That give more time for the ball throwers to do their work. More balls crashed into the sturdy gates without effect. Behind him, Danil could hear mark-leaders shouting. He looked back to see his blades and spear carriers spilling around to either side of the archers. They felt they were winning, and they wanted to bring the battle to the enemy. The tower turtles were still moving forward, but slowly, too slowly.

"Hold fast!" he yelled. "Hold your positions until the gates are down!" The parishans and flank-captains echoed his words. Danil's disciplined veterans obeyed, but there was no holding back the recently freed slaves at the front of his force. They simply didn't understand they were running into disaster. His recently promoted leaders struggled to keep their units in formation, but the tightly disciplined ranks had dissolved into a headlong rush at the forbidding walls.

*And there's nothing to do but go with them.* If he was to have any hope at all of salvaging the attack, Danil had to be at the forefront the whole way. He drew his blade, clenched his teeth and ran for the closed gates at the head of what was now no more than a rampaging mob. Another volley of balls slammed against the gates. One broke loose the top hinge on the left side, the others shattered with no more impact than any of those that had come before. A terrifying battle cry rose up from his army, and now Danil ran for no other reason than to keep those behind him from trampling him as they came forward.

Even laden down with weapons and armor the distance closed from a hundred meters to fifty in what seemed like an eye blink. Shards of baked clay sprayed past him as more balls hit the gates and the walls around them. He wiped his cheek where a piece had hit him and his hand came away red with blood. It was the same place he had been slave-branded, in a life that now seemed to belong to someone else. The gates loomed ahead of him, and he sensed his warriors start to hesitate as they realized they had nowhere to go once they reached them.

*It's going to end now.* Three more balls came over, so close that he felt the air they displaced as they went past his head. They hit the gate almost simultaneously, and more shards of clay sliced the air around him. The ball throwers would have to stop shooting at the gates now or wreak carnage among their own ranks, and he prayed their crews would realize that. *Not that it matters whether I die at the hands of friends or enemies.* The gates were still intact, and the premature attack was about to reach its logical end.

*No!* The last volley of balls had struck the upper left of the left gate, where the hinge had been broken by the earlier strike. The heavy structure was leaning backwards, pivoting on the lower hinge and the center crossbar that held both gates together and shut. That left a gap at the bottom, too small for a man to even crawl through, but enough for a man to get a grip.

"Pull it down," he shouted, and ran to the gap to haul at it. He felt the gate give slightly, and then other hands were beside his, pulling, twisting the bottom of the gate out, straining the remaining hinge.

"Heave! Heave *hard*!" he yelled and the familiar work refrain galvanized the ex-slaves fighting beside him. The gap widened, and more hands grabbed the steel-bound wood.

Deep-set bolts groaned against the vulnerable hinge plate, and then all at once something snapped. The top-heavy gate fell backwards into the temple courtyard, at the same time knocking Danil and everyone else who'd been pulling on it sprawling. He fell by the still intact right-hand gate, and feet pounded past him as his army poured into the Prophet's stronghold. He staggered to his feet, just in time to see Bran go by at the head of a half-mark of blades that had somehow maintained its formation.

"With me," he yelled, and led the small group through the gate. Inside the courtyard the horse mounted parisha that had devastated Danil's left flank had been drawn up inside, preparing, perhaps, to make another foray outside of the gate. Now they charged the expanding flood of slaves and fisherfolk pouring through the broken gates. There was no time to form a spear fence, but those soldiers closest to the attack set their weapons instinctively. The ground shook beneath the combined impact of four hundred hooves as the enemy came on.

"Double line on this angle!" Danil yelled, throwing out his arms to show the direction he needed the line to face, and Bran echoed him. There wasn't room in the crush of bodies to properly execute the maneuver, but Bran's soldiers knew what he wanted, and managed to get themselves more or less into position. They formed a solid second line behind the disorganized cluster of slave-soldiers in front of them.

"Set spears!" he commanded. Those who could obeyed, but most of Bran's half-mark carried only blades. Those with bows were shooting into the enemy ranks, but there weren't enough of them, and they weren't organized to fire proper volleys. He became aware of a presence beside him. *Annaya.*

"What are you doing here?"

"The springbows can fire on their own. This is my temple. I'm here to take it back."

Danil started to order her back, but the charge was coming and there wasn't time. He braced himself for the impact of men and horses, but as the riders drew near they slowed and balked, and suddenly the disciplined inquisitor ranks had become a milling mob just a few meters in front of Danil's front line. It took him a second to realize that it wasn't the paltry fence of spears that had stopped them, but the looming wall behind them. In the open the horses would have overridden the disorganized line without slowing down, but they'd instinctively shied away from running full tilt into an immovable obstacle.

"Take them! Take them now!" Danil shouted, but held up a hand to stop Bran's small force from joining the attack. The slaves and fisherfolk ahead of him waded into the melee, killing men and horses with savage indifference. The inquisitors on the edges of the crush broke loose and rode away, but they had nowhere to go in the confines of the courtyard and arrows rose up to follow them. More arrows rained down from the top of the wall, and Danil looked up to see the ramps of two tower turtles there where the palisade had been broken, with fisherfolk pouring over them. He realized with sudden exhulation that they were winning. Behind him the right-hand gate had been torn open as well, and his soldiers were pouring into the courtyard in a torrent. What they lacked in precision they made up for in raw ferocity, their long-repressed rage at the Prophetsy unleashed on the central symbol of of its power.

The inquisitors fell back and reformed a defensive line in front of the gallery entrances, but they were already being outflanked. Shouted commands and screams of pain and triumph overlaid the clash of steel on steel in the confined space.

"Danil, take the tower." Annaya pointed. "We can end this."

"With me, advance!" Danil called to Bran's small force, and ran for the main gallery door. The rampaging ex-slaves had already broken into the huge structure, and inside the inquisitors were fighting a desperate rearguard action. The dead and the dying lay intermingled in the corridors, the steel flooring slick with their blood.

"Here!" Annaya yanked a door open and Danil led the half-mark through it to find a set of stairs spiraling up. A red cloak behind a spear stood in his way, but he grabbed the spear shaft behind the point and pushed it out of line. He stepped inside the inquisitor's guard, brought his blade up, and then his opponent was on the ground bleeding and Danil's force was charging up the stairs. On the second floor an arrow flashed by his head, and he turned in time to see Annaya burying her blade in the archer's belly. They exchanged a glance, and he ran across the room to the opposite door where the stairway spiraled up again. He arrived at the next floor, panting hard.

The room was lavishly furnished with carved wood and elaborate wall quilts. It was the same one he'd stood in a lifetime ago, as Annaya's brother convinced the Prophet that he should have a lumber crew. *I've come full circle.*

Before he had a chance to catch his breath a half dozen inquisitors poured out of the opposite door. An arrow glanced off his blade, and he stepped back in surprise. Half a heartbeat later another arrow *zwipped* through the space he'd been standing in and took Bran in the center of his chest. Danil stepped forward to attack, but inquisitor dropped his bow and fell back to draw his own blade. Danil pressed his advantage, and swung. His adversary blocked and caught the blow on his own blade, and steel rang on steel as the impact numbed Danil's hand.

He went to swing again but the two weapons had cut into each other where they collided, and he had to wrench hard to win his blade back. He stabbed forward with a short jab and caught the inquisitor hard in his belly. The other man went down, bleeding as another inquisitor stepped forward, blade upraised. He swung, and Danil's blade fractured where the first inquisitor's strike had notched it.

Instinctively Danil dodged backwards, and one of Bran's soldiers lunged past with a spear to fend off the enemy. The inquisitor's companions came around to flank the ex-slave, and more of Bran's soldiers went to meet them. Curses, grunts, and the clash of blades filled the room, and one of the slave-soldiers fell. It seemed they should easily overpower the red cloaks, but suddenly the room was much more empty. Most of Bran's soldiers had fled when he died.

There was still enough of Danil's blade left to make a short stabbing weapon, and when Bran's spear carrier fell and his killer came forward, Danil stepped into the attack and thrust it under the inquisitor's guard. The point skidded off the man's chest armor, but dug in at his armpit. Danil shoved it home and his opponent screamed and fell to the ground clutching helplessly at the now gushing wound. Annother inquisitor stepped forward and Danil froze. *Balak!*

"So, it is you." Balak's blade was up and his eyes were locked on Danil's. "I had my suspicions about you from the beginning. God has been generous to give me this day."

Danil raised his damaged weapon, and darted his eyes to the door leading downwards, but the fighting had backed him into a corner, and there was no way he could make it. The rest of Bran's soldiers were gone now, either dead or fled and only two inquisitors were left standing, holding onto a struggling Annaya. Another man came into the room behind Balak, but Danil was so focused on the High Inquisitor that at first he didn't recognize him, until Annaya yelled, "Olen!"

"Sister." The young man's face was pale, his expression distant.

A third figure came down the stairs, heavyset and balding, this one in the formal robes of a bishop.

"Annaya." The man smile broadly. "To think of all the effort I put into finding you, and here you are coming to me." He laughed. "Announce the placement, Prophet."

"Olen, no!" Annaya shouted.

"I announce the placement of Annaya, daughter of Noah, with Redorn Nufell, Bishop of Sanctity Parish . . ."

"Olen, you miserable *sooksan*," Annaya's face was a mask of fury. "You half-bred half-wit . . ."

"Enough!" The bishop cut her off. "Kill him, Balak. We'll celebrate the wedding once he's dead."

"Kill him," echoed Olen.

"As you wish, Prophet." Balak took a step forward, blade at the ready.

Danil tightened his grip on his own blade, and his forearm ached. *I'm spent from the fighting.* He felt suddenly tired, and his weapon wavered. The High Inquisitor was relaxed and confident, and the certainty of Danil's death was written in his eyes. He advanced, blade raised to strike.

"Balak!" Annaya shouted. "Stop! I'm carrying his child."

"What?" Danil looked at her in surprise, then yanked his attention back to the High Inquisitor's blade.

"Shut her up," barked the bishop, but the red-cloaks looked to Balak. Balak held up a hand to countermand the other's order.

"No, let her speak," the High Inquisitor said. He kept his eyes locked on Danil, but withheld his attack.

"I'm carrying Danil's child, Balak, and Olen is sterile." There was an edge of desperation in Annaya's voice, but beneath it her words carried the conviction of truth. "He has my father's infertility. Noah's line flows through me." She pointed at Danil. "And through him now."

"It's not true," shouted the bishop. "Olen, tell him."

But Olen didn't answer, and Balak's eyes flicked to the young man's face. Danil followed his adversary's gaze to the young man's face and saw the truth of Annaya's words written there.

Annaya pointed at the bishop. "Take him, Balak," she said. "In Noah's name."

Balak nodded, and a slow smile crept across his features.

"I knew God would send me a sign," he said. He turned and advanced on the bishop. "I knew he would make me the instrument of purification."

He extended his blade as Danil watched in stunned amazement, and the bishop backed up, his hands held up to fend off the coming strike.

"Please don't, Balak. Please," the bishop pleaded.

Balak raised his blade to deliver the killing blow, but suddenly the bishop lunged forward, and the High Inquisitor staggered back, looking down at his belly, and at the knife handle protruding there.

The bishop was laughing, the fear he'd shown vanished. "Balak, you're still a fool. Did you really think I'd go unarmed?"

Balak fell to his knees, his face contorted in pain, but he still held his blade. The bishop kicked out and the blade clattered to the floor. Balak gasped, blood spilling from the wound.

"I'll take her," the bishop said to the stupefied inquisitors. "You take him." He pointed at Danil.

Before they could react, Danil leapt forward and drove his broken blade up into the underside of the bishop's chin, up into his brain. The man dropped, dead on the spot, and then Danil was facing the two red cloaks. The Prophet Olen had backed against the wall, his face a mask of fear.

"Now," said Danil, jerking his head at the erstwhile Prophet. "You can follow me, or you can follow him."

One of the inquisitors let go of Annaya and drew his blade. Danil tightened his grip on his own weapon, ready to receive the attack. *I can take them if they come one at a time.* If they both came, he would probably die.

"Don't be stupid, Caval," said the second inquisitor. "The High Inquisitor's dead. The bishop is dead. The temple is overrun. What do you think is going to happen here?" He let go of Annaya as well, but turned to go down on one knee before her. "My loyalty is yours, Prophetess."

The first inquisitor hesitated, then did the same.

"Go down to the gallery," she said. "Tell the inquisitors to stop fighting, on my orders. There's been enough bloodshed today."

"Yes, Prophetess," the first inquisitor answered. The two stood and went down the stairs.

Danil lowered his blade, let it fall to the blood-slick floor, and went to Annaya. He put his hands on her shoulders, looked into her eyes. "Do you really have my child?" he asked her.

She nodded, slowly.

"Why didn't you tell me?"

"There was a battle to fight. You didn't need the distraction, or to worry about me. And I certainly wasn't going to stay behind."

Danil just looked at her. He had a duty to his army, to his soldiers, to get back into the fray, to lead them in their moment of victory. *They need me.*

"Danil?" Annaya was looking up at him, and for the first time ever he saw uncertainty in her eyes. There was a question there, a question she didn't dare ask.

But the battle was ending, and the army could wait. He drew Annaya into his arms and kissed her, slowly and tenderly.

Tomorrow he would have to figure out how to govern the Prophetsy and what to do with the surrendered inquisitors. *But there's time for that tomorrow.* Annaya sighed in contentment and pulled herself closer to him, and for the first time he could remember Danil felt himself at peace.

# Intermezzo

*And he stretched forth his hand towards Heaven, and there was a thick darkness in all the land for three days.*

—Exodus 10:22

# Shipyear 5225—TURNOVER

Age had slowed him, but the High Inquisitor still liked to walk the streets of Charity, and he did so every day. It was healthy, and it got him among his people and away from the immediate cares of governance. He went down from the manuscript room tower and let the trading road lead him from the steel of the Inquisitory aftward. The road was lined with tall dougfir and spruce, and the air was moist and rich with their scent. As he walked, the suntube began to peek through the cloud overhead, and he looked up to see the brilliant line pointing the way aftward. The road trended gradually downhill, and curved as it emerged from the treed area and opened into the forefield pastures. Sheep and goats grazed contentedly, and before long he found himself in the city itself. A few people greeted him as he walked, and he stopped to talk with anyone who seemed so inclined.

*It's a mark of good leadership, to know your people.* He listened to a butcher voice concern about the rising price of slaughter cattle, complimented a new mother on her twins, encouraged a young man in his studies for the Inquisitory tests.

Eventually he came to the park that marked the center of the city. It had not always been a park. A very long time ago there had been a fire, and the buildings that had occupied the area had been destroyed. Rather than rebuild, the High Inquisitor of that era had decreed that the space be opened to the public. The trading road bordered it on the spinward side, and the elevated spillways that supplied Charity with running water ran through its middle. To antispinward the city's main church rose in a confection of spires and gables. It was gardened with low shrubs of blackberry and raspberry planted around symmetrically winding paths, an arrangement both decorative and functional. He left the main path as soon as he could, and made his way to the waterclock in the garden's center.

The clock was a brilliantly simple design. Water piped from the spillway fell to turn a steel waterwheel. Cogs on it spun a freewheel that sat in a clever frame, built so the freewheel's axis of rotation could be rotated three hundred and sixty degrees while its cogs stayed engaged with the waterwheel. The freewheel's axis was perpendicular to the suntube, and because of that its rotational momentum kept it aligned with the stars as they rotated in the foredome. Every two minutes the freewheel revolved all the way around the waterwheel's outer edge, and on every revolution a peg on the frame engaged the huge time-wheel that was the clock's reason for being, and rotated it one seven hundred and twentieth of the way around. The time-wheel was faced in thin-hammered steel, with a stylized representation of the foredome's star pattern etched onto its face and the numerals one to twenty-four surrounded its rim. The clock's heavy time-bell hung from the top of the frame, waiting patiently as the timewheel crept around to eighteen. The spilled water formed a small pool around the clock, then burbled away to join the main canal that connected Charity to the Silver River.

It was a pleasant scene, and the High Inquisitor sat down on a bench to enjoy it. The steady motion was almost hypnotic, and contemplating the clock was a good way to meditate on what he had heard from his citizens and the state of his world. *Everything depends on perception.* To him it appeared as if both the stars and the freewheel's axis of rotation was turning, but what was really happening was that the freewheel's axis was fixed in space by its rotational momentum, and the stars were fixed by their nature. The world and everything in it rotated around the suntube, and so for anyone standing inside it the stars and the wheel appeared to turn instead. It was a result only subtly different from the intuitive conclusion that the stars turned and the world was fixed, but it explained everything from the path of a thrown object to the fact that *down* was a local phenomena, and so wherever you happen to stand appeared to be at the bottom of the curve of the world. *And that's important, in more than one way.* It was as though the world was designed to underscore that basic fact of the human condition. The butcher had not been concerned about the difficulty of the Inquisitory tests. The mother had eyes only for her beautiful children, and the aspirant wasn't worried about the scarcity of cattle. *Although he will be soon enough, if he makes the grade.* It was the role of the inquisitors to understand the nature of the world, and to worry about such things if that was what was required. It was the role of the High Inquisitor to understand human nature, and so wisely adjust law to reflect both nature and humanity.

The freewheel's frame completed another revolution, and the peg on its frame pushed the time-wheel past the last notch to eighteen. That released an arm which swung to ring the time-bell. Its sonorous peal rolled out, only to be overtaken by the quieter, but deeper and richer sound of the bells at Charity church, where the time-priests carefully counted the turning stars in the foredome. The High Inquisitor smiled. The two bells were never farther apart in their sounding then they were today, synchronized exactly despite the fact that the source of the forewall bells remained a mystery, lost in the mists somewhere up that vertical kilometer of steel. It was said that once angels rang bells at the forewall, and that was considered proof of God's existence. *But those bells are silent now, if they ever existed, and the waterclock proves they don't have to be rung by angels.* Now the world still held many mysteries, but he was sure that all of them would fall to human reason, given enough time.

"High Inquisitor."

The High Inquisitor looked up to see an old friend. "Bishop, what brings you here?"

Charity's senior clergyman sat down on the bench. "The knowledge that I'd find you here."

"I'm not usually that hard to find." The bishop sat in silence for a moment, and there was a tension in his face. "Is there anything the matter?"

"Nothing the matter, but something . . . important. We've found a book."

"That doesn't sound very ominous."

"Its portentous . . ." The bishop paused, seeming unsure of how to proceed. "Well, I'd like your opinion. We've been working to translate it. . . ."

The Prophet's eyebrows went up. "What does it say?"

"Prophet, it says . . ." The bishop chewed his lower lip. "It says that our world is a ship, quite literally Noah's Ark." He could scarcely keep the excitement from his voice. "Noah was real, and this is proof."

The High Inquisitor laughed. "You had me concerned for a

moment, but I'm hardly surprised to hear that. Your Bible says as much, doesn't it? What's another book that says the same thing?"

"Nothing says it like this. This book isn't written, or even pressed. The binding, the paper, they are all unique, and of a quality I've never seen before. And the content—it describes how our world was built. Not created by God, but by men and women. Certainly one of them must be Noah. *Must be.* He had tremendous power, I can barely grasp how much." An excited light came into the bishop's eyes. "God's power, you understand. They speak of the tools they used to build the foredome, and the suntube." The bishop spread his arms wide. "I can barely comprehend what they are talking about, yet they speak of it so casually. They built this world, this ship, this Ark if you will, and then they set off on a voyage from their own world, a world so large that all of ours is like a dust speck beside it."

The High Inquisitor put a hand to his chin, thinking. "You're surprised by this? You only have to look at the Inquisitory to realize our world was built to order—buildings of solid steel, fused directly to the forewall. Look at the forewall itself, and the foredome. Dig beneath the water table and you'll find a floor smoother than polished steel, and so hard that a steel hammer can't scratch it. Nature doesn't produce things like that, people do. I've never doubted that our world was a constructed thing."

"Did you imagine that it was a ship?"

"I considered it of course; the Bible story had to come from somewhere. Proof though, that's something else."

"It's true. This book confirms it."

"Not so fast. You have a book which agrees with another book. Nothing says they're both right."

"Just because you don't believe in God doesn't mean He doesn't exist."

"Very true, but neither does belief imply proof."

"Belief costs me little, and Heaven's reward is eternal."

"Belief doesn't cost you at all, it costs your parishioners—but even if it did, what you have still isn't proof, it's only expediency." The High Inquisitor chuckled. "And if what you say in sermon is true, I don't think your Bible's God would would reward a faith so calculating anyway."

"I pray for your soul every day, my friend."

"And I appreciate it." The High Inquisitor stood up. "But no matter which of us is right about the ever-after, I'm sure your book is important today. Come and show it to me."

"Of course, I have it in the church." The bishop got up and the High Inquisitor followed him. As he turned away from the water-clock it clattered, and he looked up sharply. At first he couldn't locate the cause of the noise, but then it stopped and he saw that the freewheel had completely disconnected from the waterwheel. The clattering sound had been the cogs banging against each other as they de-meshed. There was something strange about that and it tugged at the edges of the High Inquisitor's awareness, but he couldn't quite place his finger on it. *And I have a book to look at.*

"Where did you find it?"

"A merchant was digging a well and found a box. There were several books in it, but most weren't intact enough to translate, the rest had crumbled. They must be thousands of years old. Even the box is miraculous, like nothing I've ever seen."

"I'd like to see the box first, if I may."

"Of course." The bishop led the High Inquisitor across the park and into the church, and then through a door into the small set of rooms set aside for living quarters of the lower clergy. From there a set of stairs led up the steeple tower. On the top floor was the observatory, where a series of wooden tubes were aimed at the foredome. Once upon a time the priests had kept time by careful observation of the rotation of the stars in the foredome. One room had been emptied and a low shelf installed around its perimeter, and it was here that the book was being worked on. Sheaves of paper and ink pots were carefully organized into workplaces where inksetters labored on duplication and translation.

"You must've found this some time ago."

"We've had it for a month. I wanted to be sure of what it was before I told you." The bishop went to a separate shelf. "This is what we found it in," said the bishop.

The box was built in two nearly identical halves, rectangular, and it was immediately obvious that it was like nothing the High Inquisitor had ever seen before. Its symmetry was perfect, and the material it was made from was unlike anything he'd ever seen. It wasn't wood, wasn't baked clay, wasn't steel. It was a milky, almost translucent material that felt more like beeswax than anything else, but though it flexed where he pressed on it, it didn't yield to a fingernail the way wax would. It was somewhat porous, to judge from the way the dirt had stained its outer surface, but the inside was glossy and clean, save for a darkened square on the bottom where the slow decay of the paper inside it had left its mark. He picked up one half and fitted it to the other. The seam where the two joined with so precisely made that he could *feel* them sealing together. The join would certainly be waterproof, even air-proof. There were four simple latches, one on each side, and two recessed handles on the shorter sides.

Experimentally the High Inquisitor closed the latches. They shut easily, with a satisfying *click*. He lifted the box with a certain kind of awe. It was robust, easy to carry, obviously built to protect something vulnerable against water, dirt, and rough handling. What was stunning was that someone would build something so finely for such a mundane purpose. *What must they have been capable of when they set their minds to it?* To ask the question was to answer it. The bishop believed that their world was Noah's Ark, and whether you accepted the story of Noah as literal fact or embroidered fiction it was no great leap to see that their world had been built by *someone*.

*And yet to see the evidence.* The box was far less impressive than the foredome, less impressive even than the Inquisitory, yet precisely because he could hold it in his hands it seemed a far more tangible miracle. He put it down almost reverently, and turned to the bishop. "May I see the book?"

The bishop nodded and showed the High Inquisitor to a chair at the shelf. As with the container it had been found in, it was immediately obvious that the book was different from anything else he'd ever seen. The illustration on its cover was faded almost to invisibility, but it was so precise, so sharp in its representation that it seemed he was looking at a real scene and not just a drawing of it. There was a textured cylinder in front of a larger sphere, a pair of human figures in strange armor that seemed to float above them.

"Careful," said the bishop as the High Inquisitor went to open it. "It's tremendously fragile."

The High Inquisitor carefully opened the cover. The first page was cracked down the middle, as brittle as a dry leaf. The title was *A History of the Ark Project,* but it was the lettering that drew his eye. It was as precise and clear as the picture on the cover, without a waver or uneven margin, without a misplaced smear of ink or uneven line of text. It was awesome in its perfection, even in something so mundane as the printing of words on paper. He turned to the next page, and found many of the letters familiar, if strangely different from modern script, and he could even make sense of the occasional word.

"You said you were translating it," he said.

"We are. There are a lot of words we don't know, but we got the sense of it, at least for the first chapter." The bishop put a hand on a stack of pages next to the book. "I've had my inksetters copy it all precisely, and we've been working from that."

"But you'd have to know the original language."

The bishop laughed. "I do know it—it's the Bible's language, written in the hand of God. All clergy learn it, so we can read His word. A lot of the smaller words are the same as we speak today, and many of the larger ones are recognizable. It's the written form that's difficult, the letter shapes have changed. If you're not trained to read the Bible you wouldn't recognize them."

The High Inquisitor nodded slowly. "So what does it say?"

"We came from a world called Earth, a place immensely larger than ours, and we're traveling to Heaven. The purpose is to bring human life to Heaven. The journey is supposed to take over ten thousand years; for some reason they couldn't do it faster. That's why they had to build us a world-ship, so that we could farm and raise families and keep the humanity alive until we got there." The bishop couldn't keep the excitement out of his voice. "We're Noah's children, quite literally."

The High Inquisitor looked up sharply. "The Prophetsy has been dead a thousand years, old friend. Let's not bring it back."

"The Prophets' claim to power was that they alone were Noah's descendents. This book says we *all* are." The bishop held out a sheaf of pages, more familiar rice paper with handwritten lines. "Here's what we've managed to translate."

"Simple math tells me we all share the same ancestors." The words came out more dismissively then the High Inquisitor meant them to be. He turned his attention to the translations. "Still, this is an incredible find." He leaned closer to read what was written, but found it difficult to focus. The first paragraphs had a great many words that he didn't understand, but they seemed to be talking about the goal of reaching from the world of Earth to the world of Heaven, at a place called Iota Horologi. It talked about a ship called *Ark,* but so many of the words were alien that he could only follow the gist of the text. He turned the page and it seemed the words written there were less clear. He squinted to read it, then looked up to the bishop.

"It seems dark in here."

"It does, let me open another shutter." The bishop moved to a closed window, pulled back the curtains and opened it. He was silent a long moment and the High Inquisitor could tell something was wrong. "The suntube . . ." the bishop said.

"What is it?"

"Come and see . . ."

The High Inquisitor put down the pages and went to the window. His friend's cause for concern was immediately apparent. The light outside was tinged orange, and the suntube's radiance was notably lower than it was supposed to be. Others had noticed the same thing. Beneath the window, people had spilled into the square below, standing and looking upwards, an excited buzz going through the crowd.

"What's happening?" asked the bishop.

The High Inquisitor shook his head. "I don't know."

There was a sudden knocking at the door. It opened to reveal a young man in clergy's robes.

"Bishop, the suntube . . ." The young man's voice quavered.

"We see it."

"People are coming in, they are afraid . . ."

"I'll talk to them." The bishop went out with his junior, leaving the High Inquisitor to watch the phenomenon by himself. There was no longer any doubt, overhead the suntube had perceptibly faded. Up the curve of the world the details of the houses and fields had become less distinct. At the same time it was possible to make out details almost directly overhead, details that had previously always been hidden by the suntube's glare. The process, like the rotation of the timewheel's frame in the waterclock, was so slow that it it was imperceptible from moment to moment. Only by extended observation was the change observable. *What could be happening?* The timewheel's disengagement tugged at his awareness. He had thought it a simple fault in the mechanism, but the more he thought of it the more that seemed unlikely. There was no obvious link between the two events, and yet it seemed too much a coincidence that they should occur simultaneously.

The suntube was still fading, and the crowd was growing anxious. In the distance he could hear the bishop's voice as he tried to calm his flock. The High Inquisitor went back to the sheaf of translations and brought them to the window where there was still enough light to read by. The book, whatever its contents, had been written by the world's creators, and perhaps it contained an explanation for what was happening. The effort was frivolous. There were too many words he just didn't know, and only the first chapter had been translated anyway. He put the pages down in frustration, and looked across the room at the book itself. *If only I had more time . . .* That realization brought home the reality that time might well be running out, not just time to translate the mysterious book, but time for the entire world. Plants would die, people would starve, the world would end.

The bishop came back in, visibly shaken. "I think we'll be safe, for now."

"For now?"

"They're scared, some of them are angry. That's a dangerous combination." As if to underscore his words a fight broke out in the crowded square below. It was over quickly, but a ripple had spread through the throng. The thrum of voices was louder, and the mood edgier. The potential for violence was established, and the next disturbance would set it off. "The suntube can't go out. It can't."

"I hope you're right." The High Inquisitor bit his lip. "What did you tell them?"

"I told them to have faith, to trust God's plan, and to pray."

"Good. That might buy us some time."

"For what? If the suntube fails we'll all die anyway."

"In which case it won't matter if they riot and burn the city, but if it comes back then it will matter very much."

"Do you think it will come back?"

The High Inquisitor shook his head. "I don't know. If the world is a ship it's a thing made by humans, and so it can break. Even fishing rafts break up sometimes."

"God couldn't allow that." The bishop looked worried. "He *couldn't.*"

"Have faith," said the High Inquisitor, with a trace of irony in his voice. High up on the curve of the world he could see a flare of fire in what must have been the town of Hope. The panic had already started there. He turned away from the window. "I need to *think.*"

He walked over to the book, and delicately closed its cover. There was barely enough light left to see the illustration there, the sphere, the cylinder, the two human figures floating there. *What could that mean?* It was impossible to get any sense of scale from the illustration. The center of the end of the cylinder was a lighter color than its edge, and he leaned closer to see what details he could make it.

All of a sudden the scene snapped into focus. *I'm looking at the world from the outside!* The cylinder was the world, the lighter circle was the foredome, lit from the inside by the suntube. The sphere could be anything, but the human figures could only be builders. He leaned closer, scrutinizing the image in the fading light, trying to find some clue that might explain what was happening. Whether the ancient book was proof of the existence of Noah or not, it was a link to the builders, and it might provide a clue as to what was happening. *If only I could read it.* He couldn't read it, and as the light continued to fade he knew he wouldn't get time to learn.

"In Noah's name, look," the bishop cried from the window. "The stars . . ."

The High Inquisitor looked up sharply. "What's happening?"

"They're changing," the bishop's voice held something close to awe. "*They're changing.*"

"What do you mean?" The High Inquisitor was already on his way to the window. He immediately saw what the bishop was talking about. The suntube had faded to a dull red, and its reflection in the center of the foredome had faded as well. No longer overwhelmed by its glare the stars twinkled in the great black expanse more clearly than he had ever seen them. Not only were they brighter but there were more of them, and as the suntube slowly dimmed more were becoming visible, fainter stars which had never before managed to shine past suntube's radiance. At first the High Inquisitor thought that was the change his friend meant. There were so many new stars that at first he didn't notice the more important difference in the brightest ones, the ones that had always been visible. They were still rotating steadily around the axis of the suntube, but their position was steadily shifting. Stars which had once been near the center of the axis had drifted to the edge. Some had drifted right over it and vanished, and there were new ones, not faint dots that would vanish again if the suntube ever rekindled itself, but bright-burning points as visible as any of the stars he'd known all his life. He became aware that he was staring open mouthed and closed his jaw with a conscious effort. *What can this mean?*

And all at once he understood, the image on the front of the book, and more importantly the failure of the waterclock's freewheel. The image on the front of the book *was* the world seen from outside, and the world *was* a ship, just as the bishop and the Bible believed. *And it's changing course.* The freewheel's axis was fixed in space by its rotational momentum, which was how the clock kept time and why the wheel stayed aligned with the stars, but the stars were not simply some part of the foredome that for some reason didn't rotate with the rest of the world. They were actually *outside* the world! He had a sudden vision of the world's cylinder inside a much larger sphere. The inside of the sphere was set with stars, and which stars were visible in the foredome depended on where the world—*the ship*—was headed. The ship was changing course, its axis was moving, and so the freewheel had twisted away from the waterwheel that drove it and the stars were changing. He raced back to the book in the fading light and peered again at the cover. Sure enough there was a faint scattering of faded white dots in the background of the image, certainly stars, and the large sphere behind the cylinder could well be a star seen right up close. *And if our world is a ship, then perhaps that's where we left from.* It was possible that every star in the sky was a world like Earth. Heaven would be a star as well, and . . .

Angry shouts rose from the crowd outside, and there was a crashing sound as something was overturned. The young clergy came back into the room, looking scared. "Bishop, there's fighting . . ."

"Where are the sentinels?"

"They're gone, fled."

The bishop had stepped back from the window, and more shouts and the flicker of flames followed him. "We have to go too. We'll go to the Inquisitory, we'll be safe there."

The young man didn't wait for an answer, and the sound of his fleeing footsteps echoed briefly in the hall. The High Inquisitor looked up from the book. "We can't go there, this book would never survive the trip."

"The book?" The bishop looked at his friend in stunned amazement. "I'm talking about our lives. That mob will be a flame riot before much longer."

"This book is more important than your life or mine. As for the crowd, you're right, and we can't let them burn this building, or the rest of the city either for that matter. You have to stop them, talk to them. They'll listen to you if they'll listen to anyone."

"What will I say? That the suntube is dying, that God is punishing us? They can see that, and they're looking for someone to blame. They'll kill me if I try it. We have to get out of here."

"We're not leaving, and I'll tell you what you're going to tell them." The High Inquisitor spoke quickly, his voice strong. "You're going to tell them the world is Noah's *Ark*, and it's changing course. Tell them the suntube will come back when we're on the new course. Tell them that we're halfway to Heaven and they'd better behave like angels."

"How do you know that?"

"I don't know it, but I *believe* it. If there was ever a time for faith, this is it. Whether you die or I die doesn't matter, because that's going to happen sooner or later anyway. What matters is what happens to our people, and I believe this book holds the key to that question." The High Inquisitor locked eyes with his old friend. Outside the window the light had faded to a dull red the color of fire, and the mob's shouting had risen to a crescendo. "That crowd is your flock. They will listen to you, they'll *believe* you, they'll follow you. Now go out there and do what you know you have to do."

The bishop opened his mouth, then closed it. An expression of grim determination came into his face and he left the room. The High Inquisitor looked again to the work-shelf where the fragile book still lay, reassuring himself that it was still intact. Outside the shouting grew louder still, and then fell away to a dull murmer. A single voice rose over the throng, and he recognized the bishop, though he couldn't quite make out what he was saying. *But the words aren't important, so long as they listen to him.* If they did, everything would be fine. If not . . . *He's a brave man.* Perhaps it was his faith that made him so.

For now the mob was listening, and that was a good thing. He looked around the darkening room for something he could use as a weapon, just in case they stopped listening. He found a heavy wooden ink-roller. It would serve if he needed it to, though he hoped very much that he wouldn't need it to. He hefted it experimentally, and then went back to the window to await the coming of the light.

# Exodus 11

*And thou shalt teach them ordinances and laws.*

—Exodus 18:20

# Shipyear 6266

The peregrine falcon wheeled overhead as Atyen watched, choosing its moment. It had missed its last attack, and the ground doves it had been hunting were hiding in the shade under the bushes, cooing in excitement. When it stooped the doves had scattered to shelter, and now they were peering about trying to decide if it was safe to come out again. They knew the falcon was up there, watching, but they didn't know where it was. The hunter soared patiently, and Atyen held his breath. *Soon. Very soon.* The doves were in a bigger hurry than the predator. There was food to be found, mates to be won, young to be cared for, and they couldn't wait all day. As Atyen watched a few of the braver ones came out, to gain for a minute or two an advantage over their less venturesome relatives. More followed them, and then more, and soon the entire flock was back in the tall wheat, searching out the ripe fallen grains, and squabbling over the best patches of turf. Atyen took his eyes off the falcon to watch a pair of doves carrying straw to the eaves of a nearby thresh mill to add to their nest. The mill wheel turned slowly in the sluggish canal current, and occasionally he could hear the millers doing whatever it was that millers did, but people didn't interest Atyen. He looked back to the peregrine as it circled. He had come to know its movements, its style, and he knew it was getting ready to stoop again.

*Any moment now.* Atyen exhaled slowly, as though breathing normally would somehow disrupt the unfolding drama, breathed in again, and once more held his breath. The paired doves fluttered back into the wheat, and then one came out again with more straw, followed shortly by the second. The peregrine stooped, rolling over into a vertical dive, falling so fast it was nothing but a blur against the clouds, streaking down like a bolt from an aftward storm. It spiraled as it came, and unconsciously Atyen moved his hands as though they were wings, as though he could adjust the bird's course as it came in for the kill. The peregrine pulled out of its dive and into level flight and the second dove never knew what hit it, the hunter's strike knocked it sideways and it fell. The falcon pulled up hard, trading speed for height, pivoted on a wing, and came around again, catching the injured dove before it hit the ground. Victorious, it flew off, flapping heavily with its burden, climbing up and away towards the foredome, while the doves once more vanished into cover with a massed whir of wings. Atyen breathed out again, his heartbeat pounding in his ears, as though it were his triumph and not the peregrine's. He closed his eyes to relive the moment, imagining himself up so high with the freedom to look down the world, to circle and spin in the free air, to choose his moment to swoop down and pull up. He pictured the predator's movements, each twist of its wings, and the way its flight feathers spread to ride the air currents.

*The tail is the key.* The falcon balanced itself in midair with its tail, steered with it, used it to control its lethal attack dive. He opened his eyes again, and opened the bound worksheaf that served as his journal to a half completed sketch of a soaring falcon. He opened his ink jar and dipped in his pen, concentrating on the image he had in his mind's eye. Picturing did not come naturally to him, and so he planned carefully what he would draw. The tail movements that controlled the bird's flight were so tiny and subtle when the bird was soaring that he could barely distinguish them, despite hours of watching. They were larger when it was stooping, but then so quick that he could barely catch them, or be quite sure of what he'd seen when he did. What he wanted to show in his image was not any single maneuver, but an amalgam of all that he learned about how the bird flew. *How it soars!* He looked up at the busy ground doves, once again peering out from shelter. They were easier subjects, easier to find and easier to follow with their larger numbers and slower flight. Their tail and wings were much easier to track, and indeed his journal was full of illustrations of doves flying, flapping, landing and launching themselves. They couldn't soar though, and more than anything Atyen wanted to soar. Unconciously he looked up

to the suntube, to see if he could spot the hunter again, but it
was gone. Where it had gone to was an ongoing mystery. They
lived high, high up on the forewall, up in the mists in a place
always hidden from human eyes. They only came down to the
midfields to hunt, and he'd never seen one land.

Atyen returned his attention to his journal, and carefully lined
in the falcon's tail, showing it canted to one side, as it was just
before a stoop. He took his time at it, and when he was finished
he inked in the distinctive banded bars that marked its feathers.
Such detail was not strictly necessary to understand how the
falcon flew, but it made him feel closer to them, closer to the
clouds. He shifted his position, only because he had been sitting
in one place so long that his legs had gone to sleep. His toes
tingled as blood rushed back into his lower limbs, and he held
his rendering at arm's length, considering it critically. He bit his
lower lip unconsciously. *It's accurate, but . . .* he had captured
every detail with anatomical precision, but somehow his drawing
lacked the inherent grace and power the falcons displayed. It was
still missing something. *There's something I don't understand yet.*
A dove fluttered overhead and he watched it as it dipped a wing
to circle, and braked to a halt with a flutter of wings. It was a
male, and it had chosen a female to try to impress with its mat-
ing display, bobbing its head and pirouetting to show its splayed
tail feathers. The female, uninterested, turned away.

A shadow drifted overhead, and he looked up to see fleecy
clouds spiraling their way foreward around the suntube. Aftward
the spirals billowed larger, harbingers of a storm. It occurred to
him that he was hungry, and he hadn't been paying attention
to the bells. It was probably well past the evening meal. He
gathered his journal, his ink and his pen into his belt-bag, and
headed foreward himself, following the line of the mill canal. As
he passed the mill he could see the millers had set dove-nets,
but they hadn't set them well and they were empty. Further up
the canal a troop of small girls were netting carp from the bank
and hanging their catch from a willow pole, and the sight of the
fresh fish stirred Atyen's hunger. A bridge crossed the canal where
it joined the Silver River and he went over it, not stopping as
he usually did to watch the ripples as the water met the pilings.
From there his path took him up the trading road, so ancient it
was worn a good meter below its sidehills, past the edge of the

cultivated fields and into dewy meadows beneath the foredome's permanent overcast. The forewall mists were high, and ahead the spire of the manuscript tower rose against the bulk of the forewall. He passed the low, grassy embankment that enclosed the outer courtyard, past the hammered steel plaque at the entrance to the main gallery that carried the Inquisition's watchwords. *From Knowledge to Truth to Justice.*

He went inside, nodding to the sentinels on duty. Hunger growled in his stomach, but before he could let himself eat he had to see his wings, and so he went to the studio rather than the meal hall. To one side there was a workshelf that was his space. It held his carefully inked plans, detailing every line of his dream. Kites of the various configurations hung on the walls above it, some small, some large enough to lift him, each aimed at solving a different piece of the puzzle of flight. The shelf held a model of his design an arm span wide, exact in every detail, and in front of it, taking up more room than Solender's other aspirants would prefer, stood the wings themselves, resting gently on their forming jigs. They were were beautiful and nearly complete, four meters across and carefully shaped to match the wing form of a soaring falcon. The frame was lightweight bamboo, weatherproofed with flax oil, cross braced and covered in strong flax linen, and waxed to give it a better surface for the wind. There were straps to hold them to his shoulders and his waist, and strong cords with hand loops so he could twist the wing tips down to maneuver, the way he had seen the falcons do it. They were built to fold neatly for carriage, so he could carry them up to the forewall ledge, and the joints locked with clever sleeves of his own design. Because he couldn't fold them in flight he wouldn't be able to stoop, at least at first. *But one day . . .* To fly at all was a bold and risky undertaking, to do it by slow stages was only prudent. He walked around them, critically taking in every joint and tie. They were not his first set, but his fourth. Some of his first crude attempts had shown themselves unable to support his weight, others were simply unstable in flight. These wings were built with double triangles between forward and trailing edges, the triangles themselves crisscrossed with bracing lines. The bracing lines were the key to strength, pre-stressing the rigid bamboo skeleton to resist the twisting and bending forces of flight. The wing tips were canted upwards, with controllable slots along the outer trailing edge that approximated the peregrines' flight feathers. The result was strong and light. He had tested the concept in a half a dozen kites, and it worked beautifully.

Hunger growled in his stomach, but he walked around his creation, running a hand over the finely crafted structure. He closed his eyes and imagined them on his back as he soared like a peregrine, looking down on the world below as he swooped and stooped with total freedom. He checked the joints again, this time physically testing each one for any loose play. There was none, and he smiled quietly to himself. Almost reverently he picked them up, unlocked the joints and folded them, being careful not to tangle the control lines that ran to the flight slots. As he did he realized that it was *time*. The wings have been ready for a week, but every day he had found a reason not to fly them. *No longer.* The evening meal could wait. He felt a rush of adrenaline at his decision, a mixture of anticipation and fear, and he swallowed hard as he finished the folding. Folded he could carry them like a backbag, and he shrugged his shoulders into the harness straps, knotted the cross strap into position, and went out. *Am I ready, that's the question.* There was only one way to answer that. It would be wise to tell someone what he was about to do, just in case something went badly wrong. The logical choice would be one of his fellow aspirants, but he went past the side corridor that led to their rooms and back to the main gallery, up the deeply worn and dimly lit flights of awkwardly large steel stairs that led to the top of the Inquisitory. From there another set of stairs led higher still. These were easier to climb. The railings and stringers were still steel, but the original stairs had long since worn away and been replaced by wooden ones. They were old and well-worn themselves, but smaller and easier to climb.

The wooden stairs led to the forewall ledge, a narrow shelf covered in climbing vines that ran all the way around the forewall, a hundred meters up from the ground. A cool mist hung in the air, and a few hundred meters away the outlet for the Silver River gushed silt-heavy water into the flood pool below. Part of the stream was captured in an elevated wooden spillway that angled its way back to the upper floors of the Inquisitory to provide its inhabitants with running water. The rush of falling water filled the air, and Atyen paused over the outlet to watch the falling torrent. The steel of the forewall was densely overgrown with vines, kiwi and grape among them. The constant mist and rain kept them well nourished, and some of the base trunks were as thick as his thigh. The vertical green carpet climbed a hundred meters from the ground to the ledge, spilled over it, and then climbed again to the next ledge above. The vines were rooted in a thick layer of pale soil, mostly bird droppings mixed with leaf hummus, lushly covered with grasses and low shrubs. *And suddenly all these details seem important.* He knew his sudden preoccupation with the sights and sounds around him came from that part of his brain that very much didn't want to do what he was about to do. Flocks of sparrows nested in the vines to feast on the fruit. *They'd make good prey for peregrines . . .* Except the falcons preferred to hunt further aftward, out of the mist and cloud of the forelands. On the other side of the river a family of wallpickers clung to the forewall's vines, gathering their bounty for sale in Charisy's markets. The parents were catching the birds with fine-woven nets and steady patience, while the children scampered up and down with preternatural agility, picking the ripened fruit and collecting it in the woven baskets they carried on their backs.

Atyen breathed in and out. The family didn't seem to be paying any attention to him. *And that's just fine.* They would be there to help if he fell, but unlike any of his fellow inquisitors it wouldn't matter if they witnessed his folly. Not for the first time he noticed the downdraft that carried the mists down the forewall. It wasn't large, but it was steady, and it would carry him down perhaps faster than he wanted to go. *If I jumped here the water would break my fall.* He took a deep breath and walked further, leaving the river outlet and its cushioning splash pool behind him. He didn't want to land in the water with his wings strapped to his back; he wouldn't be able to swim with them on. Instead he chose a position where the ground below was saturated and marshy, soft enough to keep him from injury if he didn't fly the way he wanted to, firm enough that he could stand up after he landed. *At least I hope it's soft enough.* He looked past the marshy section to the meadow beyond it. That was where he wanted to land, so long as he didn't wind up in the middle of a blackberry thorn. He took his wings off his back and extended them, tying down the joints, testing the knots. When they were set he strapped them back on his shoulders, buckled the tail straps to his ankles, put his arms through the outer loop supports and grabbed the control lines in each hand. He looked over to where the wallpickers were still at work, but they seemed to be paying him no heed.

And the wall was still waiting. He moved to stand on the edge and looked over. It was a long, long way down and sudden vertigo overcame him. He closed his eyes and tried to jump that way, but his legs wouldn't obey him. He opened them again, took a deep breath and held it, and then stepped back from the edge. *I can do this. I can do this.* He felt sweat trickling from his armpits, and he wondered if the falcons were ever afraid of heights. The height was dizzying, and he found himself wishing for a reason to turn back. It was one thing to imagine flying, something else entirely to throw himself bodily into the air.

"Atyen!"

Startled, Atyen looked up to see a gray beard, a double-red cross-sash. Ek Solender, Atyen's doctrinor and the world's Chief Inquisitor, was watching him.

"Flying without me?" he asked.

"Well no," Atyen paused. "And yes. Trying to anyway."

"I didn't see you in the meal hall." Solender frowned. "You need to have someone with you when you try this, in case something goes wrong." He was breathing hard, and red in the face. Solender was a portly man, and the climb to the ledge had winded him.

Atyen looked down, feeling abashed. "I know, Chief Inquisitor. I thought it might be easier alone." He stepped back from the edge. "It wasn't."

"Well, I'd watch you myself, but I'm hungry. Take those off and let's go down to eat. I've got a job for you to do before you kill yourself."

Atyen considered protesting, but didn't. Instead he shrugged himself out of the shoulder straps, at once relieved that the moment of truth had been postponed and angry at himself for not going all the way with his dream. "I saw a falcon catch a dove today," he said because he didn't want to talk about his crisis of courage. "I think I learned some more about how they use their tails."

"You think, or you know?" Solender watched him as he refolded the wings.

"I think. Only the falcon can know for sure why it's doing what it's doing."

"A good observation. We'll make an inquisitor out of you yet." Solender turned for the stairs and Atyen fell into step beside him.

"What's the job you have for me?"

"How long since you ate?"

"I brought my noon meal with me, and ate in the field." They walked in silence for a while. "You still haven't told me the job."

"Some background first." Solender pursed his lips. "The old texts tell us that the builders designed our world for a voyage, this much we can be sure of. It's supposed to take ten thousand years, more or less, and we're fairly certain we're over half way there. What we don't know is if they were gods or simply people with godlike powers."

"That seems more a question for a clergy than an inquisitor."

"So you'd think, but it's important. The church says the builder was Noah, and our world is his Ark, built at God's command. If that's true we have nothing to worry about. On the other hand, if the builders were ordinary people with extraordinary science, then we may have a problem."

"What problem?"

They came to the meal hall and found it empty of customers. "The first Inquisition fell when the suntube went out. Could it happen again?"

The cooks had gone to bed, and the cleaners were busy washing and sweeping. Solender stopped one of them just as he was about to empty out the last of a steel soup tureen into the slop bucket. The cleaner poured bowls for them both, and they went to one of the long wooden tables to sit and eat it.

"I don't know," Atyen said when they were settled.

"Some say it was our ship changing course, some say it was God's punishment on the world for abandoning him. Did the builders plan it? The truth is nobody knows what happened, or why. Nobody knows if it could happen again. Do you know the mouse experiment?"

"I don't."

"It was my doctrinor's masterwork, simple really. He put two mice in a pen, gave them all the food and water they could eat and left them alone. Soon enough two mice became ten mice, and ten became five hundred. He wanted to see if they would grow smaller generation by generation if they were crowded."

"Why would that matter?"

The Chief Inquisitor laughed. "Look around you, Atyen." The older man swung an arm to take in the meal hall, and by extension the whole structure of the Inquisitory. "Look how big the door-ways are, the halls and the rooms. This building is ancient, and built for people much larger than we are."

"And did the mice get smaller?"

"We never found out. They went crazy, some fought all the time, others just stopped eating. The mothers ate their young, or ignored them and let them starve. They all died."

"Why?"

"Like your falcon, only the mice know for sure. We tried the experiment three times and the same thing happened each time."

Atyen wrinkled his brow and thought. "Mice don't like to be crowded, that makes sense. What I don't understand is why they *all* died. Once enough of them had died to bring the population down, why didn't the rest just carry on normally?"

"That's an interesting question." Solender paused to have some more soup. "In fact, that's the key question. I think it was because they didn't know what normal was any longer. The mice who died off had all been born into a very overcrowded world. They learned how to live in that world, and when the overcrowding went away they still didn't know to mate and raise young normally."

"And you're concerned that can happen to us?"

"Charisy is overcrowded already."

Atyen nodded. "Most of the world isn't city. People could move out, if they wanted to."

"Yes, to a point, but there's more to it than that. People in the city need to eat, so we can't just move them onto farmland. It takes a lot of land to grow that much food."

"I never really thought about it." Atyen took a spoonful of soup while he considered the point. "It's obvious when you look at it. That's why we don't have big trees anymore."

Solender gave him a look. "How did you come to that conclu-sion?"

"Look at the beams here." Atyen pointed at the thick timbers that held up the ceiling, heavy and well blackened with age. "They're half a meter on a side and twenty long. I've never seen a tree that big, not a quarter that big. It must take a long time for a tree to get to that size. We're using all our land to grow food, so we don't have any to grow trees with anymore, at least none so large."

The Chief Inquisitor nodded slowly. "You know Atyen, when

you came into apprenticeship I told your mother you were too young. Even though you'd done so well in your tests, I thought you were too young." He paused, contemplating the huge roof timbers. "But I've been studying this problem for years now, and eating in this hall every day since I came here, and I never noticed that. This is important, and we're going to have to do this research." He pushed away his meal and got up. "I need you to go to the shorefields for me."

"What about my wings?"

"Take them back to the studio, you can leave after breakfast tomorrow."

"What about flying?"

"That's going to have to wait for a while." Atyen gave his doctrinor a look that must have said more than he meant it to. "Not forever, don't worry," Solender added, then paused, and Atyen could tell he was considering how much to tell him. "The shorefields are poor, and crowded. That's a dangerous combination. I need to know what's happening there. We may be running out of time faster than I thought."

"But the builders must have anticipated this. The world must be able to adapt, somehow."

Solender shook his head. "Maybe, maybe not. We don't know anything about the builders, really. Did they anticipate that we'd grow smaller over the generations? There's too much we don't know. And even if the builders have got a plan, their aims aren't the same as ours. I imagine they've tried to make sure our descendents will still be alive when we reach the end of the journey. They might not care as much that our particular generation lives in a world of culture, law, peace, and plenty." He paused, looking up at the huge roof beams made from now-vanished trees. "What's going to happen when we get as crowded as those mice? I've had the tithecounters go through their records. There's more people alive today than there have ever been. When today's children have children of their own . . ." Solender shrugged. "Maybe we're going to follow the mice." He leaned forward. "I need you to find out, Atyen."

"But I'm . . ."

"Trying to fly. I know. There's more to being an inquisitor than your masterwork. I've been lenient with you, but you need broader experience, and I need someone who can go to the shorefields."

Atyen started to protest and then stopped himself. "As you wish."

"As you wish," Solender laughed. "That's what aspirants say when they don't want to do something and can't say no."

Atyen didn't know what to say and so remained silent.

Solender's expression grew serious. "Trust me, Atyen, this is important. Maybe the most important thing you'll ever do." He took an ornately carved wooden ball from his sash pocket. "For you."

"A message ball?"

"With your name, and my symbol."

Atyen turned the small artifact over in his hands. "I'm honored. It isn't that I don't want to," Atyen hesitated, choosing his words carefully. "It's just, for something so important . . . I mean, I'm only an aspirant . . . surely the Inquisition in Tidings can . . ."

"I can't send an inquisitor, and I can't ask one. There's two sides to this. One is the reality of what's happening, or what might be happening. The other is how that reality will be perceived. I have rivals, as you know, and if I'm right about this . . . let's just say I need to have proof before I can act."

"You're Chief Inquisitor, how can you have rivals?"

Solender laughed. "Of all my aspirants, Atyen, you're the only one who could ask that question and mean it." He held up a hand before Atyen could respond. "You think the Inquisitory is all about the laws of man and nature. Well, it is, and one of the immutable laws of man is that ambition knows no limits. The higher you rise, the more ambitious the people surrounding you are." He stood up. "Now let's talk about what you need to look for."

Jens Madane looked up at the burning line of the suntube overhead and heaved the last carp off his net-raft and into the catchbox. He wiped sweat from his eyes and looked back to where Sarabee was talking to the monger. Tokens changed hands, and the monger's crew started emptying yesterday's catch from the smokeshed into their goat-cart to take to the market in Tidings. *My part is over.* From the water to the shed was his responsibility, after that someone else could deal with the fish. He let his eye climb the arch of the world, taking in the blue curve of the ocean and the patchwork fields that stretched up and around and over until they were lost in the glare of the suntube. In every field people were at work, tilling, sowing, planting, irrigating, reaping, and the ocean was dotted with fishing rafts. He looked over to Sarabee as she gathered up the children. Her belly was as round as a gourd, heavy with their fourth child. He was proud of her, but worried too. She'd already had to stop working the raft, and once she delivered there would be another mouth to feed. His father had raised four children himself, and Jens had never gone hungry growing up, but the carp were bigger back then—or at least so it seemed.

"Jens!" The fisher turned to see a familiar figure make its way down the shore to the dock, leading a snuffling sow on a leash.

"Atyen! By Noah, how long has it been?" He ran up the dock to greet his friend. "How's the Inquisitory?"

"It's good, which only means I'm not back because they failed me."

"What brings you here?"

"My feet, and the knowledge it has been too long since I've seen you." Atyen tugged the sow along, his leather sandals slapping against the moist earth, his backbag on his shoulders. "You'd think you were a farmer, you've grown such a fine crop, Jens." Atyen winked at Sarabee as the little girls clustered themselves around their mother.

Sarabee blushed. "You're too good with your words, Atyen."

"Not good enough my dear, or you wouldn't have married Jens." He knelt down and waved to Liese, the eldest, who regarded him with solemn, ten year old eyes. "My favorite butterfly, when I saw you last you were pulling my hair. Don't tell me you're shy now." Liese smiled shyly and said nothing. Atyen knelt down. "And how are you, daffodil?" Acelle, three years younger, giggled and hid behind her mother's legs, and her younger sibling copied her. Atyen gave Sarabee a hug, then offered his hand to Jens as he came up. The fisher shook it warmly and then clapped him on the back. "How have you been?"

"I've worked less for more reward, if that's what you're asking."

"Well, here's more reward for less work." Atyen tossed the sow's leash to Sarabee. "Here my dear, a gift for your unborn. Grow him strong for your husband."

"Atyen!" She caught the lead. "This is too generous . . ."

The inquisitor waved. "It's nothing. I've been pulling that leash all the way from the forewall, and she brings new meaning to

the phrase pig-headed. Trust me, this is a good excuse to get
rid of her."

"You were always smoother than shipsteel." Sarabee smiled her
radiant smile, wrapped the leash around her wrist and shooed
the children in the direction of the house. "I'll leave you two to
talk. I've got to feed these three."

The two men watched her go in silence, then Atyen spoke.
"She's a fine woman, Jens."

Jens pursed his lips, thinking carefully before he answered. "She
would have married you, if you'd wanted her."

For a moment the scholar looked away from the farmer. "No.
No she wouldn't have." He looked back. "And it's better for us
all that I didn't ask her."

"What brings you here?" Jens changed the subject before it
could become awkward.

"The question I asked. How have you been?"

"When the inquisitors come to ask that I begin to worry."

"I'm just an aspirant."

"Does that mean I shouldn't worry?"

Atyen nodded. Jens had always been a perceptive man. "Let's
sit on the shore and talk awhile."

They walked over the shore road and up onto an uncultivated
hillock where two fields met, and lay back in the long grass that
grew there, looking up at the ocean. Fishing platforms dotted the
inshore water, connected to the docks by a maze of boardwalks.
After a while Atyen spoke. "Remember when we took your father's
line-raft?"

"And sailed it to the aftwall and back." Jens laughed at the
memory. "He was less than pleased. You were always getting me
in trouble."

The aspirant picked up a random stick and threw it at the vast
silver disk that marked the end of the world. It splashed a few
meters from shore. "It's farther than it looks. It still seems close
enough to touch."

"And yet hours to sail." Jens rubbed his back reflexively. "I
thought we'd never get back."

"But we touched the aftwall. Few enough people do that, even
fishers."

"It's no big deal to us. Fishers can do it any time, so we don't
bother."

"You and I bothered."

"You're a farmer's son, and I only went because you convinced me."

"You always did blame me for everything."

"That's because everything was your fault."

Atyen laughed. "Fair enough, I suppose." He leaned back and looked up. "Ever wonder what's up there?"

"Up where?"

"At the suntube."

Jens shrugged. "God, I suppose. Heaven. That's what the Bible says."

"Does it?"

"That's what the priests say it says. Noah made wings of falcon feathers to fly to Heaven, but he was burned and fell."

Atyen pursed his lips. "It also says our world is his Ark, sent on a voyage to Heaven because God was unhappy with Earth and flooded it. If we're going to Heaven it can't be right up there. Both stories can't be true."

"You sound like Liese."

"Liese?"

"She's always asking strange questions. 'Dedka, if the wind always goes aftward, what makes the clouds go foreward?'"

Atyen laughed. "It's a good question. What did you tell her?"

"I told her she'd be an aspirant to the Inquisitory one day, and you'd be her doctrinor."

"A good answer, but nobody knows why the clouds go against the wind."

Jens shrugged. "If I were clever enough to be a priest I wouldn't be a fisher. All I know is the world can't be on a voyage to anywhere, because the world is everywhere, and if you took all the falcon feathers in it you couldn't make a man fly. As for the clouds, I'll leave them to you." He laughed. "And my ten year old."

"Maybe God pushes the clouds."

Jens looked at his friend askance. "I thought inquisitors didn't believe in God."

"Some do, to different degrees."

"And you?"

Atyen shook his head. "I did when I was little. Not anymore."

"What do you believe now?"

"That the builders built the world. People, not gods."

"Then why even have a god?"

"God is there to understand everything we don't." He smiled. "Like clouds."

"That's an answer? I should have you talking to Liese."

"Every time we learn something new, there's less for God to explain. I believe we can understand everything, if we think about it hard enough. So when we do," Atyen shrugged, "no god."

Jens laughed. "If I could think that hard, I'd be an inquisitor too." He paused, watching the waves. "So why don't you tell me why you've come. It's too long a walk from the forewall for casual visits, and I can't imagine you gave us a pig for nothing."

"How's the fishing?"

Jens shrugged. "As good as ever, not as good as I'd wish. It's harder to outwit carp than you might think."

"Are you making your full tithing?"

Jens looked at his friend askance, on the edge of being offended. "Don't tell me they've made you a tithecounter."

Atyen snorted. "I wouldn't let them if they tried."

"Why ask then?"

"It's important to know, and you're the only one who'll give me an honest answer."

The fisher thought about that for a while. "There's little enough love for inquisitors here in the shorefields, and tithing is the reason."

"I left my cross-sash at the Inquisitory on purpose, Jens. I'm asking as a friend."

"I'd wondered why you weren't wearing one."

"You thought perhaps I'd failed?"

"Not for a second, I knew there'd be another reason."

"It's because I didn't want a piece of cloth to come between us. I'm your friend, Jens, first and last. I need you to know that."

"I know you are. I've missed you, Atyen." Jens fell silent, considering. "And yes. I'm making my full tithing . . ." He paused, letting the silence drag out. "For now."

"For now?"

The fisher shrugged. "You saw Sarabee. Three children, all growing and a fourth on the way. We're just getting by as it is."

Atyen nodded. "And soon the choice will be feed your children or make your tithing."

Jens spread his hands wordlessly, helplessly. "What would you have me do?" His voice held an edge of bitterness.

"I told you I'm not here as an inquisitor. Feed your family. If the tithecounters find out it won't be from me."

"Do you remember Celese?"

"Sarabee's older sister? She was lovely."

"All the Fougere girls were," Jens smiled as he thought of his wife, then his expression darkened. "Celese married a farmer from Tidings, one of the Berkers. Two months ago they came for him, went into his barn and took all he had, and him with it. He got twelve years servitude, and Celese with five at home. Her youngest is two."

"Everyone has to tithe. If there were no penalty for holding back . . ." Atyen spread his arms wide. "Nobody would do it and our world would collapse."

"Inquisitors don't tithe, nor sentinels."

"Not in food or goods. We tithe in time, in hours given to study, to the law, to governance. That's worth something."

"Daydreaming all day, while I haul fish." Jens looked up at the suntube beseechingly. "May God's blessings fall upon me that I have to pay so."

The scholar shook his head. "Your labor feeds your family. My labor replaces mine."

"And yet you have wealth enough to gift a pig." Jens's voice held an edge.

"No, I have influence enough to gain a pig to aid my studies. I have concern enough to gift it to you."

Jens looked away, suddenly abashed. "I . . . *we* appreciate it, Atyen, we do, excuse my words. I'm worried with the new baby coming, that's all, and to a fisher your world looks easy. You did work hard for your position. I never understood . . ."

"Why I gave up on having my own family? Sometimes I don't either." Atyen looked away.

Jens bit his lip. *Sarabee was the reason, but neither of us can say that.* "You would have done well to fish, or farm. You were always the smartest of us."

"Maybe not. Look who has Sarabee and three children by her. And congratulations on the next one, by the way." Atyen paused. "I know what I have to do with my life, and this is it. I have four brothers, and my father's farm wasn't big enough to split five ways."

Jens stopped himself before he said something he might later regret. It had not always been he who'd held fate's relative favor, and neither he nor Atyen were responsible for the circumstances they'd been born to.

"Will you dine with us tonight?" he asked instead.

"How is it with Celese?" The scholar evaded the question.

Jens shrugged. "She's trying to work their land alone. Sarabee is giving them what we can spare."

"She's generous."

"She thinks I don't know. I can't bear to tell her not to. But soon enough it will be us . . ." Jens looked again to the aftwall, months of stress crystalizing into the moment, clamping down on his throat to cut off further words. "Celese should remarry. Her land is good, and she can still bear."

"Hardly fair to her husband."

"Newl." Jens shrugged. "No, but hunger isn't fair."

"And your other neighbors, are they tithing in full?" The fisher looked at Atyen sharply and the scholar raised his hands. "As a friend, Jens. I won't name names, never, but it's important to know."

"Why?"

Atyen paused. "Because the world has too many people."

Jens raised his eyebrows, concern in his face. "Are you sure?"

"You know this yourself, it doesn't take an inquisitor to see it."

"Sure, times are tight here in the shorefields, but . . ."

"It's tight everywhere, the shorefields, the midfields, the forefields, for the fishers and the millers and smiths, even in the Inquisitory." Atyen smirked. "You have no idea how hard I had to fight to get you that pig." He held up a hand before Jens could thank him again. "Are your neighbors tithing?"

"This goes no further?"

"On my father's pyre."

Jens still hesitated, despite the reassurance. *But I can trust Atyen.* "No, no they aren't. There's some who have an agreement, they arrange to share catches back and forth, so it seems there's less when the tithecounter comes, and hold the tokens back."

"And the rest of you turn a blind eye to this?"

"We all know it might be us next."

Atyen nodded. "Then it's worse than we knew. How do they know when the tithecounter is coming?"

Jens snorted. "It isn't that long since you left the shorefields. Gossip runs faster than a man can sprint." He looked out at the ocean again. A fisher family was clamming from one of the platforms, the children lithe as eels as they dove down to find the clams. "How bad is it, Atyen?"

"We don't know. I'll tell you one thing, families will have to get smaller."

"What do you mean?" Jens looked at his friend, not quite understanding, not wanting to understand.

Atyen shrugged. "Not all of this generation's children will live to grow up."

"What will you do? What will the inquisitors do?" There was a trace of fear in Jens's voice now.

Atyen pursed his lips. "Fix it, if we can. First we have to understand what's happening. That's what I'm here for."

"What can I do?"

"I need you to keep watch for me."

"Why me?"

"Because you're smart and reliable, and I can trust you as I can trust no one else."

"I'm just one man. The inquisitors must have other ways of finding these things out."

"How many from the shorefields pass the tests? This is a job for a full inquisitor, not an aspirant, but here I am. They sent me here because I'm from here, and I can move here in ways they can't. But I can't be here all the time, and you are."

"They must be desperate."

"My doctrinor is. How do you think I got the pig?"

"I wondered . . ." The fisher paused. "Yes, I'll keep watch for you. What am I watching for?"

"We don't know, exactly. Food shortages, mothers abandoning children, anything strange that might warn the system is breaking down."

"If I see anything, how do I reach you?"

Atyen took a fist-sized wooden ball from his backbag and passed it over. "Come to the Inquisitory, show this to the sentinels, or send Sarabee with it. If neither of you can come, you can put a message in this and send a messenger to the gates, it will get to me."

The ball was a puzzle, and Jens watched as Atyen showed him how to open it; a push, two twists, another push, and it came apart along a zigzagging joint concealed in the geometric patterns worked into its surface.

"I will." Jens examined the ball, assured himself he could work the puzzle. It had the shield and blade of the Inquisitory sculpted into its surface, folded into a more ornate sigil that he didn't recognize, and Atyen's full name scribed around its equator. They sat in silence for a while, and then the conversation turned to lighter things, memories of childhood, Jens's adventures in childrearing and Atyen's in the strange mix of arcane and mundane that was the world of an inquisitor. They walked together to Jens's small home, and Atyen put his head in long enough to say goodbye to Sarabee.

"Take care of yourself, Atyen," she said.

"Take care of those children!"

Sarabee was nursing the baby, and Jens saw how Atyen carefully didn't look at the curve of her breast. Suckling women didn't usually conceive, but Sarabee . . . The joke used to be she was so fertile she'd get pregnant if you masturbated thinking about her, and certainly enough of the shorefield's boys had tried to prove the theory. *I was lucky to win her.*

She blew Atyen a kiss and waved, and Jens led his friend back out. They walked in companionable silence to the shore road that led to the Tidings main road that helixed up the curve of the world to connect to the trading road, which in turn would take him home to the Inquisitory.

They came to the junction, and embraced. "We were best friends, you and I." There was regret in Jens's voice.

"We're still best friends."

"Yes, but I'm a fisher, and you're an inquisitor. You'll be Chief Inquisitor one day."

Atyen laughed. "I appreciate your confidence. And we'll still be friends even if I'm Chief Inquisitor."

Jens sighed. "Yes, I know. But friends should spend time together, and our paths have forked so far apart. I'm sorry you couldn't stay for the evening meal."

"I'll come again when I can, and stay longer."

"I hope you will." They shook hands and embraced, and parted. Jens watched his friend walking down the path until he disappeared in the distance. He had missed Atyen more than he knew, in the years since they'd finished school. It would be good to see more of him. He turned back and hiked back down the shore. He would watch, as his friend had asked, but he would also prepare. Atyen's request was also a gift, in that it gave him a warning. There might not be much he could do with it, given that he and Sarabee were already struggling, but he would do what he could. At a minimum it was time to start building up their food stores, perhaps trading fish for grain and hiding some of their surplus from the tithe collector. Outside the house he stopped and hefted the wooden ball, contemplating it. He opened the ball's catch, examined the tiny hidden space within as though it held the secret of the future. A man with family had to think for the future, there was no way around that. *Times are hard, but they aren't yet bad.* With Noah's blessing that's the way they would stay, despite what Atyen had said. His gut tightened as he contemplated the alternatives. *But worry won't feed children.* He took a deep breath to calm himself, then pushed the door open to help his wife with their new pig.

Atyen's mind was on his wings for most of the long hike back to the Inquisitory. In truth he had welcomed the delay Solender had imposed, despite his eagerness to feel the wind beneath his wings. *How can I be sure they're going to work?* The truth was he couldn't. His kites and models could only take him so far, and sooner or later he'd have to take that leap of faith. Every step forewards brought that moment closer, and Atyen was less comfortable with it than he would have liked. It was one thing to lie in a warm field and dream of soaring like a falcon, it was another entirely to stand on a windy ledge with a flimsy set of experimental wings strapped to your back and contemplate the fall. His teeth worried his lower lip as he considered what he was about to undertake, but when he finally got back to Solender's studio he found a thick pile of tithesheets waiting for him on his worksheet. There was also a note. Solender wanted him to go over the sheets to track food production and population changes. Implicit in the request was the requirement that Atyen finish the research before he went back to working on his wings. *Reprieved.*

The cost of reprieve was tedious hours of drudgework. Atyen sifted through the stack, noting with dismay that the records went back more than a thousand years. He settled down to work resignedly. The tithesheets were endless pages of numbers concerning the production of grain and chickens and barrels of fish, the births and deaths in different families, the building of houses and shops, the sale of steel from the steel-falls, and every other piece of minutia the tithecounters could imagine to record. In theory his job should have been simple, but the record keeping hadn't been standardized and so he was forced to make estimates and interpolate the numbers to derive some kind of coherent picture of the way population and economy interacted over time.

He opened a fresh worksheaf, not wanting to sully his journal with anything unrelated to flying, and sighed as he pored over a well-faded report in the archaic phrasing of some long-dead tithecounter, who thirteen hundred years previously had made measure of the farms and planted tares in Bountiful parish. There was little need, he thought, to go back so far, but the Chief Inquisitor was obsessed with thoroughness. Resignedly he pulled another stack of sheets onto his lap, noted the figures from the first page on his worksheaf in his careful hand, then turned the page to read more. The anonymous tithecounter had not bothered to provide anything so convenient as an overall total. The holdings of each farm in the parish were listed individually, together with a confirmation that the appropriate tithes had been paid, but the long dead functionary had left it to Atyen to add them up. *Or at least, I haven't found an overall total.* The ancient documents were often missing sheets, which didn't help.

Sometimes not just pages but entire references were missing, and he went up to the manuscript tower to find them. The tower rose over the Inquisitory's main gallery, and it was as old as the rest of the ancient structure. Its outer surface was deeply pitted, but inside the walls were still smooth, worn shiny and rounded in places where people might come in contact with them, still angular and matte-finished elsewhere. Atyen had always loved it, for the hush that filled its spaces and for the limitless knowledge locked up in its endless documents, the accumulated labor of countless generations of inquisitors. The reading room was on the very top floor of the tower, an almost sacred place in the inquisitor traditions, a place of concentration and of knowledge, with waxed flax sheets stretched over the huge window openings to provide light while keeping out the mists, and heavy wooden tables where eager aspirants could pore over their work. He paid little heed to his surroundings, concentrating on getting through the sheets as quickly as possible. The sooner he finished, the sooner he could get back to work on his wings. He was going over a long-faded farm census of Bountiful parish when something strange caught his eye. He called over a scriptkeeper.

"I don't know this word," he said, "What's a cattle?"

"A what?"

"A cattle." Atyen pronounced the unfamiliar word carefully. "I've found a farm here that has sixty pigs, three hundred chickens, and ten cattle, whatever they are."

"I'm not sure." The scriptkeeper frowned and came to look over his shoulder. "Show me."

Atyen pointed to the entry, and the scriptkeeper examined it with a quizzical expression. "It's not an error," she said. "Maybe a joke of some kind?"

"From a tithecounter? In an official document?" Atyen pursed his lips. "Unlikely. We'll have to find out what he meant."

"Perhaps it's just a variety of sheep, they don't seem to list many of them."

"Maybe. I'll ask around."

Atyen went on with his work, and the keeper came back a bell later. "I'm sorry," she said. "Nobody's ever heard of a cattle."

Atyen's heart sank, because he knew Solender would want to know what it was. His doctrinor had always taught him that the most important discoveries were hidden in the most trivial observations. He had been trained to look for anomalies that anyone else would dismiss as insignificant, and this was certainly one. He would have to find out for sure what *cattle* were, which in turn meant more time in the reading room and less time working on the riddles of flight. He sighed. Still, there was no point in trying to avoid the question. For every hundred who took the Inquisitory tests, six where accepted as aspirants and two of those won the coveted double-red cross-sash. He had been lucky to pass his tests as young as he was, and luckier still to be have the Chief Inquisitor himself as doctrinor. Most of the time he was free to follow his heart in his learning, so long as he kept what he did well documented. *It is an honor to be allowed to live life to learn.* Solender had told him that on his first day, and over and over again ever since. *You have to show that you're worthy of the privilege.*

Atyen idly chewed a thumbnail as he considered his next move. The major question was where to look for the information. If a *cattle* really was just a long-vanished name for some variety of sheep then he would have to find a document that recorded the transition, with more clarity than the tithesheet in front of him.

If it was something else then he need to find out what. *But what else could it be, really?* The best place to start would be in the tithesheets from the years immediately before the one he'd been looking at. In that case the inconsistent formats of the various tithecounters would be an advantage, because one of them might have recorded details that another had neglected. There was another advantage in that, which was that he already knew where to look for the relevant manuscripts.

He pushed away the sheets in front of him, got up and went down the spiralling staircase that wound around the inner wall of the tower. The tithesheets were mostly stored on musty shelves in the seldom visited back rooms of the second floor. *I hope.* It was the job of the scriptkeepers to organize the reams of information in their care, but every new generation of custodians had a different idea of how that organization should be done. Atyen crossed his fingers and went into the dim and musty stacks. Once he had found the right stack of documents it didn't take him long to discover that *cattle* were increasingly common as he went back in time. The entry he'd first found had only ten, but the previous year there had been sixteen in Bountiful, on three farms, and the year before that there were nearly a hundred on over a dozen farms. He skipped back a few years, and found a parish overflowing with cattle, every farm had at least a few, most had dozens. They were occasionally listed in three varieties, *bull, cows* and *calves.* He resolved that mystery when he found a listing for *bull calves* and *cow calves*, which implied that *bulls* and *cows* were the primary varieties of *cattle*, with *calves* being some some special subvariety. However by then he'd uncovered a deeper mystery, which was something called a *horse. Horses* stopped appearing in the records altogether the same year *cattle* got scarce, but before that there were at least four subdivisions, *mares, stallions, geldings* and *foals.* Later he found two more, *shorthorses* and *work-horses.* When they were listed simply as *horses* they usually appeared beside *cattle*, but when the subdivisions were used they were listed separately. *So they aren't just a type of cattle.* That only deepened the mystery, and since the tithesheets assumed the reader would know what a *horse* was, in all its many variations, there was no way to gain anything more from them.

He stroked his chin, considering the page in front of him. It detailed the extensive horse holdings of the Innhop farm of the

shipyear 5211. *And the deepest mystery is, where did they all go?*
Like cattle, horses had to be farm animals, if only because they
were consistently listed with pigs, ducks, goats and chickens, but
how could *another* whole category of farm animal simply vanish?
The tithesheets couldn't tell him that, and so he waded into the
depths of the manuscript room, scanning through the shelves
to find something, anything that would resolve the problem. *If
they were important enough to tithe they were important enough
to study.* Somewhere, sometime, some aspirant had to have done
a masterwork on them, the only problem was to find it. Even
deciding where to start was difficult, since the work could have
been on any of a dozen sub-topics concerning animals of which
he knew nothing. He spent bells searching through long forgotten indexes for a promising title, and then when he went to find
the manuscript that it referred to, he usually found that the filing
scheme they had been built around had long since been changed.
When he did find something that might prove useful he was then
faced with the task of deciphering it. The tithesheets hadn't been
too hard to work with. The language in them was simple and they
were mostly written using the tithecounters' preferred blood ink,
which didn't fade much. By contrast the aspirants commonly used
charcoal ink for their manuscripts, which faded steadily over the
centuries. Even when they were legible the archaic grammar and
word usage frequently strained his understanding. Usually he had
to painstakingly decipher first the letters, working from no more
than the scratches the author's pen had left on the paper. Only
then could he work on understanding the words. And inevitably
once he'd worked out enough to learn what the manuscript was
about, it was about something other than *horses* or *cattle*. As the
days began to slip past his progress differed from zero only in
the pitifully small pile of documents he'd confirmed as useless.
After a while he began to think that there had never really been
horses or cattle, except in the spiteful imaginations of a generation of tithecounters, who generated fictions intended specifically
to confound their descendants with a fruitless search for animals
that never existed.

    And then, at the start of his third week of research, he found
a treasure. It was a copyscript of a study done by an inquisitor
named Nafel. It was in blood ink, which made both text and
illustrations easy to read, and it was titled simply *The Anatomy of*

*the Horse.* Nafel had meticulously recorded the mechanics of an animal that resembled a hornless goat as much as anything else, although with heavier musculature and a larger, longer head. He turned the ancient pages carefully, puzzling out Nafel's words as the ancient scholar described the articulation of the hind limbs, the ligaments of the back and neck, the heart and lungs and digestive system, with carefully drawn illustrations of the animal's body parts. The middle of the manuscript had doubled pages, designed to fold out to provide a larger surface for a larger image, and when he reached them he opened them cautiously, fearful of tearing the fragile paper. What he saw made him freeze.

It was a triple illustration of the beast itself, shown from in front, from behind and from the side, done in exquisite detail and with every important feature of its body labelled. However the striking part was beside the main drawing, a human figure drawn to scale. Horses, in Atyen's imagination, were about the size of the goat. Now he realized, they were *huge*. The horse towered over the man beside it, and if he was of average height the animal had to be a good two meters tall. *Incredible. Solender has to see this.* He looked at the picture for a long time, amazed at what where his investigation had led him. Finally he refolded the center pages, closed the volume and reverently carried it up to the top floor. The disappearance of an animal so significant was a major finding. His doctrinor couldn't help but be pleased. At the same time he felt a sense of foreboding. If horses could vanish from the world then maybe Solender was right, and perhaps people could vanish too.

"Harder," urged the midwife, and Sarabee groaned as the contraction hit her womb. She bore down as hard as she could, grimacing against the pain. Her belly was tense, her pretty features puffy with effort and streaked with sweat in the effort of her labor.

"Harder," the midwife repeated. "A few more good ones and you'll be done." The curtains were drawn in the modest bedroom, suntubelight filtering through them to dapple the wall.

"You'd think this would get easier . . ." Sarabee panted. She would have said more, but the next contraction hit and cut her words off with another agonized groan and she bore down again. Experience told her that the harder she pushed the sooner she would be done. *And I'll have my baby.* It was the thought she used to focus herself, to hang onto as her body wracked itself. *My beautiful new baby.* The contraction passed and she breathed deep to get ready for the next one. Jens was there, his hands on her shoulders, but she was barely aware of his presence. Her entire awareness was concentrated on her belly, as her uterus strained to deliver her fourth child.

"Harder still this time!" the midwife repeated. "The head is coming down. You're almost there." Even before the woman had finished another contraction hit, and again Sarabee bore down, dizzy now with the effort and only wanting the birthing to be over. "Harder!" The child was big, bigger than any of the others had been. *A boy for sure, Jens will be pleased.* She had known in her heart it would be a boy for months now. This pregnancy had simply felt different, but she hadn't told Jens that, even as he had carefully hidden his desire for a male heir. Instead she just left him to wonder at the secret smile that came to her lips, whenever her baby kicked and reminded her that yes, this time it would be a boy. For some things it was better to wait.

"The baby's crowning. One more." As if on cue another contraction came, and Sarabee bore down for all she was worth, grunting with the effort. She felt the baby move, felt herself stretch agonizingly wide, and then, all in a rush, it was done, the baby was out, and she fell back against the pillows, exhausted. A faint cry came from the end of the bed, and the midwife was holding up her newborn, beautiful and glistening and seemingly far too tiny to have been the cause of ten bells worth of anguished labor.

"It's a boy," the midwife said. "It's a perfect little boy," and all of a sudden Jens was kissing her.

"It's a boy, my love. A boy." The midwife was cleaning the mucus and uterine fluid from the child, and Sarabee closed her eyes, breathing deep. There was another contraction, this one almost gentle compared to the ones that had been wracking her body for most of the day. *That will be the afterbirth.* She sighed, suspended somewhere between exhaustion and contentment. The birthing was done, and everything else would wait. Someone put the child on her chest, wrapped in a fresh swaddling cloth. Instinctively she pulled the tiny body up between her breasts. *It's too soon to feed him.* She knew from experience that newborns needed sleep right after being born, but this time she was wrong. He nuzzled at her breast, rooting for the nipple, found it and began suckling, his tiny mouth working hard for his first meal. Sarabee smiled to herself, her eyes still closed.

"Jerl," she heard Jens telling the midwife. "We're calling him Jerl." The name sounded warm in Sarabee's ears, comforting. It had been her father's name, and since before Liese had been born they'd planned to call their first boy Jerl. *He'd be so proud now.* It was sad that her father hadn't lived to see his first grandson born, but her boy was on her breast, and in him she felt his presence, in a way she hadn't since he'd died. The baby finished suckling, having had just a taste of pre-milk, but he felt strong as he moved inside his wrap. Sarabee smiled and drifted off to contented sleep.

The next days were filled with the bustle of visitation, as neighbors and relations came by to see the newborn. In fisher tradition Sarabee's sisters and aunts looked after the food and the child care, while her mother arranged the entertaining, giving Sarabee the time to focus exclusively on Jerl. Jens looked on with quiet pride, accepting the congratulations offered with a smile. It wasn't that anyone thought less of a man who couldn't produce a son, but everyone knew the importance of having at least one. Even Sarabee's mother deferred to him now, giving him the deeper respect she had somehow always managed to withhold even as she had meticulously observed the bare formalities due a husband. *He's such a good man.* She'd had her pick of the shorefields boys before she married, but in the end it had come down to Jens and Atyen. Atyen had been the more interesting choice, with his quick wit and shy charm, but he had also been committed to his dream of inquisitorship, his time devoted to his studies and not to her. Then too, Jens had his father's raft, and he was loyal, hard working and reliable. When he'd asked her to marry him she hadn't hesitated to say yes, and she'd never once had cause to regret that choice. *Though I sometimes wonder what would have happened if Atyen had asked me first.* It was an idle thought. Atyen had not asked, and life with Jens was too good to upset with dreams of what might have been.

Visitation was three days by tradition, and by the end of it Sarabee was exhausted, and relieved to have some time alone with just her baby and her husband. Celese stayed to help clean up, while Jens took the baby down to the shore for his first dive. That too was tradition, and he had done the same with all the girls.

It would only be a brief dunk, to bring the child good catches for the rest of his life. *And Jens needs his time with the baby too.* Still, Sarabee felt something close to panic as she watched her husband walk down to the shore with her newborn. Celese gently pulled her inside and closed the door, and Sarabee bit her lower lip and tried to focus on getting her house returned to normal after the visit. She smiled to see how Liese had taken charge of her younger sisters, ordering them about in her ten-year-old voice as though it were she and not Sarabee who was their mother. She kissed all three of them, from youngest to oldest and tried to keep her eyes from straying to the door.

It seemed to take forever for Jens to return, though it couldn't have been more than a bell. When he did it was all she could do to hold herself back from just grabbing her newborn to her breast to prove to herself that he was all right. *But Jens wouldn't let anything happen.*

"He swam like a fish." Her husband was beaming with pride in his new son.

Jerl's hair was fine and downy, plastered wet against his head, and Sarabee took him back, proud and relieved at the same time. Celese helped put the girls to bed, and then went back to her own children, leaving Sarabee and Jens with Jerl. She went to sleep in her husband's arms with her baby curled against her, tired but happy.

Jerl woke her twice to suckle, and Sarabee stroked his small head, marveling at his perfection in the dim light that filtered through the sleep-shutters. She woke again on her own, to find Jens gone and Liese asleep where he had been. Jerl's tiny body was curled up in the crook of her arm. Both children were in fresh clothes, which mean that Jens had changed the baby before he left. *He let me sleep, he's such a good man.*

Liese yawned and her eyes opened. "I'm hungry, Mamsha," she said.

"We'll get you . . ." Sarabee paused to think. Normally her internal clock could tell her the time to within half a bell, but now it was completely unset. Jens had left the sleep-cloths down. Did her daughter want breakfast or lunch? *I didn't even hear him leave . . .* "We'll get you some food soon," she said.

"I'm hungry *now*," persisted the little girl.

"Well, *soon* will be *now* before you know it," Sarabee smiled, and tweaked her daughter's nose. "My little button shrew. Sometimes I think you'll starve if I don't feed you every bell."

Liese giggled. "I'm too big to be a button shrew now."

"Maybe so. How do you like your new brother?"

The little girl pursed her lips, considering the question seriously. "I like him," she decided, and moved up to put a kiss very deliberately on the baby's forehead. "His name is Jerl."

"Yes it is." Sarabee picked up her son in one arm and her daughter in the other. "Let's go and find you something to eat."

There was no one in the kitchen, which meant the younger girls were with Celese. There was fresh yeasted bread, and a basket of fresh apples, which Celese must have brought with her when she came for the children. Sarabee sliced off a piece of the bread and cut a slice of pungent goat-cheese to go with it for Liese, added half of an apple to her daughter's plate, and ate the other half herself even though she didn't feel hungry. *I have to get my strength back, Jens needs my help.* By then the baby was stirring and hungry, and she settled down at the kitchen table to feed him. Just as she was about to start there was a knock on the door. She got up and answered it with the baby on her hip, expecting Celese but finding a trio of young men.

"Can I help you?" she asked.

"We're hungry," said the closest. He was rangy, his skin taut over muscle and bone. "Do you have any work we could do for a meal?"

Sarabee shook her head. "I don't but my husband might. He's down by the dock."

The youth was looking past her into the house. "That's a lot of apples you have there. Do you think we could have one each before we start?" She hesitated. Something subtle had shifted in the atmosphere, an aura of danger she couldn't quite put her finger on. *But the best thing to do is act normally.*

Sarabee smiled and hoped it was convincing. "Of course, just a moment."

She turned to get the apples, and in that moment her premonition of danger was realized. All three of them followed her into the house, and the leader reached past her into the apple basket with a grubby hand to pick out a fruit. "Good apples," he said, looking at her with a hunger that had nothing to do with his stomach, standing close enough to make her uncomfortable.

Sarabee resisted the urge to step backwards, and he took a bite of the apple, not taking his eyes off her.

"I'd like you to leave now," she said, keeping her gaze steady on his. Showing fear would only embolden them. The other two were helping themselves to the bread and cheese, and for a moment the leader looked uncertain, and then all of a sudden he moved, snatching Jerl from her hip and backing away.

"Jerl!" Sarabee leapt to grab him back, but the youth passed him to one of the others, and grabbed her, his hands hard as shipsteel.

"Jerl!" She brought a knee up to catch him in the groin, but he managed to evade the strike, twisting her arm up painfully behind her back.

"Gently now, sister, gently." He spun her around and held her from behind so she couldn't try the move again, forcing her up against the kitchen table. "Nothing's going to happen to your baby, just as long as you cooperate." She could feel his erection hard against her, and realized with a kind of distant shock that she was about to be raped. Time seemed to slow down, and as if from a long distance she heard her assailant still talking. "You be nice to us, and we're going to be very nice to you."

Sarabee had been afraid when she'd first sensed the menace in the leader's expression, more afraid when they'd followed her into the house, but now that the threat had become reality a strange calm came over her. *I can't get pregnant, I just gave birth.* That suddenly became vitally important. What else happened to her was irrelevant, so long as Jerl was safe and she didn't wind up carrying a bastard for Jens. *And Liese, where's Liese?* Her little girl was gone, whether she'd hidden or run away didn't matter, she was safer where she was. *I won't call for her. No need to risk two children.*

"I'll be nice," she heard her voice saying, again as though from a great distance. "Promise you won't hurt him."

"Oh, we promise," the leader said, in a voice that promised nothing. He put a hand on her milk-filled breast and squeezed, hard enough to hurt. She winced reflexively, but the pain didn't really register, her mind was entirely focused on the situation, seeing, assessing, planning. The other two were still eating bread and cheese, wolfing it down. *They really are hungry.* That fact was important, it meant they probably had come to the door looking only for food, if not for work. They were young, hungry, frustrated and angry. Raping her was a spur of the moment thing, an opportunity that had presented itself and that they'd taken, possibly not even realizing what they were doing until they were already doing it. *Which means they aren't planning to kill me, not yet.* They might later decide to, in order to keep her from accusing them, but they hadn't planned that far ahead. *Which means the longer I can keep them busy the safer I'll be.* Her eye fell on the knife she'd cut the bread with, just out of reach on the table. The leader was still pawing at her, pulling her top-blouse down and muttering obscenities in her ear, but his words didn't matter. The one holding Jerl looked sullen, relegated to babysitting duty while the leader enjoyed his new toy. He would be the tag-along, eager to be a member of the group, resentful because he was given so little power within it. The other one was watching the show with an appreciative leer as he chewed and swallowed, secure in the knowledge that his loyalty would be rewarded when his own turn came. His eyes were cruel, and he was enjoying the hurt and humiliation the leader was inflicting on her. She avoided meeting his gaze, knowing instinctively that offering any challenge would only encourage him to be rougher when he got the chance.

"That's better, sister. Just relax and enjoy it." The leader slid his hand to her thighs.

Sarabee looked away from the knife so as not to give away her thoughts. *I can move there, let him think I'm cooperating.* It would take just one quick motion to grab the knife, slide it into his belly, up between his ribs to reach for his heart. One quick motion with every last kilo of strength behind it, and in her mind she rehearsed the action. She'd never killed a man before, but she knew how to do it. *Just like gutting a fish.* She would have to deal with the second one then, the cruel one, but she'd be holding the knife at that point, and his cruelty would be a front for his cowardice—that was why he wasn't the leader himself. He would run. The third one, the one holding Jerl, lacked the yats to actually hurt the baby unless the leader told him to do it, and he would run when the other did.

"Let me turn around, I'll make it good for you," she said, keeping her voice low.

"Look, the sow likes it." The leader's voice held an edge of triumph. He relaxed his grip and Sarabee turned around, at the same time bringing the knife within reach. She looked up and gave him a gaze halfway between arousal and submission, pressing her now naked breasts against his chest. She was rewarded when he moved his hands to her waist, to her hips, to pull her groin into his. That left her own hands free, and she put them on his chest, caressing it.

"You're so strong," she said. "Take me slowly, it's better when it's slow."

He gasped then, and his face softened slightly. *He's probably never had a woman who really wanted him.* She had power now, and if she used it carefully she would gain more. She moved her right hand down to his belly, marking the place where she would drive the knife home, and flicked her eyes to the other two. They had both stopped eating, their eyes fixed on the scene in front of them with naked lust. The one holding Jerl was the key. It wasn't enough that he would run when she killed the leader, because he would probably drop the baby when he did. She didn't want to take that risk. *But sooner or later he'll put the baby down, and then . . .* Her assailant's expression relaxed more as he gave in to the pleasure of her body against his, and she slid her left hand to his groin, massaging him through his clothes. She had him where she needed him now, and she knew what she had to do to keep him there. It was only a matter of time before he'd be dead. It was a simple fact, and it raised no emotion in her. He had chosen his course of action, and that had dictated hers.

There was a small cry. Jerl had woken up and was hungry. The leader stiffened, looked behind him with annoyance. "Shut that up," he barked to the tag-along. Sarabee tensed, ready to beg for her baby's life if she had to, but the tagalong wasn't the type to give violence to a crying infant. He looked uncertain for a moment, then took her newborn into the bedroom. *He's going to put him on the bed, come back and close the door.* Sarabee moved her left hand back up to where her right hand was, to free her right to grab the knife. She again rehearsed the motion that would cut her attacker open, visualizing where the knife was, how the handle was angled on the table behind her. When she heard the bedroom door close, she would move.

The leader moaned with desire. "Don't stop, sister," he said, and put a hand over hers to push it back down to his groin. Jerl's cries had started Sarabee's milk flowing, and she felt it first leaking, then streaming from her nipples, but her assailant either didn't notice or didn't care. She fought to keep herself calm, her ears tuned to the creak of the bedroom floor, to the *clack* that would tell her the tag-along had closed the bedroom door, that Jerl was safe and that she could move. *He's probably tucking him in.* The tag-along didn't belong with the other two, he was out of his depth, doing things he wouldn't do himself just to be accepted . . .

A door opened and closed, not the bedroom door, but the front door. Suddenly Jens was in the room, his eyes wide in shock. The leader reacted instantly, shoving Sarabee to the floor and spinning to meet the threat. Her head smacked hard against one of the kitchen stools on the way down, flashing her vision white with pain, and she sprawled in a heap against the far wall.

"You're the husband." The leader grabbed up a forged steel frying pan from the table. "Pretty wife, but you picked the wrong time to come home." The cruel one turned to close ranks with the leader, and the tag-along came out of the bedroom where Jerl was still crying. Sarabee's eyes flew to where the knife was, but the cruel one was between her and the table now, even though his attention was fixed on Jens. She watched as her husband sized up the situation, his gaze moving from one youth to the next. Jerl was still crying in the bedroom and she suppressed the urge to run to get him and instead searched for another weapon. There was nothing she could get to without going through the cruel one first. *But still I can serve my son better here.* She wasn't going to leave Jens to face them three-to-one.

"Not scared, husband?" The leader advanced on Jens with the frying pan upraised. "You should be."

Jens stood his ground, his face hard, his large hands clenched into fists. "You're tough in a group. Any of you have the yats to fight me alone?"

"I'll do it," said the cruel one, too quickly. The leader stopped, and put up a hand to restrain his deputy. Sarabee bit her lip, watching the tableau play out.

"Why should I fight you?" the leader asked, his lips twisted into a smirk, "I think I've got the advantage right now."

"Because if you don't you're a coward, that's all." Jens kept his eyes locked on the leader. "Three of you against a woman and a baby. Three of you against one of me. I think I see a pattern."

Sarabee turned over, slowly, not getting up, not presenting

herself as a threat, but positioning herself to jump when the time came. Jens was smart. Even the two of them would probably lose against the three, and the leader could have ordered the others to fight Jens for him. Now her husband had made it a point of manhood. If the leader didn't face Jens alone he'd lose status in the group and the cruel one would take over.

"You think I can't take you alone, old man?" The leader spat and took a step forward, raising the frying pan to strike.

"With a weapon you can. Dare to try it barehanded?"

"Clean fight?"

"Clean fight."

"You're on." The leader held the frying pan out to the cruel one, who took it, a hard smile on his face. No matter what happened, he couldn't lose. If the leader beat Jens, he'd still get his time with Sarabee, but if Jens started winning he'd step in and finish the fight with his weapon, and get Sarabee and the leadership as well.

The leader cocked a fist and advanced on Jens, and Jens pivoted on his forward foot and drove his heel into the youth's groin. The youth went down with a grunt, writhing in pain, his hands clutched to what was probably a crushed testicle. Jens advanced over him and drove a dock boot into his face. Sarabee heard bone crunch, and the fallen man screamed, his nose smashed flat and now streaming blood. The cruel one stood in shock for a single, infinitely extended second. He hadn't expected his leader to lose at all, let alone so quickly, but he saw his opportunity, and stepped forward with the steel pan. Jens fell back to give himself room to fight, but as soon as the cruel one was out of the way Sarabee launched herself for the table. The thug caught her motion in the corner of his eye, and started to turn to stop her, aiming the pan at her head, but he was already committed to his advance on her husband. His awkward swing missed, and then she had the knife. She turned, brought it up and brought it down, but it wasn't the well rehearsed gutting stroke she'd envisioned. The blade bit into his chest, slicing muscle but skidding off bone, and then he brought the pan around again. He was aiming for her knife hand, but he caught her left wrist instead, almost knocking her sideways, and overbalancing himself in the process. They both went down in a heap and she stabbed at him again, but he'd brought his hands up to fend her off. The blade sliced into his forearm and blood gouted where she'd opened an

artery. The pan fell to the floor, and she was on top of him, raising the knife again. Panic had replaced the brutality in his face,
his eyes were wide, almost pleading with her not to kill him, but
the fear she had repressed to save her son came back as rage,
and she drove the knife down again, this time catching him right
below the ribs. She had her full weight behind the blow, and she
felt it dig into his belly, sink down until it caught in his spine.
He gasped, his face a sudden mask of pain, his hands flying to
the wound while she hauled the knife and raised it again. She
was about to drive it into his chest, but hands caught her from
behind, and Jens was pulling her up.

"Leave him," her husband said. "Leave him. Are you hurt?"

"Yes . . ." Suddenly she was trembling and his arms were around
her. "Jens, I . . ."

"We haven't got time. Where's Jerl?" The youth she'd stabbed
was doubled up on his side gasping, his eyes vacant, blood pool-
ing underneath him. The leader was still on the floor, one hand
clasped to his groin, the other to his nose, groaning in pain. The
tag-along had vanished. *Out the back door . . .* For some reason
it seemed important to understand where he'd gone.

"Where's Jerl?" Jens asked again, his voice tight.

She shook herself. "In the bedroom."

Jens nodded, his own face taut with unexpressed emotion.
"Take him to Celese, get her to send her oldest for the sentinels."

"How did you know to come?"

"Liese ran to me, crying. She's still at the dock, take her too."

Sarabee nodded, swallowing hard. *Brave Liese.* She'd have to
talk to her later, tell her she'd done the right thing. She gave her
husband one final hug, putting everything she had into it. "I love
you. I'll be back when I've got the children safe."

Jens hugged her back hard, let her go and went to take a length
of hogline from the cupboard by the door. "I'll be here with this
one." He knelt to lash the leader's arms behind his back with the
line. "Be fast."

Sarabee turned to go, suppressing the urge look at the motion-
less body on the floor. *I couldn't have killed him, not really.* She
went to the bedroom and picked up Jerl and then went out the
back door, pulling up her top-blouse as she went. Outside it was
bright and clear, an absolutely normal day with nothing to hint
at the violence that had just gone on inside her home. She saw

with sudden shock that Jerl's swaddling cloth was stained with blood, and for a single horrified instant she thought he was hurt, but then she realized she was soaked with the cruel one's blood, and some of that had gotten on her baby. At the dock Liese was peaking around a corner of the smokeshed, looking scared, and Sarabee went to her with deliberate calm, so her daughter would know the danger had passed. She took Liese's small hand in hers, and tried to stop her own hand from shaking. *But the danger hasn't passed.* The shorefields were known to be rough-and-tumble, but . . . *Nothing like this.* Something had changed in her world, changed for the worse, and in her gut she knew it had changed permanently.

Solender was very pleased by the discovery of the horse document, and released Atyen to his own devices while he delved deeper into the question of vanished farm animals. Freed from the confines of the manuscript tower, Atyen returned his concentration to the problem of flight. It should have been a simple matter of carrying his wings back up to the forewall ledge, strapping them on and taking the leap of faith. As he discovered, it wasn't. He spent a day going over them in detail, verifying every joint and tie. He went to sleep that night determined to fly the next day, but in the morning found himself strangely reluctance to commit himself to the jump. Instead he took his journal and his ink pots to the mill to watch the peregrines, but the clouds spiraled up from the aftwall, and he saw none. He tried to content himself with watching the doves, but found himself strangely restless. As the bells rolled past he went from one side of the field to the other, opened his journal and got out his pens and ink, but made neither notes nor sketches. The doves and their fluttering were irritating rather than captivating, and the skies stayed empty of peregrines. A pair of ducks distracted him briefly as they took off from the canal and winged their way aftward, but after they had vanished in the distance his eyes went forward, to the forewall and the thin line of the forewall ledge, visible only as a thickening in the green vines that covered the wall's lower reaches. There was a second green line a hundred meters above the first, though there was no way to get to the second ledge short of climbing the vertical steel surface, and a third line higher still. *They're calling me.* Atyen looked away. Above the third ledge the gray steel merged into the gray cloud mists, and somewhere above that was the secret home of the peregrines. *And I'm here, sketching doves.*

He pressed his lips together, because he wasn't even sketching doves. He knew the source of his restlessness, and it was nothing more than the conflict between the desire to realize his dream and the primal fear that gripped him when he looked over the edge. Beneath the secret relief he had felt when Solender had stopped him was an even deeper secret shame that he had hesitated and backed down at the critical moment. He bit his lip, hard, not wanting to confront what he had discovered about himself. *You're taking the easy way again, Atyen.* It was a broader truth than he was comfortable with, applying to more than an understandable reluctance to jump off a cliff. His whole life had been one of choosing the easy choice over the one he really wanted. *The Inquisitory over the farm, the Inquisitory over Sarabee.* He hadn't wanted to offend his brothers, and so gave up his claim on his father's land. He hadn't wanted to lose Jens as a friend, and so gave up on the woman he loved. Everyone had been so impressed with his intelligence, with his single-minded determination to beat the odds and earn the double-red cross-sash. He was applauded for his dedication, and his sacrifice. And it wasn't that he hadn't enjoyed the challenge, nor found satisfaction in his studies and his research. *But it wasn't what I would have chosen.*

And there was a deeper truth, as well as a broader one. He told everyone else he wanted the Inquisitory, he told himself that he chose it because it was easier. *But really, I was afraid.* Afraid to fight his brothers for the farm, afraid to fight Jens for Sarabee, afraid . . . *afraid of everything.* He looked up at the ledges again, clenching his jaw, his throat tight with emotion. For the first time in his life he was faced with something he wanted with nothing but his own fears to keep him from attaining it. If he did not fly, it would not be because flight was impossible, it would not be because Solender opposed it. If he did not fly it was because at the final moment his courage failed him. It was a truth he would have to admit to no one but himself, but it was a truth he would have to live with until he died. He would be a fraud, a shell of a man, and even if he made it to the Law Council, even if he became Chief Inquisitor, the forewall would look down on him every day and remind him that he was a coward.

*Coward,* he said under his breath, and the word was bitter in his mouth. The manuscript tower seemed to mock him. He could be in it now, safe at a table perusing dusty manuscripts. If he hadn't chosen a flight for his masterwork, he wouldn't now be facing the reality of a hundred meter plunge. *Why did I choose it?* That answer wasn't comforting either. *Because I thought it wasn't possible.* He had wanted something original, wanted more praise for his brilliant creativity, wanted to shock his doctrinor and the other aspirants with the audacity of his thought. At the same time, if he attempted the impossible, no one could fault him for failure. He had kept the belief that it could never happen carefully hidden, even from himself. *Especially from myself.* And now he had to either make the jump, or admit his cowardice. He put his head in his hands and began to weep quietly. *I can't do it, I just can't.* He could go away perhaps, find himself a place in thronging Charisy, take work as a laborer, even beg if he had to. No one would know where he had come from, or who he had been. He could just disappear.

It should've been a comforting thought, but it wasn't. The one person he couldn't hide from was himself. *At least I'm smart enough to know that.* He took a deep breath to steady himself, and at that moment it occurred to him that if he jumped from the ledge without wings he'd be killed on impact, and so relieved of his inner turmoil, free of the self-punishing thought-cycle he had fallen into. It seemed like the easy solution, but a slow smile crept into his face as he recognized the inherent illogic of embracing certain death to avoid merely risking it. *The mind is a strange thing.* He felt better at the understanding though his thoughts continued to churn, calling up scenarios of crippling injury that would be worse than death itself. The more he tried to imagine positive images the more tenaciously they gripped his consciousness. *Lal.* The friend of his older brother had been kicked in the head by a horse and reduced to idiocy. *Minsa.* The fisher-boy fell from a mast, landed badly, and lost the use of his legs because of it. *Better to die than live like that.* His early test drops had produced some spectacular wrecks. It was true a satchel of clay couldn't steer the way he hoped to, nor flare for landing the way even a dove could but . . . He clenched his teeth, trying to force the images away. *It doesn't matter.* He was going to have to jump, and he would deal with what happened after it happened.

He gathered his journal and backbag and made his way back

to the Inquisitory, his mood made foul by his internal struggle. It was after the evening-meal bell by the time he got there. He'd wasted the entire day. Hunger growled in his stomach, and so he went to get a meal. He saw Solender in the meal hall but irrational anger rose in him at his doctrinor. He didn't want to have to explain himself, and so sat at a distant table. The meal was roasted tomato with savored lamb and it smelled good, but he ate mechanically and without even really tasting the food. When he finished he went back down to the studio to look at his wings once more, to try to recapture the eagerness they had once inspired in him. They were as they had been, but now they seemed full of foreboding rather than promise. Atyen reached out and ran a hand over the familiar fabric. It hadn't changed, only his feelings had. *We create the world in our minds.* It was late, and he was tired, but he took the time unlock the joints and fold them. They would be ready the next morning, and he would carry them out to the ledge, and this time he would jump.

He left for his room. Corl nodded to him as he went out, the other aspirants didn't even acknowledge him. It was nothing new. Since the time he arrived in the Inquisitory, Solender's other aspirants had either ridiculed his chosen masterwork as impossible or slighted him for being the favored student of their doctrinor. It was partly jealousy, he knew. Solender's aspirants were among the most ambitious, and most of them had spent a long time maneuvering themselves into the Chief Inquisitor's studio, while Solender had actually sought Atyen out. Another part of it was that Atyen put no effort into currying influence within the Inquisitory's power structure, an affront to those who valued status over everything. For his part, Atyen was content to be ignored. Interacting with his fellow aspirants took time away from his wings and his beloved peregrines.

*Or so I tell myself.* Perhaps his indifference was just another mask for fear, setting himself apart, rejecting people before they could reject him. *But one issue at a time, Atyen.* He laughed at himself as he went into his room. It was an austere space just big enough for his bed, a clothes-stand and a small table. He closed the shutters, lowered the sleep-cloth and lay down, but found himself just staring at the ceiling. The internal struggle between what he was and what he wanted to be returned with the knowledge that he had delayed his test for one more day. *I haven't given up, but I need to sleep. I need to be rested to do this properly.* He whispered the words to himself, an affirmation of his commitment, but that didn't stop the niggling voice in the back of his head. *Coward*, it whispered back, and defied him to prove it wrong.

Eventually he did manage to fall asleep, but his dreams were of an endless, panicked fall, watching the ground get closer and closer until he hit. He woke with a start, breathing hard, his heart pounding in the darkness, surprised to find himself alive. He suppressed the urge to check for broken bones and closed his eyes again, but what sleep he got was shallow and fitful. The breakfast bell found him already awake, staring at the ceiling.

He was hungry and poorly rested, but rather than going to the meal hall he went back to the studio to pick up his already folded wings. There was only one way to quell the doubts that had tortured him all night, and that was to jump. His body's demands could wait until after he flew, if he didn't kill himself in the attempt. If he did, it would hardly matter. He slipped the straps over his shoulders and went to the stairs. Solender's injunction that he shouldn't try to fly alone rang in his ears, but he was loath to have any witnesses to what had become a very personal experience. It was foolish, he knew, but he would fall or fly, live or die, on his own. *And perhaps that's why I went alone the first time too.*

The stairs were long enough to be tedious, and tiring as well with the extra weight of the folded wings. He paused when he reached the forewall ledge, turned and looked down at the bulk of the Inquisitory below him. There was mist in the air, but it was clear enough to see over the great steel building, past the manuscript tower. Charisy's buildings clustered in the middle distance, and beyond that the patchwork fields faded into the blue of the ocean and the gray of the aftwall behind it. The fear that had kept him awake closed in on his throat, and he resisted the urge to press his back against the vine covered wall behind him, to get as much distance between himself and the drop as he could. The fear had not been so visceral last time he'd climbed to the ledge. *The last time I wasn't committed to jump. Not really.* Last time, Solender's appearance had given him an easy out. Last time he had not come face-to-face with himself as a coward. Not this time.

*Not this time.* Atyen took a deep breath and walked down the ledge, past the river outfall, to the place he had been when Solender had stopped him. He shrugged the folded wings from his back, unfolded them, locked them open, and then put them back on. He had a bad moment when the steady downdraft caught the fabric and nearly pulled him over the edge, but he got them under control. He attached the tail straps to his ankles, took the control loops in each hand, and looked over the edge. It was still a long, long way to fall. His wings felt flimsy and inadequate, and he felt not like a peregrine about to stoop but a very fragile human being about to plummet to his death. He took a deep breath. *I just have to jump.*

And he had planned to jump on the word jump, but his legs wouldn't obey. He closed his eyes, but it didn't help any more than it had last time. He had to leap from the ledge, forward, out and down, as hard as he could. Less than full commitment to the motion would lead to disaster, as it had with his test models that had crashed and splintered before he had learned he had to throw them rather than drop them. *Just do it.* It was an easy thing to think, a much harder thing to do. Again Atyen gathered himself for the leap, again he couldn't bring herself to actually launch. He took another breath, and clenched his teeth and his resolve together, and looked down to where he wanted to land, five hundred meters distant and a hundred down. That was a mistake because it seemed absolutely impossible that he could travel so and his knees went weak when he thought about it. His body simply didn't want to make the jump. *But I've worked for this for years, and I'm not taking these wings off and walking back down. I'm not. I'm not. I'm not.* He checked one last time to see that the control loops were still tight in his hands, looked to see that his ankles were still strapped in, took one more deep breath, and leapt.

There was a rush of wind, and the airflow yanked the tail up hard as he fell away, much faster than he had expected. Instinctively he brought his legs down to use the tail to slow down, but that pitched him even more steeply forward, until he was going straight down headfirst. Panicked, he raised his feet again, and he felt the wings take the sudden strain of his weight as he first leveled out and then pitched steeply up. The wind rush vanished and then he was falling backwards, twisting to the right.

He pulled hard on the left-hand line, to go back the other way, but it seemed to have no effect. Suddenly panicked, he pulled harder. The world spun, and all at once he was heading straight down again with the ground rushing up with ferocious speed. He released the line, pushed his legs back and up and managed to turn his vertical dive into something flatter just before he hit, still spiraling to the right. The right wing hit the ground first and crumpled, and then pain spiked through his shoulder as the ground hit him hard in the face. He was vaguely aware he was tumbling sideways as bamboo snapped around him. Something hit his head and the world flashed white.

A long time later he became aware of someone talking to him, shaking him, shouting at him. He tried to answer, but his mouth wouldn't form words. A face floated in front of him, seemingly disembodied, and the voice came again. He tried to move and suddenly everything hurt, his shoulder, his face, his legs. He heard someone moaning, and then realized that it was him. The forewall loomed up behind the face in front of him, and the ledge he had jumped from was impossibly high up. He was on his back, and when he tried to move again, more carefully this time, his legs wouldn't work. That made him fear paralysis, but then he realized he was simply wrapped up in the wreckage of his wings. *And I flew.*

"What happened?" The face over him belonged to a man he didn't recognize.

Atyen laughed, which made everything hurt more. "Did you see me fly?" He felt giddy despite the pain, or perhaps because of it.

"I saw you fall," The man started cutting away the torn fabric with his belt knife. There was a wall-picker's basket on his back. "Like a rock." He looked towards Atyen's feet and addressed someone he couldn't see. "Help me get him untangled."

"I *stooped!* Like a falcon." Atyen heard his own voice, full of excitement that overrode the pain. "I stooped and I flew, all the way down." He felt someone cutting away the fabric wrapped around his legs as the first man tried to free his arm of the arm supports.

"Call it what you want, you're lucky to be alive." The wallpickers finished cutting Atyen free. "Can you stand up?"

The man offered a hand and Atyen took it, got his feet beneath him and stood, shakily. There was a sharp pain in his calf and when he looked down he saw it impaled on a length of fractured bamboo frame, his blood soaking red into the cream colored fabric still attached to it. A slab of torn muscle hung loose. The second wallpicker was a woman, perhaps the first one's wife, and she knelt to examine it.

"You've really managed to hurt yourself, haven't you?" She gently pulled the splintered frame section from the wound, then tore a section from the ripped fabric of the wings and used it to staunch the bleeding.

Atyen winced at her touch, looking down on the wreckage. "My wings are ruined."

The man smirked. "Just be glad you're not ruined."

"I think your ankle is broken." She bound it with the torn fabric as well, and then stood up. "Don't worry, I've seen worse. Here, let us help you."

The man put Atyen's good arm around his neck and even that hurt, but he didn't care. "The tail was wrong, I can see that now. I always knew that was what most important part. We'll fix it though. . . ."

"We'll get you fixed first. Let's get you to the surgeons." They moved off. Pain shot through Atyen's ankle with every step, and in ten paces it had made him so dizzy he nearly blacked out again. He took a deep breath and stopped talking, concentrating on each step. His head was spinning with the pain, but what he felt more than anything was the exultation of success. He had taken the leap and truly *flown*. He had proved it possible. *More important, I proved myself.* He had survived, and when his body had healed he would do it again, farther, faster, better. He became aware of wetness on his face and wiped it away with his good arm. His hand came away solid red with blood. There was a dull, throbbing ache in his nose that he hadn't noticed before, and he reached up to touch it gingerly. Pain flared sharp and bright.

He drew a few looks from the sentinels as they came around into the grass courtyard of the Inquisitory but was beyond caring. The surgeon's hall was in an auxiliary building, built out from the main gallery, which was fortunate because it meant he wouldn't have to climb stairs. The wallpickers took him in. There was a brief conversation with the surgeon, and then he was helped onto an examination cot that was far more comfortable than it looked. A surgeon looked him over.

"He cracked his skull when he landed," the first wallpicker told the surgeon. "He was babbling."

The surgeon ran a hand over his ribs, held his eyelids open and looked carefully into each eye. "Did you lose consciousness?" he asked Atyen, and Atyen had to think hard to remember. Speaking seemed too much of an effort, and so he just nodded.

"How long?"

Atyen found the question strange. *How can I know how long when I was unconscious?* "I don't know," he managed to answer.

"Not long," put in the wallpicker. "He jumped from the fore-wall ledge, just spinward of the river outfall. We came running right away."

"He jumped from the forewall ledge?" the surgeon asked, disbelieving.

"I *flew*," said Atyen, in a voice that sounded distant in his own ears. His hurts seemed trivial compared to the knowledge of what he had accomplished.

"You've broken your nose," the surgeon said. "Hang on, this is going to hurt." Without waiting for him to answer, he took Atyen's nose and wrenched it sideways, hard. Atyen screamed with a sudden agony that came and went almost before he could register it. Fresh blood gouted from his nose, streaming down to soak his shirt.

"Tilt your head back, and pinch here." The surgeon showed him how.

"And drink this." A second surgeon, this one a woman, handed Atyen a mug of thick tea. It was awkward trying to drink with his head tilted back, but he managed to swallow small sips. The tea had a bitter taste, but by the time he had finished it the pain was fading. Atyen felt suddenly sleepy, and he closed his eyes, feeling his body relax.

"He jumped from . . ." The rest of the surgeon's words were too fuzzy to understand, and Atyen let himself drift away, feeling a pleasant languor coming over him. The wallpickers and the surgeon were still talking, and he caught the phrase "bleeding inside." He might be dying, he realized, which meant that if he went to sleep now he would never wake up. There was something sad in understanding that, and he wished the woman would take his hand and hold it, give him one last comfort as he passed. She was still talking to the first surgeon and the wallpickers though, and Atyen couldn't keep himself awake any longer. *But I flew, like a peregrine, I really flew.* If he died now, he would die complete, and he drifted off into the darkness remembering the rush of air beneath his wings.

He woke up much later, blearily aware of a dull pain in his calf and another in his ankle. They throbbed painfully, and he fell back asleep flushed and feverish. Much later he awoke to a sharper pain, to find the female surgeon examining his injury.

"That hurts," he complained, not fully awake.

"You've got an infection." She pursed her lips. "A bad one." A surgeon's errander brought in a steaming steel pot, and the surgeon took a small steel funnel with a long but narrow neck from a shelf of obscure equipment above Atyen's bed. She dropped it into the boiling pot, then scooped some more water from it into a clay jug. She took jars from the shelf, one at a time, and stirred their contents into the jug, though the only ingredient Danil recognized was honey. He was tempted to ask her for some but pain had quashed his hunger, and he didn't think he'd be able to keep it down.

"What's your name?" he asked. There was a pungent, rotten smell in the room, and he realized belatedly that it was coming from his leg.

"Bellile," she answered. She finished her concoction and stood up. "Wait here while I get some help." She went out of the lean-to and was back a few moments later with two more erranders.

"Lie right back," she said, easing him backwards onto the strawbed. When he was down she gave him a rag. "This will hurt. Bite this, and try not to move. It's easier if you relax." She motioned to the erranders. "Hold him."

The men knelt by Atyen's bedside, one leaning forward so his weight came onto his hips, the other extending his leg and leaning it on that so his calf and the wound were exposed for her to work on. Bellile tested the temperature of her mixture with a finger, then took a pair of wooden tongs from her rack and used them to fish the funnel out of the boiling water. She held it up while it steamed, and when it was cool enough to touch she put it to Atyen's wound. The pain was sudden and excruciating, and Atyen bit down hard, thrashing his head from side to side, and trying to overcome the instinct to yank his leg away. He was only partially successful in that, but the erranders did the rest of the job. *It's easier if you relax.* He did his best to relax, to lie limply and accept the burning throb as only a sensation.

Unbidden, an image of Sarabee came into his mind and he tried to focus on her face, on her smile, purely as a distraction from the pain. *She would be proud of me. Proud.* It lessened the hurt, to a degree, but he kept his eyes closed as Bellile poured her concoction into his wound. The flow of warm fluid stung, but it didn't hurt the way the insertion of the funnel had. He could feel the water running out of the wound on the other side. It felt as though he were bleeding, and he had to remind himself that he was not. She worked on the wound for quite some time, pushing the funnel deeper, pouring her medicine into it, and then repeating the process, and the experience alternated periods of greater and lesser pain. Finally the funnel came out, and the men let go of his shoulders. He could feel her dressing his wound again, with bandages made sticky with medicinal honey, but he didn't open his eyes to look.

"It's best to rest now," she told him when she was finished. It was unnecessary advice. A vast lethargy overcame him, and he was asleep in heartbeats.

When he awoke he had no idea how much time had passed, but his body told him it had been a long time. He felt feverish and hazy. *But I flew, I really flew.* Could it be it was only a dream? The pain in his leg was proof that it wasn't. There was a tremendous sense of liberation in that. There were some dried apples in a bowl on the shelf above him, and he managed to reach one, but when he tried to eat it he found he had little appetite. Bellile came in and changed the dressing on his wound, and beneath it in the flesh was hot and swollen. He slept fitfully that night, and when she came to see him after breakfast there was yellow fluid oozing out through the fabric. She looked concerned, and he kept his eyes on her face as she carefully unwrapped the bandage, wincing when the bandage stuck to his flesh. Her expression grew serious as she did, and the rank odor of infection hit his nose like a physical blow. He didn't want to look, but he couldn't help it. His calf was an angry red, swollen to twice its normal size and hot to the touch. The wound itself was an ugly mess, green and yellow pus mixed with the red of semi-clotted blood. Bellile squeezed gently and Atyen gasped as pain shot up his leg. Gouts of pus flowed out and dripped to the ground.

Atyen looked back to the surgeon, trying to read her eyes. "Am I going to lose it?" The euphoria of his success was fading, and a vision of the crippled fisher boy came to him. *Will that be me?*

She put her lips together, then moved her hands down to his forearm, and into his hand. "Your toes are still warm, that's a good sign. For the rest, it's too early to tell."

The treatment was the same as they had given him the day before, the boiling of the funnel, the preparation of the honey concoction, the rag to bite on and the erranders to hold him down against the pain. It hurt worse than it had the first time, hurt so badly he saw stars and his ears rang, and he thought he would bite right through the rag. It was what he had to endure if he wanted to keep his leg, and so he bit hard and squeezed his eyes shut, and held himself as still as possible so Bellile could work. At some point he must have passed out, and he dreamed he was flying again, soaring high above the clouds to find the place the falcons lived. All of a sudden his wings were gone and he was falling, watching the ground rush up to kill him. He woke in a cold sweat, to find himself trembling and feverish. The swelling now extended from his calf all the way to his foot, and his toes tingled. He tried to sit up and found the effort made him dizzy. When he lay down again he found himself unable to sleep, though too feverish to think clearly. Eventually he lapsed into a semi-waking delirium. All sense of time vanished, though at some point he was vaguely aware of Solender by his bedside, saying things Atyen couldn't understand. *Chiding me, no doubt.* Later he went through the cleaning process again, but though the pain was intense he felt strangely disconnected from it, as though he were merely watching the procedure happening to someone else. Some time after that an errander brought him soup, but he couldn't bring himself to swallow more than a couple of spoonfuls. By then the swelling had spread to his toes. They were numb now, and cold when he touched them with his other hand. Bellile examined him again and shook her head.

"It's going to have to come off. I'm sorry."

Atyen looked at her, not wanting to understand what he'd heard. "Not my leg. You can't."

"You'll die if I don't."

Bellile's expression was serious, and Atyen felt cold despair seep into his heart. "I'll be useless, what will I do?"

She smiled at him gently. "You're young and strong. You'll adapt."

He shook his head. "There must be something you can do. You can clean it again, I don't care how much it hurts."

"The honey wash is helping in the wound, but the contagion is moving beyond it, and the swelling is cutting off your circulation."

Atyen looked up at her, still not wanting to accept what she was saying. "There must be something," he repeated.

She looked at him for a long moment, considering. Finally she spoke. "I can try leeches."

"Leeches?"

"To keep blood moving through your leg. It's worked before." She paused. "It's failed before too."

"The worst that can happen is it won't work and I'll lose my leg, right?"

Bellile shook her head. "The worst that can happen is you'll die. Once the infection is in your blood, it spreads. Sometimes fast, sometimes slow. With you it's slow, so far. That can change."

"I don't want to live without my leg, surgeon."

"I'll try. First I have to see if I can catch some leeches."

She went away and Atyen waited, exhausted. Eventually he slept and dreamed dreams too fragmented to even try to reconstruct. When he woke up she still wasn't there, but his foot felt funny. When he looked at it he recoiled in horror. There was a fat leech hanging from each toe, already noticeably distended. It took an effort to stop himself from reaching down to pull them off. He looked away and tried not to think about it, but even the thought of the bloodsuckers made him nauseous. Only a long time later did he realize that it was probably a good sign that his foot felt funny rather than numb. His lower leg was still swollen though, and the infected area was still spreading up past his knee. The next days passed in a blur. He was getting worse, he could tell, and once when he moved from fitful sleep to waking delirium he vaguely recalled a conversation where Bellile was again trying to convince him to let her amputate. He had to check to see if his leg was still there, though the throbbing pain should have told him at once. *I'm not thinking clearly.* The realization was distant, and he felt oddly unconcerned with the realization that he might well be dying. Sleep was his only respite, as shallow as it was.

He woke another time to find Bellile kneeling over him.

"Drink this," she told him, and held a cup to his lips. It was some kind of broth, and he sipped it.

"Am I going to keep my leg?"

She hesitated. "It's too late to amputate." Her pause, and her expressive face told him much more than her words.

"Am I going to live?"

"Drink this." She held the cup to his lips again to stave off more questions. Her eyes told him what her words held back.

He took a few more sips and fell back, exhausted by the effort. The feverish sleep returned, and he dreamed again of soaring, and of falling. At some point he became aware of the now-familiar stabbing pain in his leg and was blearily aware of bodies over him, holding him down. He tried to struggle and found he couldn't even do that. Eventually the pain faded to a distant numbness and the dreams returned. He awoke again, some timeless time later, to find himself drenched in sweat and chilled to the bone, shaking with cold and a deep down nausea that wrenched at his gut. He had lost all track of time, by bell or even the day. Sleeping and waking merged into a feverish blur and all he could do was wish for it to be over. Eventually he even stopped caring if he recovered or if he died, either would be a release from the nightmare he was now inhabiting.

Eventually his fever broke and he fell into a deep and dreamless sleep. When he woke up he found Bellile bending over him, putting a cool cloth on his forehead.

"How are you feeling?"

Atyen tried to speak and found he couldn't. He swallowed hard and tried again, with better results. "I'm sore, and thirsty. Can I have some water?"

The surgeon nodded and went to a barrel in the corner of the room, and brought him back a mug full. He drank it down and gave it back for the surgeon to fill again. "How long have I been sleeping?"

"Three days. You had us worried for a while. Did you really jump off the forewall ledge?"

Atyen nodded, slowly and carefully so as not to worsen his headache. "Yes. I did." He considered explaining about his wings, but decided it would be too much effort. *Let her think I'm crazy, she will anyway.*

But whatever Bellile thought she kept to herself, as she deftly unwrapped the dressing on Atyen's calf. She manipulated it slowly, which made him wince. "Ouch."

"You're going to live," she told him. "And you're going to keep your leg."

"Are you sure?" he asked, surprised. He felt weak but clearheaded for the first time since the infection had taken hold.

"You'll walk with a limp, but you'll walk. Your fever is gone, the swelling is gone. I've taken off the leeches."

Atyen looked at his leg to see dark red scabs at regular intervals, where the bloodsuckers had been attached. The swelling in his calf had subsided, though it still throbbed painfully, and he didn't look too closely at the red mess where the injury was healing. "Thank you."

"It was a close thing." She untied his dressing to examine the wound. "It would have killed a lot of men. You have a strong heart." She moved up to look at Atyen's nose. "This is going to heal crooked, I'm afraid. Are you hungry?"

"Starving."

"I'll have some food brought in."

The surgeon finished her examination and went out, leaving Atyen to rest and run over his leap in his mind. Eventually an errander arrived with a rich broth of mutton and root vegetables. Atyen wolfed it down, suddenly realizing how hungry he was. The errander left and he slept again. That set the trend for the next days. He ate, slept, was examined, and all the while he fretted about the changes he wanted to make to his wings. On the first day he tried to get up and go back to Solender's studio, but his ankle was still broken and wouldn't take his weight. He considered crawling, but he wouldn't be able to work on his hands and knees and so abandoned the thought. Bellile had cut out almost half his calf muscle trying to halt the spread of infection, and it was all he could do to stand and support himself against the wall. His leg would give him trouble for the rest of his life . . . *But I might not have had it at all.* That evening meal he ate the first solid food he had since his fall, and Solender came to visit him.

"Look, I chose you because I thought you were smart. Now you're making me look foolish."

"I flew. I proved it could be done."

"You nearly killed yourself in the process. I've got a lot of years invested in teaching you to think. Good aspirants aren't so common that I can afford to lose one so easily."

"But—"

"But me no buts." Solender looked closer at Atyen's leg. "At least this will keep you on the ground, for a while." He took a thick sheaf of paper from his back bag. "Here, I brought you more tithesheets. You can make yourself useful while you heal."

Atyen sighed. "What do you need to know now?"

"I need to know why the horses died. They were work animals, not food animals, so they weren't all eaten."

"I wish I'd never heard of horses."

"Then we're even. I wish you'd never heard of peregrines."

"You could always forbid me from flying."

The Chief Inquisitor snorted. "I've already forbidden you from flying alone, but that didn't work. Will it work better if I forbid it outright? Burying you in tithesheets is the best I can do. I'm under no illusion that it'll stop you from throwing yourself off the forewall again, but at least I'll get some useful work out of you before you die."

"I won't die, I understand what went wrong."

"We all die, sooner or later. With you it's going to be sooner, if you don't learn that you shouldn't do dangerous things by yourself. What you *think* you understand is what's going to kill you." Solender dropped the tithesheets on Atyen's lap. "Consider this your penance."

Atyen started to protest, but found he had nothing to say. Solender was right, and the fact that he preferred to work on his own was little defense. He picked up the sheets. "I'll do my best," he said.

"You'd better."

Solender left, and Atyen reluctantly started working through the sheets. In two days Bellile declared him fit enough to leave, and with his calf still bandaged and walking with a staff, Atyen went back to Solender's studio. It was hard to see the wreckage of his wings, unceremoniously piled in a corner, with his blood still soaked into the torn fabric. He picked up the splintered mainspine, ran his fingers over the resin soaked sinew where the struts joined each other. None of his joints had failed in the crash, which meant they were stronger than the wood itself. He smiled to himself. *This much was successful.* Already he could see ways to improve his the design, a better tail was just the beginning. *Soon!* He turned away, looking at the mounted kites and the drawings in his corner of the workspace. His journal was in its place on his workshelf, and almost without thinking he sat down and opened it, dipped a pen in an ink jar, and sketched out a rough outline for the new tail. It was not what he should have been doing, and every time another aspirant came into the studio he found himself looking over his shoulder to see if it was Solender. *I should be in the reading room.* The work was so engrossing that it was hard even to stop for the length of time required to go to the tower, but he forced himself to. There was no need to annoy his doctrinor unnecessarily.

The stairs to the top of the tower were a challenge for his injured leg, and it occurred to him that it would be no more effort to climb to the forewall ledge that it was to go up the manuscript tower. *I could get someone else to carry the wings.* His injury wouldn't matter in the air, and bringing someone else would satisfy Solender's safety concerns, though if he crashed again he'd need help waiting on the ground, and not up on the forewall. He bit his lip, considering who he might ask for the favor. *Corl, perhaps, or Alzin.* Among the other aspirants in Solender's studio they were the ones most likely to be helpful, but even so the idea of asking for help made Atyen uncomfortable. *And that's for the future.* It was one thing to sneak sketches into his journal, but he knew Solender wouldn't let him build a new set of wings until he had made some significant progress on the question of horses. He finished his outline sketch of the new tail, and then, because he knew he'd be unable to concentrate on anything else until he had his ideas down, went over the mechanography of the wing slots. He could get more control by putting more flex into the outer trailing edge, without compromising the rigidity of the main structure.

When that was done he sighed and got down to the task at hand. Surprisingly he found it more engrossing than he might have thought. The mystery of what had become of the horses and cattles was compelling.

Since he couldn't fly, tracking down their story became Atyen's life. As he dug deeper into the archives he amassed a sizable pile of documentation to prove that they had existed. He'd discovered a great deal about cattle as well. Once they'd been used as meat beasts, like sheep and chickens, but on a much larger scale. Both horses and cattle also served as work animals, and horses in particular were far more powerful than goats. Solender went over his conclusions on the top floor of the manuscript tower, stroking his chin as he read.

"They're big," he said, when he came to the inked illustration in three views that had first impressed Atyen. "I didn't imagine they'd be so large."

"Perhaps even larger than they look, if people have grown smaller over time," Atyen said, recalling his conclusion about the stairs.

Solender nodded. "Perhaps. Why did they vanish?"

"Well, I've gone over the records." Atyen turned to his carefully annotated numbers. "There were more and more of them, at one point every farm in the world had dozens, and then all at once the numbers started dropping. In ten years they went from thousands to nothing. Once the last ones were gone . . ." He shrugged. "That was it."

"But *why*?"

"I don't know. Yet."

"Hmmph. How long did it take for the population to peak?"

Atyen ruffled through his pages, ran a finger down a column of numbers. "They were fairly stable for a long time, a hundred and twenty years before the crash is when they started increasing." He pursed his lips. "It's a pattern very close to your overpopulated mice, but over a much longer span of time."

Solender stroked his chin, thinking. "No, I don't think they're like the mice."

"Why not?"

"These are farm animals, not wild ones. If the population grew it's because people bred more of them. If the population fell it's because people bred less."

"Why would they breed fewer? They seem like such useful animals."

"I don't know." Solender paused again, thinking. "If there were as many of these things as they say there were, there must be bones somewhere."

Atyen's heart fell. "Finding them will take forever." *And I'll never get to fly. . . .*

"Don't worry, my eager peregrine," Solender answered, reading his thoughts. "This is too big to leave in your hands. I'll have to convince the Law Council to help, and *that's* what's going to take forever. In the meantime, you can go flying again."

Atyen's heart leapt at his doctrinor's words, but Solender didn't let him off right away. First, he assigned him to look through the old property surveys the tithecounters mapped out to calculate their tithe calls. What he wanted him to find was a butcher's garbage pit in Charisy, one old enough to contain the bones of ancient horses and cattles. It was a clever idea and Atyen accepted the task uncomplainingly, both because he knew complaining would do him no good, and because he didn't expect it would be hard to find the site he was looking for. He did find it too, on a map fourteen hundred years old. What he hadn't expected to find was that Charisy itself was moving. On old maps the city was foreward of where it was now, and the older the maps the farther foreward it was. The motion was considerable, an average of two meters a year. It was a baffling finding. His first thought was that it was a social phenomenom, with people abandoning the poorer foreward districts and building on the aftward side of the city, but when he looked closer he saw that while the city's road network had grown, its core hadn't significantly changed in all that time. The only possible conclusion was that the roads themselves were moving along with the buildings, which in turn meant that the very ground had to be moving. *And that's just crazy.* Solender had drilled into him that in research an explanation that seemed too complex was probably wrong, and so he went up to the tithe-counter's hall to find out how they were doing the measurements.

"It's simple enough," said the senior tithecounter, a tall, spare man with thinning grey hair and what looked to be permanent ink stains on his fingertips. "The surveyors can't be absolutely accurate, and we make allowances for that. Two meters on a kilometer section is an acceptable error."

"Yes, but it's two meters the same way each year," Atyen protested.

"The important thing is that the tithes come out properly," the tithecounter answered.

"But don't you see what this means? The ground can't be moving, you've got a systematic error in the way you do your surveys."

"Perhaps." The man looked at the maps Atyen had brought with him. His white and blue cross-sash was faded to the point that the colors were hard to distinguish in the dim light of the counter's hall. "I think these older ones are probably just badly done."

"Three kilometers badly done?"

"Perhaps. What we care about is how big a plot is, and what it's planted with. Whether it's located a little bit this way or that way is less important." The man's tone suggested that it was actually completely unimportant, and that Atyen was wasting his time. Technically Atyen's red-green cross-sash outranked his, but having an aspirant a third of his age question his methodology didn't sit well with him. "I can get you a surveyor to talk to if you like."

"I would," he said, and the tithecounter called over an errander, who took him to another part of the hall.

"The surveyors are usually out, there's only four of them," the errander told him, preparing him for dissappointment. There was a surveyor in though, bent over a workshelf, a woman in upper middle age, poring over a half-drawn map with a pair of dividers. She was happy, even eager, to show Atyen how her specialty worked. Her primary tool was what she called a measuring circle, a tripod with a wooden arm on top that moved around a scale disc inscribed with angles. The arm was equipped with small steel sighting tubes at either end, and it moved vertically against a second metal scale that measured its angle. A dangling weight was used to make sure it was level.

"You sight through the tubes to your reference point," the surveyor told him, and showed him the tables which converted angular measurements into linear distances. "Fore and aft we always use the point where the suntube intersects the foredome," "Spinward and antispinward is harder, because everything is referenced from the Inquisitory tower as a known fixed point, but most of the time you can't see it because of the mist, so we have to use intermediate points and triangulate."

"But the foredome curves inward a good kilometer. What do you do if you're foreward of its apex?"

"We work from known reference points, the same as we do for spinwise measurements. Fortunately we don't often have to, since no one farms that far foreward."

"And how accurate can you be?"

"It depends. Within five meters of where we think we should be is acceptable. Under a meter is good."

"What if the errors all come out the same way?"

"What do you mean?"

Atyen explained what he'd found and showed her the old survey maps. The surveyor looked surprised. "I'd have to see their data to know where they went wrong. It's hard to imagine a measurement error that big; it would be obvious you were out. It's probably a mistake in calculation."

"That large?"

"If they didn't check it."

"Every time, systematically?"

The surveyor shrugged. "What else could it be?"

Atyen nodded, and asked if he could borrow one of the instruments. The surveyor gave him one, and a brief demonstration on how to set it up, level it and take a sighting. She gave him a field map too, with all the most recent survey data on it. He thanked her and took it down and outside. The forewall mists were thick and chill, so he hiked aftward and out of them. His leg was still weak, and he was sore with the effort before he reached the forefields and a position where he could get a good angle on the suntube. He set up the measuring circle at the corner of a plowed field and the road, verifying on his survey map, levelled it and aimed the arm upwards to the foredome's apex.

The technique was trickier than it seemed. It was simple enough to take the sightings but when he sat down to do the calculations he found that no two measurements agreed. In two solid bells of experimentation he mostly learned that there was a great deal more skill involved in using the simple instrument than was readily apparent. After working through the math his errors in position were nowhere close to two meters, he was lucky to get within fifty. Frustrated, he sat down and unfurled the old maps of Charisy. *Does it even matter?* If the surveyors were wrong, they were wrong. If the horses were gone, they were gone. If people were taller in the past what possible impact could that have on the present? Solender was worried that an overcrowded humanity might vanish from the world as overcrowded mice vanished from a box, but was that a realistic possibility? Atyen lay down on his back and looked up at the patchwork of fields arching over the suntube. *Not likely.* People weren't mice. *But in case they are, I have to waste time doing this.* He let his imagination flow back to the exhilaration of his first flight, yearning to relive the experience. A gull flew overhead, and he sighed. He searched for a peregrine, but saw none.

Jens was a fisher, used to the water and the docks and the market in Tidings. He had never been even as far as Charisy, and he found the bustling city with its looming buildings and crowded, narrow streets intimidating. Even before he reached the bridge that marked the edge of the city proper the trading road was jammed, handcarts and pedestrians competing for space on the rough-cobbled roads, and the surrouding fields were overflowing with the improvised shelters of those who had nowhere else to go. He avoided them as much as he could, turned onto a side street as soon as he was into the city. It was a longer route, but there were fewer people and Jens felt more comfortable out of the crowd. Charisy was most prosperous on the aftward side, less so on the foreward side, and the streets grew narrower and the houses smaller as he went. Beggars were common, many of them drunk, and groups of young toughs stood in doorways, sizing up passersby. He walked quickly through them, avoiding eye contact as he passed people on the road. Soon enough he was through the city, and he breathed out unconsciously as he again found his feet on the trading road going foreward. The suntube vanished behind the forewall overcast, and the looming steel of the Inquisitory was intimidating as he drew closer. It was ringed by a low, grass-covered mound, too regular to be accidental, although he couldn't see why anyone would go to the effort to build it. An array of strange machinery filled the grassy courtyard before the main structure, and he kept his distance from it. Sentinels seemed to be everywhere, and he'd seen far too many of them since the attack on Sarabee. Though the case was clearly one of self defense the entire process of inquisition had been nerve wracking.

*But here I am* . . . He took a deep breath, and walked through the huge door that was the main entrance to the steel structure. It led to an impressive antechamber, framed in heavy wooden beams. There was a workshelf there, behind it sat a sentinel, a middle-aged woman with the red and white cross-sash of a watchkeeper.

"Your business?" she asked, her face betraying her skepticism that a fisher could have any business at all in the Inquisitory.

"I'm here for Atyen Horun," he told her, trying to sound as if he came to the Inqisitory all the time. Two more sentinels, blade armed, stood by the inner door.

Her eyebrows went up. "Oh? And who is he?"

"An inquisitor," Jens hesitated, unsure of the protocols of address. "Or rather, he's an aspirant."

"An aspirant?" The sentinel's already low assessment of Jens fell visibly. "Is he expecting you?"

"No, but he said to come if—"

She cut him off with a gesture. "Your name?"

"Jens. Jens Madane." The other sentinels were looking on with interest now, and Jens felt embarrassed and uncomfortable. *I shouldn't have come.* A fisher had no place in the halls of power.

"A moment," the woman said, and consulted some papers on her workshelf. After a moment she shook her head. "You aren't listed."

"But . . ."

"I'm afraid the aspirants are very busy. You can apply for an audience at the Hall of Inquisition in your parish." The tone of her voice told Jens the matter was closed.

*But I've come all this way.* Something told Jens that pleading wouldn't work. "He gave me this," he said, taking Atyen's message ball from a pocket and showing it to the woman. He felt embarrassed as he did, expecting her to laugh at his pathetic attempt to establish some kind of authority for his visit with a little wooden trinket. *But it's marked with the shield and blade, and it's all I've got.*

The sentinel's eyes widened as she took it from him, widened more as she examined it. "Where did you get this?"

"I told you, Atyen gave it to me."

"This is the Chief Inquisitor's mark," she said. There was suspicion in her voice, but Jens could sense that something had changed in his favor.

"Atyen gave it to me," he answered with more confidence. "He said to show it if I ever needed to see him." Not quite true, but close enough.

"I see." The woman gave the message ball back reluctantly. "Come with me."

She led Jens past the other sentinels and into the next room. There were benches in the entry area, and she gestured to them. "Wait here." Her tone was brusque. She wanted Jens to know she respected the ball's authority, not his.

*But that doesn't matter, I'm here. I'll see Atyen.* Jens went over and sat while the watchkeeper called over an errander. The errander bustled off and Jens settled himself to watch the world as it came to the Inqisitory. Almost everyone who came through the door wore a cross-sash: erranders, waterkeepers, full and half inquisitors, even his own tithecounter. They all seemed busy, going past the sentinels with only a cursory nod and then disappearing into the depths of the Inqisitory. None paid him any attention, which was fine with Jens. *Especially the tithecounter.* His last hauls hadn't been all that he had hoped, but he had tithed on even less. He'd gotten away with it . . . *And a man has to feed his family.* Still, it hadn't been a comfortable feeling, especially while he was under inquisition over the attack. He took a deep breath to relax himself, and remind himself that Atyen had promised to keep any transgression secret. He waited through two bells at least, and then the watchkeeper called him over.

"Errander Rote will take you in," she said. "Aspirant Horun is in the manuscript tower." She indicated a short, plump man with a yellow errander's sash across his chest.

The man bowed slightly. "Come with me," he said.

Jens followed him down a corridor and back out of the gallery, down a path and into the looming bulk of the huge structure. Inside it was hushed, and he was led up a set of spiraling stairs, past quiet, curtained spaces and rooms full of shelved manuscripts. On the top floor were large windows covered in waxed flax, and tables with aspirants poring over manuscripts. Atyen looked up when Jens came in. A smile spread over his face, but he put a finger to his lips.

"We have to be quiet here," he whispered. "We'll talk downstairs." He picked up a staff from the floor and led Jens back down a flight. He was walking with a limp and used the staff to help himself with the stairs, something Jens had never seen before. On the floor below were a series of small rooms, set around the outside of the tower. Each was just large enough for a table and four chairs. Atyen ushered Jens into one of them and closed the door behind them.

"We can talk here without disturbing anyone." He embraced Jens. "My friend, I'm glad you came."

"What happened to your leg?"

Atyen laughed. "I tried to fly. How is Sarabee? You must have a newborn by now."

"Three months old, a boy." Despite his discomfort Jens couldn't help but smile as he thought of Jerl. "She's well, Atyen, very well, but we've had trouble."

"Trouble? Tell me."

Jens swallowed hard, and told his friend about the invasion of his home. "The inquisitors from Tidings are investigating," he finished. "I'm worried what might happen."

"What might happen?" Atyen registered surprise. "They try to rape your wife, a woman who'd just given birth. They try to kill you in your own home. They'll get fourteen years servitude if they're lucky. You have nothing to worry about."

"I worry anyway. One of them is the son of the reeve of Tidings."

"So? The reeve has no influence on an inquisition."

"That's the way it's supposed to be, but I'm not convinced, Atyen. The reeve has power, and Sarabee has been so upset, and . . ." He hesitated, reluctant to tell Atyen everything, even though that's exactly what he had come so far to do. ". . . and I don't want a tithe collector looking too closely."

Atyen nodded slowly, biting his lip, and Jens fretted while his friend thought.

"What can I do?" Atyen asked at last.

"Can you come?"

The scholar smiled. "I'll come, Jens. Of course I'll come."

Jens bit his lip, suddenly sorry he'd asked. "I'll understand if you don't, I didn't know . . ." He made a gesture.

"About my leg? You couldn't know, and it's mostly healed anyway. The surgeon says walking is the best thing I can do."

"I'm grateful, Atyen."

"I promised I'd visit more last time I came. It's about time I made good on that." Atyen paused. "I want to say though . . . there's nothing I can really do, to help I mean. Only the Chief Inquisitor can change a verdict."

"But he's your doctrinor . . ."

"Which only means I work for him. He doesn't take my counsel on law. Or on anything. I take his, or at least I'm supposed to."

Atyen laughed the way he did when he'd told a joke meant only for himself, and Jens nodded. "I'd still like you to come, Atyen. Sarabee is beside itself, she'd feel better you were there."

"And I will, of course. I'm still shocked."

"You asked me to watch for anything strange. This is it. Fights are common enough. Young men . . ." He shrugged. "Well, fights were common when we were young too, but to break into a man's home and . . . and . . ." Jens closed his mouth, unable to finish.

"And try to rape his wife in front of his children, his newborn. And one of them the son of the reeve." Atyen shook his head. "You're right, this isn't a good sign."

"There's been more. I mean, nothing like this, but Tidings is full of young men with not enough to do. They go around looking for work; when they don't find it sometimes they steal, sometimes they fight. Sometimes they kill each other. It's just what you said last time. I hadn't noticed before, but after you left I started thinking. Things are changing. People don't trust each other as much, people don't share the way they used to. This . . . incident . . . I never had to bar my door before, but now Sarabee can't sleep if I don't. To tell the truth, I can't either."

"Mice."

"What?" Jens looked at him, not understanding.

"Nothing. Or rather, nothing definite. It seems people don't react well to being overcrowded. You said those boys asked Sarabee for food when they came to your door."

"They did."

"I can't speak for the other two, but the reeve's son wasn't missing any meals, I'll guarantee that."

"So what were they doing? I mean, other than the obvious."

"I don't know, but I need to find out. Tell me about your tithing."

"There's little to tell. There's only so many carp, my family is growing." Jens shrugged. "I won't see my children go hungry. Would you ask me to?"

"You know I wouldn't. But tell me, why did you choose to have more children when you were already struggling?"

Jens hesitated, not sure he wanted to share the intimacies of his marriage even with Atyen. *But he needs to know, and so I have to tell him.* "Sarabee wanted them," he answered. "I wanted to stop at two."

"Do you know why she wanted more?"

Jens shrugged. "She likes children. Who am I to tell her she can't have them?"

"Did you talk about how many you could support?"

"We did . . . or at least I did, but . . . well, you may remember how determined she can be when she decides she's going to do something."

"Like a force of nature." Atyen nodded. "I remember."

"I don't want you to get the wrong idea. We didn't fight about it. I love her, I love our children, she wanted a boy and I did too. I wouldn't trade one of them away. It's just . . ."

"It's just that four is a lot," Jens finished for him.

"Four is a lot to feed. It isn't so large for a family anymore. I know some with eight."

"Eight?" Atyen registered surprise. "How can anyone manage . . ."

"I don't know, but they do."

Atyen nodded slowly. "I should have expected that. The population is going up, somebody's got to be having more children." A wry smile crossed his face. "And I thought I had too many brothers. At least you've only got one son."

"That's not so important for fishers. We don't have land to divide."

"Are you having more children?"

"No, we're done, Sarabee and I agreed on that. Do you think we could really run out of food?" Jens asked. "I mean, not just one family but all of us."

"I don't know." Atyen paused, thinking. "We keep producing more food on less land, but there's got to be a limit somewhere. It isn't going to happen next year. Maybe something will change and it won't happen ever, but it's our job to think about these things. When's the inquisition being held?"

"Next week. But if it's troublesome . . ."

"I already said I would come. In truth I think I need to. It's not the best timing, but friendship and duty are both calling, and it gives me an excuse to get out of here."

Jens nodded. "What did you do to your leg, Atyen, really?"

"I tried to fly."

Jens gave his friend a look, and Atyen laughed. "No joke. I'll show you my wings."

Jens laughed with him. "Even Noah couldn't fly."

"He flew, and he fell. So did I." Atyen smiled ruefully. "Fortunately, I didn't fall too hard."

"What, you just flapped your wings and . . . ?"

"They aren't flapping wings. No, I jumped off the forewall ledge."

Jens shook his head. "I can never decide if you're brilliant or just crazy."

"Neither can I." A strange smile came across Atyen's face. "But I flew, Jens. I really flew."

"And nearly crippled yourself. You need a good woman, Atyen, she'd keep you grounded." Jens laughed at his inadvertent pun. "Both ways."

"You know inquisitors can't marry."

Jens shook his head. "You work so hard, and for what? To live under a bunch of rules that make it impossible to enjoy what you've worked so hard for. I've never understood that."

"It keeps the Inquisition honest. People with no children have no reason to bias the law." Atyen laughed. "Or at least that's the theory."

"I mean, I've never understood why you chose it."

"I used to think I knew. Now I think I was fooling myself, but I'm here now. And I really did get to fly." Atyen smiled. "I have some things to do here, but I'll be down tomorrow, or the day after at the latest." He stood up and put a hand on Jens's shoulder. "Don't worry. The reeve has no influence. It's going to be fine."

"I hope so." Jens bit his lip, relieved that Atyen was coming and at the same time reminded of the source of his worry.

"It's going to be fine."

"Maybe this time." Jens shook his head. "What kind of world are my children going to grow up in?"

"A good one. The Chief Inquisitor is the smartest man I know, and he's taking this seriously." Atyen smiled encouragingly. "The world's been around a long time. It isn't going anywhere in a hurry."

Jens nodded, finding relief in the words. "You're right, it's just . . ." He hesitated, unsure if he should say what he was about to say. "It's different when you have a family."

"I'm sure it is," answered Atyen. "I'm glad you came, Jens. It's good to see you."

Jens stood up. "It's good to see you too." He embraced the scholar. "Thank you, Atyen."


The meeting chamber of the Chief Inquisitor was a space from another time, with its heavy, polished oak table and elaborately embroidered wall quilts. Ek Solender ran a hand over its surface, polished to a high sheen by the sleeves and parchments of generations of inquisitors, and contemplated the symbolism of the ancient surface. The table was round, its top made from jointed slabs quartersawn a meter and a half across. What problems had his predecessors faced as they sat around it? Unrest in the population, plagues of mice and plagues of grain-fail, the enforcement of law and the changing of it, the ambitions of the powerful and the failings of the weak, and certainly problems he couldn't dream of. At some point some long forgotten Chief Inquisitor had gathered counsel because the last cattle had died, and the last horse. Whatever solution they had come up with, they hadn't been able to resurrect the dead.

But the world had carried on, and if it hadn't arrived at Heaven, neither had it descended into Hell. The problems had been adapted to, if not solved. *Perhaps it's only the human condition that solving one problem simply uncovers another.* Solender took his place to wait for the arrival of the others. His chair was the same as all the others, there was no ornamentation to mark him as first among equals; it was considered unseemly for inquisitors to make much of their rank. Still, he sat at the head of the table, and nobody was in any doubt as to his position. There was a subtlety there, one Solender hadn't recognized until he had joined the law council himself and learned the delicate game of power. A rank symbol had to be large enough to be recognized and no larger, and by downplaying the importance of the symbol the Inquisition only magnified the stature of the man who held the position.

His senior inquisitors filtered in and took their places, an errander came in to pour tea. Solender waited until they were all assembled, and then held up his hand for silence.

"We face a problem," he said. The assembled senior inquisitors listened attentively. "It's very simple. We either find a way to deal with our population, or we preside over the end of the Second Inquisition, and perhaps of humanity. . . ."

"I object to those words," Inquisitor Vesene harrumphed. "We know humanity started with the builders, and for all we know they built more worlds than ours. It's overdramatic to claim we'll see the end of the human race."

Solender looked at him, annoyed at the interruption. Vesene was a man who'd gained his position through diligence rather than brilliance, and he was a man who was determined to be the next Chief Inquisitor. "Overdramatic? Forgive me my sin, inquisitor. I'll take comfort in knowing that when every single person between the aftwall and the forewall is dead, then perhaps some other people in some other place might yet live on. Will you feel better if I confine my remarks to the fall of the Inquisition?"

"Accuracy is important," Vesene said, somewhat defensively. "It's the heart of knowledge."

"I'll try to be more accurate then," Solender answered, then turned his attention back to the table. "The mathematics are simple. Every year we have more people and less food. What happens when we can't feed everyone? That's a question I don't want to answer. Which means the question we must answer is, how can we stop that from happening?"

"What's your evidence?" asked Inquisitor Cela Joss, looking up from her worksheaf.

"I've had one of my aspirants digging through the records. He's found quite a lot of interesting information. First thing, there are entire species of food animal that have vanished. Second thing, for a thousand years at least the population has been stable, until the last three generations. I suspect it's been stable far longer than that, but that's as far back as we've gone, so far."

"That's hardly evidence," said Joss, pressing her lips together.

"Look around you. There are more people alive today than there have ever been."

"And so what if there are?" put in Vesene.

"So what? We can only grow so much food on a tare, inquisitor. It was hunger that ended the First Inquisition. A great hunger. Look here." Solender slid his worksheaf down the smooth tabletop. "This is what my aspirant has found. That creature on the top is called a horse. They're huge beasts, as big as five men, maybe ten."

Vesene picked up the sheaf before Joss could, looked at the drawing, put it down. "What are you talking about? There's no such creature." His tones were dismissive.

"Not anymore. They were all eaten. So was that beast on the bottom. It was called a cattle, and they were once farmed by the thousands. Turn the page."

Vesene gave Solender a look, he didn't like being told what to do by the man he wanted to replace, but he had no reason to object, and so he did.

"The chart shows food production, and the census figures, and the number of horses and cattle," Solender went on. "The period straddles the time of the collapse of the First Inquisition."

"The First Inquisition fell when the suntube went out," Joss put in. She didn't add *any fool knows that.* Her tone said it for her.

Solender hadn't expected such immediate resistance to what

he was presenting. *But Vesene is ambitious and Joss is his leashed badger.* They couldn't demonstrate their leadership by agreeing with what the Chief Inquisitor said. *But if they want to look like fools, I can help them do that.* He took a deep breath, sipped his tea to calm himself. "And what happened when the suntube went out?" he asked.

"People panicked. It started the lineage war."

"So say the histories, but that's not quite right. Look at the numbers. The suntube went out and the crops failed. People went hungry, their animals went hungry. The horses went first. They were for work, not meat, so they were starved to feed the cattle, but the cattle didn't last much longer. The orchards died, the seedstock got eaten, and suddenly there were more people than the land could support. They fought, and the fighting got in the way of farming. Maybe they ate each other. Half the population died in three years, and the Inquisition fell."

"And rose again," Vesene said. "It couldn't have been so bad, they were still keeping records. I see a lot of numbers. I don't see any proof." He passed the worksheaf down the table. Having touched it and found it wanting he had no further use for it. "For myself, I find the war explanation enough for the death rate."

"Then look closer," Solender rejoined. "Don't you see, starvation and war go hand-in-hand."

"I don't believe it. There are more people alive today than there were then, far more. We aren't starving. And unless you're predicting the suntube will go out again, I don't see what the problem is."

"People were larger then, and they shared the world with these huge animals. Maybe there were other factors as well. And our problem isn't the suntube, and it isn't the absolute numbers, it's the rate of growth. We're going to hit a limit. I don't know what it is, I do know we're closing in on it. Fast."

"With all respect," Vesene answered in a tone that carried no respect whatsoever. "I think you're exaggerating. But even if your conjecture has any weight, what are you proposing we do? Ban women from having children?"

"If necessary." Solender pursed his lips.

"If necessary?" Vesene was incredulous. "You've lost your mind. If anything can start a war, that will."

"You'd rather see mass starvation?"

"If I can interrupt . . ." Inquisitor Norlan Renn stood up. "I'm just a builder, I don't know much about crops and tithes, but this is a serious problem, if it's happening, and the solution will be equally serious, if it's necessary. I don't know if I'm convinced by your evidence, Chief Inquisitor, but with such a weighty issue I can't see how we can ignore it."

"What are you saying?" Vesene broke in before Solender could answer.

Renn turned to face him. "That we should study the problem and such prudent action as the results call for. We're inquisitors. We judge on facts, not emotions."

"Thank you, Renn," Solender said, relieved to have some support.

"Emotions, there's nothing here but emotion," Vesene said contemptuously. "I don't see a single fact, nothing but raw conjecture."

Solender sighed. "I think that common sense—"

"Common sense tells me that you've lost yours," Vesene snapped.

Solender stood up, his jaw clenching. "Inquisitor Vesene, I am the Chief Inquisitor, and if you are unwilling to accept what I am bringing before the council today, I expect you, at a minimum, to pay me and your fellows the respect of listening. I don't pretend to have all the answers, I don't pretend to even fully understand the problem, but I know it exists. As Inquisitor Renn says, we would be remiss in our duty if we ignored it."

"We'll be strung up on crosses if we try to stop people from having babies." Vesene pursed his lips. "Every sentinel in the world couldn't save us." He stood up as well. "You come in here with stories of mythical beasts, and you expect us to *believe* you? You come in here with wild tales of war? It's been twelve hundred years since the First Inquisition fell. Justice brings peace, we all know that. I can think of nothing less just than to deny people their children."

"Study the problem," Solender pointed at the worksheaf that Vesene had discarded. "You're an inquisitor, so inquire, and then tell me there's no danger. I have a bright young man from the shorefields who tells me that things are getting critical down there. The average size of a farmhold has fallen to a quarter tare, the smallest are barely an eighth."

"I've got enough inquiry to do on my own. Have one of your aspirants do it."

Solender took a deep breath, and forced himself to sit down

and take some more tea before he spoke again. When he did his voice was level. "I've already done that. That's the work I just put in front of you, if you'd condescend to read it. It shows that we have a food crisis coming in our near future. That's why I'm sharing my concerns with you now."

"And yet no one is going hungry," Joss put in.

"I've got beggars in Charisy," said Torr Toorman, Inquisitor-in-Chief for the city. "I've got organized gangs stealing food in the market. The reeve has been pushing me to hand out grain."

"Even the towns do," put in the Inquisitor-in-Chief for Tidings. "I need grain or more sentinels." His colleague from Blessed nodded in assent.

"Some harvests are better than others, that's not news," said Joss. "That's why we have granaries."

"And we're going to be living on them soon." Solender gave her a look and turned back to Toorman. "What's your assessment?"

"The food gangs create shortages sometimes, but the sentinels will handle them. I don't think we need to start handouts yet."

"And tithes, Cela?"

"They've fallen, but you know that." Joss looked annoyed. She didn't want to have to admit a point that supported her ally's rival.

"You remember the corn blight," said Vesene. "This is creating a problem out of nothing. You're losing your focus, Ek Solender."

"Crop failure is not the same as not being able to grow enough crops." Solender bit his lip and stood up again. There was nothing to be gained by arguing. "Now, I did not come here to get entangled in a debate over whether or not this is happening. I came here so we can start working on solutions. If I'm wrong, it won't cost us anything but a little time. If I'm right, then we owe it to our people to have a plan in place before it's too late. I want proposals on how we can effectively deal with this." He turned to Joss. "Inquisitor, I'm putting you in charge of the effort. Everyone else, have your work in to Joss for next month's counsel." He gave the assembled inquisitors a brief nod, pick up the last of his tea and drained it. "I'll leave you to it."

He turned and left, as the room burst into babbling behind him. Vesene's voice rose over the others, though he couldn't hear what the man was saying. *He's ambitious, and he's going to be trouble.* He allowed himself a small smile. It had been a slap in Vesene's face to appoint Joss over him, and strategically clever to put the leashed badger in charge of getting results. The Inquisitory was supposed to be devoted to justice and knowledge, and inquisitors were carefully separated from worldly temptations in order to keep their efforts focused on those lofty goals, but it would take more than merely human laws to separate vanity and ambition from the human spirit. He found his heart pounding harder than it should have been from the encounter, and his face flushed as he climbed the steel stairs to his quarters. He was out of breath by the time he reached the top, his chest heaving with the effort of inhaling. His throat tightened and he coughed, inhaled again, and he still needed air. He fell to his knees, clutching at his chest with one hand, trying to hold himself up with the other. He heard someone yelling, but couldn't understand the words. He looked up and saw feet, legs, a person, and he realized he was lying on the ground, with no understanding of how he'd gotten there. He tried to ask for help but he couldn't make his lips move. There was a ringing in his ears, and his vision faded to black. He felt hands on him, turning him over, and then nothing.

On the day of Jens's inquiry, Atyen yawned and stretched and rose from his narrow bed. He went over to push the shutters open a notch, and blinked as the suntube light streamed into the small room. The room had once been his niece's, and a child's rabbit bow and a set of carved dolls still adorned the shelf by the window. He could have stayed at the Inquisition in Tidings Parish. He chose instead to stay with Boreas, his oldest brother. It was important to avoid any appearance of interfering with the process of the inquiry on this visit, and for the same reason he couldn't stay with Jens and Sarabee, as much as he would've liked to.

*Not that it's a bad thing to spend time with family, but . . .* Boreas was sixteen years older than Atyen, and they'd never been close. Boreas's children were grown, or nearly so and had their own lives. He and his wife were preoccupied with their oldest, who had just been married and was expecting her own first child. It wasn't that Atyen was unwelcome, but neither did he fit into the household particularly well. *You choose your friends, but you're stuck with your relations.* Not for the first time he wondered why his parents had decided on another child when they had barely the land to support the ones they had. Perhaps there had been a shortage of bloodberries, the year he had been born. Perhaps if there hadn't been, he never would have been conceived.

*But there's no point in speculating over that.* He dressed quickly, went into the kitchen and had a sparse breakfast of heavy olive bread and cheese, washing it down with clay-filtered water. Boreas and his wife were still asleep, and he was careful to close the door softly on his way out. It was a full bell's walk to the Hall of Inquisition in Tidings, and his leg still ached after the long hike from the forewall. As he walked he was struck by the number of small houses, really no more than shacks of bamboo and waxed flax, that had sprung up along the narrow dirt road. Fields were subdivided by makeshift fences, sometimes just by piled dirt. It was nothing like the misery outside of Charisy, but it reeked of temporary expedience translated into long-term desperation. *Too many people, not enough land.*

He eventually arrived at Tidings. The town had spilled over its boundaries, and a whole other ring of houses now surrounded it, though at least these were better built and better cared for. *How it's changed since I've been gone!* Young children were everywhere, laughing and running around in the hour before school like the dove flocks at the thresh mill. Groups of teenagers clustered here and there, avoiding adults in their quest to leave childhood. The adults paid him no attention, but there was an undercurrent of suspicion beneath their indifference. He passed into the more established part of town, where the buildings were respectable resined-brick and even timber. The people there were better dressed and the suspicion faded. As he came through the market with its cajoling vendors and bustling customers he felt he had finally come back to the world he had known, but the impression the outskirts had left lasted. *Solender's mice, overcrowded and dysfunctional.* It might be worth it to try the mouse experiment again, just to see how crowded the mice got before they went crazy. *But people aren't mice, aren't mice, aren't mice.*

The Tidings Inquisition was old, built of huge beams and weathered brick that had been re-resined so many times you could hardly distinguish the individual bricks. The blade-and-shield sigil of the Inquisitory was cut into the wall on either side of the entrance, its offer of protection and promise of justice inherent. Inside, the main hall was simply appointed, with wooden benches for the public facing three long tables for inquisitors for the accused, for the accuser, and for the judgment. The hall was empty, and he went to the back and through a door to the offices there. Two sentinels and an errander looked up when he came in, but none of the inquisitors were in. That was fine with Atyen. To call on them was an expected courtesy, but before he spoke with any of them he wanted to understand the details of the inquiry. He asked the errander for the documents, and the functionary rummaged around on his workshelf, finally producing a leather sheaf-fold embossed with the Inquisitory seal. Atyen took an empty workshelf and sat down to read.

The picture laid out in the docket was simple enough. There was a surgeon's report on the youth Sarabee had killed, which detailed only the extent of his wounds and the fact that he died of them without drawing further conclusion. Atyen was taken aback as he read. *It's hard to imagine Sarabee killing a man like this.* Jens hadn't gone into those details when he'd told his story. But the next document was Sarabee's narrative, as told to the inquisitor-of-fact, and it confirmed what the surgeon had found. The gang leader was the reeve's son, and his narrative claimed that he and his friends had gone to the house looking for work and had been attacked without warning by Jens. Unfortunately for his testimony the inquisitor-of-fact had asked the same questions of the third youth, the one who'd run away, and he'd told a tale that supported what Sarabee and Jens had said. The reeve of Tidings had put in a defense of his son but despite Jens's concerns it would have little impact on the outcome of the inquisition. *The facts speak for themselves.* The gang leader would be put in servitude, quite probably for the rest of his life. His acolyte might get away with less. Atyen put his hand to his chin as he read over the young men's statements. The inquisitor had pressed them on the motive behind the attack, but neither one had been able to provide one. *Violence at random, violence for its own sake.*

He didn't like that conclusion, so he went back to reread the gang leader's narrative. The boy's name was Mial. As he read he tried to find some clue that would hint at the root of the violence, but there was nothing. The inquisitor-of-fact had done a workmanlike job of getting the pertinent information, but had gone no deeper. Atyen pushed the papers away. *He's the first son of the reeve.* Mial could expect a good inheritance, and perhaps to follow in his father's footsteps as the community's leader. He had far more to lose than gain with his crime. *So why would he do it?* Even Mial didn't know. *Solender's mice again.* Overcrowded mice couldn't know the self-destructive nature of their behavior, but if somehow they could have, could they've been changed in order to stave off collapse? Atyen bit his lip. *It's possible that a problem has no solution.* It was a rule he'd learned in mathematics, but it applied to human society as well.

"Young Atyen, welcome back."

Atyen looked up to see the Tidings' inquisitor-in-chief come in. He was a broad-shouldered man with a bluff, direct manner, and Atyen remembered him from the time he had come to the town to write his first inquisitorial test. He'd been sixteen years old then, and the senior inquisitor had seemed all powerful, all-knowing, almost godlike in the way he casually wore the position that Atyen longed so much to achieve. The intervening years had grayed him and thickened his frame but otherwise he seemed unchanged.

"I'm surprised you remember me," said Atyen as he rose to greet the older man.

"I never forget a shorefields face." The inquisitor stepped back and looked Atyen over. "I hear you're aspirant to Solender himself. Well done."

"I've been lucky." Atyen collected the inquiry documents back into their docket. "I've come down to watch this inquiry." He hesitated, not sure how much he should say. "Jens Madane is an old friend."

"Well, let's talk about it."

Atyen went over the details of the docket with the senior inquisitor, still hoping for some insight into the underlying motivation for the attack, but the inquiry simply hadn't gone in that direction. Still, as they talked it became clear that the senior inquisitor had first-hand experience with the changes that were so troubling Solender. Nobody was going hungry, but people were working more for less. The attack on Sarabee was just one of a dozen acts of seemingly random violence that had cropped up over the past year: a fisher family beaten and their house burned, a cloth merchant killed in the sleeping hours by a trio of girls he caught trying to steal his wares only hours before.

"What do you think of it?" he asked the older man.

"I've been around a long time. All I can say is, some are born good, some are born bad. I used to try to save the bad ones, show them what was right." He shook his head. "I can't say that I saved many. Now . . ." The inquisitor looked away. ". . . now I just get the facts, the law and find the sentence." He laughed. "Which is the nature of the Inquisition, after all. It's the clergy's business to know what's in people's hearts."

"But this kind of thing didn't happen when I was growing up."

The old inquisitor laughed. "You forget fast, young man. I can remember when you and your friend were brought in here, all bruised and bloody nosed over some scrap. These boys just took it a little too far."

"But . . ." Atyen stopped. To him it was obvious that something important was changing. When he was growing up the fights had been between youths. They sorted out who stood where in the hierarchy of adolescent toughness, and they had stopped when the point was made. These new assaults were by the young against the old, and people got badly hurt or even died, for gains that seemed almost irrelevant. He was surprised that the senior inquisitor hadn't noticed the same pattern, and he felt some sadness in realizing that this man he'd so revered when he was younger stood revealed as—only a man. He was well suited to overseeing his rough-and-tumble bailiwick, but he was completely lacking in imagination. The reality was that the Chief Inquisitor didn't send his best and brightest to administer law in the farthest reaches of the shorefields.

An errander brought them a late breakfast, with thickened goat's milk and bread still warm from the baker's oven, and they paused to eat.

Atyen knew better than to ask what judgement the senior inquisitor was considering in the upcoming inquiry, and the conversation turned to other things. At the end of the meal the other man excused himself to go and start his preparations.

Atyen went to meet Jens and Sarabee. He hiked down to the water and turned along the shore road towards Jens's dock. The ocean was dotted with jaunty rafts, and the water's edge was crowded close with net-hangers and smokesheds. He passed a landed net-raft, and exchanged a nod with the fishers. They were busily splitting their catch, tossing the entrails into the bait-sluice and hanging the gutted fish on the drying rack. Gulls swirled overhead, calling and chattering as they squabbled over a floating fish-head, and the pervasive odor of dried carp filled the air. They might have been suspicious of his cross-sash, there was none of the overt hostility that there had been in the outskirts of Tidings. *And yet* . . . Jens had all but told him that there were fishers withholding their tithe. That only made sense if catches had fallen. There were *a lot* of rafts on the water. *How many fish can there be in the ocean?* There would be an answer in the tithesheets, or least an approximation of one. Atyen pushed the thought away. He had no desire to go back to the manuscript tower to dig through more dusty documents.

He walked slowly to favor his injured leg, and it took a bell before he came to Jens's dock. The net-raft wasn't there, and Atyen bit his lip. It wouldn't be good for his friend to be late for the inquiry. He turned up the foreword path to Jens's house and quickened his pace. When he arrived his friend wasn't there either, but Sarabee was.

"Atyen!" she called when she saw him. "I've been waiting."

"Where's Jens? The inquiry is today."

"He's taking the children over to Celese's. He'll meet us at the inquisition."

"The raft isn't there."

"We took it up to the sailsmith in Cove. It's been needing some work, and we can't fish today." Sarabee's voice held a buried tension, and Atyen squeezed her shoulder reassuringly.

"You'll be fishing tomorrow, don't worry."

"Did you talk to the inquisitor?"

"I've seen the docket, and you've got nothing to worry about."

"I hope so." Sarabee breathed in and out, looked down at the ground. "I'm worried, Atyen. What if we get servitude? Who's going to look after the children?"

"You won't get servitude."

Sarabee looked up, with a vulnerability in her eyes that Atyen had never seen before. For a moment he thought he should hug her, to give her the physical reassurance of his presence, but he wasn't sure if the gesture would be welcome. The moment passed. A faint peal sounded in the distance, and a louder peal answered it from the direction of Tidings, the mid-day bell. "Well," he said. "We should get going."

They walked in silence, Sarabee tense and Atyen feeling not much use. He wanted to tell her of his triumph at the forewall, of the success of his flight, but somehow it didn't seem to be the time. He groped for something supportive to say, but everything he came up with seemed empty. Sarabee had killed a man, and however justified it was, however clear the case for self defense was, the upcoming inquiry worried her. Atyen sensed there was little point in explaining the difference between the reeve, polled in by the people to manage the community, and the inquisitors, selected by the order to oversee the laws.

The Hall of Inquisition had been a church once upon a time, and though most of the trappings of religion were long gone from the echoing space there remained a towering ironwood cross on the far wall. It was actually part of the structure, an extension of the support beams that held the roof up, and a stark reminder that the inquisition had once scourged the body as well as the mind. Jens was there waiting, and Atyen looked away when Sarabee went to embrace him. Eight sentinels stood at the back of the room, ready to act on the inquisitor-in-chief's word. An older couple sat in the back, dressed in severe and simple clothing, but most of the long wooden benches were empty. The only people who cared about the inquiry were the protagonists. Atyen took a seat with Jens and Sarabee in the front right row, and watched as the other inquisitors busied themselves with their worksheaves, preparing to present their findings. There was a brief bustle at the door and four more sentinels came in, with the accused attackers between them. Behind him came their families, including the reeve with his own erranders in attendance. The young men didn't look as dangerous as Jens had described them, they looked callow in their youth, and frightened.

"You didn't tell me they were being held in circumscription," Atyen whispered to Jens.

"I didn't know. What does that mean?"

Atyen looked at his friend, but the question was serious. "It means the inquisitor-in-chief considers them a danger."

Sarabee breathed out slowly. "I'm just glad to see they're under guard." Jens took her hand.

The youths were seated in the front left row, and the reeve sat behind them, with his erranders beside him and his wife in the row behind that. The other boy's parents and some others who seemed to be siblings and friends took the rows behind that. Once they'd settled, the inquisitor-in-chief's senior aspirant stood up and called for attention. The room quieted, and the inquisitor-of-fact began his presentation, going over the chronology of the events as it had been presented to him by the concerned parties, as well as the surgeon's report and his own findings. When the stories had been told, the inquisitor-of-law and the inquisitor-unbounded made their own presentations. Each added depth and detail to the case, but none changed Atyen's basic understanding of what had happened, or gave him insight into the critical question of motive. It took the better part of two bells to get through the whole process, and then inquisitor-in-chief called on Jens to answer the charge that he had attacked the young men when they came to ask for work.

Jens flatly denied the accusation, his voice low and even. After he sat down it was Sarabee's turn, and she spoke with a restrained passion that carried the anger and fear the attack had left in her. When they were done the inquisitor-in-chief turned to the two youths. Atyen watched the reeve while the first boy spoke; he seemed angry, lips pressed tight together, with his eyes focused on the inquisitor-in-chief. The boy had little to say, and he answered the inquisitor-in-chief's penetrating questions with sullen monosyllables. The inquisitor-of-fact had already dismissed the youth's claim that Jens had attacked them unprovoked when they had only come to ask for food, and he offered no other explanation, keeping his eyes on the floor in front of him. Mial, the reeve's son, spoke second. He had been the leader in the attack, and he used his time to accuse Jens of killing his friend, to dismiss Sarabee as a spent woman, unworthy even of rape and to denounce the inquisitor-of-fact as both biased and incompetent. His eyes glinted hard as he spoke, and his words carried depth and conviction. If Atyen didn't already know the truth, he would have been inclined to believe the boy. There was a murmur in the crowd of supporters on the left-hand side of the hall, and hard looks were directed at Jens. They *had* believed Mial. *But it doesn't matter what they believe, or what I believe, it matters what the inquisitor-in-chief believes.* The formal process of inquiry was carefully structured to avoid bias as much as possible, but ultimately it came down to a decision about what to believe in the face of conflicting evidence. Atyen watched the inquisitor-in-chief intently, trying to divine what he might be thinking, but could draw no definite conclusion.

The young man finished speaking and sat down, and the

inquisitor-in-chief stood up. "I find Sarabee and Jens Madane acted in self-defense against an unprovoked attack. The death of Jelfra Zaden came as a result of his participation in this attack, and no guilt attaches to them for it. Mial Broden and Frien Polis were willing participants in this attack, and threatened death to the persons of Jens and Jerl Madane, and both rape and death to the person of Sarabee Madane. In addition, guilt for the death of Jelfra Zaden attaches to them. For this I bind Mial Broden to life in servitude, with seven years restitution made to Jens and with seven years to Sarabee. For this I bind Jelfra Zaden to direct indenture to the Madanes for seven years, to be used as they see fit. This inquiry is closed."

There were gasps from the audience, and the reeve's face flushed red. "My son is not a criminal!"

"The inquiry is closed, reeve," said the inquisitor-in-chief. "I'm sorry."

"Father!" Mial's face turned white. "Do something!"

"Inquisitor, I insist . . ." the reeve sputtered, but an upraised hand cut him off.

"The inquiry is closed," repeated the older man. "Sentinels, take away the convicted."

"Inquisitor!" shouted the reeve, as guards took away his son and the other youth. Mial struggled and started to say something, but one of the sentinels twisted his arm up behind his back and the words came out as a squeak of pain.

"Reeve Broden." The inquisitor-in-chief's words held an edge of steel. "The inquiry is closed." Two broad-shouldered sentinels moved towards the dignitary, but he held up a hand to forestall them.

"You haven't heard the last of this," he said through clenched teeth, his eyes blazing. He turned on his heel and swept out of the room, and his entourage followed him out.

Sarabee was hugging Jens, tears of relief streaming down her face. Atyen felt awkward, as though he were intruding on something private, and stood up to give them space. The inquisitors were filing out into the inquisitor-in-chief's antechamber, the erranders and aspirants going back to their day-to-day work. In Charisy there were inquiries every day, but in Tidings there were only a few in a month. At the back of the room a woman burst into tears, and a man who might have been her husband led her out the back doors, his face tight and strained. Atyen hadn't noticed the couple before.

"The third boy," Sarabee whispered. She and Jens had stopped embracing and stood up themselves. "The one I killed. He was their son."

Atyen nodded slowly. The inquiry had seemed to drag, like every one of the inquiries he'd ever attended since he'd become an aspirant. Now that it was over, it seemed like too short a time, too small a venue to contain the intensity of the events that had poured out of it. *And that's something new.* He had always seen himself as an inquisitor into physical law—human law was too abstruse and subjective for his taste—but now he saw its importance.

"Thank you for coming, Atyen." Jens took his hand and shook it.

"I didn't really do anything."

"You were here, on our side. You saw the reeve. He would have tipped the balance if he could have."

"He has no power, and from what I saw of Tidings he won't be reeve for much longer."

Sarabee shuddered. "He's just like his son, he likes to be in charge, and he's cruel inside."

"He doesn't even have jurisdiction in the shorefields, but I'm glad I was here, and I'm glad you found it helpful."

"You have to come for a meal, Atyen. We haven't even thanked you for that pig yet."

Atyen smiled. "I'd be pleased to."

The three walked back to the shorefields, talking about the inquiry and then about other things. They stopped to collect the children from Celese, and Atyen was surprised how the young woman he'd remembered had aged. Sarabee gave him Jerl to hold while she corralled the girls, and he recognized the implicit honor in being allowed to hold her youngest. The boy looked up at him with big, curious eyes, and he found himself smiling, and surprisingly comfortable with the toddler. The small body was warm and soft, and as he walked and Jerl slowly fell asleep in his arms he found himself wondering if he had made the right decision in choosing the Inquisition for his life. *But it's too late to regret that now.* He had made his choice and now he had to live with it.

When they got home Jens put the boy to bed while Atyen played hide and seek with Liese and the younger girls. Sarabee cooked a fresh carp, served with boiled dry-corn and beans. The food was good and plentiful, and it was hard to worry about the world's problems with a full belly and good company. After dinner Sarabee closed the shutters and sent her daughters to sleep, and Atyen and Jens walked down to the shore to talk.

"It may be that this is a good thing," said Jens, as they sat down on the hillock overlooking his dock.

"How's that?"

"The inquisitor gave us each seven years restitution."

"The extra income will make a difference."

Atyen nodded. "I suppose it will."

"Do you know how much it is?"

Atyen shrugged. "Not in tokens. It's half for restitution to you, half to pay the Inquisitory for the system to make them do it. It's the usual."

"The usual?"

"The inquisitor-in-chief decided that they meant to kill you, so the law gives seven years restitution for that. He doubled it for Sarabee. I guess he decided the boy was dangerous, so he'll stay in the brickworks for life. You won't see him again."

"I suppose I knew that, more or less. I was too worried that he might decide we were murderers. How does the restitution come to us?"

"The tithecounters will take it off your tithing. If there's anything extra they'll bring you the steel."

Jens laughed. "Tithecounters *bringing* money. Now that's rich." He breathed out. "What about the other boy?"

"He got off light. If I were you I'd sell his indenture to someone in Charisy. You don't want him around."

"I'll do that." Jens took a deep breath, let it out slowly. "What a relief that it's all over."

Atyen nodded. The breeze had picked up, blowing out over the docks and rippling his hair. In the distance a raft without sails drifted towards the aftwall. "Somebody's fishing at this hour?"

"Some do. It's getting harder to get carp." Jens shaded his eyes with his hand to get a better look. "No, there's no one on it. It's broken loose." He peered harder. "Looks like Girn's. Not to worry, it'll wind up at the aftwall. I'll take him out there tomorrow." He paused. "Atyen?"

"Yes?"

"I've got another change for you. Carp are getting smaller. When I was a boy the big ones were as big as me. Now . . ." He shrugged. "I haven't seen one like that in years. I want my children to have a better life than I've had, but I'm starting to think that might not happen." Jens bit his lip. "Can I ask you another favor?"

"Of course."

"If anything happens. To me I mean, anything . . . bad." He paused. "Will you look after Sarabee, and the children?"

Atyen raised his eyebrows in surprise. "Jens, that's for your brother . . ."

"I know, but you and I are closer than brothers, and I'd rather it was you."

"I've got no land, and I'm not much of a fisher."

"You're an inquisitor."

"I am only an aspirant, and even an inquisitor would have to leave the Inquisitory to take on a family. They wouldn't let me stay."

"I know it's a lot to ask . . ."

Atyen raised a hand. "It's not too much to ask. It would be an honor. Of course I'll do it, if you want me to. I'm just not sure I'm the best choice."

"I am," Jens said.

Atyen looked at his friend. There was a calm surety in Jens's eyes. He felt proud to have earned such trust.

Inquisitor Byo Vesene hurried up the worn steel stairs to the Chief Inquisitor's quarters, concerned. He had carefully planned for Ek Solender's death, but he wasn't yet ready for it. The old man still had too much support, and his supporters were now automatically Vesene's rivals. *It's fortunate the surgeon's errander found me first.* Chief Inquisitors usually formally retired from the position with lots of notice, which gave the senior inquisitors plenty of time to perform the subtle dance of power that succession demanded. Alliances would quietly form, pacts would be made, expectations established, and when the actual day arrived the power structure would already have reoriented itself to the new realities. The transition would be made with scarcely a ripple visible to the outer world. *Not this time.* It was even possible that another group had killed Solender, that he wasn't the only one who knew the secret of foxglove extract. *And if that's true, I may already be too late.*

He was sweating when he got to the top tier of the Inquisitory, where the Chief Inquisitor's private rooms were. The antechamber was a simple space, decorated with blooming morning glory in pots set around the walls. Solender had done his masterwork on the medicinal properties of the plants, and they'd been his symbol ever since. Vesene smirked at the irony. *He was the one who taught me about foxglove, all those years ago.* There was an errander waiting, as there always was, ready to do whatever service the Chief Inquisitor might require.

"The Chief Inquisitor needs you at once," he said. The errander was a young man of slender stature, and Vesene spoke before he had a chance to say anything. "He's in the surgeon's hall, in a bad way."

"But I'm not supposed to leave—"

"He's dying, man! Hurry!"

The errander opened his mouth, closed it again, and then left. By the time he was at the door he was running. Vesene waited until the man was out of sight, and then went into the corridor where Solender's study and private rooms were. The heavy ironwood door to the study was closed and locked, and for a moment he cursed himself. Solender would have had the key on him. *But it's a delay, no more.* He drew a thin steel rod from his sash pocket, and slid it into the keyhole, probing for the fall-blocks. It was a skill he'd learned studying mechanography, and it had proved itself useful often enough. He looked furtively up and down the corridor, but there was no one there. *And hopefully there won't be.* Opportunity and crisis were opposite sides of the same token, and as long as he worked faster than any of his rivals, he would win the day. His teeth closed gently on his tongue as he probed at the lock, a half-subconscious way of focusing his attention. He found the first fall-block and levered it out of the way of the latch bar. He put tension on the latch slider to push the bar against the edge of the block and hold it in place, and went to work on the second block. He found it, gently pushed it up into its slot, and applied more pressure to the slider. There was a *clack* as the first fall-block came back down again.

Vesene cursed under his breath and moved the rod back to the first block, and carefully moved into position. Once he had it, he paused to visualize the locking mechanism. The second block could be a false one, designed not to stop the locking bar from moving but to dislodge the other blocks if someone tried what he was trying. *Or the first block could be worn and loose.* He probed for the second block again, moved it gently, keeping pressure on the latch slider, alert for any slight friction that would warn him that his movement was about to dislodge the first block. There was none, and he was rewarded with a slight tug on the latch lever to tell him that he'd properly set the second block. The third block was harder to reach, and he had to move slowly and carefully to get it properly positioned without disturbing either of the first two.

It seemed to take forever, but finally it clicked into place. The latch slid into position with an audible *click,* and the lock was open. Vesene went through the door, closed it behind him and breathed out in relief. There was no time to waste savoring his victory. His heart sank when he saw Solender's study. It was a mess—worksheaves stacked on worksheaves, shelves of old manuscripts piled without any semblance of order. He quickly rifled through the stack on Solender's workshelf. They were all related to population, land and food, Solender's current pet project. *The old goat took it seriously.* Unfortunately, they weren't what he was looking for. He moved to the shelves and found works of history and botany and anatomy, a manuscript on firing clay and another on steelsmithing. *Still nothing.* He was looking for anything that would illuminate Solender's position on his succession. The Chief Inquisitor had given no hint at his thoughts on a successor, but it was a safe bet that Byo Vesene was not among them. *Did he write anything down? That's what matters.* As soon as it was confirmed that Solender was dead the scriptkeepers would go through his documents, and anything he had recorded on the subject would become the definitive word on the selection of the next Chief Inquisitor. If someone else had killed Solender it could only be because they were fully prepared to take advantage of the situation. A written preference in Solender's own hand would be a key part of such a plan. *There must be something . . .*

He found a stack of papers written in the deep red ink that was reserved for the Chief Inquisitor's formal judgments. He leafed through them, but they were concerned with some dispute over the allocation of steel from the twice-antispinward steel-fall. The next pile described a wooden flowmeter, part of the dead man's long ago masterwork. Vesene found his hands shaking as he searched. *I only have so much time.* In his head he knew it would be a bell at least before the errander got back from his fool's quest, but there were other forces at work. The fear of discovery was clenched tight in his belly, and no amount of rationalization would stop his hands from shaking.

*What was that?* He stopped to listen, had he only imagined a footstep in the corridor outside? The sound wasn't repeated, and he went back to his frantic search, heart pounding in his chest. In his hurry he knocked over a haphazard pile of documents, and cursed. Down on his hands and knees he scanned each one as he tried to reconstruct the pile. *No one will notice, no one will notice . . .* Vesene himself kept meticulous notes on every erstwhile rival, every potential ally, and he couldn't imagine the Chief Inquisitor doing anything less. He turned to the next shelf. There was a flowmeter there, a six-bladed wheel that spun a gear to turn a dial, on another shelf was a miniature canal gate, and sundry less identifiable trinkets. He looked past them, concentrated on the papers there, but they were just manuscripts, not personal notes. *So ignore everything not scribed in red.* Most of what he saw was in plain black, a little in the blue reserved for senior inquisitors, but there was almost nothing in red. *Why is that?* For a single horrified moment he thought that Solender might have had his worksheaf with him when he died. He stopped searching for a moment to think, brought up an image in his mind of the older man as he'd seen him in the surgeon's hall. He forced himself to concentrate, slowly going over everything he had seen. *Did he have a worksheaf with him?* Vesene had been too shocked at the suddenness of death, too taken with the sudden urgency to put his half formed plan into action to pay close attention. *And what if someone's already taken it?* Who knew how many people had contact with the Chief Inquisitor's body on its way to the surgeon's hall.

And ultimately it didn't matter. He rifled through more shelves, but found nothing of interest. There was another sound from the corridor, perhaps footsteps, perhaps . . . *what?* Instinctively he ducked down behind Solender's worksheaf. Again he listened, petrified that he might be caught in his criminal trespass. Once more the sound was not repeated, and he began to doubt whether he'd really heard it at all. He wiped cold sweat from his forehead, and took a deep breath. *This is taking too long.* The room was a mass of manuscripts, and it was possible Solender had kept his notes elsewhere, perhaps in his sleeping room, perhaps in . . .

*I'm wasting time.* Vesene felt a kind of panic taking over as he went to search the workshelf once more. Making sure his rivals would find nothing to use against him among Solender's notes was only one of many things he had to take care of if he wanted control of the Inquisitory for himself. There was nothing even close to what he was looking for, and then he saw, beneath another document, a page scribed in red, and not yet finished. He snatched it up, but the Chief Inquisitor's ink jar had been resting on it, and it tipped over. The heavy fluid spilled and spread like blood, staining the papers beneath it. He cursed, and cursed louder when he realized his hands were smeared red as well. *If they catch me like this . . .* If anyone came in now it would be obvious what he was trying to do, and his enemies would seize the chance to try him for Solender's murder and exonerate themselves. He grabbed a random manuscript and tried to wipe the ink off, but his effort only served to smudge the paper without cleaning his hands. He looked at the mess with growing horror. A spilled ink jar could be explained away as Solender's fault, but if he kept searching for the Chief Inquisitor's notes he'd get red ink everywhere, and that would raise suspicion. Again he cursed the old man for dying too soon.

He couldn't wipe his hands on his own cloak, and he looked around in desperation, for a towel, for some water, for anything to get rid of the telltale stain. There was nothing that would do the job, but his eye fell on the firebowl in the corner of the room. A kind of desperate inspiration spread through him. He went to it, but it was cold, empty even of ashes. He clenched his fists in angry frustration and was about to smack the bowl across the room to relieve it when he saw the fire piston hanging from its stand. He grabbed it, took it back to the workshelf, took the piston from its cylinder, and tore a small piece of paper from one of manuscripts. His hands were trembling so much that he dropped the paper twice as he tried to fit it into the end of the piston. Finally he managed, and positioned the piston back of the entrance to the cylinder, then pumped it with a single quick stroke. When he withdrew it the paper was a burning ember. He held it to the manuscript he'd torn it from, to be rewarded a second later with a small flicker of flame. The manuscript flared up, and he held it to the stack of paper on the workshelf until it was burning too. He took the flaming page to the wallshelves, and in seconds the documents there were a wall of fire. It was time to go. He ran out into the corridor, heedless now of who might see him, barely remembering to close the door behind him. He ran to the stairs and down them, and only when he got to the bottom did he pause to breathe, trembling in reaction and feeling a strange elation over what he just done. *I'm brilliant, truly brilliant.* Not only would the fire destroy any documents that might help his enemies, but the chaos would only help him seize power. *People follow strong leaders in a crisis.* Shouts rose above him, the fire had been discovered. He paid no heed, that was a problem for someone else now, and he had his own to solve.

He went to his own quarters, closed and locked the door behind him. There was a water bowl by the window, the water scented with chamomile. He had a lot more to do in the next bells, but first he had to get the ink off his hands. He rinsed them, and the water turned red, but the thick red fluid was soaked into his pores. He scrubbed harder, scratching at his skin with his fingernails, but that only forced the ink into his nail beds. He found himself breathing too fast, and it felt as though someone were watching him, recording each movement as evidence of his guilt. The exultation he had felt moments ago vanished.

*I didn't kill Solender, I didn't* . . . He had planned it, but someone else had done it. The foxglove extract was still on his workshelf where he had left it. *It is, isn't it?* The ink still stained his hands, and the water was now blood red itself. He couldn't put it down his own drain spout, even a trace of ink left there would be enough for his enemies to use. He'd have to empty it somewhere where no one could see, somewhere it couldn't be traced back to him, and then get rid of the bowl. *Melt it down.*

He scrubbed harder, tearing at his skin, and some of the water spilled on the floor quilt. *I'll have to burn it, and my clothing.* There was something in his sash pocket, and it seemed heavy, inexorably tugging down on his cross sash. He reached in and found the foxglove jar. *And how did that get there?* He hadn't put it there himself, and he resisted the urge to tear off the sash and throw it across the room. *First I need my hands to be clean.*

When that was done he could take off his sash and get rid of the incriminating jar of foxglove powder, maybe hide it somewhere. After that he'd burn the floor quilt. *What else do I need to look after?* He'd touched the door latch to his quarters with his ink stained hands, both inside and out. He'd have to get to that before the ink dried, especially if he touched the wooden door frame as well. The ink would have soaked in by now, he'd have to scrape down into the wood to get rid of it. *Better, tear out door and frame and burn them too.* He laughed unsteadily. *Fire solves so many problems.* And the errander he'd sent to the surgeon's hall was a witness, he too would need to be silenced. *So I need to save the foxglove, for a little while.* He'd stopped washing while he thought, his hands immersed in the blood red water. He took them out. They were sore now with scouring, but still stained, a faint, diffuse redness that blended imperceptibly into the abraded skin. He looked at them despairingly. *I have no time for this.*

Inspiration dawned. He knelt and dried his hands on the floor quilt, because he had to burn it anyway, and then went to his shelves and found his formal gloves. People might wonder why he was wearing them, but they wouldn't see the stains on his hands. He slipped them on and, his guilt so concealed, went out to find Cela Joss. She wasn't in her quarters, and her errander told him she was in the reading room. He cursed and ran to the manuscript tower, up the top of the stairs, to the reading room, arriving soaked in sweat. The aspirants clustered around the tables looked up from their worksheaves, surprised in their silent study by his noisy appearance. Vesene ignored them. He couldn't see Joss.

"Cela," he called. Again the aspirants looked up, annoyed at his disregard for etiquette but too deferential to his rank to say anything. Again he ignored them. "Cela!"

Joss looked up from a workshelf by the far window, and came over. "What is it?" she asked.

He went to her table. "Solender is dead. Godstruck, the surgeons tell me. The Inquisitory is on fire."

"This is . . ." Joss paused, groping for words.

"It's an opportunity, if we can seize it. It's going to be chaos. We'll need sentinels to keep order. Our sentinels." He could hear shouts coming through the waxed flax window covers. The fire was spreading across the Inquisitory's top floors.

"I hadn't planned on this. I've got a dozen sentinels in my vaults, no more."

Vesene cursed. "Errander!" he shouted, heedless of the quiet. "Errander!" He went to one of the tables where an aspirant was looking up at the commotion. "I need this," he said. Without waiting for an answer he took the pen from the aspirant's hand and tore a page from his worksheaf. He dipped the pen in the aspirant's ink jar and scribed out a note. An errander came running as he finished, and Vesene pulled a message ball from a pocket, twisted it through its puzzle until it fell into two halves. "I need you to take this to the Inquisitor-in-Chief in Charisy," he told the errander.

"As you wish."

Vesene waved the page in the air to dry it, then folded it tightly and slid it into the message ball and reclosed it. "Go quickly," he told the errander. "It's urgent."

The errander nodded and left, hurrying, and Vesene turned back to Joss. "We have to act quickly, we have to put pressure on the senior inquisitors, make sure the right decisions are made. This will make sure it happens."

"What does the note say?"

"Torr Toorman owes me a favor, and I'm calling it in right now. We'll have five hundred of Charisy's best sentinels here, soon. To fight the fire, to keep order after it." He looked away. "You'll take charge of that, no one will question you. When I'm Chief Inquisitor, the order of Sentinels will be yours."

"The law council will object."

"Then your sentinels will discipline the law council." Joss looked away, her expression distant, then looked back. "What caused the fire?"

"God wants me to rule," Vesene held up a gloved hand, looking at the white fabric. "There's no other explanation."

Charisy was on edge when Atyen came through it. On a corner a man tiraded to a passersby about the greed of the merchants. In the market a gang of toughs beat a monger while the crowd ignored them. There wasn't a sentinel in sight, in fact there weren't any cross-sashes, and he took his own off when he realized it was drawing attention. Only when he got back on the trading road did he learn what was wrong. A cart-driver told him about the fire at the Inquisitory. Half the sentinels in the city had gone to the forewall to deal with it. The news was worrisome, and Atyen hiked foreward as fast as his injured leg would allow. He heard rumors on the way, but nothing he could confirm as a fact. The forewall mists were low, so though he could smell the smoke he couldn't see anything. It wasn't until he got there that he realized that the fire had long since burned itself out. The smoke was from funeral pyres. There were a dozen smoldering along the trading road, their residual heat fighting against the damp. The wooden top floors of the Inquisitory had burned down to the steel under-structure, and the fire must have been huge. Solender's studio was in the lower gallery, safe in steel, but even so he hurried, anxious despite himself to make sure his work hadn't been destroyed. As he drew closer the extent of the damage grew clearer. It must have been a ferocious fire. *I'm amazed they found enough left to cremate.*

There were hundreds of people gathered in the courtyard, and when he came up he could see another pyre in the center of the throng. It was big, and built not of straw but good oakwood, more usually reserved to make charcoal to forge steel. A ring of sentinels kept the onlookers at a distance. *Someone important then.*

"Whose pyre?" he asked one of the watchers, a stocky man with a timekeeper's sash.

"The Chief Inquisitor's."

"What? Solender?" *I don't believe it.*

"Solender," the man confirmed. "He died just before the fire. Probably a mercy, it would have killed him to see this." He gestured up at the ruins of the Inquisitory.

"Solender." Atyen's throat constricted. *Solender. I should have been here.* His doctrinor had done so much for him . . .

"I think they're starting," the man said.

The ceremony began with the Bishop of Charisy reading a service, though Solender had not been a believer, and then Inquisitor Vesene made a speech. "Today is a day of many tragedies," he began. "We mourn those lost in the fire that has taken so much of the Inquisitory. We mourn those lost in the fighting in the shorefields. Most of all, we mourn a great leader." The new Chief Inquisitor raised his arms to the suntube, as if imploring distant Heaven for a boon. "But we will recover. We will recover and we will find a new leader, a greater leader . . ."

The words rolled over Atyen, but he wasn't really listening. The speech ended and the priest approached the pyre again, this time with his torch upheld. He said the death-prayer, whose words Atyen could never remember, and then lowered the torch to the tinder. Flame flared, grew brighter, climbed the piled logs to lick at the body on top, and Atyen turned away, unwilling to watch. Heat grew on his back, and the fire's crackle became a roar. Smoke drifted overhead, spiralling up to meld with the mist. His doctrinor was gone, with all his knowledge and wisdom and . . . Atyen fought back tears. . . . *with all his compassion.* For perhaps the first time he realized what Solender had meant to him. In his family he had been only the youngest son, another mouth to feed for his parents, a potential land-rival to his brothers. He had never felt part of them, never felt he belonged there. Perhaps that explained why he'd spent so much time with Jens growing up, and why he'd chosen the strictures of the Inquisition rather than apprenticing for a trade. The Inquisition had offered structure at a time when he had badly needed it, and Solender had become . . . *What?* A father figure? *More than that.* His doctrinor had become his whole family. *And he wasn't that old.* Fifty perhaps, surely no more than sixty, and he'd been so full of energy, of ideas, of *life* that it seemed impossible that he was gone.

The bishop mouthed some platitude about reuniting with the Chief Inquisitor when the world arrived at Heaven, but Atyen was already walking away. Ek Solender was gone, and words wouldn't bring him back. He walked without thinking, his mind clouded with emotion and his throat tight with grief. He went into the Inquisitory, climbed the steel stairs of the manuscript tower. It was strangely empty, hushed, as though it too was mourning the absence of a close friends. He went to the reading room, and opened one of the waxed cloth windows to look out on the courtyard below. The pyre was still burning, the bishop still speaking, though at this distance Atyen could no longer make out the words. He watched the smoke rise and bit his lower lip. It seemed fitting that he should watch from a distance. He didn't want to hear anyone's comforting words, he didn't want to comfort anyone. He didn't want . . . anything. After a time the ceremony ended, and the gathered crowd dispersed. A few of them drifted into the reading room, breaking the rule of silence with buzzing with speculation over what would occur now that

Vesene had ascended to Chief Inquisitor. He ignored the chatter, and watched the pyre burn until it burned itself out, leaving only a blackened circle full of ash and charcoal. *From ashes to ashes and dust to dust.* The death-prayer's words came back. Solender was part of the world now, a part of every morsel of food, every swallow of water, every breath Atyen would take for the rest of his life. There was some comfort in that.

He went back to the studio after the ceremony and found sentinels on guard at the entrance, with blades ready and suspicious questions. They weren't Inquisitory sentinels, they were from Charisy. They let him through, eventually. Inside he saw Corl.

"What's happening?" he asked. "Why all the sentinels?"

"You haven't heard?" Corl's eyebrows went up in surprise. "They caught an errander. He started the fire on purpose."

"You're joking."

"Vesene saw him. There's a group of them, they've been planning to take over the Inquisition. They had to call in sentinels from Charisy." Corl's workspace was piled high with manuscript volumes, and he was busily piling them into heavy flax carry-bags. "He took poison when they caught him."

"The errander?"

"Who else?"

"Do you think he . . . maybe he killed Solender?"

Corl shrugged. "The surgeons said his heart failed. It happens sometimes they say, nobody knows why."

To Atyen that seemed inadequate, a failing of inquiry that such a fundamental question had no better answer, and he found himself annoyed at his colleague's apparent indifference to the death of their doctrinor. *He's like the others, eager to be the Chief Inquisitor's aspirant for no reason but the status.*

"Have you found a new doctrinor yet?" Corl asked. He was still packing volumes into bags.

"I hadn't thought of it."

"Best to hurry. It's no secret Vesene had little time for Solender."

"Why would that matter?"

"You really are an innocent, aren't you?" Corl laughed. "There aren't a lot of inquisitors who are going to make themselves unpopular with him by taking on one of Solender's aspirants. I've gotten old Stronka to take me on, but he doesn't care because he's going nowhere." He made a face. "I was going right to the top, and now I have to start all over. I'll tell you one thing. I didn't spend five years slaving here to fail my masterwork for no good reason. Stronka will do until I find better."

Atyen nodded, suddenly overcome with a great tiredness. He had meant to work on his new wing design, but instead he went out of the studio and back to his room. The future was uncertain, but he would worry about that tomorrow. He crawled into bed, exhausted, and slept without even closing the shutters. He woke up late the next day, not hungry enough to eat. Instead he went to back to the studio. The place was in chaos, with most of the other aspirants in the process of moving out, but his workspace was as he had left it, the wreckage that had been his wings was still piled in a corner, untouched since Solender had assigned him to study the tithesheets. He picked up the broken bamboo, ran a hand over the rust colored stains on the tangled cloth. *My blood.* They were beyond salvation . . . *But I can build better now anyway.* Solender's death had freed him to pursue his dream, but at the same time it had given him a strict time limit. The Chief Inquisitor had the most desirable studio in the Inquisitory, and Vesene would take it over as soon as he had his position secure.

He went to his workbench, where long bamboo poles were piled against the wall, and selected one. It was twice as thick as his thumb, with a good, mature wall. He inspected it carefully, looking for cracks and weak spots, but he'd chosen carefully when he bought it and he found nothing. It would become the mainspine of a new set of wings. He set it in the vice, and measured it for cutting, letting his hands take his mind away from his worries. He worked from the careful drawings in his journal, making modifications by instinct as he went. He needed to cant the wing tips up more, and that entailed a change in the bracing. The tail needed to be bigger, to add stability. The day passed in an eyeblink, and he worked until he was too tired to work anymore, then went to his room to sleep a deep and dreamless sleep.

He awoke even later the next day, and though he was famished he went back to his wings without pausing for food, hunger overridden by the desire to *build.* The place was already half empty, but there was no sign that Vesene had moved to fill the space with his own aspirants. No doubt the new Chief Inquisitor had his hands full dealing with the aftermath of fire and the rumors of errander conspiracy. Still the change was coming, Atyen could sense it. A steady stream of his erstwhile colleagues trickled in through the day as he worked, some sad, some angry, all collecting the last of their belongings and trudging off with them, some lucky few to begin again with new doctrinors as Corl had, most simply leaving the Inquisitory to return to whatever lives they had left out in the world. Atyen ignored them, focusing on his task with obsessive single-mindedness. He had no illusions that some other inquisitor would accept him as aspirant. His work was too out of the mainstream, even if he wasn't one of Solender's orphans. By the evening-meal bell he had the fabric cut and the frame completed. Aching hunger finally forced him to pause long enough to go for a meal. To his surprise the sentinels were gone from the studio entrance, which was a relief. *Vesene must have a use for them elsewhere.* He went to the meal hall and ate ravenously. Once he'd finished he took some cheesed bread tied in a cloth so he wouldn't have to stop again, and went right back to work. Securing the fabric to the frame meant laboriously stitching leather grommets into the heavy, waxed flax, and then lacing the fabric to the frame. He was spent by the time he'd finished, and there were sounds of life stirring in the corridors. He'd worked right through the sleeping hours. Not wanting to take the time to go back to his room, Atyen pulled a section of wing fabric over himself and lay down on the thin floor quilt that covered the steel floor. It was hardly comfortable, but he was asleep in seconds.

There was some commotion around the noon-meal bell, but nobody bothered him so he pulled his makeshift blanket tighter and managed to sleep through most of it. When he awoke the studio was quiet again, and now empty except for his corner. The last of the other aspirants departed, and the space echoed with their absence. Atyen ate the last of his bread and went back to work, testing joints, tightening fabric where it wasn't quite taut. He added a hanger and straps so he could carry his backbag with him, snugged up beneath the right wing, and another for his walking staff under the left. When he was done he folded them up, put them on his back, and went to the stairs that led to the forewall ledge. He'd forgotten how heavy they were and as he started up the effort made his damaged calf ache. He bit his lip against the pain and climbed onward, leaning hard on his staff. The stairs were busy with workers clearing away the wreckage from the top of the Inquisitory, but it was only when he got to the top himself that he realized his mistake. The frame and railings of the stairs that went from the top of the Inquisitory to the forewall ledge were steel, but the wooden steps had burned with the rest of the structure's upper floors. There was no way he could reach the ledge. He stood staring at the blackened steel for a long time. To his own surprise he wasn't angry, wasn't frustrated. The destroyed stairs were only an obstacle, and one he could overcome if he worked at it.

He went closer and examined the supports. The original steel steps had long since been worn away, but the stringers still showed the marks where they had been attached. The railings themselves were polished smooth and shiny on top by the eons of hands that had grasped them for support, mute witnesses to the wear that had forced the replacement of the original steps. He tried putting his feet on the stringers, using them for support while balancing himself with the railing. He couldn't support his injured leg with his staff that way, so he slid it in between the folds of his wings. Carefully he made his way up to the space where the first landing had been, and stood precariously, assessing his progress. His leg was sore, but the forewall ledge beckoned, and there was no reason he couldn't make it the rest of the way. He carried on and soon was on the ledge. He paused to rest, satisfied in accomplishing the climb and overcoming the problem. *But don't be too smug, Atyen. The real test is yet to come.*

When he had recovered he walked down the ledge, past the river outfall to the place he had leapt from before. He looked out over the world, and thought about his last flight. It had been more of a controlled crash than anything, but this time would be better. *If only I had more height.* His thrown kite experiments had taught him that it was the first seconds of flight, when the wing was moving slowest that control was hardest. More height would give him more time, and more speed. That would give him more control, and more distance. He turned around to look up the sheer steel cliff above him. It loomed high, thickly covered in climbing vines. A hundred meters above there was a second ledge, this one visible only as a narrow line, a horizontal interruption in the vertical texture of the vast wall. He'd never paid much heed to it, his attention had always been focused outward, on the space he dreamed of flying through. *But if I could get up there . . .*

It was something he'd never considered, but his success in climbing the burned-out stairs gave him fresh courage. *The wall-pickers do it. Why can't I?* He turned to the wall and studied it. Beneath the thick thatching of ivy the steel was deeply textured, with sculpted vertical channels eroded by the constant drip of running water. The channels braided into a complex network, and the thick ivy vines wedged themselves into them, finding support on the knobby surface and nutrients in the trickling water. Some of the trunk vines were thicker than his thigh, and climbing them looked easy. *At least the wallpickers make it look easy.* He took a deep breath, and reflexively checked to see that his wings were still secure on his back. They were, and he put a hand on a thick vine, tested its strength. It held firm, and so he started climbing. *Handhold, handhold, foothold, foothold.* He used his good leg as much as possible, and tried to use his arms to reduce the strain on his injury. He lacked the effortless ease of the wallpickers, but he was making progress. He had only meant to do a short, experimental climb, to find out how hard it would be to go up the forewall with the extra twenty-five kilos of his wings folded on his back, but it wasn't as hard as he'd feared. *As long as I pretend it doesn't hurt . . .*

Ten meters up he found a grape vine clinging to the thick ivy stems, its unripe fruit still hard and green, and ten meters above that a climbing kiwi had rooted itself in a crook filled with leaf litter. For a few meters the two fruits intertwined with the ivy, the thickness of the combined growth making it impossible to even see the steel beneath it, but then the kiwi gave up and the grape began to thin out. At thirty meters the grape was gone and the ivy was getting less substantial, and he began to have to use the forewall itself to climb. That was difficult. The water eroded channels ran mostly up and down, which meant he had to wedge his fists into the crevices to support himself. The wet steel was slippery, and it sucked the heat from his fingers until they were numb. At fifty meters he found another vine that was growing down from the ledge above, intertwining itself with the last tendrils of the ivy. The new vine thickened as the ivy thinned, and he gratefully grabbed its thick hanging loops. His bad leg was trembling with every new foothold now, so he wedged his feet into a loop of vine and rested for a while, looking out into the misty air. A swirling flock of sparrows fluttered past and were gone again.

The vine he was on had big, almond shaped leaves, but he didn't recognize it except to know that it wasn't ivy. *Not that I'd recognize grape or kiwi if they weren't bearing fruit.* The wallpickers would certainly know. He looked up at the vertical face he still had to conquer. The moisture on the vines had soaked him to his skin, and once he stopped moving he began to cool down. He looked down and shivered, not entirely due to the cold. *Do I dare go higher?* To ask the question was to answer it. He had come halfway, it would be no harder to go up than down now. His calf was burning, and his foot trembled when he put weight on it, but he reached up and took hold of the thick runners that snaked down from above. The vine had large purple flowers, and they had a rich, fragrant scent that overwhelmed his senses when he disturbed one. It was also less robust than the ivy he had just climbed. *Do I trust it?* If he wanted to fly he had to. He took a deep breath and climbed onward, using the vine when he could and the cold steel when he had to. Twenty meters up his foot slipped off a slippery steel knob, and the thin vine peeled off the wall. Adrenaline surged and he grabbed for a thicker strand, getting it just in time. For an endless moment he hung suspended, heart pounding, before his feet found purchase on the steel again. High above another vine dangled, beckoning him up. Forty meters to go, and his calf was on fire. Once he gained the second ledge there was no way he'd be able to climb down again. Going higher was an implicit commitment to use his wings.

Atyen clenched his teeth, reached up and grabbed another knob of slippery, water-smoothed steel. Again the heat was sucked from his fingers as he pulled himself up. Even his feet were cold inside the soaked leather of his soft-soled shoes, and wedging them into the crevices in the steel hurt more and more as he progressed. He came to a wall section covered in hemispherically sculpted blobs of mud and straw—swifts' nests. He tried to avoid them as he climbed, but inevitably he knocked some loose. It hurt to see the tiny white eggs falling free to shatter on the ground below. The swifts flew almost as beautifully as the peregrines—not quite so fast, but even more agile than the soaring predators. He kept climbing, and with ten meters to go found a vine thick enough to hold both his feet. He rested again, looking up to judge his final route. When he had his breath, he climbed on until he got a hand on the ledge. It didn't offer the handholds and footholds that the wall itself did, and so he had to scramble over the top by spreading his weight over a wide-spreading mat of vines and hoping he didn't pull the entire array free. Finally he got his legs over the top and for a long moment he lay there, panting. The mist layer overhead was noticeably closer now, it seemed he could almost reach out and touch it. *I could climb to it, maybe.* It would be a difficult climb, because the ivy rooted on the second ledge only went up fifteen or twenty meters. That meant he'd be using the cold, wet steel the rest of the way. Looking up he couldn't even see if there was a third ledge. Not even the wallpickers went higher than this, and he could see why.

Atyen stood up and looked out over the view, and it was both dramatic and daunting. Now he had two hundred meters of height to make his wings fly. If they wouldn't fly in that distance they wouldn't fly at all. *And I didn't come here to climb down.* He unstrapped his wings from his back, laid them carefully on the carpet of moss and ivy and unfolded them. Unlike his previous set, the two meter tail was rigidly fixed to the mainspine. He would be unable to stoop and dive the way a peregrine could, but his previous jump had shown him that he couldn't control a free tail well enough anyway. Gliding down like one of his test models wouldn't be quite the same as soaring and stooping, but it would be a first step. *And much safer, I hope.* He went to each joint and locked it, working carefully and methodically. Forgetting one would be fatal. When he was done he checked them all again, then lifted the assembled wings and secured the straps around his waist and hips. That done, he reached out to take the control lines and put his hands through the loops.

And once more there was nothing to do but jump. *There's so much I can discover, if I can make this work.* He looked over the edge. The ground was a frightening distance below, and his throbbing calf reminded him of the pain of his first bad landing. *But I flew, I really flew.* The memory of the wind beneath his wings was enough, and he leapt, launching himself out as hard as he could. There was an immediate rush of air and he pitched steeply down, diving headfirst for the ground. For a long, horrible moment it seemed that he was about to repeat his previous accident, but then he began to level off, and then all at once he was flying, even climbing. He began to roll to the right and pulled his left control line to compensate. The left wing dropped in response, and he wobbled back in that direction, still climbing. The rush of air fell silent, and then suddenly he was nose down and falling again. His descent was less steep this time, and he was ready when his speed picked up and he again leveled and began to climb as it increased. He had seen the same up-and-down behavior in test models. It happened because the wings weren't trimmed for the load properly, and he pulled in both his control lines as soon as he leveled out to deepen the wing curve. He heard the fabric flapping as the wings grabbed more air, and both his speed and descent rate stabilized. He lurched right again, slacked the right line to compensate, and then tightened it before he could slide away to the left. Keeping tension on both lines, a little less on the right than on the left, made the wobbles less violent.

And he was flying, really flying! The right wing dropped a bit. He caught it a little low, and left it there, biting his tongue in concentration as he tried to keep himself balanced. He was rewarded with a gentle turn to the right. When he had that mastered he tightened the left line and released the right to reverse the turn. Turning was tricky, because a low wing tended to fall away even more, which required him to slack the opposite line in order to compensate. He straightened himself out into more-or-less level flight, and already he was most of the way to the ground. He brought his legs forward in anticipation of landing, but that made him nose down again and he picked up speed. Startled, he pushed them back again, and leveled out. Paying attention to his legs made him forget about his control lines and as he slowly nosed up he dropped his left wing badly. He yanked the left line hard and got the wings level just in time to skid into a low thicket of blueberries. The spiny branches tore at his skin, and then he was stopped. It wasn't the most graceful landing, but he hadn't broken anything, and had only a few scratches for the effort. *I did it, I really did it.* The stillness and quiet came rushing in on him, and already the experience seemed unreal. He let go of the control lines and got to his feet, awkward with the cumbersome bulk of his wings still strapped on, to find a farmer staring at him in wide-eyed amazement. The suntube was bright overhead and he realized he'd flown right out of the forewall mists to the edge of the forefields, easily a kilometer and a half.

Atyen gave him a friendly wave and, somewhat uncertainly, the farmer waved back, then came over.

"How did you do that?" the man asked.

"I jumped, that's all," Atyen answered, as though it were that easy.

The farmer nodded slowly. "Just jumped. Well, that's something."

Atyen he looked up to the distant second ledge, amazed anew at the journey he'd taken. *I flew.* Slowly a broad smile crept across his face. *I really flew.* Still smiling, he looked up the curve of the world to the suntube. Something moving against the brilliant line. It was a peregrine circling slowly as it hunted for dinner.

"I'll be with you soon," Atyen whispered under his breath, as if a louder voice would scare the falcon away, would turn the reality of his accomplishment back into a dream. "I'll be with you soon."

Byo Vesene stood up and went to the back windows of his chamber. It had once been the reading room, the top level of the manuscript tower, but after the fire it had been necessary to find new quarters for himself. He pushed open the shutters to look across at the teams of workers rebuilding the Inquisitory's upper floors. The burnt out skeleton of the old structure had been entirely cleared away, though the underlying steel was still soot-black. The work teams were starting on a heavy bamboo scaffold to rebuild around it. Inquisitor Renn was overseeing the effort, and Vesene had ordered him to do the rebuilding in grand style, but . . . Irritated, he closed the shutters, paced to his worksvshelf, paced back. The room seemed too small. The fire that had consumed the top floors of the Inquisitory had destroyed most of the working records that ran the world, and the work-spaces of those who did the running. The manuscript tower had been pressed into service to house the displaced functionaries, the spaces normally occupied by quietly laboring aspirants were instead full of the bustle of bureaucracy, and it made Vesene feel crowded. *And I don't like to be crowded.* He took off his gloves and took a new pair from the stack beneath his workshelf. Being crowded made him feel . . . unclean. He slid the new gloves on and, feeling better, pulled over the plans for the reconstruction work, frowning. He could already see he didn't have enough space.

There was a knock on the door and looked up. "Enter."

"Chief Inquisitor?"

Vesene saw the gray beard and the double-red cross-sash. "Solender!" he gasped in shock. "You're . . ."

"Solender?" Torr Toorman laughed. "I'm afraid not."

"No, no of course not." Vesene regained his composure, annoyed that Toorman had made him lose it. Fortunately, Charisy's Inquisitor-in-Chief didn't seem to have noticed. "What do you want?"

"I need my sentinels back."

"Hmmm. I'll consider it." Vesene leaned back in his chair.

"Consider it?" Torr's eyebrows went up. "I owed you a favor. I've paid it, and now I need them back. You think Charisy's streets haven't noticed the sleep-watch is gone?"

"Yes . . ." Vesene spoke slowly, enjoying the moment. "I'm afraid they're still needed here. The erranders are still plotting." He leaned forward and lowered his voice conspiratorially. "They poisoned Solender, you know."

"Poisoned him? I thought it was natural. Godstruck, I heard."

"No, no, they poisoned him." Vesene couldn't help but run a hand over his sash-pocket, where the foxglove extract still nestled. "They want me next."

"I gave you five hundred sentinels, surely you don't need—"

"Yes, yes I do. I've made changes to the way the Inquisition runs, and there are those who resent that."

"Chief Inquisitor, I don't need to tell you things aren't good in Charisy. I'll have looters in two days and riots in three if I don't have my force back."

"Ah, but I've thought of that. I'll give you grain."

"Grain?"

"Feed your people, keep them happy. Work out how much you need, go to Cela Joss, tell her I approve it."

"You're going to just give away grain?"

"Why not? It's our job to look after our people." Vesene waved a hand expansively. "The granaries are full. You can have fifty sentinels, and all the grain you require. What else do your people need?"

"Housing, but . . ."

"Make an announcement. Tell them we're going to build houses. Nothing too fancy, but a roof for everyone."

"Are you sure we can do that? The cost will be immense."

"We're already having Renn rebuild the Inquisitory. A few houses for the people will be nothing next to that. Tell him I approve it." Vesene stood up, went back to the window, opened the shutters to look at the work in progress on the roof again, reclosed them. "Better yet, I'll tell him." He went back to the door, called down the stairs. "Get me Inquisitor Renn."

"At once," his head errander answered from below.

"There," said Vesene. "Will that do?"

"You're very generous," Torr Toorman said, though he seemed less pleased than he should have been. Charisy's Inquisitor-in-Chief took his leave, and Vesene closed the door and went back to his workshelf to wait for Renn. *I shouldn't be calling downstairs for service, and I shouldn't be waiting for anything.* There were going to have to be changes, large changes. He picked up his grooming pick and began cleaning his nails. The simple motions were soothing, and they helped him think. There would need to be houses in Charisy, but more important the plans for the new Inquisitory weren't right. *I need something grander, much grander.* He would stop the work here, order Renn to build him something in Charisy. *A proper palace.*

The frightening climb to the second forewall ledge became routine in time, and it gave Atyen opportunity to think. More and more his thoughts were occupied with his future. Most of Solender's other aspirants had curried influence since they'd arrived, with one eye on their masterworks and one on the ladder of power. Since Solender's death they'd used it to gain places with other inquisitors, but Vesene was smarter than they were. He'd used the aspirants to root out Solender's supporters, sending them out to administer law in the farthest parts of the world. Even Atyen knew what that meant. They would rise no higher, and the aspirants they took with them would be unlikely to ever finish their masterworks. So far he'd avoided their fate, perhaps just because he had kept going back to Solender's empty studio and called no further attention to himself. It had worked for over a year. *But I still need a plan.*

He worked his way up the now familiar lattice of vines. His muscles had adapted to the climb, though his injured leg still ached under the strain every time he went up the wall. He'd tamed the harder stretches by tying knots in loops of rope, then jamming the knots into the grooves in the textured wall. Properly placed they held like part of the steel. *The only problem I haven't solved is the wet.* Wool clothing held off the chill, but his hands were perpetually raw from rough use in damp conditions. When he came to the top he threw a leg over the ledge and pulled himself up, stood up and looked out over the world. *Everything is so simple from here.* It would be nice if the rest of his life were the same. Solender's studio had filled up with Vesene's aspirants, but they all assumed that Atyen was supposed to be there and said nothing. Vesene himself never came to mentor, and so Atyen was able to keep quietly working without disruption. It seemed strange to him that the news that he'd learned to fly had not made a bigger splash in the Inquisitory. *But everyone is so worried about what Vesene is going to do.* He'd had a few watchers come for his first few flights, but soon they'd drifted back to their own pursuits and left him to himself.

Which was fine with Atyen. He unfolded his wings and spread them out on the narrow ledge, carefully securing the joints and rigging the control lines. It wasn't hard to fly, once you knew how, and he spent every moment he could steal either refining his wings or leaping from the forewall ledge to test his new ideas. He gained stability by canting his wings upward, and more by sweeping them back. He learned to control his flight not only by twisting the wing tips with the control lines but by simply shifting his weight. He developed a technique of landing on the run, which saved him from the painful skidding his first efforts had involved. He learned how to turn without losing control, and how to shift backwards to brake for a smooth landing. He added length to his harness, which gave him more range to shift his weight back and forward, and added a bracing pole to the mainspine so he could shift more easily. The modifications had added some weight, and he had been afraid that would negatively impact performance, but in fact he could now fly farther and faster than he ever had before.

When he was ready he hoisted his wings onto his back, took his up the lines, and leapt. The now familiar rush of air filled Atyen's ears as he dove away from the ledge, smoothly correcting for the turbulence. The time of wobbly flight and frantic overcorrection was long gone. He had become a creature of the wind. Below him the wallpickers didn't even look up. They'd grown

used to seeing a man fly. *And perhaps one day they'll be flying
too.* As they were, his wings were little more than a toy, a way
of proving that a man could fly, but if he could improve them
to the point where he could soar to the shorefields all sorts of
possibilities opened up. He had a vision of a huge set of wings,
one that he would not wear but ride, and one that could carry
more people as well. Hours of trekking would be replaced by a
brief, comfortable flight. If he could expand them to the point
where he could carry cargo, then one day they might replace
goat-carts as the world's main trade carriers.

The muddy headwaters of the Silver River slipped underneath
him, undulating its way aftward like a grass-snake. The noisy
turbulence of the outfall pool gave way to gentle ripples, and then
a surface as smooth and reflective as polished steel. The suntube
blazed a golden line on its surface, leapfrogging across the river's
loops, a beacon-line pointing due aft. He turned to follow it, slipping silently over the marshy ground. Far ahead he could see the
buildings of Charisy, which seemed so close and yet were way
beyond his flight range. He shifted his weight backwards slightly,
and trimmed the control lines to minimize his rate of fall. He
could stretch his glide, but nowhere near far enough to reach the
city. *And that's the next problem I'll have to solve.*

The marsh turned into meadow, with sheep grazing the lush
grass, and already he had lost half his height. He came out from
beneath the forewall overcast and blinked as the full light of
the suntube hit him. Below, the meadow had become cultivated
fields, layer cropped beneath an olive tree canopy. He picked
his touchdown point, a narrow field, fallowed now with turnip
and clover. There were a few goats grazing in it, but none in
his way. He put the field under his left wing, flew over it until
it was behind him, then dropped the left wing and pivoted into
a tight turn to reverse course. He came out heading into the
steady breeze from the forewall. The headwind cut his forward
progress in half, and he tightened up on the control lines to flex
the wings and deepen their camber. The control slots fluttered
and he slowed more, as his glide angle steepened until he seemed
to be descending almost vertically. He set himself up for touchdown for the near edge of the field, held the line tension as the
wind-rush faded, and dropped towards his goal with peregrine
precision. The grass came up fast, and at the last moment he

shifted his weight backwards, and leveled out, canting the wings higher to help him brake to a stop. His feet touched down and he ran, slowed, stopped. *Beautiful!*

He breathed out with the exhilaration of a beautiful landing, pulled the straps off and set his wings down. The upswept angle he'd added to improve their stability meant they couldn't sit flat on the ground. The right wing was canted up, and he sat down in its shade, unbuckled his backbag and fished out his journal to record the flight. He leafed through the pages to the last one, found an ink jar and began to write. It was his hundredth flight, a milestone, and it had been beautiful. He recorded the details, the distance, the subtle changes in control that his last modifications had brought, the improvement in his landing technique. When he was done he bit his lip. It had been a near-perfect . . . *but* . . . He looked back to the previous page and read over what he had recorded there. That flight had been near-perfect too, and the flight before that, and before that. He was flying, but he wasn't *progressing*. If flying was to become more than an amusing distraction, if his dream of a sky full of cargo carriers was to ever be more than a dream, he had to be able to do more than glide. He lay back in the soft grass, and looked up the curve of the world. In Bountiful a message mirror was twinkling, over Blessed the spiralling clouds were dumping twisting curtains of rain. *And at the Inquisitory, Atyen Horun has mastered flight!* He could turn on a wing tip, dive to skim the ground, pull up to the vertical and pivot in midair to swoop back the way he'd come, as close to a full peregrine stoop as a man could conceivably get. *I just can't soar.* The falcons rode air currents, working the sky the way a child worked a swing. They would dive, pull up, turn, and dive again, and get higher with each cycle, but when Atyen tried the same thing he never gained height above his start point. As he climbed and slowed the wing fabric would flutter as the airflow dropped to nothing, and he would have to release the control lines and nose down again or risk the stomach-turning drop that inevitably happened when he ran out of speed in a climb. It was beginning to seem that soaring like a peregrine was as far beyond his reach as the falcons themselves were. The steady downdraft at the forewall didn't help either, though once he was launched it became a tailwind that helped extend his glide.

Movement caught his eye, a shape high up by the suntube, a

circling peregrine. There was a second one near it, facing aftward and trimmed into the wind so perfectly that it seemed to
be simply hovering. The first one came around to join it, and
they flew in loose formation. They were a mated pair, and they
were hunting. Atyen watched in frustration. He had come so far,
and yet he was still a creature of the ground, his wings giving
only temporary liberation from its relentless pull. *There must be
a way.* He reached over to pull his journal within reach, just in
case the birds gave up a clue that he might record, then went
back to watching the graceful predators fly. *How do they stay
up?* Oblivious to Atyen's frustration, the peregrines continued
their hunt, slowly descending. He watched as they came down,
and then suddenly first one, then the other dropped a wing and
dove to foreward, turned sharply aftward and pulled up, climbing each time. Even that was more effort than they often put in.
Sometimes they would just circle for hours, now climbing, now
diving, but never doing more than twitching a wing.

   *And that should be impossible.* Birds weren't magic, not even
peregrines. A wing was a simple mechanographic device, a vari-
ant on the inclined plane, changing the direction of a force.
They turned a vertical drop into a shallow glide down an invisible slope of air, but just as a ball was constrained to roll down
a slope there was no way he could hope to get higher than he
was when he started. The kites he had started with could climb
because the anchoring line allowed them to turn the horizontal
wind into vertical motion, but peregrines weren't anchored, and
a kite cut loose would fall as it drifted downwind, deprived of
the force that kept it aloft.

   It was the upward tug of a kite string that had convinced him
that he too could fly, if only he could build a kite large enough.
Overhead the peregrines were still circling in flat defiance of
everything he knew about flight. *How do you do that?* Perhaps
there were vertical air currents that the birds somehow sensed,
perhaps . . . He started to sketch a diagram of their rhythmic
climb-and-dive cycle, carefully inking the curving path. Always,
always the turn and dive was to foreward and the pull-up and
climb was to aftward. There had to be something important about
that, but what it might be was a mystery as opaque as the aftwall.
High overhead wispy clouds were spiraling up from the ocean,
not enough to threaten rain, but . . .

Ink spilled on the page as understanding blossomed. *Of course!*
On the ground the wind blew always from foreword to aftward,
but clouds moved the opposite way, drawing their majestic spirals around the suntube as they went. *It's a cycle!* Wind was just
moving air, and if the steady breeze aftward weren't balanced by
a higher wind in the other direction all the air would quickly pile
up at the aftwall. The downdraft at the forewall was caused by the
foreward-moving upper wind hitting the foredome and deflecting
downwards until it hit the ground to become the aftward-moving
lower wind. *Which means there must be an updraft at the aftwall!*
With trembling hands Atyen tore the ink-stained sketch of the
circling peregrines from his journal and threw it away. There was
enough ink left in his jar to start a new sketch, a rough cylinder
that outlined the extent of the world, with a simple line down the
middle to signify the suntube. He drew in careful arrows to trace
the wind circulation, aftward and up and foreward and down. As
he sketched another understanding came to him. *The water cycle.*
The constant mist at the forewall was water evaporated from the
ocean by the suntube, carried up the length of the world by the
upper winds, and condensed against the cold steel of the forewall.
The wind cycle and the water cycle were meshed together like
the gears of a waterclock.

That couldn't be *all* of the water cycle, the gushing outfalls
at the river sources had to come from somewhere else, but as
Atyen sketched he realized that there had to be some connection
that drained water from the ocean and somehow pumped it to
the outfalls. *Otherwise the world would fill up with water.* His
hand trembled as he drew. What he was understanding went far
beyond flight. He was touching on the fundamental nature of the
world, and sensed some unifying concept just beyond his grasp.
*Concentrate, Atyen. Cycles . . .* He looked sharply to the forewall,
to the churning brown torrent that spilled from the Silver River's
outfall. *And the land cycle . . .* Suddenly he understood the mystery of the survey errors that he had explored for Solender in
what now seemed like another lifetime. The rivers washed silt
to the ocean, and something, he couldn't imagine what, pumped
muddy bottom-water back up to the outfalls. The mud settled in
the marshy headwaters of the rivers, slowly building up over time
until the inexorably building pressure forced the very ground to
shift aftward. His hand trembled as he made notes. The wind cycle

would go around in a day or two, but it had to take years for the outfalls to move the whole ocean. *And the land cycle must take centuries, more than centuries.* He realized he could work out its parameters with the old tithing surveys. *How many more cycles are at work in the world?*

The first thing was to understand the wind cycle. Already his drawing was revealing some of its secrets. He looked up to the spiraling clouds. The air would move fast close to the ground and to the suntube, faster still at the world's endwalls, slowest along an invisible line in the sky where the aftward and the foreward winds slipped past each other. *What happens there?* Would there be no wind at all? Or would there be roiling whirlpools of air, as there were when two river currents met? Near the aftwall and the foredome there had to be an overturn, where the moving air turned back on itself, and the air would whirlpool there. He drew carefully, filling in detail and texture. He sketched in the clouds. *I'm still missing something.* What he'd drawn would not produce the spiraling cloud patterns, and he bit his tongue as he pondered what might cause them. The in-bulging curve of the foredome was another question. It had to have some effect on the flow, but it was difficult to predict what it might be. His best guess was that it would shade the forewall from the full force of the downdraft.

*But it's the aftwall that's most important.* There was an updraft there, the complement of the forewall's downdraft, and if he was right about the shading effect of the foredome it would be even stronger. If it were strong enough it might even let him climb. *If I can get into it.* Overhead, the peregrines were still circling. Despite his excitement he forced himself to work slowly, sketching the details of the clouds as he saw them, and calling up memories of other clouds to incorporate into the drawing. Clouds always started over the shorefields, and as they rose they twisted spinward, always spinward, gradually at first and then until they had wrapped the suntube in strands of spiraling fleece. The strands grew fluffier as they stretched, until by the time they reached the forewall mists they had become a uniform shroud, with a texture that only hinted at the spiral structure that had formed it. *They blend with it, but they aren't part of it.* Clouds came and went, but the forewall mists were omnipresent. Sometimes clouds brought rain, but when they did it came in heavy drops and heavy downpours, where at the forewall the mist shaded into drizzle and back again as fog rose and fell.

He finished his drawing, packed his journal and his ink jars into his back bag, folded his wings and shouldered them and headed back to the Inquisitory. As he walked his mind raced over the possibilities. There were ledges on the aftwall, if the lines of green on its surface were any clue. If he could get up on them, he could ride the aftwall updraft as high as he dared. *Noah flew to the suntube.* He had never paid much attention to the Bible, but his diagram hinted that perhaps the story was true. *Or at least possible.* Moving his work to the shorefields would require support, and that meant he needed a doctrinor to sponsor him. Like it or not, he was going to have to test the uncertain waters of Inquisitory politics. *And that might be more dangerous than jumping from the forewall.* As he walked he considered who he might approach to help him. He started to make a mental list of possibilities, but soon became bogged down in speculation and gave up, unable to come to any conclusion. The truth was he didn't know any of the senior inquisitors. It had not seemed important when Solender was his doctrinor, and now he would have to make a decision with no real evidence to base it on. *And perhaps there is no right answer.*

But he had to do something. He made his way into the building and up to the level where the senior inquisitors lived, and by the time he arrived he had a solution to his problem, of sorts. He stopped at the watchkeeper's station to get directions to Inquisitor Renn's quarters. He knew Renn, if only vaguely, and that was a start. The functionary pointed, and Atyen went down the elaborately quilted hall to the indicated door. It was shut and so he knocked, tentatively at first, and then with more confidence when the first knock was overlooked.

"Come in," a voice said, muffled through the heavy door.

Atyen entered. "Excuse me, inquisitor." Renn was a spare man with a graying beard, and his outer office was half in chaos, with paper and manuscripts piled haphazardly over the workshelf and spilling onto the floor. Carefully inked drawings of buildings adorned the walls, models of bridges sat on the walls, a miniature of a two-beam crane took up most of his workshelf.

"Atyen, isn't it?" the inquisitor asked.

"Yes, inquisitor."

Renn pushed his chair back. "Come in, come in. Sit down. You were Solender's aspirant, weren't you? The one who's been jumping off the forewall?"

"I'm learning to fly."

The inquisitor nodded. His cross sash was faded and ink stained. "And now you want to present your masterwork."

"That too, I suppose," Atyen answered. In truth he hadn't considered that a possibility any longer, and it hadn't occurred to him that it mattered. *As long as I get to fly, nothing else is important.*

Renn gave Atyen a surprised look. "You suppose? What else would an aspirant with no doctrinor want from a senior inquisitor?"

"Just the support to keep learning."

"Don't you want to be an inquisitor yourself?"

"I do, I mean . . ." Atyen hesitated, unsure of what might be appropriate to say. "I didn't think it was possible. Anymore, I mean . . ."

Renn laughed without humor. "Our new Chief Inquisitor has not been kind to those who were close to Solender. Is that what you mean?"

"I know they've all been assigned away from the Inquisitory."

Renn nodded. "Exactly. Do you know what will happen if I take you on? Vesene will send us both to the smallest village he could find, me to serve out my time as inquisitor-of-fact for petty land disputes, and you to abandon any dream of a double-red cross-sash."

"I haven't come to ask you to take me on. Only to ask you who I should ask."

Renn's eyebrows went up. "I'm not of a quality to be your doctrinor, is that it?"

"No no, it's not that," Atyen protested. "I mean . . . I've seen what happened to Solender's other aspirants, and the doctrinors they've gone to. I wouldn't put you in that position, but I don't know who to ask. I've never really gotten to know any other inquisitors."

Renn leaned back, a slow smile spreading across his face. "Very clever. You don't know who might still be foolish enough to take on one of Solender's aspirants, but you think I do."

Atyen hung his head, feeling defeated. *I didn't think I'd be so transparent.* "I'm sorry to have bothered you, inquisitor," he said, and turned to go.

"Stop!" Atyen stopped and turned around. Renn waved him back into his seat. "I thought the last of Solender's studio were gone months ago. How have you managed to work without a doctrinor for so long?"

"I've been overlooked, I think."

"Overlooked." Renn put a hand to his chin and considered Atyen as if he were a new kind of insect. "Haven't you tried to find a new place before this?"

"No. I haven't needed one."

"How does that work?"

Atyen shrugged. "Nobody's asked me to leave. I have my room, my workspace, I eat in in the meal hall. I do my work and no one bothers me."

"So why do you need a doctrinor now?"

"I can glide, but I can't soar. To do that I need to go to the aftwall."

Renn laughed. "You know, I'm starting to think you don't want to be an inquisitor."

"As long as I can keep flying it doesn't matter."

"So tell me what's at the aftwall that so important."

Atyen explained briefly what he'd figured out about the wind cycle, and the updraft he predicted at the aftwall. Renn listened patiently, but as soon as he was done began to ask questions. Atyen found himself elaborating on the water and earth cycles as well, on the flight of peregrines, on the shape of wings and the vagaries of flight control. The senior inquisitor was sharp, and inexorably zeroed in on the weak spots in Atyen's analysis. He began to sweat as Renn challenged him on his assumption that water evaporated from the ocean by the suntube would carry air with it. He had no proof that it did, and without that his whole theory would collapse. After a while the questions stopped, and Renn was silent. Atyen bit his lower lip not daring to hope that the senior inquisitor might choose to take him on.

Eventually Renn spoke. "You're the one who did the population research for Solender, aren't you?"

"Yes, inquisitor."

"Did he ever mention our new Chief Inquisitor to you?"

"No. He never spoke of any senior inquisitors. He told me he had rivals once. I can see now he was talking about Vesene."

"I see." Renn looked away, lost in thought. "So what did you think?"

"About what?"

"About our situation, our population, our food supply, our future. All those things Solender was worried about."

Atyen opened his mouth to answer, and closed it again. Certainly Solender had been worried, and Atyen had made his doctrinor's concern his own. *But this man won't be satisfied with such an unreasoned answer.*

"I don't have enough understanding to give a firm conclusion, inquisitor," he said at length.

Renn nodded slowly. "What conclusion would you give, given what you know right now?"

Atyen bit his lip. "Somewhere there's a limit to how many people the world can feed. I don't know how close we might be to that. I think it's more important to understand why the population is growing so fast now when it's been stable for so long. Will it slow down? Will it stop and reverse itself? Can we influence it?"

The senior inquisitor pursed his lips. "Insightful." He picked up a tenth-meter tacklewheel from his workshelf and contemplated it. "Byo Vesene is giving grain to the hungry in Charisy, a noble gesture. He's rebuilding the Inquisitory there, rebuilding it *grandly,* and building houses too." Renn turned the tacklewheel over in his hands, studying it as if the answers he was looking for were written on its underside. "He plans to have full employment in the city. What do you think of that?"

"Those aren't bad things . . . People need food, jobs and houses. As for the Inquisitory, I never understood why we were up here in the mists."

Renn nodded. "I sense a reservation."

Atyen shrugged. "They don't address the underlying problem. The grain has to come from somewhere, so does the bamboo for the houses, the bricks for the Inquisitory."

"Hmmm." Renn considered the tacklewheel some more. Finally he put it down. "Well, young Atyen, I'm not going to recommend an inquisitor to you. I can't see any good coming out of it."

Atyen's heart sank. *But at least I tried.* "Thank you for your time, inquisitor." For the second time he got up to leave.

"Here, take this to the aftwall." Renn reached under his workshelf and pulled out a small satchel of ornately dyed cloth. "Learn to soar, and if the learning doesn't kill you, come back and see me in a year." He dropped the satchel in front of Atyen. It hit the workshelf with a weighty *clunk*.

Atyen picked it up and nearly dropped it; it was far too heavy for its size. He opened it, reached in and brought out a metal disc, the same size and shape as a two-token, but made of something he'd never seen before, like steel but with a smoother, brighter luster and much heavier. It was embossed with the same multi-pointed circle that all tokens carried, but on the reverse it was denominated with a five instead of a two. It was exactly round where most tokens were at least a little out of true, and the embossing was nothing short of perfect. He looked closer and found tiny letters scribed around the rim, but the words had no meaning. I-O-T-A  H-O-R-O-L-O-G-I-I.

"What are these?" he asked.

"Builder tokens."

Atyen looked at the heavy disc with new reverence. "I've never seen one. What are they made of?"

"Nobody knows. They can't be melted, at least not in any forge I've tested them in. They can't be scratched, and you can see that in thousands of years they've barely been worn. Builder artifacts were supposed to be my masterwork, but I learned almost nothing that wasn't already known." Renn shrugged. "I moved on." He chuckled and picked up the tacklewheel again. "But I kept collecting tokens, I have been for forty years now."

"Builder tokens." Atyen took another disc out of the bag. This one was slightly larger, octagonal rather than round, and with different embossing. On the reverse side was the number twenty, though it was far too small for a modern twenty-token. "Why are you giving them to me?"

"They're doing no one any good here. I'm making an investment. You're going to make sure it pays off for me."

"But . . ." Atyen swallowed. "These must be priceless, I can't . . ."

"Not priceless, just valuable. Never take less than ten times the face value for one."

"Face value?"

"The numbers are the face values—you'll find they don't correspond to their steel-weights, though the five-token is close. Don't let anyone talk you into trading them by weight."

Atyen turned the twenty token over in his hand, and considered that it was worth a solid two kilos of steel. "Does this mean *you're* taking me on as an aspirant?"

"This means I think you're too valuable to be wasted. Go away, come back in a year. Things will have changed by then, if we're lucky. Maybe we'll get you a double-red cross-sash after all."

"Thank you." Atyen didn't know what else to say. "Thank you."

"Don't thank me, just don't kill yourself. We're going to need you. And Atyen?"

"Inquisitor?"

"Let's keep this just between us."

The catch-box was overflowing with flopping carp, their scales glinting in the suntube light. The early haul had been a good one. Sarabee gave Jens a kiss, and he winked at her and stepped back onto the net-raft to go out for another run. He pulled the sail up by its haul lines, the fabric flapped and billowed, then tightened as it filled with wind, and the small craft nosed its way into the gentle waves. Sarabee smiled as she watched him go. *Jens is such a good man, a good provider.* She kept watching as he deftly guided the raft through the maze of fishing platforms that clung to the shore. Jens was a deep water fisher, casting his nets a kilometer or two out into the ocean, where the carp lived deep and grew bigger. It took more skill than platform fishing, because you had to know how the fish moved, anticipate where they were going to be, and then be there before anyone else.

"Mind your brother," she told Healan. "Why don't you take him up to the smokeshed and show him how to gather grass."

"I will," her youngest daughter answered. "Come on, Jerl." She took his hand.

"String," Jerl gurgled happily. String was his new word, and his new favorite toy, and he toddled unsteadily after his sister.

"Don't go too far now," Sarabee called after them, then turned to her older girls. "Liese, Acelle, you can help me get these fish on the rack." Without waiting for an answer she grabbed one of the carp from the catch-box, slapped it on the cutting table and deftly gutted it. Proud to be allowed to help, and certain of her priority as the oldest, Liese took the split fish and hung it on the shaded drying rack where the wind could get at it. Soon the three of them had an efficient routine established. It took them the better part of an hour to work their way through the catch, by which time the girls were tired and ready for their noon meal. She sent Liese up to collect the younger children while she washed down the bloody table with buckets of water, then went up to the smokeshed herself. As she had expected they hadn't made much progress gathering grass. *But at least it kept them busy.* She opened the door to the low-roofed structure to check the progress of the fish smoking inside. They was coming along well, though the fire in the firebowl was getting a little low. She took a couple of handfuls of grass from the pile outside, mixing the older, dried blades with fresher, greener material that would smolder and smoke to preserve the fish and infuse it with its delicate flavor. The mongers gave her a premium for her product because it was so good, and her neighbors were always trying to find out what her secret was. *But really it's the way Jens built the smokeshed to draw fresh air in and use it to swirl the smoke.* His innovation cured the fish faster and more evenly, and that made all the difference.

"Sarabee," a voice called. "What do you have for me today?"

Sarabee looked up to see Pren, Cove's most successful monger. "A good batch, done by the evening bell. A hundred kilos at least."

"Mind if I take a look?" Pren was already climbing up the bank from the road. Behind him his son was bringing up a goat-cart piled high with cured carp sides.

"Of course not. Liese, take everyone up to the house. I'll be there shortly."

Her eleven-year-old herded the other children up the path, her young voice giving firm orders.

"Come see," Sarabee continued as Pren came up. She re-opened the smokeshed door and pulled out a side of fish. Expertly she sliced a hunk off for him.

He tasted it, considered it, nodded. "Very nice. Fifty tokens."

"Don't you want to wait till it's done?"

"I'll pay you now, and I'll send the boy back at evening meal."

"Seventy-five," said Sarabee.

"Sixty," he answered. "Only because I like you."

"Seventy," Sarabee countered. "You like your mother, but you'd sell her teeth in Charisy market if you could get a two-token for them."

"You malign me," Pren said, pretending to be offended. "My

mother's teeth are worth more than that. I'll give you sixty-five, though I'll take a loss on the sale."

The offer was what Sarabee had expected, and she was about to agree when a new voice broke in. "I'll give you seventy." She and Pren looked up together and saw a tall, older woman coming up the boardwalk by the docks. Csay, who usually worked the spinward shore.

"Seventy-five," countered Pren, giving the interloper an unpleasant look.

"Eighty," said Csay, out of breath. She'd been running.

"Ninety, though it's twice what they're worth. I won't let such fine fish go to this old hag."

"A full kilo. Don't let this thief cheat you, Sarabee."

"A thief am I?" The banter of bargaining wasn't meant to be personal, but Sarabee could see a hint of anger creep into Pren's eyes. The comment had struck home. "I'll give you a kilo and ten, Sarabee, and as much again for your next catch."

"A kilo and a quarter then," Csay answered. "And the same for your next three catches." She took off her backbag and pulled out a shiny ingot, five kilograms of shipsteel.

"You haven't even seen the fish," protested Pren.

"I trust the Madanes." Csay held out the ingot. "What do you say, Sarabee?"

Sarabee looked from one monger to the other, trying to keep the amazement off her face. "Pren?"

"I can't match it, not today." Pren pressed his lips together. "I'll take what she doesn't of your next catches. Same price."

"A kilo and a quarter for what she *doesn't* take?"

Pren nodded. "Do we have a bargain?"

"We do," Sarabee answered slowly. *What's happening here?* Pren put out his hand and she shook it. "I'll be back tomorrow or the next day. Good catch, Sarabee." He went back down the bank to the road where his son was waiting with the goat cart.

Sarabee turned her attention back to Csay. She looked at the offered ingot, not quite believing in it. Slowly she reached out and took it from the monger. It felt heavy, very heavy, and the steel glowed with a soft luster.

"Thank you, Csay," she said.

"Don't thank me, you should see what good fish is bringing in Tidings, let alone in Charisy."

"How much?"

Csay laughed. "Enough that I'll make a nice profit. You're lucky I got here in time. You were going to take sixty-five?"

"A good enough price." Sarabee paused. "Or so I thought."

"You haven't heard then?"

"Heard what?"

"The tithe on grain just doubled. Yesterday, the inquisitors announced it, the lazy sooksas. Doubled! Today the market was full of farmers trying to unload what they had before the tithecounters took it. You could get fifty liters of wheat for nine tokens. Then the news started spreading and everyone was buying. By the noon meal it was twenty, by the time I left it was thirty."

"That's grain, not fish."

"When bread costs what meat does, people might as well buy meat. When everyone does that, pretty soon meat costs more again. Tomorrow cured fish is going to sell like wheat did today. The other mongers haven't figured that out yet, but I'm buying what I can while I can buy it."

"Oh yes? What would you offered me if Pren hadn't been here?"

Csay smiled. "Sixty-five, I'm no fool." She turned to go back to the boardwalk. "I'll send someone for the catch later."

Sarabee nodded and watched her go, then looked at the ingot, ran a hand over its smooth, unblemished surface. It wasn't smith-cast, it was an original shipsteel ingot, a rarity in the shorefields. People usually saved them when they could, so Csay must have meant what she said about buying all the fish she could get her hands on. *And Pren . . . when has Pren ever lacked the steel to buy what he wanted?* He must've spent all he had already, and certainly his cart had been overflowing. *Not that I can complain about high prices.* Who knew how long the good fortune might last? She checked the smokeshed fire one more time, then started walking up to the house. The unexpected windfall was just in time. Her ancient stewpot, handed down from her grandmother's grandmother, had finally worn out. She hadn't had the steel to get it recast, but the ingot would make a fine new one, with enough left over to pay the smith for the forging. The old pot would make a fine set of hooks for Jens's lines. . . .

Liese had organized a snack for her sisters by the time she got home, and even Jerl was nibbling uncertainly on a piece of panbread. Sarabee's breasts were heavy, and she picked him up to nurse. He'd be weaned, soon enough, and then she and Jens would have to decide if they wanted another child. *We could have one more . . .* Sarabee had always imagined herself with a large family, but the reality was that even four was stretching them tight. *But if fish prices stay so high . . . anything might be possible.* Liese brought her a panbread stuffed with ewe's cheese and dried olives.

"Thank you, butterfly," she said, and kissed her daughter on top of her head. Liese giggled and ran off, and Sarabee watched her go proudly. Her oldest was such a delight, so helpful and mature. All her children were delights in their own way, but Liese had something special, a sly humor that spoke of maturity beyond her years. *And it doesn't hurt that she's so beautiful.* Acelle and Healan took after their father more, but Liese had Sarabee's own graceful features, and her longer, leaner proportions. She was going to break hearts when she grew up.

She finished her meal slowly as Jerl nursed. The market would be closing soon, but she still had time to get the ingot in to a smith, if she left right away. When Jerl was finished she rocked him till he fell asleep, picked up his carry-sling and slipped him into it, then collected her old and worn out pot. She called for Liese to gather the girls, and led all four children over to Celese's. Celese was full of news and gossip about the new tithe rate and the soaring price of grain, but Sarabee stayed to talk only as long as was polite. She told her sister she was on her way to get her pot fixed, but didn't mention the heavy ingot in her backbag. *There's no need to make her jealous.* Celese had given up trying to work her land and was renting it out, so she wouldn't be sharing in the market rise.

She left Jerl tucked in and the girls playing with Celese's boys and went up the road towards Tidings. There was the usual amount of traffic on the road, and that didn't worry her too much, but she kept a watchful eye on her surroundings as she came to the makeshift huts that marked the town's outskirts. Since the attack she felt nervous in open spaces, and uncomfortable alone in public. Ahead a group of youths seemed to take notice of her, and she tensed, but their attention was momentary and a few moments later she was past them without incident. *Things just aren't good in the town.* The merchants had put low walls around their stalls, to keep the urchins from stealing their wares. The sentinels were out in force and the street toughs had vanished from view, but they weren't gone, they just kept to the tangled back alleys, which had started to overflow with squatters living under makeshift canopies of discarded wood and cloth. The market was closing when she got there, the merchants putting away their wares and the customers heading for home. Every grain bin was empty, and even those who sold bread and fruit and vegetables had little work to do in closing up. *Csay was right.* The price of fish tomorrow would be high, and perhaps she'd come to regret having promised the monger three more catches at a kilo and a quarter each. *But who can know tomorrow?*

Sarabee made her way to the street of artisans. There were a dozen smiths there, including three who specialized in pots and utensils. She knew all of them by reputation but none of them in person, and so she went to all three to inspect their wares and prices, finally settling on the one in the midrange of both. The smiths were a broad-shouldered man and his talented wife and they did solid, quality work, but without the ornamental flare of the more expensive shop. She bargained with the wife, who haggled hard, but eventually she came away with what she was expecting, a fifteen liter stewpot for her five kilo ingot. She resisted the temptation to buy a new ladle to go with it. *I've been lucky today, but that doesn't make us rich.* As she was going out another woman came in, a miller to judge by the flour smeared on her clothes. She had a bag full of tokens, and she too wanted a new stewpot. Sarabee smiled to herself, she'd gotten in just in time. The price of smithwork was about to go up.

There was a lot of preparation to be done before Atyen could leave, but he threw himself into it. No longer was he hanging in limbo, existing in the margins of the Inquisitory's new order. He had a purpose, and he had a future. Jumping from the aft-wall would be different, if only because he would be landing in the ocean. He spent some time designing a quick release buckle system, so he could separate from his wings and swim away as soon as he hit the water, and more time assuring himself that the resin used to secure his bindings wouldn't lose strength when it was immersed. He took a day to go to the market in Charisy, to trade some of his builder tokens for steel and buy what he would need.

The city was much calmer than it had been last time he was through. The toughs he saw were in grain-lines, the sentinels were back in the streets. Even so he was acutely aware of the small fortune in the small satchel in his backbag, and decided not to trade any builder tokens in the market. Instead he took them around to the various trust-houses, exchanging only two at each one. He could only trade a fraction of them that way, but he still wound up with a hefty weight of steel. He used it to get himself a goat cart and three pairs of goats, more resin, sinew, best quality bamboo poles and flax fabric and beeswax, dried fruit and meat and sundry tools and equipment. When he got back he left the goats and the loaded cart in charge of the stablemaster, and went back to the studio. He wasn't able to exactly duplicate the studio's toolset, and so he made one last set of modifications to his wings using his new acquisitions, in order to confirm that he could do everything he needed to do with what he had. The experiment proved that he couldn't do without a routing plane, so he would have to make another trip to the toolsmith to get one. He gathered his forming jigs, his collected journals and brought them to the cart, then returned for his clothing, a quilt, and the meager few possessions he had in his room. It was after the evening-meal bell before he was finished, but there was no point in staying in the Inquisitory. He stirred up the goats and headed back down, taking the trading road through Charisy one more time. Even in the sleeping hours the streets were busy with builders, throwing up the bamboo frames of Vesene's new housing projects. He made it to the shorefields before the breakfast bell and knocked on Jens's door. His friend answered his knock, bleary eyed.

"Atyen!" He exclaimed, blinking against the suntubelight. "What are you doing here?"

"I left the Inquisitory . . ."

Jens embraced him. "Come in, come in, you must be exhausted." His friend led him inside, it was only when he put down his blade Atyen noticed that he'd answered the door armed. "Just in case, after last time," Jens said, following his gaze. He closed the door and cracked a sleep shutter open.

"I'd like to stay for a while, if I could, and make some use of your raft."

"You're going to be a fisher?" Jens asked, incredulous.

Atyen shook his head, and explained what happened at the

Inquisitory. "I need you to take me to the aftwall," he finished. "I'll trade you a goat cart and six goats, for as many trips as that will buy me, and straight steel for everything after that."

Jens laughed. "Once again, you're too generous, my friend. I'll get you to the aftwall. First let me find you somewhere to sleep."

There was no extra bed in the small house, but Jens piled a couple of floor quilts in the kitchen alcove by the firebowl. Together they unloaded Atyen's equipment into Jens's sailshed, then turned the goats into the small paddock. When he finally crawled into his makeshift bed he was exhausted.

The breakfast bell came all too soon, with the voices of the children and their mother. Sarabee was surprised to find him there, but welcomed him with a hug. Liese, grown a tenth-meter since last he'd seen her, looked after the younger ones while Sarabee cooked panbread. It was served steaming hot, slathered with peach honey, a rare luxury in the shorefields, and washed down with big mugs of thickened milk. After breakfast Atyen help Jens get the net-raft ready for the trip to the aftwall. He'd brought his wings, though he wasn't sure he'd get a chance to fly. The first thing he had to do was figure out how to get up to the aftwall ledge. They pushed off, and Jens raised the sail. He maneuvered them skillfully through the maze of platforms that crowded close to the shore, the net-raft's sharp nose cutting cleanly through the water. A lot of other rafts were putting out as well but some were coming in.

"They can't have filled their nets already," Atyen said.

Jens shook his head. "Those are liners, not netters, and they've been out the whole sleeping hours."

"Why would they do that?"

"Some think the fish are better when there's fewer rafts in the water. They work when we sleep, they sleep when we work." Jens shrugged. "I've done it, but it didn't make much difference to the catch. Mostly made it harder to catch the mongers, and I never saw the children or Sarabee."

"I see." Atyen fell silent, and then Jens asked him about his wings. He explained once more his theory about the wind cycle, and he couldn't tell if his friend thought he was brilliant or crazy. *Not that it matters. I'm here, I'm doing it.* He watched the graceful rafts sliding over the rippling ocean, and dangled a hand over the side, enjoying the coolness. Eventually the other

rafts began to fall behind as they dropped their nets and began
fishing. Ahead the aftwall seemed close enough to touch, but it
still took them bells to reach it. He spent the time tying lengths
of net line into knotted loops to use on the coming climb. As
he worked his mind drifted back to the last time he and Jens
had sailed to the wall. It had taken much, much longer than he
had thought it would. Eventually they were the only boat for
kilometers. The last bell he'd heard had been almost too faint to
make out, and he was sure that it had taken three at least to get
as far as they had come. Unlike the forewall, the aftwall had no
permanent cloud layer, and the gray steel surface loomed vast as
they drew closer. He could make out the thin lines that marked
the ledges, but as they came closer he could see that climbing
to them was going to be a problem. There were green patches
where vegetation clung to the sheer face, but there was nothing
like the thick, twining layers of vines that covered the forewall.
*And there certainly won't be any stairs.*

The wind dropped as they got closer, which confirmed at least
part of Atyen's theory of the wind cycle. *All I want now is to
feel an updraft.* Instead the gentle breeze fell to almost nothing.
Their progress dropped to a crawl, and Jens angled them so the
sail could make maximum use of what wind there was. Atyen
opened his journal to his carefully scaled drawing of the world
and its cycles to see if he could understand what was happening. *Perhaps it's just random variation.* After some thought he
saw a possible answer. There was an overturn where the wind
reversed itself, an invisible point halfway to the suntube where
the air would spin around itself like a whirlpool in a waterbowl,
but the wind wouldn't turn a corner at right angles. That meant
there would be overturns at the bases of the walls, and perhaps
high up near the suntube as well. He chewed on his lip as he
considered the problem. *Or perhaps I'm wrong.* There was too
much he didn't know. As they grew closer he could see gulls and
fisherbirds swinging and screaming around the vertical face, but
their swooping maneuvers held no attraction for Atyen. He put his
journal away without making any notes, and waited impatiently
to arrive at the aftwall.

Finally they slid up to the gray steel wall, the raft side bumping
gently against it with the lapping waves. "We're here," said Jens,
dropping the sail. He looked up at the vast silver-grey surface,

ran his hand over it. "Look at that, a fortune in steel just sitting there." He ran a hand over a projecting knob near the waterline. "A good axe-blow would get that off, what do you think?"

"It's been tried. You'd break your axe."

"Maybe a blade?"

Atyen shook his head. "Shaped steel is never as good as shipsteel, and the walls are harder even than shipsteel. Anyway, if you could get steel like that it wouldn't be worth so much."

"It would be if I was the only one who could get it." Jens laughed. "Of course the same would be true of carp. What now?"

"Now we'll see if I can climb it." Atyen looked up at the sheer face. It would definitely be a more challenging climb than the forewall. The aftwall carried the same vertical ripples as the forewall, and where the waves could reach the steel it was even more deeply eroded. There was no steady trickle from above though, and so a few meters up it got much smoother. None of the higher grooves were sharp-sided enough to take a knot and hold a loop. He stood up, balancing carefully against the gentle rocking of the net-raft, and experimentally grabbed a projecting knob of the surface, testing his weight on it. *It's going to be difficult.* There was no way he was going to be able to climb with his wings on his back, that was certain. *I'll have to bring a light rope, pull up a heavier one.* That would allow him to haul up whatever he needed, and if he could find a way to anchor it, it would also make climbing much easier the next time. *And I should've thought of that before I got here.* What was it Solender had taught him? *Experience is what you don't have until just after you need it.*

"Do you have a rope I could use?" he asked Jens, and explained what he was thinking.

The fisher looked up, eyeing the wall. "Not here, not that long. I do at home."

"Hmmm. Well, we're here now. Let's see if I can climb it at all before we go back." Atyen found a foothold, tested it and transferred his weight from the raft to the wall. He found a higher foothold, felt it out with his toes, and pulled himself up.

"Be careful," warned Jens, as Atyen moved past the first, easy, holds.

"I will be," Atyen said, but the reality was he had to climb or give up, and he wasn't going to give up. *And the water will cushion my fall, if I do fall.* He found a handhold just out of reach, and after a frustrating moment trying to get ahold of it, he start looking for something closer. There were none, but there was a smooth projection, not quite a handhold, but enough to brace against to give him the extra four centimeters of reach he needed. He braced, pushed, reached, and managed to grab the elusive knob of steel. His new position wasn't stable, and he had to scramble to get a better foothold before his grip failed. At least the aftwall was suntube-warm, unlike the water-chilled forewall. It made the climbing much more pleasant.

He climbed higher, handhold, handhold, foothold, foothold, and the first time he looked down he was ten meters up, higher than the net-raft's mast. The lack of good holds put more strain on his legs, and his injured calf ached already, but he felt good. *I'm doing it.* If he could keep it up for another ninety meters he'd be on the ledge. He bit his lip and climbed onwards. The next section of wall was easier than the first; some of the ripples were deep enough that vegetation had taken hold, and once he found a tiny birds' nest, long abandoned. He went up with relative ease for another ten meters, and then ran out of easy holds. There was an easier looking route off to his right, and he moved down, across, and up again to try it. There were still no good handholds, but there was a series of deeper vertical striations in the steel that he could wedge knots into. He did, and climbed on the loops until he couldn't place any more, then rested on the loops as he assessed the way higher. Up and to his left he saw what looked like a good route, and visualized how he'd tackle it, then started climbing again. His leg was burning from the strain now, but he ignored the pain and kept on.

He shouldn't have. The pain was a warning that he'd pushed the injury as far as he safely could. Had he been climbing the more deeply textured forewall he might've gotten away with it, but he wasn't. He'd gone a few more meters up his route and was reaching for a good handhold just out of reach, trying the same brace-push-reach technique he'd used at the bottom. He didn't quite make the reach, but most of his weight was supported on his injured leg, and when he came back down on it, it buckled beneath him. He slipped, clung for a heartbeat to the single handhold he still had, grabbed at the wall with his free hand, and then fell backwards. When he hit it seemed harder even than his near fatal landing after his first flight, and the pain flashed white in his vision. For an instant he thought he'd smacked the raft itself, but then the water closed over his head. The impact knocked the wind out of him and he had to fight the urge to inhale. He flailed around, disoriented, opened his eyes and swam towards the light, kicking hard, his lungs burning. It seemed to take forever to reach the surface, and his eyes were popping by the time he broke it. He gasped, sucked in water, coughed and went down. This time he had a breath and when he broke the surface again he made sure he was well above the waves before he took another one.

"Grab it," Jens was yelling, and Atyen became aware of a wooden net-float in front of him. He grabbed it and hung on, still coughing up water. The float was tied to a length of rope, and Jens pulled him over to the raft and pulled him in over the net-haul. "Are you all right?"

Atyen tried to answer and coughed up more water. Every bone in his body felt broken, even his teeth hurt, but nothing hurt more when he tried to move it, which was a good sign. "I'm . . . fine . . ." he finally managed to gasp.

"In Noah's name, I thought you were killed."

"I've . . . had worse . . ." Atyen managed to sit up, and felt himself over, just to confirm that nothing new was broken. He looked up at the place he fallen from. It seemed very high. "Water gets harder when you fall a long way."

Jens looked worried. "I'll get you back to shore."

Atyen looked up at the wall, his eyes following his path to the point where he'd slipped. Already the pain was starting to fade in his back and legs. He'd climbed nearly thirty meters, and he wanted more than anything to just get back on the wall and get back up. *But I need rope next time.* He'd learned that he could climb the aftwall, and he'd learned that it was dangerous. There was no point in trying again until he could make his success count towards his goal.

"I'm just glad you didn't drown." Jens was already raising the sail to take them back.

Atyen breathed in shakily. "Me too. We'll come back tomorrow."

Jens gave him a look. "Tomorrow? Are you out of your mind? Why would you do that again?"

Atyen shrugged. "Because I want to fly."

"You *are* out of your mind."

374        *Paul Chafe*


"Then it's a good thing I've got you to look after me." Atyen put a hand on Jens's shoulder, reawakening the pain in his punished muscles. "Thank you."

Jens's expression was unreadable, and they sailed in silence, each lost in his own thoughts. Atyen kept his eyes on the aftwall as it receded. *I can do it, I know I can.*

The voyage back took twice as long as the voyage out, because they had to work against the wind, and it was long into the sleeping hours before they were back to the dock. Sarabee and the children were asleep when they came in. Atyen hadn't broken any bones, but he'd pulled every muscle in his body and could barely sleep as a result. When Liese's young voice woke him at the breakfast bell he was so sore it was all he could do to stand up and hobble to the kitchen table. *So I'm not going back to the aftwall today.* Jens told Sarabee what had happened, and she insisted on putting him into their own bed when her husband went out to do the day's fishing. He protested, and tried to make himself useful, but every movement was painful and awkward and so he finally acquiesced to her ministrations. At the noon-meal bell he insisted on getting up to sit outside and work on his journal, sketching in the eroded steel of the aftwall and considering how he could climb better. He found no easy solution. The steel was the steel, and he could not cut handholds in it, nor attach anything to it. Without vines or enough places for climbing loops it was down to his own strength and skill, and that had already proved inadequate. He recalled an experiment he learned when he'd first studied in mechanography, where two pieces of steel rubbed together in a certain way would develop a force that made them cling tenaciously to each other or a third piece. *But that force is nowhere near strong enough to climb with.* It might be possible to find a way to increase that, but he wasn't inclined to engage in yet another side-exploration in pursuit of this goal. The wall was there. *I'm just going to have to climb it.* The one thing he could do was make sure he only had to succeed once. He had initially envisioned a simple rope, with a timber frame that he could haul up in sections to anchor it. *But I can do better than that.* He spent the rest of the day carefully planning a heavy frame with an overhanging beam that would support a carrier basket moving up and down on ropes run over tacklewheels, so he could easily haul things up and down, including himself.

They didn't return to the aftwall the next day either, or even on the third day. He felt well enough to move though, and he borrowed the goat cart he had just given Jens and took it into Tidings to buy some rope, some light bamboo and some heavy lumber, the routing plane he needed, two pairs of tacklewheels and a few other necessary sundries. The only lumber in the cutyard that met his needs had been salvaged from an old barn, and it was more much more expensive than he had thought it should be. The tacklewheel systems ran the rope top to bottom to top to bottom, which meant he needed three-hundred meters of rope for each carrier. There was nothing like that available in Tidings, so he had to go to the sailsmith in Cove and leave an order. While he was there he bought a couple of big double-geared winding drums, meant for hauling nets. They'd be easier and safer than simply hand-over-handing the ropes.

The hike to Cove and back saw him home after the evening-meal bell, but he still managed to buy a disused fisher's sailshed not far from Jens's dock. Like the lumber it was more expensive than he'd imagined, and it took a significant fraction of his token reserves to buy it. It had two rooms, one of which would serve as a small workshop, the other for a tiny living space. Jens and Sarabee had been generous in letting him stay, but they really didn't have the room with four children, and it was awkward sleeping on their kitchen floor. *And Sarabee . . .* She was bright, open, funny, generous, and as beautiful as she had always been. Living in close proximity to her aroused emotions in him that he didn't really want to deal with. *She's the wife of my best friend.*

He spent one more night with them, and then Sarabee gave him a sleeping quilt and a few domestic sundries to set up housekeeping, and he made a hammock out of some discarded sail cloth that he found in a corner. He set up his forming jigs on the workshop floor, and his tools on the workshelf. He was used to living by himself in austere circumstances, but for some reason he felt lonely in a way he hadn't since he'd first arrived at the Inquisitory. The windows had shutters but no sleep-cloth, and it was too bright inside for good sleeping. He threw his arm over his eyes to keep the light out, and eventually managed to fall asleep. When he did he dreamt he was falling again, and awoke with a start. It felt like he'd slept for only minutes, but the toll-ing of the breakfast bell from Tidings church told him he'd been asleep for hours. He got up, ate a handful of his dried fruit and got to work with the lumber he'd bought. Over the next week he built a pair of heavy frames to hold the tackle-wheels, one for the hundred-meter ledge and one for the two-hundred-meter ledge. He had designed them in sections so he could lift them in pieces and assemble them easily up on the wall. At the end of the fourth day the frames were finished, and he no longer felt lonely. *I'm accustomed to working by myself, living by myself.* It was only when he saw what Jens had that he felt what he lacked.

The sailsmith arrived with the winding drums and two heavy coils in a cart, and Atyen was amazed at their size and bulk, six hundred meters was a lot of rope. He picked one up experimentally, grunting with the effort. He had planned to bring one to the top of the aftwall and drop it over so he could haul up the frame components, but there was no way he'd be able to climb with such a weight on his back. The solution was straightforward, he sent the sailsmith back with an order for a hundred-and-twenty-meter length of light cord, strong enough to pull up the rope, which could then be used to pull up everything else. He spent the rest of the day working on the carriers, lightweight baskets of bamboo big enough to hold him and his wings, barely, each built around the drums. He added locking cleats to the ropeways for safety.

In another week the carriers were finished, and with the rope in hand he had all the components he needed. It made him impatient to get back to the aftwall, but he held himself back. The only way he would conquer the aftwall was through physical strength and climbing technique. His technique wasn't bad, he'd learned a lot on the forewall, but there was no question he could be stronger, and getting to the second ledge would take all the strength he could get. He didn't know how far he had to fall before cushioning water became hard enough to be fatal, but it couldn't be much more than the thirty meters he'd fallen so he couldn't afford another mistake. *In a way I'm lucky I fell when I did.* Very much higher and he might not have survived the experience. He cut a series of small blocks, nailed them to one wall of this workshop, and for the rest of the day he practiced climbing on them. When he was too tired to go on he set about making his small space a little more comfortable. He cut sleep-cloths from the leftover sail cloth, painted them over with some pitchfill he found in a corner and hung them.

Light still filtered around the edges, but they made the room dark enough to sleep in. He cleaned up his small room, swept the floor, and arranged his few belongings on a shelf that had once held nets and floats. When he was done he climbed his blocks again, and then again.

That set the pattern for the next weeks. With his forming jigs set up he could work on his wings, but there was little he could do to improve them until he had test-flown the current configuration. He put the rest of his time into climbing practice and long walks to build his endurance. Once he even hiked all the way to the forewall, climbed to the second ledge and back down. He spent the sleeping hours in the Inquisitory, sleeping in one of the dark and disused inner corridors, and then hiked all the way back to the shorefields. His injured leg was screaming by the end of it, but his muscles were harder than he could remember them ever being, he felt stronger and fitter than he ever had, and the entire trip back he kept his eyes on the aftwall. *I will climb, and I will fly.* Occasionally Jens would bring up dinner in covered dishes to spend the evening and talk, other times Atyen would visit to share the evening meal with him and with Sarabee. The conversations would last far past the time they should have been in bed, and Atyen found himself thriving. He hadn't had friends since he'd left for the Inquisitory, only colleagues and doctrinors. He'd forgotten how much he missed that.

And then, when he was ready, he outlined his plan and asked Jens to take him back to the aftwall.

His friend hesitated. "I'm not sure I should, Atyen. I don't want to help you kill yourself."

"Jens is right," put in Sarabee. "It's so nice to have you back in the shorefields. Come and fish with us, we could use the help . . ." She hesitated. ". . . and I wouldn't have to worry about you."

Atyen opened his mouth to answer, and closed it. *There's no way I can explain so they'll understand.* "It's what I have to do," he said finally. "I've worked on this for years now, and I'm not giving up. I have to hire someone to take me to the aftwall, and I'd rather it was you. And I'd rather it was you there if something goes wrong again."

"Atyen . . ." Jens paused.

"You can't convince me not to do it, you can only help me, or not."

"Alright," Jens breathed out. "It's your life, and your pyre."

"Thank you." Atyen looked to Sarabee and saw in her face the protest that she wasn't allowing herself to voice. "Thank you both."

The conversation turned to other topics, and then Atyen helped Liese with her mathematics lessons while Jens and Sarabee finished their chores. Sarabee set up his quilts on the floor again, and he spent the night there. The next day he and Jens took the goat cart up to his converted shed, loaded the lifting frames and sections, the carrier baskets, the rope and the tackle wheels, and his folded wings and took them down to the dock. They transferred the cargo into Jens's raft and again they set sail for the aftwall. They chatted on the journey, mostly about the children, Liese's bright curiousity, Jerl's propensity to hike off by himself with toddler boldness, Acelle's rivalry with Healan in cloth doll-making. Atyen had never seen himself as a father, but he had enjoyed helping Liese with her work, and playing with the younger siblings. He remembered Jens's advice to find himself a wife and settle down. *But how can I do that?* Even if he left the Inquisition for good he had no way to support a family.

As they got closer to the aftwall Atyen moved ahead of the sail, searching out a section of wall with more green. More vegetation would mean deeper crevices and easier climbing, or least so he hoped. Jens steered them towards the point he'd selected, and when they came to the wall he could see he'd made the right choice. The surface was noticeably more textured. He again chose handholds and footholds and started climbing. Behind him Jens pushed the net-raft off, to anchor a little distance away. Atyen had been lucky not to hit it last time he fell, and there was no use in tempting fate any further than he had to. A coiled length of light cord hung from the back of his belt. It was easier this time, his efforts at conditioning and careful choice of route had paid off, and so had the practice he'd put into more difficult climbing. His leg began to pain him halfway up, but he was able to rest with one foot on a small projection until he felt able to continue. The denser vegetation seemed to have attracted the gulls and fisherbirds as well, and they swooped and called all around him, their combined cacophony seeming to drown out the world. He made it to the top without incident, clambered onto the ledge, and breathed a sigh of relief. The aftwall ledge was wider than the one on the forewall, a good five meters. It was thickly covered in grasses, with messy looking gull's nests everywhere, interspersed with blueberry bushes picked ragged by the birds. Some distance away a fair sized tree was growing, something he'd never seen on the forewall ledge.

He went to the tree, took the cord from the back of his belt and tied it to the trunk. When the cord was secured he went to the edge and tossed it over. Far below Jens had pushed the raft away from the wall and was looking up. He paddled the raft over to grab the cord, and while he did Atyen took a moment to inspect the tree. It was an oak and huge, bigger than any he'd ever seen. Other trees just as large stood at intervals around the ledge. It seemed incredible that no one had come to harvest them. *But perhaps nobody can.* The fishers who could sail to the aftwall were fully occupied hauling their living from the ocean. The wallpickers who had the skills to climb lived at the forewall, thirty kilometers kilometers distant, and specialized in gathering food, not lumber. The timber cutters who concerned themselves with bamboo and tree-wood lived in between. No single group had the skills necessary to harvest the inaccessible trove. He ran a hand over the rough bark, marveling at it, and looked down to where its roots gripped the ground. As on the forewall ledge the soil was a pale mixture of bird droppings and decaying leaves but it was thicker and heavier, perhaps due to the much less frequent rain. There were fisherbird nests in the branches, some easily within his reach, but the birds seemed totally unafraid of him. *And why would they be? Nothing can eat them up here.* The ledge, he realized, was a completely self-contained world-within-the-world, untouched by humans for centuries, millennia, perhaps not since the Builders. *Maybe I'll find a horse up here.* Even as Atyen thought it he laughed at himself. A tree could grow from a seed that a bird could carry to the ledge, not so a horse.

"Atyen, are you all right?" Jens's voice rose faintly from below.

Atyen went to the edge and leaned over. The net-raft seemed like a toy bobbing in the ocean below. "I am! Tie on the other rope."

"It's ready, haul away."

Atyen began pulling, and soon the light cord gave way to the heavy rope that Jens had tied on. He called down again to tell Jens to attach the first of the frame parts, and then looped the rope around the tree so he could use it as a makeshift tacklewheel.

Even so it was a lot of work to haul the frame components up. He brought up the carrier last, and by the time he finished, his already tired arms were aching. Jens had put the tools he needed to assemble the frame in it: shaped wooden pegs, cast nails and his hammer. He'd designed the frame to be heavy and stable enough to support his weight by itself, but as he started to put it together he realized that he could have just used the oak to secure the upper tacklewheel and saved himself a great deal of effort. *If I'd thought of it.* On impulse, he lugged the frame components over to the tree. It didn't take long to get them assembled and nailed together, and when he was finished he cut a few meters of rope and lashed the frame to the tree's trunk as an extra safety measure. He threaded the rest of the rope through the tacklewheels, attached one to the carrier's winding drum and one to the frame, and he was done. It didn't take long to lower the carrier back down to the boat. Down below, Jens loaded the components for the second frame and carrier, and the second rope. Atyen hauled it up, unloaded it, and sent it back down so Jens could come up himself. While his friend slowly cranked himself up in the carrier, Atyen looked up to the second ledge. He was tired, but there was no point in stopping now.

"You're crazy, do you know that?" Jens said as he came over the top. "This is dangerous."

"It's what I have to do," Atyen answered.

Jens had brought a basket of dried carp, bread and fresh fruit with him, and they shared the meal in silence. The fisher was looking out over the ocean, and Atyen saw in his eyes the appreciation of the vista. *And it is beautiful.* The arching curve of the world encircled the brilliant line of the suntube, itself wreathed in spiraling clouds. The distant foredome looked like an eye, the forewall mists providing a narrow iris around a huge, black pupil, in which he could faintly see the ever-spinning stars. *The view from the forewall was never this good.*

"I'm going up again," he told Jens.

"Good luck."

Atyen untied the light cord from the oak, coiled it and attached it to the back of his belt again, checked his supply of climbing loops, found a good set of handholds and started climbing. This time he was slower, both due to the fatigue in his arms, and the soreness in his calf. The steel of the wall was even less deeply

eroded than that below, and it gave fewer good handholds, and
nowhere to wedge knots. Several times he had to go down and
sideways to find a better route up. If he fell this time he'd hit
the ledge below, and there would be no second chance. His arms
were trembling in fatigue halfway up, and his fingertips were
numb, but as he climbed higher he could feel a gentle updraft
on his back. It was what he had come for, and it put steel in
his determination to go on. The updraft strengthened steadily as
he approached the top, and when he finally scrambled ungrace-
fully onto the ledge he knew he'd come to the right place. The
knowledge washed away the pain and fatigue, and he laughed,
feeling the up-rushing air washing over his face, tugging him up
towards the suntube.

Re-energized, he once more tossed the light cord over the
edge to Jens, once more hauled up the heavy rope, and then
the components for the tacklewheel frame. He rested before he
assembled it, looking out towards the foredome again. He imagined the peregrines there, soaring and wheeling with effortless
ease. *I'm coming soon.*

This time there was no convenient tree to tie the frame to,
he would have to trust his calculations that it would be stable
enough to hold his weight without sliding off the ledge. He was
tempted to get Jens to send his wings up and test right away. *But
that wouldn't be smart.*

He was far too tired to attempt a flight, so he swung himself
into the bamboo carrier, and cranked his way down to the first
ledge. Jens had taken the opportunity to have a nap while he
worked, and Atyen woke him up. Together they got into the first
carrier and lowered themselves to the water.

Sarabee had long since put the children to sleep and gone to
bed herself by the time they got back. Atyen spent the night once
more on the kitchen floor, to save the walk back to his shed. That
proved to be a mistake when Liese stepped on him before the
waking bell. She was up to start the oven for breakfast, although
at least her early-morning eagerness gave Atyen time to get up and
make himself presentable before Sarabee came into the kitchen.

"Are you really going to fly, Atyen?" Liese asked, opening the
hearth door.

"Who told you that, butterfly?"

"Mamsha. She said that flying is very dangerous, but that you are very brilliant." Liese pronounced *brilliant* carefully, emphasizing each syllable in turn. "She said that if anyone could fly you could." She knelt by the hearth and swept the ashes from the evening meal's cooking into a wooden bucket.

"Did she?" Atyen felt himself fill with pride, and reminded himself to be modest. "Well, I am learning to fly, but it's really not that difficult. Anyone could do it if they worked at it. Here, let me help you with that." He took the bucket from her and finished sweeping out the hearth.

"Can *I* fly?" Liese, standing back to watch him work.

"Not yet, butterfly. Maybe when you're older." Atyen took tight-twisted straw fire-rolls from the stack beside the oven and arranged them in a neat pyramid.

"I like to watch the gulls, they're very graceful."

"They are. Where does your mother keep the fire-piston?"

Liese got him the utensil and he loaded it, pumped it, and got the fire going. Sarabee came in with the other children and began organizing breakfast, and soon the kitchen was full of the aroma of panbread and fried carp.

After the meal he and Jens went back to the raft and again sailed for the aftwall. Atyen had a momentary panic when he tried to pinpoint the spot on the wall they'd sailed for before and couldn't find it, but Jens was a skilled navigator and guided them unerringly back to the carrier.

"How do you do that?" Atyen asked.

"Every fisher has his marks," Jens answered, pointing out a series of notches on the mast. "The middle one is my home mark. When I'm sitting on the steering bench and it lines up with Cove, then I know home is straight ahead. Our spot on the aftwall puts the mouth of the Golden River just below the high notch."

Atyen nodded. The system was a simple but effective version of the measuring circle the surveyor had taught him to use. He had noticed the notches before, but it hadn't even occurred to him that they might have a purpose. *How much more in the world has a purpose that I can't even guess?* The ledges, for example. He was sure the Builders hadn't put them there so that one day he might jump from them. What purpose did they serve? Or were they simply artifacts left over from the creation of the world, like mold marks on poured steel, existing as evidence of the process with no function of their own?

They came at last to the hanging carrier, and Atyen clambered in with his folded wings. Cranking the carrier up on its rope was much less risky than climbing, but it was no faster and it seemed to be even more work. It seemed to take forever to get himself up to the first ledge, longer still to get to the second. When he finally arrived, he unfolded his wings, locked the joints, hoisted them back onto his back and went to the edge. He checked his control lines, verified his backbag was buckled in place. The updraft was strong in his face, and he took a deep breath and launched himself out and away from the aftwall. The upwelling airstream caught his wings and all at once he was flying. *Soaring!* He swooped down, pulled up, and was already higher than the ledge, and still climbing in the rising air. He pulled the right control line and banked around to see the net-raft. Jens was waving, shouting encouragement, though his words were too faint to make out. He banked right, banked left, headed for the distant eye of the foredome, and still he was going up, it was that easy. The raft was soon a tiny dot slipping behind him, and the world stretched out around him, laid out in a patchwork of brown and green fields.

It was exhilarating, liberating in a way that even his best forewall glide had never been. Turbulence buffeted him, but he confidently compensated with the control lines, shifting his weight forward to fly faster. Faster forward meant faster downwards, but even as the wind rushed in his ears he was still going up. He even felt lighter, and just for fun he pulled up almost vertically, dropped the left wing and fell away, pivoting to swoop down heading in the opposite direction. The maneuver left him giddy, and he laughed out loud, pulled up and did it again to the right. The pull-up-wing-drop was almost identical to a peregrine's stoop entry maneuver. All he would have to do was hold the dive as he spiraled down, down, to pull out at the last moment and skim the ground. *Soon, but not yet.* Height was distance, distance was freedom, and he wanted more. He straightened out, heading foreward again, to regain what he'd given away in the maneuvers, and to get some more space away from the aftwall.

The temperature dropped as he climbed higher, until it was cool enough to make him shiver, but he was beyond caring about physical discomfort. Once he thought he was high enough he tried the maneuver again, this time keeping his weight forward, extending the move into a nearly vertical dive. The wind built to a roar in his ears and his wings shook violently, until finally he pulled in both lines and shifted backwards to pull up and swoop again. The pull-out was so sudden that the straps cut hard into his shoulders and waist, and in an instant he was climbing vertically for the suntube. The wind rush faded to silence and for a moment he hung there, weightless and marveling at the incredible freedom he had won. Then all of a sudden he tumbled backwards as the world spun around him. Panic spiked, and he was falling, spinning out of control, and though he yanked hard on the control lines the spin only speeded up. *Oh please Noah, let me live.* All of a sudden the ocean wasn't far below, it was close, and coming up fast. He tried to shift backwards to slow down, but that didn't work either. In desperation he alternated pulling left and right, and all of a sudden the spin stopped, leaving him heading straight down, with his wings once more shaking from the strain of his speed. Ever so gently he pulled himself out of the dive, swooped up and then leveled out once more, shaking and giddy. The experience was terrifying and liberating at the same time, and the steady updraft was once more carrying him upwards.

He breathed deep to calm himself, and tried to understand what had just happened. Peregrines could stoop and pull out, turn in their own wingspan, even roll over on their backs, and he had never seen one plummet out of control the way he just had. *But peregrines are born to fly.* Atyen didn't have the same easy, instinctive control over his wings that they did. Flying was freedom, but not unlimited freedom. He couldn't fly too fast, or too slow, climb or dive too steeply. *But I stooped, or close enough.* He looked down and saw he'd made it halfway to the shorefields, easily twice as far as he'd ever flown before. He soared higher, riding the wind up towards the suntube. As he soared higher he felt strangely lighter, and his wings seemed to respond more sluggishly. *Strange . . .* The air had gotten decidedly brisk, but at the same time the suntube's heat grew more intense, radiating even through the wing fabric. Waxed flax burned easily, so he put a hand up to gauge its temperature. *Hot, but not hot enough to burn.* He could go higher but he'd have to be careful. He didn't want to wind up like Noah, falling from heaven with his wings on fire. He looked down and saw to his surprise that he was already halfway to the shorefields, and he sensed that his upward progress was slowing. He'd ridden the updraft into the foreward moving upper airstream, and it was pushing him with the clouds towards the foredome.

Mindful of the fabric temperature, he shifted his weight forward to fly faster and lose some of his height, but the rush of wind in his face was much gentler than he'd expected. He felt almost as though he was floating, though ahead and below the shore was getting noticeably closer, so his speed on the ground hadn't slowed. *The rules are different up high.* He kept his weight shifted forward until he sensed he wasn't going up any longer, then started slowly shifting it back to maintain what felt like level flight.

A billowing cloud spiraled ahead, and he turned to fly towards it. From a distance it looked like fresh fleece, solid enough to land on, but as he got closer it dissolved into diaphanous tendrils of mist. Just for fun he flew into it, but very quickly the mist closed in to envelope him in grey nothingness. He shifted forward, intending to fly out the bottom, and was reassured when the wind rush increased. It kept increasing though, and his weight built up again with alarming speed. He tried shifting back again, but nothing changed. He felt himself in a hard turn to the right and yanked on the left control line to straighten himself out. The move lurched him violently sideways, and the mainspine creaked under the strain. He yanked the other control line for lack of a better idea, and then he was tumbling, with no idea which way was up, and no clue what to do to right himself. He fell out of the bottom of the cloud going sideways and far too fast. Heart pounding, he managed to get himself leveled out, shifted back and soared up again. He was several hundred meters below the cloud by the time he'd regained control but to his surprise he found he had no trouble climbing back up underneath it; in fact, he had to shift hard forward to keep from climbing right back into it again. His speed built up slowly, and he set his course for the foredome again. Far below him he could see the shoreline, just slightly behind him now. He'd flown ten kilometers in half a bell. *Amazing!*

He flew out from under the cloud and shifting winds rocked him again. There had definitely been an updraft under it, because though he could fly fast and level beneath it once he was past its margin he began descending again, slowly at first and then with increasing speed. Below him was a sprawl of buildings that must have been Tidings, and ahead and spinward the larger sprawl that was Charisy. He'd come down as he flew, and he considered turning around to try and find the updraft beneath the cloud again, but decided to try and find home instead. He banked into a circle, scanning the ground for landmarks. The wind was still drifting him foreward, and so he had to adjust to circle, flying slower foreward and faster afterward to keep himself more-of-less stationary over the ground. It was hard to recognize anything with certainty, he was just too high. He smiled to himself. *Too much height, what a problem to have.* He'd come a long way from his first, hesitant jump from the forewall.

He was completely unprepared when the turbulence hit. It lifted one wing, dropped the other, and suddenly he was nose down and falling. He recovered as he had before, weight forward, pull against the spin until it stopped, and then ease out of the dive. *I'm learning.* The air was still rough, jostling him left and right, up and down, but he was able to compensate without getting turned over. *The wind is full of surprises.* An instant later there was a particularly violent gust, and then suddenly the wind in his face stopped and his wings, robbed of lift, stopped flying. He dropped again and started to tumble and this time recovered instinctively. *Not graceful, but effective.* He went back to his slow, circling descent and discovered another surprise though it took him a couple of turns to recognize. He was now drifting aftward as quickly as he had been going foreward before.

It was a puzzle, until he realized that he must have passed from the higher, foreward moving wind layer to the lower, aftward moving layer. He'd run out of airflow because of the direction change as he crossed the boundary. *And the turbulence is where the two winds meet.* He had predicted the swirling overturns where the wind cycle turned back on itself at the walls, but of course there would be a turbulent boundary where the two flows met and slid past each other along the whole length of the world. The drift was pushing him back out over the ocean, and he had to drop the nose and fly fast upwind to get back over land. He felt his weight coming back as he got lower, and his wings got more responsive again. *Time to pick a place to land.* He found Tidings again, followed the main road to the shore road, followed it antispinward what he judged to be a couple of kilometers. One of the docks there had to be Jens's, but he still couldn't tell which one. *Never mind, just get down.* He chose what looked like a pasture field, turned foreward into the wind, just as he had at the forewall, lined himself up, shifted back and put tension on both lines, and then he was down.

He unbuckled his wings and lay down in the long hay, looking up at the spiralling clouds. He had transcended the ground, truly soared! *Wonderful!* He looked forward to the foredome, taking its measure. Somewhere up there the peregrines nested. *And sometime soon, I'll be there.*

Byo Vesene was frustrated. Work on the grand new Inquisitory building in Charisy was going too slowly, and he was tired, tired, tired of the forewall mists, and all his inquisitors did was complain. *Why am I persecuted so?* He got up from his workshelf, went down the stairs of the manuscript tower. On the next level down his guards fell into step on either side of him, and erranders and tithecounters got out of his way as he descended. That at least was satisfying. *They recognize my greatness.* He went outside, where the gray steel of the Inquisitory faded indistinguishably into the gray fog in the distance, and walked along it. At the far end of the building there was a wooden extension to the steel structure, the receiving floor for the Inquisitory's grain vaults. Its entrance was guarded by a dozen more sentinels, but they stood back when they recognized him, and he went through. The space inside had large scales and weights, workshelves for tithecounters, bound volumes of tithesheets. The floor was dusted with spilled grain, and a rank of fifty-liter grain jars stood against the far wall, along with a small beam-crane to lift them onto the wood-decked cart that ran on steel-topped rails through a door in the steel wall and into the depths of the main Inquisitory. A couple of erranders were lounging by the workshelves, but there was no other activity. They jumped when they saw Vesene, trying to look busy, but he ignored them.

"Wait here," he told his sentinels, and followed the trolley tracks through the inner door without waiting for an answer.

The room they led to was vast and dimly lit, and heavy with the mingled scents of milled flour and dried fruits. The trolley rails branched to run between parallel lines of scaffolding that

388

Paul Chafe

held stacked ranks of grain jars. *The wealth of the Inquisition, my wealth.* There was another beam-crane there, mounted on a pair of trolley trucks and much larger than the one on the receiving floor. It was used to lift the heavy jars into position, and it should have been in busy use.

Movement flickered in a distant corner. A cat, its fur a darker black against the dim shadows, hunting the mice that came to feast on the storage vault's spillage. It padded quietly along the wall, then leapt smoothly up to the second level of the scaffold and vanished behind the jars there. Vesene watched for it to reappear, but it didn't. *Little friend, I wish my life was as simple as yours.* He walked down the trolley track to see if he could catch a glimpse of the small creature.

"Perhaps Solender was right," a voice said behind him.

Vesene jerked and whirled around. "Never say that name!"

Cela Joss was standing in the doorway from the receiving floor, her body silhouetted by the light streaming in from outside. "He was concerned about how much food the world can produce." Joss held up a sheaf of papers. "I have an answer for your question. Our grain stocks are falling."

"Solender wasn't right." Vesene bit the words off sharply. "He had it easy, he had no rabble to contend with. He was lucky to die when he did."

"As you wish. The fact remains, our grain stocks are falling. They were going down before he died, and they're going down faster now. We can't feed all of Charisy forever."

"How did you know I was here?" Vesene asked suspiciously.

"I was already here, you walked past me. I've been taking inventory, as you instructed. May we talk about the grain reserves?"

Vesene allowed himself to show irritation. "Talk then."

Joss shrugged. "We're using more than we're getting." She looked at her papers, tilted to them to catch the light. "Last month we took in two hundred cubic meters of corn, one hundred of flax seed, thirty of olives . . ."

Vesene made a dismissive gesture. "Just give me the total."

"At the end of last month we were down four hundred cubic meters, over all crops."

Vesene nodded, looking at the endless ranks of grain jars. "And tithing?" he asked.

"Up slightly, since we doubled the tithes."

Vesene clenched a fist. "The farmers are still holding out. I want the tithe patrols doubled."

"We don't have the sentinels to do that."

"Walk with me," Vesene said. He went deeper into the vault, and Joss fell into step beside him. "Why is it you defy me, Cela?"

"Me?" Joss's voice carried her surprise. "I only—"

"I'm Chief Inquisitor now. *Chief Inquisitor.* My word is law." Three walls of the vault were the original steel, the fourth was heavy timber, built to subdivide a larger space.

"Of course . . ."

"I ordered that the tithes be increased. I ordered that months ago. *Months!* Why am I only hearing we lack sentinels now?"

"It's in hand, Chief Inquisitor. Only so many apply to be sentinels, only so many of those are suitable, and then it takes time to train them . . ."

Vesene found himself getting angry. "Time. Every month we have less grain you tell me." They came to a heavy steel door in the back of the huge vault. The remains of a complicated locking wheel were still mounted in its center, but the mechanism itself was long since worn out and the door was secured by a heavy timber bar held in place with a smithed-steel lock. Vesene took a large key from his cross sash-pocket, opened it and pushed the bar out of the way. Joss started to answer him, but he held up a hand to silence her. "I gave you the order of sentinels because I thought you could use them correctly."

"I can't create trained sentinels out of nothing."

"I don't want excuses, I want results. What's a sentinel but a farmer with a blade?"

"If you want armed farmers, there is no difference. If you want good sentinels, sentinels loyal to the law, then we need the right people, and they need the right training."

"I want sentinels loyal to *me*," Vesene snapped, and then a slow smile spread across his face. "Go to the brickworks. I want the smartest, strongest there. Give them blades and shields and cross-sashes. You'll have all the sentinels you need."

"They're already sentinels."

Vesene shook his head. *Joss is useful, but she doesn't understand.* "Not the sentinels, the bound servitors."

"Criminals? We can't—"

Vesene cut her off with a gesture. "They owe service to the

Inquisition, let this be their service. As for loyalty, if they don't serve me well, they can go back into servitude and show loyalty to the bricks. The Inquisitors-in-Chief have been bothering me for more. This will quiet them."

"But . . ."

"You don't have to do it if you don't want to, Cela." Vesene shrugged, pretending indifference. "I'm sure I can find someone who will." He took a step forward, towering over her, letting his anger show. "I want this vault overflowing with grain, do you hear me? And I want it now."

Joss hesitated, took a step back. "I'll see it's done," she said, finally.

"Good." Vesene turned away from her, waited until he heard her footsteps retreating. Only then did he push open the door he'd unlocked and step through. It was almost totally dark in the room beyond, and it took a moment for his eyes to adjust to the darkness. When they did he could see shiny ingots stacked in rectangular piles around the edge of the room, raw shipsteel ingots collected from the forewall steel-falls. There were tons and tons of them, thousands and millions of tokens worth, the centuries-accumulated wealth of the Second Inquisition, stored and guarded against the day it might be needed.

Stored and guarded against the day Byo Vesene would need it. *I am at the crossroads of time, and all history has existed just to bring me here.* Just looking at it made him feel powerful, in a way he never had before. *The power of limitless riches.* It was time to put his power into use.

The peregrine turned foreward and dived, pulled up and turned aftward and Atyen followed it, feeling the rush of wind build up in the dive, hearing the mainspine creak as the wind dropped away to nothing when he shifted his weight back to turn-and-climb. The rough air of the boundary layer rocked him, and then the breeze was back in his face as he crossed into the higher, foreward moving wind belt. The fresh wind carried him higher. His turns were wider than the circling predator's, his climbs and dives longer, but he kept level with it, and there was satisfaction in that. Overturn soaring, as he'd come to call the maneuver, worked the flow difference between the lower, aftward moving wind and the higher, foreward moving

wind like a child pumping a swing. Done correctly he could
stay up indefinitely, though it was the most difficult flight skill
he'd attempted. A single misjudged turn and he'd be out of the
boundary layer and stuck in the lower wind, drifted helplessly
aftward until he could, if he was lucky, find the rising air
column that hid beneath the spiral clouds and climb back up.
*But I've mastered the boundary now.* The peregrine ignored him
and his accomplishment, concentrating on the ground below. It
was hunting. *How* it hunted was a mystery Atyen had yet to
unravel. He couldn't even make out people from the height of
the overturn, but the falcons could find a dove on the wing.

The bird swooped and circled again, and then all at once it
rolled over and stooped, accelerating down so fast that Atyen
could barely track it. In seconds it had vanished, and he transferred his eyes to the ground below. He had no hope of seeing
the peregrine's target, but he'd learned to look for the most likely
area. *There!* Most of the fields below were somewhere between
brown and green, but one was a soft gold, a ripening crop and
thus a likely place for a flock of doves to descend and feed. He
crossed his fingers in silent prayer for the peregrine's safety. Dove-
netting was becoming a popular way to put meat on the table,
and despite the predator's incredible agility they couldn't always
avoid the fine mesh in their high-speed attacks.

*But I can't worry about it now.* Whether the peregrine scored
or missed or got caught in a net Atyen would never know, and
he had indulged himself in a luxury to circle with it. He wanted
to find their hidden nests, somewhere up on the foredome, but
the wind-cycle became a downdraft there. He could never get
higher than the boundary layer, a third of the way to the suntube, and every time he'd been swept down at the foredome, once
right into the forewall mists. He frowned. That had been bad. He
had learned to stay out of clouds; no matter how hard he tried
he would almost instantly lose orientation and wind up out of
control. He'd tried to keep himself perfectly level as he'd sunk
into the mists, knowing just a few minutes would see him out,
but even that hadn't worked. He fallen out of the bottom of the
mist layer nearly upside down, with only a couple of hundred
meters to right himself. It wasn't quite enough, and he'd landed
hard, crumpled his right wing and had been lucky to avoid a trip
back to the surgeon's.

*Not what I need to be thinking about.* What he needed was to spinward, a small, fluffy cloud just starting to expand. *Perfect.* It looked like he was higher than its base, but he knew that was an illusion caused by the curve of the world, and so didn't try to fly directly for it. He'd get drifted aftward in the lower wind and end up too low and too far aft to catch it. Instead he started stretching his circles spinward, still working the overturn, slowly gaining on the cloud. He caught a flicker from the corner of his eye off to his right, moving wings. Against probability he'd caught sight of the peregrine again, foreward and below, barely more than a dot against the darkness of the foredome, and he smiled at the sight. It was flapping heavily, which meant it was carrying prey back to its hidden nest. *Good for you.* He lost sight of it on his next turn, but with luck and a following wind he'd be seeing it again soon. He returned his attention to the cloud. As he approached it billowed higher and started to extend itself foreward. The updraft beneath it would be strong, and that was what Atyen needed. He concentrated on visualizing the interacting patterns of the airflow. Somewhere far below the suntube was warming a plowed field and the moist, heated air was rising, moving aftward with the lower wind and cooling with height.

He worked the overturn layer towards the cloud until a sudden lurch upwards told him he'd found the updraft beneath it, and he abandoned his climb-turn-dive-turn pattern for a simple circle. The updraft carried him higher, and a few turns brought him to the underside of the cloud. He straightened out and sped up to fly level beneath it, following it as it extended foreward and began to spiral up the curve of the world. It was a good cloud, and he had to put the nose down, flying faster to avoid being swept up inside it. *Hopefully it's not too good.* The strongest clouds brought rain, which came with sudden, violent downdrafts. Before long he'd reached the leading edge of the spiral. The updraft ended there, but he flew out and ahead of the cloud as far as he dared. He couldn't see the top of his own cloud, but there was another white spiral halfway anti-spinward, and he checked its billowing top. The cloud's sharp edges went wispy there, and they were swept back, just a bit, as if they were starting to spiral backwards. Atyen smiled.

It was confirmation, he hoped, of what he had long suspected and was now trying to prove, a third layer to the wind cycle, this one closest to the suntube and moving aftward. If his hunch was right the forward moving layer was sandwiched between aftward moving layers, moving with them like intermeshed gears, and *that* meant there were two overturns at the foredome, one down and one up. If he could reach the upper one he could soar up and along the foredome as close to the suntube as he dared. *And there, somewhere, the falcons live.*

He turned to fly back into the cloud's updraft before he got too low to find it again. The trick would be getting to the upper overturn. Launching from the aftwall would take him only to the lower one. He would have to ride a cloud, not just forward but *up*. The updraft jostled him as he flew into it, and he circled again to regain his height. Once he had it he trimmed the left control line to hold the turn, hooking the handloop to keep it in place. Flying carefully with just the right line, he took his left arm out of the supports and carefully reached into his backbag for a hunk of dried carp. It took five solid bells for a cloud to trail its spiral all the way to the forewall, and he'd learned the hard way to drink sparingly and eat only dense, nutritious foods on long flights.

And then there was nothing to do but circle and wait as the cloud carried him steadily forward. It was cool, almost cold, but he was comfortable in a sheepskin jacket and heavy flax leggings. Charisy slid beneath him, and his cloud darkened enough that he feared it might rain, but it didn't. Ahead and below he could see the forewall mists, a horizontal wall of grey at the base of the looming foredome. *It's time.* He shifted his weight forward to build speed, flew to the front of the cloud, then shifted back, tightened both lines and swooped up, into the bottom of the cloud at its leading edge. If he did it right, he would skim back and forth in the narrow zone right at the cloud's front, inside its updraft, but able to see well enough to keep himself upright.

The cloud closed in on him as he climbed into it, but thinned again as he rose to its leading edge. He broke out into the light and felt the updraft change to a downdraft, and turned back into the cloud. The maneuver worked. The cloud rocked him with its turbulence, but every gust took him higher. He quickly fell into a steady figure-eight pattern, which let him enter the mist at a shallow angle and immediately turn out of it when he started to lose visibility. There was a strong euphoria that came with mastering nature like that, a feeling he had only vaguely imagined when he'd looked up at the soaring peregrines.

His wings got more sluggish as he got higher, and the wind slowed in his face, and he compensated with larger tugs on the lines, and shifted his weight forward to fly faster. It was a phenomena that had taken a while to understand. Control came from airflow over his wings, which came from forward speed, which came from the downward force of his weight. His weight came from the world's spin, and because there was less spin as he approached the suntube he had less weight. *Too bad understanding doesn't lessen the gusts.* As he climbed it became harder and harder to compensate for the cloud's turbulence, and soon he was being tossed around like a chase ball in a schoolyard.

*But I'm climbing!* The foredome was coming closer, and suddenly his world filled with water, big gentle drops that fell too slowly to really count as rain. *But they still count as wet.* They were cold too, and he was immediately soaked and shivering despite his warm clothing. He was high enough anyway, and he straightened out, shifted forward more to gain speed, and flew out into the clear air. The second he left the cloud the suntube's heat hit him like a fist, and he belatedly remembered how Noah had tried to fly to Heaven only to fall out of the sky on fire. Little streamers of steam wisped back from the fabric. He would be safe only until it dried, which didn't look like it would take long. The foredome loomed, huge and black and full of stars, not a kilometer away. He was higher than he'd ever been, well over halfway to the suntube. *But am I high enough?* The windrush built up in his ears, and a few minutes later he had to turn to avoid flying straight into the dome. He paralled it, heading anti-spinward, and came past one of the great, curved steel struts that spanned its diameter, an artifact he'd seen only as a distant thread before. There were patches of green and brown clinging to it, and he saw darting swifts. *Even here life takes hold.*

Up close the dome itself was streaked with droplets of water that joined into trickles snaking lazily downwards, but unlike the steel the surface was uneroded and devoid of anything living. On the other side of it were the stars, harder, sharper, clearer than he'd ever seen them before, and he stared at them, mesmerized. Several minutes later another strut came past, and he blinked, his star-focus broken. This strut carried the neat mud cones of swifts' nests, clinging to what seemed to be ladder rungs running up it. *And peregrines can eat swifts.* He felt a slow excitement swell in him at the thought, but he pushed it away. *Fly first, Atyen.* He put a hand up to check how hot the wing fabric was getting, but to his surprise it was only warm. That wasn't what he expected, so he squinted up against the suntube's brightness and saw to his surprise that it didn't actually burn all the way to the apex of the foredome, the first five hundred meters or so was a simple tube, cool and grey. As long as he stayed close to the foredome he'd be safe from its destroying heat. *Or at least safer.* He made a mental note to check the fabric temperature frequently.

Most importantly he seemed to be climbing—at least his wings were getting even more sluggish—and he shifted his weight even further forward to get enough speed to steer with. There remained the possibility that the peregrines nested down by the forewall, even down in the mists, but on seeing the swift's nests he didn't think so. They were soaring predators who hunted with keen eyes. They'd want clear air and as much height as they could get. He passed another strut, saw a few climbing vines that seemed rooted in nothing. A shape caught his eye, flying strangely. For a second he thought it might be a peregrine, but as he caught up with it he realized it was a gull. Its flight pattern was very strange though. It sailed along with its wings closed, floating through the air in defiance of common sense. While he watched, it flapped, once, twice, and closed its wings again, moving faster now and on a slightly changed trajectory. Some distance later he saw a dove, using the same flap-and-coast flight technique. He changed course and managed to catch up with it, and when he did he could see that it was subtly different from the doves he had known, with a longer, leaner body and a speckled pattern on its feathers. A second one joined it, perhaps its mate, and he followed them as they flew higher.

The updraft grew more pronounced as his weight fell away and soon he was not so much flying as drifting along in a river of air. Even with his weight shifted fully forward he could barely generate enough speed to maneuver. He checked the fabric temperature again and found it still cool, though no longer damp, and looked up at the suntube to see how close he was. His jaw dropped. There, at the apex of the foredome, at the spin-center of the world, was a mass of green, surrounded by thousands upon thousands of swarming birds. Never in his life had he seen a flock as big, not a tenth as big. Beneath the green he could make out the outlines of a structure, as big or bigger than the Inquisitory. The doves he was following were coasting leisurely towards it, and he just watched in stunned amazement as he came closer and closer. The updraft began to subside again, and he let go of the control lines, they weren't doing anything for him anyway, and got ready to grab on when the wind drifted him past.

It was easier said than done. He had no more control than a wind-lofted dandelion seed. The updraft fell further, until he was just drifting along. There was a platform of some sort extending from the bottom of a shaft that followed one of the foredome struts, some eighty meters below the central hub of the structure. He undid his waist belt and hung in the shoulder straps, bringing his legs up in front of him to get what weight he had left as far forward as possible. It gave him barely enough speed to bank for the platform, and he had the sudden realization that if he didn't manage to grab it he'd be drifted right past the structure and along the suntube's axis without enough weight to dive away. If that happened he'd be burned alive. *Perhaps that's what happened to Noah.* The story had to have come from somewhere. He managed the turn, got himself awkwardly lined up, but when he reached the platform his right wing hit the vine-covered steel first, and started him slowly tumbling. Disturbed doves fluttered around him. On the first tumble he grabbed a handful of leaves and pulled himself in so hard that he hit the platform and bounced off again, tearing the leaves away with him. On the next tumble he went over backwards without even a chance to grab on. The third tumble was his last chance before he slid past the platform and he managed to grab the vine layer. Something squished in his hands and he saw red, imagined blood, until he realized that the color wasn't quite right. *Grapes!*

At least he'd have something to eat while he figured out how to get back to the ground. The breeze had fallen to almost nothing, but he moved carefully just in case, undoing his shoulder straps with one hand and holding on with the other. When he had his wings off he tied them to a thick grape runner with one of the control lines, released his backbag and shrugged it on, and then carefully began to explore his new environment. He *did* have some weight. His wings had settled slowly to the platform deck, and his backbag tugged reassuringly down on his shoulders. At the same time he'd have to move gently or he'd launch himself right off the platform. Without wings to tug on, the breeze wouldn't be able to drift him into the suntube, but he would fall the longest possible fall in the world. *And I don't want to spend that much time dying.* The very thought gave him a strange vertigo, the way he'd felt when he'd first looked off the forewall ledge and felt the desire to fly. He resisted the urge and instead made a small, experimental push with just his toes. Just that much exertion launched him a good meter in the air, and it took several seconds for him to settle back to the platform again.

There was a building at the end of the platform, something like a warehouse with two sets of towering steel doors that seemed built to slide open in segments. He went to them, still moving carefully, as doves flocked in every direction to get out of his way. Walking was difficult, because the natural rhythm of his pace was completely mismatched to the long, slow rise and fall of his stride, and he had to move in with long, exaggerated sliding steps. The ground beneath the vines was spongy with moss that grew in a weird spiral pattern, and was everywhere dotted with bird droppings. *Which explains where the soil comes from.* The platform was bigger than it looked, and when he got close to the doors they towered high over his head. They were far too massive to shift on his own. *And probably seized shut with age.* After some exploration he found a smaller door inset in the bottom of one of the center segments, closed with a heavy latch and locking bar. He tried it, and to his surprise it moved easily. He had to rip up the overgrowing vines and dig up the ground to free the door, but once he did, it opened, and he stepped cautiously through. The space beyond was immense, at least a hundred meters square and twenty high, and lit from above by brilliant panels that shed a strange, cold light with a blue-white cast to it. The floor was covered thickly in vines, and they grew indiscriminately on every surface, even the ceiling spaces between the lighting panels, but though the floor was thick with dropping-enriched soil there didn't seem to be any birds. There *were* half a dozen large mounds, where it looked like something big had been buried by the encroaching vines.

There was also a door on the back wall and he went to it. *Or at least it looked like a door.* On closer inspection it had neither handle or hinge. There was a hand sized pad beside it, slightly raised above the steel. He tried to pull at it, in case it concealed a latch, and when it didn't move he almost instinctively pushed it. There was a soft click and then a sudden, powerful whir. The door slid open of its own accord, and Atyen jumped back in shock. He drifted helplessly backwards for meters before he finally touched down and bounced, very slowly, to the ground. By the time he'd picked himself up the door had slid shut again. He took a deep breath to calm himself, and then went cautiously back to it. He pressed the pad, and it obediently slid open. Light spilled out of the space beyond, and he went through it and on the other side found another world. He was in a corridor with walls angled to give it a hexagonal cross-section, and the air was cool and dry. The place felt uncomfortable, but in a familiar way, and it took him a moment to realize why. *Everything is oversized.* Like the Inquisitory, the structure was ancient, from a time when people grew larger than they did now. *This is a Builder place, but it shows no wear.* It had been lost at the core of the world, forgotten as the centuries slipped by, only hinted in the story of Noah, waiting for someone to rediscover it. *Waiting for me.*

The strange door slid shut behind him, and he had a moment of panic before he verified that there was another pad on his side of the door, and that it would also open it. Satisfied that he wasn't trapped, he went forward in long, gliding strides. The floor was grey and softly textured, like a floor quilt, but one that ran from one wall to the other without seam or interruption. More doors led deeper into the structure, and he chose one at random. Like the first it had an opening pad, and it was blazoned with a strange symbol in bright yellow, a hue so deep and rich it seemed to glow. He ran a hand over it and found it cool and smooth as the steel beneath it. He rubbed a finger over its edge, but there was no ridge to mark the transition from color to bare steel. The figure was not ink or dye, somehow the very fabric of the metal had been colored. All at once his perception inverted itself, and he realized that he wasn't looking at some alien glyph but simply the number eight, styled so simply he hadn't recognized it at first. Almost reverently he pressed the opening pad, but the space beyond was just another corridor, running perpendicular to the first. There were more doors, these plates beside them that carried words in a clean, simple script. Most of the letters were recognizable and the words seemed pronounceable, but they made no sense—L-O-G-I-S-T-I-C-S  D-I-R-E-C-T-O-R, E-C-O-S-Y-S-T-E-M-S, P-R-O-J-E-C-T  I-N-T-E-G-R-A-T-I-O-N.

He pressed the pad for the one labelled P-E-R-S-O-N-N-E-L, and saw a studio divided into small workspaces. Every workspace had a workshelf, made with lines so straight and clean they seemed somehow inhuman. There were chairs of strange design, made for people half again as tall as Atyen. The first workshelf held a few papers, printed in strange lettering, but when he tried to pick them up they crumbled into fragments. He found more papers at another workshelf, and this time tried to read them without touching. Most of the simple words were clear enough, but he knew only a couple of the larger ones. *But the underlying language is the same.* The conclusion was inescapable. The Builders had been giants, but they were human, and had they been able to speak he would have been able to understand them. In a third workspace he found a note, this one handwritten. It was just five words, and they seemed simple. He puzzled out the letters, formed them into words, and found to his astonishment that he was actually reading the ancient text. The message was simple. "Trude, back after breakfast. Ivo."

He read the note again, barely daring to breathe lest he destroy the fragile scrap. *Trude, back after breakfast. Ivo.* One day, countless ages ago two people had expected to meet. Were they friends? Lovers? Had Ivo ever returned? It was impossible to know. There were drawers beneath the workshelf and he slid one open. Inside were a few small pieces of something close to steel, silver wires twisted into a sort of double oval, tarnished discs the size of a fingernail with a short spike on one side. What purpose could they have served? It was impossible to know. They were all made with seemingly impossible precision. He picked up two of the double ovals to compare, and found them as identical as his eyes could discern. He was reminded of his builder tokens, made with a precision no present-day smith could hope to duplicate. *Such power they had.* He dropped one of the ovals and played with the other one, flexing it, then unbending it, testing its properties, then dropped it and watched it fall slowly back into the drawer. He closed it and move further into the studio. As he explored, it became obvious that the place had not been suddenly abandoned. Whoever they were, the ancients had not vanished all at once. They had moved out on purpose, taking most of whatever had occupied the space with them, though here and there oddly shaped knickknacks still adorned the abandoned workshelves.

Were they functional, or merely decorative? He couldn't know. He picked up one of the widgets. It was made of some smooth and light material, closer to wood than anything else, but without any obvious grain and with a soft luster to its surface. It had a square base, with a pair of cups seamlessly attached to it. It might have been an elaborate ink-jar, though it lacked lids. *Or it might be anything.* He put the piece down again, careful to replace it exactly as he had found it. The place felt strange, as though the ghosts of Trude and Ivo were watching him, and he went out without touching anything else.

Back in the corridor he went from door to door in long, gliding strides. Behind F-A-B-R-I-C-A-T-I-O-N he found a huge hall of complex machines, boxes with jointed arms that looked like they should move, but with no tacklewheels or beltropes to move them. Behind M-O-B-I-L-I-T-Y he found emptiness, just marks on the floor where equipment had once been. Further down the corridor a shaft led straight up, with handholds tempting him higher. On the ground it was an impossible jump but here . . . He jumped and caught a handhold, floating higher with gentles pushes. *Amazing.*

The shaft was circular, and the walls were covered in white fabric pads. It went up eighty meters at least, with a slight curve away from perfectly vertical. Instinctively Atyen understood that it was following the curve of the foredome up to the exact center of the world. As he floated higher the gentle downward tug of his weight faded until it was imperceptible. As he came to the top of the shaft, weirdly, it felt as if he were falling headfirst into the space above. The end of the shaft was covered with a circular metal hatch. Like the doors, it had an opening pad, but when Atyen pressed it the hatch did not slide open, but divided itself into six sections and it vanished into the walls with a sharp *hiss* and a brief gust of wind. The gust caught him unprepared and pushed him a good five meters backwards. For a brief moment it felt like he was falling, and he grabbed for a handhold harder than he needed to.

The hatch had closed itself again by the time he'd got himself back up the shaft. This time he held on with one hand while he pressed the opening pad, but this time there was no gust. He pushed himself through and into the space above, and found himself floating in an echoing cylindrical chamber twenty meters around and fifty long. The walls seemed to be spinning and sudden vertigo seized him. He closed his eyes and took a deep breath. As he opened them again he realized the walls *were* spinning. More accurately, the far end of the cylinder was rotating, and the part he was in was not. The sensation made him queasy, and so he concentrated on the hatch behind him until he felt more stable. Once he had his stomach under control he was able to look up and take in the rest of the scene. At both ends the cylinder was closed with a huge circular door divided into six sections, like the hatch he had just come through. He was drifting, floating slowly through the space, and he found that though he could look around, he couldn't change direction. Feeling somewhat silly he tried flapping his arms like a bird, but the motion had no discernible effect on his trajectory. He had to wait until he drifted into the wall.

The wall had handholds recessed into it, and when he finally got to it he grabbed one while he contemplated his next move. There was what looked like an opening panel beside each of the huge end-doors. He pushed off with his toes, aiming for the panel in the rotating section. He realized his mistake as soon as he launched and the panel moved away from his intended land-ing point. He hadn't allowed for the rotation. He had to aim for where his destination would be when he landed, not for where it was when he pushed off. He passed into the rotating section, and when he got close to the wall he grabbed a handhold. Once he had himself stopped and stabilized he looked back to where he had been, and was nonplussed to find himself stationary, while the section he had just left was now rotating. It took him a moment to realize that the apparent motion was relative. The opening panel he'd been aiming for was almost directly above him. He pushed off again, heading straight up, but as he moved the panel started to drift away from his aimpoint. Once again there was nothing he could do to change his trajectory in mid flight, and when he landed the panel had moved nearly a quarter of the way around the cylinder. Timing the rotation was harder than it looked.

Rather than try again he went around the wall from handhold to handhold. Beside the opening panel an inset square glowed red, showing words he could almost read. N-O  E-X-T-E-R-N-A-L P-R-E-S-S-U-R-E. He pressed the panel, and it clicked as the others had, but the door didn't open. Disappointed, he tried again, but still got no result. He turned to go back to the other huge door to try it, but before he could push off he noticed another small hatch, similar to the one he'd come through, at the other end of the chamber. He went to it, hand over hand, pushed its panel and was nearly sucked headfirst down the shaft behind it as air rushed past him. The air gust was over in a second, and he drifted up the shaft twice his own body length before he came to a second hatch. He opened that too, and in the space behind it he found the stars.

The room's roof was a transparent hemisphere, the same material as the foredome, but thinner and with no layer of mist or reflections from the suntube to mar the view. Every star glittered hard and bright in the ultimate blackness surrounding it, and there were far, far more of them than he would ever have imagined, scattered like sugar on a black robe. To his left was the vast curve of the foredome, and with shock Atyen realized that he was *outside* of the world, looking in through the dome's curve to the fields and rivers, roads and towns he had known his whole life. As he watched, the world rotated beneath him, and he realized that, for the first time in his life, the stars were not. All at once he understood the purpose behind the rotating cylinders he had just come through, designed to give passage between the rotating world and the strange new realm he had entered. *Or is it that the world has always been stationary, and now I'm the one who's spinning?* It was impossible to know which point of view was correct. He turned so his world was behind him, and within his field of view there were only stars. There was a stark beauty to the scene, and he felt his heart thudding in his chest. After a while he went back to watching the world turn, and it was a long time before he could tear himself away from that to even consider the room he was in.

The hatch he had come through was in the center of the floor, and the room was circular, ringed with an angled workshelf set with softly glowing squares, similar to the one by the huge door that had refused to open, but larger. He looked closer, and saw that they were covered in words and strange symbology. The one closest to him showed four circles connected by lines to a long rectangle. There were small numbers in each circle, and larger ones below the rectangle. With something close to awe he reached out a finger to touch the glowing digits, half afraid that they would burn him. What he felt was a surface as smooth and cool as steel, with nothing to betray the source of the glow beneath it. Gently he slid his hand across the surface, and his fingertips left faint smudges in the thin layer of dust that had collected on the surface.

The numbers changed as Atyen slid his finger over one of the circles and he yanked his hand back as though he'd been bitten. He looked at the changed writing in awestruck fascination, and realized he had no words to describe what he had seen. Hesitantly he extended his finger again, touched the circle, and again the numbers changed. *Living paper, what else can I call it?* It was only the vaguest of analogies, the strange surface shared no commonalities of paper at all, other than the fact that it could have words scribed on it at will. *But whose will?* He looked around, half expecting to see a godlike Builder watching him, but there was no one there. *And what is this place then?*

It occurred to him again that it might be Heaven as the Bible described it, up above the suntube, not somehow beyond it but simply foreward of it. The world was supposed to be voyaging to Heaven, but perhaps that was just a misunderstanding of the physical reality that traveling foreward was quite literally traveling towards this hidden place. It might even be that foreward and aftward were so identified because of their relative proximity to it. *What other truths might be concealed in the Bible's words?* Noah had flown to heaven on wings made of peregrine feathers. Now Atyen had done the same thing. *But if this is heaven, where is everybody?* The place had the air of long abandonment, which was not how he understood heaven was supposed to be. He would have to dig deeper into Noah's story, to tease out what was fact and what was only imagination.

He looked closer at the glowing symbols. At the top were the words F-U-E-L S-T-A-T-U-S. The larger numbers beneath the rectangle measured something called C-H-4. There were 15517927 T-O-N-N-E-S of C-H-4, whatever that meant, and then all of a sudden Atyen realized that he knew what it meant, or at least part of it. T-O-N-N-E-S were *tonnes*, the same as tonnes of wheat or yams. The glowing panel was some kind of tithesheet. The smaller numbers in the circles also counted C-H-4 in tonnes, and on a hunch Atyen started adding them up. As he suspected, the numbers in the circles amounted to the total beneath the rectangle. As he watched, one of the numbers in the circles changed, from 3844571 to 3844570, and the number in the rectangle changed as well, to 15517926. Whatever CH4 was, there was less of it now. He touched the living paper again, and it obediently changed, now counting C-H-4 P-R-E-S-S-U-R-E in the circles, which each measured 209 A-T-M. Unlike the previous display there was no grand total beneath the rectangle. Fascinated, he tapped again. Obediently the living paper changed, this time to measure CH4 F-L-O-W, which was .5842 K-G-/-S in one circle and 0 in all the others.

"Flow," he whispered the word to himself. He was actually understanding what was in front of him, a development more magical than any other wonder of the day. CH4 was something stored somewhere in prodigious volume, and it was flowing somewhere else. Somehow the living paper was able to measure that, and rewrite itself to reflect that reality. He touched again, and was rewarded with a new diagram, this one much more complicated, with interconnected lines bearing small triangles of different colors. At the top were the words PUMP STATUS, and he shook with excitement to realize that he was both reading the ancient words and confirming his hypothesis at the same time. CH4 not only *flowed,* it was *pumped,* like water. *And perhaps it is water.* Certainly there was little else in the world that came in an abundance of fifteen million tonnes. There were more numbers at different points in the diagram, but none of them made any sense. Experimentation proved that touching the living paper at different symbols could cause different changes in the information it reported, though some just made LOCKED OUT flash in red over the whole diagram for a few seconds. He realized with frustration that he didn't know how to get back to any of the reports he had seen before, and moved to the next square of living paper. It reported DRIVE WALL TEMP, which was 4403 K and CORE FIELD STRENGTH which was 1227 T, and other parameters too cryptic to even guess at. Atyen scratched his head as he contemplated the words. He'd had a burst of initial optimism with PUMP STATUS and TONNES, but though he could read these new words, they made no sense strung together the way they were. It was going to take a long time to decipher the meaning of what he was looking at.

*But that doesn't matter. Now I know what my life is for.*

"Two a token," said the monger as Sarabee looked over the onions. They were bruised and slightly shrivelled and far from the best onions she'd ever seen in Tidings market, but they were a good size, and they were what was on offer.

"Two?" She picked up the smallest, most bedraggled specimen she could find and held it up. "I wouldn't take these at six."

"Two a token, and a bargain at that." The monger gave her a big smile. "They'll make a good soup, fry nice with carp or mutton, and you won't find better here today."

Sarabee made a face and held out the injured onion like it was a dead mouse. "I'll say five a token, to save walking elsewhere. They aren't worth more."

"Three a token, only because I want to empty the box."

"Onions like these used to be twelve. Onions better than these used to be twelve."

"My wife used to be beautiful." The monger shrugged. "Not anymore. Three, if you want them."

"Look at the bruises! You can't be serious."

"Four, then."

"Four," Sarabee nodded. "I'll take twenty."

"And you'll have the best soup you've ever tasted," the monger promised, smiling as Sarabee counted out the steel disks and then counted the onions into her backbag. She left her bargaining onion on the table and took better ones. *And at least they're big.* Her bag was bulging when she was done, and she shouldered it and moved on. *But four a token for onions, it's outrageous!*

She looked over some other tables, considering what to get. Nothing was a bargain. At first she hadn't minded when the fish tithe was doubled to match the grain tithe. It only drove the carp price higher, and for a while she had so much steel she didn't know what to spend it on. The problem was the prices in Tidings market rose inexorably in the wake of the increases, until they had entirely consumed the extra profit. Worse, they ate away what they got from their restitution pay and from Atyen, and those amounts hadn't risen with the price of carp.

"Sarabee!" a familiar voice called.

She whirled around, found a face in the market crowd. "Newl!" She looked at her sister's husband in stunned amazement. "Newl! What are you doing here?"

"I'm on my way to see Celese." Her brother-by-marriage smiled, and embraced her as he came up, then held her at arm's length to look her up and down. "How are you?"

"I'm good. I'm very good now that you're here. But . . ."

"How did I get out of servitude?" Newl laughed. "I'm a sentinel now, if you can believe it."

Sarabee took a step back. "What? But that takes years."

"Not anymore." Newl was smiling broadly. "They offered a deal, take twice as many years of servitude, but do it as a sentinel." He laughed. "How could I not take that? A month's training and here I am."

"Where's your cross-sash?"

"In my backbag. Brand new. Noah, it's good to see you."

"Well, let's not stand here any longer," Sarabee enthused. "Celese will be joyous." She grabbed his hand and tugged him along, marketing forgotten. "And the children! Newl, I'm so happy!"

"How are you and Jens?"

"Good. Life continues, we fish, the children grow. But look at you, a sentinel!"

Newl smiled. "I was lucky."

"They must have chosen you."

"They've been doing it for a while." He frowned. "I'm supposed to take tithes. I'm not going to like that."

"Better that than making bricks. What are they paying you?"

He told her and she whistled. "That's ample. When do you start?"

"I'm supposed to go to the Inquisition Hall, but I'm going home first."

"Of course you are." Sarabee navigated them out of the market. "Celese wouldn't speak to me if I let you out of my sight."

She took him back to the Celese's farm, and watched with tears in her eyes as her sister ran into her husband's arms and wept. Celese's boys danced around yelling "Dadsha, dadsha!" except for the youngest who was too young to remember his father and cried. Sarabee took the little one in her arms to comfort him, while Celese gasped and exclaimed and hugged her husband yet again, and then Newl had to take out his red and blue cross-sash and model it for them. It didn't quite fit, and of course he lacked a blade and shield and the other trappings of a sentinel, but she told him he looked dashing anyway. She let the children exhaust themselves hugging their father and telling him stories, and once they'd settled down somewhat she herded them all over to her house, to give the reunited couple some time alone. Jens was there, which surprised her.

"I thought you were out with Atyen."

Her husband looked serious. "I was, he's gone flying. A long flight. He said not to expect him for a day, maybe a week."

"I have news to make you smile," she said, but Jens only looked more somber when she told him about Newl.

"What's wrong?" she asked.

"Let's talk in the bedroom."

"Liese, you're in charge," Sarabee told her eldest, not that it needed saying.

"Yes, Mamsha."

She followed her husband into the bedroom, sat on the bed while he took a deep breath. "A tithecounter came today," he said.

"A tithecounter," Sarabee's blood ran cold. "He didn't find . . ."

Jens shook his head. "No, he wasn't here to search, thank Noah."

"Then what?"

"Our restitution has been stopped."

"Oh," Sarabee paused. "Well, we'll survive, we always have. Prices have gotten so high it hardly matters. Onions today were—"

"It's not the steel that worries me," Jens interrupted her. "They stopped it because Mial Broden was released from the brickworks. The tithecounter wouldn't say why, but hearing about Newl, I think they must have made him a sentinel too."

Sarabee's mouth fell open and she stared her husband, trying to absorb what she'd just heard. The man who tried to rape her, the man who'd threatened her baby was walking free. *Not just free, but wearing a sentinel's cross-sash.* She wanted to scream, wanted to hit Jens, to beat him until he said it wasn't true, wanted to get up and run and run until she found a place Mial Broden could never find her. She did none of those things, because she found she couldn't move a single muscle. Jens came over and put his arms around her. *Onions today were four a token. Four a token . . .* It was all she could think, and it wasn't such a bad thought, but then Jens wiped away her tears and she realized she was sobbing.

The glowing panels of the builder's command center painted their reflections on the transparent dome overhead, a gentle overlay to the star-frosted darkness. Atyen floated weightless in the middle of the dome, revolving slowly as he watched them. He could spend hours staring at the view, and frequently he did. He drifted until he reached the dome, put out a hand and pushed off. The push spun him gently, and the view shifted until he was looking into the world's cylinder through the foredome. It still seemed strange to be outside the world. He had taken to calling the hidden world at the apex of the foredome Heaven, partly because it was above the suntube, as heaven was supposed to be, partly because he'd flown there as Noah was claimed to have done, but mostly because of the feeling. *Is this how God felt, looking down on his Creation?*

His gentle trajectory brought him back down to the ranks of workshelves that ringed the room, and with an effort Atyen pulled his attention away from the dome. He pulled himself back to the living-paper panel he'd been using and buckled himself into the chair. His worksheaf was clipped to the shelf with the clips the Builders had put there for just that purpose. The panel showed a minor miracle, a moving three-dimensional map of the world. He touched, slid his finger, and it obediently rotated to the angle he wanted. Already it had taught him that the suntube had a complex internal structure, and that it burned CH4. He still didn't know exactly what CH4 was, but he did know it was stored in four dimpled spheres a kilometer across, that were attached to the outside of the world below the forewall. He could actually *see* them through the room's transparent dome, out beyond the edge of the world's cylinder, proof of the map's veracity. He'd discovered that the ocean was sixty meters deep next to the aftwall, and confirmed his theory it circulated water to the river outfalls through huge tubes deep under the soil. He'd learned that the shipsteel falls were no accident but a mechanism designed to ration ingots from storehouses hidden high up on the forewall. The storehouses themselves were connected to vertical ladder shafts that ran within the forewall itself, connecting down to a huge hidden space full of mysterious machinery at the forewall base, and up to the foredome's support struts. The ladder rungs he'd seen the swifts building nests in weren't an accident. It was possible, at least in theory, to climb the forewall all the way to Heaven. *And they must have done it sometimes, for some reason, else why make it possible?*

Atyen bit his lip, comparing what the panel showed with the charcoal-sketched copy in his worksheaf. He found charcoal messy to work with, but he'd learned the hard way that it was impossible to use a pen without weight. The ink would stick to the pen tip, and come out of the jar in a single, spherical blob. Any incautious movement of the pen would detach the ink blob, sending it wobbling through the air until it touched something, at which point it would collapse into an indelible mess. *And this map isn't much better.* He frowned at his effort, turned to a blank page for a fresh start, then went back to studying the panel, spinning the world-cylinder with a finger to see what a new perspective might show, scaling in to examine the maze of the Inquisitory. He had known its back passages only as unlit tunnels that led to dank and dangerous spaces long abandoned, but the living map showed it as a living, breathing world in its own right. He was sure there were useful secrets there, but it was frustrating work trying to tease them out. Once he'd managed to get it to show words that described what he was looking at, but then he'd touched something else, and he'd never been able to bring them up again.

Atyen grew tired of the world map, and touched the symbol that made it vanish. Another touch brought up another map, the one that traced the path of the world through the star-ocean. It held its secrets even closer than the world map, but even the little Atyen had learned from it was stunning. Its very existence confirmed the Inquisition's fragmentary understanding that the world really was on a journey from one star to another. Their destination was named Iota Horologii, the same nonsense name that was etched on his Builder tokens. That strongly suggested that the same people were responsible for both Heaven and the coins, and by extension the world as a whole, and *that* confirmed the story of the Builders. *Builders indeed!*

The star map had also taught him that, surprisingly, the world was moving backwards, with the aftwall towards Iota Horologii and the foredome facing back the way they'd come. The map claimed their speed was an astonishing twenty-seven-thousand kilometers in a *second*. At first he'd thought he'd misinterpreted something, first because such a velocity was preposterous on the face of it and second because he could see with his own eyes that the stars were so firmly fixed in their positions that they might as well have been painted on the outside of the dome. It was only as he'd come to understand the mind-boggling distances between them that he realized the number could easily be correct. If it was, the world wouldn't reach its destination for another five thousand years.

*And who were these people to think on these scales?* The entire Second Inquisition was only a thousand years old, both Inquisitions together weren't more than two, and whatever had come before them was so thoroughly lost in the mists of time it was more legend than fact. Yet the Builders had launched a project meant to last five times longer than even that vast gulf of time. The audacity required was staggering! *Could they have been gods?* It wasn't the first time he'd pondered that question, but he'd seen with his own eyes that all too human scribble, "Trude, back after breakfast. Ivo." Gods wouldn't leave notes like that. The Builders were incredibly powerful, but they were human.

Atyen played with the star map some more, trying to prise out deeper secrets. What he had not yet discovered was *why* it was important to move the world from one star to another, and to his eye there seemed little enough to choose between them. He had not discovered *how* the world was propelled, or exactly what they were travelling through, or if it was even possible to choose a different path. He touched symbols, changed the map, changed the numbers overlaid on it, but found no new information, nor any new understanding of what he'd already seen. He was tired and his mind started to wander. *How long have I been doing this?* The bells didn't reach to his isolated perch and it was too easy to lose track of time. *Three days at least, maybe a week.* Long enough to fill two worksheaves anyway. He stretched and looked back up at the stars. Heaven provided food from its vines and huge bird flocks, water from the ever-dripping condensate on the foredome. Cooking had been an issue at first. For some reason fire just didn't burn well in Heaven, the flames were pale and weak no matter what he tried to burn. Fortunately he'd discovered a room with a surface that produced heat in any amount, controlled with the touch of a finger. After that the only problem was that he wasn't a very good cook.

*And you're getting nowhere, Atyen.* He stabbed a symbol and dismissed the starmap. *It's time to go back to the world.* He'd always been comfortable on his own, but in Heaven it was too easy to forgo human contact for more blissful hours of stargazing. *And that's not good for you in the long run.* He grabbed his backbag from where it was floating, unclipped his worksheaf, retrieved his charcoal scriber from the end of its string, and unbuckled himself. A gentle push took him away from the workshelf, and he guided himself over to the room's central hatchway and down the access tube to the huge half-rotating room. He launched himself across it with practiced accuracy, and laughed in midair, thinking back to his first crude attempts at flying. *Here I don't even need wings.* He threaded the complex's corridors and shafts back to what he called the vine room, the one that opened onto the landing platform. It was his best source of fresh food, because the open door that had allowed the birds to colonize it was now choked with vines growing on the rich soil layer they'd left behind. The birds couldn't get in anymore, and so he had all the fruit to himself. He kept his wings there too, because then there was not the slightest risk they'd drift off the platform, and also just to keep them from getting covered in bird droppings.

Outside on the platform he unfolded them, locked and double-checked the joints, buckled his backbag in its place, strapped them on and went to the edge facing the aftwall. The key to a good flight down was getting a solid launch; if he didn't, it took forever for his minuscule weight to build up enough speed to maneuver against the updraft. He grabbed the lip of the platform with both hands, swung himself head down, got his feet under him and pushed off as hard as he could, cutting through the whirling doves like a falcon. He put his hands through the supports and grabbed the lines, shifted his weight full forward and pitched down until he was in a vertical dive.

*And I'm flying!* It was still a thrill. His speed built up imperceptibly at first and he seemed to hang in mid-air, but as his weight gradually increased he fell faster. He held the nose down, aiming just beyond the forewall mists, and left the control lines loose, leaving the slots closed to minimize drag. The wind became a steady breeze, and he pulled in a touch of left line to counteract the antispinward drift. There was a brief burble of turbulence as he fell through the upper overturn boundary, and he compensated with a couple of quick line tugs. He accelerated faster as his weight built up and the rush grew to a roar. He held the dive until he heard the mainspine start creaking, then pulled in both lines, flexing the trailing edges down and opening the slots. Still he kept the nose in its full-down stoop, relying on the added drag to keep himself from overspeeding. The lower overturn smacked him hard, yanking him against the straps and rocking him violently, but he was through it so fast that it was gone before he could even register it. Only then did he shift his weight back, gradually pulling out of his headlong descent. The maneuver put him solidly into the lowest, aftward moving wind layer, and with the wind behind him and the speed he'd gained in his dive the world slipped past with amazing speed. Between the raft ride to the aftwall, winching himself up to the second ledge, and the lazy, spiralling flight up the world with the clouds it took most of a day to make it to Heaven, but getting back on the ground took less than a bell.

He found Charisy, halfway up the curve of the world, which put Tidings almost exactly behind the suntube. He angled anti-spinward to fly over the city, picked up Tidings from there, and as he drew closer found the place where the helixing main road met the shore. It was easy to spot Jens's house from there, and he swooped low over it, banked around into wind, trimmed out level with the lines and came down in his usual pasture, just fifty meters from his own small shed. His bad leg nearly buckled on landing, and his wings felt like they weighed twice their twenty-five kilos. It was like that every time he came down; his body seemed to forget what weight was when he was in Heaven.

"Atyen! Atyen!" Liese and Acelle had watched him come over and came running up.

"Butterfly!" He smiled as he undid his flaps. "Daffodil!" He ruffled their hair. "Shouldn't you be in school?"

"Everyone knows it's a holiday," Acelle said.

"Those are so beautiful," Liese said, running her hand over the leading edge. "I want to try."

"You can try them on. You'll have to ask your mother to actually fly them."

"You say that every time. You *know* she won't let me." Liese heaved an overdramtic sigh, but brightened up the second it was done. "Help me put them on, Acelle."

"I want to wear them too," put in the younger girl as she tried to lift the trailing edge. Atyen winced, and held the wings up so Acelle's help wouldn't tear a slot, and Liese slipped the shoulder straps on.

"They're really heavy," she said as Atyen let her take the weight. "They're supposed to carry you, not the other way around."

"My turn," put in Acelle.

Liese turned herself to face into wind and bent at the waist so the wings could grab air. "You can really feel them lifing."

"My turn," Acelle repeated, more insistent.

The older girl relinquished the wings reluctantly and Atyen held them again so her younger sister could have her turn, holding them up so she wouldn't have to carry the full weight.

"Where's your father?" he asked Liese.

"Down on the dock, working on the nets."

"You're the only inquisitor my father likes," Acelle said. "*And my mother. They said.*"

"I'm just an aspirant, I'm studying to be an inquisitor." He released the locking joints. "You can help me fold these," he said, and showed the girls how to pack the fabric into a nice neat package.

"I guess you're supposed to carry them after all," Liese observed dryly, as he slipped his arms through the shoulder straps again, and then she ran to catch Acelle who'd run off ahead.

Atyen hung the folded wings on the wall and turned to look over his next project. His forming jigs were fully occupied with the skeleton of his next experiment. The new wings were cargo carriers, with twice the span of his old set, slots in both the main wings and the tail, and a cargo basket. Fully laden they'd be too heavy to carry on his back for the leap from the ledge, so he'd designed them to launch by sliding down a pair of rails. He ran a hand over the oiled bamboo skeleton and it came away dusty. He frowned. The wing fabric was folded neatly in a corner, waiting to be strung onto the frame, but since he'd found Heaven he'd done no work on them at all.

*Because Heaven is more important.* Atyen went into his small bedroom. His workshelf was covered with stacks of journals, the distilled product of all he'd done since he'd come to the aftwall. He picked up one of the first ones, leafed past drawings of falcons, his first, clumsy concepts for wings he could really fly, even an imaginative picture of a peregrine chick. *I've even forgotten about finding a peregrine's nest. How long has it been?* Long enough that Jerl had learned to talk and was taking an interest in rafts, long enough that Liese had given up on dolls. Inquisitor Renn had

told him to come back in a year, but Renn couldn't have anticipated what Atyen would find at the foredome apex. *This is too
important to keep to myself.* There was far more to do, more to
learn in Heaven than one man ever could. It was time to bring
his findings back to the Inquisitory, teach others to fly, transform
his hard-won experience into knowledge that anyone could access.

*Time to leave the aftwall, at least for now.* It was a hard decision
to make. Jens's family had become like his own. *Closer than my
own.* He'd miss the long raft trips to the aftwall with his best friend,
miss the children, miss Sarabee. *But it has to be done.* He went to a
drawer, drew out a small bag, and headed down to the dock.

Jens was there as advertised, fixing nets.

"Atyen," he called. "When did you get back?"

"Just now." Atyen sat down, picked up a section of net to look
for holes.

"What *do* you do up there? It's been a week!"

"I learn about Heaven."

Jens laughed. "You say that every time."

"Because you ask every time." Atyen paused trying to figure out
how to explain it. "It's a whole other world, Jens. Some things so
strange I don't believe them even when I'm looking at them. You
can see stars by the thousand, float in the air. You should come."

"It terrifies me just watching you jump off that ledge, and carp
don't catch themselves." Jens shook his head. "Thanks, but I'll
float in the water, and see the stars from here."

Atyen nodded, and felt a slight sadness that his friend couldn't
share in the wonder he'd experienced. "I'd like you to watch the
shed for a while."

Jens nodded slowly, taking that in. "It's time, is it?"

Atyen nodded. "It is."

"It's been good having you Atyen. You're welcome anytime."

"I'll be back soon. I'm not done flying yet." Atyen hoped it was
true. "Here, I want you to have this." He handed over the flax bag.

Jens took it, hefted it. "What's in it?"

"Builder tokens." Atyen briefly explained what they were.
"My . . . a doctrinor gave them to me to pay for my work down
here. I don't need them anymore, and you do."

"Atyen, this is . . ."

"Don't protest. You asked me once to look after your family.
Well, now I am."

"Only if something happens to me!"

"Think of it as an advance payment."

Jens nodded in appreciation. "Thank you, Atyen. I'll save it for an emergency. Just in case."

"Good fishing."

"Safe journey."

They shook hands, and Atyen went up to the house to say goodbye to Sarabee. She wasn't there. *Probably marketing.* It was disappointing to miss the goodbye, but there was no sense in delaying. He started walking, looking wistfully up at the spiralling clouds. It had been a long time since he'd had to walk a long distance, and combined with his post-Heaven muscle fatigue his injured calf was sore in the first five hundred meters. He'd hoped to hike all the way to the Inquisitory, but he was spent before he reached Charisy. He found a traveller's house, put the cart in their stable and bought himself a surprisingly expensive meal of mutton and vegetables. For six months he'd either eaten with the Madanes or in Heaven, and prices had risen sharply since then. *I have to get back in touch with the world.*

He slept well, shared a pricey breakfast with a cart-vendor going to Bountiful parish, and left early. As he walked he went over what he'd need to do to get his masterwork finished, and he was half-surprised to find himself looking forward to his double-red cross-sash. *Heaven is too important to keep to myself, and I'm going to need aspirants to help understand it.* There were a trio of sentinels waiting at the intersection of the Tidings road and the trading road, but he paid them no heed as he considered how best to proceed. Getting people up there was going to be the difficulty. *Could I teach them all to fly?*

"Stop right there, fisher," the leader said. "Tithe-patrol."

Atyen looked up from his reverie, surprised. "I'm an aspirant."

"That so? Well, aspirant, let's just see what you've got in the cart." The voice was challenging, almost belligerent.

"I've got my cross-sash here somewhere . . ."

"I don't care. Let's see what's in the bag."

The sentinel took a step forward, so Atyen shrugged and handed over his backbag. The leader handed it to one of the others, who began rummaging through his things. Aspirants weren't subject to tithes, and he had nothing tithe-able anyway, but if they wanted to waste their time that was their affair. Still, something was wrong. He couldn't quite put his finger on it. *Maybe the challenge . . .* Aspirants technically outranked sentinels, though it was a foolish aspirant who pushed the issue. Still, sentinels were nothing if not mindful of protocol. They were trained to apply violence when necessary but they were uniformly polite when it wasn't. *And they've got no reason to be rude to me.* More than that, there was something about the way they carried themselves. One had worn his cross-sash off center, another's was wrinkled, and none of them had tucked away the draw-strings on the their backbags. *And what does that mean?* Probably nothing.

They quickly finished with his few belongings, and they seemed disappointed not to have found anything. One of them rifled through his worksheaves, tossing them to the ground once he'd proved there was no untithed grain hidden between the pages. Finally they finished, leaving Atyen to reorganize the mess they'd left in his bag. *These are sentinels?* They didn't even have a tithe-counter with them. The encounter left him shaken, and he decided to detour around Charisy on the farming roads in the hope of avoiding more like it. The cart-vendor had complained loudly about the patrols on the trading road, but he had complained loudly about a lot else and Atyen hadn't given his stories much credit. *But now I see what he meant.* As an afterthought he put his cross-sash on, just in case.

It took him several bells to get to the forewall by the longer route, and the forewall mists were cool and pleasant when he reached them. He left the goats and cart with the stablemaster, and went up to find Inquisitor Renn. When he got to Renn's quarters he found them empty. The Inquisitory was still in disarray after the fire, and nobody seemed to know where he'd gone. Finally he went down to the entry and asked the watchkeeper.

"Renn's gone to Charisy," he was told. "He's building the new Inquisitory."

Atyen sighed, and went back to the stables to get the cart.

"I'm brilliant, aren't I? Simply brilliant!" Enthusiasm radiated from Byo Vesene's words.

Renn nodded slowly. They were on an inspection tour of the new Inquisitory, his personal project and the Chief Inquisitor's eager passion. It occupied space that had once been crafter's shops on the foreward side of Charisy's main market, with the wealthy merchant district behind it and the market square proper to its front. The main building was forty meters wide, and already the central tower was twenty meters high.

"Aren't I brilliant?" prompted Vesene, not satisfied with the nod.

"You are brilliant, Chief Inquisitor," Renn answered dutifully. He couldn't see Cela Joss behind him, but he could feel her hard gaze. It was Cela's job to make sure that when Chief Inquisitor Vesene needed agreement, people agreed. "Moving the Inquisitory here is a stroke of genius." He didn't look at the Chief Inquisitor, instead running a critical eye over the work in progress. Crews of bound criminals were busily hauling bricks up the bamboo scaffolding that wound around its sides under the watchful eyes of armed sentinels, most of whom had been prisoners themselves not long ago. The main building was halfway finished, and the foundations had been laid for the wings on either side.

"It's going to be twice as high as the Inquisitory Tower," Vesene enthused, pointing up. "Twice! And away from the cursed mist. Look here." He pointed to a raised dais at what would become the entrance to the tower. "My statue will go here. Triple life size, yes."

"Triple, Chief Inquisitor," Torr Toorman answered. Renn could hear the well veiled sarcasm in Toorman's voice, but if Vesene picked it up he ignored it.

"The people will see me every day in the market. They *must* know me. The people must *love* me."

"The people do love you, Chief Inquisitor," Joss put in reassuringly.

"They'll worship me before long. You'll see. They'll worship me like a god." Vesene's face darkened, and he pointed a group of laborers unloading a goat-cart full of bricks. "They're slacking, Renn. Slacking. Get on that. I want this done quickly." He turned away before Renn could answer and clapped his gloved hands. "Carriers!"

"Carriers," Joss echoed, and a group of eight erranders came forward, bearing a travel cart with the wheels replaced with long poles so they could carry it. Renn rolled his eyes at the Chief Inquisitor's latest vanity.

The carriers lowered the cart so Vesene could climb in, and picked it up again when he was ensconced. "Home," he ordered, and they left at the trot. His honor guard of sentinels fell into formation around him and the whole procession set off for the forewall.

Toorman moved to stand beside Renn. "He says the wheels jolt him too much."

Renn laughed. "His brain has been jolted too much."

"He really is brilliant you know."

Renn gave the Inquisitor-in-Chief of Charisy a look. "Don't tell me you've lost your mind too."

"I should be so blessed. But look, everyone's working, everyone's fed." He swept an arm at the bamboo framed, waxed flax walled apartments that had sprung up as second and third stories atop the city's older buildings. "Everyone's housed, and he didn't even have to buy farmland to do it. Nobody has to beg anymore, and everyone loves him, just like he says."

Renn snorted. "Everyone's eating because his tithe patrols are squeezing the farmers to keep the grain lines open. Everyone's working because he's draining the steel vaults to build this insane palace. Everyone's housed in these ridiculous firetraps with neither water nor sewers, and your city's going to burn to the ground the next time someone kicks over a firebowl, if they don't all die of the stench first. And everyone loves him because if anyone expresses any discontent they wind up either making bricks or hauling them." Renn gestured at the servitors laboring on the growing edifice.

"Like I said, he's brilliant."

"Were you always this cynical?"

"Only since Cela Joss starting serving foxglove to anyone who spoke their mind."

Renn nodded. "Walk with me," he invited, and turned towards main avenue that led antispinward from the market square. "Cela frightens me. I don't know why she backs him up. She's smarter than that."

"Thank Noah she is. She's the only one who can talk any sense into him at all."

"That's little comfort." Renn stroked his chin. "I wonder what her motive is?"

"She likes power, and he keeps giving her more."

"Why doesn't she just take it for herself? She doesn't need him, and we'd be better off."

"I don't know." Toorman paused. "We have to do something you know. We can't let this go on."

The shopfronts crowded close on the avenue, with vendors

hawking all manner of wares. They stayed to the raised cobbling that ran beside it, ignoring the clamor. "What do you propose?" Renn asked.

"I don't know." Toorman spread his hands, palm up. "He's made all those thugs into sentinels, and turned them into his bodyguard."

"Cela did that."

"It was his idea. She objected at first, if you can believe it. So she told me anyway."

"Are they loyal to him?" Renn asked. He stopped by a quilt vendor selling pure fleece floorquilts. He needed one for his space in the new Inquisitory, and he ran a hand over the soft sheepskin, testing its texture, then laughed at himself. *How effectively I distract myself with triviality.*

"Loyal to Cela, I think." Toorman hadn't noticed Renn's brief moment of self-cynicism. "I can't believe I was glad to get my sentinels back from him." He looked up at the suntube as if imploring Noah for intervention. "What I wouldn't give for one of my own by his side right now."

"You couldn't have known." Renn waved away the vendor before he could start a sales pitch, and turned to keep walking.

Toorman snorted. "I can't believe I was stupid enough to send them to him in the first place." He shook his head sadly. "I owed him a favor."

"There was a fire, what else were you to do?"

"Perhaps." He laughed. "I thought I had street problems with half my sentinels gone. Now every beggar and thief in the world has moved here to eat free grain and live in free apartments."

"Don't remind me." Renn sighed. "If we used the brick in that palace to build real houses instead . . ."

They passed a dancehouse, and a revealingly clad young woman stood in the door, beckoning them in to enjoy the carnal delights on offer. "Just a few tokens," she called to them. "Anything you want you can have."

Toorman waved her away. They walked in silence for a while, came to the trading road and turned aftward. "Do you know he's selling women?"

"What?" Renn looked up sharply. "When did this start?"

"Just last week, in the auction hall. They're all farm wives, farm daughters. Officially it's indenture, but the sentinels are turning a blind eye to what really happens." He jerked his head back at the dancehouse. "I'm sure some of them are working in there right now."

"You're the Inquisitor-in-Chief! Can't you stop it?"

"I'm Inquisitor-in-Chief for Charisy. It all happens in the farm parishes, by the time they get here there's nothing I can do. They get squeezed for tithes, they dodge the tithes, get caught by the tithe-patrols and the whole family gets bound into servitude." Toorman shrugged. "Then the women get sent here. Their servitude is commuted to indenture, because our benevolent Chief Inquisitor is so lenient." He grimaced. "Then their indentures are auctioned off. It's all well within the law." They turned off the trading road and into Charisy's central park, pleasant paths through well groomed bushes, with the main church rising on its spinward side.

"But they're your sentinels . . ."

"Not my sentinels, Cela's." Toorman registered distate. "Thugs in cross-sashes. They're most of the buyers too, nobody else has the tokens." Toorman laughed. "Another piece of brilliance. He pays them hard steel to extract tithes and arrest farmers, then he feeds them the tithed food, sells them the farm women to get the steel back, uses it to pay for his palace and makes the farm men build it."

Renn shook his head. "That particular brilliance has Cela's sigil all over it. Vesene only cares about drowning himself in opulence. She's the one who has to find the steel to buy it."

"She has to keep the granaries full too, and this madness won't do that. How many farms has she destroyed, I wonder?"

"Too many. I'm worried. Solender was predicting we'd run out of food even before this."

"I'm not worried about food," Toorman said. "The farmers feed crops to animals to make meat. If they don't have any extra crops, they won't feed the animals." They came to the waterclock at the park's center, and he sat down on a bench to watch the water splash and the wheels spin. "So we'll all eat, we just won't eat meat." He tossed a stray stick into the pool at the clock's base. "I wonder if that's what happened to Solender's cattle and . . . what did he call the work beasts?"

"Horses."

"Horses." Toorman sighed. "You and I are just horses, did you know that? Laboring workbeasts. You're building that monstrosity to his glory, and I'm holding this city together so everyone can worship him while he wallows in it." His face showed disgust.

"Believe me, if I could get out of it with my life I'd be gone long ago. Have you talked to Charisy's reeve about this?"

Torr shook his head. "I wouldn't dare, the reeve loves him."

"Please tell me you're joking!"

"I wish I were, but the reeve is polled in. There's not a gram of his soul that isn't ruled by the people's will, and make no mistake the people do like Vesene. He gives out grain, the reeve worms himself the credit. When he builds houses, provides jobs, even when he sells women, the reeve worms himself the credit."

"Your reeve sounds like a worm himself."

"He is."

Renn had nothing to add to that, and so they sat watching the water. The flow was lower than it should have been. Charisy's new upper floor apartments were too high to draw directly from the conduit system, but their inhabitants took buckets from the public basins, and there were a lot of them. *Yet another overstretched resource. How long before something snaps?* "Shall we kill him?" he asked at last.

"We have to do something."

Renn looked at his fingernails, his expression far away. "We'd have to kill Cela too, and half the law council."

"They all have blood on their hands. Probably even Solender's."

"The law demands an inquisition."

"Are you serious?" Toorman's eyebrows went up. "You watched them make Stronka drink foxglove! And Born. And how many others have been suddenly godstruck?"

"Then they'll be convicted. Giving them an inquisition is for our benefit, not theirs. We'll show the people law means something again." Renn pursed his lips, thinking. "How many sentinels have you got, real sentinels, loyal to you over Cela?"

Toorman looked up, considering. "More than I had before. They're not happy with what Cela's done to the order."

"How many would we need to get through to him?"

"Not too many. His thugs have blades, but they aren't properly trained with them. The problem will be gaining control afterwards, that will take a lot more bodies. The poor won't like losing their grain lines and free houses, the rich won't like losing his steel. His thugs will fight and so will the law council. It could get ugly if we don't do it right."

Renn smiled. "Do we actually have a plan here?"

Toorman nodded. "The start of one. We'll have to be very careful, or we'll both end up with a mug of foxglove tea."

"Well, let's be careful then. Let's think on it, think on who we can bring in who we can trust absolutely. Can you meet here tomorrow? Say the noon bell?"

"Perfect."

Toorman offered his hand, and Renn shook it and stood up. "I'll see you then. I'm going to step into the church."

"What for?"

Renn laughed. "To pray. What else?"

"I didn't know you believed."

"I don't."

"Then why?"

"Just in case it helps." Renn smiled, feeling a great load lifted from his shoulders. *One step starts the journey.* He crossed the park to the church, and up the grand stairs. The heavy oak doors creaked open at his push. Inside it was cool and still, and he walked to the far end of the ranked ironwood benches, up past the well-worn dais and the ancient altar. At the very back was a small door, and he knocked. Footsteps sounded, and the door opened to the bishop of Charisy.

"Inquisitor Renn!" The bishop beckoned him in. "Welcome. What brings you here?"

"The sins I'm about to commit." Renn stepped through the door.

"You need forgiveness?"

"I need your help."


Sarabee was clearing the evening meal plates when there was a knock on the door. She went to answer it and it opened to Newl with his cross-sash on, with three men and a woman behind him.

"Newl, what . . . ?"

"I'm sorry, Sarabee." Newl's expression was sickly. "I'm sorry . . ."

One of the other men pushed past her brother-by-marriage. "Well, well, Sarabee. It's been a long time." The man who'd tried to rape her, Mial Broden, in a cross-sash.

She recognized him immediately. In her nightmares he terrified her, chased her, trapped her, laughed cruelly at her fear as he pawed at her body, but when she saw his face on her doorstep her instant reaction was blind rage. She screamed and leapt at him, knocking him over, her hands locking onto his throat. Her own fear was reflected in his face as he fell backwards and it only gave her strength. She would have snuffed out his life on the spot if the other two sentinels hadn't dragged her off him. They hauled her to one side, and all five came in. Acelle started crying, Healan ran into the bedroom to hide, Liese grabbed Jerl and hurried him into the kitchen.

Newl was wringing his hands together. "Sarabee, I'm so sorry."

"Newl, you get that motherless sooksa out of my house this instant," Sarabee raged, wrenching at the sentinels restraining her. "Get him out you yatsless little girl, *get him out!*"

"What's going on?" Jens strode in from the kitchen. He caught sight of Newl. "Newl, what's happening here?"

Newl started to answer, but one of the other men cut him off. "I'm tithecounter for the Tidings shorefields. This is a tithe patrol."

"A tithe patrol?" Jens looked the group over. "Well, we've got nothing to hide. What do you want to see?"

"What we're going to see . . ." Mial put in. ". . . is you and your pretty little wife in servitude." His voice was raw, and Sarabee's handprints were livid on his throat. He smiled a nasty smile at Sarabee. "And I'm going to enjoy that servitude quite a bit."

"*Sooksa!*" Sarabee spat the word, then spat at him.

"Enough!" The tithecounter raised his hand. "I see there's some history here. Inquisitor Broden, you wait outside." Mial was wiping Sarabee's spittle from his cross sash and didn't move. The tithecounter turned to face him, his voice hard. "Outside. Don't make me say it again."

Sullenly Mial went out.

"I'm so sorry," Newl repeated, still wringing his hands.

"I apologize for that," the tithecounter said. "There's no need for this to be personal."

Jens nodded, slowly. "As I said, we've got nothing to hide." He nodded to the other two sentinels. "You can let my wife go now."

"I *don't* apologize," Sarabee snapped. "And if that animal comes into my house again I'll gut him like I did his friend."

"He's not coming in, Sarabee." Jens said. "You two, let her go."

The sentinels did as Jens said, and Sarabee went to the opposite side of the room, keeping her eyes on the door.

"We'll make this as fast as possible," the tithecounter said. "This is just routine, your hauls have been low, so we have to check.

Let's just go over the figures." He pulled out a worksheaf. "Can you confirm these sales?"

Sarabee came over. "I handle the selling," she said. She took the page and scanned it. "They look right."

"Very good." The tithecounter smiled a perfunctory smile. "And you've made no sales not recorded here?"

"You've got every monger from here to Cove listed."

"Then you won't mind if we look around?"

"Do you clean up after yourself?"

"This isn't meant to be hostile, please, we're just doing our jobs."

"Go ahead," Jens said, before Sarabee could say more. He gave her a look. *Concern, love, caution.* He was doing the right thing, and there was nothing to be gained by antagonizing the tithecounter. She took a deep breath and pressed her lips together.

The sentinels who'd held her did the looking, the tithecounter just watched. Newl just stood in the corner, still wringing his hands and looking miserable. He looked like he wanted to apologize again, but Sarabee shot him a look and he wilted. The sentinels were very thorough, the woman lifting the floor quilt and checking the floorboards, the man climbing up to check the rafters. They went through the kitchen shelves, opened the drawers, dipped into the rain barrel, went through Sarabee's backbag, and counted out the tokens there, checked the beds and the walls.

"It looks fine to me," the woman reported, finally.

"And me," her partner added.

"Very good. Do you own any other buildings?" asked the tithecounter.

"Just my sailshed and my smokeshed," Jens answered. "And my raft, if you want to go through that."

The tithecounter shook his head. "I think we've disturbed your privacy enough for today. I apologize again. I didn't know there were any . . ." He coughed. ". . . issues with sentinel Broden, or I wouldn't have brought him."

Jens took a deep breath. "I appreciate your courtesy," he said, and moved to let the tithe patrol out.

The door opened before he got there. It was Mial. He held up a small bag, turned it over, dumped it out. Builder tokens spilled out onto the floor. "In the smokeshed, under the firebowl," he said, and smiled his cruel smile. "I'm going to own you, Sarabee Madane." He grabbed her wrist and she swung her fist at his face, but he jerked out of the way, and then caught her other wrist as well, spinning her around so she couldn't kick at him. "I've got her," he called.

Jens crossed the room in a blur and drove his fist into Mial's face. The impact sounded like an axe hitting wood, and the youth staggered back with his nose broken flat over, blood streaming from it. Sarabee pivoted and drove her knee into his groin and he went down in a ball, and then Jens was on top of him, driving his fist down over and over, his face contorted in fury. The other two sentinels grabbed him and hauled him off, and then the tithecounter had Sarabee from behind.

"Don't make it worse," he said in her ear as she struggled and cursed. "Don't make it worse."

Mial rolled over, groaning, hands clutched to his groin, his face a mask of hate already distorted by the swelling. He staggered to his feet, grabbed his blade from his belt, and with a sudden lunge, drove it into Jens's belly. Sarabee screamed as her husband gasped in pain, and then with dying strength he tore his arms free of the inquisitors holding him back and his hands went to Mial's throat. The youth's eyes popped and he struggled to breathe, his own hands flying to Jens's in an attempt to pry them off. He wasn't strong enough, but Jens was gouting blood and weakening, and finally his muscles went slack and he slid forward onto the floor.

"No!" Sarabee screamed, and kicked back at the tithecounter until he let go. She flew to her husband's side. "No! No! No!" She sobbed the word over and over, putting her arms around him. Mial moved towards her but the tithecounter put up a hand and the other two sentinels stepped forward to keep him away.

"Oh Sarabee, I'm so sorry." Newl had his hands clasped to his breast, half bent over. "I'll get Celese, we'll look after the children. Don't worry about the children . . ."

She ignored him, sobbing over Jens's body. Time stood still, and she seemed to be watching herself from a long, long way away. It seemed to be hours before the sentinels helped her to her feet, before they led her outside to the goat-cart, but it couldn't have been because Newl was still cringing and apologizing and promising. She wanted to spit at him, but her body wouldn't respond, and she numbly followed them where they took her. At some point she was in Tidings, at another in the basement of the

Inquisition Hall. At some point the female sentinel was undressing her, washing the blood away and at another the inquisitor-of-fact was asking her questions, though she couldn't remember what he'd asked or what she'd answered. She didn't even know if the washing came before or after the questions. The inquisitor's face did seem familiar, and a long time afterwards she realized that he was the same one who'd interviewed her after the rape attempt.

Once she heard Mial yelling in a room not far away, but they kept him away from her. At least a week passed between her arrest and her inquisition, but when Mial was called forward as a witness his face was still a bloody mass, barely recognizable as human. He couldn't visually identify her because both eyes were swollen shut, and when he spoke his speech was slurred, Jens had broken half his teeth. The realization raised the corner of her mouth a tiny fraction, the largest emotional reaction the whole process raised in her. The Inquisitor-in-Chief was the same man as before too, and he looked sad and tired as he bound her for five years servitude for tithe neglect. *The law is the law.* Sarabee was beyond caring.

The reeve was there too, and as they roped her wrists behind her back he shouted something about owning her. That didn't register either. Her only thoughts, when she had any thoughts, were for her children. *Celese will look after them.* She clung to that thought. Her sister was a good woman, and Sarabee had helped her when Newl was gone. She would stand by her family. Newl himself was irrelevant, he had removed himself from the world of men, from the world of humanity, when he'd allowed the tithe patrol to bring Mial to her door. She couldn't imagine Jens being so weak, or Atyen, or her father. *No wonder I couldn't spit at him.* He wasn't worth the spit.

They loaded her on a goat cart with a cage on the back and jolted their way foreword. She assumed they were going to Charisy, but they stopped at the bridge into the city and pulled into the courtyard of a small travelling house. A sentinel read a document at her, commuting her sentence from servitude to indenture, whatever that meant. Another woman was put in the cart at that point, her sentence commuted as well. At first Sarabee dared hope that that was a good thing, but then another woman came, and a fourth and a fifth. *Only women, and none who can't bear children.* It wasn't a positive sign, and the fear of rape began to grow in her again. They'd replaced her blood-soaked clothing with a robe at the Inquisition hall. It was a simple single-piece garment of plain flax, but it had a hood so she drew that up to hide her hair and hunched forward to de-accentuate her breasts. She kept her head down as well, avoiding eye contact and retreating as far into the fabric as she could. They waited there the from noon bell to noon bell without food or water. Several of the other women urinated in the cart and they all complained of thirst and hunger except Sarabee. Her body seemed to be totally shut down, and she was indifferent to the stench of stale urine and unwashed bodies and the heat of the suntube overhead. Finally another cart full of women joined them, another document was read, and the drivers stirred up the goats and they clattered over the bridge into the city. The sign on the travelling house read "Welcome," and for some reason that fact stuck in her mind.

Beyond the bridge was a wide road with tall, impressive houses, but their route soon took them through a bad part of the city, where cheap apartments of bamboo and waxed flax squatted on the roofs of rundown brick houses. There were men on the road, leaning out of windows, desire plain in their eyes, shouting obscene comments. Sarabee ignored them, keeping her eyes on the cart floor. There was raw sewage stinking in the street as well, something she'd never experienced in Tidings, but the smell didn't really register. It didn't take long to reach their destination, a large, low building of brick and timber. Both carts were unloaded and the women were herded into a large building of brick and timber, down a corridor and into a plain room that had been divided into a series of improvised cages with bamboo bars. Several men and a woman watched their arrival from the other side of the bars, and the prisoners were divided up among the various cells. Most of them held two or three women, but Sarabee wound up alone in hers. The cage door was closed and barred, and a sentinel stepped forward to explain that they'd be fed shortly and taken to be washed. He warned of the consequences of disobedience, smacking a heavy stick into his palm as he threatened them.

His words evidently disturbed the watching woman, dark hair and dark eyes with an inquisitor's double-red cross-sash.

"These are the Chief Inquisitor's property," she said severely. "Don't mark them."

---

Wearily Atyen threaded his way through the throng of workers swarming around Charisy's new Inquisitory. The stables were unfinished, but he managed to talk the worker in charge there into letting him leave his goats and the cart there temporarily. It was an impressive structure even with the soaring tower incomplete and the wings mere foundations. The main building was nearly finished, and already some offices were in use. *Hopefully including Renn's.* He went up into the pillared entrance and found a fountain gushing in the grand, domed entrance hall. Wide staircases spiralled up either side of it to the spacious halls on either side. There was none of the makeshift, much modified and well worn atmosphere of the old Inquisitory. There were already carvings and statuary in ornate niches, and heavily embroidered quilts cushioning the walls. *And it isn't damp.* He'd forgotten how damp it was at the forewall, how a faint scent of mildew pervaded everything, how he'd always had to wear wool to keep the chill at bay.

*Much improved.* He chose the left hand stairway at random, which led him to the left hand hall, brightly lit with well placed skylights above. It was the right decision. An errander directed him to Renn's quarters, and he found the senior Inquisitor at his workshelf.

"Well, well, young Atyen," Renn said when he turned around at Atyen's knock. "I'm surprised to see you returned."

"I've found something. I thought you'd want to know about it as soon as possible." Atyen dropped a stack of worksheaves on Renn's workshelf.

"Hmmm." Renn pulled over the top sheaf, opened it, started reading. His eyes grew big, and he looked up. "What *is* this?"

Atyen sat down, and described what he'd found in Heaven.

"And you flew there? Really flew?"

"I did."

"This . . ." Renn paged through the sheaf, reading snippets at random. "This is incredible. This is the Builders, for certain." His voice rose in excitement. "Do you realize what you've got here?"

"I think so. I hope to present it as my masterwork. That and what I've learned of flying. If it's possible . . ."

"Oh, there's no doubt of that. I'll stand as your doctrinor. We'll have your double-red cross-sash on you very soon. First, we have to solve some problems."

"You meant that I'm Solender's—"

"No, no, not that. I only wish our Chief Inquisitor were still worried about Solender's people." Renn gave a sardonic half-smile. "We have far larger problems now."

"Like what?"

"Like this building, for starters. Vesene has dumped so much steel into the market to pay for it that oranges are going for five tokens apiece, if you can find oranges. That means everyone who *isn't* being paid Inquisition steel to put this thing up can't afford to eat. He solved that problem by expanding the grain lines, only now the grain stores are empty and I don't know what's going to happen next. He's killed half the law council . . ."

"Killed?"

"Murdered them, and bought the rest. Why do you think I'm building this monstrosity in the full knowledge it's ruining the Inquisition, except to save my own fragile neck? The sentinels have been debased completely. And every day he descends from his half-finished tower to accept the grateful praise of his people."

Voices rose outside, angry and growing louder. "Ah," Renn smiled. "Here come the worshippers now."

He stood and went to the window, and Atyen followed him. Outside, work on the palace had come to a halt, as the market square filled with an angry, chanting mob. A line of sentinels had formed across the front of the structure, and there was a small gap between them and the mob, a measure of respect given to the sentinel's blades. As they watched the mob grew larger and the chanting louder, and Atyen could hear snatches of words. "Grain . . . Bread . . . Vesene . . ." Soon there were thousands in the market square, and though the narrow corridor between the crowd and the sentinels remained, it was obvious the mob could overrun them in a heartbeat if things went badly.

"What's going to—" he started to ask, but all at once the crowd quieted.

"Vesene has taken the balcony," Renn explained.

"They don't sound very worshipful."

Renn laughed. "They don't like being hungry, but watch."

The tower balcony was above Atyen and to the left, so he couldn't see the Chief Inquisitor, or make out very well what he was saying. He heard snippets. "My people . . . your love . . . grain . . . farmers . . . come together . . . faith in your leader . . . faith in your god . . ."

"It's the usual speech," Renn explained. "He's blaming the farmers, he's been doing that for months. The people think he's wonderful, so they're willing to go along with that. They just need somewhere to put their anger. Today he's got no grain to give them, so he's giving them promises."

"But if he's got no grain . . ."

"Cela Joss's tithe patrols are out right now getting it. There'll be grain tomorrow, that's what matters." Renn smirked. "Maybe not a lot, maybe not even enough, but some. They've always managed so far, and they'll keep managing until they run out of farmers to squeeze."

"What then?"

"Then there'll be promises but no grain. That'll work for a little while, they're used to waiting for promises now. When the promises won't hold anymore, he'll give them steel; he's already brought it all here from the old Inquisitory." Renn turned away from the window. "And when the people figure out there's no food to buy and they can't eat steel, there's going to be a war."

Atyen looked at the older man, aghast. "A war?"

"What will the people do? Pull down their god because he lied to them? That won't fill their bellies, and people will go a long way to avoid admitting to themselves they've been made fools of. No, they already *know* it's the farmer's fault, those evil, selfish farmers denying free food to the upstanding people of Charisy. He's told them that so often they think they've figured it out for themselves. They'll just go out into the fields and take what they want, and kill whoever gets in their way. A third of the world lives in this city. When that many people start fighting, it's a war."

Atyen nodded slowly. "I saw some hints things were getting worse in the shorefields. I had no idea it was this bad."

"The shorefields don't matter, none of the farm parishes matter, none of the towns matter, only Charisy matters. What happens here will set the outcome for the rest of the world, for better or for worse."

"Solender saw this coming."

"A lot of us saw it coming. Our shame is we didn't stop it when it was easy." Outside the window the speech came to an end, and the crowd started chanting "Vesene! Vesene! Vesene!" Their anger changed to wild enthusiasm. "Look," Renn pointed. "He's done it again."

"I should have been here myself. I didn't know . . ."

"You didn't know," Renn turned away from the window and went back to his workshelf. "Vesene would have sent you off to some tiny village, just like the rest of Solender's aspirants. Or he'd have had Cela Joss kill you, if he had the slightest thought you were dangerous. You did the right thing in going, and you'd probably be better off if you'd stayed where you were."

"Well, I'm here now. There must be something you can do."

"I'd hoped you'd say that." Renn smiled. "In fact, we're already doing something, and there's something you can do too."

Aunt Celese closed the shutters and lowered the sleep-cloth. Liese Madane lay in the darkness, staring at the ceiling and listening to the others as they said their goodnights. She, her siblings and their five cousins were crowded three to a bed in the children's room, but she was far from ready for sleep. Newl, she decided, was useless.

Beside her Jerl was already breathing deeply, and Acelle was too. There was some scuffling from the other side of the room, some low voices, a giggle as the other children settled. Normally she would have put on her stern voice and told them to be quiet, but she didn't. She was too busy being angry with Newl. *Useless!* When he'd come into the kitchen after the fight she'd asked him what was happening. He'd said nothing, just hurried her and her siblings over to Aunt Celese's house. Healan and Acelle had both been so frightened they were in tears, and he'd done nothing to comfort them, he hadn't even carried Jerl, Liese had to do that herself. When she'd later asked him again later, he'd said only that her parents were gone. *Gone!* What a word to use. It was Aunt Celese who'd had to tell her that her father was dead, that her mother was arrested.

*He was there and he didn't do anything to stop it. Useless!* The room grew quiet, and she could tell the other children were drifting off to sleep, but Liese's thoughts wouldn't still. Newl was a sentinel, so she'd asked him to bring her mother back. He'd given her some stupid words and done nothing, and since then he'd done nothing more but guzzle wine and sleep. *Useless!* The fear and frustration she'd been holding down for two days welled up in Liese's chest, but she forced it down to be angry at Newl some more. *I just want my parents back!* It wasn't fair that he did nothing, it wasn't right, and she knew she couldn't have her father again, but she wanted, needed, *had* to have her mother. She felt tears forming in her eyes and wiped them away angrily. She didn't want the other children to hear her crying. She didn't want to cry at all.

But she cried anyway. All she could do was suppress the sobs so they wouldn't wake Jerl or Acelle, and the tears rolled down her cheeks until the quilts were soaked. She hated crying. *I'm the oldest, I have to be stronger.* That thought didn't stop the tears either. She missed her mother, she missed her father, she missed her home. She reached over and pulled Jerl close to her, drawing comfort from him. He was too young to understand what was going on, so it was safe to share her secret weakness with him. Eventually she fell asleep.

The next day was the funeral for her father, and Celese put her in charge of keeping her sisters in order while the ceremony went on. She felt numb as the bishop went through the ritual, and felt no connection at all with the silent, flax-wrapped shape on top of the pyre. She didn't cry then, though her sisters did, Celese did, even Newl did, and she felt proud of herself for staying in control.

"Your father is with God now," her aunt Reane told her as the flames rose up, trying to be comforting, but the only thing Liese cared about was that he wasn't with her. It was hard not to cry then, and she squeezed her hands into fists, digging her nails hard into her palms until she felt the skin tearing. Her eyes filled, but she blinked back the tears, and got back to Celese's for the visitation. The hustle and bustle kept her distracted for a while, but gradually the flow of guests diminished until it was just the family left. Her aunt Reane had stayed as well, and all the cousins were sent out to play while the adults had a talk. They didn't tell her what it was about, but she knew they were deciding which children would go with Reane, and which would stay with Celese, and what would be done with the house and the dock and the rafts.

The last thing she felt like doing was playing, so she walked back to her house. The door was locked, but she knew how to get the bedroom shutters open from the outside and wriggle through. She picked up Jerl's favorite fleece rabbit, Healan's best cloth doll, and the painted clamshell lined with waxed flowers that Acelle had made and put above her bed. She had intended to bring something of her own as well, but as she looked over her things she couldn't bring herself to. It would be admitting that she wouldn't be coming back to her home, that things would never be the same again. *And they will be. They have to be.* Still, she wanted something to hold, to keep close her memories in the time in between. *And something to remember Dadsha.* She went to his shelves, looked over his things. Her eye fell on an ornately carved wooden sphere, the message ball Atyen had given him, and she slipped it into a pocket.

There was a noise at the front door and she jumped. A key turned in the lock. Instinctively she crouched down behind her parents' bed, heart pounding, making herself as small as possible. There were footsteps, voices, a man and a woman, and she listened, barely daring to breath. *Please don't let them come in. Please don't let them come in.* She couldn't quite make out what they were saying, but they spent a long time, walking back and forth, talking, sometimes moving things. She slowly slid herself backwards into the space between the bed and the waterbowl stand. If they did come in, they'd only see her if they came right around the bed.

Something hit her on the head and she nearly screamed. The waterbowl clattered to the floor. She'd knocked the stand over.

"What was that?" a voice asked. The bedroom door opened, a man with a cross-sash stood over her.

"What are you doing here, child?"

Liese's eyes darted to the window, but there was no way she could bolt for it over the bed without being caught. She slowly stood up, still clutching the rabbit, the shell and the doll. "It's my house, sir."

The man nodded. "I see. Well, come out from there. We aren't going to hurt you." The woman had come in and was standing behind him. "I'm Nade, Inquisitor-of-Fact in Tidings." He sat down on her parent's clothing chest. "This is my aspirant, Juna. Why don't you sit and talk to us?"

Slowly, suspiciously, Liese came around and sat on the bed.

"You just came back to get some things, is that it?"

Liese nodded silently.

"And who's looking after you?"

"My aunt, sir."

"You don't have to call me, sir."

Liese nodded, not sure what to say. An idea occurred to her. "Inquisitors are in charge of sentinels, aren't they?"

"Some are. Not all of us."

"Are you?"

"Of some sentinels."

"Can you get them to bring my mother back?"

The man's expression changed, and he looked away. After a long time he looked back. "No, I'm sorry. I wish I could, but I can't."

"Where did they take her?"

"I don't know."

"To Charisy," the woman named Juna said. Nade gave her a look and something passed between them that Liese couldn't fathom.

"Why did they come?" Liese's was no longer afraid, and her anger came flooding back. "Why did they take my Mamsha and Dadsha?"

"It's complicated . . ." Nade began.

"It's not fair!" Liese screamed, her fear suddenly turned to anger. "We didn't do anything. It's not fair!" Her tears came flooding back, this time loud and long, the sobs wracking her body. Nade sat beside her and put his arms around her, and even though she didn't like him it was comforting so she let it happen.

Eventually she stopped, exhausted, ashamed for showing weakness to strangers, and feeling lost and very small. "Come on," Juna said. "I'll take you home."

She took Liese out the back door, trying to keep her away from the place where the floor quilt was missing, where the a wide stretch of wood was stained dark. She knew it was her father's blood. *They think I'm a child, that I wouldn't notice.* She let them maintain their illusion. Mercifully Juna didn't want to talk to Aunt Celese, which saved Liese from a lecture, and just dropped Liese off at the end of the farm lane. Liese found Acelle and Healan in the barn playing tag with her cousins, and she called them aside and gave them their treasures in secret. There was no need for the adults to know where she'd been. Her cousins tried to involve her in the game, but she walked back to the house and slipped past her aunts and Newl, who were still in deep discussion, Celese with Jerl on her knee. Back in her cousin's room, back in the bed that was hers for now, she climbed under the quilts, and their enveloping warmth helped her feel a little better.

She took the message ball from her pocket and looked at it. It was ornately carved and heavy for its size, made of a hard, dark wood. ATYEN HORUN was inscribed around its equator.

The message ball had always fascinated her. She knew it could be opened, but her father had never let her play with it, and scolded her the one time she'd snuck it down from the shelf and tried to figure it out herself. All she'd learned the first time was that it was divided into thirds, and the top and bottom thirds could be twisted a half turn against the middle. She tried that, twisting and pulling this way and that, but the ball remained stubbornly closed. Eventually she tired of it. The evening-meal bell sounded, and Aunt Celese came in to call her to eat, but she wasn't hungry and refused. Celese sat with her a minute, ran her fingers through her hair.

"I know it's hard, Liese. You just have to trust that everything will work out."

"Who are you sending with Aunt Reane?"

"Jerl and Healan. You and Acelle will stay here."

"Can't we keep Jerl instead?"

Celese shook her head slowly. "He's too young, and I've got too many to look after here as it is."

"I can look after him. I already do."

"It's been decided. Why don't you come down and eat?"

Liese shook her head, and after a moment Celese left her to carry on with the rest. *It's been decided.* Just like adults to make that kind of choice without even asking. *Jerl is my responsibility now. They can't take that away from me.* Only they had, and anger grew in her until she wanted to scream and break something. The message ball was there and she picked it up with the urge to throw it across the room. She fought it down with an effort, and instead squeezed it, hard enough to make her hand hurt.

Something moved, and she opened her hand, her anger gone in an instant. She'd pushed in a small section in the middle third of the ball, and a corresponding section on the opposite side had been pushed out. She twisted the segments experimentally, and found the top third twisted further than it had before. When she did that the protruding piece was locked out, and couldn't be pushed back in. After some more experimentation she found that allowed the bottom third to twist farther too. She was stuck there for a while, until she pushed the protruding piece again. It sank back flush with the surface, and the ball fell apart along a hidden zigzag around its middle, revealing a small hollow. There was a note folded tight inside.

Liese hadn't expected that, and she picked it up and carefully opened it. It was in her father's writing, and simple. *Atyen, we need you, please come at once. Jens.* She turned it over to see if there was anything on the other side, but there was nothing. With trembling fingers she folded it up along the original lines and tucked it back in the hollow. It took her a couple of tries to reverse the steps to close the ball, but when it was closed she pressed it over her heart. For just a moment she felt her father close.

And then she had an idea. *Atyen.* Her father had faced a problem, and he'd turned to Atyen. Atyen was an inquisitor, Atyen could *fly.* If anyone could get her mother back, it was Atyen. She didn't know where he was, but the message ball would find him. That's what it was for. She'd take it to the Hall of Inquisition in Tidings, and they'd send a mirror message to get him. A small smile crept across her lips. She wasn't going to let the adults ruin her life for her. She slipped out of bed, went to her backbag, rummaged past her clothing for her school worksheaf and charcoal scriber. With them she wrote a new note. *Atyen, Dadsha has died and they took Mamsha. Please help me find her. Liese.* She folded it tight, re-opened the ball and replaced her father's message with hers. After some thought she tucked the original note into her worksheaf and put it back in her backbag.

She slept eventually, and the next day ate as much breakfast as she could. Afterwards she made sure Jerl was settled with Aunt Celese, put a bag of dried apples in her backbag and set off for Tidings. She'd only been there a few times with her mother and hadn't really been paying attention to the route, but she was set on her plan and determined to see it through. It was surprisingly simple—she recognized the important landmarks—and before long she was in Tidings market. She asked a cart-vendor where the Hall of Inquisition was, got directions and went there. There was a sentinel at the entrance, and that gave her pause. It was the sentinels who had taken her parents from her. The courage that had carried her as far as the hall doors failed her, and she turned around and went back into the street.

*You're being weak,* she admonished herself. *You've come all this way to do this. Just do it.* Still she couldn't bring herself to, and she walked around the building to build her courage, down a little alley past a claywright, through the hall's back courtyard onto the side-street and then back around to the front door. It didn't help. *But you have to do it or you're weak.* She stood herself straight, tugged her hair for luck, and walked up the stairs and inside.

"Can I help you?" the sentinel asked.

"I have a message for Inquisitor Atyen Horun," she said, trying to sound as if she delivered messages for inquisitors all the time.

"Come in, I'll see if he's here." The sentinel led her into another room, gave her a chair to sit on. "What's your name?"

"Liese," she said, and the sentinel nodded and went away. She put her backbag under her chair to wait. He was back a few minutes later. "I'm sorry, there's no one here with that name."

"I know he's not here." She held up the message ball. "I brought this. You have to send him a mirror message."

The sentinel took the ball from her, looked at it, looked back at her. "Where did you get this?"

"From my father."

"I'll be right back." He took the ball and left her waiting again. This time he was gone long enough that Liese began to fidget, bored with waiting.

Eventually he returned. "Come with me please." She picked up her bag, and he led her down a corridor to another room, where a woman sat at a workshelf. For a moment she thought it was Juna, but when she looked up it wasn't. The message ball was on the shelf in two halves, her note unfolded beside it.

"Sit down," the woman said, and Liese sat down across from her. "Liese is it?"

"Yes."

"So Liese, where did you get this ball?"

"From my father."

"Does he know you have it?"

"He's dead. The note says so."

"I'm sorry to hear that." The woman pursed her lips, thinking. "Did you write it?"

"Yes." Liese scanned the woman's face, trying to read what was going through her mind. She knew enough to know when she was in trouble with adults, and things weren't going the way she had imagined they would.

"Liese." The woman leaned forward. "You have to understand, these balls are not toys. They're for important messages."

"This is a very important message." Liese made her voice emphatic. "I need Atyen to come."

"Yes . . ." The woman paused. "Liese, I'm very sorry your father is gone. I know it must be very upsetting, but this isn't the right thing to do . . ."

She said more, but Liese wasn't listening. She could see now there would be no mirror message, they weren't going to bring Atyen, and they were going to keep the message ball. *And it's not fair, and I'm not going to let them.* If she had to find Atyen herself she would. No adult was going to stop her, ever again. She had her backbag over one shoulder, and she slipped the other arm through the strap so it was properly on her back. The woman was saying something about responsibility, the sentinel had gone somewhere else, and Liese stood up, grabbed a ball-half with each hand, and bolted from the room. The woman yelled, more in surprise than anger, but she'd have to come around the workshelf, and that would slow her down. Liese sprinted down the corridor, grabbed the corner of the doorway to make the turn out the front door past the sentinel and jumped the stairs to the street in a single leap. She didn't look to see if they were chasing her, just dodged into the alley by the claywright. The alley continued past the hall's back courtyard and so she kept running, out into the next street, and then down it. She dodged into another alley, followed it into a square, and angled across it into another street, her feet pounding on the brick cobbling until finally she was too out of breath to run further. Only when she stopped did she look back. The street was full of adults, vendors, farmers driving goat-carts, marketers with bags full of their purchases. No one was chasing her, no one was paying her any attention at all. *Thank Noah.* She still had the halves of the message ball clutched in her hands, and she took a minute to reassemble it and put it back in her backbag. That done, she looked up and down the street to get her bearings. Nothing was familiar, and it slowly dawned on her that she was lost.

Sarabee's cage was big enough for her to lie down, barely, but the floor wasn't comfortable for sleeping. The clatter of carts on the cobbles went on without interruption through the sleeping hours. The smell of raw sewage wafting in from outside assaulted her nose, and the numb disconnection she'd experienced through the whole ordeal had gradually been replaced by a desperate desire to see her children. She reminded herself that Celese would take care of them, but that did nothing to banish the feeling. There was only one sentinel, a woman, watching them from the other side of the bamboo cage door, and halfway through the night Sarabee heard her snoring. She raised herself on an elbow, and saw the woman sound asleep on a folded quilt on the other side of the steel cage door.

It was her chance, and she quickly rose and tried the cage door. The locking bar was tight and secure, and so were the hinges, but there was play in the bars, so she looked to see if she could loosen them. They were set into a heavy wooden beam that was in turn pegged solidly to the floor, and though she tried, it was beyond her strength to unseat them. *Think, Sarabee, think.* The one conclusion she came to was that if she did get out she'd open the other cages as well. Fifty escaped women running through the streets of Charisy would not remain free for very long, but they deserved their chance, and the sheer numbers would give Sarabee a better opportunity. She tried the bars again, wrenching hard at them in frustration, but they wouldn't budge. She tried to loosen the pegs on the beam, but they were too tightly seated. Finally she had to admit that she couldn't get out. She sat, staring out through the bars, unable to sleep.

The breakfast bell came and went, and the other women began to wake up. Sarabee was hungry now, but no food came. A buzz of voices began, grew steadily louder. Somewhere close by a substantial crowd was gathering. They waited in glum silence for what seemed like quite a long time, and then a squat, balding man came and talked to the sentinel at some length. After a while two more sentinels came in. A cage was opened, the women inside brought out. One of the sentinels attached a braided rope collar with a short lead line to their necks.

"Line up against that wall," the balding man barked, pointing. The women shuffled into position. The newcomer looked them over appraisingly. "You, there." He pointed again. "Then you, then you."

Another cage was opened and the process repeated, and then another. Sarabee was the second-last, by accident or design she couldn't tell, and put second-last in line. The collar was rough on her neck, but she didn't care about that. Sooner or later her chance would come, and when it did she'd get away. *Patience, Sarabee, focus on the children.* The important thing was to get home to them, everything else was secondary. They were led in a line to a heavy door, urged through it into a narrow corridor, not even wide enough to turn around in, and she found herself pressed tight against the women to either side. The last woman was herded in behind her, and the heavy door was closed. The crowd noise was in front of them, and it kept getting louder as they waited.

"Do you know what's happening?" she asked the woman in front of her.

She shook her head. "I wish I did."

The narrow space quickly grew stifling. She tried to look forward to see what was ahead, but couldn't see past the press of bodies. Suddenly the crowd noise quieted, and a single voice replaced it. She recognized the tones of the balding man, but though she strained to listen she couldn't quite make out the words. A moment later a whisper came down the line from the woman at the front. They were being *auctioned.* A deep anger came over Sarabee, and unconsciously her hands balled into fists as she remembered the words of the female inquisitor from the previous day. *I am no one's property!* She reminded herself of her decision to be patient, to show no resistance until the time was right. She'd give herself a better chance if she wasn't marked as a problem beforehand. The line of women lurched forward, and as she grew closer to the front the words of the auctioneer grew more distinct, touting the youth and beauty of each woman, her strength and supposed domestic skills. Her anger grew, as she realized that the auctioneer had put them into order of increasing sexual attractiveness. *He'll get better prices that way, that's all he cares about.* It was cold comfort that she'd been put at the end of the line, assessed as one of the more desirable.

As the line grew shorter she could see ahead a large room, lit from above by skylights. A set of stairs led to a stage, and two female sentinels stood in a curtained area at the edge, stripping the clothing of the woman to be sold off before shoving her into the center. A man there tethered her by her neck rope to an overhead pole to be displayed. The auctioneer was shouting to the crowd, calling out the bids, and a pair of erranders to the side were recording the numbers, collecting kilos of steel from the winning bidders. The auction was fast-moving, and her turn came quickly. For a moment she considered retreating to the other end of the narrow corridor and making them come to drag her out. They'd have a difficult time of it in the confined space, and she'd make them pay. *But they'll make me pay that much and more.* She abandoned the idea. It would change nothing in the end, and it was still smarter to save her rebellion for when it would make a difference. The corridor ended in a curtained space below the stairs and separated from the main auction area. One of the female sentinels grabbed her neck rope and hauled her out of the corridor.

"Strip," the other ordered. There was a pile of discarded clothing on the floor, all of it dirty and torn. Reluctantly she did as they told her, and added her own garments to the pile. On the stage the woman ahead of her was being sold, and trying to cover her nakedness with one hand across her breasts and the other over her vulva. She had her head down, her long hair covering her face. She looked like a frightened girl, vulnerable and humiliated in front of her captors. Very soon it would be Sarabee in front of the crowd, and she wasn't looking forward to it. *I can't prevent that but I'm not going to let them see I'm beaten.* All too quickly the gavel came down on the sale, and Sarabee was led by her neck rope up onto the stage. She held her head high and kept her shoulders back, standing straight and proud. The crowd applauded and whistled as she was brought to the center, and some shouted obscene comments. There were hundreds of them she saw, almost all men, some dressed well, others not, a surprising number in sentinel's cross-sashes, but all of them openly desirous. She swallowed hard and focused her eyes on the back wall, trying to ignore the whistles and catcalls that were still coming up from the throng. She fought down the urge to cover herself. *It won't change anything, and I won't let them think that they've shamed me.*

The auctioneer held up his arms for silence. "The faster you're quiet, the faster we'll have her sold to some lucky buyer. Quiet please, so we can start the sale." The room calmed down, and he began. "Look how proud this one is, she's got spirit. What do I hear for an opening bid? Five hundred tokens is not too much for a woman this fine."

"Five hundred!" yelled a man in the front row. "She's a good one." Despite herself Sarabee looked at him, then quickly looked back to the far wall. He was balding and bearded, with coarse and dirty clothing to match his demeanor, a landless worker in all likelihood, presented for the first time with the opportunity for his own woman. In some sense it didn't matter who purchased her, the entire idea was wholly repugnant. At the same time she fervently hoped that this man didn't win the bidding.

"Five hundred ten!" yelled another man. This time Sarabee didn't look.

"Increments of fifty, and no less." The auctioneer waved a hand to dismiss the bid. "I have five hundred now, who'll give me five hundred fifty?"

"Five fifty!"

"Six hundred!" It was the first voice, and Sarabee's jaw clenched reflexively.

"Six hundred. Gentleman, gentlemen, please don't insult this fine creature. Fifty is the minimum increment, but look at her breasts, look at her thighs. It's rare a woman so beautiful comes on the stage. I'd buy her myself if I were allowed. Who'll give me seven hundred?"

"Eight hundred." It was a deeper voice, firm and not excited as the others had been. Sarabee didn't look at who it might be.

"Nine hundred." The bidding went on but Sarabee stopped paying attention to it, letting her mind drift back to her children. *And I need to remember them. I need to remember that no matter how bad this is, I'm going to get back to them.* She found herself thinking of Jens. *Jens!* It was impossible to think that she'd never be in his arms again.

"Fifteen hundred and fifty!" The auctioneer banged his gavel and Sarabee looked over to him, brought back to the present moment. "Sold!" She looked out at the crowd to see who had bought her, but the bidder was anonymous in the throng.

The auctioneer unhooked her neck rope and his assistant led her off the opposite side of the stage from the one she had entered on, and gave her to an errander. There was another small curtained area there, and the errander recorded her name and her price. Behind him bags of tokens and stacks of ingots were piled into wooden boxes, more steel than Sarabee had ever seen in one place in her life. As she waited several men came forward, all with identical smocks carrying a sigil in the shape of the letter "A" with an arrow on the crossbar, and each carrying a heavy box of steel ingots. The errander took off her neck rope, gave her a white flax robe tied at the waist with a crimson sash, and then counted out the steel from the boxes. When he'd confirmed the total he turned her over to an older woman with an ornately dyed overcloak.

"Your name?" the woman asked.

"Sarabee."

"I'm Nilsa. Come with me, Sarabee." Her new caretaker led her through a side door and into a fenced compound with two gates. Three enclosed travel carts were parked there, each with a nine-goat team, and all with the same A-shaped sigil that the men had worn. She was ushered into the first one, and Nilsa followed her. The interior of the cart was lavishly appointed, the roof pillars finely carved and the seats upholstered in fine leather.

The situation was not at all what she'd been expecting. "Where are we going?" Sarabee asked the other woman.

"To my home." A man with a sigiled smock climbed up to the cart's driver's seat.

"What do you want me for?"

"To cook, to clean, to please my husband." Nilsa smiled. "We treat our servitors well. You could have done a lot worse out of that auction."

"What do you mean, 'please your husband'?"

Nilsa laughed. "What do you think? How does a woman please a man?"

"Isn't that . . ." Sarabee looked at Nilsa, unsure of what to say. ". . . isn't that your . . . I mean, he's your husband to please."

"Of course he is. And I enjoy pleasing him. It doesn't have to be just with my body, it can be with yours too."

Sarabee felt her expression grow hard. "There's only one thing you need to know. I've already killed one man who tried to rape me. If your husband so much as touches me, I'll kill him too."

Nilsa's eyes widened. The driver stirred up the goats, the gates were swung open and then they were jolting their way through Charisy's crowded streets.

Atyen crossed the market square, his staff tapping on the cobbles, heading for Charisy's central park. He had on his new double-red cross-sash, and it changed the way people reacted to him. Some gave him a subtle deference, some a subtle hostility, but few who noticed it ignored it. *It seems like cheating to wear it.* Renn had given it to him the day after he arrived at the palace. There was no grueling presentation of his masterwork, no formal challenge of his discoveries. The senior inquisitor just handed it to him and had him put it on. It was a crashing anti-climax to years of work, but there were more important things to worry about. Scholarly formalism and ceremonial recognition had to wait. The cross-sash allowed Renn to give him an official position, and as soon as he had it on he was put in charge of the new observatory, which was to be built on top of the spinward wing of the palace. However, since neither palace wing was anywhere near complete this really amounted to being in charge of nothing at all.

He did get an office, an errander loyal to the revolt being planned, and a budget of more tokens than he'd ever seen in his life, at least on paper. He was excited when he first heard the figures, but price-growth had so badly eroded the value of steel that it didn't amount to as much as he thought. *I remember Sarabee talking about the prices going up.* It hadn't had as much impact in the shorefields, where people ate the fish they caught and the vegetables they grew, but in the city the situation was desperate and getting worse. He knew, because when he wasn't working on plans for the observatory, which was ninety percent of the time, he was working on plans to feed Charisy after Vesene had been deposed.

Atyen reached the park and crossed it, heading for the city's main church. He had no idea how Renn and his cabal planned to accomplish the overthrow. The organization was completely compartmentalized, because Cela Joss had spies everywhere in the palace. Anything hinting of disloyalty would result in an audience before Vesene, and quite likely a mugful of foxglove extract in front of the law council. Atyen had already witnessed one unfortunate put to death like that, and had no desire to be the next. The only members of the cabal he knew were Renn and the Bishop of Charisy. His supposed overseeing of the observatory gave him a perfectly legitimate excuse to go to the church. Officially it was to talk to the time-priests about their star observations, but that was just an excuse to give him the chance to talk to the bishop. The bishop would be using his influence to calm the crowd, and the church organization to help with rationing in the first few days.

The church was empty when he got there, and he went up the tightly winding stairs to the steeple with its tiny observation platform and its few simple instruments aimed up at the foredome. There was a time-priest there, looking over a sighting arm and methodically recording the revolutions of the stars. Every thirty revolutions he would pull a string, which would ring a small bell on the floor below to tell the bellringer to sound the hour on the big church bells. To Atyen it seemed a mind-numbingly dull task, but the time-priests did it day in, day out, and had for thousands of years. He was tempted to tell the man about the glories of the stars seen from Heaven, but he didn't. *It would be cruel.*

He exchanged greetings with the observer, who answered him without looking up, and continued up to the belfry, where the great steel bell hung. The bishop was waiting for him there. It was the safest place to talk.

"Atyen, what's the news?"

"None from me. Renn wants to know if you're ready."

"I have been for a week. I still am. Did he say when it would happen?"

Atyen shook his head. "No. I don't know what the holdup is."

"And you?"

"As ready as I can be. I've got lists of all our indentured farmers and where they're from. Did you get the certificates of manumission?"

"I have them here, safely hidden."

"Good. We can have the farmers working again two days afterwards. It's going to take longer to get food into the system of course. I've got a citywide rationing plan ready to go. People won't like it, but they won't starve while we get the farms reestablished. We're going to take fields out of flax and wheat, put them into corn, beans and squash. That's the best, fastest yield we can get."

"And supplies on hand?"

Atyen shrugged. "Hardly anything. You've seen the market. I don't know what to say, except we'll do our best."

The bishop shook his head. "That's bad. Why doesn't Renn move?"

"Do you even know it's Renn who's in charge?"

"No." The bishop laughed. "I suppose I don't."

"Vesene is hard to get close to, and too many of the law council are on his side, from fear or expedience. Renn will move when he can. He knows the urgency better than either of us."

"I hope so."

There were footsteps on the stairs below, and the bishop's errander appeared. "Excuse me, Bishop," she said. "There's a boy here to see the inquisitor."

It took Atyen a moment to realize that he was the inquisitor she was talking about.

"He said to give you this." The errander held out a message ball.

Atyen took it, went to open it, and saw his own named scribed around the equator. "Where did you get this?" he demanded, and then left without waiting for an answer, leaping down the stairs four at a time.

The boy was waiting for him at the bottom, perhaps twelve years old. He was dirty, bedraggled and with long hair tangled into an unruly mop. He looked frightened, but beneath the fear there was a determination. He had set himself a task and he was going to accomplish it, no matter what it took.

And he seemed somehow familiar. Recognition dawned. "Liese! What are you doing here? Why are you dressed like that?"

In response she embraced him. "Atyen!" She burst into tears, hugging him so hard he could barely breathe. "Atyen, Atyen!"

"What's wrong? Liese?" He held her until the worst of her crying had passed and took her in to the church proper. He sat on one of the pews, and sat her on his knee getting her story between sobs. He kept his expression calm as he listened, not wanting to upset her, but her words cut like a blade. *Jens, gone. Sarabee bound into servitude.* It didn't bear thinking about. The bishop came down at some point, sat a little distance away, not interfering but ready to help. A short while later his errander brought in some soup, and Liese paused in her story long enough to wolf it down. She hadn't eaten a proper meal in five days.

"Can she stay here?" Atyen asked the bishop. "I have to look into this."

"The church has always been a sanctuary. You do what you have to do, we'll get her a meal, some clothes and a bath. She'll be safe here."

"Where are you going, Atyen?" Liese asked. Her tears were dry now, and she seemed more herself.

"To get your mother."

"Do you know where she is?"

"Not yet, but I will soon." Atyen gave her one last hug. "Don't worry, butterfly, I'll get her back." He got up, got his staff and backbag and went out, heading back to the palace. When he arrived he went straight up to Renn's office and outlined the situation.

"She was bound into servitude in Tidings," he finished. "How can I find out where she is?"

"Tiding's Hall of Inquisition will have the records." Renn pursed his lips. "But you can't go there."

Atyen looked at the other man. "Oh yes I can. Just watch me."

"No. Atyen . . ." Renn paused. "I shouldn't be telling you this yet, but I will. We're moving on Vesene today. Everything is set, and we have a window at the evening meal. There'll . . . Well, you don't need the details. It's going to be chaos, and we're going to need you here."

Atyen looked away. "I can be to Tidings and back by the next breakfast bell. Do it then."

"We can't. You know that. This is our chance."

"My part doesn't start until afterwards anyway. You don't need me right away."

Renn shook his head slowly. "It's going to be chaos, Atyen. We are going to have to show that we're in control of the situation immediately, or things are going to get very bad, very quickly. The law council needs to see it, the public need to see it, and our own people need to see it."

"I'm just handing out paper! What importance is that?"

"It's not only paper." Renn stood up and went to the window, gesturing out at the worksite where hundreds of bound servitors were laboring on the scaffold-clad palace wings. "Look at them. Most of them are farmers. When we get rid of Vesene's thug-sentinels, they're going to pick up and go back to their farms, no matter what we do. If we give them those manumission certificates first they leave as our supporters. If not they leave as enemies of the Inquisition. If you organize their departure it gives you the time to make sure they know the crop plan. It means they're going to know who you are and trust you when you set up the rationing. With their support, we win the support of the farm parishes, and we have a chance to turn the world around. Without it this whole thing will fall apart. You're key to this, Atyen. We need you."

Atyen's jaw clenched. *He's right, it's my part of the plan and I still can't abandon Sarabee.* He didn't want to admit that out loud, and so pressed his lips together and said nothing.

"I'm sorry Atyen, you can't go to Tidings," Renn stood up and put a hand on his shoulder. "But she may be right here in the city. A lot of bound women are . . . coming here. There's an auction hall, down by the river. I hope it's not true, for your friend's sake, but check the auction hall records."

"Why do you hope it's not true?"

"Check the records. Just remember, we need you in place before the evening-meal bell. You know what to do. The recognition signal is a square of blue cloth, the word is 'Justice.'"

Atyen nodded slowly, his jaw set, and he left. He went to his office and got Sten, his errander. Sten had grown up in the city, and Atyen got him to lead him to the auction hall.

"What happens when bound women come here?" he asked as they walked out into the market square.

"To the auction hall? Usually the dancehouses buy them."

Atyen nodded, and walked faster, ignoring the cramping in his bad leg. The auction hall was on the other side of the city, and he was walking more on his staff than his feet by the time they arrived. At the hall he spoke to the overseer, who seemed disinclined to be helpful but was unwilling to say no to an inquisitor. They were taken to a room full of cabinets and left to sort through the worksheaves that listed the various auctions. *Oh please Sarabee, please don't be here.* Better she be in the brickworks, better she have to wait until Vesene was gone, than that they'd turned her into a dancehouse girl. It was Sten who found her name in the list, two bells later. Her indenture had been sold to one Nilsa Lorn. There was an address listed, and an amount.

"Not a dancehouse," said Sten. "That area is too wealthy."

Atyen nodded, not reassured. The list told him Sarabee was worth thrice her weight in solid steel. *And they didn't pay that to have her wash quilts.*

Once more Atyen followed Sten through the crowded streets, hobbling now on his injury. It was getting close to the evening-meal bell. *But we have time, I'll make it back to the palace before then.* As they walked, the streets got wider and the houses got larger, set back behind low walls, with awning shaded windows and manicured bushes by the walkways. Eventually they came to one with its own driveway and stables. Trees showing over the roof hinted at an enclosed courtyard; whoever lived in it had wealth and power. The gatepost was marked with a sigil in the shape of an "A" with an arrow for a crossbar, and Sarabee's name on the list at the auctionhouse had been marked with a similar sigil.

Violence would be a bad idea, but he still reflexively checked for his belt knife. They went up to the house, knocked. A man in a smock marked with the same arrowed A appeared.

"I'm looking for Nilsa Lorn," Atyen said.

The man gave a slight bow. "I'll see if she's available, Inquisitor." Before he could leave another man came up behind him, with greying hair and powerful shoulders.

"I'm Yen Lorn," he said. His manner expected deference. "May I help you?"

Atyen set his jaw. "Sarabee Madane is here. We've come to take her."

Lorn raised an eyebrow. "By what right?" He was not the kind of man to be intimidated by a double-red cross-sash.

"I don't need any right. She's a free woman, and she's coming with me."

Lorn looked Atyen up and down. "I don't recognize you, Inquisitor. What's your name?"

"Atyen Horun."

"Well, Atyen Horun, I don't think I'm going to give her to you. My wife paid a great deal of steel for her, and we're going to keep her." Lorn gave a brief nod. "Good day." He started to close the door.

Atyen stuck his foot out and blocked it, and Lorn looked up, annoyed. "Sten," Atyen said, not taking his eyes off the other man. "Get the sentinels. I want them here before the next bell."

"But . . ."

"Go. Wait for me in the palace." Sten left, running, and Atyen went on. "I have no quarrel with you, Yen Lorn, but if you don't produce Sarabee before the sentinels get here, you are going to find yourself in that auction house on the wrong side of the auction."

Lorn looked over his shoulder. "Perlin, bring the other servitors up." The man in the sigiled smock bowed and disappeared into the house, and Lorn returned his attention to Atyen. "I think you're bluffing, Inquisitor. You don't have the authority, and I don't think you have sentinels either."

"No? Well, we'll see what authority the tithecounters can get for me."

"I have friends on the law council, Inquisitor." Lorn's voice held a quiet threat. Behind him Perlin returned, with two other men in identical clothing.

"If you think the law council has the power to protect you . . ." Atyen laughed a short laugh. "Well, you haven't been paying attention, have you?" He pushed the door wider with his foot. "I work for Cela Joss."

Lorn's eyes widened slightly at Joss's name, and then grew calculating. Atyen could tell Lorn still thought he was bluffing, but the Chief Inquisitor's executioner was too dangerous to risk crossing, even for a man of his wealth and status. *Perhaps especially for a man of his wealth and status.* Lorn's face darkened and he glanced over his shoulder. "Perlin, bring Sarabee." He looked back to Atyen. "This *will* be in front of the law council, Inquisitor."

"I'm sure it will."

Lorn turned on his heel and left, and Atyen waited. A few minutes later Perlin returned with Sarabee, wearing an elegant cloak in shades of red, well fitted and elaborately embroidered.

"Atyen!" She ran to hug him, and Atyen turned around before she could. *If Lorn sees we're close, he'll know it's personal. He'll know I'm not here for Cela Joss.*

"Atyen?"

"Come with me," Atyen said, keeping his voice flat. He turned and left, hoping she would follow without question. She did, and he heard the door close behind him.

"Atyen, what . . . ?"

"Wait until we're down the street," he said, but as soon they were out of sight of the house he turned to embrace her.

"Liese came to me; she told me about Jens." Atyen looked down. "I'm sorry Sarabee, I wish . . ."

"Liese came here? How is she? Where is she?"

"She went through hell to get here but she's fine. She's waiting at the church. She's a brave and resourceful girl, Sarabee. You should be proud."

"And the other girls? My baby?"

"With Celese, last Liese knew." Atyen looked Sarabee over. "You look stunning in that cloak! They must have treated you well."

"They fed me, clothed me, housed me. They didn't . . . force themselves on me. For those things I'm grateful." Sarabee frowned. "They kept my door locked, didn't let me go to my children. For that I'll never forgive them." She turned to Atyen and embraced him again. "Thank you for coming, Atyen, I didn't dare to hope . . ."

In the distance the bells rang the hour before the evening meal. "Come on," Atyen said. "We have to hurry."

He had planned to take Sarabee to the church and collect the certificates of manumission before getting back to the palace in time for Renn's planned insurrection, but there wouldn't be time for that. *I'll take her as far as the palace, give her directions, and send Sten for the certificates.* He walked as fast as he could, his leg almost numb with pain. As they approached the market the streets grew more crowded, and Atyen realized there was another food protest gathering. The mood was ugly, it had been two days since there'd been any grain for the grain lines, and the market stalls were empty. Some of the protesters carried improvised clubs, a few were carrying blades. *This is getting dangerous.* He pulled Sarabee over to a side-alley, out of the main throng, and gave her directions to the church that took her around by smaller roads and away from the market square.

"Aren't you coming?" she asked.

"There's something I have to do here. The bishop will look after you. I'll be there in a few days."

"A few days? Atyen, what's going on?"

"I can't tell you. It's safer if you don't know." He saw the doubt in her eyes. "Trust me, Sarabee, I'll be there. Now Liese is waiting for you. Go."

She hugged him, kissed his cheek, and went, and Atyen went back into the surging crowd. As they approached the jammed market square the mob thickened and it became harder to make progress. Nobody was deferring to his cross-sash now. *And maybe it's not a good thing to be recognized as an inquisitor here.* He slipped it off and put it in his backbag. He inched forward in the square, fretting over the time, until finally he could see the palace entrance, but the sentinels had already deployed across the front of the building. There was no way he'd be able to get inside, and he cursed in frustration.

*But Renn is counting on me.* Vesene would be making a speech soon, and the palace laborers had already been herded into their pens to free more sentinels for guard duty. *If I can get to the*

*pens* . . . The important thing was to get control of the farmers before they took advantage of the chaos in the wake of the
takeover and left. If he told them they were getting certificates of
manumission, they'd wait long enough for him to send Sten to
the church to get them. He started working his way backwards,
trying to get to a place where he could get around the side of
the square, to the workers' pens where his job would be when the
time came. Even that became more difficult, as more and more
people poured into the square, packing it tight. The evening-meal
bell rang before he was there, and desperation surged in him
as he struggled against the jammed-in bodies. The crowd began
chanting. "Grain! Grain! Grain! Grain!"

He made it to one of the buildings surrounding the market.
The first floor was old timber and resined brick, the floors above
new and built of bamboo and waxed flax. The crowd was thinner
there and he made better progress. The chanting grew louder as
he came around to the pens. A line of sentinels were there, both
guarding the prisoners and keeping the crowd at a distance. The
mob wasn't pressing as close to the sentinels as they were at the
main entrance, and they were more relaxed. In the distance he
heard the church bells were still tolling, but not in the evening-
meal pattern. The chanting crowd quieted, not sure what was
going on, and Atyen redoubled his pace, leaning hard on his staff
to spare the strain on his leg. Ahead of him there was a shouted
command, a flash of blades, a sudden scuffle, and suddenly half,
three quarters of the sentinels at the prisoner pen were down.
One of the ones still standing started barking orders, and the
rest closed ranks, closing their line to compensate for the sudden reduction in their numbers. Atyen pushed his way through
the last of the crowd, and found himself facing a fence of blades.

"Justice," he called. "Justice."

The blades fell away and he was brought through the line,
stepping over cross-sashed bodies. The blood was running like
water in the street, the order of sentinels had purged its ranks of
Vesene's contagion. He took a deep breath to steel himself. *The
sharp edge of power isn't pretty.* He went to the senior sentinel,
a broad-shouldered warrior with a blue scarf hastily tied around
his upper arm.

"You're our man?" the sentinel asked.

Atyen nodded. "I am. I need you to send someone into the

palace. Second floor, spinward wing, the observatory office. An errander named Sten will be there. Tell him I need the documents from the church brought here. He'll know what to do."

"It's done." The sentinel waved over another of his group and repeated Atyen's instructions. The man he'd detailed ran off at a sprint.

*We can still pull this off.* The bells were still ringing as Atyen pulled his cross-sash from his backbag and put it on. He advanced to the servitor pen. It was a flimsy structure of bamboo poles, designed only to temporarily hold its occupants while under armed supervision. There were hundreds of prisoners, and the greatly reduced ranks of the sentinels couldn't hold it if they tried to run, even if they didn't have the crowd to worry about. So far the prisoners hadn't reacted to the situation, but that wouldn't last long.

"Farmers! Freemen!" he yelled through cupped hands. "Be calm! We are taking control of the Inquisitory, and you will be freed to go back to your farms. Papers declaring your freedom are coming. Be calm! Be patient! You'll be going home shortly."

Behind him someone yelled "Vesene!" The call spread, grew and soon the entire crowd was chanting "Vesene! Vesene!" Atyen raised his voice to repeat his message, but the wall of sound behind him made it impossible. And then suddenly the chant died away, and an expectant hush descended on the square. Up on the tower balcony a figure appeared. Atyen squinted. It was difficult to tell at the distance, but . . .

Renn! *He's done it!* Renn had his arms up to still the crowd, and then as the silence grew and extended he lowered them. "People of Charisy," he said, and his voice echoed off the buildings at the back of the square. "I am sorry to have to tell you the Chief Inquisitor is dead. We are taking immediate steps—"

"Fire!" someone yelled. "Fire!" Atyen whirled, and saw flames licking up from one of the bamboo apartment structures he'd just passed by. It grew slowly, and he could see the red flickering through the waxed flax walls, and then suddenly the entire building exploded into flame. A wave of heat rolled over him, and the crowd turned as one and stampeded. Atyen found himself forced back against the flimsy bamboo fence of the servitor pen. Fortunately most of the crowd surge was away from him, and his portion of the market was empty in a few seconds. Others weren't so lucky, and screams rose across the square as people were trampled in the mob. The sentinel commander shouted orders, and his group ran with him to the dipping basin nearest the blazing building, grabbed buckets and formed a line to throw water on the burning building. Even before they got there upper floors of the next building were alight. Up in the tower balcony Renn was still speaking, shouting, imploring the crowd, but his words were lost in the screams. Another building burst into flames, and there was a splintering crash behind him. Atyen whirled around to see the palace laborers breaking out of their pen, though they were in no immediate danger from the flames.

"Stop!" he yelled. "Wait, you're safe here!"

And they were safe, at least for a while, surrounded by the bricks and dirt of the worksite, though the bamboo scaffolds might yet burn. Atyen had a momentary instinct to organize an orderly evacuation down the spinward wing of the palace, a route made awkward by the debris of construction but otherwise safe. Nobody listened to him, and the pen drained like a broken bucket, the prisoners joining the general exodus across the square. He was left standing by the broken fence. He called after them, helplessly, hopelessly, but he knew they weren't coming back. *I've failed.* The realization was bitter, but there was no time to dwell on it. At the first building the sentinels had given up on their bucket-line and retreated. The second-floor inferno was cooking the resin out of the first floor's bricks and dark rivulets were running down its sides. Overhead the leaping flames were whirling burning scraps of waxed flax upwards, to descend elsewhere and start more fires. The panicked crowd had managed to get only twenty or thirty meters away from the burning building before they became too packed to move, and those closest were screaming and pushing, pounding on the backs of those in front of them. The retreating sentinels still had cohesion and they dumped their buckets on themselves, then started grabbing people out of the crowd, directing them out of the square through an alley between two buildings where the fire wasn't yet in full blaze. A few ran for it, but most of the panicking mob refused to face the flames. They kept trying to push against the immobile throng in front of them, some even climbing up and over, stepping on heads and shoulders in their desperation to escape. Finally the sentinel commander gave up, and led his people out through the gap before it was too late.

*And I should follow them.* Atyen started in the direction of the gap, but by the time he reached it the alley had become a gauntlet of flame. Perhaps he could have sprinted through it, but his leg wouldn't let him run. He retreated back to the relative safety of the construction site, to follow the route he'd planned to take the workers out, down the length of the unfinished palace wing and past the flames. He started picking his way around piles of dirt and stacks of bricks, and then saw flame in front of him, at the far end of the palace. He couldn't tell where it came from, perhaps a flying scrap of waxed flax that managed to drift against the breeze to ignite a building further along. *And it doesn't matter.* The scaffolding at the far end of the palace was already burning, and he retreated again to his start point. The upper floors on the entire spinward side of the market were a single wall of flame now, and the streams of melted brick-resin pouring from the first floor walls were starting to smolder, swirling clouds of black, choking smoke into the square. The heat was intense even where Atyen was, and the people trapped at the back of the mob were screaming in pain as well as panic now. The only escape left was up and over the palace wall. He looked at his staff, reluctant to abandon it, but there was no choice. He dropped it, turned and clambered up the scaffolding behind him. His injured leg screamed, but he pulled himself up the way he'd climbed the forewall, hauling himself from level to level till he got to the unframed windows of the second level. By the time he got there his skin burned everywhere it was exposed to the inferno's radiated heat.

He clambered through. The floor had not yet been laid inside, so he had to balance on the floor joists, but the mass of the building shielded him from the blaze, a relief as cool and sweet as ocean water. He kept the wall between him and the worst of the blaze, and looked through the window at an angle to the chaos in the square. The crowd was still emptying from the market at the main avenues aftward and antispinward, but everywhere else it had become a living horror. In the smaller alleyways the jammed throng had gotten wedged in, trapped by the crush following them. Living walls two or three meters high had formed, with the trapped flailing madly as they tried to free themselves. Those behind weren't waiting, and were climbing over the top to jump down and flee on the other side. The center of the mob was packed too tightly to move, and burning scraps of waxed flax were drifting down. People screamed as their clothes caught fire, but they were pressed too close to raise their arms. Unable to beat out the flames, they burned where they stood. Those at the back, closest to the heart of the fire, had pushed inexorably forward in their fear, and now in their wake there were broken bodies, people who'd fallen and been crushed underfoot.

The wind was pushing the fire aftward, and as Atyen watched, it reached the aftward avenue, and seconds later crossed it. The leading edge of the exodus shrank back from the newly burning buildings, but the throng behind was still pushing forward, and people were pushed headlong into the fire. Along the palace wall a few others were climbing the scaffold to escape through the half-built structure as he was. At the main stairs the sentinels were gone, either fled or crushed, and the throng was forcing its way up the stairs. He felt a momentary urge to pick his way over the joists to the main building. His worksheaves were in the observatory office, the embodiment of months of painstaking work recording the secrets of the Builders. *You have bigger things to worry about, Atyen.* Smoke wisping through the window holes underlined the point. The fire in the scaffolding was spreading towards him. The bamboo joists were widely spaced, and springy, uncertain footing. If he missed a step he'd fall through to the floor below, which would be fatal if it disabled him so he couldn't flee. His injured leg throbbed, but it held, and he managed to gain the window on the other side, clamber through it and down the scaffolding there. There was no scaffolding at the main building, and people there were jumping from the second floor windows to the cobbles below, some to run away, some to hobble, some to lie where they fell. The first floor windows and even the back entrances were jammed with people wedged in the doorframes, forming solid walls of faces, shoulders, flailing arms. The ones on the bottom were already dead, the ones higher up were pleading with those behind them to back up. *But they can't, not with that mob behind them.* Atyen went to a door, grabbed a man's hand and tried to haul him free, but the man didn't budge. He tried another and another, but the pressure from behind was too great, and the suffering mass was stuck. There was nothing he could do. Reluctantly he turned away, to head towards the church. If there was anything to be done to forward the revolt, it would be done there. *And Sarabee is there, and Liese.* He wondered briefly what had happened to Renn.

The area behind the palace was even more expensive than the one he'd rescued Sarabee from, with large houses set back behind high walls. The calm seemed strange after the chaos of the market square, but the bulk of the palace hid the flames, and the wind carried the smoke aftward and away. The only hint of the unfolding disaster was the occasional escaper who ran past him as he limped along. He didn't know the area, so headed generally anti-spinward, hoping to skirt around the fire and the crowds. The houses grew smaller, more closely packed as he traveled, and a few times he could see red flames and smoke. The streets began to fill with people, some fleeing, some just watching the growing pall of smoke as it rose towards the suntube, moving aftwards in a gentle spiral as it did. Atyen ignored them, intent on his goal. He turned aftward, moving on side-streets, heading back towards the main avenue that led antispinward from the market, which would take him towards the church. As he approached it there were more and more people, and more and more of them were fleeing, faces blank and clothing singed, until finally it seemed he was swimming against a living river. He moved to the side, where the stream was less dense. The church steeple was closer now, just a few hundred meters away. The antispinward avenue was between him and his goal, and when he reached it he stopped.

If the side-streets were rivers, the main avenue was a flood, a vast rush of bodies, far more than he would have thought could even fit in the market square. Behind them he saw the reason. The fire had grown into a moving wall of flame, spreading inexorably towards him. As it reached each new building it spilled its inhabitants into the streets to flee as best they could. It was no place for a man who could only hobble. *But I have to do it.* He looked for an opening in the throng, found one, and stepped forward to be swept away. A man bumped him from behind and he tried to quicken his pace, hobbling, limping. His foot hit something and he stumbled, caught someone's arm to stop the fall. He'd stumbled over a body, crushed in the torrent. The man he'd grabbed gave him a look, shook off his hand, and vanished into the throng. Atyen kept moving. He'd planned to cross the avenue directly, or at least to angle his way over to the other side, to get back on the smaller streets on the other side and over to the church, but it was impossible. It was all he could do to keep up, to keep himself from being knocked over from behind and crushed underfoot. The steeple passed by and behind him, and still he could only move forward.

Finally they came to the trading road. The throng divided three ways there, aftward and foreward and straight along the avenue, and it thinned enough that Atyen could choose his route. He headed aftward until the road reached the central park, and then he broke free of the mob, turned back across the park towards the church. His blood ran cold. The fire had grown more as it fed on the close-packed housing in Charisy's center, transformed itself into a raging monster, flames shooting higher than the church steeple, spreading itself with whirling blazes of cinders. The wind was gusting, now aftward, now towards the center of the blaze as it sucked in air to stoke itself. *Sarabee!* Fear shot through Atyen and he started running, only to have his bad leg buckle. He fell, picked himself up and kept on. People were fleeing past him, all of them running now.

"This way!" a man shouted, pointing as though Atyen couldn't see for himself the wall of flame he was heading towards. Atyen ignored him, and the man ran off. The park wasn't large, but it seemed to take forever to cross it. The fire was across the street from the back of the church by the time he reached its front door, and at that distance it felt like he was standing in front of an open hearth forge.

Sarabee was there, waiting for him with Liese in hand. "Atyen, thank Noah, we were just about to go."

"You shouldn't have waited."

"Yes, I should have. Where's your staff?"

"I had to leave it."

She put her arm around him, and the three of them headed back across the park. Even with Sarabee's help Atyen couldn't move quickly, but nobody was running past them now. The green space was less flammable than the buildings around it, a refuge from the flames for at least a little while. To aftward the fire had advanced to come parallel to them and Sarabee started to head foreward.

Atyen stopped her. "No, the streets are all jammed there, we'll never get out."

"Look!" Liese shouted, pointing.

Ahead of them smoke was starting to rise. They were trapped.

"This way," Atyen said, and led them towards the center of the park. The waterclock there was no longer spinning—the fire had cut the spillways—but the pool at its base was still full. "In here."

They climbed over the side and into the cool water. The wind grew above them until it was howling, and the bushes around them started to smoke, then one after another burst into flame. It quickly grew too hot to look above the pool's rim, and after that they could see nothing but the showers of sparks that swirled overhead as the fire consumed the burning bushes. The water grew warm, and then hot, and the howl of the wind grew to an outlandish shriek. Atyen risked a look to see what was happening, but the heat seared him like he'd shoved his head in an oven, and he had to duck back. In that brief instant he saw the church transformed into a pillar of flame, rivers of fire running down its front, the very bricks burning. The world was reduced to a hell of red flames and black smoke. Sarabee clutched his hand and yelled something in his ear, but he couldn't hear her over the noise, so just squeezed her hand. Overhead the screaming wind was overtaken by a deeper roar as the firestorm took them into its heart. To Atyen it sounded like the devil laughing.

Inquisitor Norlan Renn stopped at the first travelling house foreward of Charisy, and turned to watch the city's pyre. A churning column of smoke boiled toward the suntube, lit a flickering red from below. *Could it be treachery?* It asked too much of coincidence that such a disaster had struck the moment he'd retaken control of the Inquisition. *But who could hope to gain by this?* Byo Vesene would have been crazy enough, vindictive enough, to destroy what he could not possess, but Renn had personally put the foxglove extract in Vesene's wine and watched the Chief Inquisitor die. It hadn't been Vesene? *Cela Joss?* The church bells had rung the start signal, which meant the watching time-priests had seen all the required mirror messages, including the code that meant Joss was dead. *It might have been a trick.* Joss was ruthless. She could have evaded Torr Toorman's sentinels, captured the one sent to kill her, beaten the code out of him and sent it as a deception. *Or the plot could have been betrayed.* One of his biggest worries had been that some of the old-guard sentinels might still be loyal to Cela, despite what she'd done to the order.

But even if the signal was a deception, what end could she could have hoped to achieve with it? It made no sense.

There were other refugees coming out of the city, and Renn watched them pass, first a few, and then more and more. They brought up a more immediate question. *Have I come far enough?* He'd seen fires before, never one like this. *All those apartments . . .* Waxed flax and bamboo, they couldn't have been more flammable if he'd designed them to burn. He'd known their danger, and he hadn't favored cramming so many into so small a space, that had been Vesene's idea. *But I had no idea it would be like this.* The whole city would burn, from the ancient core to the dense-packed outskirts, and there was no particular reason for the fire to stop at the last house either, the crop fields could burn just as easily. He'd come five kilometers, crossed several wide irrigation canals, but he'd seen the fire jump streets just as wide. Foreward was safer than aftward, because the winds would carry the fire aftward but . . . *Have I come far enough?* He wanted to stay close to the city, to get back into it, take control of what he'd started, begin immediately rebuilding, managing problems, but as he watched, the pillar of smoke boiled higher, and the flickering on its bottom grew larger, more intense, until finally the dark cloud was suffused with its own infernal red glow. *Soon I might not have a city to come back to.*

A family came by, father, mother, six children. They were artisans to judge by their clothes, people who worked hard and managed to get food on the table even as it grew scarce and expensive. They hadn't been part of the mob in the square, but they were fleeing too. There would be a lot like them, transformed from productive members of the social order to helpless victims in need of food and shelter. Behind them there were more people, and then more, a flood of fleeing bodies. *And I haven't come far enough, I need to be at the Inquisitory.* The realization sent a chill down his spine. The danger wasn't the fire, the danger was the deluge of city dwellers the fire had pushed out of the city. Charisy held a third of the world's population. Nearly half a million people had just been turned out into the world with nothing more than the clothes they stood in. They had no food, no shelter, and many of them were already hungry. Around the curve of the world the signal mirrors were flashing steadily, and he focused on the one in Blessings. g-r-e-a-t-f-i-r-e-i-n-c-h-a-r-i-s-y, it blinked. s-e-n-d-f-o-o-d-s-u-r-g-e-o-n-s-s-e-n-t-i-n-a-l-s.

*They aren't waiting, that's a relief.* The Inquisitors-in-Chief could be relied on to act independently, and the towns and rural parishes weren't under the kind of pressure the great city had been. They would be able to spare resources. *But will they be enough?* Charisy's half million were already spreading out in all directions, hungry, frightened, some injured, and all desperate. Whether the outcome was merely vast tragedy or an unrecoverable disaster would depend on what happened over the next few bells. He needed a plan. *The key will be to contain the human flood.* Unchecked they'd be more destructive than a swarm of mice in a grain jar, and with the food reserves gone and the farms strained to the breaking point, that could trigger the collapse of the whole Inquisition. He needed a place to put half a million people that wouldn't disrupt the farmers any more than they already had been. The only place to do that was the burnt out remains of the city itself. *We have to get them to go back.* But no one would go back to Charisy unless they could get food, water and shelter there. *More waxed flax?* Much as he was loathe to use the flammable cloth, it was cheap, readily available and easy to work with. He'd send a mirror message to Bountiful, where it was manufactured and . . .

*And they're almost out.* The apartment raising project had consumed thousands of square meters of the stuff, all of the production, and all that had been stockpiled, and most of it had just gone up in smoke. What then? Plain flax? Leaves and grass? Salvaged brick from the fire's devastation? There had to be *something*. The only place to manage *that* problem from was the Inquisitory, get the law council together and figure out what to do. *But the Inquisitory has what?* The grain reserves were exhausted, the steel reserves nearly so. The finely tuned gears of governance still hadn't recovered from the previous year's fire, and Vesene's insanity had murdered the best minds on the law council, leaving only fools and nodders. The Second Inquisition's capacity to manage an emergency on such a scale was limited. The sentinels would be effective, he hoped, but there was only one sentinel for every hundred people in the world, and they were in the midst of their own upheaval in support of the revolt. There was no effective action he could take. Slowly the realization crept up on him. *We're finished.*

He looked aftward again, to see the titanic pillar of flame blossoming over what had once been the greatest city in the world, and then stepped into the rush of the exodus once more, this time not as Norlan Renn, newly acceded Chief Inquisitor of the Second Inquisition but as just another refugee.

The firestorm raged for what seemed an eternity, and at first Atyen couldn't believe it was passing. It was though, and when the howling wind had dropped, he levered himself out of the waterclock's pool to find the world reduced to shades of black. The park was nothing but soot-streaked dirt. The grass had burned to its roots, the wind had scoured away the ashes, and in every direction the city of Charisy was gone. He traded a look with Sarabee, who looked as shocked as he did. Liese bent over to touch the ground, as if reassuring herself it was still there. Here and there a few blackened sticks still stood where buildings had been, but most were just mounds of debris. Atyen walked to where the church had been and found nothing but half a collapsed wall that was still radiating heat. In the surrounding rubble some of the bricks were intact, but many had been reduced to shards, burst by the incredible heat. He kicked one and found it clinked like fired pottery. *And it might as well be.* A larger chunk turned out to be steel, and it took him a moment to realize it had been the steeple bell, now melted into a blob. Around the edge of the city a few fires still burned, and to foreward some of the buildings looked intact. Everything else was a desolate blackness.

"We're lucky to be alive," Sarabee said.

"We are." Atyen repressed a shudder. The outside of the pool they'd sheltered in was streaked with soot and his fingers were wrinkled from immersion in the hot water. If the fire had gone on much longer they might well have been boiled alive.

"Come on," she said, "let's go home. I miss my children."

The hot water had eased the pain in Atyen's injured calf, and he was able to move without difficulty. They left the park, to find the fire had boiled the resin out of the trading road's cobbling bricks and burned it, leaving a uniform crust of congealed ash that crunched beneath their feet as they walked. Collapsed shells of buildings lined the road, and in places blackened shapes sprawled in clusters, so shrunken and distorted that it took Atyen a moment to realize they were bodies. He glanced down to Liese to see if she'd noticed them, but if she had she gave no sign. Smoke still curled from the smoldering wreckage, and the smell of it hung heavy in the air. They passed a building still burning, and just past it a woman, covered head to toe in soot, searching desperately through the burned out wreckage, calling over and over for someone named Moen.

Sarabee took his hand and squeezed it for reassurance. Atyen squeezed back and breathed deep. The woman was the only moving thing they saw in Charisy. They came eventually to the irrigation canal that marked the city's aftward edge. The bridge over it was goine, nothing left but its supports, and they were burned right down to the waterline. The field beyond had been filled with the flimsy, improvised shelters of those who hadn't yet been housed in one of Renn's apartments, now there was nothing but squares of dirt less burned than the rest. *But at least they got away with their lives.* It was more than a lot of those in the market square had managed, but the thought gave him pause. Wherever the people who'd lived there had gone, their circumstance had gone from desperate to critical. *And the living may yet envy the dead.* They swam the canal, hauled themselves out and walked on past the destroyed encampment, shoes squishing. The next field had been a high crop of corn, beans and squash, but now it was just burned stalks. It smelled vaguely appetizing, and Atyen realized he was hungry. He went into the field, picked a charcoal-black corn ear off the ground and stripped off the husk. The top kernels were burned and inedible, but the underside was still yellow and juicy. He took an experimental bite and found it not only edible but deliciously cooked. Liese was already trying a blackened squash gourd, and it too was cooked and ready to eat.

They stopped to eat, sitting by the roadside. Before they'd finished a figure approached coming back into the city on the road. As it got closer it became a well dressed man with a strange look on his face, somewhere between desperation and determination. He had fled the city and now was going back to see what he could salvage, and he appeared not to notice them as he passed. Atyen didn't have the heart to tell him there was nothing. *And perhaps it wouldn't matter.* They finished their impromptu picnic, and then went on with bellies full and their mood improved. More people passed going the other way, and then more. *What do they think they're going back to?* Atyen turned around, to see if they could see something he couldn't, but the devastation was the same. *The triumph of hope over reality.* He couldn't decide if it was inspiring or sad.

The cropland was burnt all the way to the next irrigation canal, but the fire hadn't jumped it and the trading road bridge was only scorched. On the other side the road ran through citrus groves. The fences around the trees had been broken down, and there were people under the trees, hundreds of them, even thousands. Some sat in family groups, others walked around, calling for lost loved ones, some just stood and stared out at the place where the city had been. Some had bags of possessions, a few had carts. A number were burned, and they lay on the ground moaning, being tended by friends or by strangers, Atyen couldn't tell which. The oranges weren't ripe, but a lot of people were eating them anyway. There was no sign of the farmer or the farmhands, but there was little they could have done to protect the crop anyway, there were just too many people. A noisy group of children was playing tag in the trees, laughing and squealing as if disaster hadn't just descended on them and all they knew. Reflexively Atyen looked down at Liese, holding her mother's hand, walking along. She looked far better than she had when she'd first appeared at the church. *And why wouldn't she? She's found her mother, she's eaten, and the world's problems aren't hers.*

The road got crowded after that point, some people moving farther aftward, some heading back into what was left of Charisy. Just before the intersection where the Tidings road split from the trading road someone had broken down the fence around a sheep pasture. The sheep had gotten into the road and were milling about in several small groups, baaing plaintively. A distraught farmer's child and an agitated herding dog were trying to drive them back through the fence, but the sheep were confused by the crowd and weren't cooperating. A hundred meters further a woman with a half-butchered sheep asked Atyen if he had a firepump while three small children watched from the ditch, looking hungry enough to eat the sheep raw if a fire couldn't be started soon. Atyen shook his head and went on. Around the corner they found a train of goat-carts with an escort of sentinels. The senior sentinel spotted him and waved him over.

"Inquisitor, what's the situation foreward?"

"It's not good. You saw the fire?"

"Everyone saw the fire. I've got a surgeon and ten carts full of food, quilts and supplies here. Where should I set up?"

"The people worst off are foreward two or three kilometers,

in an orchard. There's some of them burned who could use your help, but what you've got won't go far."

"There's another group coming after me. Were you planning on going to Tidings?"

"Through Tidings."

"Not today. The Inquisitor-in-Chief closed it off."

"Closed it off? Why?"

"Because we've got thousands already, we just can't take anymore. We're going to help who we can out here."

Atyen nodded slowly. "Thanks for letting me know. And for coming out."

The sentinel nodded. "Good luck."

"Good luck."

The carts moved off. "Is it bad?" asked Liese.

The last sentinel waved, and Atyen waved back. "Is what bad?"

"That they've closed Tidings?" There was worry in her young eyes.

Atyen traded a look with Sarabee. *There's no point in lying to her.* "It's all bad, butterfly, a lot of people have lost everything. But we'll be fine, don't worry. We'll just have a little further to walk." He turned to Sarabee. "We'll go straight down the trading road to the shore road, and pass aftward of Tidings."

She nodded. "That makes sense."

They moved back to the trading road and continued straight aftward with the general flow. As they went the impact of the exodus began to show itself, here a field of wheat trampled flat by hundreds of people crossing it to get water from a canal, there a corn/bean/squash field stripped bare. Farmers and farmhands had started patrolling their fences, armed with hoes and scythes, watching the human torrent go by with suspicious eyes. At one field a pair of bodies were propped against a post, mute warning for potential crop thieves. It was a sobering sight, and it put Atyen in mind of Solender's mice. *Overcrowding changes behavior.* Evidently mass disaster changed it too, and not for the better. A little way up the world's curve smoke rose from a burning farmstead. *Coincidence or hostility?* He couldn't know.

With the loss of the master bell in Charisy's church nobody was ringing the hours, but by Atyen's estimate it took them three bells to reach the ocean from the time they started walking. They went out on someone's dock to get a drink, then turned spinward. Everywhere fishers were doing a brisk business selling carp from their sheds at exorbitant prices, but neither he nor Sarabee had any tokens, so they just kept on. As they came aftward of Tidings the crowd noticeably thickened, and after a kilometer it slowed and stopped.

"Evidently we weren't the only ones with this idea," he said to Sarabee.

"Evidently not."

People spilled off the road onto the shore, others got up into the shorefields to parallel the road. An angry farmer challenged a trespasser and a fight broke out, and while it was happening some other refugees just hopped the fence and carried on.

"What's going on?" Atyen asked a fisher hawking carp.

She shrugged. "Nobody knows."

"Should we wait?" Sarabee wondered.

Atyen shook his head. "I don't think it's a good idea to be in a crowd."

"You're right, let's go the other way. I know the sailsmiths in Cove. If we ask they'll raft us around and home."

They turned around and hiked back to the intersection with the trading road, hiked past it to Cove. There were fewer fugitives from the city in that direction, and many of them had gone to sleep along the road's sidehills and ditches. They reached Cove well into the sleeping hours, but the sailsmiths welcomed them in when Sarabee knocked, fed them carp stew, gave their own bed to Sarabee and Liese, and shared the floor with Atyen. They couldn't sail them back the next day, because they didn't want to leave their shop unattended with so many strangers and so much uncertainty, but they were willing to loan their line-raft, to be brought back soon. "You've come through so much, Sarabee, it's the least we can do."

The smoke had formed a bluish haze around the suntube and drifted downward. They were all sneezing, everything smelled of smoke and Atyen's eyes watered incessantly, but at least travelling by raft was easier than walking. They angled across the wind, heading spinward in easy back-and-forth legs, and aft of Tidings they pulled up at a fishing platform and asked for news.

"They've closed the shore road on both sides, and the sentinels are patrolling the fields," the fisher said. "Nothing's getting in to Tidings, and no one smart is leaving. We're lucky the Inquisitor-in-Chief thought to close the town, luckier he extended it all the way to the ocean. There's thousands who've fled Charisy, tens of thousands. They're everywhere, wrecking fields, stealing food. People have died and I'll bet a week's haul a lot more will before this is over. It's a disaster."

Atyen thanked the fisher and they sailed on. Sarabee put out a net, and soon they had a couple of dozen small carp swimming in its confines. *At least we'll be able to eat.* The air was heavy with smoke, and here and there around the curve of the world more fires were burning. *More farmhouses?* It was impossible to know. One thing was clear, with the world already barely able to feed the city's half-million, destroying crops and killing farmers was not going to solve any problems. *Will the shorefields be safe?*

It was hard to know the time exactly with no bells, but Atyen's stomach told him the noon meal had come and gone before they pulled into Sarabee's dock. The net-raft was still there, as it had been when Jens was killed and Sarabee had been taken by the sentinels, ropes coiled neatly, sails and nets folded. They tied up the sailsmiths' raft alongside it, leaving the netted carp in the water. Atyen looked from one to the other, and to his eye there was little distinction between the net-raft and the line-raft, just the net-haul at the aft of the one, the line-riggers on the other. *There must be more to it.*

It was a question for another time, and Atyen headed up the dock. There were a few refugees wandering up and down the shore road when they put into Sarabee's dock, but far fewer than the hordes on the other side of Tidings, there was no easy way to get there from Charisy with the Tidings road blocked off. It offered the hope that they were in time, but when they got to Sarabee's house the door stood open. Inside it had been ransacked, and everything of value was gone. Even the sailshed had been broken open, though the sails were still there. The horde had gotten there before them.

"Don't worry about it," Sarabee said. "They're only things, and things can be replaced. Let's go get the children."

They walked up to Celese's farm, knocked on the farmhouse door and went in, and Atyen found himself looking at a man he didn't know. The man's face was hostile, and Atyen's blood ran cold. *This is not good.* There were more people behind him, a dozen or so, men and women all related to judge by their looks.

Sarabee came in behind him, anger on her face. "Where's my sister?" she demanded. "Where are my children?"

The man's expression was hard. "This place was empty when we got here." He shrugged, but didn't even try to make the lie convincing.

Anger flashed in Sarabee's eyes. "You're lying!" she shouted, and slapped him across the face. "What did you do? What did you do with my babies?"

She raised her arm to hit him again but Atyen grabbed her before she could strike. "Let's go outside," he said.

She rounded on him, eyes blazing. "Don't you see? They . . ."

"I see very clearly." Atyen kept his voice level. The man Sarabee had hit was looking at her with barely restrained rage, and across the room the others had stood up. "They found the house empty. Celese isn't here. The children aren't here. Liese is waiting. Let's go outside."

Sarabee's face tightened and she yanked her arm from his grip, but she turned and walked back through the door.

Atyen smiled the best smile he could manage. "I'm sorry to have bothered you," he said, and followed her out.

Outside, Sarabee grabbed him. "Atyen! Those—"

"I know, Sarabee. I know. Let's get Liese safe first, and then we'll see what we can find."

They took the girl down to Atyen's shed. The door had been broken open there too, and his half-built cargo wings dumped off the forming jigs and onto the floor. His toolshelf had been ransacked and some of his tools were missing. In his small bedroom the quilts were gone, but his ink jars and pens were still on his workshelf. The sight reminded him that he'd lost all his journals. He clenched his jaw and said nothing. *It's a small loss today.* Atyen barred the shutters and Sarabee gave Liese strict instructions to bar the door after they'd gone and not open it for anyone until they were back. Then she and Atyen walked back up to the farm. They gave the farmhouse a wide berth, and began searching through the foreward fields. It was Atyen who found them, at the edge of the olive grove, Celese and Newl, Acelle, Healan and Jerl and their cousins, lying in the long clover, shaded by sprouting turnips. Their hands had been tied behind their backs, and something blunt had smashed in their skulls. His throat constricted and he looked at the farmhouse, just a hundred meters distant, then looked to Sarabee, still walking slowly through the pasture, looking for any trace of her family. *I don't want to tell her this. I don't.* His gaze fell on Acelle. She looked peaceful, as if she were only sleeping. *Little innocent, you did nothing to deserve this, nothing.* He took a long deep breath, held it, closed his eyes to process his own anger and then let it out slowly out before he called Sarabee over.

She didn't cry when she saw, she didn't say anything, just went to Jerl and picked him up, stroking his small face. She carried him as she went to her daughters, to her sister and her nephews, touching each one, adjusting their clothing, speaking words too soft for him to hear. She didn't cry while they gathered straw for the pyre, when they added branches cut from the olive trees with his belt knife, or when they laid the bodies out. Throughout it all Atyen kept a close watch on the farmhouse. The door opened a few times, and a figure stood and watched them, but that was all. *And I understand that.* The group had been desperate when they'd come to Celese's door, still in shock from the unfolding calamity. They hadn't planned to kill, but the situation had spiralled out of control and suddenly they had a houseful of prisoners they couldn't keep and couldn't let go. Two or three of the usurpers would have taken it on themselves to solve the problem. *The rest might not even know for sure they'd murdered.* The majority would defend the house as their territory, but they wouldn't go so far as to kill in cold blood. *At least not yet.*

It was well into the sleeping hours before they'd finished, although with no bells sounding there was no way to know for sure. Atyen went to get Liese, and had to knock several times on the shutters to wake her up to open the door. He had a momentary panic when he thought his firepump had been stolen, but he found it under a forming jig after a brief search. He also found a keg of the flax oil that he used to protect the wing frames from the elements and brought it as well, in case the fire needed hastening. Liese did cry when she saw the bodies, and Sarabee held her daughter and said comforting words, but it was only when Atyen started the fire that she cried herself. Her sobs then were long and deep, and he held mother and daughter close as the flames rose high. The fire had needed no hastening.

"Ashes to ashes and dust to dust," he said, wishing he remembered more of the bishop's words at Solender's pyre, and wishing he had a bishop there to say them.

It took a long time before the fire died down to a steady crackle, and by then Sarabee's tears subsided. She once more said some words too soft for him to hear, and let him go, let Liese go. Liese went to follow her, but Atyen held her back, and Sarabee stood watching the flames by herself. After a long, long time she picked up a burning brand and the keg of flax oil, watched the flames for another long moment, and then with sudden decision turned towards the house that had been her sister's.

"Sarabee!" Atyen called. "Don't do it."

She turned. "Ashes to ashes and dust to dust. I know another line from the Bible. An eye for an eye and a tooth for a tooth." She turned again, marched straight for the house. Atyen watched, a hand on Liese's shoulder, as she emptied the flax oil over the doorstep and set it ablaze with the firebrand. Then she took it to the back and tossed it into the dried clover stacked there for the animals. The clover caught, and flames roared up. Sarabee came back and turned to watch the fire, her expression impassive. The blaze had a firm hold before they heard the first scream. Liese winced and looked away, but her mother just watched, a look of grim satisfaction on her face. There were more screams, and then a figure burst through a blazing window to run across the field, burning all the way. Finally it fell and lay still.

Eventually there were no more screams. All around the world there were more plumes of smoke, including a big one from the direction of Tidings. Atyen gave up counting at fifty. *The world is falling apart.*

"Come on," said Sarabee. "Let's go."

He headed back to the Madane's, but Sarabee's hand on his arm stopped him. "No, I don't want to sleep there. I don't want to remember. Not tonight."

They went instead to Atyen's shed. He was dizzy with hunger by the time he got there, they all were, but the thought of going to the dock, getting some of their carp, cleaning them, setting a fire and cooking was too much. They slept crowded together in his tiny shelf of a bed, Sarabee curled around Liese, and Atyen curled around Sarabee when she snuggled back against him. It was strange to have her there. She was a long-legged woman and he'd always seen her as tall, but in his arms she was tiny. *But it feels right, very right.*

It began to rain while they slept, and when they woke up it was torrenting.

"I've never seen rain like this," said Sarabee.

"It's because of all the smoke," Liese answered.

Atyen gave her a look. "Why do you say that?"

"What else can it be? What else has changed in the sky?"

"You know, you're probably right."

The rain brought refugees to the door, fortunately not aggressive ones, and Atyen directed them to Sarabee's old house.

"We can't stay here," he said. "The world is breaking down. People are already starving. The next people to come to the door might not be so restrained."

"Where can we go? It's going to be like this everywhere."

"We'll fly to Heaven. There are birds there for meat, water and every kind of vine. It'll be safe, for as long as we need it to be safe."

She looked at him askance. "Liese and I can't fly."

"I'll fly her with the cargo wings, and I'll teach you how to fly mine."

"Are you sure you can teach me?"

"I'm sure you can learn."

He found the first flaw in the plan when he opened the door to go and get the carp for breakfast. The rain was falling from a uniform overcast that stretched as far foreward as he could see. The smoke had changed the weather cycle, and without the spiralling fleece-clouds to ride to the upper overturn layer there way no way to fly to Heaven. *But that's fine, because first we have to finish the cargo wings.* He went to the raft while Sarabee improvised a firebowl and got it started, retrieved the carp and gutted them, brought them back to be cooked, then hiked up to where they'd held the pyre and dug up a handful of immature turnips. It was a basic meal, but rarely had Atyen tasted anything so good. They'd barely finished when another fugitive came to the door, attracted by the cooking smells. He was a young man, barely past adolescence, bedraggled, famished and dripping wet. It was hard to tell him there was no more food, and they let him come in to warm up. When he was somewhat recovered Atyen suggested he go up to the field to find some turnips.

"He'll be back," said Sarabee. "Where else will he go?"

"We can't take in every stray who comes along."

"If we can't fly until the rain stops, what do we do? This looks like it's going to go on forever."

Atyen put a hand to his chin, thinking. "We can live on the raft, get out in the ocean. Fish for food and wait it out."

"How will we cook?"

"We won't. We'll be eating raw fish, but we'll be eating. Make a tent out of the sails. We'll survive."

Sarabee took a deep breath. "Well, it'll be better than waiting here for the mob."

They loaded the net-raft with Atyen's wings, and the cargo wing skeleton and its wing fabric. All the tools that were left went in a box, and all the spare wing fabric in another one, and they brought the extra bamboo as well. The young man came back from the clover field with his coat full of turnips, and they gave him the shed in exchange for half the turnips, and set off with Atyen in Sarabee's raft, Sarabee and Liese in the sailsmiths'. It was thoroughly miserable travelling, soaked to the skin, and constantly having to bail out the raft. *But better here than on the shore with the horde hungry enough to kill.* They eventually made it to Cove, returned the sailsmiths' raft and gifted them with half the turnips and a netful of carp in thanks. They learned there that the situation was growing much worse. A mob had broken through the sentinel lines and ransacked Tidings, burned half of it. There were hundreds dead, maybe thousands. The mirror messages were the same from everywhere, before the rain shut them down.

"What will you do?" Sarabee asked them.

"We'll fish," said the husband. "And we'll pray."

"We're in a good spot," added his wife. "The world isn't ending, just changing."

Atyen nodded. It was a good approach to take. *Possibly the only approach.* He hauled up the sails and Sarabee steered them out again until they were well offshore, where they dropped the anchor. The sails draped over the sailpoles made an adequate tent, the only problem was they were all totally soaked before they got under it, and the rain came in the raft's uncovered fore and aft to collect in the bottom, so they had to bail constantly. Life devolved in an unending, unchanging wretchedness, huddled together under the sails to conserve body heat, constantly soaked, and constantly getting more soaked when they had to go out in the rain to bail, to haul nets or gut the fish they caught. Without shuttered windows and sleep-cloths it was too bright to sleep properly, and so time dragged by in a semi-waking misery. By the third day their skin was red and sore anywhere it made contact with anything, white and wrinkled everywhere else. By the fourth they were speaking in only the monosyllables necessary to make the raft function. By the fifth the skin was sloughing from their fingers. The chill of constant immersion had penetrated to Atyen's core, and he was shivering so badly he could barely hold the knife to divide the carp. On the sixth day he couldn't tell if the rain was slackening, or if his numbed brain was just generating a desperate illusion. *If it even is the sixth day.* Without the bells Atyen had lost all track of time. It could have been the sixteenth, for all he knew.

On the seventh day, if it was the seventh day, the rain did slack, and the suntube made a show through the clouds.

"A . . . Atyen?" Liese was shivering so hard she could barely speak. She was hollow cheeked, her skin corpse-white, her sodden, greasy hair plastered round her face. "Th-thank-you for s-saving my mother." She smiled, and was suddenly so radiant the warmth was almost physical.

Atyen's voice caught in his throat, and he took a moment to get his own shivering under some kind of control. "You're welcome."

The clouds lifted more, and they hauled up the sail and the anchor. Atyen picked their course by Jens's navigation marks up on the mast, and Sarabee steered it. After what seemed a long time, they came to the aftwall and the carrier dangling from its ropes. By then the suntube was all the way out and they were mostly dried out and feeling much better. Then it was just a matter of work, cranking themselves and all their gear up to the second ledge. Most of it was straightforward, but the mainspine of the cargo wings wasn't built to fold, and it took a lot of awkward maneuvering to get them balanced on the carrier at the bottom and unloaded at the top.

They found some dead branches in a tree that were dry enough to build a fire. Atyen cut a strip of waxed flax from the extra wing fabric to use as tinder, and they enjoyed a warm cooked meal for the first time in a week.

"If I never see carp and turnips again it'll be too soon," Atyen said as he wolfed down his portion. "But this is really good."

The next step was to get the cargo wings ready for launch. Threading the wing fabric on was straightforward, but the cargo wings needed a launch ramp, and that was more complicated.

After some thought he sacrificed the mast from the raft and laboriously sawed it in half with his belt knife. It was just long enough to make two six meter rails. He used the extra bamboo they'd brought to make support trestles to hold them in position. In between times he went over the basics of flight with Sarabee, explaining how climbing and diving interacted with speed, how to shift weight, and how to use the control lines to steer and trade momentum for lift, how to recover from the terrifying tumbles that happened when one wing stopped flying and the other didn't. He had her strap the wings on and stand at the edge of the ledge, feeling the wind tugging at them, tempting her to fly, and also getting her used to the fear of falling that had so paralyzed his early attempts. It took a solid week, as measured by waking and sleeping, to get the slide rails ready.

And in that time he realized that there was no need to undertake the risky flight to Heaven. "We can stay right here, we've got birds, fruit, fish and water. Trees to build shelter, bushes for fuel. We even have the raft, so we can check on how the world is doing."

"No," Sarabee said, surprising him. "I want to fly, and I want to see Heaven for myself."

He was about to dissuade her when he remembered his own early, frustrated yearnings as he'd watched the circling peregrines. *I've shown her the wind. I can't deny it to her now.* "Then we'll do it," he said. Beside them Liese breathed out in relief. She'd been a rapt pupil at the flight lessons, even though she wouldn't be flying herself. She wanted to see the world from above, and visit Heaven too.

*Like mother like daughter.* They spent one last day checking over both sets of wings, verifying every joint, every binding, and then went over all the flight techniques one last time, including how to maneuver to make the critical contact with Heaven's landing platform. There would be no second chances. Columns of smoke were still popping up around the world. The Second Inquisition was falling, and if they didn't make their goal they'd land right in the middle of the chaos.

And then it was time. They levered the cargo wings up on their slide rails. Liese climbed into the cargo basket, curled up tight with all their tools, and Atyen made sure Sarabee had her wings properly strapped on and the control lines taut. "Remember, leap out as hard as you can, dive for speed, when you feel the wings start to fly shift backwards, balance left and right with the control lines, level out stable and just let the updraft carry you."

She nodded tensely, and Atyen's own fears came back to him once again. *It's easy to dream of flight, hard to jump off the ledge.* He went back to the cargo carrier, put on the straps, tested the lines. "Ready back there?" he asked Liese.

"Ready!" Her voice was excited.

"Go!" he shouted to Sarabee. They had agreed that she would jump first, to avoid the possibility that he would start and she would freeze at the last second. She didn't, though; she bent at the knees and leapt. Panic shot through Atyen as she vanished over the edge, as though he had just watched her leap to certain death, but a few seconds later he saw her, wobbling slightly but climbing. He took up the slack in the lines and shouted "Release!"

Behind him Liese yanked the rope that held them up on the slide rails. There was a brief lurch, and then they were sliding, over the slope and pitching down steeply. The wings caught the air, the fabric tightened, and they were flying. He shifted back, but the cargo carrier was twice as heavy as what he was used to and it barely responded. He shifted back further, then as far as he physically could, and they slowly, slowly began to pull out. He tugged a line to counteract a slight roll, held it, and then finally they were level. He craned his neck up to spot Sarabee, already far above them. "Circle!" he called, "Slowly!"

She did, demonstrating far more control on her first flight than he had on his twentieth. *Of course, she didn't have to figure it out from zero.* She was still climbing away, and he began to fear that he'd gone down too low, that he'd fallen out of the updraft and would slowly descend until they hit the ocean. He turned, gently because steep turns cost lift, and was able to verify that they were gaining on the second ledge.

Above them Sarabee put her nose down into a gentle dive, pulled up and turned, and then dived more steeply until she was back down on their level.

"Atyen!" she called. "This is wonderful."

"It *is* wonderful," Liese enthused from the basket behind him. "That was so exciting."

*Exciting, as long as we make it.* Atyen didn't share the thought, there was no need to worry her. They continued climbing, with

Sarabee practicing the basic techniques, and Atyen adapting what he knew to the clumsy cargo carrier. They gained steadily until they were as high as they could go in the lower wind cycle. Atyen waited until a fleecy spiral cloud started to grow and extend directly in front of them, using the time to have her practice tumble recoveries and the figure-eight pattern needed to climb at the leading edge of the cloud without losing orientation in the mist. When he judged the cloud was ready he called to her, and they both shifted forward and headed for it. If he judged it right they'd fly right under its updraft and she wouldn't have to work the tricky overturn boundary.

He judged it right, and just as they crossed over the shoreline the updraft hit, and they circled, climbing upward. "Sarabee, put a bit more tension on both lines," he called. She did, and the added drag slowed her ascent to the point he could keep up. He slid up beside her until their wingtips were nearly touching and they circled in synchrony, the way peregrines sometimes did. *Flying is beautiful, flying together is heaven.* Sarabee gained confidence with every turn, and she'd mastered the basics with remarkable speed. They climbed to the cloud's underside and flew back and forth as it grew foreward, drawing its gentle spiral around the suntube as it did. They passed over the black scar that had been Charisy, but from altitude it was just a color, with nothing to show the living horror the city had become just a month ago. There were still a few fires here and there around the world, but the most notable change was the absence of twinkling message mirrors. *The Second Inquisition has fallen.* It was hard to think that the organization he'd given his life to had vanished, and perhaps with the softened view from the clouds he could have convinced himself that it hadn't. *But they trained me to reason, and the evidence is right there.* The important thing now was to get to safety. *And to keep my promise to Jens.*

"How are you doing?" he called back to Liese.

"It's still wonderful," she called back.

He smiled, and looked over to see Sarabee circling easily. The front of the cloud was approaching the foredome. It was time. "Figure eights," he called to her. "Follow me."

She turned, dove, fell in behind him, and he headed out to the front of the cloud, climbed up and into it. He was cautious at first, keeping so far forward that visibility was never in question, but there was barely enough lift to keep his heavy cargo carrier up. Gradually he worked deeper into the cloud, and he began to climb. "Stay forward," he shouted. "I need more updraft than you."

He'd made the decision out of concern, he didn't want her to get caught too deep, where the fleecy mist became a dense white shroud, where you couldn't tell up from down and the dangerous tumble became inevitable. It was a mistake, because as soon as they took different routes he lost sight of her, and he realized that if she tumbled he'd never know it.

"Sarabee!" he shouted.

"Atyen!" she answered, very faint, and it was impossible to tell the direction her voice came from.

"Sarabee!" This time he heard no answer, and he began to fret, and to look for her, trying to keep his figure eights methodical, trying frantically to spot her. *She could be above, or below or . . .* All at once she was in front, heading straight for him, and he dived on instinct, felt the rush of her passage right overhead. He banked around hard but she was already gone and he was left alone in the misty edge of the cloud. He completed the circle, a dangerous move that turned him into the advancing whiteness, and for three panicked seconds he lost sight of the ground. It came back before the tumble, but his heart was pounding hard in his chest. *Never again,* he resolved. *I've already learned that lesson.*

He went back to figure eights, gained height, and finally they met, up at the top of the cloud, with the suntube scorching their wing fabric and the foredome looming in front of them. "Foreward," he called, and they dived to meet the topmost wind cycle, and the updraft that would carry them to Heaven. They reached the dome, turned antispinward and let the updraft loft them higher. The carrier was sluggish as they lost weight, far more so than the single wings had been, and he had to work hard to steer. As the foredome's struts came past he could see the green cylinder that was Heaven getting closer overhead, with its landing platform below it, and its perpetual halo of birds. He'd been worried about Sarabee's ability to hit the platform, but soon he was concerned for his own. Even with all his weight full forward the wings lost their bite and he was drifting.

He looked back over his shoulder. "Liese, come here."

"I am here."

"No, *here,* right up front with me."

"I'll fall!"

"No, you won't, you're very light here. Hang on tight, only move one hand at a time."

She did as he asked, moved hand over hand until she was next to him. The nose dropped, and wings bit, and he tugged the lines, banked them over, and made it to the platform with the gentlest of touchdowns. He unstrapped immediately, looked around in case he had to grab Sarabee, but she guided herself in and touched down as if she'd been doing it all her life.

"Incredible," she breathed, unstrapping her wings to settle gently behind her.

Liese went to her mother. "Tiny steps," he reminded her. "You can jump right off."

"Tiny steps," the girl answered, and took her mother's hand.

"Amazing, Atyen." Sarabee laughed. "It really is Heaven. I'm not sure I really believed it before."

"It gets better inside. Real miracles."

"What's outside is enough for me right now." Sarabee came to stand beside him, moving carefully. He put his arm around her and they looked out at the spreading world below. Eventually he turned to her and, very gently, kissed her. Very gently, she kissed him back.

# Finale

*I will multiply your seed as the stars of Heaven, and all this land will I give unto your seed.*

—Exodus 32:13

# Shipyear 7583

"It's time." The young woman looked up to see her mother, looking concerned. "Are you sure you want to do this? It isn't too late."

"I'm sure," the young woman answered.

Her mother sighed. "You're so pretty. You could marry so well."

"Mother!" A note of steel crept into the young woman's voice. "It's what I want."

"I know dear, it's just . . ." Her mother hesitated. "It's just I worry for you. But I wouldn't stop you if I could." She laughed. "And I never could stop you, you're too much like your father." She straightened up, and the young woman knew she was stiffening her resolve at the same time. "Now, come on. You don't want to be late."

The young woman stood up, and let her mother help her into the fitted white fabric of her outerdress. It wasn't *a* tradition, just *their* tradition. "Here," her mother said, and handed her something. "A peregrine's claw. It was your father's. He would want you to have it."

The young woman turned the totem over, testing the razor talons with a finger. She smiled, pleased to be reminded of her father, pleased to have her mother's support. "I can't lose now."

"You can," her mother said. "But you won't."

The young woman slid the claw into a fold of her garment and her mother picked up the fired-clay wine jar that lay by the door. They came out of the tent and onto the platform together, to stand beside the steel-topped post. The crowd along the shore applauded, and the young woman bowed to her opponent, which was *a* tradition, and to the foredome, which was *the* tradition. He returned the bow, and then her mother handed her the jar

481

of wine. She raised it high and brought it down hard on the steel, shattering it and spraying the thick fluid everywhere. That was tradition too, but something more, symbolic and powerful. Her pristine outerdress was irrevocably stained with deep red blotches, symbolic of her blood, of the price she was willing to pay to win. She saw she had gotten far more of it on herself than her opponent had with his strike. *A good omen.* She knew him, knew his style; they had trained together many times. *But today he is my enemy.*

They bowed to each other again, and turned to walk down to the dock, to the swift netters that would take them to the aft-wall. The raft-captains raised sail, and they set off. The voyage to the wall was long, but she used the time to close her eyes and visualize the contest. Her opponent's netter drew ahead of hers, which shouldn't have bothered her, but it did. It didn't matter whose raft got to the wall first, except in her mind. *I am my father's daughter.* He too was too competitive, too driven to win even unimportant contests, and even imaginary ones. To take her mind off it she looked over her wings, sleek and finely crafted, the steel tip-hooks honed to a razor edge. *Today I am a falcon.*

They came at last to the aftwall, and she slung her wings and grabbed the first rungs of the dangling ladder, climbing with a sure, steady rhythm. The admonisher was waiting on the upper ledge, and he helped her up as she came over the top. Her opponent was already standing on the edge, ready to leap and looking impatient, but she took her time extending her wings and locking them, checking them. They fit her so well they became a part of her when they were on. *Or at least that's how it feels.* They were heavier than usual today, with twenty kilos of clay in a sleeve along the mainspine, her secret weapon. When she was ready she moved to the edge herself.

The admonisher put on his own wings, colored red so they couldn't be confused in the duel, and stepped to the edge. "Are you ready?" he asked. She nodded, her opponent nodded. "Jump!" he shouted.

All three launched themselves into space, and she dove, caught air, soared up, stabilized, and let the updraft carry her higher. The extra weight made the pull out deeper, her speed higher, and the extra momentum carried her farther than she was used to. She looked to see if her opponent had noticed, but she couldn't tell.

She wobbled, just in case, to let him think her uncertain and not flying well. She was half his size and so should climb faster, but she didn't because of the extra weight. *But he's arrogant, and so he'll be smug and think I fly badly, so he'll be careless.* Victory was in the balance between height and speed. More weight meant a slower climb but a faster dive, wider turns but quicker strikes. By carrying ballast she could match him in speed on the down-duel, and then dump it and beat him back up. It was a trick that would only work once. *But once should be enough.*

They climbed in silence, to the top of the first wind cycle, by then well out over the ocean, and some three hundred meters apart. She had gained a small height advantage despite her ballast and her calculated wobbles. The admonisher pierced the air with his whistle, and a long second later she heard the echo from the forewall. She turned towards her opponent and dived, to meet the obligation that they start at the same height, and to keep the speed her advantage gave her. The whistle pierced the air twice more, and the duel was on.

*Advantage to the low wing on the pass.* She aimed to pass under her opponent, it was easier to score a hit from below than above, but of course he was doing the same thing. They both dived hard, head on and the wind rush built up in her face as her pulse thrilled in her breast. At the last instant they both swerved away. She tried to catch him with a tip-hook on the way past, but was wide, far too wide. Already she was pulling up, trading dive speed for height, to circle around and come down again. He was doing the same, but already she'd detected a weakness. He'd pulled up too hard, come around too fast, and his aggressiveness had cost him meters of height. He was trying to win in the first passes, but her small advantage was now a little bit larger. She dived, more steeply this time because she had more height. The second pass was a near duplicate of the first, and again he was too aggressive on the pullout and turn, and again she gained height.

She smiled to herself. *Time to change strategy.* She dived more shallowly this time, and because she had more height was able to pass over him with the same amount of speed. She passed just too high and pulled up to the vertical. Her hope was that he'd take the bait and try for a strike, follow her up, and then run out of speed, tumble backwards and dive away. She would run out of speed too, but higher, and when she tumbled and dived she'd be behind him, chasing him down. If he tried to pull out she'd overtake him and strike at will from above. If he didn't pull out, she'd just chase him into the ocean.

Because she was climbing straight up and away she couldn't know if he'd taken the bait until she tumbled, and when she did he wasn't there. He was arrogant, but not stupid. She dived, recovered, looked around to find him, and there was a sudden rush of wings, a ripping of fabric, and then he was gone again, pulling up and around. The admonisher's whistle blew. Her opponent had scored a point. Heart pounding, the young woman checked her wings. The gash was just above the mainspine and not large, but the long, tight braid she kept her hair in had come uncoiled and was streaming out behind her. The tip hook had caught the band that held it and torn it loose. Another fraction and the tip-hook would have sliced open her scalp. *Or my head.* The duel was not lethal on purpose—a downed winger was supposed to throw her aircatcher, to billow out and slow the fall to the water below—but deaths were common enough. You could be lethally cut by a tip hook, or knocked unconscious in a collision. You could get tangled in the aircatcher's lines, or it could drag you down after you hit the ocean. There were many ways to die.

*Which is the spice.* Heart pounding the young woman turned to follow her opponent. *It's real now.* A distant part of her brain warned her of the danger of arrogance. Her opponent's flaw was also her own. *And perhaps you have to be arrogant, to duel like this in the wind.* He was climbing again, and she climbed after him. There were no intentional wobbles now, she flew as cleanly as she could. She had the slightest advantage in climb, slowly gaining a meter at a time. He knew that too of course, and so when he was high enough he dived, foreward and antispinward, a long, shallow acceleration that gradually eroded the advantage she'd won. He ended up two hundred meters in front of her, and then pulled up and turned, reversing into her for another head-to-head pass. She dived to get under him, and he let her, but when she flipped her right wing up to catch him with the tip-hook it was her wing fabric that was sliced again. He'd side-slipped and then banked so that when she made her move his hook was already there. The admonisher's whistle blew again, and she felt anger flush her face. *He will not win!* Still, he'd gained an advantage. Her sliced wing fluttered, and she had to pull opposite slots to compensate, which slowed her down. He had a speed advantage *and* a climb advantage now, not large ones, but one more mistake could bring her down. She pulled up and turned, glancing down as she did. They'd lost half the height they'd started the duel with. If she was going to win she'd have to do it quickly.

*Time for the secret weapon.* She yanked the cord that released the knots holding her ballast bag, and it tumbled away. He was definitely faster now, but she had an advantage back in at least one domain, and she pulled up, shooting towards the suntube. He had turned for another pass, started his dive, and so he had to switch to a climb to follow her. He must have expected to beat her, but he started to fall behind. She watched for the moment that he realized it, pushing forward out of his climb back into a dive, and at that moment she dropped a wing and stooped, slots closed, the wind-rush hard in her face. The torn fabric in her right wing flapped, vibrated, drummed, and then it ripped all the way back to the trailing edge. She ignored it, totally focused on her prey.

He could out-dive her, but for a short time her height advantage could be turned into a speed advantage, and because he had to pass under her she had less distance to cover. She overtook him, forcing him to steepen his dive, following when he did, and the wind howled through the tears in her wings. Still she overtook him, dipped the left wing, snagged his fabric with the tip-hook, and pulled slots on both sides. The sudden deceleration ripped the hook through the length of the wing surface, and then caught on the bamboo backspine on the trailing edge. There was a tremendous wrench and then they were both falling, tied together at that point. The world gyrated crazily, and she saw him frantically yanking on his lines, trying to free himself, trying to regain control. The blue of the ocean came up fast. There was nothing she could do but hold full slots. Her mainspine groaned under the strain.

And then he was gone, harness released, aircatcher thrown, drifting down. *Defeated!* But her victory wouldn't count if she couldn't land it, and his wings were still attached to her tip-hook, dragging her down sideways. She closed the slots to fall faster, then popped the right slots full. She was wrenched violently sideways and something snapped in mainspine, but his wings were still there. *One more time.* She was already dangerously close to the water. She repeated the maneuver, and again was wrenched sideways. Her left wing came up, slightly, and then something snapped, and her tip-hook was wrenched right off her wingtip. She popped the other line as well, killed her speed and pulled up with a hundred meters to spare. Her pulse pounded in her ears and she found she was shaking. Her right wing was badly torn, the end-joints on the left were broken, and the backspine juddered against the mainspine. *But I've won, I've won.* Her pull-up took her to a hundred and fifty meters, enough height to catch the updraft again, barely. She rode it up while she recovered herself, and saw her opponent in the distance, coming down in the water. One of the netters was already heading in his direction.

She regained her height, regained her composure, and set herself up for the glide back to shore. She turned, set up the approach, slid it in and managed to make the landing look smooth, right in front of the platforms. The crowd had seen almost nothing of the duel, it was too high, too far away, but they knew the meaning of her damaged wings and they erupted into applause. She saw her mother waiting there, looking proud and relieved. *First duel victory.* It was hers now forever. She smiled, and bowed to the foredome, which was *the* tradition and the applause redoubled itself. She had her place as a winger now, a guardian angel of the Builder's secret Heaven. She slid her hand into the fold in her garment, found her father's peregrine claw. The crowd came to get her, to lift her on their shoulders, to celebrate her bravery, but she only had eyes for the foredome's apex, the place she had finally earned.

*Oh yes, Father, I'll be there very soon.*